ADVANCED VOCABULARY
英文字彙王

進階單字 4001~6000

Levels 5 & 6

序

本系列套書依據大學入學考試中心於 109 年 7 月頒布之「高中英文參考詞彙表」重新編修，將原先的單字依使用者文化背景、日常用語及教學層面高頻用字考量，去除詞頻低、口語型詞彙及部分縮寫字與專有名詞等，將單字以**使用頻率**適度排序，另增補學習必備、各類考試重要字詞，除自學外，也適用**學測**、**高中英語聽力測驗**、**全民英檢中～中高級**、**新制多益**……等考試，並為**雅思**及**托福**的基礎必備單字。

內容方面，每單元單字除提供 K.K. 音標、詞性、實用例句、中文解釋外，亦嚴選補充該單字重要的**片語**、**衍生字**、**近似字**、**反義字**、**比較用字**、**延伸用法**及**文法說明**等，讓讀者在日常英語閱讀、聆聽、口說、寫作能力養成上，都能靈活運用這些字詞。

音檔設計上，我們特請專業美籍老師朗讀單字及例句，且為了結合科技、響應環保，全書採用 **"QR Code"**，讀者可依使用習慣，自由選擇聆聽**分頁式音檔**或**一次完整下載音檔**，邊聽邊朗讀單字及例句，可大幅改善發音並增進口語能力。

本系列《英文字彙王》套書，依單字難易程度分為基礎單字 2000（Levels 1 & 2）、核心單字 2001 ~ 4000（Levels 3 & 4）、進階單字 4001 ~ 6000（Levels 5 & 6）三套書，方便讀者循序漸進規劃學習。祝各位學習成功！

每 1～2 頁皆有 QR Code 可下載該頁音檔分段學習，另有一個單元一個完整音檔，皆可於小書名頁掃描 QR Code 下載。

單字背熟後，可在框內打勾。

0710-0716

10 rigid [ˋrɪdʒɪd] *a.* 堅固的，不易彎曲的；死板的，嚴格的 ☐

似 (1) unbending [ʌnˋbɛndɪŋ] *a.* 不易彎曲的；不妥協的
(2) strict [strɪkt] *a.* 嚴格的 ②

反 flexible [ˋflɛksəbḷ] *a.* 可彎曲的；可變通的 ④

▸ The shopping mall was constructed out of rigid steel and a lot of concrete.
這個購物中心是由堅固的鋼鐵及大量混凝土所建造而成。

▸ Congress has asked the President to adopt a rigid position on illegal immigration.
國會要求總統對非法移民的問題採取嚴格的立場。

補充單字的難度級數

與單字相關的重要片語、衍生字、近似字、反義字、比較用字、延伸用法及文法說明等補充。

代號說明

- 三 動詞三態
- 複 名詞的複數形
- 片 片語
- 衍 衍生字
- 似 近似字（含形音義）
- 比 多個近似字比較說明
- 反 反義字
- 用法 重要文法說明
- 延伸 相關補充
- [美] 美式英語
- [英] 英式英語

索　引

A	
abbreviate	237
abide	238
abnormal	8
abolish	8
aboriginal	325
abortion	7
abound	355
abrupt	67
abstraction	348

頁數

目 錄

Level 5

Unit 01 → 1
Unit 02 → 10
Unit 03 → 20
Unit 04 → 30
Unit 05 → 39
Unit 06 → 49
Unit 07 → 58
Unit 08 → 67
Unit 09 → 77
Unit 10 → 85
Unit 11 → 95
Unit 12 → 104
Unit 13 → 113
Unit 14 → 122
Unit 15 → 132
Unit 16 → 142
Unit 17 → 152
Unit 18 → 161
Unit 19 → 170
Unit 20 → 180
Unit 21 → 189
Unit 22 → 198
Unit 23 → 207
Unit 24 → 216
Unit 25 → 225

Level 6

Unit 01 → 235
Unit 02 → 245
Unit 03 → 255
Unit 04 → 265
Unit 05 → 275
Unit 06 → 285
Unit 07 → 295
Unit 08 → 305
Unit 09 → 315
Unit 10 → 325
Unit 11 → 335
Unit 12 → 345
Unit 13 → 354
Unit 14 → 364
Unit 15 → 373
Unit 16 → 383
Unit 17 → 392
Unit 18 → 401
Unit 19 → 411
Unit 20 → 420
Unit 21 → 429
Unit 22 → 438
Unit 23 → 447
Unit 24 → 456
Unit 25 → 465
索 引 → 475
附 錄 → 496

Level 5

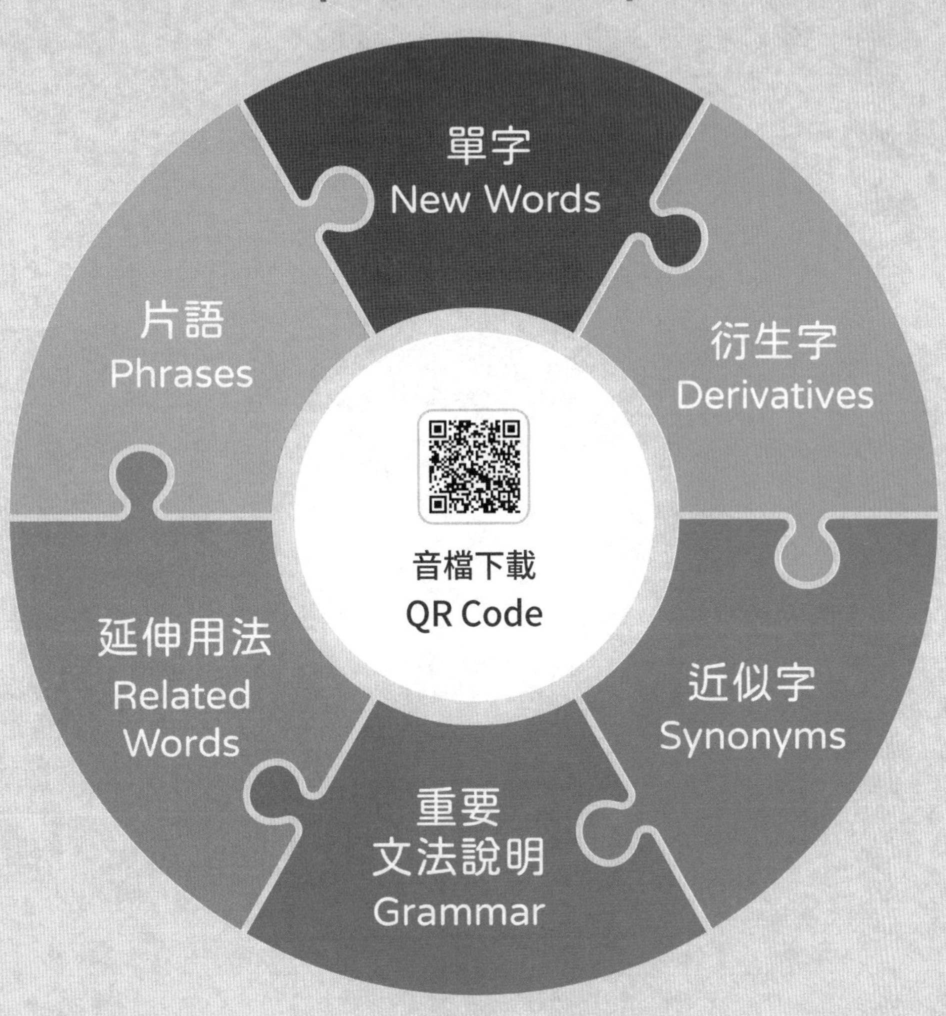
單字
New Words
衍生字
Derivatives
近似字
Synonyms
重要
文法說明
Grammar
延伸用法
Related
Words
片語
Phrases
音檔下載
QR Code

0101-0103

1 federal [ˋfɛdərəl] *a.* 聯邦的（指美國的聯邦政府時常大寫）

片 (1) federal funding 聯邦政府的資助
(2) the Federal Government of the United States 美國聯邦政府

衍 federation [ˌfɛdəˋreʃən] *n.* 聯盟；聯邦

▸ This publishing company relies mainly upon federal funding.
這家出版社主要是依賴聯邦政府的資助。

▸ The federal government will donate $1 billion to those states that need money for their economic development.
聯邦政府將捐贈 10 億美元給有經援需求的幾個州讓他們發展經濟。

2 stock [stɑk] *n.* 股票〔美〕；存貨，庫存；貯存（物）& *vt.* 儲存

片 (1) the stock market 股市
(2) (be) in stock 有庫存
(3) (be) out of stock 無庫存
(4) a stock of... 存貨 / 備有⋯⋯
(5) stock up (on sth) 大量購買 / 囤貨（某物）

似 share [ʃɛr] *n.* 股份；股票〔英〕①

▸ Stock prices fell due to rumors of a company merger.
因為公司合併的傳聞甚囂塵上，股價便下跌了。
*merger [ˋmɝdʒɚ] *n.*（公司）合併

▸ I'm sorry, but we no longer have that book in stock.
很抱歉，那本書我們現在沒有貨。

▸ We have a huge stock of quality sportswear on sale.
我們庫存了許多質料不錯的運動休閒服來賣。

▸ We have a good stock of snacks in the cupboard—please help yourself.
我們的櫥櫃裡儲備了很多零食 —— 請自取。

▸ This shop stocks a wide range of outdoor equipment.
這家店備有多種的戶外用品。

▸ There's a typhoon coming, so we should stock up on bottled water.
颱風要來了，所以我們要多囤積些瓶裝水。

shareholder [ˋʃɛrˌholdɚ] *n.* 股東〔英〕

似 stockholder [ˋstɑkˌholdɚ] *n.* 股東〔美〕

▸ Shareholders will hold a meeting to vote on the proposed merger with KGM Co.
股東將召開會議投票表決與 KGM 公司的合併案。

3 series [ˋsiriz] *n.* 系列；（電視）系列節目

複 單複數同形

片 (1) a series of + 複數名詞 一系列的⋯⋯
(2) TV series 電視影集

衍 serial [ˋsɪrɪəl] *n.*（電視）連續劇（的一集）⑥

▸ There have been a series of burglaries on the east side of the town.
城鎮的東區發生了一連串的竊盜案件。
*burglary [ˋbɝglərɪ] *n.* 竊盜

▸ A new television series called *Charming Betty* will be starting next month.
新的電視連續劇《迷人的貝蒂》將於下個月開始播出。

4 saint [sent] *n.* 聖人 & *vt.* 承認（某人，尤為死者）為聖徒

用法 若為大寫 Saint，則通常用在某位聖徒名字前，縮寫為 St 或 St.。

▸ No one is a saint. In other words, no one is perfect.
誰都不是聖人。換言之，沒有人是完美無缺的。

▸ The Irish people drink beer and wear green clothes on March 17th in celebration of St. Patrick.
愛爾蘭人在 3 月 17 日會喝啤酒，並穿著綠衣以紀念聖者派翠克。

▸ Maria was sainted for her role in the civil rights movement.
瑪麗亞因她在民權運動中擔任的角色而被認為是聖者。

5 corporation [ˌkɔrpəˋreʃən] *n.* 企業

似 (1) cooperation [koˌɑpəˋreʃən] *n.* 合作 ④
(2) company [ˋkʌmpənɪ] *n.* 公司 ②
(3) enterprise [ˋɛntɚˌpraɪz] *n.* 企業 ⑤

▸ Mr. Smith runs a major corporation.
史密斯先生經營一家大公司。

corporate [ˋkɔrpərɪt] *a.* 企業的

▸ We need some corporate sponsors for our event.
我們的活動需要一些企業的贊助。

6 commission [kəˋmɪʃən] *n.* 佣金；委任 & *vt.* 委任

片 (1) get a commission on sth 拿某事物的佣金
(2) on commission 以拿佣金的方式；以委任的方式

似 (1) assign [əˋsaɪn] *vt.* 指派 ④
(2) authorize [ˋɔθəˌraɪz] *vt.* 授權 ⑤

▸ You'll get a 15% commission on everything you sell.
你所賣出的東西都可以抽成 15%。

▸ Alex received a commission to build a memorial park.
艾力克斯被委託建造一座紀念公園。

▸ The museum commissioned the artist to make a sculpture in remembrance of the curator.
博物館委任這名藝術家製作一座雕像紀念該館長。
*in remembrance of... 以紀念……
curator [kjʊˋretɚ] *n.* 館長

7 conduct [kənˋdʌkt] *vt.* 處理；指揮（樂團）& [ˋkɑndʌkt] *n.* 行為（不可數）

片 conduct an investigation / experiment 進行調查 / 實驗

衍 (1) conductor [kənˋdʌktɚ] *n.*（樂團）指揮 ④
(2) misconduct [mɪsˋkɑndʌkt] *n.* 不當行為（不可數）

似 behavior [bɪˋhevjɚ] *n.* 行為（不可數）④

▸ Police have conducted an investigation into the case.
警方已就該案件進行調查。

▸ The local orchestra was conducted by my piano teacher, Mr. Evans.
本地的管絃樂團是由我的鋼琴老師艾文斯先生擔任指揮。

▸ Theo's conduct in class is always excellent.
西奧在班上的行為舉止總是很得體。

8 recommend [ˌrɛkəˋmɛnd] *vt.* 建議

片 (1) recommend sb to V
建議某人做某事
(2) recommend that + S + (should) + V 建議……（此時 recommend 屬意志動詞，助動詞 should 可予以省略）

似 (1) suggest [səˋdʒɛst] *vt.* 建議 ②
(2) advise [ədˋvaɪz] *vt.* 建議 ③

延伸 意志動詞為表『建議、要求、命令、規定』等的動詞，例如：recommend（建議）、advise（建議）、ask（要求）、require（要求）、regulate（規定）等。

▸ I'm going to try the seafood paella because Josie highly recommended it.
我要去吃吃看西班牙海鮮燉飯，因為喬西超**推薦**它。
*seafood paella [pɑˋelja] 西班牙海鮮燉飯

▸ The teacher recommends us to read the questions twice before answering them.
老師**建議**我們在回答問題前要把問題先看兩遍。

▸ The manager recommended that the meeting (should) be put off.
經理**建議**將會議時間延期。

recommendation
[ˌrɛkəmɛnˋdeʃən] *n.* 建議；推薦信

衍 (1) recommendable
[ˌrɛkəˋmɛndəbḷ] *a.* 可推薦的
(2) recommendatory
[ˌrɛkəˋmɛndəˌtorɪ] *a.* 推薦的

似 (1) advice [ədˋvaɪs] *n.* 建議 ②
(2) suggestion [səˋdʒɛstʃən] *n.* 建議 ④

▸ I'm not sure what to do. What's your recommendation?
我不知道該怎麼做，你有什麼**建議**嗎？

▸ Could you write me a recommendation for my university application?
你可以為我的大學入學申請寫一封**推薦信**嗎？

9 grant [grænt] *vt.* 授予，給予；承認，同意 & *n.* 撥款，補助金

片 (1) grant sb sth 給予某人某物
(2) take it for granted that...
認為……是理所當然的
(3) take (sb/sth) for granted
認為（某人 / 某事物）是理所當然的

▸ My father was granted a pension after retirement.
我父親退休後**領有**退休俸。

▸ I grant that the apartment is not cheap, but it's in a perfect location.
我**承認**這間公寓並不便宜，但它所在地點絕佳。

▸ Larry thought he had been working hard all year round, so he took it for granted that he would get a year-end bonus at work.
賴瑞認為他一年到頭都很努力，因此他**認為**自己會拿到年終獎金**是理所當然的**事。

▸ The company gave Robert a grant to conduct further research into the drug.
這間公司給羅伯特一筆**補助金**，以對該藥物進行更深入的研究。

0110-0116

10 interpretation [ɪn͵tɝprɪ`teʃən] *n.* 詮釋；口譯

衍 (1) interpret [ɪn`tɝprɪt] *vt.* 詮釋 & *vi.* 口譯 ④
interpret A as B　將 A 解釋為 B
(2) interpreter [ɪn`tɝprɪtɚ] *n.* 口譯員 ⑥

似 translation [træns`leʃən] *n.* 翻譯（尤指筆譯）④

▸ Molly said this dance was an interpretation of a poem by Frost.
茉莉說這支舞蹈是對佛洛斯特一首詩的詮釋。

▸ Simultaneous interpretation is an art that takes years of practice.
同步口譯是需要多年的練習才能成就的一門本領。
*simultaneous [͵saɪml̩`tenɪəs] *a.* 同時發生的

11 communist [`kɑmjʊnɪst] *n.* 共產主義者 & *a.* 共產（主義）的

反 capitalist [`kæpətl̩ɪst] *n.* 資本主義者 & *a.* 資本（主義）的 ④

▸ Communists believe in a classless society and equal distribution of wealth.
共產主義者篤信無階級的社會以及財富的公平分配。

▸ There is a detailed description about how a communist society works in this book.
本書詳細說明共產主義的社會是如何運作的。

communism [`kɑmjʊ͵nɪzm̩] *n.* 共產主義（不可數）

反 capitalism [`kæpə͵tl̩ɪzm̩] *n.* 資本主義（不可數）④

▸ The main ideas of communism can be found in *The Communist Manifesto* by Karl Marx.
共產主義的中心思想可以在卡爾．馬克思的著作《共產主義宣言》裡找到。
*manifesto [͵mænə`fɛsto] *n.* 宣言

12 mount [maʊnt] *vt.* 爬上；騎在……上 & *vi.* 增加 & *n.* 山

片 (1) mount a ladder　爬上梯子
(2) mount a horse / bicycle　騎上馬 / 腳踏車

反 dismount [dɪs`maʊnt] *vt.* 下（馬或車等）
dismount a horse　下馬

用法 mount 作名詞時，通常置山名前，且須大寫，縮寫為 Mt 或 Mt.。

▸ Mr. Conway mounted the stage and gave his opening speech.
康威先生登上舞臺並給予開場致詞。

▸ John mounted his horse and rode off.
約翰騎上馬便飛奔而去。

▸ After Sophie lost her job, her debts started to mount quickly.
蘇菲失業後，她的債務快速增加。

▸ George has finally fulfilled his lifelong dream of climbing Mount Everest.
喬治終於完成他這一生的心願，攀爬喜馬拉雅山。

13 saddle [`sædl̩] *n.* 馬鞍；車座 & *vt.* 裝上馬鞍

片 saddle (up) a horse　替馬裝上馬鞍

延伸 (1) spur [spɝ] *n.* 馬刺 ⑥
(2) harness [`hɑrnəs] *n.* 馬具 ⑥
(3) rein [ren] *n.* 韁繩

▸ It's not easy to ride a horse without a saddle.
沒有馬鞍騎馬很困難。

▸ Sam adjusted the saddle and checked the brakes before he rented the bike.
山姆調整坐墊和檢查剎車後才租了這臺腳踏車。

▸ Peter was saddling up his horse in the stable.
彼得在馬廄裡替馬裝上馬鞍。

14 confront [kən`frʌnt] *vt.* 使面對

片 be confronted with... 面對……
= be faced with...

▸ What would you do if you were confronted with such a problem?
面對這樣一個難題，你將怎麼做？

confrontation [ˌkɑnfrʌn`teʃən]
n. 對峙；對抗

▸ Mike wanted to avoid confrontation with the bully at school.
邁可想避免在學校對抗這名惡霸。

15 personnel [ˌpɝsṇ`ɛl] *n.* 人員，員工（集合名詞）；人事部

片 the personnel department
人事部

衍 (1) person [`pɝsṇ] *n.* 人 ①
(2) personal [`pɝsṇḷ]
a. 個人的；私人的 ②

似 human resources 人事部

用法 personnel 表『人員，員工』時為集合名詞，指所有的 workers（員工）或 employees（受僱者），視為複數名詞。作主詞時，動詞應使用複數形動詞。

▸ All sales personnel are to be properly trained to increase sales.
所有業務人員均應受到適當的訓練以增加銷售業績。

▸ The personnel department is located on the sixth floor of this building.
人事部位在這棟建築的六樓。

16 distinction [dɪs`tɪŋkʃən] *n.* 卓越（不可數）；區別，差異

片 (1) graduate with distinction
以卓越的成績畢業
(2) a distinction between A and B
A 與 B 之間的差異

衍 distinct [dɪ`stɪŋkt]
a. 清楚的，明顯的；有區別的 ④

似 (1) excellence [`ɛksḷəns] *n.* 卓越 ③
(2) difference [`dɪf(ə)rəns] *n.* 差異 ②

▸ Marvin graduated from Harvard with distinction.
馬文以卓越的成績自哈佛畢業。

▸ There is a clear distinction between Anna and Sherry. The former is outspoken, whereas the latter is tactful.
安娜與雪莉兩人之間有明顯的差異。前者直言不諱，後者則很圓滑。
*outspoken [aut`spokən] *a.* 直言的
tactful [`tæktfəl] *a.* 圓滑的

distinctive [dɪ`stɪŋktɪv]
a. 獨特的，特別的

似 (1) special [`spɛʃəl] *a.* 特別的 ①
(2) unique [ju`nik] *a.* 獨特的 ③
(3) distinguishing [dɪ`stɪŋgwɪʃɪŋ]
a. 顯著的

▸ The policemen of this city wear a distinctive uniform, so they are easily recognized.
該市的警察穿的制服很特別，因此很容易認出來。

0117-0124

17 entitle [ɪnˋtaɪtl̩] *vt.* 給予權利 / 資格；給……命名

片 (1) entitle sb to V　使某人有資格……
(2) be entitled to V　有資格做……
(3) be entitled to sth
有資格獲得某物（此處 to 為介詞）

衍 (1) title [ˋtaɪtl̩] *n.* 頭銜；標題 ②
(2) entitlement [ɪnˋtaɪtl̩mənt]
n. 應得的權利；津貼

▸ Kane's good academic performance in college entitled him to study at a famous graduate school.
大學時期優異的成績使康恩得以在一所知名的研究所深造。

▸ You're not entitled to check out any books from the library unless you're a student of our school.
除非你是本校的學生，否則沒有資格從圖書館借書。

▸ You are entitled to a pension once you reach sixty-five.
你滿 65 歲便有資格支領退休金。

▸ Nick entitled his paper, "Perceptions of Masculinity and Honor in the Gangster Genre."
尼克為他的論文下標題：《在黑幫電影中對男子氣概和榮譽的看法》。

18 rifle [ˋraɪfl̩] *n.* 來福槍，長槍 & *vt.* & *vi.* (尤指為了拿或偷而) 快速翻找

片 rifle through sth　快速翻找某物

似 (1) pistol [ˋpɪstl̩] *n.* 手槍
(2) handgun [ˋhændɡʌn] *n.* 手槍

▸ Rifles are designed to shoot things at long distances.
來福槍被設計為長距離射擊用。

▸ Suzanne rifled the documents on her desk in a desperate search for the important form.
蘇珊在桌上迅速翻找文件，急著想找到那張重要的表格。

▸ The burglar rifled through the drawers, looking for anything valuable.
竊賊快速翻抽屜在找任何有價值的東西。

19 meantime [ˋminˏtaɪm] *n.* & *adv.* 期間

片 (1) in the meantime
同時；在此期間
= in the meanwhile
(2) for the meantime　暫時
= for now

似 meanwhile [ˋminˏ(h)waɪl] *n.* & *adv.* 期間 ③

▸ I'll do the cooking. In the meantime, you can do the laundry.
= I'll do the cooking. Meantime, you can do the laundry.
= I'll do the cooking. Meanwhile, you can do the laundry.
我來煮飯。在此期間，你可以洗衣服。

20 adore [əˋdɔr] *vt.* 喜愛；崇拜

衍 adoration [ˏædəˋreʃən] *n.* 喜愛；崇拜

似 (1) admire [ədˋmaɪr] *vt.* 欣賞 ③
(2) worship [ˋwɝʃɪp] *vt.* 崇拜 ⑤
(3) think highly of...　對……高度讚揚

▸ Aria has 10 grandchildren, and she adores all of them very much.
艾瑞亞有 10 個孫子，每個她都很疼愛。

▸ We adore Connor for his integrity and brilliant academic accomplishments.
我們敬重康納的正直和輝煌的學術成就。

adorable [əˋdorəbḷ]
a. 可愛的，討人喜歡的

似 (1) cute [kjut] *a.* 可愛的 ①
(2) lovable [ˋlʌvəbḷ] *a.* 討人喜歡的

▶ Sadie keeps an adorable little puppy as a pet.
莎蒂養了一隻可愛的小狗當寵物。

21 abortion [əˋbɔrʃən] *n.* 墮胎

片 have / get an abortion
接受流產手術

衍 abort [əˋbɔrt] *vt.* 墮胎；(計畫) 中止

▶ The legislators are discussing whether they should make abortion legal.
立法委員正在討論是否應該將墮胎合法化。

22 barefoot [ˋbɛr͵fut] *a.* 光腳的 & *adv.* 赤著腳地 (= barefooted [ˋbɛr͵futɪd])

片 walk barefoot 光腳走路
= walk barefooted

似 bare [bɛr] *a.* 裸露的 ③

▶ The barefoot boy fell into a pit accidentally.
這光腳的小男孩不小心掉到坑裡去了。

▶ A bunch of kids walked barefoot into the park.
一群小孩光腳走進公園裡。

23 fluency [ˋfluənsɪ] *n.* 流利，流暢

衍 (1) fluent [ˋfluənt] *a.* 流利的 ④
(2) fluently [ˋfluəntlɪ] *adv.* 流利地

▶ The fluency of Andrea's English surprised the visiting foreign guests.
安德雅流利的英文使那些來訪的外賓很驚訝。

24 foul [faul] *a.* 骯髒的；惡劣的 & *vt.* 弄髒 & *n.* & *vt.* & *vi.* 犯規 & *adv.* 違反規則地

片 (1) be in a foul mood 心情很糟
(2) by fair means or foul
不擇手段 (foul 之後省略了 means)
= by hook or by crook
(3) commit a foul 犯規
(4) personal foul
侵人犯規 (籃球術語)
(5) technical foul
技術犯規 (籃球術語)
(6) foul up sth 搞砸某事

▶ Garbage dumps emit a foul smell that is revolting.
垃圾堆散發出的臭味真令人噁心。
*emit [ɪˋmɪt] *vt.* 發出
revolting [rɪˋvoltɪŋ] *a.* 令人噁心的

▶ Peter vowed to attain his goal by fair means or foul.
彼得誓言要不擇手段達到目的。

▶ The company was accused of fouling the environment by dumping its waste in the countryside.
這間公司被指控把廢棄物丟在鄉間而汙染環境。

▶ The player committed another foul and was sent off by the referee.
這名球員再度犯規，被裁判送出場。

▶ Tom lost the ball when he was fouled by the other team's best player.
敵隊最佳球員對湯姆犯規時，他錯失了球。

▶ Once again, the weather has fouled up our plans for the weekend.
天氣又再度破壞了我們週末的計畫。

▶ The coach warned the team that he would not tolerate anyone playing foul.
教練警告球隊，他不容許任何人違反規則。

25 abnormal [æb`nɔrml̩] *a.* 不正常的，異乎尋常的

似 unusual [ʌn`juʒuəl] *a.* 不尋常的
反 normal [`nɔrml̩] *a.* 正常的 ③

▶ John's abnormal behavior can be seen as a sign of mental stress.
約翰異常的行為可視為心理壓力的徵兆。

26 abolish [ə`bɑlɪʃ] *vt.* 廢除

衍 abolishment [ə`bɑlɪʃmənt] *n.* 廢除
似 do away with... 廢除……

▶ The protesters called on the government to abolish the death penalty.
抗議群眾呼籲政府廢除死刑。

27 commentary [`kɑmən͵tɛrɪ] *n.* 評論；(系統性的) 註解；(電視或電臺上的) 解說，實況報導

片 (1) a play-by-play commentary
(球賽的) 現場講評
(2) a running commentary
實況報導
衍 (1) comment [`kɑmɛnt] *n.* 評語，批評 & *vi.* 評論 (與介詞 on 並用) ④
(2) commentate [`kɑmən͵tet]
vi. 評論 (與介詞 on 並用)

▶ This commentary on the election is worth reading.
這則選舉評論值得一讀。

▶ I had no idea what the author was trying to say in this poem until I read the commentaries.
在讀過這些註解前，我不知道作者透過這首詩想表示什麼。

▶ The broadcaster is doing a lousy commentary on the ball game. Let's switch to another channel.
這名播報員的球賽講評有夠爛。我們轉到其他頻道吧。

commentator [`kɑmən͵tetɚ]
n. (電視或電臺的) 評論家，解說員
似 (1) critic [`krɪtɪk] *n.* 評論家 ④
(2) observer [əb`zɝvɚ] *n.* 觀察家 ⑤

▶ Richard used to be a political commentator on an evening news program.
理察曾是一名晚間新聞節目的政治評論家。

28 diplomatic [͵dɪplə`mætɪk] *a.* 外交的；說話圓滑的

片 (1) establish diplomatic relations
建交
(2) break off diplomatic relations
斷交
衍 (1) diplomatically [͵dɪplə`mætɪklɪ]
adv. 外交上；圓滑地
(2) diplomat [`dɪpləmæt]
n. 外交官 ④
(3) diplomacy [dɪ`ploməsɪ]
n. 外交；外交手腕 ⑥

▶ That nation broke off diplomatic relations with the US last Friday.
那個國家上週五和美國斷絕外交關係。

▶ The government official gave a diplomatic response to the reporter's questions.
這名政府官員給了個圓滑的答案回應記者的問題。

29 innovation [ˌɪnəˋveʃən] *n.* 創新 (不可數)

衍 innovate [ˋɪnəˌvet]
vt. & *vi.* 創新，改革

▸ Innovation is the key to success in the fast-changing business world.
在這個瞬息萬變的商場上，創新是成功的關鍵。

innovative [ˋɪnəˌvetɪv] *a.* 創新的
似 creative [krɪˋetɪv] *a.* 有創意的 ③

▸ The manager has come up with an innovative way to cut costs.
經理想到了一種可以降低成本的創新辦法。

30 perceive [pɚˋsiv] *vt.* 察覺；認為

片 perceive A as B　把 A 認為是 B
似 (1) notice [ˋnotɪs] *vt.* 察覺 ①
(2) discern [dɪˋsɝn] *vt.* 察覺

▸ The mother perceived a subtle change in her daughter's behavior.
這位母親察覺到女兒的行為有微妙的變化。

▸ This kind of gossip magazine is often perceived as superficial.
這種八卦雜誌通常被認為很膚淺。
*superficial [ˌsupɚˋfɪʃəl] *a.* 膚淺的

perception [pɚˋsɛpʃən]
n. 感知，感覺 (不可數)；洞察力 (不可數)；觀點 (可數)
衍 (1) perceptive [pɚˋsɛptɪv]
a. 知覺敏銳的
(2) perceptible [pɚˋsɛptəbl̩]
a. 可察覺的

▸ I'm not very good at parking the car because I have a poor sense of perception.
我不太擅長停車，因為我的感知力很差。

▸ Rachel has excellent powers of perception for such a young girl.
對這麼年輕的女孩來說，瑞秋有極佳的洞察力。

▸ My perception of the meaning of life is different from yours.
我對生命意義的觀點和你的不同。

31 proclaim [proˋklem] *vt.* 宣稱；宣布，昭告

片 (1) proclaim that...　宣稱……
(2) proclaim sb (to be) sth
宣告某人為……；表明某人是……
衍 proclamation [ˌprɑkləˋmeʃən]
n. 宣布，公布

▸ The defendant proclaimed that he was innocent of the charges.
被告宣稱他在這些指控中是清白的。

▸ The young prince was proclaimed (to be) king shortly after his father's death.
年輕的王子在父親過世後旋即被宣布為國王。

32 diaper [ˋdaɪ(ə)pɚ] *n.* 尿布 & *vt.* 為……襯尿布

▸ Using cloth diapers is better for the environment than disposable diapers.
使用布尿布要比免洗尿布環保。

▸ Help me diaper the baby, will you?
幫我替寶寶包尿布，好嗎？

Unit 02

0201-0207

1 maintenance [ˋmentənəns] *n.* 維持；維修，保養（皆不可數）

片 (1) car maintenance
汽車維修 / 保養
(2) a maintenance fee / worker / check 維修費 / 工人 / 檢查

衍 maintain [menˋten]
vt. 維持；維修，保養 ②

▸ This organization is responsible for the maintenance of international peace.
維持世界和平是這個組織的責任。

▸ A thorough maintenance check had been carried out before the plane took off.
該班機起飛前先進行了一次徹底的維修檢查。

2 substantial [səbˋstænʃəl] *a.* 大量的；堅固的

片 a substantial meal / house
令人飽餐的一頓飯 / 一棟堅固的房子

衍 (1) substance [ˋsʌbstəns]
n. 物質；本質 ③
(2) substantially [səbˋstænʃəlɪ]
adv. 相當多地

似 considerable [kənˋsɪdərəbḷ]
a. 相當多 / 大的 ③

▸ Nowadays, you can earn a substantial amount of income by selling goods online.
現在，你可以藉由上網賣東西賺取大筆收入。

▸ The building is substantial enough to withstand a direct hit from a tornado.
這棟建築物夠堅固，足以抵擋龍捲風的直接侵襲。
*withstand [wɪðˋstænd] *vt.* 抵擋
tornado [tɔrˋnedo] *n.* 龍捲風

3 prospect [ˋprɑspɛkt] *n.* 可能（性）；前途（常用複數）& *vi.* 探勘（黃金、礦物等）

片 prospect for sth 探勘某物

衍 (1) prospective [prəˋspɛktɪv]
a. 預期的 ⑥
(2) prospecting [ˋprɑspɛktɪŋ]
n. 探勘
oil prospecting 石油探勘

似 (1) possibility [ˌpɑsəˋbɪlətɪ]
n. 可能性 ②
(2) probability [ˌprɑbəˋbɪlətɪ]
n. 可能性

▸ Ned looks forward to the prospect of being admitted to his favorite college.
奈德期待能獲得錄取就讀他最喜歡的大學。

▸ This four-day course is designed to improve your career prospects.
這個為期 4 天的課程設計的目的就是要讓你在職場更有前途。

▸ The economic depression of the 1930s saw a huge increase in people prospecting for gold in the US.
美國三〇年代的經濟大蕭條，想要探勘黃金的人大幅增加。

4 justify [ˋdʒʌstəˌfaɪ] *vt.* 證明……是合理的，使合理化

三 justify, justified [ˋdʒʌstəfaɪd], justified

片 justify oneself 為自己的行為做解釋

衍 (1) just [dʒʌst] *a.* 公正的 ①
(2) justice [ˋdʒʌstɪs] *n.* 公平 ②

▸ The ends justify the means.
結果能使手段合理化 / 為達目的不擇手段。—— 諺語

▸ I can't justify taking a day off to stand in line for a magic show.
請一天假去排隊看魔術表演，我不認為這樣做是有道理的。

(3) justified [ˋdʒʌstəfaɪd]
a. 有正當理由的；情有可原的
be justified in + V-ing
做……是合理的

▸ The boy was too naughty, so his dad was justified in punishing him.
這孩子太過調皮，因此他老爸處罰他是有道理的。

▸ I do not have to justify myself to you. Just do as you are told!
我沒必要向你解釋。你只要聽話照做就對了！

justification [ˏdʒʌstəfəˋkeʃən]
n. 正當的理由（與介詞 for 並用）

似 (1) reason [ˋrizṇ] *n.* 原因 ①
(2) excuse [ɪkˋskjuz] *n.* 理由，藉口 ②

▸ There is no justification at all for killing animals to make fur coats.
為了做毛外套而殺害動物，這種做法根本沒有道理。

5 contemporary [kənˋtɛmpəˏrɛrɪ] *a.* 現代的；同時期的 & *n.* 同時期的人

片 (1) contemporary art / music / dance / literature
當代藝術 / 音樂 / 舞蹈 / 文學
(2) a contemporary of sb/sb's
和某人是同時期的人

似 modern [ˋmɑdɚn] *a.* 現代的 ①

反 ancient [ˋenʃənt] *a.* 古代的 ②

▸ Although it was built a long time ago, the bridge still has a little contemporary touch.
雖然這座橋是很久以前建造的，它還是有一點現代化的風格在裡面。

▸ Nearly all of the contemporary accounts of the battle suggested that the outcome was unavoidable.
幾乎所有關於這場戰役同時期的報導都暗指著這樣的結果是無可避免的。

▸ Christopher Marlowe was a contemporary of William Shakespeare's.
克里斯多夫．馬羅和威廉．莎士比亞是同時代的人。

6 league [lig] *n.* 聯盟 & *vi.* 結盟；聯合

似 (1) union [ˋjunjən] *n.* 聯盟 ③
(2) association [əˏsosɪˋeʃən] *n.* 聯盟 ④
(3) alliance [əˋlaɪəns] *n.* 聯盟 ⑤
(4) federation [ˏfɛdəˋreʃən] *n.* 聯盟

▸ The baseball league is seeking corporate sponsors to help weather its financial difficulties.
棒球聯盟正在尋求企業贊助來協助他們度過財務困難。
*weather [ˋwɛðɚ] *vt.* 度過（困難）

▸ The two parties leagued together to ensure that the important bill passed unopposed.
兩黨結盟以確保該重要法案能在無人反對下通過。

7 notion [ˋnoʃən] *n.* 想法，見解；一時興起的想法

片 (1) have a clear / vague notion of...
對……有清楚 / 模糊的概念
(2) have a notion to V 突然想做……

似 idea [aɪˋdɪə] *n.* 想法 ①

▸ I reject the notion that greed motivates people.
貪婪能給人動力，這種想法我不接受。

▸ I missed a few key points, so I only had a vague notion of what the professor had just said.
我錯過了幾個重點，因此教授剛才說的話我不甚清楚。

▸ Trevor had a notion to ask the girl out, but he got cold feet at the last minute.
崔佛**突然**想約那個女孩出去，但他在最後一刻臨陣退縮了。
*get cold feet　臨陣退縮

8 alter [ˋɔltɚ] *vt.* & *vi.* 改變 & *vt.* 修改（衣服）

片 have / get + 衣物 + altered
把某衣物拿去修改（使其更合身）

似 (1) altar [ˋɔltɚ] *n.* 祭壇
(2) change [tʃendʒ] *vt.* 改變 ①

▸ The internet has altered the way we seek information.
網路已**改變**了我們尋找資訊的方式。

▸ No matter how many years go by, my love for you will never alter.
無論過了多少年，我對你的愛永遠不會**變**。

▸ I need to have the pants altered to fit me well.
我得**把**這條褲子**拿去修改**，好合我的身。

---

alteration [͵ɔltəˋreʃən]
n. 改變；改動，修改

片 make alterations to sth　修改某物

似 change [tʃendʒ] *n.* 改變 ①

▸ The pants didn't fit, so I took them to the tailor for alterations.
這條長褲不合身，所以我把它拿去裁縫師那兒**修改**。

▸ The secretary made some alterations to the document to make it better.
祕書**修改**這份文件讓它變得更好。

9 supreme [səˋprim] *a.* 至高無上的；最大程度的

片 the supreme court　最高法院

延伸 the district court　地方法院

▸ The Constitution endows the President with supreme authority.
憲法賦予總統**至高無上的**權力。
*endow [ɪnˋdaʊ] sb with sth　賦予某人某物

▸ Joe made a supreme effort to lose weight, but in vain.
喬盡了**最大的**努力去減肥，卻徒勞無功。

10 execute [ˋɛksɪ͵kjut] *vt.* 執行；處死

片 (1) execute a plan　執行 / 實行計畫
(2) execute sb for sth
因某事處死某人
= sb be executed for sth

似 carry out　執行

▸ Make sure our plan to reduce costs is executed with great precision.
務必確定我們降低成本的計畫被精確**執行**。

▸ The soldier was executed on the spot for treason.
這名士兵因為叛國罪而當場被**處死**。
*treason [ˋtrizn̩] *n.* 叛國罪

---

executive [ɪgˋzɛkjutɪv]
a. 執行的；行政的 & *n.* 主管

片 (1) chief executive officer
首席執行長（縮寫為 CEO）

▸ The executive committee consists of the directors of the company.
執行委員會由該公司的董事組成。

(2) the executive power 行政權
(3) the executive （政府的）行政部門

▸ Marian is working as senior executive in a computer firm now.
瑪麗安現在正在一家電腦公司擔任資深**主管**。

execution [ˌɛksɪˋkjuʃən]
n. 執行，實行；處決

片 put sth into execution
執 / 實行某事

似 (1) implementation
[ˌɪmpləmɛnˋteʃən] *n.* 履行，執行
(2) capital punishment 死刑

▸ The execution of this plan requires a large amount of time and money.
執行這項計畫需要大量的時間和金錢。

▸ The execution of the murderer will be carried out tomorrow morning.
這位殺人犯的**處決**將於明天早上進行。

11 submit [səbˋmɪt] *vt.* 遞交 & *vi.* 屈服，服從

三 submit, submitted [səbˋmɪtɪd], submitted

片 (1) submit sth to sb
遞交某物給某人
(2) submit to... 向……屈服
= yield to...
= surrender to...
= succumb to...
= give in to...

▸ It's a requirement that all applicants submit their resumes to the personnel manager no later than October 1st.
依規定，所有求職者最晚在 10 月 1 號以前要**向**人事經理**遞交**履歷表。

▸ John refused to submit to the school bully.
約翰拒絕**向**那名學校惡霸**低頭**。

submission [sʌbˋmɪʃən]
n. 屈服，投降

片 force / starve sb into submission
迫使某人屈服 / 讓某人餓到投降

似 surrender [səˋrɛndɚ]
n. 屈服，投降 ④

▸ The strategy of siege warfare is to starve your enemy into submission.
包圍戰的策略就是**讓**敵軍**餓到投降**。
*siege warfare [sidʒ ˋwɔrˏfɛr] 包圍戰

submissive [sʌbˋmɪsɪv]
a. 服從的，順從的

片 (1) a submissive person 溫順的人
(2) be submissive to... 服從……
= be obedient to...

似 obedient [əˋbidjənt] *a.* 服從的 ④

▸ James does everything that his wife asks of him; he is quite submissive to her.
老婆向他要求什麼詹姆士都照辦；他**對**她**言聽計從**。

12 estate [ɪsˋtet] *n.* 地產；資產，財產

片 (1) real estate 房地產
(2) a real estate agent 房仲

▸ By investing in real estate, Tom made a huge fortune.
湯姆投資**房地產**賺翻了。

0212-0218

似 property [ˋprɑpɚtɪ] *n.* 房地產；財產 ③

▸ Upon the singer's death, his estate was worth in excess of one billion dollars.
這名歌手去世後，他的財產價值超過 10 億元。

13 interior [ɪnˋtɪrɪɚ] *a.* 內部的 & *n.* 內部

片 interior design 室內設計

似 (1) inside [ɪnˋsaɪd] *a.* 裡面的 ①
(2) internal [ɪnˋtɝnḷ] *a.* 內部的 ②
(3) inner [ˋɪnɚ] *a.* 內部的 ③

▸ The interior walls of the building were painted white.
這棟建築物的內牆被漆成白色的。

▸ The car's interior is very comfortable. It's equipped with leather seats.
這輛車的內部很舒適。它配有皮製座椅。

---

exterior [ɪkˋstɪrɪɚ]
a. 外部的 & *n.* 外部；外表

似 (1) outside [aʊtˋsaɪd] *a.* 外部的 ①
(2) outer [ˋaʊtɚ] *a.* 外面的 ③
(3) external [ɪkˋstɝnḷ] *a.* 外部的 ⑤
(4) appearance [əˋpɪrəns] *n.* 外表 ②

▸ The exterior walls of the building are made of glass and steel.
這棟建築物的外牆是由玻璃和鋼鐵搭建而成。

▸ The exterior of the house needs painting.
這間房子的外部需要油漆粉刷了。

▸ Underneath that pleasant and gentle exterior, Jane is actually quite ruthless.
在珍親切和藹的外表下，她其實很無情。
*ruthless [ˋruθləs] *a.* 無情的

14 scheme [skim] *vt.* & *vi.* 策劃，密謀 & *n.* 詭計，陰謀

片 (1) scheme to V 密謀要……
= plot to V
(2) scheme against... 密謀對抗……

似 plot [plɑt]
vt. & *vi.* 策劃，密謀 & *n.* 陰謀 ④

▸ Kevin has been scheming to get that promotion since the day he joined the firm.
自凱文進公司的那天起，他就一直想辦法要奪得那個位置。

▸ The finance minister has been scheming against the prime minister for months now.
財政部長密謀對抗總理已數個月了。

▸ The company owner was fined for an illegal scheme to avoid paying taxes.
這家公司的老闆因為非法圖謀逃漏稅而被罰款。

15 partly [ˋpɑrtlɪ] *adv.* 部分地

衍 (1) part [pɑrt] *n.* 部分 ①
(2) partial [ˋpɑrʃəl]
a. 偏心的；部分的 ④
(3) partially [ˋpɑrʃəlɪ]
adv. 部分地；偏袒地

片 entirely [ɪnˋtaɪrlɪ] *adv.* 完全地

用法 partly 常與 because of 或 due to 並用。

▸ I didn't enjoy the trip very much partly because of the bad weather.
我不太喜歡這次旅行，部分是因為壞天氣。

16 purchase [ˋpɝtʃəs] *vt.* & *n.* 購買

片 purchase sth　購買某物
= make a purchase of sth
= buy sth

▸ I purchased some face masks and hand sanitizer at the store.
= I made a purchase of some face masks and hand sanitizer at the store.
= I bought some face masks and hand sanitizer at the store.
我在店裡買了些口罩和乾洗手。
*hand sanitizer [ˋsænəˏtaɪzɚ]　乾洗手

▸ You need proof of purchase to claim a refund.
你需要**購買**證明才能要求退款。

17 cite [saɪt] *vt.* 引用；引……為證

片 cite A as B　引用 A 為 B 的例證
衍 citation [saɪˋteʃən] *n.* 引用

▸ The author cited a passage from Lincoln's Gettysburg speech in her new book.
這位作者在她的新書中引用了林肯蓋茨堡演說中的一段。

▸ Marcus cited his heavy workload as the main reason for his resignation.
= Marcus referred to his heavy workload as the main reason for his resignation.
馬可斯**指出**龐大的工作量**就是**他辭職的主因。

18 proportion [prəˋpɔrʃən] *n.* 比例；部分 & *vt.* 使成比例

片 (1) the proportion of A to B
A 和 B 的比例
(2) be in proportion to...
與……成比例
(3) be out of proportion with...
和……不成比例
(4) be proportioned to...
與……成比例
衍 (1) proportional [prəˋpɔrʃənl̩]
a. 成比例的
(2) proportionate [prəˋpɔrʃənet]
vt. 使成比例

▸ The proportion of boys to girls at the elementary school is about three to one.
這所小學的男生和女生的比例大約是 3 比 1。

▸ In this picture, the head is out of proportion with the body.
在這幅圖畫裡，頭和身體**不成比例**。

▸ Women and children make up a large proportion of the population in this village.
這個村莊內女人和小孩的數量占了人口的很大一部分。

▸ The amount of your bonus is proportioned to the number of sales you make.
你的獎金**和**你的銷售量**成正比**。

---

ratio [ˋreʃo] *n.* 比例
片 the ratio of A to B　A 和 B 的比例
似 percentage [pɚˋsɛntɪdʒ]
n. 比例；百分比 ④

▸ What is the ratio of men to women in your department?
你們部門男、女性的比例是多少？

19 yield [jild] *vt.* 出產；讓出 & *vi.* 屈服 & *n.* (農作物等的) 產量；收益，利潤

片 (1) yield sth to sb　讓出某物給某人
(2) yield to...　屈服於……
= submit to...
= surrender to...
= succumb to...
= give in to...

似 produce [prəˋd(j)us] *vt.* 生產 ②

▸ I believe this investment should yield a reasonable return.
我相信這項投資會**產生**合理的收益。

▸ Please yield your seat to elderly, pregnant, or disabled passengers.
請把你的座位**讓給**年老、懷孕、行動不便的乘客。

▸ Carlos is a man of strong character; he never yields to threats.
卡洛士的個性堅強，他從來不會**屈服於**威脅。

▸ Due to the long, dry summer, our yield of olives increased greatly this year.
由於今年漫長又乾燥的夏季，我們橄欖的**產量**巨幅增加。

▸ Investing in this company involves a greater risk but should lead to a higher yield.
投資這間公司涉及很大的風險，但應該會帶來更高的**收益**。

20 hence [hɛns] *adv.* 因此

似 (1) therefore [ˋðɛr,fɔr] *adv.* 因此 ②
(2) consequently [ˋkɑnsə,kwɛntlɪ] *adv.* 因此
(3) as a result　因此

▸ Charles didn't study hard. Hence, he failed the test.
查爾斯沒有用功念書。**因此**，他考試不及格。

21 prevail [prɪˋvel] *vi.* 勝過；普遍，盛行

片 (1) prevail over / against sth
勝過某事物
(2) prevail in / among...
在……很普遍 / 盛行
(3) prevail on / upon sb to V
說服某人做……
= persuade sb to V

▸ Our school basketball team prevailed over their rivals in a tough game.
我們的籃球校隊在一場艱困的比賽中**戰勝了**對手。

▸ Those kinds of superstitions still prevail in certain areas.
那種迷信在某些地區還是**很普遍**。

▸ Tom's mother prevailed on him to finish college before getting a job.
湯姆的母親**說服**他完成大學學業再找工作。

prevailing [prɪˋvelɪŋ]
a. 普遍的，盛行的

▸ The prevailing opinion is that the economy will not rebound until the fourth quarter.
普遍的看法為要一直到第四季經濟才會重振。
*rebound [rɪˋbaʊnd] *vi.* 重新振作

22 overall [ˋovɚ͵ɔl] *a.* 全部的 & *adv.* 總體上 & *n.* (連身) 工作褲 (恆為複數)

片 a pair of overalls　一件連身工作褲

似 entire [ɪnˋtaɪr] *a.* 全部的 ②

▸ The principal thought that the overall result of the exams was quite satisfactory.
校長認為考試**整體**結果是很令人滿意的。

▸ Overall, imports account for half of our economy.
= In general, imports account for half of our economy.
大體而言，進口貿易占了我們一半的經濟。

▸ I thought John was wearing overalls to protect his clothes, but it turns out they were a fashion statement.
我以為約翰穿**連身工作褲**來保護他的衣服，但結果那只是一種時尚。
*a fashion statement　(宣揚個人的) 時尚主張

23 awe [ɔ] *n.* 敬畏 & *vt.* 使敬畏

片 (1) hold sb in awe　令某人敬畏
(2) be in awe of...　對……感到敬畏

衍 awed [ɔd] *a.* 充滿敬畏的

▸ The spectacular view of the valley really held me in awe.
山谷的壯麗景色實在**令我震懾**。

▸ I was often in awe of my grandmother when I was little.
我還小的時候常**對**祖母**感到敬畏**。

▸ Maya's confidence and beauty awe me; I wish I could be like her.
瑪雅的自信和美麗**使我震懾**；我希望我能像她一樣。

24 barren [ˋbærən] *a.* 荒蕪的；(女性) 不孕的

似 (1) infertile [ɪnˋfɝtḷ] *a.* 不孕的
(2) sterile [ˋstɛrəl] *a.* 不孕的

反 fertile [ˋfɝtḷ] *a.* 肥沃的；能生育的 ④

▸ We just drove through a barren desert with no plants in it.
我們剛開車經過一片沒有植物的**貧脊**沙漠。

▸ Judy had learned early in her marriage that she was barren.
茱蒂結婚後不久便得知她**不能生育**。

25 vendor [ˋvɛndɚ] *n.* 小販

似 peddler [ˋpɛdlɚ] *n.* 小販

▸ On Saturday nights, this famous night market is always crowded with vendors and shoppers.
每逢星期六夜晚，這個知名夜市總是擠滿了**攤販**和購物者。

26 scenario [sɪˋnɛrɪ͵o] *n.* 可能發生的情景 / 局面

片 a best-case / worst-case scenario
最好 / 壞的情況

▸ During the job interview, Tim was asked how he would solve problems in several difficult scenarios.
提姆在工作面試時，被問及面臨幾種困難的**情形**時他會如何解決問題。

27 sophisticated [sə`fɪstə,ketɪd] *a.* 世故的，圓滑的；(機器、系統) 精密的

似 advanced [əd`væːnst] *a.* 先進的 ③

▸ Even sophisticated diplomats may have trouble dealing with that problem.
即使是精明老練的外交官處理這個問題也會有困難。

▸ This machine is very sophisticated. Therefore, it should only be run by professionals.
這臺機器很精密。所以最好由專業人士來操作。

naïve [nɑ`iv] *a.* 天真的
似 innocent [`ɪnəsn̩t]
a. 天真的；無罪的 ③

▸ Don't be so naïve as to believe what Joseph said!
別天真到相信喬瑟夫說的話！

28 attribute [ə`trɪbjut ] *vt.* 將……歸因於 & [ `ætrə,bjut] *n.* 特質，特性

片 attribute A to B　將 A 歸因於 B
= ascribe A to B
似 quality [`kwɑlətɪ] *n.* 特質 ②

▸ Terry attributes his success to hard work and a little bit of luck.
泰瑞將他的成功歸因於努力以及一絲運氣。

▸ Organizational ability is the most important attribute for a good manager.
組織能力是稱職的經理所需具備最重要的特質。

29 transit [`trænsɪt] *n.* 運輸 (不可數) & *vt.* 通過

片 (1) in transit　運送途中
(2) the mass / public transit system　大眾 / 公共運輸系統

▸ My brother made an insurance claim for his luggage that was lost in transit.
我哥的行李在運送途中遺失了，所以他去申請了保險理賠。

▸ The ship is currently transiting the Panama Canal and will arrive in five hours.
這艘船現正通過巴拿馬運河且將在五小時後抵達。

transition [træn`zɪʃən] *n.* 轉變
片 (1) the transition from A to B
從 A 轉變為 B
(2) be in transition　正在轉變
衍 transitional [træn`zɪʃənl̩]
a. 轉變的，過渡的

▸ The transition from high school to college can be difficult for students.
從高中到大學的轉變對學生而言可能很難適應。

▸ The country is in transition as it adapts to a new system of government.
這個國家正在轉型，因為它正在適應新的政府體制。

30 unprecedented [ʌn`prɛsə,dɛntɪd] *a.* 史無前例的

▸ The mayor was elected for an unprecedented fourth term.
這位市長於第 4 屆連任選舉中獲勝是史無前例的。

31 whatsoever [ˌ(h)watsoˋɛvɚ] *adv.* 無論怎樣

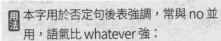

用法 本字用於否定句後表強調，常與 no 並用，語氣比 whatever 強：

no + N + whatsoever

一點點……都沒有

▸ I have no money whatsoever to lend you.

我沒有一點錢可以借你。

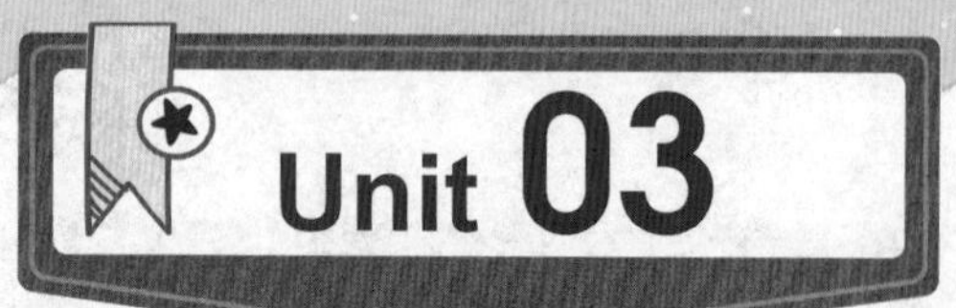

0301-0305

1 bureau [ˋbjʊro] *n.* (政府機構的) 局，處；辦事處，聯絡處

複 bureaus (美) / bureaux [ˋbjʊroz] (英)

片 (1) the Tourism Bureau
交通部觀光局
(2) the Federal Bureau of Investigation
美國聯邦調查局 (簡稱 FBI)
(3) an employment bureau
求職介紹所

似 agency [ˋedʒənsɪ] *n.* 局 ④

▶ Mrs. Jones reported her son's disappearance to the Missing Persons Bureau of the Los Angeles Police Department.
瓊斯太太把她兒子失蹤的事通報給洛杉磯警察局失蹤人口處。

bureaucracy [bjʊˋrɑkrəsɪ]
n. 官僚制；繁文縟節 (不可數)

衍 (1) bureaucrat [ˋbjʊrə͵kræt]
n. 官僚；官僚主義者 ⑥
(2) bureaucratic [͵bjʊrəˋkrætɪk]
a. 官僚主義的

似 red tape 繁文縟節，繁瑣手續

▶ My visa application is tied up in red tape at the embassy.
我的簽證申請因為繁瑣手續還卡在大使館。

▶ When Johnson applied for his business license, the amount of government bureaucracy frustrated him.
強森申請營業執照時，政府的**繁瑣程序**令他感到氣餒。

▶ We should do everything we can to reduce bureaucracy in our company.
我們應竭盡所能減少公司內部的**繁文縟節**。

2 categorize [ˋkætəgə͵raɪz] *vt.* 將……分類

片 (1) be categorized as...
被歸類為……
= be classified as...
(2) be categorized into A and B
被區分為 A 和 B
= be classified into A and B

衍 (1) category [ˋkætə͵gorɪ]
n. 種類；範疇 ④
(2) categorization [͵kætəgəraɪˋzeʃən]
n. 分類

似 classify [ˋklæsə͵faɪ] *vt.* 將……分類 ④

▶ The author's latest work cannot be categorized as a novel.
這位作者最新的作品不能**被歸類為**小說。

▶ The participants in this study are categorized into adult and teenage groups.
這項研究的參加者**被區分成**成人組和青少年組。

3 massive [ˋmæsɪv] *a.* 巨大的；大量的

衍 (1) mass [mæs] *n.* 團，塊；大量 ②
(2) massiveness [ˋmæsɪvnəs] *n.* 巨大

似 (1) huge [hjudʒ] *a.* 巨大的 ②
(2) gigantic [dʒaɪˋgæntɪk] *a.* 巨大的 ④
(3) immense [ɪˋmɛns] *a.* 巨大的 ⑤

▸ The bookstore was massive, with five floors, two coffee shops, and thousands of books.
這間書店很大，有五層樓、兩間咖啡店及數千本書。

▸ The typhoon caused a massive increase in vegetable prices.
颱風造成了蔬菜價格暴漲。

4 extension [ɪkˋstɛnʃən] *n.* 擴大；延期；伸展；(電話) 分機

衍 extend [ɪkˋstɛnd] *vt.* & *vi.* 延長；延期 ④

似 (1) increase [ˋɪnkris] *n.* & [ɪnˋkris] *vt.* & *vi.* 增加 ②
(2) expansion [ɪkˋspænʃən] *n.* 擴大 ④
(3) enlargement [ɪnˋlɑrdʒmənt] *n.* 擴大 ④
(4) delay [dɪˋle] *n.* 延遲 ②
(5) postponement [postˋponmənt] *n.* 延期 ③

▸ When the extension to the subway system is completed, it will stretch to the edge of the city.
地鐵擴建完成後，將會延伸到城市的邊緣地區。

▸ Can I request an extension on the deadline to submit my thesis paper?
我可否要求延長繳交論文報告的截稿期限呢？

▸ Due to his injury, full extension of his left arm was impossible for Mark.
由於馬克受傷，他的左手臂要完全伸展是不太可能的。

▸ Call our main number at 1122-3344, and ask for my office extension, 21.
打我們的主機號碼 1122-3344，並要求轉接我辦公室的分機號碼 21。

extensive [ɪkˋstɛnsɪv]
a. 廣泛的；大量的

似 (1) comprehensive [ˏkɑmprɪˋhɛnsɪv] *a.* 廣泛的 ⑥
(2) considerable [kənˋsɪdərəbḷ] *a.* 相當多的 ③
(3) substantial [səbˋstænʃəl] *a.* 大量的 ⑤

▸ Professor Johnson possessed extensive knowledge in the field of natural science.
強森教授在自然科學的領域擁有廣泛的知識。

▸ The typhoon has caused extensive damage to the city.
這次的颱風對這座城市已造成極大的損害。

5 versus [ˋvɝsəs] *prep.* 對抗 (縮寫為 vs.)

▸ The Foreman vs. Ali fight was one of the best in boxing history.
福爾曼對抗阿里之戰是拳擊史上最精彩的拳賽之一。

0306-0310

6 strain [stren] *n.* & *vt.* & *vi.* 拉緊 & *n.* 緊張，壓力 & *n.* & *vt.* (肌肉) 拉傷，損傷 & *vt.* 盡力

片 (1) be under (the) strain
在拉力 / 緊張狀態下
(2) face the stresses and strains
面對緊張和壓力
(3) (a) muscle strain 肌肉拉傷
(4) strain to V 盡力去做……
(5) strain one's eyes
某人盡力睜眼，費力去看

似 sprain [spren]
n. & *vt.* 扭傷 (手腕、腳踝)
▸ Grant sprained his ankles while playing basketball.
葛藍特打籃球時扭傷了腳踝。

▸ Although strong, bones will break if placed under enough strain.
骨頭雖然硬，但若拉力夠大骨頭還是會斷掉的。

▸ The rope strained to pull the heavy weight so much that it finally broke.
繩子拉重物拉得過緊，導致它最後斷掉了。

▸ The editors are under great strain because the deadline is approaching.
編輯們因為截稿期限快到了，所以現在很緊張。

▸ Reading in low light can put an uncomfortable strain on a person's eyes.
在昏暗的燈光下閱讀可能會給人的眼睛造成不舒服的損害。

▸ Jason strained a muscle in his back carrying those heavy boxes.
傑森因為搬了那些很重的箱子而拉傷某塊背肌。

▸ I strained my eyes to read those tiny words on the blackboard.
我竭盡眼力想把黑板上的小字唸出來。

7 legislation [ˌlɛdʒɪsˋleʃən] *n.* 立法 (程序)；法規 (皆不可數)

衍 (1) legislate [ˋlɛdʒɪsˏlet] *vi.* 立法
(2) legislator [ˋlɛdʒɪsˏletɚ]
n. 立法委員 ⑥
(3) legislature [ˋlɛdʒɪsˏletʃɚ]
n. 立法機關

似 (1) lawmaking [ˋlɔˏmekɪŋ] *n.* 立法
(2) regulation [ˏrɛgjəˋleʃən]
n. 規定，規則 ④

▸ Legislation of a new trade agreement will be difficult and will take time.
新貿易協定的立法程序會很困難且耗時。

▸ The new legislation on abortion will be enacted next year.
有關墮胎的新法規將於明年制定。
*enact [ɪnˋækt] *vt.* 制定 (法案)

---

legislative [ˋlɛdʒɪsˏletɪv] *a.* 立法的

片 the Legislative Yuan 立法院

延伸 (1) the Executive Yuan 行政院
(2) the Control Yuan 監察院
(3) the Judicial Yuan 司法院
(4) the Examination Yuan 考試院

▸ Congress is a legislative branch of the US government.
國會是美國政府的立法部門。

---

lawmaker [ˋlɔˏmekɚ] *n.* 立法者

衍 lawmaking [ˋlɔˏmekɪŋ] *n.* 立法

似 legislator [ˋlɛdʒɪsˏletɚ] *n.* 立法委員 ⑥

▸ The Cancer Society joined the lawmakers' efforts to pass the smoking ban.
癌症協會與立委共同努力要促成該禁菸法案的通過。

8 specialist [ˋspɛʃəlɪst] *n.* 專家（與介詞 in 並用）

片 a specialist in... 在……方面的專家

衍 special [ˋspɛʃəl] *a.* 特別的 ①

似 expert [ˋɛkspɝt] *n.* 專家 ②

▶ Dr. Nilson is a specialist in contemporary linguistics.
尼爾森博士是位當代語言學的專家。
*linguistics [lɪŋˋgwɪstɪks] *n.* 語言學

specialize [ˋspɛʃəl,aɪz] *vi.* 專攻

片 specialize in... 專攻／專門從事……

▶ Professor Lee specializes in English sentence structure analysis.
李教授專精於英文句構分析。

▶ That Chinese restaurant specializes in Sichuan cuisine.
那家中式餐廳專賣四川菜。

specialty [ˋspɛʃəltɪ] *n.* 專長；名產
（= speciality〔英〕）

似 strength [strɛŋθ] *n.* 長處

▶ Truffle risotto is the chef's specialty.
松露燉飯是這位廚師的專長。
*truffle [ˋtrʌfl] *n.* 松露
risotto [rɪˋsɔto] *n.* 義式燉飯

▶ Pineapple cake is a Taiwanese specialty.
鳳梨酥是臺灣名產。

9 resume [rɪˋzum] *vt.* & *vi.* 重新開始 & *vt.* 重返

片 (1) resume + N/V-ing 重新開始……
(2) resume one's seat
某人重新回到位子上

▶ The speaker paused for a moment to take a sip of water and then resumed speaking.
講者停頓了一下喝口水，接著就繼續開始發表談話。

▶ For a while, Josh appeared to be satisfied, but later his complaining resumed.
喬許似乎心滿意足了一下子，但他接著又繼續抱怨。

▶ The show will continue in just a few minutes, so please resume your seats.
表演將於幾分鐘之後繼續，所以請諸位回到位子上。

resumé [ˋrɛzə,me] *n.* 履歷表
（亦可寫作 resume 或 résumé）

▶ To apply for this job, please send your resumé to our personnel department.
要應徵這份工作，請你將履歷表寄到本公司人事部。

10 enterprise [ˋɛntɚ,praɪz] *n.* 企業

片 (1) a public / private enterprise
公／私營企業
(2) small and medium-sized enterprises
中小型企業

▶ The tax reduction policy is aimed at helping small and medium-sized enterprises.
這項減稅政策旨在幫助中小型企業。

entrepreneur [ˌantrəprəˋnɝ]
n. 企業家

似 businessman [ˋbɪznəsmən]
n. 企業家 ②

▸ The entrepreneur started his own business selling beauty products.
這名企業家自行創業販賣美容產品。

11 observer [əbˋzɝvɚ] *n.* 觀察員

衍 (1) observe [əbˋzɝv]
vt. 觀察；注意到；遵行；慶祝 ③
(2) observation [ˌabzɝˋveʃən]
n. 觀察 ④
(3) observatory [əbˋzɝvəˌtorɪ]
n. 天文臺

▸ The United Nations sent a team of observers to monitor the progress of the peace talks.
聯合國派遣了一組觀察員前往監控和談的進展。

12 index [ˋɪndɛks] *n.* 索引；指數，指標 & *vt.* 為……編索引

複 indexes [ˋɪndɛksɪs] / indices [ˋɪndəˌsiz]

片 (1) the Dow Jones index　道瓊指數
(2) an index finger　食指

似 indicator [ˋɪndəˌketɚ] *n.* 指標

▸ You can search the library database for author and title indexes.
你可以到該圖書館的資料庫裡查詢作者和書名的索引。

▸ The economic indices in this magazine suggest that the economy is recovering.
雜誌裡的幾項經濟指標顯示經濟正在復甦。

▸ The photographer has indexed thousands of photographs according to subject and date.
這名攝影師依主題和日期為數千張照片編索引。

13 residence [ˋrɛzədəns] *n.* 住宅；居住 (不可數)；合法居住資格 (不可數)

片 (1) a three-story residence
三層樓的住宅
(2) a place of residence　居住地
(3) permanent residence
永久居留權

衍 reside [rɪˋzaɪd]
vi. 居住 (與介詞 in 並用) ⑥

似 residency [ˋrɛzədənsɪ] *n.* 居住

▸ The White House is the official residence of the President of the United States.
白宮是美國總統的官方住所。

▸ Please write down the address of your current place of residence on the form.
請在此表格上寫下你現行居住地的地址。

▸ Since Johnny had committed crimes in the past, he was refused residence in the foreign country.
由於強尼過去曾犯罪，外國拒絕讓他定居。

resident [ˋrɛzədənt]
n. 居民；住院醫生 & *a.* 居住的

片 (1) a (legal) resident of...
……的 (合法) 居民

▸ After visiting Canada, Tim hoped that one day he could become a resident of that country.
提姆到訪加拿大後，希望有一天能成為該國的居民。

(2) a foreign resident 外國定居者
(3) be resident in... 居住於

▶ Julia is a first-year resident in pediatrics at Boston Hospital.
茱莉亞是在波士頓醫院服務第一年的小兒科**住院醫生**。
*pediatrics [ˌpidɪˋætrɪks] *n.* 小兒科

▶ Susan has been resident in Germany since she was a teenager.
蘇珊自青少年時就一直**居住在**德國。

residential [ˌrɛzəˋdɛnʃəl]
a. 居住的，住宅的

片 a residential area 住宅區

▶ We're against the proposal of changing a section of the national park into a residential area.
我們反對將國家公園的某一部分改建為**住宅**區的提案。

14 prior [ˋpraɪɚ] *a.* 在前的；優先的 & *adv.* 在前 & *n.* 修道院副院長

片 prior to... 在……之前
= before...

衍 priority [praɪˋɔrətɪ] *n.* 優先考慮的事（可數）；優先權（不可數）④

似 previous [ˋprivɪəs] *a.* 先前的 ③

▶ No prior knowledge of Spanish is required for the course.
修這堂課你不必**先**具備任何關於西班牙語的知識。

▶ Make sure you have the report ready prior to the meeting.
務必確定你**在**會議**之前**要把報告準備好。

▶ After many years of service in the church, Benedict was promoted to the position of prior.
班尼迪克在教會服務多年後，他的職位被提升為**副院長**。

15 setting [ˋsɛtɪŋ] *n.* 環境；背景

似 background [ˋbækˌgraʊnd]
n. 背景 ③

▶ The company decided a beach resort was an ideal setting for its annual meeting.
該公司決定濱海度假村會是他們年度會議的理想**環境**。

▶ Nancy rewrote a scene from *Romeo and Juliet* with a contemporary setting.
南希以現代的**場景**重新編寫了《羅密歐與茱麗葉》的其中一幕。

16 insecure [ˌɪnsɪˋkjʊr] *a.* 不安全的；沒自信的

片 be / feel insecure about...
對……感到沒自信

似 unsafe [ʌnˋsef] *a.* 不安全的

反 secure [sɪˋkjʊr]
a. 安全的 & *vt.* 獲得；弄牢 ④

▶ Though well trained, Kevin still felt insecure about his ability to handle the job.
雖然受過良好訓練，凱文還是**對**他處理該工作的能力**感到沒自信**。

17 particle [ˋpɑrtɪkl̩] *n.* 微粒；粒子

▸ The surface of the desk was covered with particles of dust.
書桌的表面布滿了灰塵微粒。

▸ Electrons and protons are atomic particles.
電子和質子都是原子粒子。

molecule [ˋmɑləˏkjul] *n.* 分子
衍 molecular [məˋlɛkjələ˞] *a.* 分子的

▸ A water molecule consists of two hydrogen atoms and one oxygen atom.
一個水分子包含兩個氫原子和一個氧原子。

18 worship [ˋwɝʃɪp] *vt.* & *n.* 崇拜；信仰（上帝或神）

三 worship, worshipped / worshiped, worshipped / worshiped

片 worship the ground sb walks on
拜倒在某人的腳 / 石榴裙下

似 warship [ˋwɔrʃɪp] *n.* 戰艦

▸ Peter is so madly in love with Hailey that he'll do anything for her. He really worships the ground she walks on.
彼得瘋狂愛上海莉，因此他願意為她付出一切。他真的是拜倒在她的石榴裙下了。

▸ The church is the traditional place for people to worship God.
教堂是人們敬奉上帝的慣例場所。

▸ Julia's worship of the movie star is so great that she's put his posters all over her room.
茱莉亞非常崇拜這位電影明星，所以她房裡擺滿了他的海報。

▸ Worship usually takes the form of praying or singing in praise of God.
做禮拜通常會採用禱告或是歌頌的方式來讚美上帝。

▸ Andy's whole family is Christian, so morning worship on Sundays is routine for them.
安迪一家都是基督徒，所以每週日的晨間禮拜對他們來說是例行公事。

19 fabric [ˋfæbrɪk] *n.* 布料；結構

片 (1) cotton fabrics　棉布料
(2) the fabric of society　社會結構

衍 fabricate [ˋfæbrɪˏket] *vt.* 捏造
fabricate a story　杜撰故事

似 structure [ˋstrʌktʃə˞] *n.* 結構 ③

▸ We will display our new range of fabrics at the exhibition.
我們將在展覽中陳列出我們各式的新款布料。

▸ Our social fabric is being threatened by crime and a bad economy.
我們的社會結構正遭受犯罪和經濟蕭條的威脅。

20 weird [wɪrd] *a.* 奇怪的

衍 weirdo [ˋwɪrdo] *n.* 怪人

似 (1) strange [strendʒ] *a.* 奇怪的 ①
(2) eccentric [ɪkˋsɛntrɪk] *a.* 古怪的 ⑥

▸ Did you hear any weird noises coming from the basement?
你有沒有聽到地下室傳來的**奇怪聲音**？

bizarre [bɪˋzɑr] *a.* 奇怪的

片 under bizarre circumstances
離奇地

似 (1) weird [wɪrd] *a.* 奇怪的 ⑤
(2) unusual [ʌnˋjuʒuəl] *a.* 不尋常的

▸ A soccer player was found murdered in his home under bizarre circumstances.
一名足球員被發現在自己家中被**離奇地**謀殺。

21 accommodate [əˋkɑmə͵det] *vt.* 容納；提供膳宿

似 have room / capacity for...
可容納……

▸ The newly built auditorium can accommodate 2,000 students.
= The newly built auditorium has room for 2,000 students.
這座新蓋的禮堂**可容納** 2 千名學生。

▸ The hotel can accommodate up to 1,000 tourists.
這間飯店可以**提供** 1 千名遊客**住宿**。

accommodation [ə͵kɑməˋdeʃən]
n. 住宿（美式英語中常用複數）

似 lodging [ˋlɑdʒɪŋ] *n.* 寄宿；住所

▸ Accommodations in Taipei are much cheaper than in Tokyo.
在臺北**住宿**遠比東京來得便宜。

22 blush [blʌʃ] *vi.* & *n.* 臉紅

似 flush [flʌʃ] *vt.* & *vi.* （使）臉紅 ④

▸ I'm quite shy, so I blush easily.
我很害羞所以很容易**臉紅**。

▸ When it was revealed that Jenny had lied, a blush of shame could be seen on her face.
珍妮被揭發說謊時，可以看到她因羞愧而**臉紅**了。

23 boost [bust] *vt.* 增加，提升 & *n.* 促進，推動

片 (1) boost sb's confidence / morale / ego
提升某人的信心 / 士氣 / 自尊
(2) give sb a boost　讓某人信心大增

▸ Beating thousands of competitors and getting this job boosted Lauren's confidence a lot.
打敗上千名對手爭取到這份工作**讓蘿倫的自信大增**。

▸ The President-elect gave these businessmen a boost in saying that he would devote himself to raising the economic growth.
總統當選人說他會致力於提升經濟成長，**讓這些商人信心大增**。

24 deadly [ˋdɛdlɪ] *a.* 致命的 & *adv.* 非常

片 a deadly poison / weapon
致命的毒藥 / 武器

衍 (1) dead [dɛd] *a.* 死亡的 ①
(2) death [dɛθ] *n.* 死亡 ①

似 (1) fatal [ˋfetl̩] *a.* 致命的 ④
(2) lethal [ˋliθəl] *a.* 致命的 ⑥
(3) extremely [ɪkˋstrimlɪ] *adv.* 非常

▸ Dioxin is possibly one of the most deadly substances known to mankind.
戴奧辛可能人類所知最**致命的**有毒物質之一。

▸ Some people thought Ken's comment was a joke, but he was actually being deadly serious.
有些人認為肯的評論只是個玩笑，但他其實是**非常**認真的。

25 compensate [ˋkɑmpən͵set] *vt.* 賠償 & *vi.* 彌補

片 (1) compensate sb for sth
賠償某人某物
(2) compensate for... 彌補……

▸ The authorities promised to compensate the victims of the flood for their injuries and property losses.
當局承諾要**補償**洪水受災戶的身體損傷及財產損失。

▸ Jessica's hard work compensates for her lack of experience.
潔西卡的努力**彌補**了她經驗上的不足。

compensation [͵kɑmpənˋseʃən]
n. 補償（不可數）

片 (1) claim / demand / seek compensation for...
為……要求補償
(2) in compensation 作為補償
= in damages

似 damages [ˋdæmɪdʒɪz]
n. 賠償金（恆用複數）

▸ The union is seeking compensation for the injured workers.
該工會正為受傷的工人**尋求賠償**。

▸ The plaintiff was rewarded $10,000 in compensation.
= The plaintiff was rewarded $10,000 in damages.
那位原告獲得一萬美元**作為賠償**。
*plaintiff [ˋplentɪf] *n.* 原告

26 attorney [əˋtɝnɪ] *n.* 律師

似 lawyer [ˋlɔjɚ] *n.* 律師 ①

比 lawyer 與 attorney 均指『律師』，兩字一般可通用。惟 lawyer 多指通過律師檢定考試持有執照的律師。而 attorney 多指委託訴訟的律師。

▸ I refuse to answer any questions until my attorney arrives.
在我**律師**到達前，我拒絕回答任何問題。

27 epidemic [͵ɛpəˋdɛmɪk] *n.* 傳染病，流行病 & *a.* 傳染（病）的

片 a flu epidemic 流感傳染病

似 (1) pandemic [pænˋdɛmɪk]
n.（全球性的）大流行病

▸ The outbreak of a flu epidemic has caused the government to take quick action to protect the most vulnerable, mainly children and the elderly.
流感傳染病的爆發已使政府迅速採取行動以保護那些最容易受影響的人，主要是兒童和老年人。

(2) contagious [kən\`tedʒəs]
a. 感染性的 ⑤
(3) infectious [ɪn\`fɛkʃəs]
a. 傳染的 ⑥

▶ Car theft in this area has reached epidemic proportions.
這個區域的汽車竊盜已達到像是**傳染病**的程度了。

28 essence [\`ɛsn̩s] *n.* 要素，本質；萃取物，精華 (不可數)

片 in essence 本質上
= essentially
衍 essential [ɪ\`sɛnʃəl]
a. 必要的；本質的 ④

▶ The very essence of Christianity is love.
基督教的**要旨**就是愛。

▶ In essence, a good design is the perfect unity of function and beauty.
基本上而言，好的設計就是功能性與美感完美的結合。

▶ If you add some lavender essence to the wax, your candle will give off a pleasant smell.
如果你在蠟裡面加一點薰衣草的**香精萃取物**，你的蠟燭就會散發香味。
*lavender [\`lævəndɚ] *n.* 薰衣草

29 galaxy [\`gæləksɪ] *n.* 星系；一群出色的人

複 galaxies [\`gæləksɪz]
片 (1) the Galaxy
(地球所處的) 銀河 (系)
= the Milky Way
(2) a galaxy of people
一群出色的人

▶ There are two trillion galaxies in the universe; Earth's is called the Milky Way.
宇宙有兩兆個**星系**；地球所在的星系被稱作銀河系。

▶ A galaxy of Hollywood stars are present at the charity ball.
一群好萊塢明星出席了慈善舞會。

Unit 04

0401-0406

1 architect [ˋɑrkə͵tɛkt] *n.* 建築師

▶ This building is designed by Timothy Lee, a world-renowned architect.
這棟建築是由一位名叫提摩西・李的世界知名建築師所設計。
*world-renowned [wɝldrɪˋnaʊnd] *a.* 世界知名的

architecture [ˋɑrkə͵tɛktʃɚ]
n. 建築（風格）；建築學（不可數）

衍 architectural [͵ɑrkəˋtɛktʃərəl]
a. 建築（學）的

似 (1) building [ˋbɪldɪŋ] *n.* 建築物 ②
(2) structure [ˋstrʌktʃɚ]
n. 建築物；結構 ③
(3) construction [kənˋstrʌkʃən]
n. 建築物 ④

▶ Baroque architecture is characterized by grandeur and magnificence.
巴洛克式建築的特色就是雄偉壯麗。
*grandeur [ˋgrændʒɚ] *n.* 雄偉
magnificence [mægˋnɪfəsn̩s] *n.* 壯麗

▶ The teacher told Benny that because of his good drawing skills and love of design, he should study architecture.
老師告訴班尼，由於他良好的繪畫技巧及對設計的熱愛，他應該研讀建築學。

2 whereas [(h)wɛrˋæz] *conj.* 而；但是

用法 whereas 作對等連接詞可用以連接兩個對稱的主要子句，用法與 while 相同。

▶ The wise take advantage of mistakes, whereas the stupid only regret mistakes they have made.
聰明的人從錯誤中學習，而愚者只知後悔犯下的錯。

nonetheless [͵nʌnðəˋlɛs] *adv.* 然而

似 (1) however [haʊˋɛvɚ] *adv.* 然而 ①
(2) nevertheless [͵nɛvɚðəˋlɛs]
adv. 然而 ④

▶ The final exams are coming; nonetheless, Frank is still fooling around as usual.
期末考將至，然而法蘭克仍如往常到處瞎混。

3 nowhere [ˋno͵(h)wɛr] *adv.* 任何地方都不 & *pron.* 沒有什麼地方

片 (1) get / go nowhere
不成功；沒有任何進展
(2) get sb nowhere
對某人毫無幫助
(3) out of nowhere
不知從哪冒出來的
(4) in the middle of nowhere
在荒郊野外

用法 nowhere 為否定副詞，置句首時其後採倒裝句。

▶ After his parents died, Anthony had nowhere to go.
他父母親過世之後，安東尼沒有地方去。

▶ Nowhere can you find such a beautiful girl as Madison.
你去哪兒都找不到像玫迪森這麼漂亮的女孩。

▶ Trevor tried to convince his parents to buy him a motorcycle, but he got nowhere because they hated the idea.
崔佛試圖說服他的父母買一輛摩托車給他，但他沒有成功，因為他的父母厭惡這個想法。

▸ Tommy's crying and yelling got him nowhere; his mother still refused to buy the toy for him.
湯米的哭吼毫無用處，他媽媽仍拒絕買玩具給他。

▸ My car broke down in the middle of nowhere, and I had to walk all the way to the nearest bus stop.
我的車在荒郊野外拋錨了，只好一路走到最近的公車站。

4 vein [ven] *n.* 靜脈

似 vain [ven] *a.* 徒勞的；愛慕虛榮的，自負的 ④

延伸 (1) artery [ˋɑrtərɪ] *n.* 動脈
(2) a blood vessel 血管

▸ Amanda's fever was gone shortly after the nurse injected some medicine into her veins.
護理師把一些藥注射進亞曼達的**靜脈**裡沒多久，她就退燒了。

5 sustain [səˋsten] *vt.* 維持（生命）；支撐，承受；遭受（傷害、損失）

似 (1) maintain [ˌmenˋten] *vt.* 維持 ②
(2) suffer [ˋsʌfɚ] *vt.* 遭受 ③
(3) undergo [ˌʌndɚˋgo] *vt.* 經受 ⑤

▸ Thomas has to work very hard in order to sustain his family.
為了**維持**家計，湯瑪斯得非常努力工作。

▸ The shelf collapsed because it couldn't sustain the weight that had been put on it.
這個櫃子倒塌，因為它**支撐**不住放在它上面的重量。

▸ The company sustained a great loss due to the bad investment.
公司由於該項失敗的投資案**蒙受**很大的損失。

sustainable [səˋstenəbl̩]
a. 可維持的；可持續的

片 sustainable energy resources
永續能源資源

衍 sustainability [səˌstenəˋbɪlətɪ]
n. 持續性

▸ Experts doubted that the rapid increase in the stock market was sustainable and warned values would likely decline soon.
專家懷疑股市快速上漲是否能**維持**，並警告股價可能很快會下跌。

▸ Solar and wind power are two examples of sustainable energy resources that have become more common over the years.
太陽能和風能是兩個這幾年來越見普遍的**永續能源**例子。

6 motive [ˋmotɪv] *n.* 動機，目的

片 a motive for... 做……的動機／目的

衍 (1) motivate [ˋmotəˌvet]
vt. 給……動機 ④
(2) motivation [ˌmotəˋveʃən]
n. 幹勁，動力 ④

▸ The police are puzzled about the teenager's motive for killing his younger sister.
警方對於該名青少年殺死親妹妹的**動機**感到十分不解。

0407-0414

似 motif [moˋtif]
n. (文學、電影中重複出現的) 主題
▸ Revenge is a very common motif in action movies.
復仇是動作片常見的**主題**。

7 impulse [ˋɪmpʌls] *n.* 衝動

片 (1) have an impulse to V
有做……的衝動
(2) on (an) impulse　衝動地
(3) an impulse buy / purchase
衝動購買的東西
(4) impulse buying　衝動購物
衍 impulsive [ɪmˋpʌlsɪv] *a.* 衝動的

▸ Whenever I step into a department store, I have the impulse to buy things.
每當走進百貨公司，我就**有購物的衝動**。
▸ You will get into a lot of trouble if you act on impulse.
如果你**衝動**行事，很容易就會惹上許多麻煩。

8 sacred [ˋsekrɪd] *a.* 神聖的

似 holy [ˋholɪ] *a.* 神聖的 ③

▸ Cows are considered to be sacred animals in India.
牛在印度被視為是**神聖的**動物。

9 extraordinary [ɪkˋstrɔrdn̩,ɛrɪ] *a.* 非凡的

衍 extraordinarily [ɪkˋstrɔrdn̩,ɛrəlɪ]
adv. 非常
似 (1) remarkable [rɪˋmɑrkəbl̩]
a. 非凡的 ④
(2) exceptional [ɪkˋsɛpʃənl̩]
a. 卓越的 ⑤
反 ordinary [ˋɔrdn̩,ɛrɪ] *a.* 平凡的 ②

▸ In Jason's eyes, Diane is a girl of extraordinary beauty.
在傑森眼中，黛安是個**非常**美的女孩。

10 suspend [səˋspɛnd] *vt.* 中斷，中止；吊銷 (執照)；垂掛，懸掛

片 be suspended from school
被停學
衍 suspension [səˋspɛnʃən]
n. 中止；懸掛 ⑥
似 (1) stop [stɑp] *vt.* 停止 ①
(2) interrupt [,ɪntəˋrʌpt] *vt.* 中斷 ③
(3) hang [hæŋ] *vt.* 把……掛起來 ①
反 resume [rɪˋz(j)um] *vt.* 繼續 ⑤

▸ The meeting was suspended because of the blackout.
因為停電，會議被**中斷**了。
▸ Toby was suspended from school because he got caught cheating on a test.
托比因為考試作弊被抓到，所以**被停學**了。
▸ Peter's license was suspended for drunk driving.
彼得因為酒駕，駕照被**吊銷**了。
▸ As part of the exhibition, the museum suspended dozens of large paintings by wires from the ceiling.
作為展覽的一部分，博物館從天花板上用金屬線**懸掛**數十幅大型畫作。

11 sentiment [ˋsɛntəmənt] *n.* 情緒；意見，觀點

片 public sentiment 公眾意見

似 opinion [əˋpɪnjən] *n.* 意見 ②

▸ There is little room for sentiment in business.
做生意不能**感情**用事。

▸ Recent research has shown what public sentiment is on the issue.
最近的研究顯示**大眾**對於該議題**的觀點**。

sentimental [ˏsɛntəˋmɛntḷ]
a. 感情用事的；感傷的，多愁善感的

片 (1) be sentimental about...
對……有所感傷
(2) for sentimental reasons
出於情感的緣故

似 emotional [ɪˋmoʃənḷ] *a.* 感情的 ③

▸ Laurence is too sentimental to be a good leader.
勞倫斯太**感情用事**了，無法成為一個好領導者。

▸ Juliet kept all the movie tickets for sentimental reasons.
茱莉葉保存這些電影票是**出於感情**。

12 porch [portʃ] *n.* 門廊，陽臺（專指西式洋房一樓的陽臺，多有屋簷，陽臺上多舖木板，可在上面喝咖啡或晒太陽）

▸ The old man is sitting on his porch watching the sunset.
那個老人坐在**陽臺**上看著夕陽。

corridor [ˋkɔrɪdɚ] *n.* 走廊，通道

似 hallway [ˋhɔlˏwe] *n.* 走廊 ③

▸ All candidates were told to wait outside in the corridor before the job interviews.
所有求職者被告知待在外面的**走廊**等候面試。

13 exceed [ɪkˋsid] *vt.* 超過

似 surpass [sɚˋpæs] *vt.* 超過 ⑥

▸ Don't exceed the speed limit when driving.
開車時不要**超**速。

excessive [ɪkˋsɛsɪv] *a.* 過多的

片 excessive drinking / eating
暴飲 / 食

衍 excess [ɪkˋsɛs] *n.* 超過，過量 ⑥

反 moderate [ˋmɑdərɪt] *a.* 適度的 ④

▸ Crops were damaged by the excessive rainfall last week.
上週降雨**過多**，農作物都遭到破壞。

14 flawless [ˋflɔləs] *a.* 完美的，無瑕疵的

衍 flaw [flɔ] *n.* 缺點 ⑥

似 (1) perfect [ˋpɝfɪkt] *a.* 完美的 ②
(2) impeccable [ɪmˋpɛkəbḷ]
a. 完美的

▸ Maggie's flawless skin is the envy of every girl at school.
瑪姬**完美無瑕的**肌膚讓全校女生羨慕。

15 lump [lʌmp] *vt.* 歸併在一起 & *vi.* 結塊 & *n.* 團，塊；隆起，腫塊

片 (1) lump sb/sth together
把某人 / 某事物歸併在一起
(2) Like it or lump it.
要就要，不要就拉倒。
(3) a lump of... 一團 / 塊⋯⋯
(4) a lump in sb's throat
某人喉嚨有一個腫塊（喻某人想哭）

似 swelling [ˋswɛlɪŋ] *n.* 腫起；腫塊

▶ You cannot just lump every type of student together.
你不能隨便將每一種學生都歸成同一類。

▶ The manufacturer recommended turning the mattress over from time to time to stop it from lumping.
製造商建議不時把床墊翻面，以防止它結塊。

▶ I grabbed a lump of soil as a souvenir at Yellowstone National Park.
在黃石國家公園內，我抓了一把泥土當作紀念。

▶ There is a lump on my head because I fell off the bike and hit the curb.
我的頭腫了一塊，因為我從腳踏車上跌下來撞到人行道路緣。

▶ There was a lump in my throat when I saw those skinny children on TV.
我看到電視上那些骨瘦如柴的孩子們時感到一陣鼻酸。

16 pyramid [ˋpɪrəmɪd] *n.* 金字塔

片 the Pyramids 埃及金字塔
（P 須大寫）

▶ I hope one day I can take a trip to Egypt and see the great Pyramids there.
我希望有一天能去埃及旅遊，看看那裡雄偉的金字塔。

17 generate [ˋdʒɛnəˏret] *vt.* 產生（光、電、熱）；造成，引起

衍 generative [ˋdʒɛnəˏrətɪv]
a. 有生產力的

似 (1) produce [prəˋdus] *vt.* 生產 ②
(2) create [krɪˋet] *vt.* 創造 ②

▶ The dam generates electricity for the local community.
該座水壩發電供當地社區使用。

▶ Tourism generates more income for the seaside resort.
旅遊業為濱海勝地帶來較多的收入。

generator [ˋdʒɛnəˏretɚ] *n.* 發電機

片 an emergency generator
緊急發電機

▶ The hospital has two emergency generators in case of a power failure.
這家醫院有兩座緊急發電機，以供停電時使用。

18 accelerate [əkˋsɛləˏret] *vt.* & *vi.* （使）加速

衍 acceleration [ækˏsɛləˋreʃən] *n.* 加速

似 speed up 加速

反 decelerate [diˋsɛləˏret]
vt. & *vi.* （使）減速

▶ The candidate proposed measures to accelerate the rate of economic growth.
候選人提出加速經濟發展的辦法。

▶ The sports car can accelerate to a speed of 100 km per hour in just a few seconds.
這輛跑車可以在幾秒之間加速到時速 100 公里。

19 digestion [daɪˋdʒɛstʃən] *n.* 消化作用

衍 digest [daɪˋdʒɛst] *vt.* & *vi.* 消化 ④
反 indigestion [ˏɪndəˋdʒɛstʃən] *n.* 消化不良

▶ Drinking this tea after dinner is good for digestion.
飯後喝這種茶有益消化。

20 exotic [ɪgˋzɑtɪk] *a.* 異國風味的

衍 foreign [ˋfɔrɪn] *a.* 外國的 ①

▶ Frank was attracted to the exotic scenery of the tropical island.
法蘭克被那座熱帶島嶼的異國風景所吸引。

21 institute [ˋɪnstəˏtjut] *n.* 機構；學院（尤指理工學院）& *vt.* 開始；制定

片 institute a system 建立制度
= establish a system
= set up a system
似 (1) organization [ˏɔrgənəˋzeʃən] *n.* 機構 ②
(2) academy [əˋkædəmɪ] *n.* 學院 ⑥

▶ This research institute is dedicated to finding cures for AIDS.
這間研究機構致力找尋愛滋病的治療方式。

▶ MIT is short for Massachusetts Institute of Technology.
MIT 是麻省理工學院的縮寫。

▶ The new mayor instituted stricter law enforcement as soon as he took office.
新市長一上任就開始更嚴厲執法。
*take office 就任

institution [ˏɪnstəˋtjuʃən] *n.* 機構

似 organization [ˏɔrgənəˋzeʃən] *n.* 機構 ②

▶ Universities are institutions of knowledge and higher learning.
大學是知識和進階學習的機構。

22 administration [ədˏmɪnəˋstreʃən] *n.* 管理，行政（不可數）；管理部門 / 人員（可數）；政府（可數）

比 administration 與 government 均可表『政府』，但在美國，administration 專指『某人執政時期的政府』，因此 administration 之前必須置定冠詞 the，之後再置總統的姓氏；而 government 則指國家政府。
(1) the Biden administration 拜登政府
(2) the US government 美國政府

▶ Some experience in school administration is necessary for this job.
這份工作要求具有若干學校行政經驗。

▶ The decision of who to hire or fire is the responsibility of administration.
僱用或開除哪些人的決定由管理階層的人作主。

▶ The Bush administration failed to create more job opportunities for the American people.
布希政府未能為美國人民創造更多的工作機會。

administrative [ədˋmɪnəˏstretɪv] *a.* 管理的；行政的

片 the administrative section / department 行政部門

▶ For those who are interested in the job, please contact the administrative section for application forms.
凡對此工作有興趣者，請與行政部門接洽索取申請書。

0422-0429

administrator [əd`mɪnə,stretə]
n. 管理人員；行政人員

似 executive [ɪg`zɛkjʊtɪv] *n.* 執行者 ⑤

▸ I was quite impressed with the competence of the administrator.
這位行政人員的能幹讓我印象深刻。

23 component [kəm`ponənt] *n.* 要素；(機器、電腦等) 零件 & *a.* 組成的

片 (1) a key / vital / major component of sth 某事物的重要構成要素
(2) component parts 零件

衍 compose [kəm`poz] *vt.* 組成 ④

似 (1) element [`ɛləmənt] *n.* 要素，成分 ③
(2) ingredient [ɪn`gridɪənt] *n.* 要素 ④

▸ Economic diplomacy has been a key component of India's foreign policy.
經濟外交一直以來都是印度外交政策重要的一部分。

▸ The company made and sold computer components to various manufacturers in Asia.
這間公司製造和販賣電腦零件給亞洲不同的製造商。

▸ Jason works as a sales manager for a company that sells automotive component parts.
傑森在一間銷售汽車零件的公司擔任業務經理。

24 derive [dɪ`raɪv] *vt.* 取得 & *vi.* 源自

片 (1) derive A from B 從 B 取得 A
(2) derive from... 源自……
= originate from...
= stem from...
= come from...

▸ John derives a lot of pleasure from reading adventure stories.
約翰從閱讀冒險故事中得到許多樂趣。

▸ The story derives from an old legend.
這篇故事源自一則古老傳說。

25 originality [ə,rɪdʒə`nælətɪ] *n.* 獨創性 (不可數)

衍 (1) original [ə`rɪdʒənḷ] *a.* 有獨創性的 ③
(2) originate [ə`rɪdʒə,net] *vt.* 發明 & *vi.* 來自 ⑥

似 (1) creativity [,krie`tɪvətɪ] *n.* 創造力 ④
(2) innovation [,ɪnə`veʃən] *n.* 創新 ⑤

▸ John's work does not show much originality.
約翰的作品沒有什麼原創性。

26 ultimate [`ʌltəmɪt] *a.* 最終的 & *n.* 終極，極點

片 be the ultimate in... 是……方面的極致

似 final [`faɪnḷ] *a.* 最終的 ②

▸ The ultimate decision regarding whom to hire will be made by the boss.
僱用的人選將由老闆做最後決定。

▸ The movie star's home is the ultimate in luxury.
這名影星的住宅豪華到了極點。

27 faculty [ˋfækḷtɪ] *n.* 教職員（集合名詞，不可數）；能力（可數）

片 have a faculty for... 有……的才能

似 ability [əˋbɪlətɪ] *n.* 能力 ①

用法 faculty 表『教職員』時為集合名詞，故使用時不可說：
thirty faculties (×)
a faculty of thirty (○)
= thirty faculty members
30 名教職員

▸ That school is famous for its competent faculty and sound facilities.
那所學校以堅強的師資陣容和健全的設備聞名。
*sound [saʊnd] *a.* 健全的

▸ Tom has a great faculty for learning languages easily.
湯姆很有學習語言的天分。

28 presume [prɪˋzum] *vt.* 推測，認為；冒昧 & *vi.* 占便宜

片 (1) presume that... 推測 / 認為……
(2) presume to V 冒昧做……
(3) presume on / upon...
占……的便宜，利用……

衍 presumption [prɪˋzʌmpʃən] *n.* 推測

似 assume [əˋs(j)um] *vt.* 推測 ③

比 assume 與 presume 均可表『推測』或『猜測』，前者較謹慎，後者較大膽。

▸ From the way that lady talks, I presume that she is your secretary.
從那位女士說話的方式看來，我推測她應該是你的祕書。

▸ May I presume to tell you that you are wrong on that point?
我可以冒昧告訴你，關於那一點你說錯了嗎？

▸ Don't presume on Miss Lin's good nature by constantly asking for money.
不要利用林小姐的善良，而經常向她要錢。

presumably [prɪˋzuməblɪ]
adv. 大概，可能

▸ Presumably, Jacob will accept the job offer because the salary is good and the company is located near his home.
雅各大概會接受這份工作邀約，因為薪水不錯，公司離他家也很近。

assumption [əˋsʌmpʃən] *n.* 推測

片 make assumptions about...
對……做出推測

衍 assume [əˋs(j)um] *vt.* 推測 ③

▸ It's my assumption that gas prices will decline.
我推測油價會下跌。

▸ We too often make assumptions about others based on previous experience.
我們太常倚靠過去的經驗來對他人做出推測。

29 session [ˋsɛʃən] *n.* 講習會；開會

片 be in session 開會中

似 meeting [ˋmitɪŋ] *n.* 會議 ①

▸ A training session will be held for new employees on October 8.
10 月 8 日將舉辦一場新進員工培訓會。

▸ The city council is now in session.
市議會現在正在開會。

🔊 0430-0431

30 phase [fez] *n.* 階段，時期 & *vt.* 分段實行

片 (1) phase... in / phase in...
逐漸採用，逐步實施
(2) phase... out / phase out...
逐漸淘汰，逐步撤出

似 stage [stedʒ] *n.* (進展的) 階段 ②

▸ We're entering a new phase in communication technology.
我們正進入傳播科技的新階段。

▸ Many teachers agreed to phase in this book as a basic textbook for students.
很多老師同意逐步採用此書，作為學生的基本教材。

▸ With new technology, society has generally phased radios out.
隨著新科技的發展，社會逐漸淘汰收音機。

31 radiation [ˌredɪˋeʃən] *n.* (核) 輻射；放射，散發

片 ultraviolet [ˌʌltrəˋvaɪəlɪt] radiation 紫外線放射物

衍 radiate [ˋredɪˌet] *vt.* 發射 & *vi.* 散發

▸ There was a radiation leak at a nuclear power plant last week.
上週某座核能電廠發生了輻射外洩事件。

▸ Sunscreen protects you from harmful ultraviolet radiation.
防晒乳保護你不受紫外線放射物所害。
*sunscreen [ˋsʌnˌskrin] *n.* 防晒乳

0501-0502

1 convert [kən`vɝt] vt. & vi. 轉變；皈依（宗教）

片 (1) convert A into B 將 A 變成 B
= change A into B
= transform A into B
= turn A into B
(2) convert (sb) to Buddhism / Catholicism / Christianity
（讓某人）皈依佛教 / 天主教 / 基督教

似 (1) change [tʃendʒ] vt. & vi. 改變 ①
(2) transform [træns`fɔrm] vt. 改變 ④

▸ I'd like to convert some dollars into pounds, please.
我想要把一些美元換成英鎊，麻煩你。

▸ After many years of using a Microsoft-based system, the company converted to Apple hardware and software.
這間公司使用微軟系統多年後，決定換用蘋果的硬體和軟體。

▸ Paul converted to Buddhism from Christianity five months ago.
保羅五個月前由基督教皈依佛教。

conversion [kən`vɝʃən] n. 轉變

似 (1) change [tʃendʒ] n. 改變 ①
(2) transformation [ˌtrænsfɚ`meʃən] n. 轉變 ⑤

▸ The conversion of my old room into an entertainment room is going to take me about one week.
將我的舊房間改建成娛樂室大約要花我一個禮拜的時間。

2 vague [veg] a. 模糊的

片 have a vague idea about...
對……有模糊的概念

衍 vaguely [`veglɪ] adv. 模糊地，依稀地

似 (1) obscure [əb`skjur] a. 朦朧的 ⑤
(2) unclear [ʌn`klɪr] a. 不清楚的
(3) hazy [`hezɪ] a. 朦朧的

反 clear [klɪr] a. 清楚的 ①

▸ The mayor gave only a vague outline of the anti-corruption campaign.
市長對於於肅貪運動的大綱只是含糊帶過。

▸ I have only a vague idea about modern US history.
我對現代美國歷史只有模糊的概念。

blur [blɝ] vt. & vi. (使) 模糊 & n. 模糊的事物

三 blur, blurred [blɝd], blurred

片 blur sb's eyes / vision
使某人視線不清

衍 blurred [blɝd] a. 模糊的

▸ The heavy rain blurred my vision while I was driving on the highway.
大雨使我在高速公路上駕車行駛時，視線一片模糊。

▸ For some people, the difference between right and wrong begins to blur in certain situations.
對一些人來說，在某些情況下是非的區別會變得模糊。

▸ In the heavy snowstorm, the view through his windshield was a blur, so Max had to stop the car.
在暴風雪中，擋風玻璃前的視野一片模糊，因此麥可斯只好把車停下。

0503-0507

3 cling [klɪŋ] *vi.* 緊抓，緊握住；堅守(原則、信念等)

三 cling, clung [klʌŋ], clung

片 (1) cling to / onto... 緊抓住……
(2) cling to... 堅守……
= stick to...

似 grasp [græsp] *vt.* 緊抓 ③

▸ Grandma had to cling onto the railing tightly when she tried to climb the stairs.
奶奶爬樓梯的時候必須**緊緊抓著**欄杆。

▸ Whatever I do, I cling to my principles.
= Whatever I do, I stick to my principles.
不管做什麼事，我都會**緊守**原則。

grip [grɪp] *vt.* 緊握；吸引(注意力) & *n.* 緊握；理解

三 grip, gripped [grɪpt], gripped

片 (1) grip sb's attention
引起某人的注意
(2) loosen / tighten one's grip
某人鬆手 / 手緊抓
(3) get a grip on sth 理解某事
= understand sth

似 grasp [græsp] *vt.* 緊抓 ③

▸ Nancy gripped my hand unconsciously when we were watching the horror movie.
我們看恐怖片的時候南希不由自主地**抓緊**我的手。

▸ The novel failed to grip Brian's attention; in fact, he found it a bit boring.
這本小說沒有**吸引到**布萊恩，事實上，他覺得這本小說有點無聊。

▸ The girl escaped when the kidnapper loosened his grip.
那女孩趁綁架犯**手一鬆**的時候逃走了。

▸ I just couldn't get a grip on what Gary said.
我真是**搞不懂**蓋瑞在講什麼。

snatch [snætʃ] *vt.* 抓住，奪取 & *n.* (音樂、談話等的) 片段

片 (1) snatch sth away 將某物奪走
(2) a snatch of the conversation / music 談話 / 音樂的片段

似 (1) grab [græb] *vt.* 抓取；奪取 ③
(2) take hold of... 抓住……

▸ The little girl snatched the chocolate bar right out of her brother's hand.
小女孩從她哥哥手中把巧克力棒**搶過來**。

▸ Emma burst into tears when her brother Johnny snatched her toy away.
艾瑪被哥哥強尼**搶走**玩具後嚎啕大哭。

▸ Since Judy only heard a snatch of Jill and Jack's conversation, she didn't understand what they were talking about.
茱蒂不知道吉兒和傑克在談論什麼，因為她只有聽到他們談話的**片段**。

4 acknowledge [əkˋnɑlɪdʒ] *vt.* 承認

片 (1) acknowledge that... 承認……
(2) be acknowledged as...
被公認為……

似 admit [ədˋmɪt] *vt.* 承認 ②

▸ David acknowledged that his mistake had led to the failure of the mission.
大衛**承認**他的疏失導致這次任務的失敗。

▸ Mozart was acknowledged as a musical prodigy in his early childhood.
莫札特在很小的時候就**被公認為**音樂神童。
*prodigy [ˋprɑdədʒɪ] *n.* 奇才，天才

acknowledgement
[əkˋnɑlɪdʒmənt] *n.* 承認；致謝
(= acknowledgment)
片 in acknowledgement of...
以感謝 / 為表彰……

▸ The army gave Ryan a medal in acknowledgement of his brave deed.
為表彰萊恩的英勇行徑，軍方頒給了他一面獎牌。

5 storage [ˋstɔrɪdʒ] *n.* 儲藏（空間）（不可數）

片 (1) in (cold) storage 在（冷）儲藏中
(2) storage space 收納空間
(3) have (some more) storage for sth 有（更多）儲藏某物的空間
= have (some more) space for sth
衍 store [stɔr] *vt.* 儲藏 ①

▸ Many of the items Peter bought at the auction are still in storage.
彼得從拍賣會上買來的物品有許多**仍堆著**。

▸ Fish and meat have to be kept in cold storage so they don't spoil.
魚與肉類應**冷藏**以免腐敗。

▸ Stop buying new clothes! There's no more storage available for them in the closet.
別再買新衣服了！衣櫥內已經沒有**空間**可放了。

▸ I like this apartment very much because there is a lot of storage space.
我喜歡這間公寓，因為它有很多**收納空間**。

6 document [ˋdɑkjəmənt] *n.* （書面或電腦）文件 & [ˋdɑkjə͵mɛnt] *vt.* 記錄

似 record [ˋrɛkɚd] *n.* 紀錄 & [rɪˋkɔrd] *vt.* 記錄 ②

▸ These confidential documents must be kept in a safe place instead of just lying on your desk.
這些機密**文件**得放在安全的地方，而不是放你桌上。

▸ This movie documented the disaster in detail.
這部電影詳細**記錄**了這場災難。

documentary [͵dɑkjəˋmɛntərɪ]
a. 文件的；紀錄的 & *n.* 紀錄片
片 (1) documentary evidence / proof 書面證明
(2) a documentary film 紀錄片

▸ A documentary film is worthless if it is not based on the truth.
紀錄片若無事實根據就沒有價值了。

▸ This documentary was shot in the small town where the story happened.
這部**紀錄片**是在故事發生的那個小鎮拍攝的。

7 reverse [rɪˋvɝs] *vt.* 推翻；使反向 & *a.* 顛倒的，相反的 & *n.* 相反；（硬幣、文件等的）背面

片 (1) in reverse order 以顛倒順序的方式
(2) on the reverse side 在背面
(3) the reverse of... ……的相反

▸ The manager reversed his own decision the next day.
經理第二天就**推翻**了自己的決定。

▸ Ian reversed the old photo to check if there was a date on the back.
伊恩把這張舊照**翻過來**確認照片後方是否有日期。

0507-0515

衍 reversal [rɪˋvɝsḷ] *n.* 翻轉；顛倒

似 (1) reserve [rɪˋzɝv] *vt.* 預定（房間、位子）③
(2) overturn [ˏovɚˋtɝn] *vt.* 使翻轉 ⑤
(3) back [bæk] *n.* 背部 ①

▸ Miss Murray asked the students to repeat the words in reverse order.
莫瑞老師請學生以相反的順序複誦這些字。

▸ John's version of what happened last night is exactly the reverse of Paul's.
約翰對昨晚發生何事的說法恰恰是保羅的相反。

▸ On one side of the coin is the Queen and on the reverse is a beaver.
這枚硬幣一面是女王，背面是海狸。

8 widespread [ˋwaɪdˏsprɛd] *a.* 普遍的；廣泛的

片 widespread support 廣泛的支持

似 (1) general [ˋdʒɛnərəl] *a.* 普遍的 ②
(2) universal [ˏjunəˋvɝsḷ] *a.* 普遍的 ④

▸ The widespread use of computers has made it more convenient to communicate.
電腦的廣泛使用讓溝通更加方便了。

▸ The new policy has received widespread support.
新的政策受到廣泛支持。

9 frontier [frʌnˋtɪr] *n.* 邊疆，邊境

片 (1) on the frontier 在邊境
(2) the frontier between A and B A 和 B 的邊境

似 (1) border [ˋbɔrdɚ] *n.* 邊界，邊境 ②
(2) boundary [ˋbaʊnd(ə)rɪ] *n.* 邊界 ⑤

▸ The government set up a checkpoint on the frontier.
政府在邊疆設立一處檢查哨。
*checkpoint [ˋtʃɛkˏpɔɪnt] *n.* 檢查站

▸ We were stopped and questioned by the guards when we drove through the frontier between Germany and France.
當我們開車經過法德邊境時，衛兵把我們攔下來問問題。

10 undoubtedly [ʌnˋdaʊtɪdlɪ] *adv.* 無庸置疑地

衍 (1) doubt [daʊt] *n.* 懷疑 ②
(2) undoubted [ʌnˋdaʊtɪd] *a.* 無庸置疑的
(3) doubtless [ˋdaʊtləs] *adv.* 無疑地

▸ Edgar is undoubtedly the most dedicated worker in our company.
= Edgar is, without (a) doubt, the most dedicated worker in our company.
= Edgar is no doubt the most dedicated worker in our company.
= Edgar is doubtless the most dedicated worker in our company.
愛德格毫無疑問是我們公司最忠於職守的員工。

11 stain [sten] *vt.* & *vi.* 沾汙 & *vt.* 敗壞 & *n.* 汙點

片 stain glass 彩繪玻璃

▸ When Hal spilled his glass of red wine, it stained the white rug in the living room.
海爾把紅酒灑出來時，弄髒了客廳的白色地毯。

衍 stainless [ˋstenləs] *a.* 無汙漬的；不生鏽的
stainless steel　不鏽鋼

▶ Several businesses have had their reputation stained by this report.
好幾間企業因為這則報導而信譽大損。

▶ Do you know how to get a coffee stain out of a shirt?
你知道怎麼把襯衫上的咖啡汙漬弄掉嗎？

12 specimen [ˋspɛsəmən] *n.* 標本；樣品，樣本

似 (1) example [ɪgˋzæmpl̩] *n.* 樣本；例子 ①
(2) sample [ˋsæmpl̩] *n.* 樣品，樣本 ②

▶ Rodney has a collection of rare insect specimens.
羅德尼收藏了若干稀有昆蟲的標本。

▶ The tree specimen was chosen for its features that were typical of its species.
選擇這個樹木樣本是因為它具有該種樹的典型特徵。

13 circuit [ˋsɝkɪt] *n.* 一圈，一周；電路

片 (1) an electrical circuit　電路
(2) a short circuit　短路
(3) a circuit board　電路板
(4) a circuit breaker
斷路器；(股市) 熔斷機制

▶ It takes 15 minutes to make a circuit around the lake.
繞湖一圈要 15 分鐘。

▶ Twenty engineers worked together to design this electrical circuit.
20 名工程師合作設計出了這組電路。

▶ A short circuit caused the machine to malfunction.
短路造成這臺機器發生故障。
*malfunction [mælˋfʌŋkʃən] *vi.* 發生故障

14 myth [mɪθ] *n.* 神話；迷思，錯誤的想法

片 Contrary to the general myth, ...
與一般傳統想法不同的是，……

似 (1) legend [ˋlɛdʒənd] *n.* 傳說 ④
(2) mythology [mɪˋθɑlədʒɪ] *n.* 神話 (不可數)

▶ Contrary to the general myth, pigs are actually animals that love to be clean.
與一般傳統想法不同的是，豬其實是愛乾淨的動物。

▶ The story in the magazine is just a myth. There's not a single grain of truth in it.
雜誌裡的這則報導不過是無稽之談。毫無事實根據。
*a grain of...　一點兒……

15 enthusiastic [ɪnˏθjuzɪˋæstɪk] *a.* 熱心的；熱情的

片 be enthusiastic about...
對……很熱心

衍 (1) enthusiasm [ɪnˋθjuzɪˏæzm̩] *n.* 熱心 ④
(2) enthusiastically [ɪnˏθjuzɪˋæstɪkl̩ɪ] *adv.* 熱心地；熱情地

▶ Nowadays many people are enthusiastic about charitable work.
現今許多人對慈善工作都很熱心。
*charitable [ˋtʃærətəbl̩] *a.* 慈善的

0516-0523

(3) enthusiast [ɪnˋθjuzɪ͵æst] *n.* 熱衷者
似 (1) eager [ˋigɚ] *a.* 熱切的 ③
(2) zealous [ˋzɛləs] *a.* 熱情的

16 rail [rel] *n.* 鐵路；欄杆，扶手 (= handrail [ˋhænd͵rel])

片 (1) by rail　搭火車
= by train
(2) be as thin as a rail　像竹竿一樣瘦
似 (1) railroad [ˋrel͵rod] *n.* 鐵路 ②
(2) railway [ˋrel͵we] *n.* 鐵路 ②

▸ We went from London to Paris by rail.
我們從倫敦**搭火車**前往巴黎。

▸ Please hold onto the rail when you are going downstairs.
下樓梯的時候請抓住**扶手**。

17 condemn [kənˋdɛm] *vt.* 譴責

片 condemn sb for sth　譴責某人某事
似 criticize [ˋkrɪtə͵saɪz] *vt.* 批評 ④

▸ The doctor was condemned by many for neglecting his patients' needs.
該醫師被許多人**譴責**忽視病患的需求。

18 ceremony [ˋsɛrə͵monɪ] *n.* 典禮

片 (1) a wedding / graduation ceremony　婚禮 / 畢業典禮
(2) an opening ceremony　開幕典禮
(3) stand on ceremony　拘謹，講究禮節
衍 (1) ceremonial [͵sɛrəˋmonɪəl] *a.* 典禮的，儀式的
(2) ceremonious [͵sɛrəˋmonjəs] *a.* 如典禮般的；拘於禮節的

▸ The principal awarded five outstanding students during the ceremony.
校長在**典禮**上頒獎給 5 位優秀學生。

▸ Don't stand on ceremony; please make yourself at home.
不要**拘束**，自己來別客氣。

19 ragged [ˋrægɪd] *a.* (衣服) 破爛的；(人) 不整潔的

片 (1) a ragged coat / shirt / dress　破爛的大衣 / 襯衫 / 洋裝
(2) a ragged person　衣衫襤褸的人
衍 rag [ræg] *n.* 抹布 ③

▸ The hobo dressed in a ragged coat was asking people for some spare change outside the supermarket.
這位遊民穿著**破外套**在超市外向人乞討零錢。
*hobo [ˋhobo] *n.* 遊民

20 scramble [ˋskræmbl̩] *vi.* & *n.* 搶奪；(快速) 爬行 & *vt.* 倉促做；炒 (蛋)

片 (1) scramble for sth　搶奪某物
(2) scramble up...　爬上……
(3) scramble to V　倉促做……

▸ All the players scrambled for the ball when the game started.
比賽一開始所有球員就拼了命**搶**球。

似 (1) crawl [krɔl] *vi.* 爬行 ③
(2) clamber [ˋklæmbɚ] *vt.* & *vi.* 爬，攀登

延伸 (1) a scrambled egg 炒蛋
(2) a poached egg 荷包蛋
(3) a boiled egg 水煮蛋

▸ During the flood, many animals scrambled up the hillside to escape the rising water.
水災發生期間，許多動物**快速爬上**山坡以避開上升的水位。

▸ When the man dressed as Santa Claus entered the room, there was a scramble by the kids to get the presents.
裝扮成聖誕老人的男子進房時，孩子們**爭先恐後**來拿禮物。

▸ I'm bored of sunbathing. Let's go for a scramble over those rocks!
我厭倦做日光浴了。我們去**爬**那些岩石吧！

▸ Waking up late, Danny scrambled to put his clothes on.
丹尼醒來晚了，**倉促**地把衣服穿上。

▸ Marnie scrambled four eggs, added some milk and vegetables, and then fried them up.
瑪妮**炒**了四顆蛋、加了些許牛奶和蔬菜，然後再把它們全部一起油炒。

21 server [ˋsɝvɚ] *n.* 伺服器；服務生

衍 serve [sɝv] *vt.* 服務；供應 ②
似 (1) waiter [ˋwetɚ] *n.* 男服務生 ②
(2) waitress [ˋwetrɪs] *n.* 女服務生 ②

▸ There was a virus in the server, so we had to shut it down.
伺服器中毒了，所以我們把它關掉。

▸ Always make sure to tip your server at least 10 percent.
要記得給你的**服務生**至少 10% 的小費。

22 memo [ˋmɛmo] *n.* 備忘錄 (為 memorandum [ˏmɛməˋrændəm] 的縮寫)

▸ Did you get the memo about the new dress code?
你有收到關於新服裝規定的**備忘錄**嗎？

23 meddle [ˋmɛdḷ] *vi.* 干涉

片 meddle in / with... 干涉……
= interfere in...
= intervene in...

似 (1) middle [ˋmɪdḷ] *n.* 中間 & *a.* 中間的 ①
(2) interfere [ˏɪntɚˋfɪr] *vi.* 干涉 ④
(3) intervene [ˏɪntɚˋvin] *vi.* 干涉 ⑥

▸ Don't meddle in our business, or you'll get into trouble.
= Don't interfere in our business, or you'll get into trouble.
= Don't intervene in our business, or you'll get into trouble.
別**干涉**我們的事，不然你麻煩可大了。

0524-0530

24 stew [st(j)u] *vt.* & *vi.* (用小火) 煮，燉 & *n.* 燉的食物

似 simmer [ˋsɪmɚ] *vt.* & *vi.* & *n.* 小火煨煮

- Mother was busy stewing some tomatoes in the kitchen.
  媽媽正在廚房忙著燉番茄。
- While the beef stewed on the stove, Julia prepared some vegetables for dinner.
  牛肉在爐上燉煮時，茱莉亞準備了一些晚餐要吃的蔬菜。
- My favorite food is my granny's beef stew.
  我最喜歡吃的就是我奶奶做的燉牛肉。

25 decline [dɪˋklaɪn] *vt.* & *vi.* 婉拒 & *vi.* & *n.* 下跌

片 (1) decline to V　婉拒／謝絕做……
(2) decline sb's invitation
婉拒某人的邀請
(3) be on the decline　下降中
= be in decline

似 decrease [dɪˋkris] *vt.* & *vi.* 下降 & [ˋdikris] *n.* 下降 ③

反 (1) rise [raɪz] *vi.* & *n.* 上漲 ①
(2) increase [ɪnˋkris] *vt.* & *vi.* 增加 & [ˋɪnkris] *n.* 增加 ②

- Bob declined to join Judy's dinner party.
  鮑伯婉拒出席茱蒂的晚宴派對。
- I offered to give Tina a ride after the party, but she declined.
  舞會結束後我提議讓蒂娜搭便車，但她婉拒了。
- Car sales declined by 5% in the second quarter.
  汽車銷售量在第 2 季下降了 5%。
- Street violence seems to have been on the decline ever since the new mayor was sworn in.
  新市長上任後，街頭暴力事件似乎已在減少中。

26 conceive [kənˋsiv] *vt.* & *vi.* 構思，設想；懷孕

片 (1) conceive of sth　想像某事
(2) conceive of A as B　把 A 看作 B
(3) conceive a baby / child
懷了一個小孩

似 imagine [ɪˋmædʒɪn] *vt.* & *vi.* 想像 ②

- John conceived a plan that we all supported.
  我們都支持約翰所構思的計畫。
- An underwater wedding? Really, who would conceive of such a thing?
  水中婚禮？說真的，誰會想到這種主意？
- A woman usually gives birth ten months after conceiving a child.
  女性通常懷胎十月才生下孩子。

conception [kənˋsɛpʃən] *n.* 看法，觀念；概念；懷孕

似 concept [ˋkɑnsɛpt] *n.* 概念 ④

- Such an old conception about women should be forgotten.
  這樣一個對女性的老舊看法應該被棄絕。
- They had no conception that the Earth orbits the Sun.
  他們對於地球繞太陽運轉一事毫無概念。
- The premature baby was born only seven months after its conception.
  那名早產兒是在懷孕僅 7 個月後就生下來的。

27 inevitable [ɪnˋɛvətəbl̩] *a.* 不可避免的，必然的

片 (1) It is inevitable that... ……是不可避免的
(2) an inevitable consequence / result 不可避免的結果

衍 (1) inevitably [ɪnˋɛvətəblɪ] *adv.* 不可避免地
(2) inevitability [ˌɪnɛvətəˋbɪlətɪ] *n.* 不可避免之事

似 unavoidable [ˌʌnəˋvɔɪdəbl̩] *a.* 無法避免的

▸ That lazy guy's failure is inevitable.
那個懶惰蟲的失敗是必然的。

▸ It is inevitable that natural resources will be used up one day.
自然資源有天會被使用殆盡是不可避免的。

▸ The accident was seen as an inevitable result of parental negligence.
該起意外被視為是由於父母親疏失所造成無可避免的結果。
*negligence [ˋnɛglɪdʒəns] *n.* 疏忽

28 variable [ˋvɛrɪəbl̩] *a.* 多變的 & *n.* 變數，可變因素

衍 (1) variability [ˌvɛrɪəˋbɪlətɪ] *n.* 變化性
(2) variably [ˋvɛrɪəblɪ] *adv.* 變化地

▸ Prices are variable according to the rate of exchange.
價格隨匯率而變動。

▸ We should take all the variables into account before we make the final decision.
在做出最後決定前，我們應把所有變數考慮進去。

variation [ˌvɛrɪˋeʃən] *n.* 變化；變動（常與介詞 in 並用）

衍 (1) vary [ˋvɛrɪ] *vi.* 變化 ③
(2) variety [vəˋraɪətɪ] *n.* 變化 ③
(3) various [ˋvɛrɪəs] *a.* 各式各樣的 ③

▸ The barometer measured slight variations in pressure.
氣壓計測量到了大氣壓力的些微變化。
*barometer [bəˋrɑmətɚ] *n.* 氣壓計

29 undergo [ˌʌndɚˋgo] *vt.* 經歷；接受（治療、訓練）

三 undergo, underwent [ˌʌndɚˋwɛnt], undergone [ˌʌndɚˋgɔn]

似 (1) experience [ɪkˋspɪrɪəns] *vt.* 經歷 ①
(2) go through 經歷

▸ Phoebe underwent a lot of setbacks before becoming what she is today.
菲比經歷了許多挫敗才有今天的成就。
*setback [ˋsɛtˌbæk] *n.* 挫折

▸ The hospital requires that interns undergo extensive training.
這間醫院要求實習醫生接受大量的訓練。
*intern [ˋɪntɝn] *n.* 實習醫生；實習生

30 senator [ˋsɛnətɚ] *n.* 參議員

▸ Only three senators voted for the bill.
只有 3 名參議員投票支持該法案。

31 sponsor [ˋspɑnsɚ] *n.* 贊助商 & *vt.* 資助，贊助

似 (1) support [səˋpɔrt] *vt.* 支持 ②
support sb/sth
支持某人 / 某事物
(2) finance [faɪˋnæns]
vt. 向……提供資金 ④

▸ Those college students are seeking corporate sponsors to finance their project.
那些大學生正在尋求企業**贊助廠商**來資助他們的企畫。

▸ There were few businesses that were willing to sponsor the program.
沒什麼企業願意**贊助**這項計畫。

sponsorship [ˋspɑnsɚ͵ʃɪp] *n.* 贊助

▸ The sponsorship agreed to by the corporation allowed it to display its advertising at concerts at the stadium.
這間公司同意以在體育場的音樂會上刊登廣告來**贊助**。

▸ The sports club is looking for sponsorship of its competition so it can afford to buy some nice prizes.
這間運動俱樂部正在尋找比賽的**贊助**，好讓他們買得起一些不錯的獎品。

32 jury [ˋdʒʊrɪ] *n.* 陪審團

延伸 (1) judge [dʒʌdʒ] *n.* 法官 ②
(2) prosecutor [ˋprɑsɪ͵kjutɚ]
n. 檢察官

▸ The jury found the suspect not guilty, but the prosecutor disagreed.
陪審團認定這名嫌犯無罪，不過檢察官卻不認同。

33 convict [͵kənˋvɪkt] *vt.* & *vi.* (使) 定罪 & [ˋkɑnvɪkt] *n.* 囚犯

片 be convicted of... 被判有……的罪

反 acquit [əˋkwɪt] *vt.* 宣告……無罪
acquit sb of... 宣告某人無……的罪

▸ The jury acquitted O.J. Simpson of murdering his wife.
陪審團宣告 O. J. 辛普森謀殺妻子的**罪**名不成立。

▸ The man was convicted of theft and sentenced to two years in prison.
這名男子**被判**竊盜**罪**，處以兩年有期徒刑。

▸ The police were confident that they had gathered enough evidence to convict.
警方確信他們蒐集了足夠的證據來**定罪**。

▸ The convicts were given time each day to exercise in the prison yard.
囚犯每天有在監獄庭院運動的時間。

conviction [͵kənˋvɪkʃən] *n.* 定罪；信念

片 It is sb's conviction that...
某人堅信……
= It is sb's belief that...

似 belief [bɪˋlif] *n.* 信念 ②

▸ The court affirmed the man's conviction and sentenced him to life in prison.
法庭判定該男子的**罪行**，處以無期徒刑。
*affirm [əˋfɝm] *vt.* 證實

▸ It is our firm conviction that the economy will get better after the pandemic.
我們**堅信**疫情過後經濟很快就會好轉。

0601-0605

1 fiber [ˋfaɪbɚ] *n.* 纖維

▸ Fruit and vegetables are good sources of fiber, which is good for your health.
水果和蔬菜都是攝取**纖維**的好來源，對人的健康有益。

2 correspondent [ˏkɔrəˋspɑndənt] *n.* (報社、通訊社) 特派員

片 a war correspondent
戰地特派記者

衍 correspond [ˏkɔrəˋspɑnd] *vi.* 通信 ④

▸ Our war correspondent sent this story from Iraq.
我們的**戰地特派記者**從伊拉克傳回這則報導。

3 gathering [ˋgæðərɪŋ] *n.* 聚會

片 a social / family gathering
社交 / 家庭聚會

衍 gather [ˋgæðɚ] *vi.* 聚集 ②

似 get-together [ˋgɛttəˏgɛðɚ] *n.* 聚會

▸ There will be a small gathering tonight at Victor's house to celebrate his retirement.
今晚在維克多家將有一場小型**聚會**，慶祝他退休。

rally [ˋrælɪ] *n.* 集會 & *vt.* & *vi.* 集合，召集

三 rally, rallied [ˋrælɪd], rallied

片 hold / attend a rally
舉行 / 參與集會

似 assembly [əˋsɛmblɪ] *n.* 集會 ④

▸ Nearly 20,000 people attended the rally in front of the city hall last Saturday.
上星期六有將近 2 萬名民眾**參與**了市政府前的**集會**。

▸ The politician gave a speech in order to rally people to vote for him.
這名政客發表演說，以**召集**人民將票投給他。

▸ Unemployed workers rallied in front of the factory, ready to launch a demonstration.
失業的員工**聚集**在工廠前，準備發動示威。

4 eternal [ɪˋtɝnḷ] *a.* 永恆的

衍 eternity [ɪˋtɝnətɪ] *n.* 永恆 ⑥

似 (1) everlasting [ˏɛvɚˋlæstɪŋ] *a.* 永恆的
(2) perpetual [pɚˋpɛtʃuəl] *a.* 永恆的

▸ This wedding ring is a symbol of my eternal love for you.
這只婚戒象徵我對你**永恆的**愛。

5 bound [baund] *a.* 必然的；前往……的 & *n.* 跳躍；界限 (恆用複數) & *vi.* 跳躍

片 (1) be bound to V 很可能會……
= be sure to V
= be certain to V
= be destined to V

▸ Luke, who's been working so hard over the past 10 years, is bound to succeed as an outstanding scientist.
路克過去 10 年來都很勤奮，**注定會**有所成就，成為傑出的科學家。

0605-0611

(2) be bound for + 地方　前往某地
(3) by leaps and bounds　大幅度
(4) know no bounds　無止境

衍 bind [baɪnd] *vt.* 綁；束縛 ③

比 be doomed to...　注定要……（通常與表『失敗、死亡』等負面的字詞並用）

▶ Such a lazy man is doomed to fail.
這樣的懶人注定要失敗。

▶ I'm afraid you've taken the wrong train. This train is bound for New York, not Chicago.
恐怕你搭錯火車了。這班火車開往紐約，並非芝加哥。

▶ Thanks to Mr. Wilson's instruction, Jane's English has improved by leaps and bounds.
由於威爾遜老師的教導，珍的英文已大幅進步。

▶ Human imagination knows no bounds.
人類的想像力沒有極限。

▶ Lucy was so happy to get her birthday presents that she bounded across the room.
露西收到生日禮物很開心，所以她在房裡跳來跳去。

boundless [ˋbaʊndləs] *a.* 無限的，無窮的

似 (1) infinite [ˋɪnfənɪt] *a.* 無限的 ⑤
(2) unlimited [ʌnˋlɪmɪtɪd] *a.* 無限的
(3) endless [ˋɛndləs] *a.* 無限的

▶ Little kids are active and seem to have boundless energy.
小朋友都很好動，似乎精力無窮。

boundary [ˋbaʊnd(ə)rɪ] *n.* 邊界，分界線；界限

似 border [ˋbɔrdɚ] *n.* 邊界 ②

▶ The boundaries between countries are commonly known as international borders.
國與國之間的分界線通常被稱作國界。

▶ Prior to the interview, the mayor tried to establish the boundaries of the topics to be discussed.
在訪談前，市長試圖訂定討論主題的範圍。

6 diameter [daɪˋæmətɚ] *n.* 直徑

片 be... in diameter　直徑是……

延伸 radius [ˋredɪəs] *n.* 半徑 ⑥

▶ The diameter of this circle is 5 cm.
= This circle is 5 cm in diameter.
這個圓的直徑是 5 公分。

7 agricultural [ˏægrɪˋkʌltʃərəl] *a.* 農業的

片 an agricultural society　農業社會

衍 agriculture [ˋægrɪkʌltʃɚ] *n.* 農業 ③

▶ The scholars discussed agricultural issues in the Third World at the conference.
學者們在會議上討論第三世界的農業問題。

8 gross [gros] *a.* 總共的；噁心的 & *vt.* 總收入為 & *n.* 總額，總收入

片 (1) the Gross National Product (GNP)　國民生產毛額
(2) the Gross Domestic Product (GDP)　國內生產總值

▶ The gross profit of the company reached 5 million dollars last year.
該公司去年的毛利達到 500 萬美元。

▶ Fiona has a gross habit of biting her nails.
費歐娜有咬指甲的噁心習慣。

(3) the gross income / profit 總收入 / 毛利

(4) gross (sb) out 使(某人)噁心

似 disgusting [dɪsˋgʌstɪŋ] *a.* 噁心的

延伸 net [nɛt] *n.* 淨利 ①

▶ In his new job, Frank grosses about US$100,000, but the amount he keeps is much less than that.
法蘭克的新工作總收入約為 10 萬美元，但他拿到的比那筆金額還少多了。

▶ Gloria saw a cockroach run across a table in the restaurant, which totally grossed her out.
葛洛莉雅看到一隻蟑螂爬過餐廳的桌子，讓她感到噁心極了。

▶ The film's gross was US$150 million in the United States, and nearly US$370 million internationally.
這部影片在美國的總票房為 1 億 5 千萬美元，國際上約為 3 億 7 千萬美元。

9 elaborate [ɪˋlæbərɪt] *a.* 精緻的 & [ɪˋlæbəˏret] *vi.* & *vt.* 詳細說明，闡述

片 elaborate on... 詳細說明……

衍 elaboration [ɪˏlæbəˋreʃən] *n.* 詳細闡述；精緻

▶ Mandy was dressed in a blue suit with elaborate embroidery on the shoulder.
曼蒂穿著一襲肩上飾有精緻刺繡的藍色套裝。
*embroidery [ɪmˋbrɔɪdərɪ] *n.* 刺繡

▶ Just tell us the result. You don't have to elaborate on the process.
只要把結果告訴我們就好了，過程你就不必詳述了。

▶ The scientist attempted to elaborate his theories through a series of experiments.
科學家試圖透過一系列實驗來闡述他的理論。

10 fraction [ˋfrækʃən] *n.* 小部分；微量

片 a (small) fraction of... 一小部分 / 些微的……

▶ Vicky spends only a small fraction of her earnings on clothes.
薇琪只花一小部分的收入在衣服上。

11 straighten [ˋstretn̩] *vt.* & *vi.* (使) 變直 & *vt.* 整頓，整理

片 straighten out sth / straighten sth out (成功) 解決某事

衍 (1) straight [stret] *a.* 直的 ①
(2) straightforward [ˏstretˋfɔrwɚd] *a.* 坦率的 ⑤

▶ I fractured my left shoulder bone in a car accident 10 years ago. Even today, I still can't fully straighten my arm.
10 年前的一起車禍中，我左肩骨折。甚至到今天，我還無法把手臂打直。
*fracture [ˋfræktʃɚ] *vt.* 使碎裂

▶ Tanya wasn't happy with her curly hair, but it wasn't easy to straighten.
潭雅不滿意自己的捲髮，但要把它弄直不容易。

▶ I must straighten out the situation before I can tell you what to do.
我得先釐清這情況才能告訴你要怎麼做。

12 patent [ˋpætn̩t] *n.* 專利（權）& *vt.* 取得專利 & *a.* 專利的

片 (1) apply for a patent (for...)
申請（……的）專利
(2) a patent number 專利號碼

▸ Polly applied for a patent for her 3-dimensional puzzle to protect her intellectual property.
波莉為她的立體拼圖申請專利以保障她的智慧財產權。

▸ You should patent your new invention as soon as possible to prevent piracy problems.
你應該儘快為你的新發明取得專利以避免盜版問題。
*piracy [ˋpaɪrəsɪ] *n.* 盜版行為

▸ Once John had developed his invention, he started looking for a good patent lawyer.
約翰完成他的發明後，便開始尋找一位好的專利律師。

copyright [ˋkɑpɪˌraɪt] *n.* 版權；著作權 & *vt.* 取得版權

延伸 royalty [ˋrɔɪəltɪ] *n.* 版稅（常用複數）

▸ The copyright on the book had expired, so anyone could use it in any way they wanted.
這本書的著作權到期了，所以任何人都可以用任何他們想要的形式使用這本書。

▸ In the United States, one good way to copyright material is to register it with the Library of Congress.
在美國，取得素材版權的一項好方法是到國會圖書館註冊。

13 poetic [poˋɛtɪk] *a.* 充滿詩意的；詩的

衍 (1) poem [ˋpoɪm]
n.（一首）詩（可數）②
(2) poet [ˋpoɪt] *n.* 詩人 ②
(3) poetry [ˋpoɪtrɪ]
n. 詩（總稱，不可數）②

▸ The words the writer used to describe the scenery are beautiful and poetic.
這個作家用來描述這片風景的文字既優美又充滿詩意。

14 substitute [ˋsʌbstəˌt(j)ut] *vt.* & *vi.* 代替 & *n.* 代替品 / 者

片 (1) substitute A for B 用 A 取代 B
= replace B with A
(2) substitute for... 代替……

衍 substitution [ˌsʌbstəˋt(j)uʃən]
n. 代替

似 replace [rɪˋples] *vt.* 替換 ③

▸ You can substitute apple sauce for oil when baking a cake.
做蛋糕時，你可以使用蘋果醬替代油。

▸ Who is going to substitute for you while you are on vacation?
你休假時誰來代理你的職位？

▸ Honey is a good substitute for sugar because it is healthier.
蜂蜜是代替砂糖很好的東西，因為它比較健康。

15 sensitivity [ˌsɛnsəˋtɪvətɪ] *n.* 體貼，細膩體會；敏感

片 the sensitivity to... 對……很敏感

▸ Adam's tenderness and sensitivity won Eve's heart.
亞當的溫柔與心思細膩贏得伊芙的芳心。

衍 sensitive [ˋsɛnsətɪv] *a.* 敏感的 ②
be sensitive to 對……很敏感

▸ Due to his sensitivity to criticism, Roger often gets angry and has lost some friends as a result.
由於羅傑對批評很敏感，所以他經常生氣，也為此失去了一些朋友。

---

sensation [sɛnˋseʃən] *n.* 感覺，知覺；轟動（的事情）

片 cause a sensation 引起轟動

▸ Following the car accident, Rose lost the sensation in two fingers on her left hand.
車禍後，蘿絲左手的兩根手指失去了知覺。

▸ The news that the famous Korean band would play a concert in Taipei caused a big sensation.
該知名韓國樂團會在臺北辦演唱會的消息造成了一場大轟動。

---

sensational [sɛnˋseʃənəl] *a.* 轟動的

似 (1) amazing [əˋmezɪŋ] *a.* 令人吃驚的
(2) startling [ˋstartḷɪŋ] *a.* 驚人的

▸ The sensational discovery of oil stimulated economic growth in this area.
石油的驚人發現帶動該區的經濟發展。

16 boredom [ˋbɔrdəm] *n.* 無聊（不可數）

片 out of boredom 出於無聊

衍 (1) bored [bɔrd] *a.* 感到無聊的 ①
(2) boring [ˋbɔrɪŋ] *a.* 令人無聊的 ①
(3) bore [bɔr] *vt.* 使無聊 & *n.* 無聊的人 / 事 ③

▸ For Blair, every day is just working, eating, and sleeping. Life is full of boredom for her.
對布萊兒來說，每天就是工作、吃飯和睡覺。對她來說，人生真是無聊。

▸ James sat in front of the TV all day and ate junk food out of boredom.
詹姆士整天因為無聊就坐在電視機前吃零食。

17 banner [ˋbænɚ] *n.* 旗幟，長布條

似 flag [flæg] *n.* 旗子（尤指國旗）②

▸ There are banners everywhere in the city during the festival.
慶典期間，城市中到處都插滿了旗幟。

18 chubby [ˋtʃʌbɪ] *a.* 圓胖的

似 plump [plʌmp] *a.* 胖嘟嘟的

▸ This baby boy has rosy cheeks and chubby legs.
這個小寶寶有紅潤的雙頰和胖嘟嘟的雙腿。

19 perspective [pɚˋspɛktɪv] *n.* 觀點 & *a.* 透視的

片 (1) a perspective on...
對……的觀點
(2) from sb's perspective
從某人的觀點

▸ The accident gave me a whole new perspective on life.
這場意外讓我對生命有全新的觀點。

0619-0626

(3) from a(n) + adj. perspective
從……的觀點

(4) from the perspective of...
從……的觀點

▶ This novel is written from a blind person's perspective.
= This novel is written from the perspective of a blind person.
這本小說是從一位盲人的觀點寫的。

似 (1) opinion [əˋpɪnjən] *n.* 看法 ②
(2) viewpoint [ˋvju,pɔɪnt] *n.* 觀點 ⑤
(3) point of view 觀點

▶ The art teacher told Heather that she needed to learn more about perspective drawing.
美術老師告訴海瑟她需要多加學習透視畫。

20 anticipate [ænˋtɪsə,pet] *vt.* 期待，預期（常用名詞或動名詞作受詞）

比 anticipate 與 expect 均表『期待』，但 anticipate 需用名詞或動名詞作受詞，expect 則用名詞或不定詞片語作受詞。

▶ The law firm anticipates having dozens of applicants for the job.
= The law firm expects to have dozens of applicants for the job.
那家律師事務所預計將有數十人應徵該職缺。

21 version [ˋvɝʒən] *n.* 譯本；版本；（文藝作品的）改編形式

延伸 edition [əˋdɪʃən] *n.*（刊物、書籍的）再版 ②

▶ A Chinese version of that novel is going to be published next year.
那本小說的中譯本預計明年出版。

▶ Have you bought the latest version of the software?
你買了這套軟體的最新版本嗎？

▶ I prefer the film version of *Little Women*.
我比較喜歡電影版的《小婦人》。

22 undertake [,ʌndɚˋtek] *vt.* 承接，進行；承諾，保證

三 undertake, undertook [,ʌndɚˋtuk], undertaken [,ʌndɚˋtekən]

片 (1) undertake a project / research / study 承接一項計畫 / 調查 / 研究
(2) undertake to V 承諾做……

衍 undertaking [,ʌndɚˋtekɪŋ] *n.* 工作，任務

▶ Constructing a tunnel through the mountains can be a very difficult undertaking.
穿梭群山蓋隧道是項十分艱鉅的任務。

▶ Prof. Smith undertook a project of writing a book on zoology.
史密斯教授接下了撰寫動物學專書的計畫。

▶ I cannot undertake to finish the job by Friday.
= I cannot promise to finish the job by Friday.
我無法擔保星期五之前可以完工。

23 assert [əˋsɝt] *vt.* 堅稱；維護，堅持

片 (1) assert that... 堅稱……
(2) assert one's rights / authority 維護某人的權利 / 權威
(3) assert oneself 堅持自己的意見

▶ Frank asserted that he did not steal the money from the company.
法蘭克堅稱自己沒從公司偷錢。

▶ My boss rarely asserts his authority over his employees unless necessary.
若非必要，我的老闆很少會在員工面前維護自己的權威。

▶ You should have asserted yourself during that meeting.
那場會議中，你真該堅持己見。

24 interval [ˋɪntɚvḷ] *n.* 間隔(的時間)

片 (1) at intervals of + 時間 每隔若干時間
= at + 時間 + intervals
(2) at (regular) intervals 每隔一段固定時間

▶ The buses here run at intervals of 10 minutes.
= The buses here run at 10-minute intervals.
這裡的公車每隔 10 分鐘一班。

▶ Buses and trains from New Jersey to New York run at regular intervals.
從紐澤西到紐約有定時的公車和火車開出。

25 integrate [ˋɪntəˏgret] *vt.* 使整合

片 integrate A into B 將 A 與 B 整合
似 (1) combine [kəmˋbaɪn] *vt.* 使結合 ②
(2) incorporate [ɪnˋkɔrpəˏret] *vt.* 使併入 ⑤

▶ The manager decided to integrate my proposal into the company's marketing strategies.
經理決定把我的提議納入公司行銷策略中。

integration [ˏɪntəˋgreʃən] *n.* 整合

片 (1) the integration of A and B A 和 B 的融合
(2) the integration of A into B A 融合進 B
似 (1) combination [ˏkɑmbəˋneʃən] *n.* 結合 ④
(2) incorporation [ɪnˏkɔrpəˋreʃən] *n.* 融入

▶ The composer's music is the integration of hip-hop and Asian-American culture.
這位作曲家的音樂融合了嘻哈音樂和亞裔美人的文化。

26 regardless [rɪˋgardləs] *adv.* 無論如何 & *a.* 不留心的

片 regardless of... 不論……
= despite...
= in spite of...

▶ Everyone is required to attend the meeting regardless of the typhoon.
儘管有颱風，每個人還是被要求出席會議。

▶ Tony's regardless actions have gotten him into a lot of trouble recently.
最近東尼漫不經心的舉動替他招來許多麻煩。

0627-0635

27 opponent [əˋponənt] *n.* 對手

似 rival [ˋraɪvḷ] *n.* 敵手 & *vt.* 與……匹敵 ⑤

▶ The boxer knocked his opponent out in the second round.
拳擊手在第二回將他的對手擊倒。

28 opposition [ˌɑpəˋzɪʃən] *n.* 反對

片 (1) be met with fierce opposition 遭遇強烈的反對
(2) the opposition party 反對黨

衍 (1) oppose [əˋpoz] *vt.* & *vi.* 反對 ④
(2) opposed [əˋpozd] *a.* 反對的
(3) opposite [ˋɑpəzɪt] *a.* 相對的；相反的 & *prep.* 在……對面 ③

▶ The plan to set up a branch office in Japan was met with fierce opposition.
要在日本設立分公司的計畫遭逢強烈的反彈。

29 alternate [ˋɔltɚˌnet] *vt.* & *vi.* 交替，輪流 & [ˋɔltɚnɪt] *a.* 間隔的；交替的 & *n.* 代替者

片 (1) alternate A with B 時而 A 時而 B
= alternate between A and B
(2) on alternate Mondays / weekends 隔週週一 / 週末
(3) in alternate turns 輪流地

衍 alternative [ɔlˋtɚnətɪv] *n.* 選擇 & *a.* 替代的 ④

▶ Peter alternated working here with doing research abroad.
彼得時而在這裡工作，時而出國考察。

▶ I visit my grandmother on alternate weekends.
我隔週的週末都會去看我外婆。

▶ Like many games, Monopoly is played in alternate turns, with players rolling dice.
像許多遊戲一樣，大富翁是玩家擲骰子輪流著玩。

▶ Ray was dissatisfied with being chosen as an alternate on the team.
雷對自己被選為隊上的候補成員感到不滿。

30 dimension [dɪˋmɛnʃən] *n.* 面向，方面；(長、寬、高等的) 尺寸，面積 (常用複數)；(問題的) 嚴重性 (常用複數)

片 add a new dimension to sth 增加某事的新面向

衍 dimensional [dɪˋmɛnʃənḷ] *a.* 尺寸的

似 aspect [ˋæspɛkt] *n.* 方面 ④

延伸 three-dimensional 三度空間的 (= 3D)

▶ I think you have neglected another important dimension of the problem.
我認為你忽略了該問題的另一個重要面向。

▶ We need to know the exact dimensions of the living room before we buy the furniture.
買傢俱之前，我們得確定客廳的尺寸是多少。

▶ I didn't realize the dimensions of this problem.
= I didn't realize the seriousness of this problem.
我並未意識到這個問題的嚴重性。

31 render [ˋrɛndɚ] *vt.* 使成為；提供；翻譯

片 (1) render sb/sth + 形容詞
使某人／某物變得……
(2) render A into B 將 A 翻譯成 B
= translate A into B

▶ Thousands of people were rendered homeless by the flood.
這次的水災使上千人無家可歸。

▶ That store renders excellent service to its customers.
= That store offers excellent service to its customers.
那家店提供顧客很棒的服務。

▶ David is well trained in rendering English into Chinese.
大衛在英翻中方面受過良好的訓練。

32 revenue [ˋrɛvənju] *n.* (政府) 稅收；(公司) 收入

片 tax revenue(s) 稅收

▶ The government has a huge need for tax revenue.
政府有強大的稅收需求。

33 core [kɔr] *n.* (水果) 果核；核心

片 (1) an apple core 蘋果核
(2) the core of the problem
問題的核心
(3) be rotten to the core
(人) 壞透了；(物) 爛透了

▶ The lack of funding for this project is the core of the problem.
缺少資金才是這個企畫案問題的核心。

▶ Billy is rotten to the core! Money is the only thing he cares about.
比利這個人爛透了！他眼裡只有錢。

34 transaction [trænˋzækʃən] *n.* 交易

衍 transact [trænˋzækt] *vt.* 交易
transact a deal 進行交易

▶ Each transaction at the ATM is subject to an additional charge.
自動櫃員機的每筆交易都要額外收費。
*ATM 自動櫃員機 (為 automated teller machine 的縮寫)

35 integrity [ɪnˋtɛgrətɪ] *n.* 正直

片 (1) a man of integrity 正直的人
(2) sb's artistic / personal integrity
某人的藝術／個人操守

▶ Jerome has always been regarded as a man of integrity.
傑若姆向來被大家視為正人君子。

Unit 07

0701-0709

1 denial [dɪˋnaɪəl] *n.* 否認；拒絕

衍 deny [dɪˋnaɪ] *vt.* 否認；拒絕 ②
deny + N/V-ing　否認……
deny sb sth　拒絕某人某物

似 refusal [rɪˋfjuzḷ] *n.* 拒絕 ④

▸ Despite official denials, rumors about the mayor's death kept spreading.
儘管官方否認，有關市長死亡的謠言不斷在散播。

▸ The factory is in trouble for its denial of workers' rights.
這間工廠因否定員工權益而惹禍上身。

2 compel [kəmˋpɛl] *vt.* 迫使

三 compel, compelled [kəmˋpɛld], compelled

片 compel sb to V　強迫某人做……
= force sb to V

似 (1) force [fɔrs] *vt.* 強迫 ②
(2) oblige [əˋblaɪdʒ] *vt.* 迫使 ⑥

▸ Kevin's illness compelled him to drop out of school.
凱文的疾病迫使他輟學。

3 freight [fret] *n.* (運送的) 貨物 (集合名詞，不可數) & *vt.* 運送 (貨物)

片 (1) a freight train / car　貨運火車 / 車廂
(2) air freight　空運的貨物
(3) sea freight　海運的貨物
(4) rail freight　鐵路運輸的貨物

▸ Air freight is a lot faster but more expensive than sea freight.
= Freight carried by air is a lot faster but more expensive than freight by sea.
空運貨物要比海運快多了，但較昂貴。

▸ We always pay extra to freight the goods by airplane.
我們總是額外付費空運貨物。

4 whisk [(h)wɪsk] *vt.* 攪 (蛋，麵粉等) & *n.* 攪拌器

片 an electric whisk　電動攪拌器

▸ Whisk the egg whites in a bowl until they're very stiff.
把碗裡的蛋白攪拌到黏稠為止。
*stiff [stɪf] *a.* 黏稠的

5 ally [ˋælaɪ] *n.* 同盟者 / 國 & [əˋlaɪ] *vt.* 使結盟

複 allies

三 ally, allied [əˋlaɪd], allied

片 (1) the Allies　(二次世界大戰期間的) 同盟國
(2) ally oneself with sb　與某人結盟

衍 allied [əˋlaɪd] *a.* 結盟的

▸ During World War II, Great Britain and the USA were allies.
二次世界大戰期間，大英帝國和美國是同盟國。

▸ We must ally ourselves with other countries to fight terrorism.
我們必須聯合其他國家對抗恐怖主義。

alliance [əˋlaɪəns] *n.* 結盟

片 (1) form / make an alliance with... 與……結盟
(2) be in alliance with... 聯合……

▸ Small countries usually protect themselves by forming an alliance with their stronger neighbors.
小國常以跟鄰近強國結盟的方式來自保。

6 affection [əˋfɛkʃən] *n.* 喜愛，鍾愛；愛慕之情 (恆用複數)

片 have (an) affection for... 喜愛……
衍 affectionate [əˋfɛkʃənət] *a.* 充滿深情的 ⑥
似 (1) love [lʌv] *n.* 愛 ①
(2) fondness [ˋfɑndnəs] *n.* 喜愛

▸ Mrs. Smith has a great affection for her family, including the stray dog she has kept for almost ten years.
史密斯太太深愛她的家人，包括那隻她養了 10 年的流浪狗。

▸ The two knights competed for the affections of the beautiful princess.
兩名騎士爭奪美麗公主的愛。

7 declaration [ˌdɛkləˋreʃən] *n.* 宣告；聲明

片 make / issue a declaration 發表聲明
衍 declare [dɪˋklɛr] *vt.* 宣告 ④

▸ The US Declaration of Independence was signed on July 4, 1776.
美國獨立宣言是在 1776 年 7 月 4 日簽訂的。

8 ethic [ˋɛθɪk] *n.* 道德標準

片 (1) a code of ethics 道德規範
(2) work ethics 職業道德 (常用複數)
似 moral [ˋmɔrəl] *n.* 道德 (恆用複數) ③

▸ The reporter violated the ethics of his profession by revealing the source's identity.
這名記者因透露消息來源的身分而違反了職業道德。

▸ The progress of science is often restricted by a code of ethics.
科學的發展常被道德規範給限制住。

ethics [ˋɛθɪks] *n.* 道德學，倫理學

▸ Sophie is taking a PhD in philosophy and specializing in ethics.
蘇菲正攻讀哲學博士學位且專攻倫理學。

ethical [ˋɛθɪkḷ] *a.* 道德的

衍 ethically [ˋɛθɪkḷɪ] *adv.* 道德上
似 (1) ethnic [ˋɛθnɪk] *a.* 種族的 ④
(2) moral [ˋmɔrəl] *a.* 道德的 ③

▸ There are many ethical issues involved in human cloning.
複製人類牽涉許多道德問題。
*clone [klon] *vt.* 複製

9 statistical [stəˋtɪstɪkḷ] *a.* 統計 (學) 的

衍 (1) statistic [stəˋtɪstɪk] *n.* 統計數字 ④
(2) statistically [stəˋtɪstɪkḷɪ] *adv.* 就統計數字來說

▸ A wide range of statistical analysis software will help us shape our marketing strategy.
各類型的統計分析軟體將有助於我們制定行銷策略。

0710-0716

10 rigid [ˋrɪdʒɪd] *a.* 堅固的，不易彎曲的；死板的，嚴格的

似 (1) unbending [ʌnˋbɛndɪŋ]
a. 不易彎曲的；不妥協的
(2) strict [strɪkt] *a.* 嚴格的 ②

反 flexible [ˋflɛksəbl̩] *a.* 可彎曲的；可變通的 ④

▸ The shopping mall was constructed out of rigid steel and a lot of concrete.
這個購物中心是由**堅固的**鋼鐵及大量混凝土所建造而成。

▸ Congress has asked the President to adopt a rigid position on illegal immigration.
國會要求總統對非法移民的問題採取**嚴格的**立場。

11 province [ˋprɑvɪns] *n.* 省

片 the provinces　外地，外省
（首都以外的地方）

衍 provincial [prəˋvɪnʃəl] *a.* 省的 ⑥

▸ The province of Alberta, Canada is magnificent.
加拿大的亞伯達**省**很美。

12 constitutional [ˌkɑnstəˋt(j)uʃənl̩] *a.* 憲法的 & *n.* 健身散步

片 a constitutional amendment
憲法修正案
= an amendment to the constitution

衍 (1) constitution [ˌkɑnstəˋt(j)uʃən]
n. 憲法 ④
(2) constitute [ˋkɑnstəˌt(j)ut]
vt. 構成；制定 ④

▸ Freedom of speech is a constitutional protection in a truly democratic country.
在真正的民主國家中，言論自由會受到**憲法的**保護。

▸ Even at the age of 93, Betty still goes for her morning constitutional every day.
即使貝蒂 93 歲了，她仍每天早上都去**健身散步**。

13 stumble [ˋstʌmbl̩] *vi.* 絆倒；踉蹌；結巴 & *n.* 絆倒

片 (1) stumble on / over sth
被某物絆倒
= trip over sth
(2) stumble at / over...
結結巴巴地說……

似 (1) trip [trɪp] *vi.* 絆倒 ①
(2) stagger [ˋstægɚ] *vi.* 蹣跚而行 ⑥
(3) stutter [ˋstʌtɚ] *vi.* & *n.* 結巴 ⑥
(4) stammer [ˋstæmɚ] *vi.* & *n.* 結巴

▸ While running on the beach, I stumbled over a log and sprained my ankle.
= While running on the beach, I tripped over a log and sprained my ankle.
在沙灘上跑步時，我**被**一塊木頭**絆倒**，扭傷了腳踝。

▸ That guy who is stumbling down the street must be drunk.
那個沿街**踉蹌而行**的傢伙一定是喝醉了。

▸ Dianne stumbled over her words a few times, finding it hard to make a speech in front of the class.
黛安講話**結巴**了幾次，她發現要在全班面前演講是件困難的事。

▸ The marathon runner took a stumble but managed to keep going.
那名馬拉松跑者**絆了一下**但繼續跑步。

14 rear [rɪr] *n.* 後部 & *a.* 後部的 & *vt.* 撫養

片 (1) the rear of... ……的後部 / 後面
(2) the rear door / window 後門 / 窗

似 raise [rez] *vt.* 撫養 ①

延伸 a rearview mirror （車輛）後視鏡

▶ There are emergency exits at both the front and rear of the movie theater.
這家電影院的前**後**都有緊急逃生出口。

▶ The racehorse broke one of its rear legs during the race.
這匹賽馬在比賽時摔斷了其中一隻**後**腿。

▶ The career woman reared a family of five on her own.
這名職業婦女靠自己獨立**撫養**了一家 5 口。

15 stake [stek] *n.* 風險；股份；利害關係；賭金（恆用複數）& *vt.* 以……打賭

片 (1) be at stake 在危險關頭
(2) have a stake in... 與……有利害關係
(3) stake A on B 在 B 上以 A 打賭
= bet A on B

似 (1) risk [rɪsk] *n.* 風險 & *vt.* 冒……的風險 ③
(2) share [ʃɛr] *n.* 股份 ①
(3) bet [bɛt] *n.* 賭金 & *vt.* 以……打賭 ③

▶ We cannot afford to take risks when somebody's life is at stake.
當某人的生命**有危險**時，我們承擔不起風險。

▶ The workers are automatically given a stake in the company.
員工們自動獲得公司的**股份**。

▶ Many a government official has a stake in private enterprises.
許多政府官員**與**私人企業**有利害關係**。

▶ Andrew thinks there's no point in playing poker if the stakes are low.
安德魯認為如果**賭注**很低，那就沒有玩撲克牌的意義了。

▶ The prime minister staked his reputation on the success of the vaccination program.
總理**對**疫苗計畫的成功**賭上**他的名譽。

16 plead [plid] *vi.* 懇求 & *vt.* 承認（有或無罪）

三 plead, pled [plɛd] / pleaded, pled / pleaded

片 (1) plead (with sb) for sth 懇求（某人）某事
(2) plead with sb to V 懇求某人做……
(3) plead guilty 認罪
(4) plead not guilty 辯稱無罪

▶ The soldier was on his knees, pleading for mercy.
這名士兵雙膝跪地，**懇求**寬恕。

▶ The little boy pleaded with his parents not to ground him.
這名小男孩**懇求**父母不要禁足他。

▶ The man pled guilty to the crime.
這男子對這項罪行**俯首認罪**。

---

plea [pli] *n.* 懇求；抗辯（常用單數）

片 make a plea for sb (to V) 懇求某人（做……）

▶ The farmers made a plea for the government to promote domestic produce.
這些農夫**懇請**政府加強促銷國內的農產品。

0716-0723

▸ Everyone in the courtroom was shocked when the defendant changed his guilty plea.
法庭上的每個人對被告推翻其有罪的陳述感到震驚。

17 contend [kən`tɛnd] *vt.* 堅稱（接 that 子句作受詞）& *vi.* 競爭

片 (1) contend that... 堅稱……
(2) contend for sth 爭奪某物
= compete for sth

衍 contention [kən`tɛnʃən] *n.* 主張；爭奪 ⑥

似 (1) content [kən`tɛnt] *vt.* 使滿足 & *a.* 滿足的 & *n.* 滿足 ④
(2) compete [kəm`pit] *vi.* 競爭 ③

▸ The lawyer contended that his client was not at the scene when the crime was committed.
這名律師堅稱案發當時他的當事人並不在現場。
*client [`klaɪənt] *n.* 客戶，委託人

▸ The two countries are contending for sovereignty over the small island.
這兩個國家正在爭奪這座小島的主權歸屬。
*sovereignty [`sɑvrɪntɪ] *n.* 主權

18 erect [ɪ`rɛkt] *vt.* 建立；使豎立 & *a.* 豎直的

似 (1) set up 建立
(2) establish [ə`stæblɪʃ] *vt.* 建立 ④
(3) upright [`ʌp,raɪt] *a.* 筆直的 ⑥

▸ We erected a monument to honor the martyrs.
= We set up a monument to honor the martyrs.
= We established a monument to honor the martyrs.
我們建立一座紀念碑，以記念這些烈士。
*martyr [`mɑrtɚ] *n.* 烈士

▸ The organizers are erecting a tent to protect people from the rain.
籌辦者們正搭起帳篷來供人們避雨。

▸ Jane sat erect, nervously waiting for her test results.
珍坐得直挺挺的，緊張地等待她的檢查結果。

erection [ɪ`rɛkʃən] *n.* 建立

似 establishment [ɪ`stæblɪʃmənt] *n.* 建立 ④

▸ The erection of the building took longer than expected.
這棟大樓的建造花的時間比預期的久。

19 tribute [`trɪbjut] *n.* 敬意

片 (1) pay tribute to sb/sth
向某人／某事物致敬
(2) be a tribute to sb/sth
是某人／某事物（優秀、良好）的證明

▸ Thousands of people gathered at the funeral to pay tribute to the late Princess Diana.
數千名的群眾聚集在喪禮上向已故黛安娜王妃致敬。

▸ Kevin's success in life is a tribute to his hard work and dedication.
凱文人生中的成功是他的努力和貢獻的最佳證明。

20 olive [ˋalɪv] *n.* 橄欖 (樹) & *a.* 橄欖 (色) 的

片 (1) olive oil　橄欖油
(2) an olive tree　橄欖樹
(3) olive green　橄欖綠色

▸ The olive branch represents peace and prosperity.
橄欖樹的樹枝代表著和平和繁榮。

21 triple [ˋtrɪpl̩] *vt.* & *vi.* (使) 成為三倍 & *a.* 三倍的 & *n.* (棒球) 三壘打

▸ Ashley decided to stay on when the boss tripled her monthly salary.
老闆將艾希莉的月薪加到 3 倍時，她就決定繼續待在公司了。

▸ The number of people unemployed has tripled over the past year.
失業人數在過去一年裡已增至三倍。

▸ I'll pay triple the market price to purchase that piece of land.
我會付市價 3 倍的價格買下那塊土地。

▸ The crowd cheered when the baseball player hit a triple.
這名棒球選手擊出三壘打時全場觀眾歡呼。

22 update [ʌpˋdet] *vt.* 使更新；為……提供最新消息 & [ˋʌpdet] *n.* 更新 (消息)

片 (1) update sb on sth
告知某人某事的最新消息
(2) an update on sth
某事的更新 (消息)

▸ We're going to update our computer software next month.
我們將於下個月更新我們的電腦軟體。

▸ We'll update you on the latest development of the murder trial.
我們會讓你知道這起謀殺審判發展的最新消息。

▸ Coming up next on this station is our news update.
本臺接下來進行的是即時新聞。

23 controversy [ˋkɑntrəˏvɝsɪ] *n.* 爭議

片 cause / arouse controversy over / about sth　引起關於某事的爭議

▸ The new policy has caused heated controversy over the rights of employees.
這項新政策引起關於員工權利的激烈爭論。
*heated [ˋhitɪd] *a.* 激烈的

controversial [ˏkɑntrəˋvɝʃəl]
a. 有爭議的

片 be highly controversial
具高度爭議的

▸ Religion and politics are highly controversial subjects and, if possible, shouldn't be talked about in public.
宗教和政治是極具爭議的話題，如有可能就不要公開談論。

0724-0735

24 illusion [ɪˋluʒən] *n.* 錯誤的觀念；錯覺，幻覺

片 (1) be under the illusion that...
誤以為……
(2) have no illusions about sth
很清楚某事，對某事不抱幻想

延伸 mirage [məˋrɑʒ] *n.* 海市蜃樓

▶ Fred was under the illusion that he could finish his work on time.
佛萊德**誤以為**他會準時完工。

▶ We had no illusions about winning any design awards in the first place.
我們打從一開始就**很清楚**我們無法獲得任何設計獎。

▶ The mirrors in the small apartment give the illusion that it is spacious.
這間小公寓裡的鏡子製造了一種空間很寬敞的**錯覺**。

25 equation [ɪˋkweʃən] *n.* 方程式

衍 equate [ɪˋkwet] *vt.* 使相等 ⑥

▶ We're going to learn some basic equations in today's math class.
今天上數學課時我們將會學習一些基本**方程式**。

26 equivalent [ɪˋkwɪvələnt] *a.* 相等的 & *n.* 相等物

片 (1) be equivalent to... 相當於……
= be equal to...
(2) the equivalent of sth
某物的相等物

▶ One kilogram is equivalent to a thousand grams.
1 公斤等於 1,000 公克。

▶ There is no Chinese equivalent of this English word.
中文裡並沒有和這個英文字**相對應的詞**。

27 specify [ˋspɛsə͵faɪ] *vt.* 明確說明

三 specify, specified [ˋspɛsə͵faɪd], specified

衍 specific [spəˋsɪfɪk] *a.* 明確的 ③

▶ The contract specifies that the work should be finished by the end of June.
這份合約**明確說明**了工程應該要在 6 月底前完工。

28 virtual [ˋvɜtʃuəl] *a.* 幾乎的；虛擬的

片 (1) a virtual impossibility
幾乎是不可能的事
(2) It's a virtual impossibility to V
做……幾乎是不可能的
= It's almost impossible to V
(3) virtual reality 虛擬實境

▶ It's a virtual impossibility to find a place to park in Taipei.
要在臺北找到停車的地方**幾乎不可能**。

▶ The website offers you a chance to take a virtual tour of outer space.
這個網站讓你有機會踏上**虛擬的**外太空之旅。

29 neutral [ˋn(j)utrəl] *a.* 中立的 & *n.* (汽車的) 空檔

片 (1) remain / stay neutral 保持中立
(2) put / leave the car in neutral
把車打空檔

▶ I didn't take sides during their fight. I tried to remain neutral.
他們爭吵時我沒偏袒任何一方。我試著**保持中立**。
*take sides (with sb) 偏袒 (某人)

▶ Make sure you put the car in neutral before you start the engine.
你啟動引擎時要確定**把車子打到空檔**。

30 veteran [ˋvɛtərən] *n.* 退伍軍人；老手，經驗豐富的人

似 veterinarian [ˏvɛtərəˋnɛrɪən] *n.* 獸醫（縮寫為 vet）⑥

▶ Jason is a veteran of the Vietnam War.
傑森是位在越戰服役過的**退伍軍人**。

▶ Jack will show you the ropes. He's a ten-year veteran of the company.
傑克會告訴你要領。他是在這間公司待了 10 年的**老手**。
*show / teach sb the ropes　告訴某人要領 / 訣竅

31 implication [ˏɪmpləˋkeʃən] *n.* 暗示

片 by implication　透過暗示
衍 imply [ɪmˋplaɪ] *vt.* 暗示 ④

▶ The basketball player criticized his teammates and, by implication, his coach, too.
這名籃球員批評他的隊友，**透過暗示**，也批評了他的教練。

32 insight [ˋɪnˏsaɪt] *n.* 洞察力（不可數）；深入理解，深刻見解

片 (1) a man of great insight
很有洞察力的人
(2) give an insight into...
為……提供深刻見解
(3) gain insight into...　深入理解……

▶ Eric is a man of great insight.
艾瑞克是個**很有洞察力的人**。

▶ Amy Tan's novels give an insight into the lives of Chinese Americans living in the US.
譚艾美的小說帶我們**深入了解**華裔美國人在美國的生活。

33 highlight [ˋhaɪˏlaɪt] *n.* 最精彩的部分 & *vt.* 突顯，強調

片 the highlight of...
……最精彩的部分，……的亮點
衍 highlighter [ˋhaɪˏlaɪtɚ] *n.* 螢光筆
似 emphasize [ˋɛmfəˏsaɪz] *vt.* 強調 ②

▶ Our stay in Paris was certainly the highlight of our trip.
我們在巴黎停留的期間絕對是此行**最精彩的部分**。

▶ You should highlight your work experience in the resume.
你應該在履歷表中**突顯**你的工作經驗。

34 thereby [ðɛrˋbaɪ] *adv.* 因此

▶ Paul knocked over the red wine and thereby stained the tablecloth.
保羅打翻了紅酒**而**把桌布弄髒。
*tablecloth [ˋteblˏklɔθ] *n.* 桌布

35 doctrine [ˋdɑktrɪn] *n.*（宗教的）教義；教條

似 principle [ˋprɪnsəpl̩] *n.* 原則 ②

▶ It is the doctrine of our company that we manufacture quality products only.
我們公司的**教條**是：我們只生產高品質的產品。

36 removal [rɪˋmuvl̩] *n.* 移除（不可數）

片 the removal of sth　移除某物

衍 remove [rɪˋmuv] *vt.* 移除 ②

▸ Gary had surgery for the removal of a tumor.
蓋瑞動了手術移除腫瘤。

37 sequence [ˋsikwəns] *n.* 順序；一連串 & *vt.* 按順序排，排序

片 (1) in (a / an...) sequence
按（……的）順序
(2) out of sequence　不按順序
(3) a sequence of...　一連串的……

衍 consequence [ˋkɑnsə,kwəns] *n.* 結果；重要性 ④

似 order [ˋɔrdɚ] *n.* 順序 ①

▸ A good business letter should contain information given in a logical sequence.
一封好的商業書信內容陳述應有邏輯順序。

▸ These documents are out of sequence.
這些文件並沒有按照順序排放。

▸ Those foreign laborers launched a sequence of campaigns against racial discrimination.
那些外籍勞工發起了一連串抗議種族歧視的運動。

▸ At her manager's request, Chloe sequenced the speeches from shortest to longest.
克羅伊按經理的要求，把這些演講依最短到最長排序。

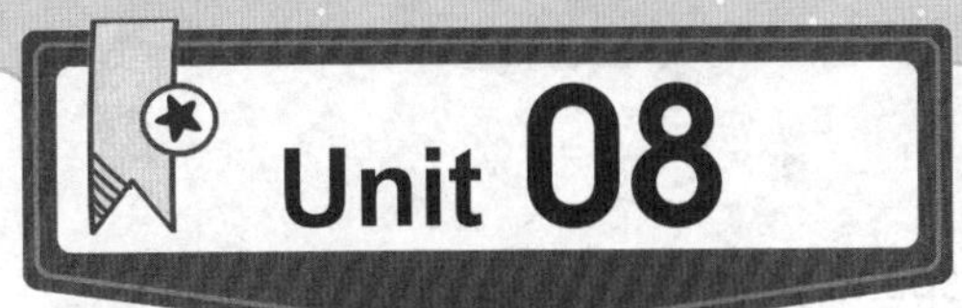

0801-0804

1 abrupt [ə`brʌpt] *a.* 突然的，唐突的

衍 (1) abruptly [ə`brʌptlɪ] *adv.* 突然地
(2) abruptness [ə`brʌptnəs] *n.* 突然

似 (1) sudden [`sʌdn̩] *a.* 突然的 ②
(2) unexpected [ˏʌnɪk`spɛktɪd] *a.* 出乎意料的

▸ Many employees in that company felt confused about the abrupt change in policy.
那間公司許多員工對於政策**突然**轉變都感到很疑惑。

2 patch [pætʃ] *n.* 一小塊（土地、汙漬等）；補釘 & *vt.* 修補

片 (1) a patch of... 一塊……
(2) patch things up (with sb) （和某人）重修舊好
= make up (with sb)
= bury the hatchet (with sb)
*hatchet [`hætʃɪt] *n.* 短柄小斧

▸ There is only one small patch of grass in his front yard.
他的前院裡只有一小**塊**草皮。

▸ The jacket Tom was wearing had two patches at the elbows.
湯姆穿的這件外套在手肘處有兩處**補釘**。

▸ The man patched his jacket because he didn't want to buy a new one.
這名男子**修補**他的夾克，因為他不想買新的。

▸ I had a fight with my brother yesterday, but I patched things up with him this morning.
我昨天和弟弟吵架，但我今早**和他合好**了。

3 crystal [`krɪstl̩] *n.* 水晶 & *a.* 水晶（製）的；清澈的

片 (1) a crystal ball 水晶球
(2) a crystal brook 清澈的小溪

延伸 crystal clear 清澈的；極為清楚的

▸ We have no more questions. Your explanation is crystal clear.
我們沒任何問題了。你的解釋很清楚。

▸ Even though her ring only has a crystal on top, Julie tells people it's a diamond.
儘管茱麗的戒指上只有一顆**水晶**，她卻告訴別人那是鑽石。

▸ Peter has a fine collection of crystal glasses.
彼得珍藏了許多高級**水晶**酒杯。

4 worthy [`wɝðɪ] *a.* 值得的

衍 (1) worth [wɝθ] *prep.* 有……的價值 & *n.* 價值 ②
(2) worthless [`wɝθləs] *a.* 沒有價值的

片 be worthy of + N/V-ing 值得……
= be worth + N/V-ing

▸ The best seller is worthy of reading.
= The best seller is worth reading.
這本暢銷書**值得**一讀。

▸ This article I found in the magazine is worthy of your attention.
我在雜誌上看到的這篇文章**值得**你留意。

0804-0811

worthwhile [ˋwɝð͵(h)waɪl]
a. 值得的

片 It's worthwhile to V
做……是很值得的

▸ You should spend your weekend doing something more worthwhile rather than just lying on the sofa and watching TV.
你週末應該做點更值得的事，而不是光躺在沙發上看電視。

▸ It's worthwhile to spend your leisure time reading, instead of watching TV.
把閒暇時間用來閱讀而不是看電視，這是很值得的一件事。

5 colonial [kəˋlonjəl] *a.* 殖民的 & *n.* 殖民地居民

衍 (1) colony [ˋkɑlənɪ] *n.* 殖民地 ③
(2) colonist [ˋkɑlənɪst] *n.* 殖民者；殖民地居民

▸ It took the country almost fifty years to rid itself of colonial rule.
該國花了幾乎 50 年才擺脫殖民統治。

▸ Before the American War of Independence, the colonials were forced to pay taxes to the British government.
在美國獨立戰爭之前，殖民地居民被迫納稅給英國政府。

6 midst [mɪdst] *n.* 中間 & *prep.* 在之中

片 (1) in our / your / their midst
在我們 / 你們 / 他們之中
= among us / you / them
(2) in the midst of...
在（時間、地區）的中間
= in the middle of...

▸ There is probably a spy in our midst.
= There is probably a spy among us.
我們之中八成有人是間諜。

▸ A lot of students fell asleep in the midst of the boring speech.
許多學生在那場無聊的演講中紛紛睡著了。

7 startle [ˋstɑrtḷ] *vt.* & *vi.* (使) 驚訝

衍 (1) startling [ˋstɑrtḷɪŋ] *a.* 令人吃驚的
(2) startled [ˋstɑrtḷd] *a.* 驚訝的

似 take sb by surprise 嚇某人一大跳
= take sb aback [əˋbæk]

▸ Steven startled me when he broke into my room without knocking on the door first.
= Steven took me by surprise when he broke into my room without knocking on the door first.
= Steven took me aback when he broke into my room without knocking on the door first.
史提芬沒先敲門就闖進我房裡，嚇了我一大跳。

▸ Martin is a very nervous guy; he startles easily.
馬丁是個神經兮兮的傢伙，他容易受驚。

8 devotion [dɪˋvoʃən] *n.* 獻身，奉獻

片 one's devotion to sth
某人對某事的奉獻
= one's dedication to sth

▸ Col. Dawson's devotion to his country is well worthy of our respect.
道森上校對國家的奉獻很值得我們敬佩。

衍 (1) devote [dɪˋvot] *vt.* 貢獻 ④
devote A to B 將 A 奉獻於 B
(2) devoted [dɪˋvotɪd] *a.* 奉獻的
be devoted to sth 致力於某事

似 dedication [ˏdɛdəˋkeʃən]
n. 獻身致力 ⑥

9 thrust [θrʌst] *vt.* & *vi.* & *n.* 猛刺；猛推

三 三態同形

片 (1) thrust A into B 將 A 刺入 / 推入 B
(2) thrust at... （用武器）刺向……

似 (1) shove [ʃʌv] *vt.* & *vi.* 推擠 ⑤
(2) lunge [lʌndʒ] *vt.* & *vi.* （用刀劍）刺，戳

▸ The knight thrust the spear into the boar's body and killed it on the spot.
騎士將長矛刺進了野豬的身體，當場殺了牠。
*boar [bɔr] *n.* 野豬

▸ Angered by what the stranger said, Raymond thrust at him with his fist.
雷蒙德被陌生人說的話激怒，因此向他揮拳。

▸ I ducked my head just in time to dodge my opponent's thrust.
我及時低下頭來，躲過了對手的擊刺。
*duck [dʌk] *vt.* 突然低下（頭）

10 modify [ˋmɑdəˏfaɪ] *vt.* 修改

三 modify, modified [ˋmɑdəˏfaɪd], modified

似 (1) change [tʃendʒ] *vt.* 改變 ①
(2) revise [rɪˋvaɪz] *vt.* 修改 ④
(3) amend [əˋmɛnd] *vt.* 修訂 ⑤

▸ Some of the terms in the contract have to be modified before I sign it.
在我簽名之前，本合同中的若干條款必須修改。

modification [ˏmɑdəfəˋkeʃən]

n. 修改

片 make a modification to / of...
對……做了修改

似 (1) change [tʃendʒ] *n.* 改變 ①
(2) revision [rɪˋvɪʒən] *n.* 修改 ④
(3) amendment [əˋmɛndmənt] *n.* 修訂

▸ We made a few modifications to the original plan to make it more effective.
我們對原先計畫做了些修改，讓它更為可行。

11 layer [ˋleɚ] *n.* 層 & *vt.* 按層排列 / 擺放

片 (1) a layer of... 一層……
(2) the ozone layer 臭氧層

▸ We found that all the furniture in the house was covered with a fine layer of dust.
我們發現屋子裡的所有傢俱都覆蓋著一層細灰。
*fine [faɪn] *a.* 細微的

▶ When making sandwiches, Glen likes to layer the meat with cheese on brown bread.
葛倫製作三明治時，喜歡將肉和起司層層疊放在黑麵包上。

12 despair [dɪˋspɛr] *n.* 絕望（不可數）& *vi.* 絕望

片 (1) be in despair 陷入絕望
(2) be the despair of sb
令某人絕望，使某人頭痛

▶ Paula was in despair when her husband left her for another woman.
老公跟別的女人跑了之後，寶拉陷入了絕望。

▶ During the terrible war, it was hard for Carmen not to despair.
在恐怖的戰爭期間，卡門很難不感到絕望。

13 overwhelm [ˏovɚˋ(h)wɛlm] *vt.* 戰勝；（因強烈的情感）使不知所措；淹沒

片 be overwhelmed by...
對……招架不住；被（水、事情等）淹沒

似 defeat [dɪˋfit] *vt.* 擊敗 ④

▶ We overwhelmed the enemy with superior weapons.
我們用精良的武器大敗敵軍。

▶ Helena was overwhelmed by grief when her puppy died in an accident.
= Grief overwhelmed Helena when her puppy died in an accident.
海蓮娜的小狗狗意外喪生之後，她傷心極了。

▶ The small village was soon overwhelmed by the flood; fortunately, all the local people were evacuated in advance.
小村子很快就被洪水淹沒；幸運的是當地民眾已事先被撤離。
*evacuate [ɪˋvækjʊˏet] *vt.* 撤退

overwhelming [ˏovɚˋ(h)wɛlmɪŋ] *a.* 壓倒性的

片 (1) score an overwhelming victory
獲得壓倒性的勝利
(2) an overwhelming majority (of...) 壓倒性多數／絕大多數（的……）

▶ The opposition party scored an overwhelming victory in this election.
在野黨在這次的選舉中獲得壓倒性的勝利。

▶ An overwhelming majority of the staff members were opposed to the new regulation.
絕大多數的職員都反對這項新規定。

14 embrace [ɪmˋbres] *vt.* & *vi.* & *n.* 擁抱

片 (1) embrace sb 擁抱某人
= give sb an embrace
= hug sb
= give sb a hug

▶ The mother embraced her baby, tenderly coaxing it to sleep.
母親溫柔地擁抱著寶寶，哄他入睡。
*coax [koks] *vt.* 哄

(2) hold sb in a(n)... embrace ……地抱著某人

似 hug [hʌg] *vt.* & *n.* 擁抱 ③

▶ When Patricia saw her good friend Herman on the street, they embraced.
派翠西亞在街上遇到好友赫曼時，他們**抱**了一下。

▶ The young couple held each other in a long embrace, apparently losing all track of time.
這對年輕情侶久久地**摟抱著**彼此，似乎忘了時間流逝。

15 ranch [ræntʃ] *n.* (尤指美國的大) 農 / 牧場 & *vi.* 在農 / 牧場工作，經營農 / 牧場

片 a cattle ranch 牛牧場

衍 rancher [ˋræntʃɚ] *n.* 農場主人，農場經營者

似 farm [fɑrm] *n.* 農場 ①

▶ Due to mad cow disease, many cattle ranches have suffered great losses.
由於狂牛症的緣故，許多**牛牧場**都蒙受嚴重損失。

▶ George makes his living by ranching in the US state of Nevada.
喬治在美國的內華達州**經營牧場**維生。

16 shortage [ˋʃɔrtɪdʒ] *n.* 不足，匱乏

片 a shortage of... ……的短缺

衍 (1) short [ʃɔrt] *a.* 短的 ①
(2) shorten [ˋʃɔrtn̩] *vt.* & *vi.* 變短 ③

▶ There was a severe water and food shortage in this area after the earthquake.
地震發生之後，這個地區的水和食物嚴重**短缺**。

▶ Years of civil war have led to an acute shortage of labor in this country.
多年的內戰已造成該國當地勞動人口嚴重**短缺**。
*acute [əˋkjut] *a.* 劇烈的

17 ridge [rɪdʒ] *n.* 山脊 & *vt.* & *vi.* (使) 成脊狀

延伸 (1) peak [pik] *n.* 山頂 ②
(2) summit [ˋsʌmɪt] *n.* 山頂 ③
(3) gorge [gɔrdʒ] *n.* (小而深的) 峽谷

▶ Our car broke down shortly after we got to the ridge.
我們開到**山脊**不久車就拋錨了。

▶ The location where the ground ridges into interesting formations attracts many tourists each year.
地面**隆起**形成有趣形狀的地方每年都吸引了許多遊客。

18 patrol [pəˋtrol] *n.* & *vt.* 巡邏

三 patrol, patrolled [pəˋtrold], patrolled

片 (1) be on patrol 巡邏中
(2) a patrol car 巡邏車

▶ Five squads are on patrol day and night to keep the enemy at bay.
日夜都有五個小隊**巡邏**，確保敵軍無法接近。
*keep sb at bay 使某人無法接近

▶ We all feel very safe with the police patrolling the street.
警察在街上**巡邏**，使我們大家都感覺很安全。

0819-0826

19 lest [lɛst] *conj.* 以免，免得

用法 lest 引導的副詞子句結構如下：
lest + S (should) + V　以免……
(should 可省略)
= for fear that + S + may / might V
(may / might 不可省略)

▸ You should get up early lest you miss the train.
= You should get up early for fear that you may miss the train.
你應該早點起床，以免趕不上火車。

20 destiny [ˋdɛstənɪ] *n.* 命運，天命

衍 destined [ˋdɛstɪnd] *a.* 命中注定的 ⑥
be destined for...　注定要……

似 fate [fet] *n.* 命運 ②

▸ Without determination and hard work, how can you be the master of your own destiny?
若無決心和努力，你怎能成為自己命運的主宰呢？

destination [ˏdɛstəˋneʃən] *n.* 目的地

片 a holiday / tourist destination
觀光勝地

▸ The train was delayed, so we were 10 hours late when we got to our destination.
火車延誤了，因此我們到達目的地時晚了 10 個小時。

▸ Hawaii has always been a hot-spot tourist destination.
夏威夷一直是個熱門的觀光勝地。

21 prey [pre] *vi.* 捕食 & *n.* 獵物 (集合名詞，不可數)

片 (1) prey on...　捕食……
(2) fall prey to...　成為……的受害者
= fall victim to...

似 (1) pray [pre] *vi.* 祈禱 ②
(2) predator [ˋprɛdətɚ] *n.* 掠食者 ⑤

▸ Eagles prey on small animals for food.
老鷹會捕食小動物。

▸ Rabbits and squirrels are often prey for larger animals.
兔子和松鼠通常是大型動物的獵物。

▸ Ironically, human beings today are falling prey to unrestrained economic development.
諷刺的是，人類如今漸漸成了毫無節制的經濟發展的受害者。
*unrestrained [ˏʌnrɪˋstrend] *a.* 無限制的

22 flip [flɪp] *vt.* 翻轉；擲 (硬幣) & *n.* 空翻

三 flip, flipped [flɪpt], flipped

片 (1) flip through...　快速翻閱……
(2) flip a coin　擲硬幣

▸ Owen flipped the paper over to read the words on the back.
歐文把紙翻過來讀後面的字。

▸ I flipped through the phone book for John's number.
我快速翻閱電話簿找約翰的電話號碼。

▸ We flipped a coin to decide who would go first.
我們擲硬幣來決定先後順序。

▸ The acrobat did 5 backward flips in a row and the audience all applauded.
雜技演員連續後空翻了 5 次，觀眾都鼓起掌來。
*acrobat [ˋækrəbæt] *n.* 雜技演員

23 obligation [ˌabləˋgeʃən] *n.* (道德上、法律上的) 義務，責任

片 (1) be under an / no obligation to V 有 / 無義務要……
(2) have an obligation to V 有做……的義務

衍 obligatory [əˋblɪgəˌtorɪ] *a.* 有義務的

▸ We are under no obligation to answer any of your questions.
我們沒有義務要回答你的任何問題。

▸ All parents have an obligation to take good care of their children.
= All parents are under an obligation to take good care of their children.
所有父母都有義務要妥善照顧他們的孩子。

24 authorize [ˋɔθəˌraɪz] *vt.* 授權；認可

片 authorize sb to V 授權某人做……

衍 (1) authority [əˋθɔrətɪ] *n.* 權威 (不可數)；當局 (恆用複數)；權威人士 (可數) ④
(2) authoritative [əˋθɔrəˌtetɪv] *a.* 權威的

▸ I have authorized Matthew to act for me while I'm abroad.
我已授權馬修在我出國期間代理我的職務。
*act for... 代理 / 代表……

25 presidency [ˋprɛzədənsɪ] *n.* (總統的) 職位；任期

衍 president [ˋprɛzədənt] *n.* 總統；公司總裁 ②

延伸 the president-elect 已當選但尚未就任的總統

▸ Joe Biden was elected to the presidency of the United States.
喬・拜登當選美國的總統。

▸ During the Trump presidency, the unemployment rate surged after the outbreak of COVID-19.
在川普總統任內，新冠肺炎爆發後，失業率激增。
*surge [sɝdʒ] *vi.* 激增

presidential [ˌprɛzəˋdɛnʃəl] *a.* 總統 (選舉) 的

片 a presidential candidate 總統選舉候選人

▸ The two presidential candidates had a heated debate on TV last night.
這兩位總統候選人昨晚在電視上有一場激烈的辯論。

26 utility [juˋtɪlətɪ] *n.* 水電瓦斯 (常用複數)；效用 (不可數)

片 (1) a public utility 公用事業公司 (如電力公司、自來水公司)
(2) utility bills 水電瓦斯帳單

▸ Our utilities were shut off for repair, so we couldn't take a bath.
我們的水電瓦斯因為維修而被切斷，所以我們沒辦法洗澡。

▸ I usually receive my utility bills near the end of the month.
我通常在快到月底時收到水電瓦斯的帳單。

▸ Tests have proven the utility of this product.
試驗結果證實了這項產品的效用。

0826-0833

utilize [ˋjutḷ͵aɪz] *vt.* 利用

似 use [juz] *vt.* & *n.* 利用 ①
make use of... 利用……

▶ Scientists utilize waterfalls to generate electricity.
科學家利用瀑布發電。

27 commitment [kəˋmɪtmənt] *n.* 承諾；奉獻（不可數）

片 (1) make a commitment to + V/N/V-ing 對……做承諾
(2) sb's commitment to + N/V-ing 某人對……的奉獻
= sb's dedication to + N/V-ing
(3) family commitments （承諾做到的）家庭責任 / 義務

衍 commit [kəˋmɪt] *vt.* 犯（罪、錯誤）；奉獻 ④

▶ The company makes a commitment to provide quality products to its customers.
該公司承諾提供給客戶高品質的產品。

▶ Peter's commitment to work has won the respect of his colleagues.
彼得對工作的奉獻贏得了同事的尊敬。

28 deliberate [dɪˋlɪbərɪt] *a.* 故意的；謹慎的 & [dɪˋlɪbə͵ret] *vt.* & *vi.* 深思熟慮

衍 deliberately [dɪˋlɪbərɪtlɪ] *adv.* 故意地
= on purpose

似 (1) intentional [ɪnˋtɛnʃənḷ] *a.* 故意的
(2) careful [ˋkɛrfəl] *a.* 小心的 ①

反 (1) accidental [͵æksəˋdɛntḷ] *a.* 意外的 ④
(2) unintentional [͵ʌnɪnˋtɛnʃənḷ] *a.* 不是故意的，不小心的

▶ Police have confirmed that the power failure was caused by a deliberate act of sabotage.
警方證實這次停電是因蓄意破壞的行為所導致。
*sabotage [ˋsæbə͵tɑʒ] *n.* 破壞

▶ The government is taking deliberate actions to lower food prices.
政府正採取謹慎的行動降低食物價格。

▶ The committee deliberated the reporter's question for a short time and then provided a vague answer.
委員會思考了一會該名記者的問題，然後給了一個模稜兩可的答案。

▶ After hearing the evidence, the jury deliberated for several hours before making a decision.
陪審團在聆聽證據後，沉思了好幾個小時才做出決定。

29 profound [prəˋfaʊnd] *a.* 深遠的；很有深度的

片 (1) have a profound influence on... 對……影響深遠
(2) have a profound knowledge of... 很懂……

反 superficial [͵supəˋfɪʃəl] *a.* 膚淺的 ⑥

▶ Globalization has a profound influence on human life.
全球暖化對人類生活影響深遠。

▶ My friend Joe is no expert, but he does have a profound knowledge of plants.
我的朋友喬不是什麼專家，但他真的很懂植物。

30 persist [pɚˋsɪst] *vi.* 堅持；持續

片 persist in + N/V-ing 堅持……

衍 (1) persistent [pɚˋsɪstənt]
a. 堅持不懈的；持續的 ⑥

(2) persistence [pɚˋsɪstəns]
n. 堅持；持續 ⑥

似 insist on + N/V-ing

▸ Eleanor persisted in learning to play the piano, even though she found it very difficult.
儘管艾莉諾覺得彈鋼琴很難，她仍然**堅持**要學。

▸ Go find a doctor if your headache persists.
如果你頭痛一直**持續**，還是去找個醫生吧。

31 mechanism [ˋmɛkə͵nɪzəm] *n.* 機械裝置；制度，體制；機制

片 (1) a mechanism to V
關於做……的制度
= a mechanism for + N/V-ing

(2) defense / survival mechanism
防禦 / 生存機制

衍 (1) mechanical [məˋkænɪkḷ]
a. 機械的 ④

(2) mechanic [məˋkænɪk] *n.* 技工 ④

▸ This watch is equipped with a delicate timing mechanism.
這只手錶配備有精細的計時**機械裝置**。

▸ Government officials are setting up new mechanisms to help the unemployed.
= Government officials are setting up new mechanisms for helping the unemployed.
政府官員正在建立新**制度**來幫助失業民眾。

▸ A feeling of physical pain serves as a natural defense mechanism.
肉體的痛覺是天生的**防衛機制**。

32 texture [ˋtɛkstʃɚ] *n.* (料子、紡織物的) 質地，觸感；(食物、飲品的) 口感 & *vt.* 形成 (不平滑、粗糙的) 紋理

片 (1) a smooth / soft / rough texture
光滑 / 柔軟 / 粗糙的觸感

(2) a crunchy / creamy texture
鬆脆 / 似奶油般濃稠的口感

▸ This scarf is made of 100 percent cashmere and has a very smooth texture.
這條圍巾是 100% 喀什米爾毛料做成，**觸感**非常柔軟。

▸ The baker used a knife to texture the icing on the cake into an unusual pattern.
烘焙師傅用刀子將蛋糕上的糖霜**刷成**不尋常的紋路。
*icing [ˋaɪsɪŋ] *n.* 糖霜

33 canvas [ˋkænvəs] *n.* 帆布；油畫 (布) & *vt.* 用帆布覆蓋

三 canvas, canvassed [ˋkænvəst], canvassed

片 (1) a canvas bag 帆布袋

(2) canvas shoes 帆布鞋

▸ I bought a canvas bag for Serene as her birthday present.
我買了一個**帆布袋**給瑟琳做生日禮物。

▸ The museum has a collection of canvases by Salvador Dali.
博物館收藏了若干薩爾瓦多．達利的**帆布畫作**。

▸ To save money, the shelter was made by canvassing over a wooden frame.
為了省錢，這個棲身處是**用帆布蓋在**木頭架上搭建而成。

34 initiate [ɪˋnɪʃɪ,et] *vt.* 開始；傳授基本知識；接納新成員 & [ɪˋnɪʃɪɪt] *n.* (尤指會被告知祕密的) (新) 加入者 & *a.* 新加入的

片 initiate sb into + N/V-ing 使某人初步了解某事；使某人加入某組織

衍 (1) initial [ɪˋnɪʃəl] *a.* 開始的，最初的 & *n.* 名字的開頭字母 ④
(2) initiator [ɪˋnɪʃɪ,etɚ] *n.* 發起人

▸ Management decided to initiate a new marketing strategy.
管理階層決定**展開**一套新的行銷策略。

▸ My father initiated me into the art of diplomacy.
父親**帶領**我**初步認識**了外交上的藝術。

▸ Carl was initiated into a fraternity right after entering college.
卡爾進大學後馬上就**加入**了一個兄弟會。
*fraternity [frəˋtɝnətɪ] *n.* 兄弟會

▸ Only the initiates of the organization really knew its deep, dark secrets.
只有這個組織的**新成員**知道該組織深沉、黑暗的祕密。

initiative [ɪˋnɪʃətɪv] *n.* 自發性，進取心 (不可數)；主動 (權)；倡議，新措施 & *a.* 開始的

片 (1) on one's own initiative 某人自發地
(2) show / lack initiative 展現 / 缺少進取心
(3) take the initiative (in + N/V-ing) 採取主動態度 (做……)

▸ Part of Mike's problem is that he lacks initiative.
麥克一部分的問題出在他**缺乏進取心**。

▸ The US took the initiative in repairing relations with Canada.
美國**主動**與加拿大修復關係。

▸ One of the initiatives that the government began last year was to build more shelters for homeless people.
政府去年開始實施的其中一項**措施**是建造更多收容所給遊民。

35 metropolitan [,mɛtrəˋpɑlətən] *a.* 大都市的 & *n.* 住在大都市者

衍 metropolis [məˋtrɑpḷɪs] *n.* 大都市；首都

▸ Metropolitan Miami covers a much larger area than the city of Miami itself.
邁阿密**大都會區**比邁阿密市本身涵蓋的範圍還要大很多。

▸ Despite growing up on a farm, Brent has become a true metropolitan since moving to the big city.
雖然布藍特在農場長大，但自從搬到大城市後，他就真正成了**住在大城市的人**。

Unit 09

0901-0904

1 sheriff [ˋʃɛrɪf] *n.* 警長

似 marshal [ˋmɑrʃəl] *n.* 警長局長；統帥

▸ The sheriff stopped Michael because he ran the red light.
邁可闖紅燈被警長攔了下來。

2 housing [ˋhaʊzɪŋ] *n.* 住屋（總稱，不可數）

片 (1) public housing 公共住宅，國宅
(2) housing costs / prices 房價

▸ The government will increase the budget for public housing to benefit the poorest in the country.
政府將增加**國宅**的預算以嘉惠該國的貧苦民眾。

3 treaty [ˋtritɪ] *n.* 條約，協定

複 treaties [ˋtritɪz]
片 sign a peace treaty 簽訂和平條約
似 agreement [əˋgrimənt] *n.* 協議 ①

▸ The government and the leader of the rebel troops finally signed a peace treaty to end the 10-year civil war.
政府與叛軍領袖終於**簽署和平條約**，終止這場為期十年的內戰。

---

accord [əˋkɔrd] *n.* 協定 & *vi.* 一致
（常與介詞 with 並用）

片 (1) sign a peace accord
簽訂和平條約
(2) be in accord with... 與……一致
= accord with...
(3) of one's own accord
自動自發地
= of one's own free will
衍 accordance [əˋkɔrdn̩s] *n.* 一致 ⑥

▸ The two countries signed a peace accord last July.
這兩個國家去年 7 月**簽訂和平條約**。
▸ What Peter does is in accord with what he says.
= What Peter does is in agreement with what he says.
彼得言行**一致**。
▸ I've had a hard time believing that John resigned of his own accord.
我很難相信約翰是**自願**辭職的。
▸ The two suspects' stories did not accord with the evidence.
那兩位嫌犯的說法和證據不符。

4 combat [ˋkɑmbæt] *n.* 戰鬥 & [kəmˋbæt] *vt.* 打擊

三 combat, combated / combatted, combated / combatted
片 (1) be in combat 戰鬥中
(2) combat crime / inflation
打擊犯罪 / 對抗通貨膨脹
似 (1) fight [faɪt] *n.* 戰鬥 & *vt.* 與……作戰 ①
(2) battle [ˋbætl̩] *n.* 戰鬥 & *vt.* 與……作戰 ②

▸ The troops of the two countries were exhausted after eight years of fierce combat.
經過八年的**激戰**，兩國的部隊都已筋疲力竭。
▸ The government took effective measures to combat crime in the city.
政府採取有效措施**打擊**該市的**犯罪**。

0904-0912

warrior [ˋwɔrɪɚ] *n.* 戰士

似 fighter [ˋfaɪtɚ] *n.* 戰士 ③

▶ The samurai were considered great warriors in traditional Japanese society.
傳統的日本社會認為武士是偉大的**戰士**。
*samurai [ˋsæmə,raɪ / ˋsæmʊ,raɪ] *n.* 日本武士

5 destructive [dɪˋstrʌktɪv] *a.* 破壞的

衍 (1) destructively [dɪˋstrʌktɪvlɪ] *adv.* 破壞地
(2) destroy [dɪˋstrɔɪ] *vt.* 破壞 ③
(3) destruction [dɪˋstrʌkʃən] *n.* 破壞 ④

反 constructive [kənˋstrʌktɪv] *a.* 建設性的 ④

▶ A very destructive typhoon left hundreds of people homeless on the island.
一場極具**破壞力**的颱風讓島上數百名民眾無家可歸。

▶ The greenhouse effect is destructive to the ecology of the Arctic area.
溫室效應對北極地區的生態**具有破壞性**。

6 supervise [ˋsupɚ,vaɪz] *vt.* 監督，管理

衍 supervisory [,supɚˋvaɪzərɪ] *a.* 監督的，管理的

似 monitor [ˋmɑnətɚ] *vt.* 監控 ④

▶ The UN is supervising the distribution of relief supplies to refugees.
聯合國正在**監督**救濟物資發放給難民的工作。

supervisor [ˋsupɚ,vaɪzɚ] *n.* 監督者，主管

似 director [dəˋrɛktɚ] *n.* 主任；主管 ②

▶ My dad has a full-time job as a supervisor at that factory.
我父親在那間工廠擔任全職**主管**的工作。

supervision [,supɚˋvɪʒən] *n.* 監督，管理（不可數）

片 under sb's supervision 在某人的監督管理之下
= under the supervision of sb

▶ These orphans are under the supervision of qualified social workers.
這些孤兒**由**合格的社工人員**監護**。

7 mumble [ˋmʌmbḷ] *vt.* & *vi.* 含糊地說 & *n.* 含糊，咕噥

片 speak in a mumble 含糊說話

似 (1) murmur [ˋmɝmɚ] *n.* 低語聲 & *vt.* & *vi.* 低語說 & *vi.* 私下抱怨 ④
(2) mutter [ˋmʌtɚ] *vt.* & *vi.* 低聲嘀咕 & *n.* 咕噥

▶ Tom mumbled an insincere apology, which made Katie all the more angry.
湯姆**含糊其詞**地道了無誠意的歉，使凱蒂更加生氣。
*all the + 比較級 更加……

▶ Jane said something, but Tina didn't understand her because she mumbled.
珍說了些話，但蒂娜聽不懂因為她**說得很含糊**。

▶ Whenever Karen's boyfriend speaks in a mumble, she reminds him to talk more clearly.
凱倫的男友**說話含糊**時，她就會提醒他話講清楚點。

8 lumber [ˋlʌmbɚ] *n.* 木材（不可數）

衍 lumberjack [ˋlʌmbɚˏdʒæk] *n.* 伐木工人

似 timber [ˋtɪmbɚ] *n.* 木材〔英〕；樹木（皆不可數）③

延伸 (1) wood [wʊd] *n.* 木頭（不可數）②
(2) log [lɔg] *n.* 圓木（一棵樹去掉頂部與樹根部分，中間剩下的樹幹主部分，可數）③

▸ The cost of paper went up because lumber was in short supply.
因為木材短缺，所以紙價上漲了。

9 segment [ˋsɛgmənt] *n.* 部分 & [ˋsɛgˏmɛnt] *vt.* 分割

片 (1) a segment of... 一部分的……
= a part of...
= a portion of...
(2) segment A into B 把 A 分割成 B

▸ A large segment of the teenage population has internet access in this country.
該國大部分的青少年人口都可上網。

▸ If a task seems too difficult, try segmenting it into smaller parts.
如果任務看起來太過困難，試著把它分成小部分進行。

10 realm [rɛlm] *n.* 領土；（知識、興趣的）範圍

片 (1) in the realm / area / field of... 在……的範圍 / 領域內
(2) be beyond the realm(s) of possibility 不可能

▸ Henry is an expert in the realm of gardening.
在園藝的領域中，亨利是個專家。

▸ Life existing on other planets is not beyond the realm of possibility.
生命存在於其他星球並非不可能的事。

11 mode [mod] *n.* 模式，方法

似 pattern [ˋpætɚn] *n.* 模式 ②

▸ Floods damaged the train tracks so travelers had to find alternate modes of transportation.
因為洪水損壞了火車鐵軌，旅客必須找尋其他替代的交通方式。

12 exclude [ɪkˋsklud] *vt.* 排除；不包括

片 exclude A from B 從 B 中排除 A

衍 exclusion [ɪkˋskluʒən] *n.* 排除；不包括 ⑥

反 include [ɪnˋklud] *vt.* 包括 ②

▸ Peter deliberately excluded Edward from the group.
彼得故意不讓艾德華加入這個團體。

▸ All those under twenty years of age are excluded from bar activities.
所有 20 歲以下的人不得參加和酒吧有關的活動。

excluding [ɪkˋskludɪŋ] *prep.* 不包括……在內

反 including [ɪnˋkludɪŋ] *prep.* 包括 ④

▸ My living expenses, excluding rent and utilities, are around 500 dollars.
我的生活開銷，不包含房租跟水電瓦斯費，約 500 美元。

🔊 0912-0920

exclusive [ɪkˋsklusɪv] *a.* 不包括的；(新聞、商品) 獨家的，專用的 & *n.* 獨家新聞

片 (1) exclusive of... 不包括……
(2) exclusive access / rights 獨家使用權
(3) an exclusive report / interview / coverage 獨家報導 / 訪談 / 新聞報導
(4) be exclusive to... 給……專用

反 inclusive [ɪnˋklusɪv] *a.* 包含的 ⑥

▸ This price is for meals only, exclusive of accommodations.
= This price is for meals only, excluding accommodations.
= This price is for meals only, accommodations excluded.
本價格只含餐點，不包含住宿。

▸ Our company has the exclusive rights to distribute that product.
我們公司有運銷那項產品的獨家代理權。

▸ The special offer is exclusive to the readers of this magazine.
這項特別優惠只由本雜誌讀者獨享。

▸ Because of Tom's reputation as a journalist and his good connections, he was able to get an amazing exclusive.
由於湯姆作為記者的聲譽和好人脈，他可以拿到驚人的獨家新聞。

13 scar [skɑr] *n.* 傷疤 & *vt.* 使留下疤痕

三 scar, scarred [skɑrd], scarred

似 wound [wund] *n.* 傷口 & *vt.* 使受傷 ②

▸ Jason has a scar on his left cheek, which is very easy to identify.
傑森的左臉頰有一道疤，很容易認出來。

▸ The burns scarred Peter's skin, leaving a permanent mark.
灼傷在彼得的皮膚上留下永久的疤痕。

14 tile [taɪl] *n.* 磁磚；瓦片 & *vt.* 貼磁磚；鋪瓦

▸ The tiles on the roof are at least 100 years old, many of which need to be replaced.
這座屋頂上的瓦片至少有 100 年以上的歷史，其中有許多片必須要更換了。

▸ After she tiled the bathroom walls and floor, Leah took a break for an hour.
莉雅貼好浴室牆上和地板的磁磚後，她休息了一小時。

15 plunge [plʌndʒ] *vi.* & *n.* 跳入 & *vi.* 驟降

片 (1) plunge in / into... 跳入……；(快速) 投入……
(2) take the plunge (經長時間考慮過後) 冒險一試，決定行動

▸ The lifeguard plunged / jumped into the river and saved the drowning boy.
救生員跳入河中，救起即將溺斃的男孩。

▸ One should not plunge into marriage. Take time to get to know your partner first.
不要貿然投入婚姻。應先花時間了解對方。

似 plummet [ˋplʌmɪt] *vi.* 暴跌

▸ Lilly decided to take the plunge and set up a design studio of her own.
莉莉決定**放手一搏**，要成立自己的設計工作室。

▸ During COVID-19, Bill expected housing prices to plunge, but they stayed about the same.
新冠肺炎期間，比爾預期房價會**驟跌**，但房價仍維持不變。

16 prolong [prəˋlɔŋ] *vt.* 延長

似 (1) lengthen [ˋlɛŋθən] *vt.* & *vi.* 延長 ④
(2) extend [ɪkˋstɛnd] *vt.* 延長 ④

▸ Having a good time, we decided to prolong our stay in Los Angeles by another week.
我們玩得很愉快，因此決定在洛杉磯**多停留**一星期。

17 civic [ˋsɪvɪk] *a.* 市民的

片 (1) a civic duty 公民義務
(2) a civic center 民眾服務中心；市民中心

▸ It is your civic duty to pay your taxes honestly according to what you earn.
確實按照你的所得報稅是你應盡的**公民義務**。

18 citizenship [ˋsɪtəzn͵ʃɪp] *n.* 公民身分 (不可數)

片 (1) US / French citizenship 美國 / 法國國籍
(2) dual citizenship 雙重國籍

▸ Raymond hadn't lived in the country long enough to obtain citizenship, but next year he could apply for it.
雷蒙德住在該國的時間還不長，還不能取得**公民身分**，但明年他就可以申請了。

19 spectator [ˋspɛk͵tetɚ] *n.* (比賽、活動等的) 觀眾

似 audience [ˋɔdɪəns] *n.* 觀眾 (集合名詞，不可數) ③
an audience of + 數字 若干名觀眾

▸ Fighting broke out among spectators in the third quarter.
比賽進行到第 3 節時，便爆發了**群眾**衝突。

viewer [ˋvjuɚ] *n.* (電視) 觀眾

衍 view [vju] *vt.* 觀賞 ②

▸ The following program may contain violent scenes that are not suitable for viewers under 12 years old.
以下節目可能包含暴力影像，不適合 12 歲以下的**觀眾**。

20 viewpoint [ˋvju͵pɔɪnt] *n.* 觀點 (= point of view)

片 from sb's viewpoint 從某人的觀點看來
= from sb's perspective
= from sb's point of view

似 perspective [pɚˋspɛktɪv] *n.* 觀點，看法 ⑤

▸ From the voter's viewpoint, the state of the economy is far more important than who is elected president.
= From the voter's point of view, the state of the economy is far more important than who is elected president.
從選民的**觀點來看**，經濟情況遠比誰當選總統來得重要。

21 ample [ˋæmpl̩] *a.* 充分的，充足的

似 (1) enough [ɪˋnʌf] *a.* 足夠的 ①
(2) sufficient [səˋfɪʃənt] *a.* 足夠的 ③
(3) abundant [əˋbʌndənt] *a.* 充裕的 ⑤

▸ There is ample evidence that sea levels around the world are rising.
有充分的證據顯示，全球的海平面正在上升。

22 shatter [ˋʃætɚ] *vi.* & *vt.* (使) 粉碎，破滅，打碎

片 (1) shatter into pieces　碎成碎片
= break into pieces
(2) shatter sb's dreams / illusions
某人的美夢 / 幻想破滅

似 smash [smæʃ] *vt.* 使粉碎 ⑤

▸ The earthquake shook the building, causing the mirror to fall from the wall and shatter into pieces.
地震搖晃著建築物，使得牆上的鏡子掉到地上碎成碎片。

▸ An unpleasant meeting shattered Peter's illusions about the joint venture.
一場不歡而散的會議粉碎了彼得對合資案的幻想。
*a joint venture　合資企業

23 batch [bætʃ] *n.* 一組，一批

片 a batch of...　一批……
= a group of...

似 patch [pætʃ] *n.* 補釘 ⑤

▸ Please sort these letters into three batches according to date and put them on my desk.
請將這堆信件按日期分成 3 組然後放在我桌上。

24 mattress [ˋmætrɪs] *n.* 床墊

片 a hard / firm / soft mattress
硬 / 穩固 / 軟的床墊

延伸 mat [mæt] *n.* 小墊子 (可放盤子、杯子或置於門口保持鞋底乾淨用) ②

▸ You need to use a firm mattress to support your back.
你需要用穩固的床墊支撐你的背部。

25 inquiry [ɪnˋkwaɪrɪ] *n.* 詢問 (與介詞 about 並用)；調查 (與介詞 into 並用)

片 (1) make an inquiry about...
詢問……
(2) launch / set up / hold an inquiry into...　對……展開調查

似 (1) question [ˋkwɛstʃən] *n.* 問題；詢問 ①
(2) query [ˋkwɪrɪ] *n.* 詢問
(3) investigation [ɪnˏvɛstəˋgeʃən] *n.* 調查 ④

▸ A family friend just rang up and made an inquiry about my father's health.
= A family friend just rang up and made a query about my father's health.
一位家族朋友剛剛來電，詢問家父健康。

▸ The authorities concerned agreed to hold an inquiry / investigation into the plane crash.
有關當局同意對這起墜機事件展開調查。

26 morality [məˋrælətɪ] *n.* 道德 (觀)

片 public / private morality
公共 / 個人的道德

▸ Mr. Morrison is giving a lecture on how to improve the standards of public morality.
莫利森先生正就如何提升公共道德水準進行授課。

衍 (1) moral [ˋmɔrəl] *a.* 道德的 & *n.* 道德規範 (恆用複數) ③
(2) morally [ˋmɔrəlɪ] *adv.* 道德上

反 immorality [ˌɪmɔˋrælətɪ] *n.* 不道德

27 characterize [ˋkærəktəˌraɪz] *vt.* 描繪……的特性；具有……的特色 (常用被動語態)

片 (1) characterize A as B　描繪 A 為 B
(2) be characterized as...　(被認為) 有……的特色

衍 (1) character [ˋkærəktɚ] *n.* 角色；性格 ②
(2) characteristic [ˌkærəktəˋrɪstɪk] *n.* 人格特質 ④

▶ Scenes of rural life characterized the painter's early works.
該畫家早期畫作**的特徵是**農村生活景象。

▶ The author characterized his protagonist as confident and ambitious.
作者**把**他的主角**描繪成**一位有自信且野心勃勃的人。
*protagonist [proˋtægənɪst] *n.* 主角

▶ This dictionary is characterized as being reader-friendly and comprehensive.
這本字典的**特色**是易讀與內容豐富。
*comprehensive [ˌkamprɪˋhɛnsɪv] *a.* 全面的

28 collector [kəˋlɛktɚ] *n.* 收集者，收藏家

片 (1) a stamp collector　集郵者
(2) a ticket collector　收票員
(3) a garbage collector　垃圾清潔工

衍 (1) collect [kəˋlɛkt] *vt.* 收集；收藏 ①
(2) collection [kəˋlɛkʃən] *n.* 收藏品 ③

▶ Tony has been a stamp collector for many years.
東尼**收集郵票**多年了。

collective [kəˋlɛktɪv] *a.* 集體的，共同的 & *n.* 集體企業

延伸 (1) collective interests　集體利益 (常用複數)
(2) collective memory　集體記憶 (一個民族共同的歷史記憶)

▶ The board has reached a collective decision on the matter.
董事會已就該議題做出了**共同的**決定。

▶ The store is run by a collective, with the profits being shared among all the staff.
這間店由**集體企業**營運，利潤由所有員工共享。

29 subsequent [ˋsʌbsəkwənt] *a.* 隨後 (發生) 的

片 subsequent to...　在……之後 (視作片語介詞，相當於 after)

似 consequent [ˋkansəkwənt] *a.* 隨之發生的 ④

反 previous [ˋpriviəs] *a.* 先前的 ③

▶ The mistakes were corrected in a subsequent edition of the dictionary.
字典中的這些錯誤在**之後的**版本都更正過來了。

▶ I wonder what happened subsequent to the accident.
我想知道那起意外**之後**發生的事。

30 municipal [mjuˋnɪsəpḷ] *a.* 市立的

片 a municipal transportation system　市立交通系統

▸ There is a municipal parking lot near the city hall.
市政府附近有一座市立停車場。

31 comprise [kəmˋpraɪz] *vt.* 包括；組成

片 be comprised of...　由……組成
= be composed of...
= be made up of...
= consist of...

▸ Our company's product line comprises 30 different items.
我們公司的產品線有 30 種不同的產品。

▸ This class comprises 50 students.
= This class is comprised of 50 students.
= This class is made up of 50 students.
= This class is composed of 50 students.
= This class consists of 50 students.
這個班級由 50 位學生所組成。

32 credibility [ˏkrɛdəˋbɪlətɪ] *n.* 可信度（不可數）

衍 credit [ˋkrɛdɪt] *n.* 信譽；信用 ③
似 reliability [rɪˏlaɪəˋbɪlətɪ] *n.* 可靠度

▸ Tom's poor judgment has already damaged his credibility as CEO of this company.
湯姆差勁的判斷力已經損害了他作為公司執行長的信譽。

33 miniature [ˋmɪnɪətʃɚ] *a.* 小型的 & *n.* 小模型

片 in miniature　縮小的，微型的
似 tiny [ˋtaɪnɪ] *a.* 微小的 ②

▸ Sally bought a miniature chair to put in her doll house.
莎莉買了一張小椅子放在她的玩具屋裡。

▸ Irene has made Polly a doll house, with the furniture in miniature.
艾琳做了一個玩具屋給波莉，裡頭有小模型傢俱。

34 unfold [ʌnˋfold] *vt.* & *vi.* 攤開，打開 & *vi.*（隨時間或故事的）展開

反 fold [fold] *vt.* 對摺（常與介詞 up 並用）③

▸ I watched Tiffany's expression as she tore open the envelope and unfolded the letter.
蒂芬妮撕開信封並攤開信時，我看著她臉上的表情。

▸ As the event unfolded that day, more and more problems came up.
那天隨著活動展開，越來越多問題浮現。

▸ The writer wrote the novel in such a way that as the story unfolds, the suspense builds.
這名作家寫這本小說的方式為，懸疑感隨著故事展開而增加。

Unit 10

1001-1003

1 indispensable [ˌɪndɪˋspɛnsəbḷ] *a.* 不可或缺的

片 be indispensable to sb/sth
對某人 / 某物是不可或缺的
= be essential to sb/sth

似 essential [ɪˋsɛnʃəl] *a.* 必要的 ④

反 dispensable [dɪˋspɛnsəbḷ]
a. 非必要的 ⑥

▸ A good dictionary is indispensable to anyone who wants to have a good command of English.
若你想要把英文學好，一本好的字典是不可或缺的。

2 poke [pok] *vt.* & *vi.* 戳；突出 & *n.* 戳

片 (1) poke (at) A with B　用 B 戳 A
(2) poke out　突 / 露出
(3) give sb a poke　戳一下某人

似 jab [dʒæb] *vt.* & *vi.* & *n.* 戳，刺
三態為：jab, jabbed [dʒæbd], jabbed

▸ I poked (at) the bug with a stick to see if it was still alive.
我用一根棒子戳一下這隻蟲，看看牠是否還活著。

▸ The dog poked its nose out of the open window of the car so it could sniff the fresh air.
狗狗把鼻子伸出打開的車窗外，好呼吸點新鮮空氣。

▸ The box was bigger than the bag, so the top of it poked out.
箱子比袋子還要大，所以箱子的上方突出來了。

▸ Alan gave me a poke with his elbow, reminding me that it was time to leave.
艾倫用手肘頂了我一下，提醒我該是離開的時候了。

3 fascinate [ˋfæsṇˌet] *vt.* 使著迷

片 be fascinated with / by...
對……著迷

衍 fascination [ˌfæsṇˋeʃən] *n.* 著迷 ⑥

似 (1) charm [tʃɑrm] *vt.* 使著迷 ③
(2) infatuate [ɪnˋfætʃυˌet] *vt.* 使著迷

▸ The animal from Australia was such a strange sight to the children that it fascinated them.
這隻來自澳洲的動物對小朋友們來說是這般奇特的景象，讓他們被這隻動物迷住。

▸ Tim was fascinated by the girl's sweet and tender voice on the phone.
電話中這位女孩的聲音甜美又溫柔，把提姆給迷住了。

fascinating [ˋfæsṇˌetɪŋ] *a.* 迷人的

似 (1) charming [ˋtʃɑrmɪŋ]
a. 令人著迷的
(2) appealing [əˋpilɪŋ] *a.* 有吸引力的

▸ The book had a dull name, but after I read it, I found it quite fascinating.
這本書的書名很無趣，可是在我讀過之後，我發現它很吸引人。

4 exclaim [ɪk`sklem] *vi.* 驚叫

片 exclaim in shock / delight
驚叫出聲 / 高興地驚呼

衍 exclamation [ˌɛksklə`meʃən] *n.* 驚叫
an exclamation mark　驚嘆號

▶ "Oh, no!" Jane exclaimed in shock as she heard about the death of her husband.
『噢，不！』珍在聽到她先生死亡的消息時，**驚叫出聲**。

5 contemplate [`kɑntəmˌplet] *vt.* & *vi.* 深思，仔細考慮

片 contemplate + V-ing　仔細考慮……
= consider + V-ing

衍 contemplation [ˌkɑntəm`pleʃən]
n. 深思，仔細考慮

似 (1) consider [kən`sɪdɚ] *vt.* 考慮 ②
(2) ponder [`pɑndɚ]
vt. & *vi.* 仔細考慮 ⑥

▶ Amy is contemplating quitting her job and spending a year traveling in Europe.
艾咪**考慮**辭掉工作到歐洲旅行一年。

▶ Sometimes, Richard likes to sit in the university library and just contemplate.
理查有時候喜歡坐在大學圖書館內**沉思**。

6 sprint [sprɪnt] *vi.* & *n.* 短跑；衝刺

片 make a sprint for...　為……衝刺

衍 sprinter [`sprɪntɚ] *n.* 短跑選手

似 dash [dæʃ] *vi.* 衝刺 ③

延伸 trot [trɑt] *vi.* & *n.* 小跑

▶ All the runners sprinted as fast as they could during the track and field event.
所有短跑者在田徑賽時都盡全力地**衝刺**。

▶ Kate made a desperate sprint for the train and almost tripped over a suitcase.
凱特**衝去趕**火車，差點被一個行李箱絆倒。

7 smash [smæʃ] *vt.* & *vi.* 打碎 & *n.* 轟動 / 成功的事物；碎裂聲

片 (1) smash to pieces　裂成碎片
(2) a smash record　暢銷的唱片
(3) a smash hit　熱門歌曲 / 電影 / 戲劇

似 shatter [`ʃætɚ] *vt.* 粉碎 ⑤

▶ The boy hit the baseball hard with the bat, and it smashed the neighbor's window.
小男孩用棒球棒用力擊球，而球**打破**了鄰居家的窗戶。

▶ Out of rage, Jack threw the vase against the wall, and it smashed to pieces.
傑克一氣之下把花瓶往牆壁丟，整個花瓶**裂成碎片**。

▶ The singer's new single quickly became a smash hit and stayed in the top 5 on the billboard for weeks.
這名歌手的最新單曲馬上成為**熱門歌曲**，好幾週都蟬聯排行榜前 5 名。

▶ Hearing a loud smash outside his home, Rudy wondered what had happened.
魯迪聽到屋子外頭傳來很大的**碎裂聲**，好奇發生了什麼事。

8 slap [slæp] *vt.* & *n.* 打耳光；用手掌打 & *adv.* 正好

三 slap, slapped [slæpt], slapped

片 (1) slap sb across / in the face 賞某人一個耳光
(2) give sb a slap 賞某人一巴掌
(3) a slap in the face 侮辱

▶ Mary slapped her boyfriend across the face when he said something insulting to her.
瑪莉賞了他男友一巴掌，因為他說了汙辱她的話。

▶ Olivia gave her brother a slap because he had snuck out gambling again.
奧莉薇亞打了她弟弟一巴掌，因為他又偷跑出去賭博。

▶ When a less experienced coworker got promoted instead of her, it was a slap in the face to Tina.
當獲得升遷的不是蒂娜，而是一位較無經驗的同事時，這對蒂娜來說是個侮辱。

▶ While looking down at his smartphone, Ralph walked slap into a wall.
雷夫看著智慧型手機的同時，就直接撞上牆了。

9 exceptional [ɪkˋsɛpʃənl̩] *a.* 卓越的；異常的，不尋常的

衍 (1) exceptionally [ɪkˋsɛpʃənl̩ɪ] *adv.* 異常地
exceptionally beautiful 美若天仙的
(2) except [ɪkˋsɛpt] *prep.* & *conj.* 除了 ①
(3) exception [ɪkˋsɛpʃən] *n.* 例外 ④

似 (1) outstanding [ˌaʊtˋstændɪŋ] *a.* 傑出的 ④
(2) unusual [ʌnˋjuʒuəl] *a.* 不常見的

▶ Alex showed an exceptional talent in art at a very young age.
艾立克斯很小的時候就展露出他非凡的藝術天分。

▶ Joe's ability to remember details is exceptional; not many people have a memory like his.
喬記得細節的能力很出色，很少人能有像他一樣的記憶力。

10 curriculum [kəˋrɪkjələm] *n.* 課程

複 curricula [kəˋrɪkjələ] / curriculums

片 a school / an undergraduate curriculum 學校 / 大學課程

衍 (1) curricular [kəˋrɪkjələ˞] *a.* 課程的
(2) extracurricular [ˌɛkstrəkəˋrɪkjələ˞] *a.* 課外的

似 course [kɔrs] *n.* (單一) 課程 ①

▶ The new curriculum will offer students chances to develop their creativity.
新的課程將提供學生許多開發創意的機會。

11 loop [lup] *n.* 圈，環

片 (1) (be) in the loop 是 (圈內) 知情人士

▶ This road is straight except for a loop near the highway.
除了在高速公路附近有個環道之外，這條路是很直的。

1011-1019

(2) (be) out of the loop
(圈外) 不知情人士

似 coil [kɔɪl] *n.* 圈

▸ Because she was not in the loop, Monica didn't know much about what was going on in the company.
因為莫妮卡不是決策圈內人士，所以不太清楚公司內發生了什麼事。

12 venture [ˋvɛntʃɚ] *n.* 投機事業 & *vi.* & *vt.* 冒險

片 (1) a joint venture　合資事 / 企業
(2) venture to V　冒險去做……
(3) venture into + 地方　冒險去某地

▸ The Ford company has invested a huge sum of money in a joint venture.
福特公司投資了一大筆金額在合資事業上。

▸ Although he was nervous, Mark walked into the boss's office and ventured to ask for a raise.
儘管馬克很緊張，他還是走進老闆的辦公室冒險問看看是否能加薪。

▸ Harry packed his food and gear, ready to venture into the unknown.
哈利打包好他的食物和裝備，準備好要往未知的地方探險。

▸ Nothing ventured, nothing gained.
不入虎穴，焉得虎子。—— 諺語

13 penetrate [ˋpɛnə͵tret] *vt.* 穿透

衍 penetrating [ˋpɛnə͵tretɪŋ] *a.* 滲透性的

似 pierce [pɪrs] *vt.* 刺破，刺入

▸ Luckily, the bullet missed the bodyguard's artery by an inch when it penetrated his chest.
很慶幸的是，這顆子彈穿透該保鑣的胸膛時，以一英寸之差偏離了動脈。

penetration [͵pɛnəˋtreʃən] *n.* 穿透

▸ Plastic materials resist water penetration.
塑膠材質可以阻擋水的穿透力。

14 steer [stɪr] *vt.* & *vi.* 駕駛 & *vt.* 帶領 & *n.* 閹牛

延伸 a steering wheel　方向盤

▸ When driving, always be sure to keep both hands on the steering wheel.
開車時，沿路要將雙手放在方向盤上。

▸ The captain was praised for steering the ship to safety in the bad weather.
船長因在惡劣環境中安全地駕駛船隻而獲讚賞。

▸ Chad owns a sports car and thinks it's very easy to steer.
查德擁有一輛跑車，也覺得它很容易駕駛。

▸ Mr. Howard steered / guided the company through the recession.
霍華先生帶領這間公司度過了不景氣。

15 compound [ˋkɑmpaʊnd] *n.* 合成物 & *a.* 合成的，複合的 & [kɑmˋpaʊnd] *vt.* 混合

片 (1) a compound of...　……的合成物

▸ Water is a compound of hydrogen and oxygen.
水是氫與氧的合成物。

(2) a compound sentence 複合句
(3) a chemical / an organic compound 化學 / 有機合成物

似 combine [kəmˋbaɪn] *vt.* 結合 ②

▶ A sentence made up of two or more main clauses is called a compound sentence.
由兩個或兩個以上的主要子句構成的句子稱為**複合句**。

▶ The pharmacist compounded several medicines according to the prescription.
藥劑師按照處方把好幾種藥**混合**在一起。
*pharmacist [ˋfɑrməsɪst] *n.* 藥劑師

16 confession [kənˋfɛʃən] *n.* 承認，坦承

片 make a confession to sb
向某人坦承

衍 confess [kənˋfɛs] *vt.* 自白；承認；招供；告解 ④

▶ Jim made a confession to his wife that he had lost all his money gambling.
吉姆**向**老婆**承認**他把所有的錢都輸光了。

17 trait [tret] *n.* 特質，特點

片 a personality / character trait
人格特質

似 (1) characteristic [ˌkærəktəˋrɪstɪk] *n.* 特徵 ④
(2) attribute [ˋætrəˌbjut] *n.* 特質 ⑤

▶ Arrogance and laziness are two of Bill's most annoying personality traits.
傲慢和懶散是比爾最令人討厭的其中兩項**人格特質**。

18 overhead [ˌovəˋhɛd] *a.* 頭頂上的 & *adv.* 在高空中 & [ˋovəˌhɛd] *n.* (公司) 經常性開支 (不可數)

片 an overhead compartment / bin
(機位上方的) 頭頂置物櫃

用法 overhead 作名詞表「經常性開支」時視作不可數名詞，此為美式用法；在英式用法中，則恆為複數 overheads。

▶ Nancy put her carry-on bags in the overhead compartment as soon as she got on the plane.
南西一上飛機就把隨身攜帶的行李放入**頭頂置物櫃**中。

▶ On his way to work, the witness saw the plane flying dangerously low overhead.
該目擊者在上班途中，看見飛機危險地從**頭上**低空飛過。

▶ The company decided to move to a different area of the city because the overhead was cheaper there.
公司決定搬去城市的另一區，因為在那裡**開支**會比較便宜。

19 clarity [ˋklærətɪ] *n.* 清楚，清晰 (不可數)

片 with clarity 清楚地

衍 clarify [ˋklærəˌfaɪ] *vt.* 說明 ④

▶ Some people can always assess a situation with great clarity.
有些人總是能以**清晰**的思路來判斷情況。

▶ Since Jerome bought such an expensive stereo system, it's not surprising the clarity is so good.
由於傑洛姆買的音響系統是如此昂貴，因此它的音質有絕佳的**清晰度**一點也不讓人意外。

1020-1025

20 surplus [ˋsɝpləs] *n.* 過剩；盈餘 & *a.* 多餘的

片 (1) a surplus of... 過剩的……
(2) a budget surplus 預算盈餘
(3) a trade surplus 貿易順差（出口多於進口）

▸ The company had a surplus of five million dollars last year.
這家公司去年**盈餘** 5 百萬美金。

▸ The company is forecasting a large budget surplus this year.
該公司預測今年會有很多**預算盈餘**。

▸ Nora invested large sums of surplus cash in the bond market.
諾拉把大筆的**剩餘**現金投資在債券市場。
*bond [bɑnd] *n.* 債券；關係

deficit [ˋdɛfəsɪt] *n.* 赤字

片 (1) be in deficit / the red 呈現赤字
(2) a trade deficit 貿易逆差（進口多於出口）
(3) a deficit of + 數字 若干金額的虧損

似 shortfall [ˋʃɔrt͵fɔl] *n.* 赤字

▸ The US trade balance has been in deficit for the past few years.
過去幾年來，美國的貿易收支都**呈現赤字**的狀態。

▸ The United States is currently running a trade deficit with China.
美國目前對中國呈現**貿易逆差**。

21 concede [kənˋsid] *vt.* (不情願地) 承認 & *vi.* & *vt.* 認輸 & *vt.* (不情願地) 讓與

片 (1) concede that... 承認……
(2) concede (defeat) 承認失敗
(3) concede A to B 把 A 讓給 B
(4) concede to... 對……讓步
= give in to...

衍 concession [kənˋsɛʃən] *n.* 讓步 ⑥

▸ I concede that we should have spent more time planning before we started the project.
我**承認**我們在計畫開始前本應該要花更多時間來規劃。

▸ With the team losing the baseball game so badly, it decided to concede.
球隊在棒球比賽中輸慘了，因此決定**認敗**。

▸ At first, the American president refused to concede power, but eventually he did so.
起初這位美國總統拒絕**讓權**，但最後他還是這麼做了。

▸ The defending champions conceded ten points to the challengers in the first few minutes of the game.
衛冕冠軍隊在比賽開始後的幾分鐘就**讓**挑戰隊得了 10 分。

▸ By no means will I concede to Peter's demands.
我絕對不會**對**彼得的要求**讓步**。

22 coordinate [koˋɔrdn̩͵et] *vt.* 協調 & *vt.* & *vi.* 相稱 & [koˋɔrdənət] *n.* 座標；成套服裝 (恆用複數) & *a.* 同等重要的

片 coordinate with... 與……相稱

▸ The boss appointed a new manager to coordinate the advertising and marketing department.
老闆指派一名新的經理以**協調**廣告部和行銷部。

衍 (1) coordinated [koˋɔrdn̩ˏetɪd]
a. 協調一致的
(2) coordination [koˋɔrdn̩ˏeʃən]
n. 協調
(3) coordinator [koˋɔrdn̩ˏetɚ]
n. 協調者

▶ This white skirt coordinates your sky blue sweater well!
這件白裙真襯你的天藍色毛衣。

▶ People who care about fashion make sure their colors and styles coordinate.
關注潮流的人會確保他們的顏色和風格相配合。

▶ The planes spotted the enemy ship and reported the coordinates to the captain.
飛機發現敵軍船隻，並將座標回報給隊長。

▶ The sales clerk showed the customer several sets of coordinates.
銷售員展示幾套套裝給顧客看。

▶ Under the law, the separate branches of the government were all coordinate.
在法律之下，政府的各個分支部門都同等重要。

23 uncover [ʌnˋkʌvɚ] *vt.* 揭露，發現

似 (1) discover [dɪsˋkʌvɚ] *vt.* 發現 ②
(2) detect [dɪˋtɛkt] *vt.* 發現，察覺 ③

▶ Police have uncovered a plot to assassinate the president during his visit to Indonesia.
警方揭露了一項要在總統訪問印尼期間刺殺他的陰謀。
*assassinate [əˋsæsəˏnet] *vt.* 刺殺

24 suburban [səˋbɝbən] *a.* 市郊的，郊區的

衍 suburb [ˋsʌbɝb] *n.* 郊區 ③
in the suburbs 在郊區

延伸 (1) urban [ˋɝbən] *a.* 都市的 ③
(2) rural [ˋrʊrəl] *a.* 鄉下的 ④

▶ The market for suburban houses of medium and small size is now more active than ever before.
市郊的中小型房屋市場現在是前所未有的活躍。

25 dedicate [ˋdɛdəˏket] *vt.* 奉獻；(音樂作品、書等) 獻給

片 (1) dedicate oneself to + N/V-ing
某人致力於……
= devote oneself to + N/V-ing
= be dedicated to + N/V-ing
= be devoted to + N/V-ing
(2) dedicate sth to sb
將某物獻給某人

▶ Hailey dedicated herself to helping the poor.
海莉致力於幫助窮人。

▶ I'd like to dedicate this song to my dear wife, who has been supporting my singing career over the past 20 years.
我想把這首歌獻給我摯愛的太太，過去這 20 年來她一直支持我的歌唱事業。

26 tactic [ˋtæktɪk] *n.* 策略；戰術（常用複數）

片 (1) a delaying tactic　拖延策略
(2) change / switch tactics　改變策略

▶ The manager uses psychological tactics in her advertising campaigns.
經理在廣告宣傳活動中使用了心理學的策略。

▶ The general's tactics helped him capture the city without the loss of a single life.
這位將軍的戰術使他不費一兵一卒就攻下這座城市。

strategic [strəˋtidʒɪk] *a.* 戰略（上）的（= strategical [strəˋtidʒɪkl]）
衍 strategy [ˋstrætədʒɪ] *n.* 戰略；謀略 ③

▶ South and Central Asia are regions of great strategic importance.
南亞和中亞是戰略上極為重要的區域。

27 successor [səkˋsɛsɚ] *n.* 繼承者

片 (1) a successor to...　……的繼承者
(2) a successor to a throne　王位繼承人
反 predecessor [ˋprɛdə,sɛsɚ] *n.* 前任者 ⑥

▶ Most people think the assistant manager will be the successor to the general manager when she retires.
大部分的人都覺得副理會是總經理退休後的接棒人。

28 scope [skop] *n.* 範圍

片 (1) in scope　範圍上來說
(2) beyond / outside the scope of...　超過……的範圍
(3) within the scope of...　在……的範圍內
似 bounds [baʊndz] *n.* 範圍，界線（恆用複數）

▶ The problem is small in scope and won't take long to fix.
這個問題不算大，不用很長的時間就可以解決。

▶ I'm afraid your questions are outside the scope of our lecture today.
恐怕你的問題不在我們今天演講的範圍內。

29 dilemma [dəˋlɛmə] *n.* 進退兩難

片 (1) be in a dilemma　處於進退兩難之境
(2) face a dilemma　面臨兩難

▶ Sophie is in a dilemma about whether to quit her job or not.
蘇菲在是否要辭職的決定當中進退兩難。

30 descend [dɪˋsɛnd] *vi.* & *vt.* 下降

片 be descended from sb/sth　是某人的後裔；從某事物演變而來
反 ascend [əˋsɛnd] *vi.* 上升 & *vt.* 攀登 ⑥

▶ The captain announced that the plane would start to descend in a few minutes.
機長宣布幾分鐘後飛機就要開始下降。

▶ John's family is said to be descended from a great emperor.
約翰的家族據說是一位偉大皇帝的後代。

31 preliminary [prɪˋlɪmə͵nɛrɪ] *a.* 初步的 & *n.* 開端，初始活動

複 preliminaries

似 initial [ɪˋnɪʃəl] *a.* 最初的 ④

▸ Preliminary results show that this skin care product can lead to cancer, but this has to be confirmed in further medical trials.
初步結果顯示此肌膚保養品會導致癌症，但這還得靠進一步的醫學實驗來證實。

▸ The meeting was only a preliminary; the main event would begin afterwards.
這場會議只是個開端，主活動之後才會開始。

32 exploration [͵ɛkspləˋreʃən] *n.* 探險，探測；研究，調查

片 space exploration 太空探測

衍 (1) explore [ɪkˋsplɔr] *vt.* 探尋，探討 ③
(2) explorer [ɪkˋsplɔrɚ] *n.* 探險家

▸ Space exploration has taught us how insignificant our planet is in the universe.
太空探測讓我們知道我們的地球在宇宙中多麼渺小。
*insignificant [͵ɪnsɪgˋnɪfəkənt] *a.* 微不足道的

▸ This documentary is an exploration into the human mind.
這部紀錄片深入探討了人腦。

33 competent [ˋkɑmpətənt] *a.* 有能力的，勝任的

片 (1) be / feel competent to V 有能力做……
(2) be competent for sth 能勝任某事

反 incompetent [ɪnˋkɑmpətənt] *a.* 不能勝任的，無能力的

▸ I don't feel competent enough to comment on the director's new movie.
我覺得我的能力不足以為導演的這部新電影作評論。

▸ I doubt if John is competent for that job.
我懷疑約翰是否勝任那份工作。

competence [ˋkɑmpətəns] *n.* 能力 (不可數) (= competency [ˋkɑmpətənsɪ])

片 competence in sth 在某事方面的能力

反 incompetence [ɪnˋkɑmpətəns] *n.* 無能 (不可數)

▸ Martha has reached a high level of competence in both languages.
瑪莎對這兩種語言的掌控能力已達到相當高深的境界。

34 swap [swɑp] *vt.* & *vi.* & *n.* 交換

三 swap, swapped [swɑpt], swapped

片 (1) swap A for B 用 A 交換 B
(2) do a swap 做交換

似 exchange [ɪksˋtʃendʒ] *vt.* 交換 ③

▸ I swapped my bicycle for a guitar with my friend.
我用我的腳踏車和朋友換了一把吉他。

▸ I'm finished with this magazine. If you're done with yours, can we swap?
我已經看完這本雜誌了。如果你看完了你的，我們可以交換嗎？

▸ Let's do a swap. I give you this dress and you give me that bag.
我們做個交換吧。我給妳這件洋裝，妳給我那個包包。

35 discrimination [dɪˌskrɪməˋneʃən] *n.* 歧視；區別，辨識力

片 (1) racial / sex / religious discrimination
種族 / 性別 / 宗教歧視
(2) discrimination against...
對……的歧視

▸ Even today, racial discrimination is still prevalent in this country.
即使到了現在，**種族歧視**在這個國家還是很普遍。
*prevalent [ˋprɛvələnt] *a.* 普遍的

▸ Discrimination against others on the basis of race, sex, or age is never acceptable.
基於種族、性別、年紀對他人**的歧視**是絕不被容許的。

▸ Children from age three to eight develop their ability of shape and color discrimination.
孩童在 3 到 8 歲時會發展他們對形狀與顏色的**辨識力**。

---

discriminate [dɪˋskrɪməˌnet]
vt. & *vi.* 區別 & *vi.* 歧視

片 (1) discriminate A from B
區別 A 與 B
= discriminate between A and B
(2) discriminate against...
歧視……

似 differentiate [ˌdɪfəˋrɛnʃɪˌet]
vt. 區別 ⑥

▸ John was born color-blind so he can't discriminate red from green.
= John was born color-blind so he can't discriminate between red and green.
約翰有先天性色盲，因此無法**區別**紅色和綠色。
*color-blind 色盲

▸ It's illegal to discriminate against women in the workplace.
在職場上**歧視**女性是違法的。

36 racism [ˋresɪzəm] *n.* 種族主義；種族歧視

衍 (1) race [res] *n.* 種族 ①
(2) racial [ˋreʃəl] *a.* 種族的 ③
(3) racist [ˋresɪst] *n.* 種族主義者

▸ People who believe in racism regard themselves as superior.
篤信**種族主義**的人會認為自己的族類是優人一等的。

▸ The Holocaust was the tragic outcome of extreme racism.
納粹對猶太人的大屠殺是極度**種族歧視**的悲慘結果。
*the Holocaust [ˋhɑləˌkɔst]（二次大戰納粹對猶太人的）大屠殺

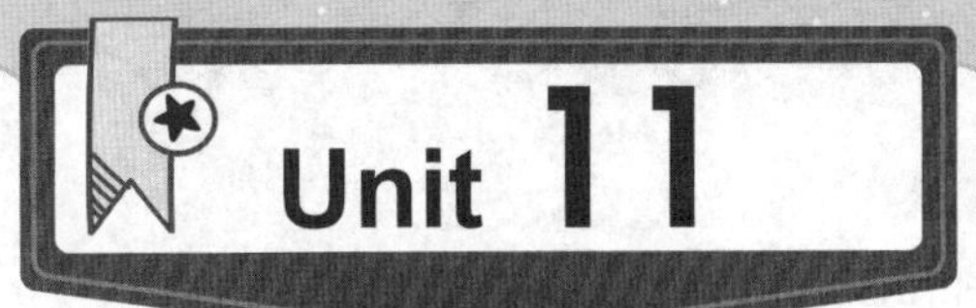

1101-1103

1 workshop [ˋwɝk͵ʃap] *n.* 研討會；工作室

似 (1) seminar [ˋsɛmə͵nar] *n.* 研討會 ⑤
(2) studio [ˋst(j)udɪ͵o]
n. (尤指藝術家的) 工作室 ③

▸ A three-day writing workshop will be hosted by the renowned author Mr. Miller.
為期 3 天的寫作**研討會**將由知名作家米勒先生主辦。

▸ The carpenter transformed the garage into a workshop for hand-made furniture.
這名木匠將車庫改裝成一間製作手工傢俱的**工作室**。

2 behalf [bɪˋhæf] *n.* 代表

片 (1) on sb's behalf 代表某人
= on behalf of sb
(2) in sb's behalf 為了某人的利益
= in behalf of sb

▸ On behalf of our company, I would like to make a toast to the newlyweds.
本人謹**代表**公司向結婚的新人敬酒。
*toast [tost] *n.* 敬酒

3 sole [sol] *a.* 單獨的，唯一的 & *n.* (單腳) 腳底；鞋底 & *vt.* 替 (鞋) 換底

似 (1) only [ˋonlɪ] *a.* 唯一的 ①
(2) single [ˋsɪŋgl̩] *a.* 單一的 ②

▸ Our sole objective is to restore public confidence in our products.
我們**唯一的**目標就是重拾大眾對我們產品的信心。

▸ Ken likes his new shoes because they have thick rubber soles, which makes them comfortable.
肯很喜歡他的新鞋，因為它們有厚橡膠**底**，穿起來很舒適。

▸ Rather than purchase new shoes, Randy paid someone to sole his old pair.
蘭迪沒有買新鞋，而是付錢請人幫他**換鞋底**。

solely [ˋsollɪ] *adv.* 單獨地，唯一地；僅僅

似 (1) simply [ˋsɪmplɪ] *adv.* 僅僅
(2) merely [ˋmɪrlɪ] *adv.* 僅僅
(3) exclusively [ɪkˋsklusɪvlɪ]
adv. 僅僅；專門

▸ The publisher is solely responsible for the inappropriate content of the magazine.
出版商應為該雜誌中不合宜的內容**獨自**負起責任。

▸ Kelly plays the guitar solely for her own enjoyment; she is too shy to perform for others.
凱莉彈吉他**只是**因為興趣，她太害羞所以不敢在其他人面前表演。

solo [ˋsolo] *n.* 獨唱 (曲)；獨奏 (曲) & *a.* 單獨的 & *adv.* 單獨地

片 a solo exhibition / performance / album 個展 / 單獨表演 / 個人專輯

衍 soloist [ˋsoloɪst] *n.* 獨唱者；獨奏者

▸ Howard's piano solo was so impressive that he received a standing ovation.
霍華的鋼琴**獨奏**非常精彩，獲得觀眾起立鼓掌。
*a standing ovation [oˋveʃən] 起立鼓掌

▸ The young artist is having his first solo exhibition at the art museum.
這名年輕的藝術家目前正在美術館舉行第一次**個展**。

▸ Because her husband was busy that night, Louise went to the event solo.
因為露易絲的老公那天晚上太忙，所以她獨自去參加活動。

4 optimism [ˋɑptəmɪzəm] *n.* 樂觀主義

衍 (1) optimistic [ˏɑptəˋmɪstɪk] *a.* 樂觀的 ③
(2) optimist [ˋɑptəmɪst] *n.* 樂觀主義者

▸ In times of economic prosperity, everyone showed great optimism about the future.
經濟欣欣向榮之際，每個人對未來都很樂觀。

pessimism [ˋpɛsəmɪzəm] *n.* 悲觀主義

衍 (1) pessimistic [ˏpɛsəˋmɪstɪk] *a.* 悲觀的 ④
(2) pessimist [ˋpɛsəmɪst] *n.* 悲觀主義者

▸ A recent survey shows that pessimism about the economy continues to grow.
新近調查指出，對整體經濟抱持悲觀的看法持續蔓延。

5 scan [skæn] *vt.* & *vi.* & *n.* 掃描 & *vt.* & *vi.* 粗略地看

三 scan, scanned [skænd], scanned
片 (1) scan sth into the computer 將某物掃描進電腦
(2) scan through... 快速瀏覽……
衍 scanner [ˋskænɚ] *n.* 掃描器
似 skim [skɪm] *vt.* & *vi.* 瀏覽，略讀 ⑥
skim through... 瀏覽……

▸ Could you help me scan these old photographs into the computer?
你能不能幫我把這些老照片掃描進電腦裡？

▸ Before the document could be emailed, it first had to be scanned.
需要先掃描文件後，才能用電子郵件寄出。

▸ The scan showed that the cancer cells had spread, and the patient needed an immediate operation.
掃描結果顯示病患的癌細胞擴散了，需要立即動手術。

▸ Peter scanned the Yellow Pages looking for the number of a plumber.
彼得概略看過工商電話簿，找尋水電行的電話。
*the Yellow Pages 黃頁，工商電話簿

▸ Every morning, Jake likes to scan through the newspaper while eating breakfast.
傑克每天早上都喜歡邊瀏覽報紙邊吃早餐。

6 commodity [kəˋmɑdətɪ] *n.* 商品

複 commodities [kəˋmɑdətɪz]
片 daily commodities 日常消費品（常用複數）

▸ Our company recently imported a lot of electronic commodities from Germany.
我們公司最近從德國進口許多電子商品。

7 mainstream [ˋmenˏstrim] *n.* (思想等) 主流 (前須置定冠詞 the)

衍 stream [strim] *n.* 溪流 ②

▸ Clubhouse might become the mainstream method of communication among teenagers.
社交平臺 Clubhouse 可能成為青少年溝通的主流方式。

8 indifferent [ɪnˋdɪf(ə)rənt] *a.* 冷漠的

片 be indifferent to... 對……漠不關心
= be callous to...

衍 indifference [ɪnˋdɪf(ə)rəns] *n.* 漠不關心，冷漠 ⑥

似 callous [ˋkæləs] *a.* 冷漠的

▸ Jennie was very angry because her husband is indifferent to her complaints.
珍妮很生氣，因為她先生對她的抱怨漠不關心。

9 caution [ˋkɔʃən] *n.* 小心，謹慎 & *vt.* & *vi.* 警告

片 (1) with caution 小心謹慎
= cautiously
(2) caution sb to V
警告某人要做……
(3) caution (sb) against...
警告 (某人) 不要……

似 warn [wɔrn] *vt.* & *vi.* 警告 ③

▸ All drugs should be used with caution.
= All drugs should be used cautiously.
所有的藥物都應謹慎使用。

▸ The park rangers cautioned us to avoid entering the park after dark.
公園管理員警告我們天黑後避免進入園區。

▸ Joe's doctor cautioned against smoking or drinking because of Joe's poor health.
喬的醫生警告他健康欠佳，所以不要吸菸或飲酒。

---

cautious [ˋkɔʃəs] *a.* 小心的，謹慎的

片 be cautious about... 謹慎處理……
= be careful about...

衍 cautiously [ˋkɔʃəslɪ] *adv.* 小心地，謹慎地

似 careful [ˋkɛrfəl] *a.* 小心的，謹慎的 ①

▸ A cautious person thinks twice before making an important decision.
謹慎的人做重要的決定之前都會三思。

▸ Andy is very cautious about making commitments.
安迪對於做承諾這件事非常謹慎。

---

precaution [prɪˋkɔʃən] *n.* 預防措施

片 take a precaution (to V) / (against...)
採取預防措施 (以……) /
採取預防 (……的) 措施
= take a preventive measure (to V) / (against...)

衍 precautionary [prɪˋkɔʃənˏɛrɪ] *a.* 預防的

▸ When going outdoors, you should take precautions to protect your skin from the sun.
到戶外時，你應該採取預防措施，保護皮膚免受太陽晒。

10 fatigue [fəˋtig] *n.* 疲勞（不可數）& *vt.* 使疲勞

片 with fatigue　很累

衍 (1) fatigued [fəˋtigd] *a.* 疲勞的
(2) fatiguing [fəˋtigɪŋ] *a.* 令人疲憊不堪的

似 exhaustion [ɪgˋzɔstʃən] *n.* 疲勞

▸ John was pale with fatigue after working all night with only one hour of sleep.
約翰工作了一整晚只睡了一個小時，累得臉色發白。

▸ The tough climbing fatigued Meg, and thus she had to take a break.
費力地登山讓梅格累極了，所以她得休息一下。

11 verbal [ˋvɜbḷ] *a.* 言語的；口頭的 & *n.* 動狀詞

片 (1) verbal abuse　言語虐待
(2) a verbal attack　口水戰

衍 (1) verb [vɜb] *n.* 動詞
(2) verbally [ˋvɜbḷɪ] *adv.* 言語上；口頭地
(3) nonverbal [ˏnɑnˋvɜbḷ] *a.* 非語言的

似 oral [ˋorəl] *a.* 口頭的 ③

▸ Though verbal abuse leaves no signs of visible harm, some people consider it worse than physical abuse.
言語虐待雖然沒有明顯的傷痕，有些人認為這種虐待卻比身體虐待更嚴重。

▸ Local authorities have given the construction company verbal approval to begin the project.
地方當局口頭上已經准許該建築公司開工。

▸ I'm sick of the politicians' verbal attacks on each other.
我對政客間的口水戰已經覺得很厭煩了。

12 peasant [ˋpɛzṇt] *n.*（尤指較為貧窮的）農夫

似 (1) farmer [ˋfɑrmɚ] *n.* 農夫 ①
(2) farmhand [ˋfɑrmˏhænd] *n.* 農場工人

▸ Little did I expect that the millionaire used to be a poor peasant.
我一點都沒想到這位百萬富翁以前曾是個窮農夫。

13 contempt [ˏkənˋtɛmpt] *n.* 輕視，藐視

片 treat... with contempt
輕視地對待……

衍 contemptuous [kənˋtɛmptʃuəs] *a.* 藐視的

似 scorn [skɔrn] *n.* 輕蔑 ⑥

▸ When the impressionist painters first exhibited their work, many people treated the artists with contempt.
當印象派畫家第一次展覽他們的畫作時，許多人都很輕視他們。

14 conceal [kənˋsil] *vt.* 隱藏

片 conceal sth from sb
不讓某人知道某事

似 hide [haɪd] *vt.* 隱藏 ①

▸ I realized from Maureen's tone of voice that she was concealing something from me.
從莫琳的語調中，我發現她有事正瞞著我。

disclose [dɪsˋkloz] *vt.* 揭露

片 disclose sth to sb 揭露某事給某人

衍 disclosure [dɪsˋkloʒɚ] *n.* 揭發 ⑥

似 reveal [rɪˋvil] *vt.* 洩漏 ③

▸ The minister refused to disclose details of the agreement to the press.
部長拒絕向媒體**透露**該協定的細節。

15 tempt [tɛmpt] *vt.* 引誘

片 (1) tempt sb to V 引誘某人做……
= tempt sb into + V-ing
(2) be tempted to V 很想做……

衍 tempting [ˋtɛmptɪŋ] *a.* 誘人的

似 seduce [səˋd(j)us] *vt.* 誘惑 ⑥

▸ Robert tempted me to bet money on horse racing.
= Robert tempted me into betting money on horse racing.
羅伯特**引誘**我玩賽馬賭錢。

▸ Having been scolded by her boss, Giselle was tempted to quit.
吉賽兒被老闆罵，因此**很想**離職。

temptation [ˏtɛmpˋteʃən] *n.* 誘惑

▸ Scott resisted the temptation of the beautiful girl's invitation and was faithful to his girlfriend.
史考特對女友忠貞，拒絕了這名美女邀約的**誘惑**。

16 infinite [ˋɪnfənət] *a.* 無限的

衍 infinity [ɪnˋfɪnətɪ] *n.* 無限

似 (1) unlimited [ʌnˋlɪmɪtɪd] *a.* 無限的
(2) endless [ˋɛndləs] *a.* 無盡的

反 finite [ˋfaɪnaɪt] *a.* 有限的 ⑥

▸ Life is finite, but knowledge is infinite.
生也有涯，知也**無涯**。── 諺語

▸ Little kids seem to have an infinite amount of energy and are curious about everything around them.
小孩子似乎有**無窮的**精力，對身邊的事物充滿了好奇。

17 pier [pɪr] *n.* 碼頭

似 (1) dock [dɑk] *n.* 碼頭；船塢 ③
(2) wharf [(h)wɔrf] *n.* 碼頭 ⑥

▸ For passengers taking the bay cruise, please board at Pier 24 at 4 p.m.
搭乘港灣郵輪的旅客請於下午 4 點在第 24 號**碼頭**登船。

18 pledge [plɛdʒ] *n.* 誓言 & *vt.* 發誓

片 (1) make a pledge that...
誓言要……
= pledge that...
(2) make a pledge to V 誓言要……
= pledge to V

似 swear [swɛr] *vt.* 發誓 ③

▸ The new mayor made a pledge that he would reduce the city's crime rate.
= The new mayor pledged that he would reduce the city's crime rate.
= The new mayor made a pledge to reduce the city's crime rate.
= The new mayor pledged to reduce the city's crime rate.
新市長**誓言要**降低該市的犯罪率。

19 shove [ʃʌv] *vt.* & *vi.* & *n.* 推擠

衍 shovel [ˋʃʌvḷ] *n.* 鏟子 ③
似 push [pʊʃ] *vt.* & *vi.* & *n.* 推擠 ①

▸ The rude young man shoved the old man aside in order to get on the bus.
這粗魯的年輕人為了要上公車而把老先生推開。

▸ When getting onto a bus or train, it is rude to shove.
上公車或火車時，推擠是很不禮貌的。

▸ After getting a shove from behind, Larry was surprised to see that a little old lady had done it.
賴瑞的背被推了一下後，很訝異發現是一名小個子的老太太推他的。

20 straightforward [ˏstretˋfɔrwɚd] *a.* 直接的；易懂的

衍 (1) straightforwardly
[ˏstretˋfɔrwɚdlɪ]
adv. 直接地；易懂地
(2) straightforwardness
[ˏstretˋfɔrwɚdnəs]
n. 直率；簡單易懂
似 frank [fræŋk] *a.* 直率的 ③
反 complicated [ˋkɑmpləˏketɪd]
a. 複雜的

▸ Don't beat around the bush. Mr. Lin is a very straightforward man. You can talk openly with him.
不要拐彎抹角的。林先生是很直接的人。你可以很坦率地跟他說話。
*beat around the bush　拐彎抹角

▸ The installation of this software is pretty straightforward. All you need to do is follow the instructions step by step.
安裝這套軟體很容易。你只要一步步跟著指示就行了。

21 random [ˋrændəm] *a.* 任意選擇的，隨機的

片 (1) random sampling　隨機取樣
(2) at random　任意地，隨機地
衍 randomly [ˋrændəmlɪ] *adv.* 任意地

▸ Political analysts often use random sampling when doing a poll.
政治分析家在做民意測驗時常會隨機取樣。

▸ Thirty students were selected at random to take part in the experiment.
30 名學生經隨機抽樣選中參與這項實驗。

22 sphere [sfɪr] *n.* 球體；領域

片 the political / economic sphere
政治 / 經濟領域

▸ From space, the Earth looks like a big blue and white sphere.
地球在外太空中看起來像是個大型藍白相間的球體。

▸ Thomas has been involved in the political sphere since he was young.
湯瑪士自年輕時就投身政治領域。

23 symbolic [ˌsɪmˋbɑlɪk] *a.* 象徵性的

片 be symbolic of... 象徵……
= symbolize...

衍 (1) symbol [ˋsɪmbḷ] *n.* 象徵 ②
(2) symbolize [ˋsɪmbḷˌaɪz] *vt.* 象徵 ⑥
(3) symbolically [ˌsɪmˋbɑlɪklɪ] *adv.* 象徵性地

▸ The use of the color blue in the film is symbolic of the misery and depression of the main character.
= The use of the color blue in the film symbolizes the misery and depression of the main character.
這部電影中使用的藍色象徵主角的不幸與憂鬱。

24 merge [mɝdʒ] *vt.* & *vi.* (使) 合併

片 merge with... 與……合併

衍 (1) merger [mɝdʒɚ] *n.* 合併
(2) emerge [ɪˋmɝdʒ] *vi.* 浮現 ④

似 combine [kəmˋbaɪn] *vt.* & *vi.* (使) 結合 ②

▸ The scientist merged two existing theories and added some new ideas to come up with his new model.
這名科學家融合兩個現有理論，並加入新想法來完成他的新模型。

▸ The two banks merged in order to become more competitive in their industry.
這兩家銀行合併以便在該行業裡更具競爭力。

25 criterion [kraɪˋtɪrɪən] *n.* (評斷、批評的) 標準

複 criteria [kraɪˋtɪrɪə]

片 (1) a sole criterion 唯一條件
(2) meet the criterion for... 符合……的標準

似 standard [ˋstændɚd] *n.* 標準 ②

▸ A strong educational background is not the sole criterion we use for selecting suitable new staff.
高學歷背景不是我們用來選擇適合員工的唯一條件。

26 norm [nɔrm] *n.* 常態；平均水準 (均須置定冠詞 the)；規範 (常用複數)

片 (1) be below / above the norm 在水準之下 / 上
(2) social norms 社會規範

衍 normal [ˋnɔrmḷ] *a.* 正常的 ③

▸ Sending kids to daycare centers is gradually becoming the norm in modern society.
把孩子送到托兒所在現代社會已經逐漸變成一種常態。

▸ This student's reading ability is above the norm for her age group.
這個學生的閱讀能力超過她年齡群的標準。

▸ Social norms are different throughout the world, so it's best to do a little research before traveling.
每一個國家的社會規範都不一樣，所以旅行前最好做一些研究。

27 capability [ˌkepəˋbɪlətɪ] *n.* 能力；軍事武力

片 (1) have the capability to V
有能力從事……
= have the capability of + N/V-ing
= have the ability to V
(2) beyond / within one's capability 超越某人的能力 / 在某人能力範圍內
(3) military / nuclear capability
軍事 / 核子武力

衍 capable [ˋkepəbl̩] *a.* 有能力的 ③

▸ With his background in Latin, John has the capability to learn Italian quickly.
= With his background in Latin, John has the capability of learning Italian quickly.
由於約翰有拉丁文的基礎，因此他可以很快就學會義大利文。

▸ I can understand German in daily conversations, but understanding technical discussions is beyond my capability.
我可以聽得懂德文的日常會話，但是若要聽懂專業的對話對我來說就太難了。

▸ It is reported that the nation is trying to develop its nuclear capability.
據報導該國正在發展核子武力。

28 diminish [dəˋmɪnɪʃ] *vt.* & *vi.* 減少；降低（重要性）

似 (1) reduce [rɪˋd(j)us] *vt.* 減少；降低；減輕 ③
(2) decrease [dɪˋkris] *vt.* & *vi.* 減少 ③
(3) lessen [ˋlɛsn̩] *vt.* & *vi.* (使) 變少

▸ The new policy is expected to diminish the cost of health care.
這項新政策可望降低健康照護的成本。

▸ The political influence of the former president diminished with time.
前總統的政治影響力隨著時間的流逝而慢慢減弱。

29 density [ˋdɛnsətɪ] *n.* 密集度；密度

衍 dense [dɛns] *a.* 稠密的 ④

▸ Tokyo is a city of high population density.
東京是人口密集度高的城市。

▸ Aluminum is low in density.
鋁的密度低。

30 propaganda [ˌprɑpəˋgændə] *n.* 宣傳，鼓吹（以左右人心）(不可數)

片 a propaganda campaign
宣傳活動（表達某政治組織的立場）

▸ The anti-war groups launched a propaganda campaign against the ruling party.
許多反戰團體發起政治宣傳活動，要大家對抗執政黨。

31 recruit [rɪˋkrut] *vt.* & *vi.* 招募（員工、新兵）& *n.* 新成員；新兵

片 (1) be recruited into the army 被徵召入伍
(2) a new / raw recruit 新成員

衍 recruitment [rɪˋkrutmənt] *n.* 招募

▶ The job fair offers companies a chance to recruit new staff members.
求職博覽會提供商家**招募**新員工的機會。

▶ My brother was recruited into the army soon after he graduated.
我弟弟畢業後沒多久就**被徵召入伍**了。

▶ New recruits were sent to the headquarters in New York for training.
新員工被送去位於紐約的總部接受訓練。

32 heritage [ˋhɛrətɪdʒ] *n.*（歷史所留下的傳統、文化、語言等）遺產（不可數）

片 cultural / musical / literary heritage 文化 / 音樂 / 文學遺產

似 inheritance [ɪnˋhɛrətəns] *n.*（從別人那裡獲得的）繼承物，遺產

▶ Vienna is hosting a classical music festival to celebrate its musical heritage.
維也納目前正舉辦古典音樂季，頌揚其**音樂遺產**。

33 vicious [ˋvɪʃəs] *a.* 殘忍的，惡毒的

片 (1) a vicious attack 殘忍的攻擊
(2) a vicious circle 惡性循環

似 (1) brutal [ˋbrutl̩] *a.* 殘忍的 ④
(2) malicious [məˋlɪʃəs] *a.* 惡毒的

▶ Why do you have to be so vicious? Can't you just say something kind?
你為什麼非得要這般**惡毒**呢？你就不能說點友善的話嗎？

34 spacious [ˋspeʃəs] *a.* 寬敞的

衍 space [spes] *n.* 空間；太空 ①

似 roomy [ˋrumɪ] *a.* 寬敞的，空間大的

▶ The living room is spacious and has many French windows to let a lot of sun in.
這個客廳很**寬敞**，加上又有很多落地窗可以讓陽光照進來。
*French windows 落地窗（常用複數）

35 erupt [ɪˋrʌpt] *vi.*（暴動、感情等）爆發

片 (1) erupt / burst into / with laughter 突然笑出來
(2) erupt in applause 猛地鼓掌

衍 (1) eruption [ɪˋrʌpʃən] *n.* 爆發
(2) eruptive [ɪˋrʌptɪv] *a.* 爆發的

▶ After the protest, the police feared that a riot would erupt anytime.
= After the protest, the police feared that a riot would break out anytime.
那場抗議之後，警方擔心暴動隨時會一觸即發。

▶ After a pause, the entire room erupted into laughter and applause.
停頓了一下後，整個房間的人**突然大笑**並且鼓掌叫好。

Unit 12

1201-1207

1 sober [ˋsobɚ] *a.* 清醒的，沒醉的 & *vi.* & *vt.* (使) 變得冷靜 / 嚴肅

片 (1) stay sober 保持清醒
(2) be stone-cold sober 十分清醒
(3) sober (oneself) up
（使某人）醒酒 / 清醒

反 drunk [drʌŋk] *a.* 喝醉的 ③

▸ Michael has a serious drinking problem. He is seldom sober.
麥可有嚴重的酗酒問題。他很少有清醒的時候。

▸ You should wash your face with cold water if you want to stay sober.
你若要保持清醒，應該用冷水洗把臉。

▸ Although the conversation began in a humorous manner, the tone sobered when Bob mentioned a friend who had cancer.
儘管這段對話是以幽默的方式開始，但在鮑伯提到一位罹癌的朋友時語調就變得嚴肅了。

▸ Debbie drank two cups of coffee to sober herself up and decided not to drive home.
黛比喝了兩杯咖啡來讓自己清醒一點，並決定不要開車回家。

2 ridiculous [rɪˋdɪkjələs] *a.* 可笑的，荒謬的

衍 ridicule [ˋrɪdɪkjul] *vt.* & *n.* 嘲弄，揶揄

似 (1) funny [ˋfʌnɪ] *a.* 好笑的；奇怪的 ①
(2) comical [ˋkɑmɪkḷ] *a.* 滑稽的

▸ The hat Tim wore at the party last night was absolutely ridiculous.
昨晚派對上提姆戴的那頂帽子超可笑的。

▸ I would never do that! That's ridiculous!
我是不會那麼做的！那實在太荒謬了！

absurd [əbˋsɝd] *a.* 不合理的，荒謬的

衍 absurdity [əbˋsɝdətɪ] *n.* 荒謬

▸ The idea that the number 13 brings bad luck seems absurd to me.
認為 13 這個數字會帶來噩運的想法在我看來似乎頗荒謬。

3 beloved [bɪˋlʌvɪd / bɪˋlʌvd] *a.* 心愛的，受鍾愛的 & *n.* 心愛的人

片 be beloved of / by... 被……所愛戴

▸ Mrs. Hunter is beloved of all her students.
= Mrs. Hunter is loved by all her students.
杭特老師受她所有學生愛戴。

▸ The woman's beloved broke her heart, and now she is too sad to date anyone else.
女子的愛人讓她心碎，她現在太難過而沒辦法和其他人約會。

4 continental [ˌkɑntəˋnɛntḷ] *a.* 洲的，大陸的

片 a continental breakfast
歐陸式早餐

▸ A continental breakfast is a light breakfast that usually contains no meat but bread and butter.
歐陸式早餐通常指一頓輕量的早餐，沒有肉，只有麵包跟奶油。

衍 continent [ˋkɑntənənt]
n. 洲，大陸 ③
on the European / Australian continent　在歐洲 / 澳洲大陸

5 sturdy [ˋstɝdɪ] *a.* 堅韌的，耐用的；健壯的

似 robust [roˋbʌst] *a.* 堅固的；健壯的 ⑥
反 (1) fragile [ˋfrædʒəl] *a.* 脆弱的 ④
(2) delicate [ˋdɛləkət] *a.* 纖弱的 ④

▸ The sturdy brick house here was the only one in the neighborhood that didn't fall in the earthquake.
這邊這棟堅固的磚頭房屋是這一帶唯一一棟沒在地震中倒塌的房子。

▸ My cousin Tony is quite sturdy. He can do 100 push-ups nonstop and doesn't even break a sweat.
我的表哥東尼很健壯。他可以連續不停做 100 個伏地挺身，不流一滴汗。
*nonstop [ˌnɑnˋstɑp] *adv.* 不間斷地

stout [staʊt] *a.* (身材) 結實的；堅固的

似 (1) strong [strɔŋ] *a.* 強壯的 ①
(2) stocky [ˋstɑkɪ] *a.* 矮壯結實的

▸ When I was a child, I was very afraid of the stout old lady next door who always gave me the evil eye.
我小時候很怕隔壁那位健壯的老太太，她總是帶著不懷好意的眼光瞧我。

▸ I suggest you buy a pair of stout shoes for mountain climbing.
要登山的話，我建議你買雙堅固耐用的鞋子。

6 structural [ˋstrʌktʃərəl] *a.* 結構的

衍 (1) structure [ˋstrʌktʃɚ] *n.* 結構 ③
(2) structurally [ˋstrʌktʃərəlɪ]
adv. 結構上

▸ Jimmy's essay was structurally sound but lacked an in-depth discussion of the topic in question.
吉米的論文結構上井井有條，但欠缺對該討論議題的深入探討。

▸ Fortunately, the typhoon only caused minor structural damage to the buildings.
幸好颱風僅造成建築物結構輕微的損害。

7 preference [ˋprɛf(ə)rəns] *n.* 偏愛

片 have a preference for A over B
喜歡 A 勝於 B

衍 (1) prefer [prɪˋfɝ] *vt.* 較喜愛 ②
(2) preferable [ˋprɛfərəbl̩]
a. 更合意的

▸ Fewer parents these days have a preference for baby boys over baby girls.
現今偏好生男寶寶而非女寶寶的父母越來越少了。

8 haul [hɔl] *vt.* & *n.* (用力) 拖運，拖拉 & *n.* (費力、艱苦的) 旅程，路途

片 a long haul　艱苦且耗時的路程

延伸 haul 作名詞亦可表『(偷、收集或贏來的) 一大批東西』，因此在 YouTube 上也會看到有 YouTuber 將自己血拼的戰利品開箱拍成 "a shopping haul"，也就是開箱一大批戰利品的意思。

▸ The ship was hauled to the beach where the launching ceremony was to take place.
那艘船被拖到海濱，在那裡要舉行下水典禮。
*launch [ˋlɔntʃ] *vt.* (船) 下水

▸ Paul attached a thick rope to the heavy box and pulled it, but the haul tired him out too much.
保羅在沉重的箱子上綁了一條粗繩並拉它，拖著箱子讓他累到不行。

▸ It was a long haul, but we finally made it to the top of the mountain.
歷經千辛萬苦，我們總算成功攻頂。

9 bulk [bʌlk] *n.* 大部分；大量

片 (1) the bulk of sth　某事物的大部分
(2) in bulk　大量地

衍 bulky [ˋbʌlkɪ]
a. 笨重的；體型龐大的 ⑥

▸ The bulk of the book is about how to use your money wisely.
這本書大部分內容是關於如何聰明理財。

▸ It's cheaper when you buy food in bulk.
大量購買食物會比較便宜。

10 via [ˋvaɪə / ˋvɪə] *prep.* 經由 (= through)

▸ You can access our library's database via the internet.
你可以透過網路進入我們圖書館的資料庫。

11 patron [ˋpetrən] *n.* (老) 顧客；贊助者

衍 patronize [ˋpetrə͵naɪz] *vt.* 光顧；資助
▸ We used to patronize the Chinese restaurant around the corner. The food there was just incredible.
我們過去常光顧附近那家中式餐廳。那裡的食物好吃得不可思議。

似 (1) customer [ˋkʌstəmɚ] *n.* 顧客 ②
(2) sponsor [ˋspɑnsɚ] *n.* 贊助者 ⑤

▸ Patrons of that restaurant were all dismayed to learn that it was going to be closed.
那家餐廳的老主顧得知該店即將關門大吉，都感到十分失落。
*dismay [dɪsˋme] *vt.* 使沮喪

▸ The millionaire is the patron of many famous artists.
這位百萬富翁是許多知名藝術家的贊助者。

12 orchard [ˋɔrtʃɚd] *n.* 果園

似 grove [grov] *n.* 果園；小片樹林

▸ I like to pick oranges in the orchard early in the evening.
我喜歡傍晚的時候去果園採柳丁。

13 compromise [ˋkamprə͵maɪz] *n.* & *vi.* 妥協 & *vt.* 危害（名譽、原則）

片 (1) reach a compromise with sb on sth 與某人就某事達成協議
(2) make a compromise 妥協
(3) compromise with... 與⋯⋯妥協
(4) compromise on... 就⋯⋯上妥協

▸ After several days of negotiations, we finally reached a compromise with our business partners on certain issues.
經過幾天的談判，我們終於就若干事項與我們的生意夥伴達成協議。

▸ We all have to make compromises in life despite ourselves.
我們在生活中都必須不得不做出妥協。
*despite oneself 不得不

▸ Management refused to compromise with the union members.
資方拒絕跟勞方妥協。

▸ Dylan would rather be shot than compromise his principles.
狄倫是寧死也不肯違背自己的原則。

14 sow [so] *vt.* & *vi.* 播種

三 sow, sowed [sod], sown [son] / sowed
似 (1) sew [so] *vt.* 縫（衣服）
(2) plant [plænt] *vt.* 種植 ①

▸ Farmers started sowing their seeds in the spring.
農人春天開始播種。

▸ As you sow, so shall you reap.
一分耕耘，一分收穫。—— 諺語

15 odds [ads] *n.* 機率；不利情況（皆恆用複數）

片 (1) (the) odds are that... 很有可能⋯⋯
(2) against all (the) odds 在不利的情況下
(3) be at odds (with sb over sth) （與某人在某事上）意見不合
(4) odds and ends 零星雜物，雜七雜八的小東西
衍 odd [ad] *a.* 奇怪的；奇數的 ③
an odd number 奇數
似 probability [͵prabəˋbɪlətɪ] *n.* 可能性；機率

▸ The odds are that Frank will mess it up again.
= Chances are that Frank will mess it up again.
法蘭克很可能又會搞砸。

▸ Against all odds, the Thunderbirds, which were considered a weak team, won the championship.
儘管在不利的情況下，被認為很弱的雷鳥隊仍贏得了冠軍。

▸ Paul is always at odds with his wife over how to educate their children.
有關如何教育孩子，保羅總是和他的妻子意見不合。

▸ My grandmother left me some odds and ends when she passed away.
我的奶奶過世之後留給我一些零星雜物。

16 bruise [bruz] *n.* 瘀青 & *vt.* & *vi.* （使）瘀青

▸ How did you get that bruise on your arm?
= How did you bruise your arm?
你手臂上的瘀傷是怎麼造成的？

▸ While her brothers never get injured, Jolene bruises easily.
喬琳的弟弟們從沒有受傷過，但她卻很容易瘀青。

17 apt [æpt] *a.* 有……傾向的

片 be apt to V　易於……
= be prone to V
= be inclined to V
= be liable to V
= tend to V

▸ Fred is apt to talk ceaselessly when he gets nervous.
= Fred is prone to talk ceaselessly when he gets nervous.
= Fred is inclined to talk ceaselessly when he gets nervous.
= Fred is liable to talk ceaselessly when he gets nervous.
= Fred tends to talk ceaselessly when he gets nervous.
佛瑞德一緊張話**就容易**講個不停。

18 blast [blæst] *n.* 一陣強風 / 氣流；爆炸 & *vt.* & *vi.* 爆破

片 (1) a blast of wind / cold air
　一陣強風 / 冷空氣
(2) in the blast　在爆炸中
(3) blast away at...　爆破……
(4) blast off　（火箭、太空船等）升空

似 (1) gust [gʌst] *n.* 強風
　a gust of wind　一陣強風
(2) explosion [ɪkˋsploʒən] *n.* 爆炸 ④
(3) explode [ɪkˋsplod] *vt.* & *vi.* (使) 爆炸 ③

▸ A sudden blast of wind blew my hat away and I had to run after it.
突然**一陣強風**把我的帽子吹走，讓我得追著它跑。

▸ It is reported that there were 20 people killed in the blast.
據報導，有 20 人在**此爆炸中**喪生。

▸ We blasted the door open with a bomb.
我們用炸彈把門**炸**開了。

▸ The workmen tried to blast away at the road surface, but to no avail.
工人們試圖**爆破**路面，但徒勞無功。

▸ We watched the spaceship blast off on TV.
我們在電視上看見太空船**升空**。

19 doorway [ˋdɔr͵we] *n.* 門口

片 in the doorway　在門口
似 gateway [ˋget͵we] *n.* 入口處，通道
延伸 doorstep [ˋdɔr͵stɛp] *n.* 門階

▸ The policeman stood in the doorway, blocking my way out.
那個警察站**在門口**，擋住我的去路。

driveway [ˋdraɪv͵we] *n.* (私人) 車道
(指在美國私人住宅通往公共街道的一小段路)

▸ There is a beautiful sports car parked in the driveway.
車道上停了一臺漂亮的跑車。

20 jug [dʒʌg] *n.* 壺，罐〔英〕；一壺 / 罐的容量 & *vt.* 用陶罐燉煮（兔子等打獵所獵到的動物）

三 jug, jugged [dʒʌgd], jugged

▸ The water spilled when I poured it into the jug.
我把水倒進**壺**裡時，水濺了出來。

片 a jug of... 一壺……

似 pitcher [ˋpɪtʃɚ] *n.* 壺，罐〔美〕⑤

▸ The cook wanted to serve the guests something unusual, so he jugged a rabbit for them.
廚師想要提供點不一樣的東西給客人，所以他用陶罐燉煮兔肉給他們。

21 artifact [ˋɑrtɪ͵fækt] *n.* 歷史文物，古物（可數）

比 handicraft 指的是一般的『手工藝品（常用複數）』，而 artifact 則指具有考古學或文化上意義、由過去的人所做的『歷史文物』。

▸ This ancient Greek artifact is extremely valuable.
這件希臘古物價值連城。

22 inherent [ɪnˋhɪrənt] *a.* 固有的；與生俱來的

片 be inherent in... ……本身就有的

衍 inherently [ɪnˋhɪrəntlɪ] *adv.* 固有地；天性地

▸ It is inevitable that there are inherent risks in every operation.
任何手術本身具有風險，這是不可避免的。

▸ Disappointment, at least for some participants, is inherent in competition as not everyone can win.
至少對一些參賽者來說，比賽本來就會伴隨失望，因為不是每個人都可以當贏家。

23 slavery [ˋslevərɪ] *n.* 奴隸身分；奴隸制度

衍 slave [slev] *n.* 奴隸（與介詞 to 並用）③
a slave to money 金錢的奴隸

▸ In the early nineteenth century, many African Americans fled from the South to the North to escape slavery.
19 世紀早期，許多黑人為了躲避奴隸制度而從南方逃向北方。

24 abuse [əˋbjuz] *vt.* & [əˋbjus] *n.* 虐待，辱罵；濫用

片 (1) abuse one's position 濫用某人職位
(2) child abuse 兒童虐待
(3) verbal abuse 言語上的辱罵
(4) abuse of power 權力的濫用
(5) alcohol / drug abuse 酒精 / 藥物的濫用

衍 abusive [əˋbjusɪv] *a.* 辱罵的

▸ Most Asian-American teenagers have the experience of being verbally abused at school.
大部分的亞裔美國青年在學校都曾有遭到言語辱罵的經驗。

▸ Charles abused his position as manager to steal money from the company.
查爾斯濫用其經理的職位從公司竊取錢財。

▸ The man was arrested on a charge of child abuse.
這名男子因虐童罪名而遭逮捕。

▸ Frodo suffered from brain damage due to long-term drug abuse.
佛拉多因為長期濫用藥物導致腦部受損傷。

25 valid [ˋvælɪd] *a.* 有效力的；令人信服的

片 (1) a valid credit card 有效的信用卡
(2) a valid argument / reason
令人信服的論點 / 理由

衍 (1) validity [vəˋlɪdətɪ] *n.* 效力
(2) validate [ˋvæləˏdet] *vt.* 使有效

反 invalid [ɪnˋvælɪd] *a.* 無效的

▸ This train ticket is valid for three days.
這張火車票 3 天內**有效**。

▸ The manager had valid reasons for thinking that the plan was not workable.
經理有**令人信服的**理由來解釋為何他認為該計畫不可行。
⋆workable [ˋwɝkəbḷ] *a.* 可行的

26 fluid [ˋfluɪd] *n.* 流體 & *a.* 不固定的，不穩定的

似 (1) unstable [ʌnˋstebḷ] *a.* 不穩固的
(2) unsteady [ʌnˋstɛdɪ] *a.* 不穩固的

延伸 (1) liquid [ˋlɪkwɪd] *n.* 液體 ②
(2) gas [gæs] *n.* 氣體 ③
(3) solid [ˋsɑlɪd] *n.* 固體 ③

▸ For the good of the patient, the doctor suggested that he take only fluids for 3 weeks after the operation.
為了病人好，醫師建議病人在手術過後 3 個星期都吃**流質**食物。

▸ Tourists were warned against visiting that country because its political situation was still somewhat fluid.
遊客被警告避免至該國旅遊，因為該國的政治局勢仍有些**不穩定**。

27 hazard [ˋhæzɚd] *n.* 危險，隱憂 & *vt.* 冒險做

衍 hazardous [ˋhæzɚdəs] *a.* 有危險的；冒險的

似 (1) danger [ˋdendʒɚ] *n.* 危險 ②
(2) risk [rɪsk] *n.* 危險 & *vt.* 冒風險 ③
(3) venture [ˋvɛntʃɚ] *n.* 冒險 & *vt.* 使冒險 ⑤

▸ That bumpy road is a constant safety hazard.
那條崎嶇不平的道路一直是安全的一大**隱憂**。
⋆bumpy [ˋbʌmpɪ] *a.* 崎嶇不平的

▸ During the meeting with his boss, Frank hesitated to hazard an opinion.
法蘭克與老闆開會的期間猶豫是否要**大膽**提出自己的看法。

28 reinforce [ˏriɪnˋfɔrs] *vt.* 加強；補強（建築物）；增援

衍 reinforcement [ˏriɪnˋfɔrsmənt] *n.* 加強；增援

似 (1) strengthen [ˋstrɛŋθən] *vt.* 加強，增強 ④
(2) fortify [ˋfɔrtəˏfaɪ] *vt.* 加強，增強 ⑥

▸ Roger's rude remarks merely reinforced my dislike of him.
羅傑粗魯的言論只是**加深**了我對他的反感。

▸ The storm is coming, so I think it's a good idea that we reinforce our house a little bit.
既然暴風雨要來了，我覺得**補強**一下房子是個不錯的主意。

▸ Two battalions of soldiers were sent to reinforce the fort.
兩個營的兵力被派去**增援**該要塞。
⋆battalion [bəˋtæljən] *n.*（軍）營

29 subtle [ˋsʌtl̩] *a.* 微妙的，細微的

似 (1) slight [slaɪt] *a.* 輕微的 ④
(2) imperceptible [ˏɪmpɚˋsɛptəbl̩] *a.* 察覺不出的

反 obvious [ˋɑbvɪəs] *a.* 明顯的 ②

▸ These two pictures look the same at first glance, but there exist subtle differences.
乍看之下這兩張照片似乎一樣，但是仍有細微差異。

30 dissolve [dɪˋzɑlv] *vt.* & *vi.* 溶解

片 (1) dissolve A in B
使 A 溶解於 B 之中
(2) dissolve in sth 溶解於某物

衍 dissolution [ˏdɪsəˋluʃən] *n.* 分解，溶解

▸ Dissolve the tablets in warm water before you take them.
把藥片投入溫水中溶解後再服用。

▸ The instant coffee powder didn't completely dissolve because the water was not hot enough.
因為水溫不夠高，即溶咖啡粉末並未完全溶解。

31 assess [əˋsɛs] *vt.* 評估；對……估價

片 (1) assess the effectiveness / impact / effect / extent of sth
評估某事物的效用 / 衝擊 / 影響 / 程度
(2) assess sth at + 金錢
估價某物為若干金額

似 evaluate [ɪˋvæljuˏet] *vt.* 評估 ④

▸ More clinical trials are needed before pharmacologists can assess the effectiveness of this new drug.
藥理學家需要更多的臨床實驗才能評估這個新藥物的效用。
*pharmacologist [ˏfɑrməˋkɑlədʒɪst] *n.* 藥理學家

▸ The damage caused by the earthquake was assessed at 50 million dollars.
地震造成的損害估計達 5 千萬美元。

assessment [əˋsɛsmənt] *n.* 評估

片 make an assessment of...
對……做出評估

似 evaluation [ɪˏvæljuˋeʃən] *n.* 評估 ④

▸ What's your assessment of the team's chances of winning?
你看該隊勝算如何？

▸ It would be prudent to make a comprehensive assessment of the situation before we make any plans.
在我們制訂任何計畫前，保險的作法應是先對局勢做全盤的評估。
*prudent [ˋprudnt] *a.* 審慎的

32 coincidence [koˋɪnsədəns] *n.* 巧合

片 (1) what a coincidence! 真巧！
(2) by (pure / sheer) coincidence
碰巧

▸ What a coincidence! I'm going shopping, too.
真巧啊！我也正要去購物。

▶ By sheer coincidence, Mr. Johnson was in the shop, too, when I was there speaking ill of him with my friends.
真夠巧的，我在那家店裡跟朋友說強森老師壞話的時候，老師也在裡面。

33 deputy [ˋdɛpjətɪ] *n.* 副手，代理人

片 a deputy chairman / governor / mayor　副主席 / 州長 / 市長

似 vice [vaɪs] *prefix.* 副手的，代理的 ⑥

▶ Richard was promoted to deputy director of our company at the age of 25.
理查 25 歲就被拔擢為我們公司的副主任。

34 certainty [ˋsɜtn̩tɪ] *n.* 確定性 (不可數)；確定的事 (可數)

片 with certainty　確定地

衍 certain [ˋsɜtn̩] *a.* 確定的，確信的 ①

▶ I can't say with certainty whether or not Susan will come to the party.
我沒有把握蘇珊是否會來參加派對。

▶ The only certainty is that we need more time to evaluate the situation.
唯一確定的一件事是，我們需要更多時間來評估情勢。

35 suite [swit] *n.* 套房

片 a honeymoon suite　蜜月套房

▶ I'd like to reserve a suite for about one week, starting from the first of April.
我想訂一間套房，住 1 個禮拜左右，從 4 月 1 日起。

attic [ˋætɪk] *n.* 閣樓

片 an attic bedroom　閣樓臥房

▶ Old furniture and boxes of toys were stacked in the attic.
老傢俱跟裝滿玩具的箱子被堆放在閣樓。

36 regime [reˋʒim] *n.* 政權，政體

▶ The military regime began its reign of terror soon after it seized power.
這個軍事政權在掌權後不久就開始恐怖統治。
*reign [ren] *n.* 統治

37 viable [ˋvaɪəbl̩] *a.* 可實施的；可以養活 / 生長發育的

衍 viability [ˌvaɪəˋbɪlətɪ] *n.* 可行性；能生長發育

似 (1) practical [ˋpræktɪkl̩] *a.* 可實施的 ③
(2) feasible [ˋfizəbl̩] *a.* 可實行的 ⑥
(3) workable [ˋwɜkəbl̩] *a.* 可行的

▶ Kelly didn't think the plan was viable because it would be too expensive and difficult to carry out.
凱莉覺得這個計畫無法實施，因為它成本過高且難以執行。

▶ As the seeds had been damaged, they were not viable and could not develop into a plant.
因為種子被破壞了，所以它們無法長成一株植物。

1301-1304

1 manifest [ˋmænəˏfɛst] *vt.* 表現；顯示 & *a.* 明顯的，清楚的

衍 (1) manifesto [ˏmɛnəˋfɛsto] *n.* 宣言
(2) manifestation [ˏmænəfɛsˋteʃən] *n.* 表示，顯示

▸ The disease is usually manifested in acute stomachaches at its initial stages.
疾病初期表現通常為劇烈胃痛。

▸ Although Bruce didn't say a word, his anger was clearly manifest in his face.
儘管布魯斯不發一語，他的怒氣在臉上顯而易見。

2 commute [kəˋmjut] *vi.* & *n.* 通勤

片 (1) commute from A to B
從 A 通勤到 B
(2) commute between A and B
在 A 與 B 之間來回通勤

▸ Leticia commutes between Taipei and Taoyuan by train every weekday.
莉蒂西亞每天上班日坐火車在臺北與桃園之間來回通勤。

▸ Since Irene lives more than 50 kilometers from her place of work, she has a long commute.
艾琳的住所離上班地點有五十多公里遠，因此她通勤時間很長。

commuter [kəˋmjutɚ] *n.* 通勤者

▸ Over 10,000 commuters were affected by the strike.
超過 1 萬名通勤者受到該起罷工事件的影響。

3 comply [kəmˋplaɪ] *vi.* 遵守，順從

三 comply, complied [kəmˋplaɪd], complied
片 comply with... 遵守……
= conform to...
= abide by...
= obey...

▸ There will be serious consequences if you don't comply with the regulations in this lab.
若你不遵守這間實驗室的規定，將有嚴重後果。

▸ It's important that you comply with the law.
守法很重要。

conform [kənˋfɔrm] *vi.* 遵守（規則、習俗）

片 conform to / with... 遵守……

▸ You'd better conform to the school regulations to avoid trouble.
你最好遵守校規，避免麻煩事。

4 wither [ˋwɪðɚ] *vi.* 枯萎

衍 withered [ˋwɪðɚd] *a.* 枯萎的
似 shrivel [ˋʃrɪvl̩] *vi.* 萎縮
反 flourish [ˋflɝɪʃ] *vi.* 茂盛；興旺 ⑥

▸ Plants will wither if not watered.
植物若不澆水會枯萎。

1305-1311

5 indulge [ɪnˋdʌldʒ] *vt.* & *vi.* (使) 沉溺，縱容

片 indulge (oneself) in...　(使自己) 沉溺於……

衍 indulgence [ɪnˋdʌldʒəns] *n.* 放縱

似 (1) spoil [spɔɪl] *vt.* 寵壞，溺愛 ③
(2) pamper [ˋpæmpɚ] *vt.* 縱容

▶ Elsie's grandparents always indulge her and give her everything she asks for.
艾爾希的祖父母一直很寵溺她，所以她有求必應。

▶ Sophia absolutely loves chocolate, but she tries to control herself and not indulge her desires to avoid becoming fat.
蘇菲亞十分愛吃巧克力，但她試著克制自己、不放縱慾望以免變胖。

▶ Shortly after his wife left him, Tom began to indulge in drinking.
湯姆的太太離他而去後不久，他便開始酗酒了。

6 consent [kənˋsɛnt] *n.* & *vi.* 同意 (作名詞時不可數)

片 (1) by common consent 大多數人同意
(2) consent to + N/V-ing　同意……
(3) consent to V　同意做……

似 (1) permission [pɚˋmɪʃən] *n.* 同意，許可 (不可數) ③
(2) permit [pɚˋmɪt] *vi.* 同意，允許 ③

▶ You can't just take other people's stuff without their consent / permission. That's stealing!
你不能不經同意就拿走別人的東西。那算偷竊！

▶ Robert's photograph was, by common consent among the panel of judges, the best, so he won the competition.
評審團大部分的人都同意羅伯特拍攝的照片最棒，所以他贏得了比賽。

▶ My girlfriend's father finally consented to our marriage.
我女朋友的父親終於同意了我們的婚事。

▶ Professor Davis consented to give Laurie more time to complete her assignment.
戴維斯教授同意給蘿蕊多一點時間來完成她的功課。

7 briefcase [ˋbrif͵kes] *n.* 公事包

似 suitcase [ˋsut͵kes] *n.* 皮箱，行李箱 ⑥

▶ Passengers on the plane were all terrified when the man claimed that there was a bomb in his briefcase.
當那名男子聲稱公事包內有炸彈時，機上乘客全嚇壞了。

8 hostile [ˋhɑstaɪl / ˋhɑstḷ] *a.* 有敵意的，不友善的；(生長條件) 惡劣的

片 be hostile to / toward(s) sb 對某人有敵意

似 (1) unfriendly [ʌnˋfrɛndlɪ] *a.* 不友好的
(2) unfavorable [ʌnˋfev(ə)rəbḷ] *a.* 不利的

▶ The government's project to build a nuclear plant was met with a hostile reception from locals.
政府興建核電廠的計畫遭到當地居民惡意回應。

▶ After James and Lisa broke up, he was hostile towards her and often said bad things about her.
詹姆士和麗莎分手後對她懷有敵意，還經常說她的壞話。

反 (1) friendly [ˋfrɛndlɪ] *a.* 友善的 ①
(2) favorable [fev(ə)rəbl̩] *a.* 有利的 ④

▸ No plants can possibly grow in such a hostile environment.
在如此**惡劣**的環境中植物很難生長。

hostility [hɑsˋtɪlətɪ] *n.* 敵意

片 have hostility to / toward(s) sb
對某人懷有敵意

似 grudge [grʌdʒ] *n.* 怨恨
bear a grudge against sb
對某人心存怨恨

▸ Edward has borne a grudge against Joe since Joe beat him in a game of tennis.
艾德華在網球賽輸給喬後就一直對他心存怨恨。

▸ I have no idea why John has so much hostility toward me.
我不明白約翰為何**對**我**有**這麼強烈的**敵意**。

9 agony [ˋægənɪ] *n.* 痛苦

片 in agony 痛苦地，身處痛苦之中

衍 agonize [ˋægəˏnaɪz] *vt.* & *vi.* (使) 痛苦萬分

似 pain [pen] *n.* 痛苦 ②

▸ Daniel screamed in agony after the drunken man attacked him with a bat and broke his leg.
丹尼爾被該酒醉男子持球棒攻擊打斷腿後，發出**痛苦**的慘叫聲。

10 quest [kwɛst] *n.* 探索，尋覓

片 (1) in one's quest / search for...
尋找⋯⋯ (通常為某項艱鉅任務)
(2) in quest / search of... 尋找⋯⋯

▸ The quest for the Holy Grail is a recurrent theme in many medieval tales.
探索聖杯是許多中世紀故事裡常出現的情節。
*the Holy Grail [grel] 指傳說中耶穌在最後的晚餐所使用的杯子

▸ These scientists worked day and night in their quest for a cure for the disease.
這些科學家日以繼夜地工作**以尋求**治療該疾病的良方。

▸ Peter set off in quest of adventure.
彼得出發去**尋找**冒險。

11 muscular [ˋmʌskjələ˞] *a.* 肌肉的；肌肉發達的，健壯的

片 muscular pain 肌肉疼痛

衍 muscle [ˋmʌsl̩] *n.* 肌肉 ③
tone up one's muscles
鍛鍊某人的肌肉

▸ Maria likes men who are tall and muscular. That's why she married Hank.
瑪莉亞喜歡高大的**肌肉**男。所以她嫁給了漢克。

12 ego [ˋigo] *n.* 自尊心，自我

複 egos

片 (1) boost sb's ego 增強某人的信心
(2) bruise sb's ego 傷某人的自尊心

衍 (1) egoism [ˋigo͵ɪzəm] *n.* 利己主義，自私自利
(2) egoist [ˋigoɪst] *n.* 自我中心者
(3) egoistic [͵igəˋɪstɪk] *a.* 利己的，自私自利的

▸ Roger is a man of average intelligence, but he does have a strong ego.
羅傑才智平庸，但自尊心奇強。

▸ Kathy is popular among her male colleagues because she really knows how to boost their egos.
凱西很受男同事歡迎，因為她很懂如何增強他們的自信心。

▸ My ego was bruised when Lilly called me a loser.
莉莉說我是沒用的人，讓我自尊心很受傷。

13 resort [rɪˋzɔrt] *n.* & *vi.* 訴諸 & *n.* 度假勝地

片 (1) as a last resort 作為最後的手段
(2) resort to + N/V-ing 訴諸於……
(3) a summer / ski resort 避暑 / 滑雪勝地

▸ As a last resort, the debtor went to Canada to hide out.
作為最後的手段，債務人跑去加拿大躲了起來。

▸ We'll resort to legal action if you fail to pay the debt by Friday.
如果星期五之前你無法還清債務，我們將採取法律行動。

▸ The Lake District in Northwest England is a world-famous summer resort.
英格蘭西北邊的湖區是世界知名的避暑勝地。

14 immense [ɪˋmɛns] *a.* 巨大的

片 be of immense value to... 對……極具價值

似 enormous [ɪˋnɔrməs] *a.* 巨大的 ④

衍 (1) immensely [ɪˋmɛnslɪ] *adv.* 巨大地
(2) immensity [ɪˋmɛnsətɪ] *n.* 巨大

▸ Your hard work has been of immense value to this company. I hereby promote you to general manager.
你的辛勤工作對本公司極有價值。所以我在此拔擢你為總經理。
*hereby [͵hɪrˋbaɪ] *adv.* 特此，以此方式

15 carbon [ˋkɑrbən] *n.* 碳

片 carbon dioxide [daɪˋɑksaɪd] 二氧化碳

▸ Plants absorb carbon dioxide and produce oxygen.
植物吸收二氧化碳並且製造氧氣。

16 applause [əˋplɔz] *n.* 鼓掌（不可數）

片 a round of applause 一陣掌聲

衍 applaud [əˋplɔd] *vi.* & *vt.* 鼓掌 ⑥

似 clap [klæp] *n.* & *vt.* & *vi.* 鼓掌 ②

▸ The speaker received a big round of applause when she finished her speech.
這位講者演講結束時，獲得一陣熱烈掌聲。

17 assault [əˋsɔlt] *n.* & *vt.* 攻擊，襲擊

片 (1) make / launch an assault on... 對……發動攻勢
(2) under assault 遭受攻擊

似 attack [əˋtæk] *n.* & *vt.* 攻擊 ①

▶ The assault was considered premeditated, because there was not a single fingerprint left at the crime scene.
該攻擊案被認為是事先預謀好的，因為犯罪現場沒留下任何指紋。
*premeditated [prɪˋmɛdə͵tetɪd] *a.* 預謀的

▶ The man was caught on the spot by police when he tried to assault the woman.
此男子企圖攻擊該女子時，被警方當場逮捕。
*on the spot 現場；馬上

18 corruption [kəˋrʌpʃən] *n.* 腐敗，貪汙

▶ The intellectuals in this country are deeply concerned about the widespread corruption within the government.
該國的知識分子都很憂心政府內部氾濫的貪腐問題。

corrupt [kəˋrʌpt] *a.* 腐敗的，貪汙的 & *vt.* 使腐敗

▶ The corrupt officer was put in jail for taking bribes.
那位腐敗的官員因為收賄被捕入獄了。
*bribe [braɪb] *n.* 賄賂

▶ Violence on TV may corrupt the minds of young children.
電視上的暴力可能會殘害幼童的心靈。

19 glee [gli] *n.* 快樂（不可數）

片 with glee 快樂地

似 delight [dɪˋlaɪt] *n.* 快樂 ④

衍 gleeful [ˋglifəl] *a.* 快樂的
a gleeful smile 快樂的微笑

▶ David told me with glee that he was going to be a father.
大衛很高興地告訴我他要當爸爸了。

20 stalk [stɔk] *vt.* 跟蹤 & *n.* 莖，梗

片 a flower stalk 花梗

衍 (1) stalker [ˋstɔkɚ] *n.* 跟蹤者
(2) stalking [ˋstɔkɪŋ] *n.* 非法跟蹤

似 (1) follow [ˋfɑlo] *vt.* 跟蹤 ①
(2) trail [trel] *vt.* 追蹤 ③

▶ Tina rushed into the police station and reported that someone had been stalking her.
蒂娜衝進警局，檢舉有人在跟蹤她。

▶ Remember to trim the stalks before you put the flowers into the vase.
把花放進花瓶之前，記得先修剪花梗。

1321-1329

21 realism [`rɪə͵lɪzəm] *n.* 實際情況；(繪畫、文學等) 現實主義 (皆不可數)

衍 (1) reality [ri`ælətɪ] *n.* 現實 ②
(2) realistic [rɪə`lɪstɪk] *a.* 現實的，實際可行的 ④
(3) realist [`rɪəlɪst] *n.* 現實主義者，務實的人；現實主義畫家 / 作家等

▸ Larry prefers to focus on the realism of their financial situation while his wife considers it to be no big deal.
賴瑞想要就他們財務狀況的**實際面**來考量，但他老婆覺得事情沒那麼嚴重。

▸ Picasso was famous for his abstract paintings, which feature little or no sense of realism.
畢卡索因抽象畫而為人熟知，他的畫幾無或完全沒有**現實主義**風格的特色。

22 episode [`ɛpə͵sod] *n.* (單一或一連串) 事件，一段經歷；(電視劇的) 一集

片 an episode of... ……的一集
似 incident [`ɪnsədənt] *n.* 事件 ④

▸ The latest episode of the political scandal shocked the whole society.
這樁政治醜聞的最新**發展**震驚了整個社會。

▸ The last episode of the drama series will be broadcast this evening.
這部連續劇的最後**一集**將於今晚播出。

23 dome [dom] *n.* 圓屋頂 & *vt.* 把圓屋頂蓋在……上

▸ The dome of the church was severely damaged during the war.
這座教堂的**圓屋頂**在戰時受到了嚴重的損壞。

24 minimal [`mɪnəml̩] *a.* 最小的

衍 minimum [`mɪnəməm] *n.* 最少量 ④
a minimum of + 數字 至少……
反 maximal [`mæksəml̩] *a.* 最高的，最大量的

▸ The house survived the fire with only minimal damage.
這棟房子逃過這場火災，只受到**極小**的損害。

minimize [`mɪnə͵maɪz]

vt. 使降到最低；輕描淡寫

反 maximize [`mæksə͵maɪz]
vt. 使增至最大限度

▸ To maximize your time, you should study on your way to and from school.
為充分利用時間，你要在往返學校的途中念書。

▸ The medicine the doctor gave you should minimize your pain.
醫生給你的藥應該可以將你的疼痛**降至最低**。

▸ Tom tends to minimize his health problems because he doesn't want others to worry about or feel sorry for him.
湯姆往往對他的健康問題**輕描淡寫**，因為他不想讓別人替他擔心或難過。

25 prescribe [prɪˋskraɪb] *vt.* 開立（藥方）；規定

片 (1) prescribe sb + 藥物
給某人開某藥物
(2) prescribe A for B　為 B 開立 A
(3) prescribe that...　規定……

▸ The doctor prescribed some medicine for my bad cough.
醫生為我嚴重的咳嗽**開**了一些藥。

▸ Our office rules prescribe that all staff members should wear a white collared shirt to work.
我們的辦公室守則**規定**所有員工都應該要穿白領襯衫來上班。

prescription [prɪˋskrɪpʃən]
n. 處方，藥方

片 (1) write (sb) a prescription (for...)
（給某人）開（……的）處方
(2) fill a prescription
（藥劑師）依處方配藥

▸ The doctor wrote me a prescription for antibiotics and handed it to me.
醫生**開了**一張抗生素的**處方箋給**我。
*antibiotic [ˏæntaɪbaɪˋɑtɪk] *n.* 抗生素

▸ You can have this prescription filled at the pharmacy.
你可以憑此**處方箋**去藥房**配藥**。
*pharmacy [ˋfɑrməsɪ] *n.* 藥房

26 legendary [ˋlɛdʒəndˏɛrɪ] *a.* 傳說的，傳奇的

衍 legend [ˋlɛdʒənd] *n.* 傳說 ④

▸ A fairy tale is a legendary story involving some imaginative characters and is often passed down from one generation to the next.
童話故事是包含一些虛幻角色的**傳奇**故事，通常會代代相傳。

27 organism [ˋɔrgənˏɪzəm] *n.* 有機體

衍 (1) organ [ˋɔrgən] *n.* 器官 ②
(2) organic [ɔrˋgænɪk] *a.* 有機的；有機物的 ③

▸ Scientists have to study the minute organisms in the polluted river to understand the cause of its pollution.
科學家必須研究這條受汙染河流當中的**微生物**，以了解汙染的原因。
*minute [maɪˋn(j)ut] *a.* 微小的

28 explicit [ɪkˋsplɪsɪt] *a.* 明確的

似 clear [klɪr] *a.* 清楚的 ①
反 implicit [ɪmˋplɪsɪt] *a.* 暗指的 ⑥

▸ The police officer gave me very explicit directions on how to get to the train station.
警察告訴我前往火車站的**明確**方向。

29 stimulate [ˋstɪmjəˏlet] *vt.* 刺激；促進；激勵

片 stimulate sb to V　激勵某人去做……
衍 stimulation [ˏstɪmjəˋleʃən] *n.* 刺激；激勵 ⑥

▸ Since coffee stimulates him, Jason always has a cup of it in the morning.
由於咖啡讓傑森**提神**，他早上總會來一杯咖啡。

1329-1335

似 encourage [ɪnˋkɝɪdʒ] *vt.* 鼓勵 ②

▸ Congress is considering tax cuts in order to stimulate investment.
國會正在考慮減稅方案以促進投資。

▸ Good teachers should ask questions that stimulate students to think.
稱職的老師應該要問能夠激勵學生去思考的問題。

stimulus [ˋstɪmjələs] *n.* 刺激；激勵

複 stimuli [ˋstɪmjəˏlaɪ]

似 stimulant [ˋstɪmjələnt] *n.* 刺激物

▸ Tourism has acted as a stimulant to the island's economic growth for a long time.
觀光業長久以來振興了著這座小島的經濟成長。

▸ To provide assistance during the tough times, the government developed an economic stimulus that helped both people and businesses.
為了在艱困時期提供協助，政府開創了經濟刺激方案來幫助人民和企業。

▸ A teacher's praise is the best stimulus for students to keep learning.
老師的讚美是讓學生持續學習的最好鼓勵。

30 spectrum [ˋspɛktrəm] *n.* 光譜

複 spectra [ˋspɛktrə] / spectrums

片 the political spectrum 政治光譜

▸ Newton divided the spectrum into seven colors.
牛頓把光譜區分成 7 種顏色。

▸ The purpose of the political spectrum is to show the differences in ideologies.
政治光譜的目的是要顯示出意識型態的差異。
*ideology [ˏaɪdɪˋɑlədʒɪ] *n.* 意識形態

31 intervention [ˏɪntɚˋvɛnʃən] *n.* 干預

片 military / government intervention 軍事 / 政府干預

衍 intervene [ˏɪntɚˋvin] *vi.* 干涉 ⑥

似 interference [ˏɪntɚˋfɪrəns] *n.* 干涉 ⑤

▸ The Mexican president has appealed to the UN for intervention in the global distribution of coronavirus vaccines.
墨西哥總統呼籲聯合國介入全球新冠肺炎疫苗的分配事宜。

32 sibling [ˋsɪblɪŋ] *n.* (其中一個) 兄弟姊妹

延伸 offspring [ˋɔfˏsprɪŋ] *n.* 子孫 ⑥

▸ How many siblings do you have?
你有幾個兄弟姊妹？

33 ritual [ˋrɪtʃuəl] *n.* 儀式；例行公事 & *a.* 儀式的

片 (1) a religious ritual 宗教儀式
(2) a daily ritual of... 做……的例行公事
(3) a ritual dance 儀式 / 傳統舞

▸ The priest performed a ritual of blessing at the altar.
這位牧師在祭壇上進行祈福代禱的儀式。

▸ Reading an English newspaper has become part of my morning ritual.
閱讀英文報紙已經成為我晨間例行公事的一部分。

似 rite [raɪt] *n.* 儀式

▸ As part of the ceremony, Joseph and the other men must perform a ritual dance.
作為典禮的一環，喬瑟夫和其他男子必須表演**儀式**舞。

▸ Important events such as weddings and funerals are full of ritual activities.
諸如婚禮和喪禮等的重要活動有很多**儀式性**活動。

34 offering [ˋɔfərɪŋ] *n.* (獻給上帝的) 奉獻；祭品

▸ Jeannie helped her mother lay out fruit and snacks as offerings to the gods.
金妮協助她媽媽把給神明的水果、零食**祭品**擺放好。

35 chaos [ˋkeas] *n.* 混亂 (不可數)

片 be in chaos 混亂

衍 chaotic [keˋatɪk] *a.* 混亂的

▸ Leave Tom alone. He is in a chaotic state of mind right now.
讓湯姆靜一靜。他現在心情很亂。

▸ I spent the whole afternoon tidying up my room because it was in chaos.
我花了一整個下午整理房間，因為它很**亂**。

Unit 14

1401-1407

1 slam [slæm] *vt.* & *vi.* 猛地關上 & *n.* 砰的一聲

三 slam, slammed [slæmd], slammed

片 (1) slam a door closed / shut 猛地把門關上
(2) a door / window slam (shut) 門 / 窗戶碰地關上

延伸 (1) slam-dunk [ˋslæm,dʌŋk] *vt.* & *vi.* 灌籃
(2) a slam dunk 灌籃

▸ After our argument, my wife stormed into the bedroom and slammed the door shut.
我們爭吵之後，我老婆便氣沖沖地走進房間並用力把門關上。

▸ As soon as I walked into the big house, I heard the door slam shut behind me.
我一走進這棟大房子內，就聽到後面的門猛然關上。

▸ The slam of the car door was a sign that George was mad about something.
車門砰的一聲關上是喬治對某件事大發雷霆的跡象。

2 currency [ˋkɝənsɪ] *n.* 貨幣

片 (1) foreign currency 外幣
(2) hard / soft currency 強 / 弱勢貨幣

衍 current [ˋkɝənt] *a.* 當前的 & *n.* 水流，氣流 ②

▸ How much foreign currency did you take with you when you went abroad?
你出國時帶了多少外幣？

3 likelihood [ˋlaɪklɪ,hʊd] *n.* 可能性

片 (1) in all likelihood 很 / 極有可能地
(2) There is a great / strong likelihood that... 很有可能……

衍 likely [ˋlaɪklɪ] *a.* 可能的 ②

似 probability [,prɑbəˋbɪlətɪ] *n.* 可能性

▸ In all likelihood, the staff meeting will be put off until next Tuesday.
員工會議很有可能會被延到下星期二舉辦。

▸ There's a great likelihood that it's going to rain this afternoon.
今天下午很有可能會下雨。

4 shiver [ˋʃɪvɚ] *vi.* & *n.* (寒冷、害怕地) 發抖

片 (1) shiver with cold / fear / anger 冷 / 怕 / 氣得發抖
(2) send shivers up (and down) sb's spine 令某人不寒而慄

似 (1) tremble [ˋtrɛmbḷ] *vi.* & *n.* 發抖 ④
(2) shudder [ˋʃʌdɚ] *vi.* & *n.* (寒冷、害怕地) 發抖

▸ Dennis shivered with cold while waiting for the bus in the snow.
丹尼斯在雪裡等公車時冷得發抖。

▸ The strange sound from the basement sent shivers up my spine.
從地下室傳來的奇怪聲響令我不寒而慄。

quiver [ˋkwɪvɚ]
vi. & *n.* (因寒冷或強烈情緒而) 顫抖

▸ Nick's bottom lip quivered with fear and then he burst into tears.
尼克的下嘴唇因恐懼而顫抖，接著他就哭了出來。

片 quiver with cold / fear / rage
因寒冷 / 恐懼 / 盛怒而顫抖

▸ Julie felt a quiver run through her, but she wasn't sure if it was excitement or fear.
茱麗感到一陣發抖，但她不確定那是因為興奮還是害怕。

5 counsel [ˋkaʊnsḷ] *n.* 忠告 (不可數) & *vt.* 勸告，建議

三 counsel, counseled〔美〕/ counselled〔英〕, counseled / counselled

片 counsel sb (not) to V
建議某人 (不要) 做……
= advise sb (not) to V

衍 counseling [ˋkaʊnsḷɪŋ] *n.* 諮商

似 (1) council [ˋkaʊnsḷ] *n.* 議會 ④
(2) advice [ədˋvaɪs] *n.* 建議 ②
(3) advise [ədˋvaɪz] *vt.* 建議 ③

▸ We should listen to wise counsel so that we can make proper decisions.
我們應該要聽從明智的忠告，以便能做出適當的決定。

▸ The attorney counseled his client not to accept the settlement.
= The attorney advised his client not to accept the settlement.
律師建議他的當事人不要接受和解。

counselor [ˋkaʊnslɚ] *n.* 顧問；輔導員

片 a marriage counselor 婚姻顧問

▸ The school counselor and I talked about which courses I should take.
學校的輔導老師和我談論該修哪些課程的事宜。

6 vertical [ˋvɝtɪkḷ] *a.* 垂直的 & *n.* 垂直線 / 面

片 (1) vertical integration
垂直整合 (指公司全面掌控原料生產、產品生產及出售等)
(2) a vertical line 垂直線

衍 vertically [ˋvɝtɪklɪ] *adv.* 垂直地

▸ Nowadays many firms are seeking vertical integration to increase productivity.
現今有很多公司正在尋求垂直整合，以提升生產力。

▸ The artist said that the verticals in his paintings represent people's connection to Heaven.
這位藝術家說他畫中的垂直線代表人們和天堂之間的連結。

horizontal [ˌhɔrəˋzɑntḷ] *a.* 水平的 & *n.* 水平線 / 面

片 a horizontal line 水平線，橫線

衍 (1) horizon [həˋraɪzn̩] *n.* 地平線 ④
(2) horizontally [ˌhɔrəˋzɑntḷɪ] *n.* 水平地

▸ Draw a horizontal line at the bottom of the page and sign your name above it.
在這一頁的底部畫一條橫線，並在線上簽署你的名字。

▸ Most of the paintings of this painter are full of horizontals.
這名畫家大部分的畫作都充滿水平線。

7 scrap [skræp] *n.* 一小片 (紙、布)；少量，一點點 & *vt.* 丟棄，廢除

三 scrap, scrapped [skræpt], scrapped

▸ Please write your phone number on this scrap of paper.
請把你的電話寫在這張小紙條上。

1407-1414

片 (1) a scrap (piece) of paper　小紙條
(2) a scrap of...　一點點……
(3) scrap a plan　放棄計畫

似 (1) scrape [skrep] *vt.* 刮；擦傷 & *n.* 輕微擦傷 ⑤
(2) shred [ʃrɛd] *n.* 少量；碎片 ⑥

▸ There's not a scrap of evidence to suggest that he murdered his wife.
絲毫沒有任何證據可以指出他謀殺了妻子。

▸ We are considering scrapping our plan to set up another branch due to lack of funding.
由於資金不足，我們正考慮**放棄**設立另一家分公司的**計畫**。

8 dialect [ˋdaɪə͵lɛkt] *n.* 方言

▸ The characters in the movie spoke in a Scottish dialect.
這部電影裡的角色講蘇格蘭**方言**。

9 understandable [͵ʌndɚˋstændəbl̩] *a.* 可理解的

衍 understand [͵ʌndɚˋstænd] *vt.* 了解 ①

似 comprehensible [͵kɑmprɪˋhɛnsəbl̩] *a.* 可了解的

▸ Lucy's disappointment was understandable because she tried really hard but didn't win the contest.
露西的失望是**可以理解的**，因為她真的很努力但沒有贏得比賽。

10 creek [krik] *n.* 小溪

片 up the creek (without a paddle)
陷入困境

似 stream [strim] *n.* 小河 ②

▸ This creek used to be a large river teeming with fish and aquatic plants.
這條**小溪**過去曾是一條滿是魚類和水生植物的大河。
*teem with...　充滿著……
aquatic [əˋkwætɪk] *a.* 水生的

▸ Herman knew that he was up the creek without a paddle because of his big mistake.
赫曼明白因為他犯的大錯而讓自己**陷入困境**了。

11 squat [skwɑt] *vi.* & *n.* 蹲，蹲下 & *a.* 矮胖的

三 squat, squatted [skwɑtɪd], squatted

片 squat down　蹲下來

似 (1) crouch [krautʃ] *vi.* & *n.* 蹲下
(2) stocky [ˋstɑkɪ] *a.* 矮胖的

▸ The mechanic squatted down and examined the front wheel of the car.
技工**蹲下來**檢查這輛車子的前輪。

▸ The poster of the missing dog described the animal as being squat with short legs.
走失狗狗的海報描繪這隻狗**矮矮胖胖的**、腿也短短的。

12 delegate [ˋdɛləgət] *n.* 代表 & [ˋdɛlə͵get] *vt.* & *vi.* 委派，委託

片 delegate sth to sb
把某事委派 / 託給某人

▸ The delegates have discussed the problem for days without coming to a consensus.
代表們討論這個問題已好幾天了，仍未達成共識。

似 (1) representative [ˏrɛprɪˋzɛntətɪv] *n.* 代表 ③
(2) assign [əˋsaɪn] *vt.* 指派 ④
(3) authorize [ˋɔθəˏraɪz] *vt.* 授權 ⑤

▸ Mr. Thompson delegated many of the day-to-day details to his assistant.
湯普森先生將許多例行小事**委派給**他的助理處理。

▸ A good manager needs to be able to delegate; otherwise, he or she won't be effective.
一名優秀的經理要能夠**下放權力**，不然他或她就沒有效率可言。

---

delegation [ˏdɛləˋgeʃən] *n.* 代表團 (可數)；委任，授權 (不可數)

似 (1) assignment [əˋsaɪnmənt] *n.* 分配；指派 ④
(2) authorization [ˏɔθərəˋzeʃən] *n.* 授權

▸ The president sent a delegation to the conference.
總統派遣**代表團**出席該會議。

▸ Delegation is not one of Rupert's strong points; he seems to want to do everything himself.
委派任務不是魯伯特的強項之一，他似乎想自己做每件事情。

13 bid [bɪd] *vt.* & *vi.* & *n.* (在拍賣中) 出價，競標

目 三態同形

片 (1) bid + 金額 + for sth
出價若干金額買某物
(2) bid against sb for sth
與某人競標爭取某物

衍 bidding [ˋbɪdɪŋ] *n.* 出價；命令

延伸 bid 作及物動詞時，亦有『打招呼，致意』之意，此時動詞三態為三態同形，或為：bid, bade [bæd], bidden [ˋbɪdn̩]。

▸ A foreign collector bid $5,000 for an antique vase at the auction.
一名外國收藏家在拍賣會上**出價** 5,000 美元**競標**一個古董花瓶。

▸ Another company is now bidding against us for the contract.
另一家公司現在正和我們**競標**取得那份合約。

▸ At the auction, the highest bid for the antique vase was $5,000.
在拍賣會上，這個古董花瓶的最高**競標價格**是 5 千美元。

14 profile [ˋprofaɪl] *n.* 側面像 & *n.* & *vt.* 簡介

片 (1) in profile　側面
(2) keep a low / high profile
保持低 / 高調

▸ On the wall was a drawing of the former mayor in profile.
牆上掛的是前任市長的**側面**畫像。

▸ The lawmaker has kept a low profile since the scandal broke out.
醜聞爆發後，這名立委始終**保持低調**。

▸ Job profiles can be found on the company's website.
你可以在這家公司的網站找到工作**簡介**。

▸ In his latest report, Jackson profiled the vice president of the country.
傑克森在最新的報告中**簡介**了該國的副總統。

15 grim [grɪm] *a.* 令人不快 / 沮喪的；嚴肅的

衍 (1) grimly [ˋgrɪmlɪ] *adv.* 討厭地；可怕地；嚴肅地
(2) grimness [ˋgrɪmnəs] *n.* 可怕；嚴肅

似 (1) grin [grɪn] *vi.* 咧嘴大笑（與介詞 at 並用）③
(2) gloomy [ˋglumɪ] *a.* 令人憂鬱的 ⑤
(3) stern [stɝn] *a.* 嚴厲的

▶ After entering the building, Sergeant Smith came across the grim sight of a dead body.
進入該棟建築後，史密斯警官竟撞見了一具屍體的**可怕**景象。

▶ The manager looked grim. I could tell something was wrong.
經理面色**嚴肅**。我可感覺出有狀況發生了。

16 clinical [ˋklɪnɪkḷ] *a.* 臨床的

片 (1) a clinical trial 臨床試驗
(2) clinical training 臨床訓練

衍 clinic [ˋklɪnɪk] *n.* 診所 ③

▶ The doctors held a clinical trial to test the drug for side effects.
醫生們進行**臨床試驗**，測試這種藥物的副作用。

▶ Receiving clinical training is an important part of becoming a doctor.
接受**臨床訓練**是成為醫師很重要的一環。

17 spectacular [spɛkˋtækjələ˞] *a.* 壯觀的；驚人的 & *n.*（活動）壯觀場面；（表演）盛大演出

衍 spectacle [ˋspɛktəkḷ] *n.* 景觀；眼鏡（恆用複數）⑥

似 (1) striking [ˋstraɪkɪŋ] *a.* 驚人的 ⑤
(2) stunning [ˋstʌnɪŋ] *a.* 震驚的
(3) sensational [sɛnˋseʃənḷ] *a.* 引起轟動的

▶ This is the most spectacular fireworks show I've ever seen in my life.
這是我這輩子看過最**壯觀**的煙火表演。

▶ The writer's latest work of fantasy literature has been a spectacular success.
這名作家最新的奇幻文學作品**大獲成功**。

▶ The circus performers put on a true spectacular for the audience.
馬戲團表演者們為觀眾獻上一場非常**盛大的演出**。

18 fabulous [ˋfæbjələs] *a.* 很棒的

似 wonderful [ˋwʌndə˞fəl] *a.* 很棒的 ①

▶ We had a fabulous dinner last night.
我們昨天晚上吃了很**豐盛**的一餐。

19 toll [tol] *n.* 過路費；傷亡人數 & *vi.*（鐘聲）響起

片 (1) a toll bridge 有收過路費的橋
(2) pay a toll 付過路費
(3) take a heavy toll 造成嚴重傷亡
(4) the death toll 死亡人數

衍 tollgate [ˋtolˏget] *n.*（高速公路的）收費站

▶ Hannah just got a job collecting tolls on the freeway.
漢娜剛找到一份在高速公路上收**過路費**的工作。

▶ The hurricane took a heavy toll, causing the death of hundreds of people.
該颶風**造成重大傷亡**，導致數百人死亡。

▸ The church bell tolled in mourning for those who died in the accident.
教堂的鐘聲響起，為在該起意外中死亡的人哀悼。

20 complexity [kəm`plɛksətɪ] n. 複雜性（不可數）；複雜之處（常用複數）

複 complexities [kəm`plɛksətɪz]

片 a problem of great complexity
極為複雜的問題

衍 complex [`kɑmplɛks] a. 複雜的 & n. 複合式建築 ②
a shopping complex　購物區

▸ The complexity of the problem is far beyond my imagination.
這個問題的**複雜程度**遠超出我的想像。

▸ Our aim is to help the public understand the complexities of the city's financial problems.
我們的目標是幫助大眾了解該城市財務問題的**複雜之處**。

complication [͵kɑmplə`keʃən]
n. 複雜，困難；併發症

片 (1) add a further complication to sth　使某事更加困難
(2) develop complications
產生併發症

衍 complicate [`kɑmplə͵ket]
vt. 使複雜 ④

▸ The long distance added a further complication to the couple's relationship.
遠距離**使**這對情侶的感情關係**更加複雜**。

▸ John developed complications after his heart transplant surgery.
約翰在心臟移植手術過後**產生了併發症**。

21 betray [bɪ`tre] vt. 背叛；（無意中）暴露

片 betray sb/sth (by...) to...
（藉由……）把某人 / 某事出賣給……

衍 betrayal [bɪ`treəl] n. 背叛

▸ That man betrayed his wife to the secret police.
那個男子將老婆**出賣給**了祕密警察。

▸ Eric tried to look calm, but his clenched fist betrayed his anger.
艾瑞克故作冷靜，但他緊握的拳頭**洩漏**了他的憤怒。
*clenched [`klɛntʃt] a. 緊握的

traitor [`tretɚ] n. 叛徒

似 betrayer [bɪ`treɚ] n. 背叛者

▸ My friends called me a traitor, simply because I refused to help them cheat on the exam.
我朋友說我是**叛徒**，只因為我拒絕幫他們考試作弊。

22 radical [`rædɪkḷ] a. 激進的；基本的 & n. 激進分子

片 a radical change / reform
根本上的改變 / 改革

衍 radically [`rædɪklɪ] adv. 激進地；根本地；徹底地

▸ I was surprised at Mark's radical views on politics.
我對於馬克**激進的**政治理念很驚訝。

▸ During the meeting, some professors pointed out the crucial need for radical changes in the current education system.
會議中，有些教授指出當前的教育體制急需**徹底改變**。

似 fundamental [ˌfʌndəˋmɛntḷ]
a. 根本的 ④

反 conservative [kənˋsɝvətɪv]
a. 保守的 ④

▸ This writer was labeled a left-wing radical.
該作家被歸類為左派**激進分子**。
*left-wing [ˌlɛftˋwɪŋ] *a.* (政治) 左派的

23 legitimate [ləˋdʒɪtəmət] *a.* 合理的；合法的；合法婚生的 & [lɪˋdʒɪtəˌmet] *vt.* 使合法化，使合理化

片 a legitimate heir / company
合法繼承人 / 公司

衍 (1) legitimize [ləˋdʒɪtəˌmaɪz]
vt. 使合理化，使正當化

▸ The author was accused of legitimizing violence in his novels.
這位作家遭人指控在小說裡將暴力**合理化**。

(2) legitimacy [ləˋdʒɪtəməsɪ]
n. 合法性；合理性

似 legal [ˋligḷ] *a.* 合法的 ②

反 illegitimate [ˌɪlɪˋdʒɪtəmət] *a.* 非法的，不正當的

▸ Kelly's boss didn't think that going to bed at 3 a.m. was a legitimate excuse for arriving late to work.
凱莉的老闆認為凌晨三點才睡覺不是上班遲到的**正當**藉口。

▸ Hank wasn't sure whether or not the company was really legitimate.
漢克不確定這間公司是否真的**合法**。

▸ Since Gina is Mr. Parker's legitimate child, she is by law a potential heiress to his estate.
既然吉娜是帕克先生的**合法婚生**子女，她在法律上是可以成為他財產的繼承人。
*heiress [ˋɛrəs] *n.* 女繼承人

▸ George is trying to legitimate his own selfish behavior again.
喬治又在試圖為自己自私的行為**自圓其說**了。

24 exploit [ɪkˋsplɔɪt] *vt.* 剝削；利用 & [ˋɛksplɔɪt] *n.* 功績 (常用複數)

衍 (1) exploiter [ɪkˋsplɔɪtɚ] *n.* 剝削者
(2) exploitation [ˌɛksplɔɪˋteʃən]
n. 剝削行為
(3) exploitable [ɪksˋplɔɪtəbḷ]
a. 可利用的

似 (1) utilize [ˋjutḷˌaɪz] *vt.* 利用 ⑤
(2) feat [fit] *n.* 功績

▸ This factory owner exploited his workers by making them work a lot of unpaid overtime.
這位工廠老闆**剝削**他的員工，要他們常常加班又不給加班費。

▸ Melissa hoped her son would stop being so lazy and one day exploit his abilities.
梅莉莎希望她的兒子不要再這麼懶惰，且有天能好好**發揮**他的能力。

▸ The novel depicts the main character's heroic exploits during his journey to save the princess.
這本小說描述了主角在拯救公主的途中所展現的**英勇事蹟**。

25 monopoly [məˋnɑplɪ] *n.* 壟斷；獨占 (權)；專賣 (權)

片 have a monopoly on / of / over...
壟斷……；有……的獨占 / 專賣權

衍 monopolize [məˋnɑplˌaɪz] *vt.* 壟斷；獨占

▸ The government used to have a monopoly on tobacco sales.
過去政府曾**壟斷**了菸草的銷售量。

延伸 遊戲『大富翁』的英文名稱就稱作 *Monopoly*。

▸ The government should take measures to prevent good medical care from becoming a monopoly solely for the rich.
政府應該制訂措施來防止醫療資源全被有錢人給**獨占**。

▸ At one time, Microsoft had a monopoly on the computer software business.
微軟曾經**獨占**電腦軟體市場有一陣子。

26 installation [ˌɪnstəˋleʃən] *n.* 安裝（不可數）；設備；就職（典禮）

片 installation cost　安裝費用

衍 install [ɪnˋstɔl] *vt.* 安裝 ④

▸ Installation of the security system will take two days.
安裝保全系統要花上兩天時間。

▸ The whole heating installation needs to be replaced.
全部的暖氣**設備**都需要更換。

▸ The ceremony for the new mayor's installation was held last May.
新任市長**就職**典禮於去年 5 月舉行。

27 tumor [ˋt(j)umɚ] *n.* 腫瘤

片 a benign / malignant tumor
良 / 惡性腫瘤

衍 tumorous [ˋt(j)umərəs] *a.* 腫瘤的

▸ My mind went blank when I heard my uncle was diagnosed with a malignant tumor.
當得知我叔叔被診斷出長了**惡性腫瘤**時，我腦中一片空白。

28 coverage [ˋkʌvərɪdʒ] *n.* 新聞報導（不可數）；保險（範圍）；涵蓋範圍

片 (1) media / press coverage
媒體新聞報導
(2) news coverage　新聞報導

衍 cover [ˋkʌvɚ] *vt.* 掩蓋，隱瞞；採訪，報導 & *n.* 封面 ①
a cover story　頭版新聞；封面故事

▸ The news coverage about this young man was strongly biased.
關於這位年輕人的**新聞報導**嚴重偏頗。

▸ My insurance policy provides coverage against fire and theft.
我的保險單提供**承保**了火災和竊盜險。

▸ This reference book provides comprehensive coverage of the subject we're talking about.
這本工具書涵蓋了我們現在所談論的題材所有的**面向**。

29 missionary [ˋmɪʃəˌnɛrɪ] *n.* 傳教士 & *a.* 傳教士的

複 missionaries [ˋmɪʃəˌnɛrɪz]

片 a missionary school / hospital
教會學校 / 醫院

衍 mission [ˋmɪʃən] *n.* 任務 ③

▸ When he was in his 20s, Vincent traveled to Taiwan to work as a missionary.
文森二十多歲時到臺灣擔任**傳教士**。

▸ Many young members of the Mormon church spend time doing missionary work.
摩門教會的許多年輕成員花時間來**傳教**。

1430-1437

30 decent [ˋdisənt] *a.* (人) 正直的，正派的；(東西) 像樣的

片 a decent job / meal
像樣的工作 / 一頓飯

反 indecent [ɪnˋdisənt] *a.* 不像話的；不禮貌的

▶ Henry is a decent man. He'll never do things like that.
亨利是個**正直的**人。他絕對不會做那種事。

▶ Stop fooling around and go find a job! You have to lead a decent life, or others will look down upon you.
別再鬼混，快找份工作吧！你得活得**像樣**一點，不然大家都會瞧不起你。

31 rational [ˋræʃənl̩] *a.* 理性的；合理的

片 a rational explanation / argument / decision 合理的解釋 / 論點 / 決定

衍 rationality [ˌræʃəˋnælətɪ] *n.* 理性

似 reasonable [ˋriznəbl̩] *a.* 合理的 ③

反 irrational [ɪˋræʃənl̩] *a.* 無理性的；不合理的

▶ A rational person will never behave like that.
理智的人絕不會那樣做。

▶ The authorities concerned have yet to find a rational explanation for the accident.
有關當局仍在設法為該起意外找尋**合理的解釋**。

32 sovereignty [ˋsɑvrəntɪ] *n.* 統治權，主權 (不可數)

片 claim sovereignty over sth
宣稱擁有某物的主權

▶ These actions were interpreted as a threat to national sovereignty.
這些行徑被解讀為威脅到了國家**統治權**。

▶ Many Native American tribes have claimed sovereignty over parts of the US.
許多美洲原住民部落**聲稱**他們**擁有**部分美國土地的**主權**。

33 lawsuit [ˋlɔˌsut] *n.* 訴訟

片 file / initiate a lawsuit (against...)
(對……) 提出訴訟

似 suit [sut] *n.* 訴訟 ②

▶ Local residents filed a lawsuit against the construction company over noise pollution.
當地居民因為噪音汙染的緣故，而對該建築公司**提出告訴**。

34 likewise [ˋlaɪkˌwaɪz] *adv.* 同樣，也

片 do likewise 照著做

似 (1) similarly [ˋsɪmələlɪ] *adv.* 同樣地
(2) by the same token 同樣地

▶ I will respect your privacy. Likewise, I hope you will respect mine.
我會尊重你的隱私。**同樣**，我也希望你會尊重我的隱私。

▶ Terry is a salesman and likewise his brother is in the same profession.
泰瑞是一名業務，而他弟弟**也**做同樣的職務。

▶ The teacher wrote the names of three animals on the board and told the students to do likewise.
老師在黑板上寫了 3 種動物的名字，然後要學生**照著做**。

35 consumption [kən`sʌmpʃən] *n.* (能源、資源) 消耗 (量)；攝取 (食物)；消費 (皆不可數)

衍 (1) consume [kən`sum] *vt.* 消耗；消費；攝取 (食物) ④
(2) consumer [kən`sumɚ] *n.* 消費者 ④

▸ The rapid increase in oil consumption has led scientists to search for alternative energy.
石油消耗量的快速增加促使科學家找尋替代能源。

▸ After my liver operation, Dr. Peterson warned me to stop all alcohol consumption.
我動完肝臟手術後，彼得森醫師警告我要停止攝取酒精。

▸ When consumption increases, businesses make more money and the economy improves.
消費增加時，企業就賺更多錢，經濟也會改善。

36 productivity [ˏprodʌk`tɪvətɪ] *n.* 生產力

衍 (1) product [`prɑdʌkt] *n.* 產品 ③
(2) production [prə`dʌkʃən] *n.* 生產 ②
(3) productive [prə`dʌktɪv] *a.* 有生產力的 ④

▸ Computers have greatly increased productivity in offices.
電腦大幅提升辦公室的生產力。

37 windshield [`wɪndˏʃild] *n.* (汽車等的) 擋風玻璃

片 a windshield wiper (擋風玻璃) 雨刷 (常用複數)

衍 shield [ʃild] *n.* 盾牌；防護物 ⑤

▸ The windshield is dirty and it definitely needs to be washed.
這塊擋風玻璃實在太髒了，當然要好好清洗。

Unit 15

1501-1507

1 parallel [ˋpærə͵lɛl] *a.* 平行的；(經常同時發生且) 相似的 & *n.* 相似 (處) & *vt.* 與……平行；與……相似

片 (1) be / run parallel to sth
與某物平行
(2) parallels between A and B
A 與 B 間的相似處
(3) be without parallel
舉世無雙，無可匹敵
= have no parallel

似 (1) similar [ˋsɪmələ˞] *a.* 相似的 ②
(2) similarity [͵sɪməˋlærətɪ] *n.* 相似 ③
(3) resemble [rɪˋzɛmbḷ] *vt.* 像，類似 ④

▸ The road and the canal run parallel to each other for about 40 miles.
這條道路和運河彼此平行約 40 英里。

▸ Parallel concerts took place in London, Tokyo, and New York.
類似的演唱會同時在倫敦、東京和紐約舉辦。

▸ There are several parallels between the lives of the two celebrities. For instance, both were child stars who quit acting as adults.
這兩位名人的生平有一些相似處。例如，他們倆都是童星，但長大後就不再演戲了。

▸ The breakthrough is without parallel in medical history.
= The breakthrough has no parallel in medical history.
這項突破性進展在醫學史上是舉世無雙的。

▸ The two roads parallel each other for several kilometers before turning in different directions.
這兩條路並列好幾公里後才分開往不同的方向。

▸ To many performers, nothing parallels the excitement of performing on stage in front of an audience.
對許多表演者來說，沒有什麼比上臺在觀眾面前表演來得更令人激動了。

2 stack [stæk] *n.* (整齊的) 一堆 / 疊 & *vt.* 把……(整齊地) 堆疊起來 & *vi.* (整齊地) 堆 / 疊

片 (1) a stack of sth　一堆 / 疊某物
(2) stack (up)...　把……堆疊起來

▸ There is a tall stack of newspapers next to the back door that needs to be recycled.
後門旁有很高的一疊報紙要被回收。

▸ Ted is responsible for pricing the items and stacking them on the shelves.
泰德負責為商品貼上標價，並整齊地堆疊到架上。

▸ The boxes are made to stack quite nicely, with edges that match up and create stability.
這些箱子被設計成容易堆疊的形式，它們的邊都能相接而更穩固。

3 noticeable [ˋnotɪsəbḷ] *a.* 顯著的

衍 notice [ˋnotɪs] *vt.* & *n.* 注意 ①
似 (1) obvious [ˋɑbvɪəs] *a.* 明顯的 ②
(2) conspicuous [kənˋspɪkjʊəs] *a.* 明顯的

▶ There has been a noticeable increase in sales since we adopted the new strategies.
自從我們採用新策略之後，業績就有了**顯著的**成長。

4 cluster [ˋklʌstɚ] *n.* 群；串；束 & *vi.* 聚集

片 (1) a cluster of... 一群 / 串 / 束⋯⋯
a cluster of grapes 一串葡萄
(2) a flower cluster 花束
(3) cluster around... 聚在⋯⋯周圍

▶ There was a cluster of fans surrounding the K-pop idol, asking for his autograph.
這位韓國偶像的身旁圍繞著**一群**粉絲，向他索取簽名。

▶ The old man's grandchildren clustered around him to listen to tales about his childhood.
老先生的孫子們**圍繞**在他身旁，聽他講述童年的故事。

5 tournament [ˋtɝnəmənt] *n.* 巡迴賽，錦標賽

延伸 a tennis / golf tournament
網球 / 高爾夫錦標賽

▶ The world-class tennis player was eliminated from the tournament in the first round.
這名世界級的網球選手在**錦標賽**第一輪就遭淘汰。

6 asset [ˋæsɛt] *n.* 資產 (常用複數)；有用的人 / 物 / 特質

片 be an asset to sb/sth
對某人 / 某事是個優點

▶ A company's assets consist of buildings, equipment, cash, and specialist knowledge.
公司的**資產**包含建築物、設備、現金和專業知識。

▶ Tina has been a great asset to our company since she started working here.
自從蒂娜開始在這兒工作以來，她就一直是本公司的**寶貴人才**。

7 journalism [ˋdʒɝnḷˏɪzəm] *n.* 新聞業 / 學

片 the Department of Journalism
新聞系
衍 (1) journal [ˋdʒɝnḷ] *n.* 期刊；日記 ②
(2) journalistic [ˏdʒɝnḷˋɪstɪk] *a.* 新聞工作的

▶ The position is open to applicants who majored in journalism while in college.
這份職缺供大學主修**新聞學**的求職者申請。

journalist [ˋdʒɝnəlɪst] *n.* 新聞工作者

延伸 此字包含 reporter [rɪˋportɚ] (記者)、editor [ˋɛdɪtɚ] (編輯)、anchorman [ˋæŋkɚˏmæn] (主播)、newscaster [ˋnuzˏkæstɚ] (新聞廣播員)。

▶ According to a recent survey, most journalists think they're working under too much pressure.
根據一項最近的調查，大多數的**新聞從業人員**認為他們的工作壓力過大。

1508-1514

8 mock [mɑk] *vt.* (常指藉模仿) 嘲笑 & *a.* 假裝的；模擬的 & *n.* 嘲笑 (的對象)；模擬考試〔英〕(常用複數)

片 (1) mock sb　取笑某人
= make fun of sb
(2) a mock test　模擬考
= a simulated test

衍 mocking [mɑkɪŋ] *a.* 嘲弄的

似 (1) jeer [dʒɪr] *vt.* & *vi.* & *n.* 嘲笑
jeer (at) sb　嘲笑某人
(2) taunt [tɔnt] *vt.* & *n.* 嘲笑辱罵

▶ Those students are always mocking their teacher for the way he speaks.
那些學生老是模仿嘲笑他們老師講話的方式。

▶ Although he knew about the birthday party, Charlie wore an expression of mock surprise when his friends greeted him.
雖然查理知道生日派對的事，但當他朋友迎接他時，他還是假裝很驚訝。

▶ The high school student prepared for her final exams by taking a mock test at home.
這名高中生透過在家做模擬考來準備期末考。

9 intent [ɪnˋtɛnt] *n.* 意圖，目的 & *a.* 專心致志的

片 be intent on / upon + N/V-ing
專心致志於……
= be determined to V

衍 (1) intend [ɪnˋtɛnd] *vt.* 打算 ④
(2) intention [ɪnˋtɛnʃən] *n.* 意圖 ④

似 determined [dɪˋtɝmɪnd]
a. 已下決心的

▶ It was not my intent to spend half of the morning on the phone.
= It was not my intention to spend half of the morning on the phone.
我不是有意要花半個早上在講電話。

▶ Henry is intent on going abroad to further his studies.
= Henry is determined to go abroad to further his studies.
亨利已下定決心要出國深造。

10 soak [sok] *vt.* & *vi.* & *n.* 浸泡

片 (1) soak A in B　將 A 泡在 B 裡
(2) soak up sth　吸乾某物 / 吸收某事

衍 soaking [ˋsokɪŋ] *a.* 溼透的
be soaking (wet)　溼透的

▶ I was caught in a heavy rain without an umbrella and ended up (being) soaking wet.
我被困在大雨中又沒帶傘，結果全身溼透了。

▶ You should soak beans in cold water overnight before boiling them.
煮豆子前應該要在冷水中浸泡一夜。

▶ In order to relax, I soaked in the tub for a while.
為了放鬆，我在浴缸裡泡了一會兒。

▶ Young children are like sponges because they can soak up information incredibly quickly.
幼童就像海綿，吸收資訊的速度快得驚人。

▶ Before washing the dishes, Millie decided to let them have a soak in hot, soapy water.
米莉決定洗碗前先把這些碗盤浸在熱泡泡水中。

11 tin [tɪn] *n.* 錫 (不可數) & *vt.* 在……上鍍錫

三 tin, tinned [tɪnd], tinned

片 a tin can　錫罐頭

▶ How should we dispose of these empty tin cans?
我們該如何處置這些空的錫罐頭？

延伸 zinc [zɪŋk] *n.* 鋅（不可數）

▸ In the manufacturing process, the steel is tinned in order to help prevent it from getting rusty.
在製造過程中，鋼鐵被鍍錫以防生鏽。

bronze [brɑnz] *n.* 青銅 & *a.* 青銅製 / 色的

延伸 (1) brass [bræs] *n.* 黃銅 & *a.* 黃銅製 / 色的 ③
(2) copper [ˋkɑpɚ] *n.* 銅 & *a.* 銅製的 ④

▸ The metals gold, silver, and bronze are commonly used as medals to symbolize first-, second-, and third-place victories.
金、銀和銅常被用來當作代表第一、二、三名的獎牌。

▸ A bronze statue stands in the middle of the park.
公園中央佇立了一座青銅像。

12 trim [trɪm] *vt.* & *n.* 修剪（頭髮、樹枝等）& *a.* 整齊的；健康苗條的

三 trim, trimmed [trɪmd], trimmed
片 (1) give sth a trim 修剪某物
(2) a trim figure 身材苗條
衍 trimmer [ˋtrɪmɚ] *n.* 修剪器
似 slim [slɪm] *a.* 苗條的 ①

▸ It took me about four hours to mow the lawn and trim the hedges.
鋤草和修剪籬笆花了我大約 4 個小時的時間。

▸ My hair is not too long, so just give it a trim, please.
我的頭髮並不會太長，因此請稍加修剪就行了。

▸ Unlike his brother, who is a very messy person, Jasper likes to maintain a trim appearance.
賈斯柏喜歡維持整潔的外表，這點和他髒亂的弟弟不一樣。

▸ Franklin keeps trim by jogging three times a week and occasionally going to the gym near his home.
法蘭克林一週慢跑三次、偶爾去家附近的健身房來保持精瘦的身材。

prune [prun] *vt.* 修剪（樹枝）

似 clip [klɪp] *vt.* 修剪 ③

▸ The gardener pruned the long branches of the tree.
園丁把這棵樹木的長樹枝修剪掉。

13 thigh [θaɪ] *n.* 大腿

似 calf [kæf] *n.* 小腿

▸ Many women are concerned about the ratio of muscle to fat on their thighs.
許多女性很關心她們大腿上肌肉和脂肪的比例。

14 arena [əˋrinə] *n.*（比賽、競爭的）場地，競技場

片 (1) a sports arena 體育場
(2) the political arena 政界

▸ Kevin entered the political arena as an aide to the mayor.
凱文因擔任市長的助手而進入了政界。
*aide [ed] *n.* 助手

15 alien [ˋelɪən] *a.* 外國的；外星人的；陌生的 & *n.* (住在他國的) 僑民；外星人

片 (1) an alien spaceship
外星人太空船
(2) be alien to sb 對某人而言很陌生
= be unfamiliar to sb
= be foreign to sb

衍 (1) foreign [ˋfɔrɪn] *a.* 外國的；陌生的 ①
(2) unfamiliar [ˌʌnfəˋmɪljɚ] *a.* 不熟悉的
(3) extraterrestrial [ˌɛkstrətəˋrɛstrɪəl] *a.* 外星人的 & *n.* 外星人

▸ There are an estimated 50,000 alien residents in this country.
該國估計有 5 萬名外僑。

▸ That practice is alien to us.
那個習俗對我們而言很陌生。

▸ Before becoming a US citizen, Roy was labeled an alien by the government.
羅伊成為美國公民前，被政府歸類為外國人。

▸ Do you believe in aliens from outer space?
你相信外太空有外星人的存在嗎？

16 stereotype [ˋstɛrɪəˌtaɪp] *n.* 刻板印象 & *vt.* 對……有成見 / 刻板印象

片 (1) conform to a stereotype of...
符合對……的刻板印象
= fit a stereotype of...
(2) a cultural / gender stereotype
文化 / 性別刻板印象

衍 (1) stereotyped [ˋstɛrɪəˌtaɪpt] *a.* 刻板的
(2) stereotypical [ˌstɛrɪəˋtɪpɪkḷ] *a.* 老套的

▸ Scott, who is always casually dressed, doesn't conform to the stereotype of a Wall Street banker.
史考特衣著一向很隨便，不符合一般人心目中華爾街銀行家的形象。

▸ Those who stereotype other people often base their opinions on what they have heard, not actual experience.
那些對他人有刻板印象的人，常以他們所聽到的，而非實際經驗來做評論。

17 nominate [ˋnɑməˌnet] *vt.* 提名

片 nominate A as B 提名 A 擔任 B

▸ We unanimously nominated Jerry as chairman of the committee.
我們一致推舉傑瑞擔任委員會主席。
*unanimously [ʊˋnænəməslɪ] *adv.* 一致地

nomination [ˌnɑməˋneʃən] *n.* 提名

片 (1) win the nomination as...
贏得……的提名
(2) receive a Grammy nomination
獲葛萊美提名

▸ After a fierce competition, John won the nomination as candidate for mayor.
經過激烈的競爭後，約翰贏得了市長候選人的提名。

nominee [ˌnɑməˋni] *n.* 被提名者

▸ The nominees in this year's Academy Awards Best Director category were announced this morning.
今年奧斯卡最佳導演的入圍者名單於今早宣布。

18 thorn [θɔrn] *n.* 刺

衍 thorny [ˋθɔrnɪ] *a.* 長滿荊棘的；棘手的
a thorny problem　棘手的問題

▸ Most cacti are filled with thorns.
大多數的仙人掌都布滿了刺。
*cactus [ˋkæktəs] *n.* 仙人掌（複數為 cacti [ˋkæktaɪ] / cactuses）

19 cathedral [kəˋθidrəl] *n.* 大教堂

似 (1) church [tʃɝtʃ] *n.*（一般）教堂；教會 ①
(2) basilica [bəˋzɪlɪkə] *n.*（古羅馬）長方形教堂

▸ St. Patrick's Cathedral stands tall on New York City's Fifth Avenue.
聖派翠克**大教堂**聳立在紐約市第五大道上。

20 braid [bred] *vt.* 把頭髮綁成辮子 & *n.* 辮子

片 wear one's hair in braids
把頭髮綁成辮子

▸ Mary braids her hair in the summer because it helps her stay cool.
瑪莉夏天時會**綁辮子**，因為那能讓她保持涼爽。

▸ Jenny used to wear her hair in braids, but now she prefers to let it down.
珍妮過去都是**綁辮子**，但她現在比較喜歡把頭髮放下來。

21 crude [krud] *a.* 粗略的；粗糙的；粗俗的 & *n.* 原油（= crude oil）（不可數）

片 a crude joke / language
粗俗的笑話 / 語言

似 (1) approximate [əˋprɑksəmət] *a.* 大約的 ⑥
(2) vulgar [ˋvʌlgɚ] *a.* 低級的；粗俗的

▸ Currently, I can only give you a crude estimate of the number of victims who died in this terrorist attack.
目前，關於這次恐怖攻擊的死亡人數，我只能給你一個**大約的**數字。

▸ This crude bridge was built for temporary use during the typhoon.
這座**簡陋的**橋是颱風期間臨時搭建使用的。

▸ Paul's crude jokes embarrassed the girls in the group.
保羅**粗俗的**笑話讓隊裡的女孩子感到很尷尬。

▸ The government is concerned that the surging crude oil prices will lead to inflation.
政府擔心**原油**價格急速上漲會引發通貨膨脹。

22 symptom [ˋsɪmptəm] *n.* 症狀

片 a symptom of...　……的症狀
似 indication [ˌɪndəˋkeʃən] *n.* 徵兆 ④

▸ A high fever, a sore throat, and a runny nose are all symptoms of the flu.
發高燒、喉嚨痛以及流鼻水都是流行性感冒的**症狀**。

1522-1531

syndrome [ˋsɪn͵drom] *n.* 併發症，症候群

▸ Alice in Wonderland syndrome is a condition in which people's perceptions are distorted due to problems with the brain.
愛麗絲夢遊仙境症是一種由於大腦有問題，而導致人們的感知有扭曲的情況。

23 obscure [əbˋskjʊr] *a.* (意思) 模糊的，難懂的；不出名的 & *vt.* 使看不清楚；使難以理解

片 be obscured by... 被……遮住

比 obscure、vague 及 ambiguous 作形容詞皆有『含糊不清的』之意，惟 obscure 表某意思因解釋不清或需要特殊知識而難以理解；vague 是指說明、解釋不夠具體而導致意思模糊不清；ambiguous 則是指語意上模稜兩可而導致意思模糊不清。

▸ I found Professor Johnson's lecture on modern art very obscure.
我覺得強森教授針對現代藝術所做的演講**很難理解**。

▸ This year's national literary award was given to an obscure writer.
今年全國性的文學獎頒給了一名**沒沒無聞的**作家。

▸ The airport and runways were obscured by the heavy fog, so our plane could not land.
機場與跑道**被**濃霧**遮住**了，所以我們的班機無法降落。

▸ The recent increase in stock prices has obscured the fact that the company is going through financial difficulties.
最近股價上漲**掩蓋**了這家公司正有財務困難的事實。

24 questionnaire [͵kwɛstʃənˋɛr] *n.* 問卷，調查表

片 fill out / fill in / complete a questionnaire 填問卷

▸ Please turn in your questionnaire as soon as you fill it out.
問卷填好後請馬上交上來。

25 voucher [ˋvautʃɚ] *n.* (代替現金用的) 禮券，憑證

似 coupon [ˋkupɑn] *n.* 優惠券，折價券 ⑥

▸ In the lucky draw, Kevin won a voucher worth NT$20,000, so he bought some furniture with it.
凱文摸彩贏得價值新臺幣 2 萬元的**禮券**，因此他用禮券買了些傢俱。

26 progressive [prəˋgrɛsɪv] *a.* 進步的；逐漸的 & *n.* 進步分子，革新主義者

片 (1) a progressive decline 逐漸下降
(2) a progressive tense （文法）進行式

衍 progress [ˋprɑgrɛs] *n.* 進步；進展 ②
make progress 有進步；有進展

▸ One can't be a good leader without progressive ideas.
唯有**進步的**思維才配當一個優秀的領導人。

▸ People suffering from Alzheimer's disease experience a progressive decline in language abilities.
患有阿茲海默症的病人語言能力會**逐漸**退化。

▸ Rupert was definitely not a conservative person; in fact, he could easily be described as a progressive.
魯伯特絕非保守的人，事實上，可以很肯定地說他是革新分子。

27 contradiction [ˌkɑntrəˋdɪkʃən] *n.* 矛盾

片 a contradiction between A and B　A 和 B 之間的矛盾

衍 contradict [ˌkɑntrəˋdɪkt] *vt.* 相矛盾 ⑥

▸ Tim is a hypocrite. There are always contradictions between what he says and what he actually does.
提姆是個偽君子。他說的與他實際做的總是互相矛盾。
*hypocrite [ˋhɪpəkrɪt] *n.* 偽君子

28 narrative [ˋnærətɪv] *a.* 敘事的 & *n.* 故事；記敘文

片 a narrative poem　敘事詩

衍 (1) narrate [ˋnæret] *vt.* 講述 ⑥
(2) narrator [ˋnæretɚ] *n.* 解說員；敘述者 ⑥

▸ Jane composed a narrative poem depicting the beauty of nature.
珍寫了一首敘事詩描繪大自然的美麗。

▸ The famous author has written a gripping narrative of his time in the army.
這位名作家寫了有關他當兵時的故事，很引人入勝。

29 pitcher [ˋpɪtʃɚ] *n.* (棒球) 投手；大水壺

片 a pitcher of water　一水壺的水

衍 pitch [pɪtʃ] *vt.* 扔；擲 ③

延伸 batter [ˋbætɚ] *n.* (棒球) 打擊手 ⑥

▸ The strong boy shows great promise as a baseball pitcher.
這個強壯的男孩大有希望成為一名棒球投手。

▸ A waiter poured water from a pitcher into my glass.
服務生把水從水壺倒進我的杯子。

30 depict [dɪˋpɪkt] *vt.* 描述，描繪

片 depict A as B　將 A 描述為 B
= describe A as B

衍 depiction [dɪˋpɪkʃən] *n.* 描繪

延伸 describe [dɪsˋkraɪb] *vt.* 描述 ②

▸ This novel depicts the extravagant life of the upper class.
這本小說描繪了上流社會奢侈浪費的生活。
*extravagant [ɪkˋstrævəgənt] *a.* 奢侈浪費的

▸ Some Hollywood movies depict dark-skinned people as dangerous and violent, but this is not the case at all.
一些好萊塢電影把深色皮膚的人描繪成危險暴力分子，不過實際上根本就不是這麼一回事。

31 theoretical [θiəˋrɛtɪkḷ] *a.* 理論上的

衍 theoretically [θiəˋrɛtɪkḷɪ] *adv.* 理論上地

反 practical [ˋpræktɪkḷ] *a.* 實際上的 ③

▸ The formula is still only theoretical and has not been tested yet.
這道公式還只是理論性的，還尚未受到檢測。

32 expedition [ˌɛkspəˋdɪʃən] *n.* 遠征；探險隊

片 go on an expedition to + 地方
遠征至某地方，到某地方探險

▸ We went on an expedition to the North Pole to take photos of the icebergs.
我們**遠征**到北極拍攝冰山。
*iceberg [ˋaɪsˌbɝg] *n.* 冰山

▸ Five members of the expedition were killed in an avalanche.
這支**遠征隊**的 5 名成員在雪崩時喪生。
*avalanche [ˋævḷˌæntʃ] *n.* 雪崩

33 vulnerable [ˋvʌlnərəbḷ] *a.* 脆弱的；(生理或心理) 易受傷的

片 be vulnerable to sth 易受某事物的攻擊 / 傷害
= be susceptible to sth

衍 (1) vulnerability [ˌvʌlnərəˋbɪlətɪ] *n.* 弱點
(2) vulnerably [ˋvʌlnərəblɪ] *adv.* 易受傷地

似 susceptible [səˋsɛptəbḷ] *a.* 易受影響的

▸ Judy looked rather vulnerable standing in the corner on her own.
茱蒂獨自一人站在角落裡，看來非常**柔弱**。

▸ Dorothy's behavior left her vulnerable to her schoolmates' attacks.
桃樂絲的行為讓她**飽受**學校同學的攻擊。

▸ Newborn infants are particularly vulnerable to the flu.
初生的嬰兒特別**容易被**傳染感冒。

34 prone [pron] *a.* 有……的傾向，易於……；俯臥的

片 (1) be prone to + N/V-ing 容易……
= be prone to V
= be inclined to V
= be likely to V
= tend to V
(2) (be) lying prone on... 俯臥在……上
= (be) lying face down on...

延伸 (1) accident-prone [ˋæksədəntˌpron] *a.* 容易發生意外的
(2) injury-prone [ˋɪndʒərɪˌpron] *a.* 容易受傷的

▸ Workers are prone to accidents if they are not familiar with the working environment.
工人若對工作環境不熟悉，就很**容易**發生意外。

▸ Grace is prone to lie to people. Take what she says with caution.
葛瑞絲很**容易**撒謊。要小心她說的話。

▸ The police found Jenny lying prone on her bed with a knife in her back.
= The police found Jenny lying face down on her bed with a knife in her back.
警方發現珍妮**俯臥在**床上，背上插了把刀。

35 evolve [ɪˋvalv] *vi.* 進化；發展為

片 (1) evolve from... 由……進化 / 演變而來
(2) evolve into... 逐漸發展成為……

▸ The artist's idea for the masterpiece evolved from a casual conversation with a neighbor.
這名藝術家對這傑作的構想是**從**他和鄰居一段隨興的對話**演變來**的。

▸ Through months of teamwork, our idea finally evolved into a feasible plan.
藉由數個月的團隊合作，我們的想法終於**化為**可行的計畫。
*feasible [ˋfizəbl̩] *a.* 可行的

evolution [ˏɛvəˋluʃən] *n.* 進化；發展

片 the theory of evolution　進化論

似 (1) progress [ˋprɑgrɛs] *n.* 發展，進展 ②
(2) development [dɪˋvɛləpmənt] *n.* 發展 ②

▸ We learned about Darwin's theory of evolution in today's biology class.
我們在今天的生物課學了達爾文的**進化論**。

▸ The twentieth century witnessed the evolution of computer technology.
二十世紀見證了電腦科技的**進展**。

36 anonymous [əˋnɑnəməs] *a.* 匿名的

片 (1) an anonymous donor
匿名捐贈者
(2) an anonymous letter / phone call　匿名信件 / 電話

衍 (1) anonymously [əˋnɑnəməslɪ] *adv.* 匿名地
(2) anonymity [ˏænəˋnɪmətɪ] *n.* 匿名

似 unnamed [ʌnˋnemd] *a.* 匿名的

▸ The diamond ring was sold to an anonymous bidder for one million.
那枚鑽戒以 1 百萬美元賣給一位**匿名的**競標者。
*bidder [ˋbɪdɚ] *n.* 競標者

▸ The general manager received an anonymous letter accusing an employee of embezzlement.
總經理接到一封**匿名信函**，信中指控某位員工盜用公款。
*embezzlement [ɪmˋbɛzl̩mənt] *n.* 挪用公款

Unit 16

1601-1610

1 salmon [ˋsæmən] *n.* 鮭魚 & *a.* & *n.* 鮭肉色 (的)，鮭魚粉色 (的)

複 salmon / salmons

片 salmon pink　鮭魚粉色（帶橘調的粉紅色）

延伸 carp [kɑrp] *n.* 鯉魚

▸ After years at sea, adult salmon swim back to the place of their birth to reproduce.
在海裡生活多年後，成年的鮭魚會游回牠們出生的地方產卵。
*reproduce [ˌriprəˋd(j)us] *vi.* 繁殖

▸ When asked if the color of her living room walls was orange, Clara replied that they were salmon pink.
克萊拉被問到她臥室牆壁的顏色是否為橘色時，她回答是鮭魚粉色。

tuna [ˋt(j)unə] *n.* 鮪魚

複 tuna / tunas

片 (1) a can of tuna　一罐鮪魚罐頭
(2) canned tuna　罐裝鮪魚

▸ Tuna is an excellent source of vitamins, minerals, and protein.
鮪魚是維他命、礦物質和蛋白質的極佳來源。

2 undergraduate [ˌʌndɚˋgrædʒuət] *n.* (在學) 大學生

片 an undergraduate student / course　大學生 / 課程

反 graduate [ˋgrædʒuət] *n.* (高中、大學) 畢業生 & *a.* 研究所的 ③

▸ The loan is available for undergraduates who qualify for financial aid.
凡合乎獎助金資格的大學部學生皆可申請這筆貸款。

3 framework [ˋfremˌwɝk] *n.* 架構，構造

衍 frame [frem] *vt.* 裝框 & *n.* 框架；結構 ④

似 structure [ˋstrʌktʃɚ] *n.* 結構 ③

▸ Every thesis has to be written within a certain framework, or it will be too general.
每篇論文必須在某一架構範圍內撰寫，否則內容會太大而化之。

4 notify [ˋnotəˌfaɪ] *vt.* 通知，告知

三 notify, notified [ˋnotəˌfaɪd], notified

片 (1) notify sb of sth　告知某人某事
= inform sb of sth
(2) notify sb that...　告知某人……
= inform sb that...

衍 notification [ˌnotəfəˋkeʃən] *n.* 通知

▸ The receptionist will notify you of the arrival of your guests.
有您的客人到達時，櫃檯人員會通知您。

▸ Sarah was notified by mail that she was admitted to Cambridge University.
莎拉被以信件告知她已獲准進入劍橋大學就讀。

5 transparent [træns`pɛrənt] *a.* 透明的

衍 transparency [træns`pɛrənsɪ] *n.* 透明（度）

反 opaque [o`pek] *a.* 不透明的

▸ We used transparent packaging so that customers can see what is inside the box.
我們使用**透明**材質包裝，因此顧客看得見盒子裡面的東西。

6 novelty [`nɑvl̩tɪ] *n.* 新奇（不可數）；新奇的事物（可數）

衍 novel [`nɑvl̩] *a.* 新奇的 & *n.* 小說 ②
a novel idea 新奇的點子

▸ The novelty of having new clothes wears off quickly. That's why women want to buy so many.
買新衣服的**新奇感**消失得很快，這就是女性會想買很多衣服的原因。

▸ Back in the late 19th century, the camera was a great novelty.
在 19 世紀末當時，相機是個**新奇的事物**。

7 outsider [ˌaut`saɪdɚ] *n.* 外人，局外人

衍 outside [aut`saɪd] *n.* 外面 & *prep.* 在……之外 & *a.* 外面的 ①

反 insider [ˌɪn`saɪdɚ] *n.* 內部的人

▸ William felt like an outsider because he could not get along well with his work team.
威廉覺得自己像個**局外人**，因為他和他的工作團隊相處不來。

8 wrongdoing [`rɔŋˌduɪŋ] *n.* 惡行

▸ The wrongdoing of an adult may become a youngster's excuse to do the same.
成年人的**惡行**可能會成為年輕人做壞事的藉口。

9 contagious [kən`tedʒəs] *a.* 有傳染性的

片 a contagious disease 傳染病

似 infectious [ɪn`fɛkʃəs] *a.* 傳染（性）的 ⑥

▸ People with COVID-19 symptoms should be quarantined because the virus is highly contagious.
有新冠肺炎症狀的人須被隔離，因為這種病毒極具**傳染性**。
*quarantine [`kwɔrənˌtin] *vt.* 使隔離

10 decay [dɪ`ke] *vt.* & *vi.* & *n.* 腐爛，侵蝕（作名詞時為不可數名詞）

片 (1) tooth decay 蛀牙
(2) fall into decay 衰敗

似 (1) rot [rɑt] *vt.* & *vi.* 腐爛 ③
(2) decompose [ˌdikəm`poz] *vt.* & *vi.* 腐爛
(3) deterioration [dɪˌtɪrɪə`reʃən] *n.* 惡化

▸ Air pollutants have gradually decayed the façade of the cathedral.
空氣中的汙染物質逐漸**侵蝕**這座大教堂的正面。
*façade [fə`sɑd] *n.* 建築物的正面

▸ Sugar can cause teeth to decay if people don't look after them by brushing them regularly.
如果大家不經常刷牙照顧好牙齒，糖可能會讓牙齒**蛀掉**。

1610-1619

延伸 a decayed tooth　一顆蛀牙

▶ Due to a lack of maintenance, the buildings in that area have fallen into decay.
由於缺乏保養維修，那個地區的建築物都**損壞**了。

11 tick [tɪk] *vi.* 發出滴答聲 & *n.* 滴答聲；勾〔英〕(= check〔美〕)

片 (1) tick away / by / past （時間）漸漸消逝
(2) put a tick　打勾〔英〕
= put a check〔美〕

▶ The living room was silent, except for the old grandfather clock in the corner, which ticked constantly.
客廳很安靜，除了在角落的落地鐘，它一直**發出滴答聲**。

▶ The last minutes ticked away, and I still couldn't think of a good way to solve the problem.
最後幾分鐘**漸漸消逝**，而我卻仍想不到解決這問題的好方法。

▶ The automatic machine made a loud tick as it operated, which bothered some of the employees.
這臺自動機器運轉時發出很大的**滴答聲**，打擾到了一些員工。

▶ Put a tick in the box next to the items you want to order.
請在您欲購買物品旁的方框裡**打勾**。

12 rip [rɪp] *vt.* & *vi.* 撕破 & *n.* 裂口，裂縫

三 rip, ripped [rɪpt], ripped
片 (1) rip up sth　把某物撕掉
= tear up sth
(2) be ripped off　被敲竹槓
似 (1) tear [tɛr] *vt.* & *vi.* 撕破 & *n.* 撕裂處 ②
三態為：tear, tore [tɔr], torn [tɔrn]
(2) split [splɪt] *vt.* & *vi.* 撕裂 & *n.* 裂縫 ④

▶ Daniel ripped up the letter angrily and threw it into the garbage can.
丹尼爾生氣地**把信撕掉**，丟進垃圾桶裡。

▶ John knew he was ripped off when he later found the watch he bought was much more expensive than the same one I bought.
約翰後來發現他買的那只錶比我買的同一只錶貴了許多時，他知道他**被敲竹槓**了。

▶ When he was putting on his tight pants, Vince noticed there was a large rip in them.
文斯穿上緊身褲時發現褲子有一條很大的**裂縫**。

13 prohibit [prəˋhɪbɪt] *vt.* 禁止

片 prohibit sb from + N/V-ing　禁止某人……
= ban sb from + N/V-ing
= restrain sb from + N/V-ing
衍 prohibition [ˌproəˋbɪʃən] *vt.* 禁止 ⑥

▶ Smoking is strictly prohibited in hospitals.
醫院**嚴禁**吸菸。

▶ The strict parents prohibited their teenage daughter from staying out later than 9:30 p.m. on weekdays.
這對嚴厲的父母**禁止**他們青春期的女兒平日晚上在外面待超過 9:30。

14 fleet [flit] *n.* 艦隊；(車、飛機等運輸工具的) 隊伍

片 a fleet of ships / aircraft
船隊 / 機隊

▶ Honolulu is a major port for the US naval fleet.
檀香山是美國海軍**艦隊**的主要集散港口。

▶ American Airlines owns a large fleet of aircraft.
美國航空公司擁有數量龐大的**機群**。

15 habitat [ˋhæbə͵tæt] *n.* (動物) 棲息地

片 a natural habitat 自然棲息地

▶ Wildlife in Taiwan has lost large areas of natural habitat because of urban sprawl.
由於城區肆意擴展，臺灣的野生動物失去了大片的**自然棲息地**。
*sprawl [sprɔl] *n.* 雜亂無章擴展的地區

16 coherent [koˋhɪrənt] *a.* 連貫的，前後一致有條理的

片 a coherent account / explanation / argument 連貫一致的陳述 / 解釋 / 論點

衍 coherence [koˋhɪrəns] *n.* 連貫性

反 incoherent [͵ɪnkoˋhɪrənt] *a.* 不連貫的

▶ Hank's lecture was clear and coherent, so students understood him easily.
漢克講課清楚又**連貫**，所以學生很容易瞭解。

▶ The next section of this chapter will teach you how to write a coherent essay.
本章的下一節將會教你如何撰寫**條理清晰的**文章。

17 sheer [ʃɪr] *a.* 完全的，純然的 & *adv.* 陡峭地

片 sheer luck / nonsense
全然的運氣 / 完全是廢話

似 (1) pure [pjʊr] *a.* 純粹的 ③
(2) absolute [ˋæbsə͵lut] *a.* 完全的 ④

▶ Michael's suggestion is sheer nonsense.
邁可的建議**全是廢話**。

▶ Rising up sheer from the ocean, the cliff was a dramatic feature of the wild coastline.
這座懸崖**陡峭地**聳立在海上，成了這荒蕪海岸線的鮮明特色。

18 intact [ɪnˋtækt] *a.* 完整的，完好無缺的

片 remain intact 完好如初

似 (1) undamaged [ʌnˋdæmɪdʒd]
a. 未受損害的
(2) untouched [ʌnˋtʌtʃt]
a. 沒被動過的

▶ After the terrible earthquake, the historic building still remained intact.
可怕的地震過後，該歷史建築物依舊**完好如初**。

▶ The celebrity emerged from the scandal with his reputation intact.
這位名人從這次的醜聞全身而退，名譽**未受影響**。

19 fragment [ˋfrægmənt] *n.* 碎片；片段 & [ˋfræg͵mɛnt] *vt.* & *vi.* (使) 破碎

片 (1) break into fragments 摔成碎片
= break into pieces
(2) a fragment of... 片段的……

▶ Susan dropped the glass on the floor, and it broke into fragments.
蘇珊不小心把杯子摔在地上，杯子**碎**了滿地。

衍 (1) fragmented [ˋfrægmɛntɪd]
a. 成碎片的
(2) fragmentation [ˌfrægmənˋteʃən]
n. 破碎

▸ I happened to hear a fragment of their conversation in the bathroom.
我碰巧聽到他們在廁所的一段對話。

▸ In her anger, Miley fragmented the plate into many pieces by throwing it on the kitchen floor.
麥莉一怒之下把盤子丟到廚房地板上摔碎了。

▸ Due to a variety of disagreements over the years, Bob and Ted's once strong friendship fragmented.
由於過去幾年來的種種爭執，鮑伯跟泰德曾經深厚的友誼已破碎了。

20 metaphor [ˋmɛtəfɚ] *n.* 隱喻

片 a metaphor for... ……的隱喻
衍 metaphorical [ˌmɛtəˋfɔrɪkl̩]
a. 用隱喻的

▸ The author uses magic as a metaphor for power.
這位作者用魔法來比喻權力。

21 acquisition [ˌækwəˋzɪʃən] *n.* 獲得（不可數）；添購的物品；收購

衍 acquire [əˋkwaɪr] *vt.* 獲得 ④

▸ The acquisition of new knowledge enables you to keep pace with changing trends.
獲得新知可以使你跟上不斷在改變的潮流。

▸ My parents' latest acquisitions are a dishwasher and a blender.
我父母親最近買了一臺洗碗機和果汁機。

▸ The company's acquisition of Fuji Tech will help it compete in the software market.
該公司收購富士科技將有助他們在軟體市場上競爭。

22 unlock [ʌnˋlɑk] *vt.* 開鎖；揭開

片 unlock the secret / mystery of sth
揭開某事的祕密
衍 unlocked [ʌnˋlɑkt] *a.* 沒有上鎖的
似 reveal [rɪˋvil] *vt.* 揭露 ③
反 lock [lɑk] *vt.* 鎖上 & *n.* 鎖 ③

▸ Mary unlocked the jewelry box with a key.
瑪莉用鑰匙打開珠寶箱。

▸ The experiment was conducted to unlock the secrets of the aging process.
進行這項實驗是為了揭開老化過程的祕密。

23 acute [əˋkjut] *a.* 敏銳的；急性的；嚴重的

片 (1) an acute sense of smell
敏銳的嗅覺
(2) an acute disease 急性病
(3) an acute shortage of water
嚴重缺水

▸ Dogs have an acute sense of smell.
狗兒有敏銳的嗅覺。

▸ Mark's daughter developed acute appendicitis last week.
馬克的女兒上星期患了急性闌尾炎。
*appendicitis [əˌpɛndəˋsaɪtɪs] *n.* 闌尾炎

▸ The long drought caused an acute shortage of water in West Africa.
長期乾旱造成西非地區**嚴重缺水**。

chronic [ˋkrɑnɪk] *a.* 慢性的
片 a chronic disease　慢性病

▸ Kevin has been suffering from chronic arthritis for two years.
凱文罹患**慢性**關節炎已經兩年了。
*arthritis [ɑrˋθraɪtɪs] *n.* 關節炎

24 pension [ˋpɛnʃən] *n.* 退休金，養老金 & *vt.* 給……退休金〔英〕

片 (1) a pension plan　退休金計畫
(2) receive a pension　領退休金
(3) pension sb off　發給某人退休金

▸ Once I retire, I'll have to live on my pension.
一旦我退休後，就靠**養老金**過活了。

▸ Each month, Tom pays six percent of his salary into a pension plan.
湯姆每個月將薪資的 6% 存起來做為**退休金**。

▸ Because the company needed to cut salary costs, several long-term employees were pensioned off at the beginning of the year.
因為這間公司要縮減薪資支出，幾位久任員工在今年初被**支付退休金**退休了。

25 disapprove [ˌdɪsəˋpruv] *vt.* 駁回 & *vi.* 反對

片 disapprove of + N/V-ing　反對……
衍 disapproving [ˌdɪsəˋpruvɪŋ] *a.* 反對的
反 approve [əˋpruv] *vt.* 批准 & *vi.* 同意 ③

▸ The teacher disapproved the students' plan for a party.
老師**駁回**學生們的舞會計畫。

▸ My parents strongly disapprove of my going out with that girl.
我爸媽強烈**反對**我和那女孩出去約會。

26 foster [ˋfɔstɚ] *vt.* 培養，促進；收養 & *a.* 收養的

片 a foster family　寄養家庭
似 (1) rear [rɪr] *vt.* 養育 ⑤
(2) nurture [ˋnɝtʃɚ] *vt.* 培育；養育 ⑥
(3) cultivate [ˋkʌltəˌvet] *vt.* 培育 ⑥
比 foster 是指『在某段時間內養育某個孩童，卻沒有成為其法定的父母親』，而 adopt 則是指『領養某孩童且成為其法定父母親』。

▸ This meeting's aim is to foster friendly relations between our two companies.
這次會議旨在**促進**我們兩家公司之間的友好關係。

▸ Judy has fostered three children from Africa during the past five years.
茱蒂過去 5 年來已經**收養**過 3 位來自非洲的孩童。

▸ A social service agency placed the orphan with a foster family.
社福機構將這名孤兒安置在一個**寄養家庭**中。

27 rebellion [rɪˋbɛljən] *n.* 叛亂，暴動

片 (1) rise in rebellion against... 群起反叛……
(2) suppress / put down / crush a rebellion 鎮壓叛變

衍 rebel [ˋrɛbḷ] *n.* 叛徒 & [rɪˋbɛl] *vi.* 反叛 ④

似 uprising [ˋʌpˌraɪzɪŋ] *n.* 起義；叛亂 ⑥

▸ The farmers rose in rebellion against the corrupt ruler.
農夫**群起反叛**腐敗的統治者。

▸ The government took extremely brutal measures to suppress the rebellion.
政府採取極度殘忍的手段來**鎮壓叛變**。

28 breakthrough [ˋbrekˌθru] *n.* 突破

片 make / achieve a breakthrough in... 在……上有所突破

衍 break through 突破；克服

▸ Scientists think they are beginning to break through in the fight against cancer.
科學家認為他們在對抗癌症上開始有所突破了。

▸ Everyone is expecting doctors to make a breakthrough in cancer treatment.
大家都希望醫生能**在**癌症治療**上有所突破**。

29 threshold [ˋθrɛʃhold] *n.* 門檻；開端

片 be on the threshold of... 在……的開端 / 起點

▸ Stepping on the threshold is deemed impolite in Chinese culture.
在中國文化裡，踩在**門檻**上被認為是不禮貌的。
*deem [dim] *vt.* 認為

▸ After being admitted to Harvard, Gary felt as if he were on the threshold of a new life.
獲得哈佛大學的入學許可後，蓋瑞感覺他就像是要**展開一段**新生活似的。

30 prejudice [ˋprɛdʒəˌdɪs] *n.* 偏見 & *vt.* 使有偏見（常以過去分詞作形容詞用）

片 (1) racial prejudice 種族偏見
(2) have a prejudice against... 對……有偏見
= be prejudiced against...

▸ Some people have a deep prejudice against people of certain races.
某些人**對**特定的種族**存有**很深的**偏見**。

▸ Before anti-discrimination laws were passed, judges were often prejudiced against blacks.
在反種族歧視法通過之前，法官常**對**黑人**存有偏見**。

31 stability [stəˋbɪlətɪ] *n.* 穩定(性)(不可數)

衍 (1) stable [ˋstebḷ] *a.* 穩定的；牢固的 ③
(2) stabilize [ˋstebḷ͵aɪz] *vt.* & *vi.* (使) 穩固

反 instability [͵ɪnstəˋbɪlətɪ] *n.* 不穩定

▸ The country had enjoyed many years of stability, but all that changed when enemy forces attacked the government.
該國**穩定**地度過好幾年，但一切在敵軍攻擊政府後全變了。

▸ It is John's stability that makes him such a reliable friend.
正是約翰**穩重**的個性使他成為值得信賴的朋友。

32 provoke [prəˋvok] *vt.* 引發；激怒

片 provoke sb into + N/V-ing 激怒某人……

衍 provocative [prəˋvɑkətɪv] *a.* 挑釁的

▸ Yeast can provoke allergic reactions in some people, particularly skin disorders.
酵母可能會**引發**某些人的過敏反應，尤其是皮膚病變。
*yeast [jist] *n.* 酵母

▸ Peter's rudeness provoked Linda into slapping his face with all her might.
彼得的粗魯**激怒**琳達而使她用盡全力打了他一耳光。
*might [maɪt] *n.* 力量

33 investigator [ɪnˋvɛstə͵getɚ] *n.* 調查者

片 a private investigator 私家偵探
= a private detective
= a private eye

衍 investigate [ɪnˋvɛstə͵get] *vt.* 調查 ③

▸ Rosa hired a private investigator to find out whether her husband was cheating on her.
羅莎僱了一名**私家偵探**調查她丈夫是否對她不忠。

34 consultation [͵kɑnsəlˋteʃən] *n.* 諮商(會)

衍 (1) consult [kənˋsʌlt] *vt.* 請教；查閱 & *vi.* 諮商(與介詞 with 並用) ④
(2) consultant [kənˋsʌltənt] *n.* 顧問 ④

▸ I chose my career path during a consultation with my parents and Professor Johnson.
我**諮詢**過爸媽以及強森教授的意見後才選定我的職涯方向。

35 donate [ˋdonet / doˋnet] *vt.* & *vi.* 捐獻(金錢、物資等)；捐贈(器官、血液等)

片 (1) donate A to B 將 A 捐給 B
(2) donate blood 捐血

▸ Mr. and Mrs. Smith donated one million dollars to a local charity.
史密斯夫婦**捐**了 100 萬美元給當地的慈善機構。

▸ People lined up to donate blood which would be sent to soldiers overseas.
民眾排隊**捐**要給海外士兵的**血**。

▸ The charity asked people to donate to help the victims of the natural disaster in South America.
該慈善機構請大家**捐助**，以幫助南美洲的天災受難者。

donation [do`neʃən] *n.* 捐贈，捐贈物

片 (1) make a generous / large / small donation to...
慷慨 / 巨額 / 小額捐給……
(2) blood / organ donation
捐血 / 器官捐贈

▸ Jonathan makes a generous donation in his father's name to a local church every Christmas.
喬納森每年聖誕節都會以父親的名義**慷慨捐錢給**當地的一所教會。

▸ Some people do not support organ donation because of their religion.
有些人因為信仰的關係，所以不支持**器官捐贈**。

---

donor [`donɚ] *n.* 捐贈者

片 (1) a blood donor 捐血者
(2) an organ donor 捐贈器官者

似 (1) contributor [kən`trɪbjətɚ] *n.* 捐贈者
(2) giver [`gɪvɚ] *n.* 贈予人

▸ The heart donor was a 16-year-old boy who had died in a car accident that morning.
心臟**捐贈者**是一名 16 歲的男孩，他在那天早上因為車禍過世了。

36 transmission [træns`mɪʃən] *n.* 傳送（電視訊號）；傳播（疾病）

片 transmission of disease
疾病的傳播

衍 transmit [træns`mɪt] *vt.* 傳送 ⑥

▸ The five-minute interruption in our transmission yesterday was due to technical malfunction.
由於技術故障，昨天我們**傳送**的訊息斷了 5 分鐘。
*malfunction [mæl`fʌŋkʃən] *n.* 故障

▸ The state government took action to prevent the transmission of disease between hospitals.
州政府採取行動，防止各醫院間相互**傳播疾病**。

37 slot [slɑt] *n.* 投幣孔；（時間表等的）時段 & *vt.* 放入狹槽 / 長孔中

三 slot, slotted [slɑtɪd], slotted

片 (1) a slot machine 吃角子老虎機
(2) a time slot 時段
(3) slot A into B 把 A 放入 B 中

似 timetable [`taɪm,tebl̩] *n.* 時間表

▸ John inserted the coins into the slot and selected the beverage he wanted.
約翰把硬幣投入**投幣孔**，接著選擇他想喝的飲料。

▸ If your band still wants to perform at the fair, there's a slot open at 7 o'clock.
如果你的樂團還想在園遊會中表演，7 點有一個空的**時段**。

▸ The carpenter slotted the leg of the table into the top and then inserted screws to secure it.
木匠把桌腳**嵌入**頂端，接著鎖入螺絲來固定它。

38 resemblance [rɪ`zɛmbləns] *n.* 相似

片 (1) bear little / no resemblance to sb/sth
和某人 / 某物一點都不相似

▸ Though Kathy and Joan are sisters, they bear no resemblance to each other.
凱西和瓊恩雖然是姊妹，卻**一點也不像**。

(2) bear a close / striking / strong resemblance to sb/sth
和某人／某物極為相似

衍 resemble [rɪ`zɛmbḷ] *vt.* 和……相似④

似 similarity [ˌsɪmə`lærətɪ] *n.* 相似(處)③

▶ That suit you're wearing bears a close resemblance to the one I just bought.
你身上穿的那件西裝和我剛買的那件很像。

39 respondent [rɪ`spɑndənt] *n.* 應答者，答覆者

衍 (1) respond [rɪ`spɑnd] *vt.* & *vi.* 回答②

(2) response [rɪ`spɑns] *n.* 回答③

▶ Although thousands of surveys were sent out, the number of respondents was only about 300.
雖然發出去了數千份調查，但答覆的人數只有大約 3 百位。

Unit 17

1701-1706

1 compact [kəm`pækt ] *a.* 小巧的；密實的 & *vt.* 壓縮，擠壓 & [ `kɑmpækt] *n.* 粉盒；小型轎車（= compact car）

片 (1) a compact car 小型轎車
(2) a powder compact 粉盒

衍 compactness [kəm`pæknəs] *n.* 小巧；緊實

似 compress [kəm`prɛs] *vt.* 壓緊，壓縮

▸ I just moved into a new apartment that's quite compact and cozy; and most importantly, the rent is pretty cheap.
我剛剛搬進一間小巧舒適的新公寓；最重要的是，房租很便宜。

▸ The ground was quite compact, so it was difficult to dig a hole in it.
這片土地十分密實，所以很難在上面挖洞。

▸ All the rubbish will have to be compacted and stored for future disposal.
所有垃圾必須被壓縮並儲存留待日後處理。

▸ Louise opened her purse, took out her compact, and applied some makeup.
露易絲打開她的手提包、拿出粉餅盒上了點妝。

2 juvenile [`dʒuvənḷ / `dʒuvənaɪl] *a.* 青少年的 & *n.* 青少年

片 (1) juvenile delinquency [dɪ`lɪŋkwənsɪ] 青少年犯罪
(2) a juvenile delinquent [dɪ`lɪŋkwənt] 不良少年

▸ Juvenile delinquency is a deep-seated problem in almost every country.
幾乎在每一個國家中，青少年犯罪都是根深蒂固的問題。
*deep-seated [`dip,sitɪd] *a.* 根深蒂固的

▸ In most cases, juvenile delinquents come from troubled families.
少年犯大多來自問題家庭。

▸ The number of juveniles arrested for committing crimes has doubled over the last decade.
過去十年內，因犯罪被捕的青少年人數已增加一倍了。

adolescent [ædḷ`ɛsṇt] *a.* 青春期的；青少年的 & *n.* 青少年

衍 adolescence [ædḷ`ɛsṇs] *n.* 青春期 ⑥

▸ Adolescent stress is an issue parents and school authorities shouldn't ignore.
青春期壓力是個父母及校方應該正視的議題。

▸ Tommy is over thirty but he still acts like an adolescent.
湯米已年過 30，但行為還是像個青少年。

3 dough [do] *n.* 麵糰；錢（不可數）

片 be rolling in dough 在錢上打滾，非常富有

▸ You can make dough by adding some water to the flour.
加點水進麵粉裡你就能做出麵糰了。

衍 doughnut [ˋdonʌt] *n.* 甜甜圈 (= donut) ③

▶ Dude, 5,000 bucks is a lot of dough! I don't have that much money to lend you.
老兄，5 千美元可是一大筆**錢**耶！我沒那麼多錢借你。

▶ Once we win the lottery, we'll be rolling in dough!
一旦我們中樂透頭獎，就**發財**了！

4 stall [stɔl] *n.* (尤指露天的) 小攤位 & *vt.* & *vi.* (使) 引擎熄火

片 a hot dog stall / stand 熱狗攤

似 stand [stænd] *n.* (尤指露天的) 小攤位 ①

▶ We saw a few stalls selling exotic food in the outdoor market.
我們在露天市集上看見有幾個**攤位**販賣異國食品。

▶ The pilot of the small plane stalled the engine by climbing too steeply and too high.
這架小飛機的駕駛員因為攀升地太陡峭、太高而**使引擎熄火**了。

▶ My car stalled this morning, and I had no money with me, so I had to walk all the way to work.
今天早上我的車子**熄火**了，同時我身上沒有錢，因此只好一路步行去上班。

5 booth [buθ] *n.* 亭子

片 (1) a ticket booth 售票亭
(2) a telephone booth 電話亭
(3) a voting booth 投票亭

▶ An old lady kept rushing me when I was in the telephone booth making an urgent call. It was so annoying!
當我在**電話亭**內打一通緊急電話時，一位老太太不斷催促我。真是煩死人了！

6 skeleton [ˋskɛlətən] *n.* (整具的) 骨骼

片 a skeleton in the / one's closet 不為人知的祕密，難言之隱〔美〕
= a skeleton in the / one's cupboard〔英〕

▶ Archeologists dug out a few skeletons from the site that were estimated to be more than 3,000 years old.
考古學家挖出了幾具**骨骸**，推估有超過 3 千年之久。

▶ We all have one or two skeletons in our closets, things that are too embarrassing to talk about.
我們都有一些**不為人知的祕密**，也就是那些太難堪而令人不願提起的事。

skull [skʌl] *n.* 頭骨

片 get it into / through one's (thick) skull 搞懂，弄清楚

▶ Police discovered several skulls and bones in Jim's backyard that belonged to the victims.
警方在吉姆家後院找到幾片受害者的**頭骨**跟骨頭。

▶ When will Eddie get it into his thick skull that Ellie has a crush on him? He's hopeless!
艾迪幾時才會**開竅**，知道艾莉對他有好感呢？他真是沒救了！

spine [spaɪn] *n.* 脊椎（骨）

衍 spineless [ˋspaɪnləs] *a.* 無脊椎的；懦弱的

似 backbone [ˋbæk͵bon] *n.* 脊椎（骨）⑥

▸ Bad posture can cause spine injury or back problems when you age.

不良的姿勢在你上了年紀時會造成**脊椎**受傷或背部問題。

*posture [ˋpɑstʃɚ] *n.* 姿勢

---

rib [rɪb] *n.* 肋骨 & *vt.* 調侃

三 rib, ribbed [rɪbd], ribbed

片 rib sb about sth 就某事調侃某人
= tease sb about sth

似 tease [tiz] *vt.* 調侃 ③

延伸 rib eye steak 肋眼牛排

▸ According to the Bible, Eve was created from Adam's rib.

根據聖經記載，夏娃是由亞當的一根**肋骨**所化成。

▸ George's classmates ribbed him about the love letter he got from the girl.

喬治班上的同學拿女孩給他情書這檔事**調侃**他。

7 wilderness [ˋwɪldɚnəs] *n.* 荒野，野外

片 in the wilderness 在野外
= in the wild

似 wild [waɪld] *n.* 荒野，荒地 & *a.* 野生的；野外的 ②

▸ Wendy got lost in the mountains while hiking and spent three days wandering in the wilderness before she was finally found by the rescue team.

溫蒂登山健行時迷了路，花了 3 天**在野外**流浪才終於被救難隊找到。

---

wildlife [ˋwaɪld͵laɪf] *n.* 野生動物（集合名詞，不可數）

片 (1) endangered wildlife 瀕臨絕種的野生動物
(2) a wildlife preserve 野生動物保護區

▸ Some endangered wildlife will become extinct within years if we don't take action.

如果我們再不行動，幾年之內有些**瀕臨絕種的動物**就要滅絕了。

8 nobility [noˋbɪlətɪ] *n.* 貴族；高貴（不可數）

片 the nobility 皇家貴族

衍 noble [ˋnobl̩] *a.* 貴族的；高貴的 ④

似 (1) aristocracy [͵ærəsˋtɑkrəsɪ] *n.*（泛指所有）貴族
(2) aristocrat [əˋrɪstə͵kræt] *n.*（一位）貴族

延伸 (1) duke [d(j)uk] *n.* 公爵
(2) earl [ɝl] *n.* 伯爵
(3) baron [ˋbærən] *n.* 男爵
(4) marquis [ˋmɑrkwəs] *n.* 侯爵

▸ I was astonished to know that Jack, a man I've known for ages, is actually descended from French nobility.

我很驚訝地發現傑克，一位我認識多年的男子，竟是法國**貴族**的後裔。

▸ We shouldn't doubt the nobility of his intentions. This man is trying to help us!

我們不該懷疑他**崇高**的心意。這人是想幫我們忙吶！

9 torment [tɔrˋmɛnt] *vt.* 使痛苦，折磨 & [ˋtɔrmɛnt] *n.* 痛苦，折磨（不可數）；讓人頭痛的人 / 事 / 物（可數）

片 (1) be tormented by... 受……折磨
(2) be in torment 身在痛苦之中

似 (1) torture [ˋtɔrtʃɚ] *vt.* & *n.* 折磨 ④
(2) anguish [ˋæŋgwɪʃ] *vt.* & *vi.* (使)極度痛苦 & *n.* 極度的痛苦
(3) agonize [ˋægə͵naɪz] *vt.* & *vi.* (使)痛苦，折磨

▸ I've been tormented by a sense of guilt ever since I broke Jay's precious digital camera.
自從我把傑伊的高價數位相機弄壞後就一直受罪惡感**折磨**。

▸ Because of the terrible war in her country, Melody lived a life of torment.
由於祖國可怕的戰爭，美樂蒂過著**痛苦**的一生。

▸ It's been a torment to travel around with Alice, who literally lacks any concern for other people's feelings.
跟愛麗絲旅行真是一大**折磨**，她對別人的感受一點也不在意。
*literally [ˋlɪtərəlɪ] *adv.* 實在地，簡直

10 chord [kɔrd] *n.* 和弦

片 (1) play the B chord 彈 B 和弦
(2) strike / touch a chord with sb 與某人看法一致，令某人贊同

▸ That guitar player played the wrong chord twice, but nobody seemed to notice it.
吉他手彈錯了**和弦**兩次，但似乎沒有人注意到。

▸ That candidate's speech struck a chord with the voters.
候選人的一席演講**令**選民**深表贊同**。

choir [kwaɪr] *n.* 合唱團

衍 chorus [ˋkorəs] *n.* 合唱團；副歌 ④

▸ When I was a kid, I used to be a member of the local church choir.
我小時候曾是地方教堂**合唱團**的成員。

11 attendance [əˋtɛndəns] *n.* 出席

片 (1) in attendance 出席
(2) attract / draw full attendance 引來滿場觀眾

衍 attend [əˋtɛnd] *vt.* 出席 & *vi.* 照顧（與介詞 to 並用）②

▸ We are honored to have the mayor in attendance.
我們很榮幸能請到市長**出席**。

▸ The speech last night was quite successful. It attracted full attendance even though there had not been much advertisement for it.
昨晚的演講相當成功。雖然之前沒做太多廣告宣傳，還是**吸引滿場觀眾**前來。

12 agenda [əˋdʒɛndə] *n.* 議程；工作事項

片 (1) be on the agenda 在議程 / 工作事項內
(2) set the agenda 排定議程

▸ My boss always has a full agenda.
我的老闆的**行程**總是滿檔。

▸ What's on the agenda this morning?
今早的**議程**為何？

▸ It's only natural that the boss sets the agenda of the weekly meetings.
由老闆來**擬訂**週會的**議程**才是正常的。

13 aisle [aɪl] *n.* (教堂、飛機與火車內座椅間的) 走道

片 (1) an aisle seat 靠走道的座位
(2) walk / go down the aisle 結婚
= get married

▸ The Nobel Prize winner's speech drew so many people that some had to sit in the aisles.
諾貝爾獎得主的演講引來許多人，有人甚至得坐在**走道**上。

▸ In two months, Belinda will walk down the aisle, so she has lots to do to prepare for her wedding.
兩個月後貝琳達就要**結婚**了，所以她要做很多事來籌備婚禮。

14 allergy [ˋæləˌdʒɪ] *n.* 過敏

複 allergies [ˋælədʒɪz]
片 have an allergy to... 對……過敏

▸ I have a severe allergy to dust and cat hair.
我**對**灰塵和貓毛有嚴重的**過敏**。

allergic [əˋlɝdʒɪk] *a.* 過敏的
片 be allergic to... 對……過敏

▸ My son is allergic to pollen.
我的兒子**對**花粉**過敏**。
*pollen [ˋpalən] *n.* 花粉

15 shrewd [ʃrud] *a.* 精明的

衍 shrewdness [ˋʃrudnəs] *n.* 精明

▸ A shrewd man like David is not going to buy it. Let's try our tricks on Chris! He is much more gullible.
像大衛那樣**精明的**人是不會上當的。我們來騙騙克里斯吧！他好騙多了。
*gullible [ˋgʌləbḷ] *a.* 易受騙的

16 rim [rɪm] *n.* (常指圓形物品的) 邊緣 & *vt.* 裝邊於

三 rim, rimmed [rɪmd], rimmed
片 (1) the rim of... ……的邊緣
(2) be rimmed with...
被框以……的邊
似 (1) edge [ɛdʒ] *n.* 邊緣 ②
(2) brim [brɪm] *n.* (容器的) 邊緣

▸ There was still lipstick on the rim of the coffee cup where Penny had drunk from.
潘妮喝過的咖啡杯**邊緣**留有口紅印。

▸ This watch is rimmed with pure gold.
這只錶的**邊緣是**純金的。

17 diagnose [ˋdaɪəgˌnos] *vt.* 診斷

片 (1) be diagnosed as... 被診斷為……
(2) diagnose sb as / with + 疾病
診斷某人罹患某疾病

▸ Ellen's condition was diagnosed as Alzheimer's disease.
艾倫的病情**經診斷之後判定為**阿茲海默症。

▸ The doctor diagnosed the infant with jaundice.
醫生**診斷**這名嬰兒**罹患**黃疸。
*jaundice [ˋdʒɔndɪs] *n.* 黃疸

diagnosis [ˌdaɪəgˋnosɪs] *n.* 診斷

複 diagnoses [ˌdaɪəgˋnosiz]

片 make a diagnosis 做出診斷

▸ Our goal is to make an accurate diagnosis as early as possible.
我們的目標是要儘早**做出**準確的**診斷**。

18 abundant [əˋbʌndənt] *a.* 充裕的

片 (1) be abundant in... 有充裕的……
(2) abundant opportunities for... 許多……的機會
(3) an abundant supply of sth 某物充分的供應量

似 plentiful [ˋplɛntɪfəl] *a.* 充裕的 ④

▸ The river is abundant in salmon at this time of the year.
這條河在每年此時都會**有大量的**鮭魚。

▸ As long as you perform well at the company, you'll have abundant opportunities for promotion.
只要你在公司表現良好，升遷的**機會多的是**。

19 incentive [ɪnˋsɛntɪv] *n.* 動機，動力 & *a.* 作為動力的

片 an incentive (for sb) to V （某人）做某事的動力

▸ A full scholarship provides a strong incentive for students to do well in school.
全額獎學金是促使學生努力讀書的**強大動力**。

20 compatible [kəmˋpætəbḷ] *a.* (電腦) 相容的；可共存的

片 be compatible with sth （電腦）可和某物相容；可和某物共存

衍 compatibility [kəmˌpætəˋbɪlətɪ] *n.* (電腦) 相容性

▸ The new software is not compatible with our computer system.
新的軟體和我們的電腦系統不**相容**。

▸ Aaron can't donate bone marrow to Sophie because their types aren't compatible.
艾倫不能捐骨髓給蘇菲，因為類型不合。
*marrow [ˋmæro] *n.* 髓

21 advocate [ˋædvəˌket] *vt.* & *vi.* 主張，提倡 & [ˋædvəkət] *n.* 支持者，擁護者

片 (1) advocate + N/V-ing 主張 / 提倡……
(2) advocate for... 主張 / 提倡……
(3) an advocate of sth 某事的支持者

▸ The mayor advocates building more libraries and schools.
市長**主張**多蓋圖書館和學校。

▸ Worried about air pollution, the group advocates for greater use of solar and wind energy.
該團體擔心空汙問題，所以**提倡**多加使用太陽能和風能。

▸ The most prominent advocate of this theory is Dr. Andrews.
這項理論最著名的**支持者**是安德魯斯博士。

22 confidential [ˌkɑnfəˋdɛnʃəl] *a.* 保密的，機密的

片 (1) confidential information / documents 機密資訊 / 文件
(2) keep sth confidential 保密某事
(3) highly / strictly confidential 極機密的

▸ Recycling confidential documents instead of shredding them may cause a leak in information.
若**機密**文件不用碎紙機銷毀而是拿去回收，可能會造成資訊外洩。
*shred [ʃrɛd] *vt.* 用碎紙機銷毀

▸ All patients' medical records and personal information will be kept confidential.
所有患者的就醫紀錄與個人資料都將**保密**。

▸ These files are strictly confidential.
這些是**極機密**檔案。

23 outlet [ˋaʊtˌlɛt] *n.* 宣洩的途徑；銷路，通路；打折暢貨中心

片 (1) an outlet for... ……的宣洩方式
(2) a retail outlet 零售店
(3) an outlet mall 打折暢貨中心

▸ Exercise provides people with an outlet for negative emotions and built-up stress.
運動提供大家一個**宣洩**負面情緒和累積壓力的**管道**。

▸ The company has nearly 30 retail outlets in Taiwan alone.
這家公司光是在臺灣就有近 30 處的**零售據點**。

▸ Frank spends most of his spare time shopping at the outlet mall.
法蘭克大部分空閒的時間都在**打折暢貨中心**購物。

24 transformation [ˌtrænsfəˋmeʃən] *n.* 變形，轉型

片 (1) undergo / experience a transformation 經歷轉變
(2) transformation from A to / into B 從 A 轉型成 B

衍 transform [trænsˋfɔrm] *vt.* 使改變 ④

▸ The country's political status has experienced a dramatic transformation in recent years.
這些年來，該國政局**經歷**了戲劇化的**轉變**。

▸ Today's topic is India's transformation from poverty to prosperity.
今天的主題是印度**從**貧窮**轉型到**富裕的過程。

25 cemetery [ˋsɛməˌtɛrɪ] *n.* 公墓

似 graveyard [ˋgrevˌjɑrd] *n.* 墓地

▸ Don's parents were buried in the cemetery in which his grandparents were buried.
唐恩的雙親和他的祖父母葬在同一座**公墓**。

---

coffin [ˋkɔfɪn] *n.* 棺材，靈柩

似 casket [ˋkæskət] *n.* 棺材

延伸 hearse [hɝs] *n.* 靈車

▸ The workers dug a hole and lowered the coffin into the grave.
工人們挖了一個坑，然後把**棺材**放進墓裡。

burial [ˋbɛrɪəl] *n.* 葬禮；埋葬

片 (1) a state burial 國葬
(2) a burial site 埋葬之地

衍 bury [ˋbɛrɪ] *vt.* 埋葬 ③

延伸 (1) interment [ɪnˋtɝmənt] *n.* 土葬
(2) cremation [krɪˋmeʃən] *n.* 火葬
(3) a sea burial 海葬

▸ The soldier was given a state burial in honor of sacrificing his life for his country.
這位士兵獲得**國葬**禮遇，紀念他為國犧牲。

▸ The burial site of the renowned writer has become a hot tourist spot.
那位名作家的**葬身地點**已成了熱門觀光景點。

26 shed [ʃɛd] *vt.* (樹葉、蛇皮等) 脫落 & *n.* (尤指用來儲藏的木製) 小屋

三 三態同形

片 (1) shed tears / blood 流淚 / 流血
(2) shed light on sth 闡明某事
(3) a tool shed 工具屋

▸ How often does a snake shed its skin?
蛇多久**脫**一次皮？

▸ Harry shed tears emotionally as he watched the sad movie.
哈利看這部悲傷的電影時，情緒激動地**落淚**。

▸ A recent study has shed light on the causes of climate change.
最近的一項研究**闡明**了氣候變遷的成因。

▸ Hank built a shed to keep all his garden tools in.
漢克建造了一間**小屋**來放他所有的花園用具。

27 biological [ˏbaɪəˋlɑdʒɪkḷ] *a.* 生物 (學) 的

片 biological parents / father / mother 親生父母 / 父親 / 母親

衍 (1) biology [baɪˋɑlədʒɪ] *n.* 生物學 ④
(2) biologist [baɪˋɑlədʒɪst] *n.* 生物學家
(3) biologically [ˏbaɪəˋlɑdʒɪkḷɪ] *adv.* 生物學上

▸ Mr. Todd is carrying out a biological experiment in room 806.
陶德先生正在 806 室做**生物實驗**。

▸ Jamie is an adopted child and is eager to know who her biological parents are.
潔咪是被收養的小孩，她渴望知道誰是她的**親生父母**。

28 raid [red] *n.* & *vt.* 突襲；(警方) 突然搜查

片 (1) carry out / launch a raid on... 對……展開突襲
(2) an air raid 空襲
(3) a police raid on... 警方突襲搜查……

似 attack [əˋtæk] *n.* & *vt.* 攻擊 ①

▸ The US army launched an air raid on the enemy's ammunition depot as night fell.
美軍在入夜後**對**敵軍彈藥庫**展開空襲**。
*ammunition [ˏæmjəˋnɪʃən] *n.* 彈藥
depot [ˋdipo] *n.* 儲藏處

▸ A large amount of heroin was found last night during a police raid on the farmhouse.
警方在昨晚一場**突襲**農場的行動中查獲大量的海洛因。

▸ Police raided the drug dealer's house in the early morning.
警方一大早就**突襲**毒販的房子。

1729-1733

29 riot [ˋraɪət] *n.* & *vi.* 暴動

似 uproar [ˋʌpˌrɔr] *n.* 騷亂，騷動

▶ A riot broke out in that area, but it was soon suppressed by the police.
該區發生暴動，不過很快就被警方鎮壓了。
*suppress [səˋprɛs] *vt.* 鎮壓

▶ These people are rioting because of the discrimination they face on a daily basis.
這些人暴動是因為他們每天面對的歧視所引起的。

30 aggression [əˋgrɛʃən] *n.* 侵略，攻擊（不可數）

衍 (1) aggressive [əˋgrɛsɪv]
a. 具侵略性的；積極的 ④
(2) aggressively [əˋgrɛsɪvlɪ]
adv. 侵略地；積極地

▶ Angry yelling and hitting things with one's fists are signs of aggression.
生氣地吼叫和用拳頭打東西是攻擊的表現。

31 analyst [ˋænlɪst] *n.* 分析師

衍 (1) analyze [ˋænlˌaɪz] *vt.* 分析 ④
(2) analysis [əˋnæləsɪs] *n.* 分析 ④
(3) analytical [ˌænlˋɪtɪkl] *a.* 分析的 ⑥

▶ Mike works as a financial analyst in a multinational corporation.
麥可在一家跨國企業裡擔任財經分析師的工作。
*multinational [ˌmʌltɪˋnæʃənl] *a.* 跨國的

32 autonomy [ɔˋtɑnəmɪ] *n.* 自主（權）；自治（權）（皆不可數）

衍 autonomous [ɔˋtɑnəməs] *a.* 自治的
似 anatomy [əˋnætəmɪ] *n.* 解剖學

▶ The three companies belonged to the same group, but the individual managers had autonomy to make their own decisions.
這三間公司隸屬同一個集團，但是各個經理有自行做決議的自主權。

▶ Demonstrators demanded greater autonomy for the province.
示威運動者要求該省獲得更多的自治權。

33 volcano [vɑlˋkeno] *n.* 火山

複 volcanos / volcanoes [vɑlˋkenoz]
衍 volcanic [vɑlˋkænɪk] *a.* 火山的

▶ The volcano erupted in 1947 and many villagers were killed.
這座火山於 1947 年爆發，造成許多村民喪生。

1801-1804

Level 5 Unit 18

1 antique [æn`tik] *n.* 古董 & *a.* 古董的

片 an antique shop / dealer
古董店／古董商

▸ That valuable piece of artwork is an antique.
那件值錢的藝術品是件**古董**。

▸ This store deals in antique furniture.
這家商店從事**古董**傢俱的買賣。

2 shield [ʃild] *n.* 盾牌 & *vt.* 保護

片 shield A from B　保護A免受B所害
= protect A from B

▸ The police officers carried shields to protect themselves from the bottles and rocks being thrown.
這些警察手持**盾牌**來保護自己不被扔過來的瓶罐和石塊擊傷。

▸ The ozone layer shields the Earth from the Sun's ultraviolet rays.
臭氧層**保護**地球**免受**太陽的紫外線所害。
*ozone [`ozon] *n.* 臭氧
ultraviolet [͵ʌltrə`vaɪəlɪt] *a.* 紫外線的

3 ass [æs] *n.* 驢子

片 make an ass of oneself
使某人出洋相

似 donkey [`daŋkɪ] *n.* 驢子 ③
(現代英語中，若指『驢子』，多使用 donkey 一字)

▸ When Hank drinks too much, he makes an ass of himself.
漢克酒喝多時，會**使**自己**出洋相**。

4 astonish [ə`stanɪʃ] *vt.* 使驚訝

似 (1) amaze [ə`mez] *vt.* 使驚訝 ③
(2) astound [ə`staʊnd] *vt.* 使震驚

衍 (1) astonished [ə`stanɪʃt]
a. 感到驚訝的
(2) astonishing [ə`stanɪʃɪŋ]
a. 令人驚訝的

▸ Lydia's answer astonished Paul: How could she not know the name of the capital of her own country?
莉迪雅的回答讓保羅**很震驚**：她怎麼會不知道自己國家首都的名稱？

▸ What astonishes me is that the little girl can sing so beautifully at such a young age.
令我**驚訝**的是，這名小女孩年紀輕輕就能把歌唱得這麼好。

astonishment [ə`stanɪʃmənt]
n. 驚訝

片 (1) To sb's astonishment, ...
令某人驚訝的是，……
(2) in astonishment　訝異地

似 amazement [ə`mezmənt] *n.* 驚訝 ③

▸ Much to everyone's astonishment, the diamond on display was stolen.
令大家大吃一驚的是，展示中的鑽石被偷了。

▸ We all watched Danny's amazing performance in astonishment.
我們都**驚訝地**看著丹尼精彩的表演。

1805-1812

5 ballot [ˋbælət] *n.* 選票；(不記名) 投票 & *vi.* 投票表決

片 (1) cast a ballot for sb　投票給某人
= cast a vote for sb
(2) (a) secret ballot　不記名投票
(3) ballot for...　投票表決……

似 vote [vot] *n.* & *vi.* & *vt.* 投票 ②

▸ For the upcoming election, make sure to cast a ballot for the candidate of your choice.
關於即將來臨的這場選舉，務必要**將選票投給**您心目中的候選人。

▸ Most people wanted the voting to be done by secret ballot, but a few wanted to know who everyone supported.
大多數人想要採**不記名投票**，但有少部分人想要知道每個人支持的是誰。

▸ The new student union president was selected by students at the college balloting for one of two candidates.
新的學生會會長由該所大學的學生從兩位候選人中**投票表決**選出一位。

6 ban [bæn] *vt.* 下令禁止 & *n.* 禁令

三 ban, banned [bænd], banned

片 (1) ban sb from + N/V-ing
禁止某人做……
= prohibit sb from + N/V-ing
(2) impose a ban on sth
對某事施以禁令
(3) lift a ban on sth　取消某事的禁令

似 prohibit [prəˋhɪbɪt] *vt.* 禁止 ⑤

▸ The law bans motor boats from entering within a 10-mile radius of this island.
法律**禁止**快艇進入這座島嶼周圍半徑 10 英里的範圍內。

▸ Most students were unhappy when the school decided to impose a ban on their hairdos.
校方決定**對**學生的髮型**實施禁令**時，大部分的學生都很不悅。

▸ The government lifted the ban on imported beef from Canada recently.
政府最近**取消**了從加拿大進口牛肉的**禁令**。

7 belongings [bəˋlɔŋɪŋz] *n.* 所有物 (恆用複數)

片 personal belongings
個人隨身攜帶物品

衍 belong [bəˋlɔŋ] *vi.* 屬於
(與介詞 to 並用) ①

似 possession [pəˋzɛʃən] *n.* 所有物 ④

▸ When getting off the train, don't forget to take all your personal belongings with you.
下火車時，別忘了將全部的**隨身物品**帶下車。

8 beneficial [ˏbɛnəˋfɪʃəl] *a.* 有益的

片 be beneficial to / for...　對……有益

衍 benefit [ˋbɛnəfɪt] *n.* 利益 & *vt.* 有益於 & *vi.* 獲益 (與介詞 from 並用) ③

反 (1) harmful [ˋhɑrmfəl] *a.* 有害的 ③
(2) detrimental [dɛtrəˋmɛntl̩]
a. 有害的

▸ Exercising on a daily basis is beneficial to your health.
每天運動**對**你的健康**有好處**。

9 beware [bɪ`wɛr] *vi.* 當心

片 beware of + N/V-ing　小心……

▶ A large sign on the door with red lettering told visitors to beware of the dog.
門上寫有紅色字體的大標示告訴遊客要**小心**這隻狗。

▶ Beware of falling asleep while driving late at night.
深夜開車要**小心提防**不要睡著。

wary [`wɛrɪ] *a.* 小心的，警惕的
片 be wary of...　對……小心提防
似 cautious [`kɔʃəs] *a.* 謹慎的 ⑤

▶ Claire told her children to be wary of strangers who offer to buy them candies.
克萊兒跟她的孩子們說，要**小心提防**那些主動請他們吃糖果的陌生人。

10 blueprint [`blu,prɪnt] *n.* 藍圖

片 a blueprint for...　……的藍圖 / 計畫

▶ The government has hammered out a blueprint for economic reform.
政府擬定了一套經濟改革**計畫**。
*hammer out...　擬定……

11 bolt [bolt] *n.* 門栓；螺栓；一道 (閃電) & *vi.* 快速移動；逃走

片 (1) a bolt of lightning　一道閃電
= a lightning bolt
(2) a bolt from the blue
出乎意料之外的事情
= a bolt out of the blue

▶ I slid the bolt back and opened the restroom door.
我把**門栓**推開，打開廁所的門。

▶ A bolt came off the bike, causing the wheel to come loose.
螺栓從腳踏車上脫落，造成車輪鬆脫。

▶ A bolt of lightning suddenly flashed and lit up the sky.
一道閃電劃過天際點亮了天空。

▶ The news that Larry was marrying a woman he had just met came like a bolt out of the blue.
賴瑞要和一位他剛認識的女子結婚，這個消息**出乎**大家的**意料之外**。

▶ The scared cat bolted out of the room and then disappeared when it heard someone coming.
受到驚嚇的貓聽到有人進來房間時，**快跑**出去消失了。

12 bonus [`bonəs] *n.* 獎金；紅利

比 bonus 是指在固定薪水以外的『特別獎金』，通常是對員工在工作上特殊的表現給予的獎勵；而 dividend [`dɪvə,dɛnd] 則是指公司的盈餘發配給股東們的『股息』。

▶ Dean received a bonus of NT$5,000 last month due to his excellent performance.
迪恩工作上有良好的表現，上個月收到臺幣 5 千元的**獎金**。

13 boom [bum] *n.* & *vi.* 突趨繁榮，迅速增長

片 (1) a baby boom 嬰兒潮
(2) a boom in... ……迅速增長

似 (1) prosper [ˋprɑspɚ] *vi.* 繁榮 ④
(2) flourish [ˋflɝɪʃ] *vi.* 繁榮 ⑥

反 slump [slʌmp] *n.* & *vi.* 暴跌 ⑥

▸ This year has seen a boom in car sales in India.
今年印度的汽車銷售量**大增**。

▸ Our business is booming this year because of the rising demand for our products in the market.
我們今年生意**興隆**，因為市場對我們產品的需求量升高。

thrive [θraɪv] *vi.* 繁榮，興隆；繁茂地生長

三 thrive, thrived / throve [θrov], thrived / thriven [ˋθrɪvən]

▸ The company began to thrive after a new CEO took charge.
公司在新的執行長上任後**生意日益興隆**。

▸ The cactus is one of the few plants that can thrive in the desert.
仙人掌是少數可以在沙漠中**繁茂地生長**的植物。

14 gut [gʌt] *n.* 勇氣，膽量 (恆用複數) & *vt.* 毀壞 (建築、房屋) 內部

三 gut, gutted [ˋgʌtɪd], gutted

片 have the guts to V 有勇氣做……
= have the courage to V
= have the nerve to V

似 courage [ˋkɝɪdʒ] *n.* 勇氣 ②

▸ The manager didn't have the guts to admit that he had made a bad decision.
經理沒**勇氣**承認他做了一個差勁的決定。

▸ The owner of the old home told the workers that he wanted them to gut the kitchen and rebuild it.
這棟舊屋的主人告訴工人們，他想要他們**拆掉**廚房的**內部**並且重建。

15 boxer [ˋbɑksɚ] *n.* 拳擊手

衍 boxing [ˋbɑksɪŋ] *n.* 拳擊 ⑥

▸ It is said that this boxer always knocks his opponents out in the first round.
據說這位**拳擊手**總在第一輪就將對手擊昏。

16 bully [ˋbʊlɪ] *vt.* 欺負，霸凌 & *n.* 霸凌者

三 bully, bullied [ˋbʊlɪd], bullied

複 bullies

▸ The recent survey shows that one out of every five students is bullied at school.
最近一項調查顯示，學校裡每 5 名學生中就有 1 人被**霸凌**。

▸ Jason gave in to the school bully and gave him all his money.
傑森向這名學校**惡霸**低頭，把所有的錢都給了他。

17 canal [kəˋnæl] *n.* 運河

片 the Panama Canal 巴拿馬運河

延伸 strait [stret] *n.* 海峽 ⑥

▸ The Panama Canal connects the Caribbean Sea with the Gulf of Panama.
巴拿馬運河連接加勒比海和巴拿馬灣。

18 celebrity [səˋlɛbrətɪ] *n.* 名人（可數）；名聲，名氣（不可數）

衍 celeb [səˋlɛb] *n.* 名人

▸ The writer's best-selling book made him an instant celebrity.
那位作家的暢銷書使他一時間成了名人。

▸ Celebrity can be fun and exciting, but it also has its disadvantages, including a lack of privacy.
出名這件事或許既有趣又刺激，但也有缺點，包含缺乏隱私。

19 certificate [sɚˋtɪfəkət] *n.* 證明；證書 & [sɚˋtɪfə͵ket] *vt.* 發證書給

片 a birth / marriage certificate
出生證明 / 結婚證書

▸ Doris received a certificate after she completed the course.
桃樂絲上完這堂課後獲得了一份證書。

▸ The institution certificates accountants who take their training programs and score sufficiently high enough on their exams.
這個學院會發證書給完成訓練課程且在考試上得分夠高的會計師。

20 check-in [ˋtʃɛk͵ɪn] *n.* （旅館）辦理住房手續；（機場）辦理登機手續

▸ When is the check-in time for the flight?
這班飛機是什麼時候開始受理登機手續？

checkout [ˋtʃɛk͵aʊt] *n.* （旅館）辦理退房手續；結帳處，收銀臺

▸ This hotel's checkout time is 12:00 p.m.
這家飯店退房時間是中午 12 點。

▸ The sign above the checkout stated that it was for customers who were purchasing not more than eight items.
該結帳處上方的告示說明這是給購買八樣物品以下的顧客用的。

21 speculate [ˋspɛkjə͵let] *vi.* & *vt.* 臆測

片 (1) speculate about / on sth
對某事加以臆測
(2) speculate that... 臆測……

衍 speculation [͵spɛkjəˋleʃən] *n.* 臆測
▸ There is speculation that the two banks will merge in the near future.
有人臆測這兩家銀行最近就會合併。

▸ The political analyst refused to speculate about why the finance minister stepped down.
這位政治分析師拒絕臆測財政部長下臺的原因。

▸ Some people have speculated that this Hollywood couple will break up within a year.
有些人臆測這對好萊塢情侶一年之內會分手。

1822-1831

22 comparable [ˋkɑmpərəbl̩] *a.* 可相比的

片 be comparable to / with...
可與……相比

衍 (1) compare [kəmˋpɛr]
vt. & *vi.* 比較 ②

(2) comparison [kəmˋpærəsn̩]
n. 比較 ③

▸ A small car is not comparable to a large one for comfort.
在舒適性上，小車是無法與大車相比的。

23 undermine [ˌʌndɚˋmaɪn] *vt.* (逐漸) 損壞

似 (1) damage [ˋdæmɪdʒ] *vt.* 破壞 ②
(2) spoil [spɔɪl] *vt.* 破壞 ③
(3) ruin [ˋruɪn] *vt.* 破壞 ④

▸ Some people tried to undermine the celebrity's reputation by spreading rumors about his private life.
有些人想藉由散布關於這個名人私生活的謠言來破壞他的聲望。

24 conservation [ˌkɑnsɚˋveʃən] *n.* (動植物) 保護；(自然資源) 保存 (皆不可數)

片 wildlife conservation
野生動物保育

衍 conserve [kənˋsɝv] *vt.* 保護；保存 ⑥

▸ Not only does energy conservation reduce your energy bills, but it also helps the environment.
能源節約不但能降低電費，也可拯救環境。

25 script [skrɪpt] *n.* 腳本，劇本 & *vt.* 替……寫腳本

衍 scriptwriter [ˋskrɪptˌraɪtɚ] *n.* 編劇

似 screenplay [ˋskrinˌple] *n.* 電影劇本

▸ Nick was chosen to write the script for a TV series about the Vietnam War.
尼克被選中撰寫一齣關於越戰的電視連續劇腳本。

▸ As a member of the writing team, Joyce is responsible for helping to script the popular TV program.
喬伊絲身為編寫團隊的一員，她負責替這檔熱門電視節目寫腳本。

26 crucial [ˋkruʃəl] *a.* 決定性的，重要的

片 (1) It is crucial that...
……是很重要的
(2) be crucial to... 對……極為重要
(3) play a crucial role in...
在……扮演重要的角色

似 (1) critical [ˋkrɪtɪkl̩] *a.* 關鍵的 ④
(2) vital [ˋvaɪtl̩] *a.* 極為重要的 ④

▸ It is crucial that the doctor (should) perform an immediate operation on the badly injured man.
醫師立即為這名嚴重受傷的人動手術是很重要的。

▸ Your dedication is very crucial to the success of our company.
= Your dedication plays a crucial role in the success of our company.
你的奉獻對本公司的成功來說極為重要。

trivial [ˋtrɪvɪəl] *a.* 瑣碎的，不重要的

衍 trivia [ˋtrɪvɪə] *n.* 瑣事

似 trifling [ˋtraɪflɪŋ] *a.* 瑣碎的

▸ I don't know why Joe got so upset about something trivial.
我不知道喬為何對瑣事感到心煩。

petty [ˋpɛtɪ] *a.* 瑣碎的，不重要的

片 petty cash （公司的）小額現金

▶ We have wasted too much time on petty issues at the meeting.
我們開會時浪費太多時間在討論**瑣碎的**議題上了。

▶ Purchases like toilet paper are usually paid for out of the petty cash.
諸如衛生紙等物品的採購通常由**小額現金**支付。

27 unemployment [ˏʌnɪmˋplɔɪmənt] *n.* 失業（不可數）

片 the unemployment rate 失業率

▶ The unemployment rate has increased over the past year since the outbreak of COVID-19.
自新冠肺炎爆發後，過去一年來**失業率**已增加。

28 projection [prəˋdʒɛkʃən] *n.* 推測，預估；投射

衍 (1) project [prəˋdʒɛkt] *vt.* 預估；投射 & [ˋprɑdʒɛkt] *n.* 計畫 ②
(2) projector [prəˋdʒɛktɚ] *n.* 投影機

▶ Due to the inefficiency of the production department, our company failed to achieve last year's sales projections.
由於生產部門沒有效率，本公司未能達到去年**預估**的銷售量。

▶ The equipment allows the projection of an image from devices such as smartphones, computers, and tablets.
這個設備能讓如智慧型手機、電腦及平板等裝置**投射**影像。

29 therapy [ˋθɛrəpɪ] *n.* 療法

似 treatment [ˋtritmənt] *n.* 治療 ①

▶ After suffering from emotional problems since he was a child, Don finally decided to get some therapy.
唐恩自小受情緒問題所苦，他最終決定接受**治療**。

therapist [ˋθɛrəpɪst] *n.* 治療師

片 a speech therapist 語言治療師

▶ Kevin has an appointment with his speech therapist at four this afternoon.
凱文今天下午 4 點和他的**語言治療師**有約。

30 squad [skwɑd] *n.* 小隊，小組

片 a bomb squad 防爆小組

▶ A bomb squad was called in to defuse a bomb placed underneath the official's car.
防爆小組被召集來拆除被安置在官員車下的炸彈。
*defuse [diˋfjuz] *vt.* 拆除（炸彈的雷管）

31 prosecution [ˏprɑsɪˋkjuʃən] *n.* 起訴

衍 prosecute [ˋprɑsɪˏkjut] *vt.* & *vi.* 起訴 ⑥

▶ Prosecution for minor offenses rarely leads to imprisonment.
因輕微罪行而被**起訴**的幾乎很少要被關。
*offense [əˋfɛns] *n.* 過錯，犯法
imprisonment [ɪmˋprɪzn̩mənt] *n.* 監禁

32 outfit [ˋaut,fɪt] *n.* 全套服裝 / 裝備 & *vt.* 提供全套服裝

三 outfit, outfitted [ˋau,fɪtɪd], outfitted

片 (1) a superman / cowboy outfit
全套超人 / 牛仔裝
(2) a ski outfit 全套滑雪裝備
(3) outfit sb with...
為某人提供 (全套服裝)

▸ I'm considering wearing a superman outfit to the costume party.
我正考慮要穿**全套超人裝**去那場變裝派對。

▸ The clothing brand quickly rose to fame by outfitting celebrities.
該服裝品牌藉由**提供**名人**全套服裝**的穿著而快速嶄露頭角。

33 squash [skwaʃ] *vt.* 壓扁 & *vt.* & *vi.* 擠入 & *n.* 擁擠

片 (1) squash A in / into B 把 A 擠入 B
(2) squash in / into... 硬擠進……

似 (1) flatten [ˋflætṇ] *vt.* 使平坦
(2) squeeze [skwiz] *vt.* & *vi.* 擠 & *n.* 擁擠 ③

▸ Fred accidentally sat on a woman's bag of groceries and squashed a box of eggs.
佛萊德不小心坐在那名女子裝滿雜貨的袋子上，**壓扁**了一盒雞蛋。

▸ The people on the bus were packed in like sardines, but the woman at the bus stop insisted on squashing herself in.
公車裡的人擠到不行，但站牌的這名女子堅持要**擠上去**。
*be packed (in) like sardines 擁擠不堪

▸ The four of us squashed into the back seat of his car.
我們 4 個一同**擠進**他車子的後座。

▸ It was a squash to fit into the elevator, but Jackie just managed to squeeze into it.
進入電梯內很**擁擠**，但傑奇還是想辦法擠進去。

34 irony [ˋaɪrənɪ] *n.* 諷刺 (不可數)

衍 ironic [aɪˋranɪk] *a.* 諷刺的 ⑥
似 sarcasm [ˋsarkæzṃ] *n.* 諷刺 (不可數)

▸ "Thanks a bunch, dude. You really saved me a lot of trouble," said George with irony.
喬治**諷刺**地說：『老兄，真多謝。你讓我省了好多麻煩吶』。

35 domain [doˋmen] *n.* 屬地，領土；領域，範圍

片 (1) outside / within sb's domain
超出某人的 (研究) 領域 / 在某人 (研究) 領域之內
(2) be in the public domain
對外開放

似 (1) territory [ˋtɛrə,torɪ] *n.* 領土 ③
(2) realm [rɛlm] *n.* 領土；領域 ⑤
(3) field [fild] *n.* 領域 ②
(4) sphere [sfɪr] *n.* 領域 ⑤

▸ This forest is the king's domain. Trespassers are subject to severe penalties.
這片樹林是國王的**領地**。闖入者將遭嚴懲。
*trespasser [ˋtrɛ,spæsɚ] *n.* 擅闖者

▸ I'm afraid I won't be of much help. Your research subject is outside of my domain.
很抱歉，我可能幫不上忙。你的研究主題**在我的領域之外**。

▸ This information is not in the public domain. Only a handful of people know about it.
這消息還未**對外公開**。僅有少數幾個人知情。

36 **upgrade** [ˌʌpˋgred] *vt.* & [ˋʌpgred] *n.* 升級

片 a software / system upgrade
軟體 / 系統升級

衍 upgradable [ˌʌpˋgredəbḷ] *a.* 可升級的

反 downgrade [ˋdaʊnˌgred] *vt.* 降級

▶ We need to upgrade our office equipment to improve efficiency.
我們的辦公室設備需要**升級**以提升效率。

▶ The engineer has made some upgrades to the computer.
工程師已經幫這臺電腦做了一些**升級**。

Unit 19

1901-1908

1 mustard [ˋmʌstɚd] *n.* 黃芥末

似 wasabi [waˋsabɪ] *n.* 綠芥末

▸ Would you like ketchup, mustard, or sauerkraut on your hotdog?
你的熱狗要不要加點番茄醬、芥末醬或是酸黃瓜？
*sauerkraut [ˋsaʊr͵kraʊt] *n.* 酸黃瓜

2 clause [klɔz] *n.* 條款；子句

▸ The legislator suggested that a clause be added to the bill to ensure immigrants' rights at the workplace.
這名立法委員建議該法案加入一項**條款**以確保移民者在職場上的權利。

▸ In English grammar, a clause is part of a sentence that consists of a subject and a verb.
在英文文法中，**子句**是完整句的一部分，由一個主詞與動詞組成。

3 comedian [kəˋmidɪən] *n.* 喜劇演員

衍 (1) comic [ˋkamɪk] *a.* 喜劇的；好笑的 & *n.* 漫畫 ②
(2) comedy [ˋkamədɪ] *n.* 喜劇 ④

▸ Jim Carrey is no doubt one of the greatest comedians of our time.
無庸置疑地，金凱瑞是我們這個時代最偉大的**喜劇演員**之一。

4 compliment [ˋkamplə͵mɛnt] *vt.* & [ˋkampləmənt] *n.* 讚美，恭維

片 (1) compliment sb (on sth) 讚美某人 (某事)
(2) pay / give sb a compliment (on sth) 讚美某人 (某事)

衍 complimentary [͵kampləˋmɛntərɪ] *a.* 讚美的；免費的

▸ The chocolates are complimentary of this hotel.
這些巧克力是本飯店**贈送的**。

似 (1) complement [ˋkamplə͵mɛnt] *vt.* 補足 & [ˋkampləmənt] *n.* 補充物 ⑥
(2) praise [prez] *vt.* & *n.* 讚美 ②

▸ Anthony complimented his date on her elegant red gown.
安東尼**稱讚**他約會對象優雅的紅色禮服。

▸ Guests paid Catherine a compliment on her newly furnished house.
客人**對**凱瑟琳新裝潢的房子**表示稱讚**。

5 comprehend [ˌkɑmprɪˋhɛnd] *vt.* 了解

似 understand [ˌʌndɚˋstænd] *vt.* 理解，了解 ①

▸ It's difficult for such a young student to comprehend the underlying meaning of this novel.
要年紀這麼輕的學生了解這部小說隱含的意義是有困難的。
*underlying [ˌʌndɚˋlaɪɪŋ] *a.* 隱含的

comprehension
[ˌkɑmprɪˋhɛnʃən] *n.* 理解（力）

片 (1) reading / listening comprehension 閱讀 / 聽力理解
(2) beyond sb's comprehension 某人無法理解

衍 (1) comprehensive [ˌkɑmprɪˋhɛnsɪv] *a.* 全面的 ⑥
(2) comprehensible [ˌkɑmprɪˋhɛnsəbl̩] *a.* 可理解的

似 understanding [ˌʌndɚˋstændɪŋ] *n.* 了解

▸ My comprehension of our environment greatly changed after I saw the documentary.
看過這部紀錄片後，我對我們環境的了解大大地改變了。

▸ I think the reading comprehension is the most difficult part of the test.
我認為這次考試最難的部分是閱讀測驗。

▸ When Dr. Bannon began talking about physics, what he said was beyond Simon's comprehension, and he quickly got confused.
當貝農醫生開始談論物理時，賽門聽不懂他說的並很快感到困惑。

6 contaminate [kənˋtæməˌnet] *vt.* 汙染

衍 (1) contaminated [kənˋtæməˌnetɪd] *a.* 受到汙染的
(2) contamination [kənˌtæməˋneʃən] *n.* 汙染

似 pollute [pəˋlut] *vt.* 汙染 ③

▸ The waste water discharged from the factories has contaminated the river.
從工廠排放出的廢水汙染了河流。
*discharge [dɪsˋtʃardʒ] *vt.* 排放（液體、氣體）

7 custody [ˋkʌstədɪ] *n.* 監護（權）；拘禁（皆不可數）

片 (1) receive custody of... 獲得……的監護權
(2) grant custody to... 監護權判給……
(3) joint custody 共同監護權
(4) be held in custody 遭到監禁

▸ Jennifer received custody of her twin daughters after the divorce.
離婚後，珍妮佛取得她那對雙胞胎女兒的監護權。

▸ John is being held in police custody in connection with the theft.
約翰因為與這起失竊案有關聯而遭警察拘禁。

8 deceive [dɪˋsiv] *vt.* 欺騙

片 deceive oneself 自欺欺人

衍 (1) deceit [dɪˋsit] *n.* 欺騙；不誠實
(2) deceitful [dɪˋsitfəl] *a.* 欺騙的；不誠實的

▸ Rita is deceiving herself by believing Paul is secretly in love with her, because he has no interest in her.
瑞塔相信保羅偷偷愛慕著她，但這是在自欺欺人，因為他對她一點興趣都沒有。

似 (1) cheat [tʃit] *vt.* 欺騙 ②
(2) con [kɑn] *vt.* 欺騙
(3) swindle [ˋswɪndl̩] *vt.* 詐騙
(4) defraud [dɪˋfrɔd] *vt.* 詐騙

▸ The blind woman was deceived by the young man who claimed to be her son.
這名盲眼的婦人被一名自稱是她兒子的年輕男子給**欺騙**了。

---

deception [dɪˋsɛpʃən] *n.* 欺騙
似 fraud [frɔd] *n.* 詐欺 ⑤

▸ The company owner was found guilty of obtaining money using lies and deception.
這名公司老闆因**詐欺**騙錢而定罪。

---

deceptive [dɪˋsɛptɪv] *a.* 騙人的
似 misleading [mɪsˋlidɪŋ] *a.* 騙人的；使人誤解的

▸ What Mark said was deceptive: He left out some important information so that people would not fully understand the situation.
馬克所說的話是**騙人的**：他忽略一些重要的訊息，所以大家無法全面理解狀況。

▸ Appearances are sometimes deceptive. Charles wears designer suits and drives a luxurious sports car, but in fact, he is seriously in debt.
外表有時可以**騙人的**。查爾斯身穿名牌服裝，並開高級跑車，但事實上，他嚴重負債。

9 deploy [dɪˋplɔɪ] *vt.* 調動，部署（部隊等）

片 deploy troops　派遣軍隊
衍 deployment [dɪˋplɔɪmənt] *n.* 部署

▸ The Minister of National Defense agreed to deploy another five hundred troops to guard this region.
國防部部長同意再**派遣** 500 個**軍隊**來保衛這個地區。

10 enchant [ɪnˋtʃænt] *vt.* 使著迷

片 be enchanted by...　著迷於……
= be fascinated by / with...
= be attracted by / to...
衍 enchantment [ɪnˋtʃæntmənt] *n.* 著迷

▸ Miranda was deeply enchanted by the handsome guy's smile.
米蘭達深深**被**這名帥氣男孩的笑容**所著迷**。

11 mammal [ˋmæml̩] *n.* 哺乳動物

延伸 (1) reptile [ˋrɛptl̩] *n.* 爬蟲類 ⑥
(2) amphibian [æmˋfɪbɪən] *n.* 兩棲類

▸ The largest mammal is the blue whale.
最大的**哺乳類動物**是藍鯨。

12 throne [θron] *n.* 王位，王權（前須置定冠詞 the）；王座

片 (1) succeed sb to the throne
繼承某人的王位

▸ The throne of England commands respect but does not command armies.
英國的**王權**只享有尊榮但無兵權。

(2) come to / ascend the throne 登上王位

似 thorn [θɔrn] *n.* 刺

▸ Queen Elizabeth II ascended the throne at the age of 25 after her father, King George VI, died in 1952.
伊莉莎白二世在父親喬治六世於 1952 年逝世後**登基**時年 25 歲。

▸ The king sat on his throne, listening to several presentations by people who had come to meet him.
國王坐在他的**王位**上，聆聽幾場前來會見他的人民做的報告。

13 strand [strænd] *n.* 一股 / 縷（線、頭髮）& *vt.* 使擱淺

片 a strand of... 一股 / 縷……

似 beach [bitʃ]
vt. 使擱淺；把（船）拖上岸 ①

▸ Peter brushed a strand of hair from his forehead, cleared his throat, and began to speak.
彼得撥開前額上的**一撮**頭髮，清了清喉嚨，開始演講。

▸ The ship was stranded by a typhoon; fortunately, all the crew members were rescued.
這艘船因颱風而**擱淺**，所幸所有船員都獲救了。

14 strap [stræp] *n.* 帶子 & *vt.* 捆住，綁上

三 strap, strapped [stræpt], strapped

片 (1) a watch strap 錶帶
(2) be strapped in 繫上安全帶

似 fasten [ˋfæsn̩] *vt.* & *vi.* 繫上 ④

▸ Fasten the straps on your suitcases before they go in for X-ray inspection.
在接受 X 光檢查前請把你們皮箱上的**帶子**捆緊。

▸ Make sure everyone is strapped in before we hit the road.
我們上路前請先確定大家都**繫上了安全帶**。

15 sniff [snɪf] *n.* & *vt.* & *vi.* 聞 & *n.* & *vi.* 大聲吸氣

片 sniff at... 聞……；對……不屑一顧

似 (1) smell [smɛl] *vt.* & *vi.* 聞 ①
(2) inhale [ɪnˋhel] *vt.* & *vi.* 吸
(3) whiff [(h)wɪf] *n.* 一股味道

▸ Sean took a quick sniff of his shirt to see if he should wear it or wash it.
尚恩快速**聞了一下**襯衫來確認是否要穿上它，還是把它拿去洗。

▸ Lori gently took the pretty rose in her hand and sniffed it to enjoy the nice fragrance.
蘿蕊小心地把這朵漂亮的玫瑰花拿在手上，並**聞了聞**來享受玫瑰的芬芳。

▸ The dog first sniffed at the food and then devoured everything in less than a minute.
小狗先是**聞了聞**食物的味道，然後不到一分鐘就把東西吃個精光。

▸ With a frown, Mike sniffed at the man's low offer to purchase his used car.
麥可皺著眉頭，對男子開出低價購買他二手車的提議**嗤之以鼻**。

▸ Peter cleared his throat and gave a loud sniff before he began talking.
彼得清了清喉嚨，用力**吸了口氣**，然後才開始說話。

▸ As Rocky had a bad cold, he couldn't stop sniffing and wiping his nose.
洛奇得了重感冒，他不停地**抽鼻子**和擦鼻子。

16 vocal [ˋvokḷ] *a.* 聲音的，歌唱的 & *n.* (樂曲) 演唱部分 (常用複數)

片 vocal music 聲樂

衍 voice [vɔɪs] *n.* 聲音 & *vt.* 發聲 ①

▸ Which do you prefer, vocal or instrumental music?
聲樂跟純演奏音樂，你喜歡哪種？
*instrumental [ˏɪnstrəˋmɛntḷ] *a.* 純樂器演奏的

▸ In general, Valerie enjoyed the band's music, but she thought the vocals could be improved.
總體而言，薇洛莉喜歡該樂團的音樂，但她覺得**演唱部分**可以再改進。

17 photographic [ˏfotəˋgræfɪk] *a.* 攝影 (用) 的

片 a photographic memory
過目不忘的記憶力

衍 (1) photograph [ˋfotəˏgræf] *n.* 照片 (= photo) ①
(2) photography [fəˋtɑgrəfɪ] *n.* 攝影 ④
(3) photogenic [ˏfotəˋdʒɛnɪk] *a.* 上相的

▸ Paul began to take an interest in photography a few months ago, and since then he's spent a lot of money buying photographic equipment.
保羅在數月前開始對攝影產生興趣，從那時起他就花了不少錢購買**攝影**器材。

▸ Emily has a photographic memory. She can recite an entire book after she finishes it.
艾蜜莉有**過目不忘的本領**。她一本書看完後可以整本背出來。

18 graphic [ˋgræfɪk] *a.* 生動的，寫實的；(電腦) 繪圖的 & *n.* (書籍、電腦上的) 圖像 (恆用複數)

片 (1) in graphic detail 寫實地，詳盡地
(2) computer graphics 電腦圖像

似 vivid [ˋvɪvɪd] *a.* 寫實的，栩栩如生的 ③

▸ This film described the war in graphic detail.
這部電影**寫實地**描繪了戰爭場景。

▸ My sister is experienced in graphic design.
我老姊在**圖案**設計方面很有經驗。

▸ Justin works as an editor, so part of his job is arranging the graphics that accompany the stories.
賈斯汀擔任編輯，所以他工作的一部分是安排搭配故事的**圖片**。

19 allocate [ˋæləˏket] *vt.* 撥出 (經費)；配給，分配

片 allocate sth to sb
將某物分配給某人

▸ The government has allocated US$50,000 to Dr. Nicolas for his research.
政府**撥出** 5 萬美元的經費**給**尼可拉斯博士，以資助他的研究。

▸ Dozens of hobos lined up in front of the refuge, waiting to be allocated food.
幾十位遊民在收容所外排隊，等候食物**配給**。
*hobo [ˋhobo] *n.* 遊民

20 accessible [ækˋsɛsəbl̩] *a.* 可到達的；易取得的；易理解的

片 be accessible to sb
對某人而言容易取得 / 理解的

衍 access [ˋæksɛs] *n.* 門路，方法 ④
have access to sth　使用某物的機會 / 權利

反 inaccessible [ˌɪnækˋsɛsəbl̩]
a. 難以到達的；不易取得的

▸ That tropical island is not easily accessible.
那座熱帶小島不易**到達**。

▸ Confidential military documents are not accessible to the public.
一般大眾無法**取得**機密的軍事文件。

▸ Aaron's poetry is accessible to people of all ages.
艾倫寫的詩大人小孩都**看得懂**。

21 premium [ˋprimɪəm] *n.* 保險費；溢價 & *a.* 高級的

片 (1) (health) insurance premiums
(健) 保費
(2) be at a premium　稀少
(3) put / place a premium on sth
認為某事物很重要
(4) premium gas / gasoline
高級汽油

▸ Officials promised that health insurance premiums would not increase this year.
官員保證今年的**健保費**不會上漲。

▸ Jude paid a premium for that house because of its beautiful view.
因為那棟房子的視野極佳，所以茱德以**高於行情的價格**收購。

▸ We should've reserved a room because vacancy is at a premium during high season.
我們應該先訂房的，因為在旅遊旺季時旅館空房一間**難求**。

▸ Colleges that put a premium on education quality tend to have higher endowments.
注重教育品質的大學容易獲得較多的捐贈金。
*endowment [ɪnˋdaʊmənt] *n.* 捐贈金

▸ Do you know how much it costs for a gallon of premium gas now?
你知道目前一加崙的**高級汽油**要價多少嗎？

22 inject [ɪnˋdʒɛkt] *vt.* 注射 (藥物)；投注 (心力、資金)

片 inject A into B
將 A 注射到 B / 將 A 投注在 B

衍 injector [ɪnˋdʒɛktɚ] *n.* 噴射器

▸ Susan told Mr. Owens to remain calm while she injected the medicine into his arm.
蘇珊告訴歐文斯先生，當她**將藥注射進**他的手臂時要保持冷靜。

▸ The enterprise decided to inject more funds to save the market.
該企業決定**投注**更多資金挽救市場。

injection [ɪnˋdʒɛkʃən] *n.* 注射；打針

片 give sb an injection　給某人打針

似 shot [ʃɑt] *n.* 注射 ②

▶ After the injection, Mrs. Williams felt sleepy, and in a few minutes, she was completely asleep.
威廉斯女士被注入藥物後昏昏欲睡，幾分鐘過後她就完全睡著了。

▶ The young doctor gave that child who had a fever an injection.
這名年輕醫師幫那個在發燒的小孩打針。

23 endorse [ɪnˋdɔrs] *vt.* 為（票據）背書；為（產品）代言；贊同

片 endorse a check　在支票上背書

▶ Would you endorse the check, please?
請你為本支票背書，好嗎？

▶ This brand has been selling like hot cakes since the basketball player began endorsing it.
自從這位籃球選手開始代言該品牌後，它就一直熱銷至今。

▶ The President is likely to endorse a ban on smoking in public places.
該總統有可能贊同公共場所禁菸的禁令。

endorsement [ɪnˋdɔrsmənt] *n.* 簽署；代言，業配；支持，認可

▶ Since the check lacked endorsement, the bank couldn't cash it.
由於這張支票沒有簽名，所以銀行無法兌現。

▶ Some people think celebrities shouldn't make money from endorsements of products they don't even use.
有些人認為名人不該代言他們自己也沒用過的產品來賺錢。

▶ The project was still waiting for endorsement from the government, and it could not proceed until then.
這份計畫仍在等待政府的許可，獲准後才可以繼續進行。

24 accounting [əˋkaʊntɪŋ] *n.* 會計（學）（不可數）

衍 accountant [əˋkaʊntənt] *n.* 會計師；會計人員 ④

▶ Eddie sued the accounting company for having mismanaged his funds.
艾迪控告該會計公司不當處置他的資金。

25 auction [ˋɔkʃən] *n.* & *vt.* 拍賣

片 at the auction　在拍賣會上

▶ This famous painting by Picasso was sold for 4.4 million dollars at the auction.
畢卡索這幅知名油畫在拍賣會上以 440 萬美元賣出。

▶ The costumes from that famous movie were auctioned to raise money for charity.
那部知名電影裡的服裝被拿去拍賣，為慈善機構募款。

26 arrogant [ˋærəgənt] *a.* 傲慢的

衍 arrogance [ˋærəgəns] *n.* 傲慢

似 (1) cocky [ˋkɑkɪ] *a.* 驕傲自大的
(2) haughty [ˋhɔtɪ] *a.* 高傲的

▶ The arrogant young man shows no respect for the senior colleagues of the company.
那個**傲慢的**年輕人對公司的資深同事不尊重。

27 adverse [ædˋvɝs] *a.* 不利的，負面的

片 (1) have an adverse effect on...
對……有不利影響
(2) adverse weather conditions
不利的天氣條件

衍 adversity [ədˋvɝsətɪ] *n.* 逆境
in the face of adversity 面對逆境

▶ Gary was admired for his courage in the face of adversity.
蓋瑞因他面對逆境時的勇氣而受到讚賞。

▶ Experts fear the merger of the two companies will have adverse effects on stock prices.
專家擔心這兩家公司的合併將會**對**股價**有不利的影響**。

▶ All flights to L.A. have been canceled due to adverse weather conditions.
所有前往洛杉磯的班機都因為**天候條件不佳**而取消。

28 alcoholic [ˌælkəˋhɔlɪk] *a.* 酒精的 & *n.* 酗酒的人

片 an alcoholic beverage
含酒精的飲料

衍 (1) alcohol [ˋælkəˌhɔl] *n.* 酒精 ④
(2) non-alcoholic [ˌnɑnælkəˋhɔlɪk]
a. 不含酒精的
a non-alcoholic drink
非酒精飲料
= a soft drink

▶ Pregnant women should avoid drinking alcoholic beverages.
孕婦應避免喝**有酒精的飲料**。

▶ Helen's husband used to be an alcoholic, but he's turned over a new leaf.
海倫的先生以前是個**酒鬼**，但他現在改過自新了。

29 alongside [əˌlɔŋˋsaɪd] *prep.* 沿著……旁邊 (= alongside of) & *adv.* 靠邊地 (= along)

▶ The police car slowed down and pulled up alongside the curb.
= The police car slowed down and pulled up alongside of the curb.
這輛警車放慢速度，並**緊靠**路邊停了下來。
*curb [kɝb] *n.* 路邊

▶ A black limousine drew up alongside, and a man wearing a black suit and a pair of sunglasses stepped out.
一臺黑色禮車**靠邊**停下，一名身穿黑色西裝、帶著太陽眼鏡的男子走下車來。
*limousine [ˋlɪməˌzin] *n.* 大型豪華轎車

30 articulate [ɑrˋtɪkjələt] *a.* 善於表達的，口才好的 & [ɑrˋtɪkjə͵let] *vt.* 明確表達；清楚地發音

似 express [ɪkˋsprɛs] *vt.* 表達 ②

反 inarticulate [͵ɪnɑrˋtɪkjələt] *a.* 口齒不清的

- The audience was fascinated by the professor's articulate speech.
  觀眾深受這名教授的好口才所吸引。
- Sometimes I find it hard to articulate the complicated feelings I have.
  我有時候很難表達我所感受到的複雜情緒。
- It can be troublesome for learners of a foreign language to correctly articulate the sounds of that language.
  對於學習外語的人來說，要正確清晰地發出某語言的發音可能會很麻煩。

eloquent [ˋɛləkwənt] *a.* 口才好的

- Rod is a very promising salesperson. He's not only eloquent, but well-versed in the art of persuasion.
  羅德是個很有前途的售貨員。他不但口齒清晰，又精通推銷的藝術。
  *well-versed [͵wɛlˋvɝst] *a.* 熟知的

31 calcium [ˋkælsɪəm] *n.* 鈣（不可數）

片 be rich / high in calcium　富含鈣質

- Dairy products are rich in calcium, which helps to strengthen our bones and teeth.
  乳酪製品富含鈣質，幫助強化我們的骨骼以及牙齒。

32 cruise [kruz] *vi.* （乘船、飛機）航行；（車緩慢）巡行，巡邏 & *n.* 乘船遊蕩

片 take a cruise　乘船遊蕩

衍 (1) cruising [ˋkruzɪŋ] *n.* 乘遊輪遊覽
(2) cruiser [ˋkrusɚ] *n.* 遊輪；（海軍）巡洋艦

- The airplane is now cruising at an altitude of 30,000 feet.
  飛機現在正在 3 萬英尺的高度航行。
- We spent the whole night cruising down the highway in our truck.
  我們整晚開著小卡車在公路上閒晃。
- A police car cruised through the street each night.
  每晚都有輛警車在街上巡邏。
- My dream is to take a round-the-world cruise.
  我的夢想是搭船航遊全世界。

33 ecology [ɪˋkɑlədʒɪ] *n.* 生態環境

衍 ecologist [ɪˋkɑlədʒɪst] *n.* 生態學者

- Plans to build a nuclear plant could endanger the delicate ecology of this area.
  核電廠的興建計畫可能會危害該區脆弱的生態環境。

ecological [ˌɛkəˋlɑdʒɪkḷ / ˌikəˋlɑdʒɪkḷ] *a.* 生態(學)的

衍 ecologically [ˌikəˋlɑdʒɪkḷɪ] *adv.* 在生態方面

▸ The accident of Chernobyl was one of the most serious ecological disasters recorded in human history.
車諾比事故是人類史上所載最嚴重的**生態**浩劫之一。

ecosystem [ˋɛkoˌsɪstəm / ˋikoˌsɪstəm] *n.* 生態系統

▸ Although small, the pond was a rich ecosystem full of numerous species of plant life, aquatic animals, and insects.
這個池塘雖然小，但有一個豐富的**生態系統**，充滿數不清的植物、水生動物和昆蟲。

34 cocaine [koˋken] *n.* 古柯鹼

▸ Cocaine trafficking in this country is punishable by death.
在該國走私**古柯鹼**可判處死刑。
*trafficking [ˋtræfɪkɪŋ] *n.* 走私
punishable [ˋpʌnɪʃəbḷ] *a.* 可依法懲處的

35 directory [dəˋrɛktərɪ] *n.* 簿；冊；名錄

片 a telephone directory 電話簿
= a phone book

▸ The Yellow Pages is a classified telephone directory that lists the numbers of companies and individuals who offer services.
《黃頁》是分類的**電話簿**，裡頭列了公司行號跟提供各式服務人員的電話。

2001-2008

1 exile [ˋɛksaɪl / ˋɛgzaɪl] *n.* 流放，流亡（不可數）；流亡者（可數）& *vt.* 放逐

片 in exile 遭流放

似 (1) banish [ˋbænɪʃ] *vt.* 放逐
(2) outcast [ˋaʊt͵kæst] *n.* 被放逐的人

▸ Due to political reasons, the scholar was forced to flee his own country and live in exile.
由於政治因素，這位學者被迫逃離自己的國家，流亡過活。

▸ The famous political activist recently published a book about his life as an exile.
這位著名的政治運動家最近出版了一本關於他流亡生活的書。

▸ The dictator was exiled soon after the military coup.
這位獨裁者在軍事政變後不久就被流放了。
*coup [ku] *n.* 政變

2 extinct [ɪkˋstɪŋkt] *a.* 絕種的

片 (1) become extinct 滅絕，絕種
(2) an extinct volcano 死火山
（已無爆發可能的火山）

▸ Scientists warn that several species of whales are going to become extinct if illegal whaling continues.
科學家警告，若不法獵捕鯨魚的情況持續下去，數種鯨魚將面臨絕種。

extinction [ɪkˋstɪŋkʃən] *n.* 絕種

片 be on the verge / edge / brink of extinction 瀕臨絕種，即將消逝

▸ Many languages in the world are on the verge of extinction.
世界上有許多語言即將消逝。

3 format [ˋfɔrmæt] *vt.* 格式化；編排 & *n.* (電腦檔案) 格式；(書籍、電視節目) 形式，安排

三 format, formatted [ˋfɔrmætɪd], formatted

似 (1) arrange [əˋrendʒ] *vt.* 安排；排列 ②
(2) arrangement [əˋrendʒmənt] *n.* 安排，布置 ②

▸ You will have to format your disk to get rid of the virus.
要除掉病毒，你得要將硬碟格式化才行。

▸ The reference book is easy to use, because its layout is formatted in a reader-friendly manner.
這本工具書很好用，因為它的版面是以便利讀者的方式所編排的。

▸ An updated version of this program enables it to support up to fifteen different music file formats.
該程式的升級版本使它能支援多達 15 種不同的音樂檔案格式。

▸ According to the company's website, all of the books are available in either print or electronic format.
根據該公司的網站，所有書籍皆可以印刷本或電子檔的形式購買。

4 gloomy [ˋglumɪ] *a.* 陰暗的；不樂觀的，洩氣的

衍 gloom [glum] *n.* 陰暗；沮喪 ⑥
似 (1) dim [dɪm] *a.* 陰暗的 ③
(2) pessimistic [ˏpɛsəˋmɪstɪk] *a.* 悲觀的 ④
(3) depressed [dɪˋprɛst] *a.* 消沉的

▸ The scholar spent most of his life doing research in this small, gloomy lab.
這位學者花費半生在這間窄小陰暗的實驗室做研究。

▸ The doctor seemed to have a rather gloomy attitude about the patient's chance of recovery.
醫生似乎對病人的康復機率抱持著相當不樂觀的態度。

5 gorgeous [ˋgɔrdʒəs] *a.* 美麗的；極棒的

衍 gorgeously [ˋgɔrdʒəslɪ] *adv.* 美麗地
似 (1) beautiful [ˋbjutəfḷ] *a.* 美麗的 ①
(2) fabulous [ˋfæbjələs] *a.* 極好的 ⑤

▸ Sammy looks gorgeous in that white dress.
珊米穿那件白色洋裝看來美極了。

▸ The weather has been quite rainy and unpleasant for the past few days, but today it is absolutely gorgeous.
過去幾天的天氣不太好一直在下雨，但今天的天氣真的好極了。

6 gravity [ˋgrævətɪ] *n.* 地心引力；嚴重性（皆不可數）

片 the gravity of... ……的嚴重性
衍 (1) grave [grev] *a.* 嚴重的，重大的 ④
(2) gravitation [ˏgrævəˋteʃən] *n.* 萬有引力
似 seriousness [ˋsɪrɪəsnəs] *n.* 嚴重性

▸ We are able to walk on the ground because of gravity.
我們因為有地心引力才能在地面上行走。

▸ Apparently our boss did not understand the gravity of the situation.
我們老闆似乎並不了解情況的嚴重性。

7 greed [grid] *n.* 貪心（不可數）

衍 greedy [ˋgridɪ] *a.* 貪心的 ③
似 avarice [ˋævərəs] *n.* 貪婪

▸ That official has paid a dear price for his greed. He was sentenced to 10 years in prison for taking bribes.
該位官員因為貪心付出慘痛的代價。他拿了賄款，被判了 10 年徒刑。
*dear [dɪr] *a.* 昂貴的

8 moan [mon] *vi.* 哀嚎 & *vt.* & *vi.* 抱怨 & *n.* 哀嚎聲

片 moan about... 抱怨……
似 groan [gron] *vi.* 哀嚎 & *vt.* & *vi.* 抱怨 & *n.* 哀嚎聲 ⑥

▸ Everyone in the office moaned when Frank began to tell the same old jokes.
當法蘭克又重複講同樣的笑話時，辦公室內每個人都哀哀叫。

▸ "I hate to work, but I need the money," Lisa moaned.
莉莎抱怨道：『我討厭工作，但我需要錢』。

▸ Tired of hearing her friend moan about the problems in his life, Bonnie told him to quit complaining.
邦妮厭倦聽她朋友抱怨自己生活中的問題，因此告訴他別再訴苦了。

- The rescuers heard a low moan from beneath the debris of the collapsed building.
  搜救人員聽見從倒塌的建築物廢墟中傳來的微弱**呻吟聲**。

whine [(h)waɪn] *vi.* 哀鳴 & *vt.* & *vi.* 抱怨 & *n.* 哀鳴聲

片 whine about... 抱怨……

- The puppy whines in fear when it hears loud noises.
  這隻小狗聽到大聲的噪音時會害怕地**哀鳴**。
- "Can I have a Big Mac instead of spaghetti for lunch?" Johnny whined.
  強尼**抱怨道**：『我午餐可不可以不要吃義大利麵，改吃大麥克呢？』。
- When his daughter started to whine about having to do her homework, Steven told her to do it immediately.
  當史蒂芬的女兒開始**抱怨**要做家庭作業，他就叫她馬上去做。
- The whine of the dogs in the middle of the night gave me the creeps.
  大半夜狗的**哀鳴聲**讓我毛骨悚然。
  *give sb the creeps 使某人毛骨悚然

9 guideline [ˋgaɪdlaɪn] *n.* 行動綱領，指導方針（常用複數）

衍 (1) guide [gaɪd] *n.* 指南；導遊 & *vt.* 指導 ②
(2) guidance [ˋgaɪdn̩s] *n.* 指導，引導 ③

- I think we'll need a new set of guidelines for the staff members to improve their work efficiency.
  我想公司職員需要一套新的**行動綱領**，好改善他們的工作效率。

10 handicapped [ˋhændɪˌkæpt] *a.* 殘障的

片 the handicapped （泛指）殘障人士（後接複數動詞）

衍 handicap [ˋhændɪˌkæp] *vt.* 使有障礙 & *n.* 不利的條件 ⑥

似 (1) crippled [ˋkrɪpl̩d] *a.* 跛的
(2) disabled [dɪsˋebl̩d] *a.* 有缺陷的

延伸 由於 handicapped 與 crippled 均帶有歧視意味，現今多用 physically challenged 表示『行動不便的』，以 people with disabilities 表示『行動不便人士』。

- It is generally considered impolite to call people with disabilities "handicapped."
  以殘障稱呼身心障礙人士通常被視為無禮。

11 lame [lem] *a.* 跛腳的，瘸的；沒說服力的

片 (1) a lame excuse / explanation 一個沒說服力的藉口 / 理由
(2) a lame duck 跛腳鴨（任期即將結束而變得較無影響力的官員）

▸ Ever since a car accident when she was young, Heather had been lame in her right leg.
海瑟小時候經歷一場車禍後，她的右腳就瘸了。

▸ Matt always makes up lame excuses when he is late for work.
麥特上班遲到時總是會編造一些**爛理由**。

▸ The governor is pretty much a lame duck now. There's only one month left before the newly elected governor takes office.
這位州長現在真的是**跛腳鴨**了。距離新當選的州長赴任只剩一個月。

12 heir [ɛr] *n.* 繼承人

片 the heir to... 為……的繼承人
= the successor to...

衍 heiress [ˋɛrəs] *n.* 女繼承人

似 successor [səkˋsɛsɚ] *n.* 繼承人 ⑤

▸ To everyone's surprise, the heir to the throne turned out to be the king's illegitimate son.
出乎眾人意料之外，王位的**繼承人**結果是國王的私生子。
*illegitimate [ˌɪlɪˋdʒɪtəmət] *a.* 私生的

13 herb [(h)ɝb] *n.* 藥草

衍 herbal [ˋ(h)ɝbḷ] *a.* 藥草的

▸ Some people are skeptical about the medicinal effects of certain herbs.
有些人對某些**藥草**的醫療效果存疑。
*skeptical [ˋskɛptɪkḷ] *a.* 懷疑的
medicinal [məˋdɪsənḷ] *a.* 用於治療的

14 hostage [ˋhɑstɪdʒ] *n.* 人質

片 hold / take sb hostage 扣押某人當人質（此片語中的 hostage 恆為單數）

似 captive [ˋkæptɪv] *n.* 俘虜 ⑥

▸ All the hostages were released after the police met the demands of the terrorists.
在警方滿足恐怖分子的要求後，所有的**人質**都被釋放了。

▸ The bank staff and customers were taken hostage by the robbers.
銀行行員跟顧客都被搶匪**挾持作為人質**。

15 idiot [ˋɪdɪət] *n.* 白痴

似 fool [ful] *n.* 笨蛋 ①

▸ The character of Benjy Compson in *The Sound and The Fury* is often referred to as an idiot.
《喧嘩與騷動》中班傑．康普森這個角色常被說成是**白痴**。

16 mint [mɪnt] *n.* 薄荷（不可數）

片 be in mint condition　全新的

延伸 mint 亦有『造幣廠』之意，從造幣廠剛印好出來的錢完全無缺點，固有上列片語。

▸ Mint is often used as a seasoning that adds flavor to food.
薄荷常用來做調味料，增添食物風味。
*seasoning [ˋsizṇɪŋ] *n.* 調味料

▸ I can't believe that this record is still in mint condition. It's a real bargain!
我不敢相信這張唱片還是全新的。真是撿到便宜貨了！

17 tangle [ˋtæŋg!] *vt.* & *vi.* (使) 糾結 & *n.* 糾結 (的一團)

片 (1) get tangled up in...
捲入某件（不好的）事情中
(2) tangle with sb
與某人爭吵，招惹某人
(3) a tangle of...　糾結的一團……

反 untangle [ʌnˋtæŋg!] *vt.* 解開

▸ When Bart put his earphones in his pocket, he tangled the wires badly.
巴特把耳機放進口袋時，把耳機線亂捲在一起。

▸ My hair tangles every morning when I wake up. It takes me a long time to untangle it.
每天早上醒來我的頭髮都糾在一起。要梳開來需要很長一段時間。

▸ How did that old lady get tangled up in the company's financial fraud? Wasn't she just a cleaner?
那位老太太怎麼會跟該公司金融詐欺案扯上關係？她不就只是個清潔工嗎？

▸ You may get hurt if you tangle with those people. They're extremely dangerous.
你去招惹那些人恐怕會受傷。他們非常危險。

▸ Jerry's brain was filled with a tangle of emotions when he learned that Mr. & Mrs. Wilson were not his biological parents.
當傑瑞知道威爾遜夫婦不是他的親生父母時，他腦子裡充滿各種糾結的情緒。

18 columnist [ˋkɑləmnɪst] *n.* 專欄作家

衍 column [ˋkɑləm] *n.* 專欄 ③

▸ The columnist's witty style combined with black humor made him extraordinarily popular among readers.
該專欄作家結合黑色幽默的風趣文筆使他大受讀者的歡迎。

19 witty [ˋwɪtɪ] *a.* 機智的；風趣的

衍 wit [wɪt] *n.* 機智；風趣 ④

似 (1) humorous [ˋhjumərəs]
a. 幽默的 ③
(2) amusing [əˋmjuzɪŋ] *a.* 有趣的

▸ We were all entertained by Raymond's witty remarks over dinner.
晚餐時大家都因為雷蒙風趣的談吐而感到十分愉快。

20 consecutive [kən`sɛkjutɪv] *a.* 連續(不斷)的

似 (1) successive [sək`sɛsɪv] *a.* 連續的 ⑥
(2) in a row　連續地

延伸 for hours / days / weeks on end 接連數小時 / 天 / 星期不停(此片語與 on end 並用，hours、days 或 weeks 之前不可再加上數字)

▸ Lisa didn't sleep well for days on end.
麗莎**好幾天**沒睡好了。

▸ The euro has appreciated in value for two consecutive weeks.
= The euro has appreciated in value for two successive weeks.
= The euro has appreciated in value for two weeks in a row.
歐元已經**連續**升值了**兩個星期**。
*appreciate [ə`priʃɪ,et] *vi.* (土地、貨幣) 升值

21 consensus [kən`sɛnsəs] *n.* 共識

片 reach a consensus (on...) (就……) 達成共識

似 agreement [ə`grimənt] *n.* 同意 ①

▸ So far we haven't reached any consensus on that matter.
到目前為止我們尚未就那件事**達成**任何**共識**。

22 debris [də`bri] *n.* 廢墟，殘垣斷瓦(不可數)

似 (1) ruin [`ruɪn] *n.* 廢墟 ④
(2) relic [`rɛlɪk] *n.* 遺物；遺跡；遺俗 ⑥
(3) remains [rɪ`menz] *n.* 殘留物；遺跡(恆用複數)

▸ The church was reduced to a pile of debris in the earthquake.
教堂在那次地震中化為一片**廢墟**。
*be reduced to...　淪為 / 化成……

23 debut [də`bju / `debju] *n.* & *vi.* 初次登臺

片 make one's debut　某人初次登臺

▸ Ryan made his debut on the big screen in 2020.
萊恩**初次**在大銀幕上**演出**是 2020 年。

▸ The new TV drama series is going to debut at 8 p.m. tonight.
這齣新的電視連續劇將在今晚 8 點**初次放映**。

24 expertise [,ɛkspɚ`tiz] *n.* 專業知識(不可數)

片 the expertise in... 在……方面的專業知識

衍 expert [`ɛkspɝt] *n.* 專家 ②

似 know-how [`no,hau] *n.* 知識技能

▸ Sharon has remarkable expertise in the history of wars.
雪倫有戰爭史**方面的專業知識**。

25 facilitate [fəˋsɪlə͵tet] *vt.* 促進，幫助

衍 facilitation [fə͵sɪləˋteʃən] *n.* 促進

似 assist [əˋsɪst] *vt.* 幫助 ③

▸ The new policies are expected to facilitate economic growth.
這些新的政策預期會帶動經濟成長。

26 genetic [dʒəˋnɛtɪk] *a.* 基因的；遺傳(學)的

片 a genetic disease　遺傳性疾病

衍 (1) gene [dʒin] *n.* 基因 ④
(2) genetically [dʒəˋnɛtɪklɪ] *adv.* 從基因方面
genetically modified food
基因改良食物(常縮寫成 GM food)

▸ The doctor suggested I do a genetic test so he could understand my disease better.
醫師建議我做基因測試檢查以更了解我的疾病。

genetics [dʒəˋnɛtɪks] *n.* 基因學(不可數)

▸ The study of genetics has made the prevention of birth defects possible.
基因學的研究可預防先天性缺陷。

27 immune [ɪˋmjun] *a.* 免疫的

片 (1) be immune to...　對……免疫
(2) the immune system　免疫系統

反 susceptible [səˋsɛptəbl̩] *a.* 易患(某疾病)的
be susceptible to...　容易感染……

▸ After you receive this vaccine, you will be immune to the contagious disease.
你打過這劑疫苗後就會對這個傳染病免疫。
*vaccine [ˋvæksin] *n.* 疫苗

28 drought [draʊt] *n.* 乾旱

▸ The change of climate has resulted in the most severe drought in one hundred years.
氣候變遷造成百年來最嚴重的一次乾旱。

29 kidnap [ˋkɪdnæp] *vt.* 綁架

三 kidnap, kidnaped / kidnapped [ˋkɪdnæpt], kidnaped / kidnapped

衍 kidnapping [ˋkɪdnæpɪŋ] *n.* 綁架

似 abduct [æbˋdʌkt] *vt.* 誘拐；綁架

▸ The gangster kidnapped the daughter of the millionaire and demanded a ransom.
歹徒綁架了這名百萬富翁的女兒並要求贖金。
*ransom [ˋrænsəm] *n.* 贖金

30 forum [ˋfɔrəm] *n.* 論壇

片 a forum on...　有關……的論壇

▸ Thousands of people attended the forum on environmental protection.
上千人出席這場有關環保的論壇。

31 grill [grɪl] vt. (用烤架) 烤 & n. 烤架

似 barbecue [ˋbɑrbɪkju] vt. & vi. 在戶外烤肉 ②

延伸 (1) bake [bek] vt. & vi. (用烤箱) 烤，烘 ②
(2) roast [rost] vt. & vi. (用炭火) 烤 ③
(3) broil [brɔɪl] vt. & vi. (用瓦斯爐或烤架) 烤 ⑥

▸ Our beef is grilled to perfection and topped with fresh onions.
我們的牛肉烤得恰到好處，也在上面加上新鮮的洋蔥。
*top [tɑp] vt. 在表面上放……

▸ Grill the sausages until they are sizzling and then remove them from the pan.
把香腸烤到熟得茲茲響，然後把它們從平底鍋拿起。
*sizzle [ˋsɪzl̩] vi. (熱油) 發出嘶嘶聲

▸ Since chicken takes longer to cook on a barbecue than other meat, Glen put the chicken on the grill first.
由於烤肉時雞肉要花比其他肉類更多的時間來烤，所以葛倫先把雞肉放在烤架上。

32 implement [ˋɪmplə͵mɛnt] vt. 實施 & [ˋɪmpləmənt] n. 工具，用具

片 (1) implement a plan 實施計畫
= carry out a plan
(2) garden / farming implements 花園 / 農業用具

▸ The authorities concerned have implemented a plan to help control traffic.
有關當局已實施了一項計畫來協助管制交通。

▸ In his grandfather's basement, Adam found some strange implements and assumed they were used in farming.
亞當在爺爺的地下室發現一些奇怪的工具，並認為它們是農用的。

33 insane [ɪnˋsen] a. 瘋狂的

衍 insanity [ɪnˋsænətɪ] n. 瘋狂
似 crazy [ˋkrezɪ] a. 瘋狂的 ①
反 sane [sen] a. 精神正常的；明智的

▸ It would be insane to go fishing when a strong typhoon is approaching.
在強颱來臨前跑去釣魚是瘋狂的行為。

34 recession [rɪˋsɛʃən] n. (經濟) 蕭條

片 (an) economic recession 經濟蕭條
衍 recede [rɪˋsid] vi. 後退
似 depression [dɪˋprɛʃən] n. (經濟) 蕭條 ④

▸ The economy has suffered so much recently that many people believe there will soon be a deep recession.
最近經濟承受許多打擊，很多人都認為不久後就會有很嚴重的經濟衰退。

35 nutrition [n(j)uˋtrɪʃən] n. 營養 (不可數)

衍 nutritious [n(j)uˋtrɪʃəs] a. 有營養的 ④
似 nourishment [ˋnɝɪʃmənt] n. 營養 (不可數) ⑥

▸ Proper nutrition is essential for patients if they want to have a quick recovery.
適當的營養對於希望早日康復的病患來說是很重要的。

🔊 2035-2039

反 malnutrition [ˌmæln(j)uˋtrɪʃən]
n. 營養失調

---

nutrient [ˋn(j)utrɪənt] *n.* 養分 & *a.* 營養的，滋養的

▸ Most plants absorb minerals and essential nutrients directly from the soil as they grow.
大部分的植物在成長時，會直接從土壤吸收礦物質和必要的養分。

▸ The nutrient value of fruits and vegetables is high; in contrast, it is low in desserts and junk food.
蔬果的營養價值很高，相反地，甜點和垃圾食物的營養價值很低。

36 migration [maɪˋgreʃən] *n.* 遷移

衍 migrate [ˋmaɪˌgret] *vi.* 遷移

▸ The scientist attached a tracking device to the bird to track its seasonal migration route.
科學家在這隻鳥身上安裝追蹤器以追蹤它的季節性遷徙路線。

37 optional [ˋɑpʃənl̩] *a.* 可選擇的；選修的

衍 option [ˋɑpʃən] *n.* 選擇 ④
反 compulsory [kəmˋpʌlsərɪ] *a.* 必修的；強迫的 ⑤

▸ Some of the following courses are compulsory, while others are optional.
下列課程有一些是必修的，而其他則是選修的。

38 medication [ˌmɛdɪˋkeʃən] *n.* 藥物

片 take medication / medicine 服藥
衍 medicine [ˋmɛdəsən] *n.* 藥物 ①

▸ The doctor advised Tim to take medication for his stomach ulcer.
醫師勸告提姆服藥以治療胃潰瘍。
*ulcer [ˋʌlsɚ] *n.* 潰瘍

39 vinegar [ˋvɪnɪgɚ] *n.* 醋

延伸
(1) sugar [ˋʃʊgɚ] *n.* 糖 ①
(2) salt [sɔlt] *n.* 鹽 ①
(3) MSG 味精（為 monosodium glutamate 的縮寫）

▸ This dish will taste better if you add some vinegar.
如果你加點醋的話，這道菜會更好吃。

2101-2105

1 landlord [ˋlænd,lɔrd] *n.* 房東

延伸 tenant [ˋtɛnənt] *n.* 房客 ⑥

▸ My landlord wouldn't fix the air conditioner for me; instead, he told me to make do with the fan.
我的房東不願修理我的冷氣機；他要我電風扇湊合著用。
*make do with... 將就著……，湊合……

2 mansion [ˋmænʃən] *n.* 豪宅

似 manor [ˋmænɚ] *n.* 莊園

▸ The billionaire's mansion is located in Beverly Hills, where many Hollywood stars live.
這位億萬富翁的豪宅位於許多好萊塢明星居住的比佛利山莊。

3 masculine [ˋmæskjəlɪn] *a.* 男性的，男子氣概的 & *n.* 陽性詞

似 (1) male [mel] *a.* 男性的 & *n.* 男性 ②
(2) manly [ˋmænlɪ] *a.* 有男子氣概的
(3) macho [ˋmɑtʃo] *a.* 大男人作風的

反 feminine [ˋfɛmənɪn] *a.* 女性的 & *n.* 陰性詞 ⑥

▸ Peggy looks rather masculine with her new short haircut.
佩姬的短髮新造型讓她看起來很像男人。

4 mentor [ˋmɛntɔr] *n.* 導師，良師

似 teacher [ˋtitʃɚ] *n.* 老師 ①

▸ Mr. Johnson has been a mentor and a good friend to many of his students.
強森先生一直是他許多學生的良師益友。

5 nasty [ˋnæstɪ] *a.* 令人反感的；惡劣的，不友善的；嚴重的；惡毒的

似 (1) unpleasant [ʌnˋplɛzn̩t] *a.* 令人不快的
(2) disgusting [dɪsˋgʌstɪŋ] *a.* 噁心的
(3) mean [min] *a.* 刻薄的 ①
(4) unkind [ʌnˋkaɪnd] *a.* 刻薄的
(5) severe [səˋvɪr] *a.* 嚴重的 ④
(6) offensive [əˋfɛnsɪv] *a.* 冒犯的；令人不快的 ④

▸ Stinky tofu smells nasty but tastes great.
臭豆腐聞起來很糟但很好吃。

▸ When Paula saw the news on TV, she was shocked and wondered how some people could be so nasty to their own flesh and blood.
寶拉看見電視上那則新聞時很震驚，不解為何有人能對自己的親骨肉如此惡劣。
*flesh and blood 親骨肉

▸ I had a nasty headache when I woke up, so I took sick leave this morning.
我醒來時頭痛得厲害，所以早上請了病假。

2105-2114

▸ Frank's habit of making nasty remarks about people's appearances made him a pain in the neck to everyone in the office.
法蘭克習慣對別人外貌做**惡毒的**評論，所以辦公室每個人都覺得他很惹人厭。
*a pain in the neck　令人討厭的人 / 事

6 vow [vaʊ] *vt.* 發誓 & *n.* 誓言

片 (1) vow to V　發誓……
= make a vow to V
(2) vow that...　發誓……
= make a vow that...
(3) marriage / wedding vows
結婚誓詞

似 (1) swear [swɛr] *vt.* 發誓 ③
(2) oath [oθ] *n.* 誓言 ⑥

▸ Gary vowed to cherish and support his wife in the rest of his life.
= Gary made a vow to cherish and support his wife in the rest of his life.
蓋瑞**發誓**會用餘生珍惜與支持他的太太。

▸ The police inspector vowed that he would track down the killer and put him in jail.
= The police inspector made a vow that he would track down the killer and put him in jail.
該巡官**發誓**要找到凶手下落並送他去吃牢飯。

7 participant [pɑrˋtɪsəpənt] *n.* 參加者

衍 (1) participate [pɑrˋtɪsəˏpet]
vi. 參加（與介詞 in 並用）②
(2) participation [pɑrˏtɪsəˋpeʃən]
n. 參與 ④

▸ Participants of the convention include congressmen, retired generals, and senior government officials.
大會的**參加者**包括國會議員、退休將領及政府高階官員。

8 pulse [pʌls] *n.* 脈搏；（強烈且規律的）節拍 & *vi.*（強烈且規律地）拍動，跳動

片 (1) feel / take sb's pulse
量某人的脈搏
(2) a strong / weak pulse
脈搏很強 / 弱

▸ The doctor took my pulse and wrote me a prescription.
醫生幫我量**脈搏**、開立處方。

▸ Regina moved to the center of the dance floor, dancing to the pulse of the rhythm.
蕾吉娜移動到舞池正中央，隨著節奏的**節拍**跳舞。

▸ The computer screen pulsed with light, illuminating the darkness in the empty office.
電腦螢幕閃著光，照亮了空無一人的黑暗辦公室。
*illuminate [ɪˋluməˏnet] *vt.* 照亮

9 reminder [rɪˋmaɪndɚ] *n.* 提醒用的物品

片 a reminder of...　作為……的提醒
衍 remind [rɪˋmaɪnd] *vt.* 提醒，使想起 ③

▸ Before Jerry left for Europe, he gave me this watch as a constant reminder of our friendship.
傑瑞出發前往歐洲前給了我這只手錶，**使**我能時刻**想起**我們的友誼。

10 refuge [ˋrɛf judʒ] *n.* 避難 (不可數)；避難處 (可數)

片 (1) take / seek refuge (from...) in...
在……尋求庇護 (以躲避……)
(2) a wildlife refuge
野生動物保護區

衍 refugee [ˏrɛf jʊˋdʒi] *n.* 難民 ④

▸ The travelers took refuge from the rain in the deserted hut.
旅人**在**廢棄的小屋裡**躲**雨。

▸ This part of the mountain was declared by the government as a site of wildlife refuge.
這塊山地被政府公告為**野生動物保護區**。

11 vegetation [ˏvɛdʒəˋteʃən] *n.* 植物 (總稱，不可數)

似 plant [plænt] *n.* 植物；盆栽 (可數) ①

▸ There used to be abundant vegetation near the lake.
那座湖邊原本有很多**植物**。

12 scent [sɛnt] *n.* 氣味 & *vt.* 聞到，嗅出；(使) 充滿芳香

片 (1) a scent of... ……的氣味
(2) be scented with...
充滿……的芳香

似 smell [smɛl] *n.* 氣味 & *vt.* 聞到 ①

▸ The shampoo has a light scent of herb extracts.
這種洗髮精有一股淡淡的藥草精油**味**。
*extract [ˋɛkstrækt] *n.* 萃取物，精華

▸ Jason's dog scented the snake before his owner and began barking to warn him.
傑森的狗比主人先**聞到**蛇的氣味，並吠叫以警告牠的主人。

▸ The banquet hall was scented with candles and flowers before the wedding began.
婚禮開始前，宴會廳裡**充滿**著蠟燭和花朵**的芳香**。

13 sponge [spʌndʒ] *vt.* (用海綿) 擦拭 & *n.* 海綿

衍 sponger [ˋspʌndʒɚ] *n.* 米蟲，光吃飯不辦事的人

▸ Bob sponged the spilled juice off the table.
鮑伯把桌上濺出來的果汁**用海綿擦乾**了。

▸ I always keep a clean sponge by the sink.
我總會在水槽旁擺一塊乾淨的**海綿**。

14 premier [prɪˋmɪr] *n.* 總理，首相 & *a.* 首要的

似 (1) premiere [prɪˋmɪr] *n.* 首映 ⑥
(2) prime minister [ˏpraɪm ˋmɪnɪstɚ]
總理，首相

▸ The premier declared a state of national emergency in his televised address.
該**總理**在電視演說中宣布國家進入緊急狀態。

▸ Wimbledon hosts one of the premier international tennis tournaments every year.
溫布頓每年主辦**重要的**國際網球錦標賽事之一。

15 rental [ˋrɛntl̩] *n.* 出租

片 (1) a car rental company　租車公司
(2) a rental car　租來的車
= a rental

衍 rent [rɛnt] *n.* 租金 & *vt.* 出租 ②

▸ Our company has been one of the top car rental agencies in town ever since it was founded in 2010.
自從 2010 年創辦以來，我們公司就一直是城裡汽車出租公司的佼佼者。

16 superb [suˋpɝb] *a.* 極好的

似 excellent [ˋɛksələnt] *a.* 絕佳的，出色的 ①

▸ This course offers you a superb opportunity to enhance your interpersonal skills.
這門課程是你加強人際關係技巧的極好機會。
*interpersonal [ˌɪntɚˋpɝsənl̩] *a.* 人際的

17 theft [θɛft] *n.* 偷竊（案）

似 burglary [ˋbɝglərɪ] *n.* 破門盜竊

▸ Taking other people's stuff without their permission is not borrowing. It's theft.
未經許可拿走別人的東西不叫借用，而是偷竊。

▸ There have been quite a few thefts in the hotel since the beginning of the holiday season.
自從假期開始之後，該飯店已發生了好幾件竊案。

18 spouse [spaus] *n.* 配偶

▸ Staff members were warned not to discuss the matter, even with their spouses.
職員遭警告不得與他人，即便是配偶，討論此事。

19 undo [ʌnˋdu] *vt.* 解開；消除

三 undo, undid [ʌnˋdɪd], undone [ʌnˋdʌn]

▸ I undid the bag and took out the books.
我打開包包，取出書本。

▸ The company is trying to undo some of the damage caused by the scandal.
公司正試圖消弭該醜聞所帶來的傷害。

▸ What is done cannot be undone.
已經做過事的沒法消除 / 木已成舟。── 諺語，喻追悔過去犯下的錯誤於事無補

20 rehearsal [rɪˋhɝsl̩] *n.* 排演，練習

片 a dress rehearsal（正式演出前）最後一次的彩排

衍 rehearse [rɪˋhɝs] *vt.* & *vi.* 彩排，排演 ⑥

▸ The singer is wearing makeup for the dress rehearsal.
這位歌手正在上妝，準備最後的彩排。

21 rhetoric [ˋrɛtərɪk] *n.* 辭令，空洞不實的言論；修辭學（皆不可數）

衍 rhetorical [rɪˋtɔrɪkḷ] *a.* 修辭（學）的

▸ The mayor's promise to rid the city of corruption was regarded by some commentators as mere political rhetoric.
市長終結該市貪汙的承諾被某些評論家認為只是政治性修辭。

▸ Rhetoric is about how to use language effectively.
修辭學是關於如何有效使用言詞。

22 seminar [ˋsɛməˏnɑr] *n.* 研討會，講座

片 (1) attend / hold a seminar 出席 / 舉辦研討會
(2) a seminar on... ⋯⋯的研討會 / 講座

似 (1) meeting [ˋmitɪŋ] *n.* 會議 ①
(2) discussion [dɪˋskʌʃən] *n.* 討論 ②

▸ Experts from a diverse range of research fields attended the seminar.
這場研討會有各個研究領域的專家出席。

▸ The company regularly holds seminars on health issues.
該公司會定期舉辦健康議題講座。

23 vomit [ˋvɑmət] *vi.* & *vt.* 嘔吐 & *n.* 嘔吐物（不可數）

似 (1) throw up 嘔吐
(2) puke [pjuk] *vi.* & *vt.* 嘔吐 & *n.* 嘔吐物（不可數）

▸ I was so ill last week that whenever I tried to eat, I vomited.
我上禮拜病得很厲害，只要我吃東西就會吐出來。

▸ After a night of heavy drinking, Meghan spent the next morning vomiting the contents of her stomach into the toilet.
梅根經過一晚狂飲後，隔天早上對著馬桶狂吐腹中物。

▸ Tim didn't realize his cat was sick until he noticed the vomit on the kitchen floor.
提姆直到看見廚房地板上的嘔吐物才發現他的貓生病了。

24 distract [dɪˋstrækt] *vt.* 使分心

片 distract sb from sth
使某人在某事上分心

衍 distraction [dɪˋstrækʃən] *n.* 分心 ⑥

▸ Noise from the street distracted the writer from his work.
街上的吵雜聲讓這名作家無法專心工作。

25 activist [ˋæktəvɪst] *n.* 激進分子

衍 activism [ˋæktəvɪzəm] *n.* 激進主義

▸ The animal rights activists protested against the killing of stray animals.
動物權益分子抗議撲殺流浪動物的行為。

26 chunk [tʃʌŋk] *n.* (肉、木材等的) 一大塊

片 a chunk of　一大塊……

▸ Cut the pork into chunks and dip them in the sauce.
把豬肉切成塊，放進醬汁裡浸泡。

27 contractor [ˋkɑntræktɚ] *n.* 承包商

衍 contract [ˋkɑntrækt] *n.* 契約 & [kənˋtrækt] *vt.* 感染 ②
contract a disease　感染疾病

▸ The contractor provides a complete home renovation at a reasonable price.
這家**承包商**以合理的價格提供完善的房屋修繕服務。
*renovation [ˏrɛnəˋveʃən] *n.* 修繕

28 lounge [laundʒ] *n.* 會客廳，休息室 & *vi.* 懶散地躺 / 坐；消磨時間

片 (1) a lounge bar
（具放鬆、慵懶氣氛的）酒吧
(2) lounge music　沙發音樂
(3) the departure lounge　候機室

▸ Students are not allowed to enter the teachers' lounge unless there is an emergency.
除非有緊急狀況，否則學生不准進教師**休息室**。

▸ After a long day at work, Steven was eager to enjoy a cold drink while lounging in his beach chair.
史蒂芬經過一天漫長的工作後，迫不及待想要**躺**在他的海灘椅上享用一杯冷飲。

▸ With so many comfy sofas, the café is a great place to lounge on a Saturday afternoon.
這間咖啡廳有這麼多舒適的沙發，是個可以在週六午後**消磨時間**的好地方。
*comfy [ˋkʌmfɪ] *a.* 舒服的

29 eligible [ˋɛlədʒəbl̩] *a.* 合格的

片 (1) be eligible for...　有……的資格
= be qualified for...
(2) be eligible to V　有資格去做……
= be qualified to V

衍 ineligible [ɪnˋɛlədʒəbl̩] *a.* 沒資格的

▸ To be eligible for this promotion, candidates must meet the following requirements.
要**具備**升遷**資格**，應徵者必須達到下列需求。

▸ Both domestic and foreign companies are eligible to bid for the building contract.
國內和國外的公司都**有資格**投標爭取這個營建合約。

30 hormone [ˋhɔrmon] *n.* 荷爾蒙

衍 hormonal [hɔrˋmonl̩] *a.* 荷爾蒙的

▸ Symptoms of hormone imbalance in women may be early signs of many things, such as pregnancy or the onset of menopause.
女性體內**荷爾蒙**不均衡的症狀可能是許多事的前兆，像是懷孕或是更年期的開始。
*onset [ˋɑnˏsɛt] *n.* 開始
menopause [ˋmɛnəˏpɔz] *n.* 更年期

31 fraud [frɔd] *n.* 詐騙，詐欺；騙子

衍 fraudulent [ˋfrɔdʒələnt] *a.* 詐欺的

似 (1) deception [dɪˋsɛpʃən] *n.* 欺騙
(2) deceit [dɪˋsit] *n.* 欺騙；不誠實

▸ Convicted of credit card fraud, the American was sentenced to three years in prison.
信用卡**詐欺**罪名成立後，這位美國人被判刑 3 年。

▸ Brendan claimed to be a psychic, but most people recognized him as a fraud.
布蘭登自稱是通靈者，但大部分的人都覺得他是個**騙子**。
*psychic [ˋsaɪkɪk] *n.* 靈媒，通靈者

32 premature [ˌpriməˋtʃʊr] *a.* 過早的；早產的

片 a premature baby 早產兒

衍 (1) mature [məˋtʃʊr] *a.* 成熟的 & *vi.* 成熟 ②
(2) immature [ˌɪməˋtʃʊr] *a.* 不成熟的

▸ The spokesman said it was still too premature to comment on the progress of the peace talks.
發言人指出，要針對和談的進展做出評論還言之**過早**。

▸ Two months before her due date, the woman went into labor and gave birth to a premature baby boy.
預產期兩個月前，這名女子分娩並生下了一名**早產兒男嬰**。

33 manipulate [məˋnɪpjəˌlet] *vt.* 操縱

衍 manipulation [məˌnɪpjəˋleʃən] *n.* 操縱

似 (1) control [kənˋtrol] *vt.* 控制 ②
(2) maneuver [məˋnuvɚ] *vt.* 操縱

▸ Throughout her political career, Linda has successfully used her charm to manipulate the media.
琳達在政治生涯中很成功地使用個人魅力去**操控**媒體。

34 recipient [rɪˋsɪpɪənt] *n.* 受領者 & *a.* 接受的

片 a recipient of... ……的受領者

▸ Marie Curie was the first female recipient of the Nobel Prize.
居禮夫人是第一位**獲得**諾貝爾獎的女性。

35 overturn [ˌovɚˋtɝn] *vt.* (使) 翻倒；打翻 & *vt.* & *n.* 推翻

似 knock over sth 打翻某物

▸ During the burglary, many of the desks and shelves in the office had been overturned.
辦公室被入門盜竊期間，許多桌子和架子都被**翻倒**了。

▸ Amy overturned a bottle of milk by accident.
艾咪不小心**打翻**了一瓶牛奶。

▸ The convict's life sentence was overturned by the Supreme Court.
該囚犯的無期徒刑在最高法院被**推翻**了。

2136-2143

36 pathetic [pəˋθɛtɪk] *a.* 可憐的，可悲的

似 pitiful [ˋpɪtɪfəl] *a.* 可憐的

▸ It's a pathetic sight to see the former millionaire reduced to begging for change.
看到這名百萬富豪淪落到在路邊討錢，真令人感到可悲。

37 pedestrian [pəˋdɛstrɪən] *n.* 行人 & *a.* 行人的；單調乏味的

比 pedestrian 指的是任何在街道上行走的人，而 passerby [ˏpæsɚˋbaɪ] 則指經過某街 / 路的路人，其複數為 passersby。

▸ Drivers should yield to pedestrians when they come to a crosswalk.
行駛至行人穿越道時，駕駛應禮讓行人先行。

▸ Barriers were installed on the street to separate the pedestrian walkways from vehicular traffic.
路障被安置在街上以區分行人走道和車輛交通。
*vehicular [vɪˋhɪkjəlɚ] *a.* 車輛的

▸ The pop star's new album was hailed as revolutionary, but John found it quite pedestrian.
這個明星的新專輯被譽為革新之作，但約翰覺得它很索然無味。

38 pipeline [ˋpaɪpˏlaɪn] *n.* 管線，輸油管

衍 pipe [paɪp] *n.* 輸送管；菸斗 ①
smoke a pipe 抽菸斗

▸ A few oil pipelines were destroyed by the rebels during the war.
有幾條輸油管在戰爭中被叛軍破壞了。

39 retail [ˋritel] *n.* & *vt.* & *vi.* 零售 & *a.* 零售的 & *adv.* 以零售方式

片 retail at / for + 金額 零售價格為……

延伸 wholesale [ˋholˏsel] *n.* & *vt.* & *vi.* 批發 & *a.* 批發的 & *adv.* 以批發方式 ⑥

▸ Many young people will gain early work experience in retail or in a restaurant.
許多年輕人會初步在零售業或餐廳獲得工作經驗。

▸ Best Buy is a major chain in the US that retails home electronics and computer products.
百思買是美國主要的連鎖店，零售販賣家電和電腦產品。

▸ This perfume retails at $50 a bottle, but you can buy it here for just $40.
這罐香水零售價是一瓶 50 美元，但在這裡買只要 40 美元。

▸ Our store buys products from the factory and earns a profit by selling them at a higher retail price.
本店向工廠購買產品，再以較高的零售價出售它們以賺取利潤。

▸ The stereo Trevor bought retail cost US$300, but it is on sale at a cheaper price online.
崔佛買的音響零售價為 300 美元，但現在網路上的特賣價更低。

40 soar [sɔr] *vi.* 急升，飛漲；翱翔

似 (1) rise [raɪz] *vi.* 上升 ①
(2) ascend [əˋsɛnd] *vi.* 上升 ⑥
(3) fly [flaɪ] *vi.* 飛行 ①

▸ Because of the energy crisis, the price of gasoline has soared in recent months.
因為能源危機的問題，汽油價格最近幾個月急速上漲。

▸ Jimmy took a picture of an eagle soaring high in the sky.
吉米拍了一張老鷹在天空翱翔的照片。

41 trauma [ˋtrɔmə] *n.* (情感的) 創傷

衍 (1) agony [ˋægənɪ] *n.* 痛苦 ⑤
(2) distress [dɪˋstrɛs] *n.* 悲傷；痛苦 ⑥
(3) ordeal [ɔrˋdiəl] *n.* 折磨 ⑥

▸ It took John a long time to recover from the trauma of his parents' death.
經過很長時間，約翰才從父母逝世的傷痛中恢復過來。

42 trigger [ˋtrɪgɚ] *vt.* 引發 & *n.* 扳機；引發物

片 pull the trigger　扣扳機

▸ The dust in the air triggered David's allergy.
空氣中的灰塵引發大衛過敏。

▸ The policeman negotiating with the gunman asked him to remove his finger from the trigger.
警察和持槍者談判，要求他把手指從板機上移開。

▸ Fireworks displays and thunder are common triggers for anxiety among combat veterans.
煙火和雷聲是引起老兵們焦慮的常見因素。

43 verdict [ˋvɝdɪkt] *n.* (陪審團的) 裁決，裁定；意見，評論

片 (1) reach a verdict of (not) guilty
判定 (沒) 有罪
(2) sb's verdict on...
某人對於……的評論

似 (1) judgment [ˋdʒʌdʒmənt] *n.* 判決；意見，看法 ②
(2) opinion [əˋpɪnjən] *n.* 意見，看法 ②

▸ Much to the surprise of people who thought the man was guilty, the jury reached a verdict of not guilty.
陪審團判定這名男子無罪，這讓認為他有罪的人感到很訝異。

▸ Simone's verdict on the movie was that while it had an interesting plot, the acting was horrible.
席蒙對於這部電影的評論是，雖然情節很有趣，但是演技很警腳。

Unit 22

2201-2210

1 rival [ˋraɪvḷ] *n.* 競爭者，對手 & *vt.* 與……匹敵 & *a.* 競爭的

片 have no rival　無人能敵
= have no match
= have no equal

衍 rivalry [ˋraɪvḷrɪ] *n.* 競爭 ⑥

似 (1) match [mætʃ] *n.* 對手 & *vt.* 敵得過 ②
(2) equal [ˋikwəl] *n.* 相等的人 & *vt.* 敵得過 ②

▶ When it comes to negotiation skills, Robert has no rival.
= When it comes to negotiation skills, Robert has no match.
= When it comes to negotiation skills, Robert has no equal.
說到談判技巧，沒人比得上羅伯特。

▶ For Roy, no other sports can rival basketball for excitement.
對羅伊來說，沒有其他運動能比籃球更刺激。

2 scandal [ˋskændḷ] *n.* 醜聞

片 (1) cause / create a scandal　成為醜聞
(2) a political / sex scandal　政治 / 性醜聞
(3) a scandal breaks　醜聞爆發

▶ The musician's behavior during the live performance caused a scandal for the television network.
該音樂家在現場表演的行為成了電視網絡上的醜聞。

▶ News of the political scandal broke at the beginning of the election campaign.
這樁政治醜聞的新聞在選舉活動一開始時爆發開來。

3 sandal [ˋsændḷ] *n.* (一隻) 涼鞋

片 a pair of sandals　一雙涼鞋

▶ These leather sandals became widely popular soon after they hit the market.
這種皮涼鞋一上市就廣受喜愛。

4 superstition [ˌsupəˋstɪʃən] *n.* 迷信

衍 superstitious [ˌsupəˋstɪʃəs] *a.* 迷信的 ⑥

▶ An Irish superstition says that you will have seven years of bad luck if you break a mirror.
愛爾蘭的迷信有此說法：你若打破了鏡子就會有 7 年的壞運。

5 tackle [ˋtækḷ] *vt.* 處理 (問題)

片 tackle a problem　處理問題
= deal with a problem
= cope with a problem
= handle a problem

▶ The government is determined to take immediate measures to tackle inflation.
政府決心採取立即的行動處理通貨膨脹的問題。

6 thrill [θrɪl] *vt.* 使興奮 & *n.* 興奮

衍 (1) thrilled [θrɪld] *a.* 非常興奮的
(2) thrilling [ˋθrɪlɪŋ] *a.* 令人興奮的

似 (1) excite [ɪkˋsaɪt] *vt.* 使興奮 ②
(2) excitement [ɪkˋsaɪtmənt] *n.* 興奮 ②

▸ Having a chance to meet Renee's favorite singer in person thrilled her.
能有機會見到自己最喜歡的歌手本人讓蕾妮很興奮。

▸ Flying in an airplane for the first time really gave Tommy a big thrill.
第一次搭乘飛機真的令湯米非常興奮。

thriller [ˋθrɪlɚ] *n.* 驚悚電影 / 小說

▸ The thriller released on DVD last week sold 2 million copies in its first day on the shelves.
這部驚悚片的 DVD 上星期發行第一天就賣掉了 200 萬片。

7 milestone [ˋmaɪlˏston] *n.* 里程碑

片 mark an important milestone (in...)
(在……方面) 記下一個重要的里程碑

▸ The navigator's voyage around the globe marked an important milestone in history.
這名航海探險家環繞地球的航行在歷史上記下重要的里程碑。
*navigator [ˋnævəˏgetɚ] *n.* 航海家

8 tuition [t(j)uˋɪʃən] *n.* 學費 (不可數)

片 tuition fees　學費 (複數)

▸ The tuition of private colleges is much higher than that of public colleges.
私立大學的學費要比公立大學的學費貴得多。

9 underline [ˏʌndɚˋlaɪn] *vt.* 在……下面劃線；強調 & *n.* 底線

似 (1) undermine [ˏʌndɚˋmaɪn] *vt.* (逐漸) 損壞 ⑤
(2) emphasize [ˋɛmfəˏsaɪz] *vt.* 強調 ②
(3) stress [strɛs] *vt.* 強調 ②
(4) highlight [ˋhaɪˏlaɪt] *vt.* 強調 ⑤

▸ All the underlined words are the most important ones in the article.
所有畫底線的字都是本篇文章中最重要的。(underline 為過去分詞作形容詞用)

▸ The increasing crime rate underlines the importance of recruiting more police officers.
犯罪率的升高凸顯了徵募更多警員的重要性。

▸ Daniel marked the most important parts of the text with a red underline.
丹尼爾在正文中用紅底線標記最重要的部分。

10 unforgettable [ˏʌnfɚˋgɛtəbl̩] *a.* 難忘的

似 memorable [ˋmɛmərəbl̩] *a.* 令人難忘的 ④

反 forgettable [fɚˋgɛtəbl̩] *a.* 易被忘記的

▸ I had a whale of a time during my stay in Paris. It was really an unforgettable experience.
我在巴黎時玩得很愉快。那真是個難忘的經歷。

11 visa [ˋvizə] *n.* 簽證

片 (1) a work / student / tourist visa 工作 / 學生 / 旅遊簽證
(2) renew / extend sb's visa 更新某人的簽證，某人加簽
(3) apply for a visa 申請簽證

▸ I came to Taiwan on a student visa, but it has expired. Therefore, I have to renew it this afternoon.
我拿學生簽證來臺灣，但簽證已經過期了。因此，我今天下午得去加簽。

12 whereabouts [ˋ(h)wɛrə͵bauts] *n.* 下落 & *adv.* 在哪裡 (= where)

似 (1) position [pəˋzɪʃən] *n.* 位置 ②
(2) location [loˋkeʃən] *n.* 位置 ③

用法 whereabouts 作名詞時，其後使用單數動詞或複數動詞皆可。

▸ John wants to know the whereabouts of his brother.
約翰想知道他弟弟的下落。

▸ Ever since Tom left for vacation last month, his whereabouts have been a total mystery.
自湯姆上個月離開去度假後，他的行蹤就成謎了。

▸ Frank turned to the woman and asked her, "Whereabouts in the city do you live?"
法蘭克轉向那名女子並問她：『妳住在城市的哪裡呢？』

13 wig [wɪg] *n.* (女用) 假髮

似 toupee [tuˋpe] *n.* (男用) 假髮

▸ The leading actress wore a blonde wig over her naturally brown hair for the role.
這名女主角為了這個角色戴上金色的假髮，以蓋過她天生的棕髮。

14 yacht [jat] *n.* 遊艇 & *vi.* 乘遊艇

▸ Since winning the lottery, Fred has bought two yachts which he sails in his spare time.
自從贏了樂透彩，佛萊德就買了兩艘遊艇，閒暇時會駕駛。

▸ Wealthy families in New England often yacht from island to island during the summer months.
新英格蘭的有錢家庭經常在夏季月份乘遊艇造訪不同島嶼。

15 bodyguard [ˋbadɪ͵gard] *n.* 保鑣

延伸 (1) lifeguard [ˋlaɪf͵gard] *n.* (海上、游泳池) 救生員 ④
(2) safeguard [ˋsef͵gard] *vt.* 保衛

▸ The billionaire is always accompanied by his bodyguards.
這位億萬富翁一直有保鑣陪在身邊。

16 browse [brauz] *vi.* & *vt.* & *n.* 隨便看看 & *vt.* 瀏覽 (網頁)

片 browse through... 隨便翻閱……

衍 browser [ˋbrauzɚ] *n.* (電腦) 瀏覽器

▸ I was browsing through a magazine at the bookstore when I noticed Sarah.
我在書店裡隨意翻閱一本雜誌時看到了莎拉。

似 (1) scan [skæn] *vt.* 粗略地看；瀏覽 ⑤
(2) skim [skɪm] *vt.* & *vi.* 瀏覽 ⑥

▸ Melissa had some time before class, so she decided to browse the books in the university library.
梅莉莎在上課前還有點時間，所以她決定到大學圖書館裡瀏覽書籍。

▸ When a new music store opened in town, Ben and Anne decided to go there for a browse.
鎮上新開了一間音樂商店，班和安決定去看一下。

▸ Many people use Google Chrome to browse the internet, but there are other options.
很多人用 Google 瀏覽器來瀏覽網頁，但也有其他選擇。

17 rattle [ˋrætl̩] *vi.* 發出咯咯聲 & *n.* 咯咯聲 ☐

延伸 (1) quack [kwæk] *vi.* (鴨子) 呱呱叫 & *n.* 鴨叫聲
(2) crunch [krʌntʃ] *vi.* 嘎吱作響 & *n.* (食物或東西碎裂的) 嘎吱聲
(3) rumble [ˋrʌmbl̩] *vi.* 隆隆響 & *n.* 隆隆聲

▸ There is a railroad near my house, so every time a train passes by, my windows rattle.
我家附近有條鐵路，所以每當火車經過，窗戶就被**震得咯咯響**。

▸ Judging from the rattle of the old car's engine, Bill realized he would need a new one soon.
從這臺老車引擎發出的**咯咯聲**來看，比爾知道他很快會需要買一臺新車了。

18 prodigy [ˋprɑdədʒɪ] *n.* 天才 ☐

片 a child prodigy 神童
似 genius [ˋdʒinjəs] *n.* 天才 ④

▸ The child prodigy attended university at the age of 12.
這名**神童** 12 歲時就念大學了。

19 stink [stɪŋk] *vi.* 發臭 & *n.* 惡臭 ☐

三 stink, stank [stæŋk] / stunk [stʌŋk], stunk
片 the stink of sth 某物的惡臭味

▸ You stink! You need to take a bath right away.
你**好臭**！你得馬上去洗澡。

▸ Barry's mother was not ready for the stink that emerged when she opened her son's gym bag.
貝瑞的媽媽打開她兒子的運動背包時，沒有料到會有一股**惡臭**從中散發出來。

▸ As a vegetarian, Linda was very sensitive to the stink of cooked meat in the steakhouse.
琳達是一位素食者，她對牛排餐廳散發出煮熟的肉**臭味**很敏感。

stinky [ˋstɪŋkɪ] *a.* 臭的 ☐
似 smelly [ˋsmɛlɪ] *a.* 臭的

▸ Many foreigners in Taiwan are afraid to try stinky tofu.
許多在臺灣的外國人很害怕嘗試吃**臭豆腐**。

20 depress [dɪˋprɛs] *vt.* 使沮喪，使消沉

衍 (1) depression [dɪˋprɛʃən] *n.* 沮喪 ④
(2) depressed [dɪˋprɛst] *a.* 沮喪的

似 (1) dishearten [dɪsˋhɑrtn̩] *vt.* 使氣餒
(2) sadden [ˋsædn̩] *vt.* 使悲傷

▸ It depresses me that everything has changed.
人事已非使我感到沮喪。

21 appliance [əˋplaɪəns] *n.* 用具（尤指家電用品）

衍 (1) an electrical appliance 電器
(2) an household / domestic appliance 家電用品

▸ They sell all kinds of electrical appliances at the shop, including TV sets, refrigerators, and microwave ovens.
這家店販售各種電器用品，包括電視機、冰箱、微波爐等。

22 acquaint [əˋkwent] *vt.* 使熟悉；使認識

片 (1) acquaint sb with...
使某人熟悉 / 認識……
= familiarize sb with...
(2) be acquainted with...
熟悉 / 認識……
= be familiar with...

似 familiarize [fəˋmɪljə,raɪz] *vt.* 使熟悉

▸ I must acquaint myself with the new laboratory system.
我必須熟悉新的實驗室系統。

▸ The two men are acquainted with each other.
這兩個人彼此認識。

23 genre [ˋʒɑnrə] *n.* 類型，體裁，風格

▸ Rock is the music genre that Jacob likes the most, but he also enjoys listening to jazz.
搖滾樂是雅各最喜歡的音樂類型，但他也很喜歡聽爵士樂。

24 sector [ˋsɛktɚ] *n.*（經濟的某一）部門，領域，產業

片 the industrial / agricultural sector
工 / 農業領域

▸ COVID-19 has had a particularly big impact on the tourism and hospitality sectors.
新冠肺炎對旅遊和接待服務業的影響尤其大。
*hospitality [,hɑspɪˋtælətɪ] *n.* 款待

25 bias [ˋbaɪəs] *n.* 偏見 & *vt.* 使有偏見

複 biases [ˋbaɪəsɪz]

片 (1) have a bias against...
對……有偏見
= be biased against...
= be prejudiced against...
(2) gender bias 性別偏見

▸ It is clear that this company has a strong bias against women.
這家公司顯然對女性存有強烈的偏見。

▸ Female employees often fall victim to gender bias in the workplace.
女性員工在職場上常會受到性別偏見所害。

衍 biased [ˋbaɪəst] *a.* 存有偏見的

似 prejudice [ˋprɛdʒədɪs] *n.* 偏見 & *vt.* 使有偏見 ⑤

▸ Weeks of negative news coverage before the trial had biased the public against the defendant.
審判前好幾週的負面新聞報導讓大眾對被告懷有成見。

26 sparkle [ˋspɑrkḷ] *vi.* 發出火花，閃爍 & *n.* 閃耀

片 sb's eyes sparkle with...
某人的眼睛散發出……

▸ Julie's new necklace sparkled in the sun.
茱莉的新項鍊在陽光下閃閃發光。

▸ When Nancy saw me, her eyes sparkled with love.
南希看見我時，她的眼神散發著愛意。

▸ There was a beautiful sparkle in Kelly's eyes the day she got married.
凱莉結婚的那一天，她的眼中閃爍著美麗的光芒。

27 sensor [ˋsɛnsɚ] *n.* 感應器

衍 (1) sense [ˋsɛns] *n.* 感覺 & *vt.* 感覺到 ②
(2) sensory [ˋsɛnsərɪ] *a.* 感覺的

▸ The light has a sensor on it, so it will automatically turn on when someone passes near it.
這盞燈有感應器，所以有人走靠近時，它就會自動打開。

28 testify [ˋtɛstə͵faɪ] *vi.* & *vt.* 作證；證實

片 (1) testify to...
為……作證；為……作見證
(2) testify against...
對……作不利的證明
(3) testify that... 證實……

▸ I'd like to testify to the boy's good behavior.
我願意為這男孩的良好行為作證。

▸ The success of our plan testified to the importance of teamwork.
我們計畫的成功為團結合作的重要性作了見證。

▸ All the witnesses testified against the woman.
所有證人都對這名女士作不利的證詞。

▸ Can anyone testify that Cheryl was at the scene of the crime?
有人可以證實雪蘿當時人在案發現場嗎？

29 trophy [ˋtrofɪ] *n.* 獎杯

複 trophies [ˋtrofɪz]

▸ On the wall, Daniel displayed the trophies he had won in his athletic career.
丹尼爾將他在運動生涯中所獲得的獎杯在牆上展示出來。

30 flexibility [͵flɛksəˋbɪlətɪ] *n.* 彈性（不可數）

衍 flexible [ˋflɛksəbḷ] *a.* 有彈性的 ④

似 suppleness [ˋsʌpḷnəs] *n.* 柔軟性

▸ Practicing yoga can improve your flexibility.
做瑜珈能改善你身體的柔軟度。

▸ The reason I enjoy being my own boss is the flexibility.
我喜歡做自己的老闆是因為有彈性。

31 salon [sə`lɑn] *n.* (與美髮、美容相關的) 店，廳，院

片 a hair / beauty salon 美髮 / 容院

▶ Judy went to a salon near her home to get her hair cut and washed before the weekend.
週末前，茱蒂到家裡附近的**美髮院**剪和洗髮。

32 franchise [`fræn,tʃaɪz] *n.* 特許經營權；投票權 & *vt.* 給予特許經營權

片 (1) a franchise holder
特許經營權擁有者
(2) a fast-food franchise
速食加盟店

衍 franchisee [,fræntʃaɪ`zi]
n. 特許經營者，加盟者

▶ Companies like McDonald's and KFC make lots of money by offering franchises to individuals who want to own restaurants.
像麥當勞和肯德基等的公司靠著提供**特許經營權**給想開餐廳的人而賺了很多錢。

▶ Before the American Civil War, blacks in the United States were not able to participate in the franchise.
在美國內戰之前，美國黑人沒辦法參與**投票**。

▶ The reason there are so many 7-Elevens is that the company franchises its stores in many countries.
有很多間 7-11 的原因是該公司在很多國家**開設加盟店**。

33 forge [fɔrdʒ] *vt.* 打 (鐵)；(很努力) 形成，產生；偽造

片 (1) forge a relationship / friendship / alliance
建立關係 / 建立友誼 / 形成同盟
(2) forge a signature / check
偽造簽名 / 支票

似 fake [fek] *vt.* 偽造 ③

▶ The company forges high-quality tools that are sold in hardware stores across the country at expensive prices.
這間公司**打造**高品質的工具，並以高價販售於全國各地的五金行。

▶ Over the years, Ben and Simon have forged a strong friendship built on trust and respect for one another.
多年來，班和賽門在互相信任和尊重的基礎上**建立**了深厚的**友誼**。

▶ The thief forged a signature on a stolen check and bought several items from a department store.
這名小偷在一張偷來的支票上**偽造簽名**，並在某間百貨公司買了好幾樣商品。

34 smog [smɑg] *n.* 煙霧，霧霾 (不可數)

衍 smoggy [`smɑgɪ] *a.* 煙霧彌漫的
▶ It's smoggy today. If possible, do not go out.
今天**煙霧彌漫**。如有可能，不要外出。

延伸 smog 是 smoke 及 fog 結合而成的字，指汽車及工廠排放出來，升至天空籠罩城市的髒空氣。

▶ The heavy industry in the region regularly blankets the capital city with smog.
該地區的重工業使首都經常被**霧霾**壟罩著。

35 sob [sɑb] *vi.* & *n.* 抽泣，啜泣

三 sob, sobbed [sɑbd], sobbed
似 (1) cry [kraɪ] *vi.* 哭泣 ①
(2) weep [wip] *vi.* 哭泣 ③

▸ Jenny sobbed uncontrollably after hearing the bad news.
聽到這個壞消息，珍妮無法控制地抽泣起來了。

▸ The old couple let out a sob while watching the destruction of the old building.
這對老夫婦看到老建築被毀壞時便啜泣起來。

36 soften [ˋsɔfn̩] *vt.* & *vi.* (使) 軟化

衍 (1) soft [sɔft] *a.* 柔軟的；細嫩的 ②
(2) softness [ˋsɔftnəs] *n.* 柔軟

▸ Mr. Wilson is strict with his children, and he has never softened his attitude toward them over the years.
魏爾遜先生對孩子很嚴，多年來他對他們的態度從未軟化過。

▸ The noodles will soften quickly, so don't leave them in the boiling water for too long.
麵條很快就會軟化，所以別把它們放在沸水裡太久。

37 venue [ˋvɛnju] *n.* (舉辦) 場所，地點

片 a venue for... ……的場所

▸ The venue for Mike's birthday party was a hotel with a swimming pool and an outdoor bar.
麥克生日派對的地點是在一間附有游泳池、室外吧檯的飯店。

38 confine [kənˋfaɪn] *vt.* 監禁；限制 & [ˋkɑnfaɪn] *n.* 界限；範圍 (皆恆用複數)

片 (1) be confined to... 僅限……
(2) (be) within / beyond the confines of...
在……的界限 / 範圍之內 / 外
似 (1) detain [dɪˋten] *vt.* 監禁，拘留 ⑥
(2) restrain [rɪˋstren] *vt.* 限制 ⑥

▸ That man was confined in prison for many years.
那名男子被關在牢裡很多年了。

▸ Lunch time is confined to only thirty minutes in our company.
我們公司的午餐時間僅限 30 分鐘。

▸ The poet's name became known far outside the confines of his hometown.
這位詩人的名氣從他的家鄉遠播四方。

▸ The problem is beyond the confines of our understanding.
這個問題超出我們所能理解的範圍。

39 defy [dɪˋfaɪ] *vt.* 反抗，違抗；激，惹

三 defy, defied [dɪˋfaɪd], defied

片 defy sb to V　激某人做……

衍 defiance [dɪˋfaɪəns] *n.* 違抗 ⑥

似 disobey [ˏdɪsəˋbe] *vt.* & *vi.* 違抗

▸ If a soldier decides to defy an order, he or she will likely be in serious trouble.

假若一名士兵**違抗**命令，他或她很可能麻煩就大了。

▸ Shelly defied her brother to prove that he was a better dancer and singer than she was.

雪莉**激**她弟弟去證明他是比她更好的舞者和歌手。

40 constraint [kənˋstrent] *n.* 限制，約束

片 (1) financial / political constraints
財務 / 政治限制

(2) be free from constraints
不受約束

衍 constrain [kənˋstren] *vt.* 限制，約束

衍 (1) restriction [rɪˋstrɪkʃən] *n.* 限制，約束 ④

(2) limitation [ˏlɪməˋteʃən] *n.* 限制 ④

▸ Due to the company's financial constraints, the manager was unable to hire any new employees last year.

由於公司的**財務受限**，該經理去年無法聘請任何新員工。

▸ Felix was told that he would be free from constraints in his new role as executive vice president.

菲立克斯被告知他作為副總裁的新身分將**不會受到任何約束**。

41 correlation [ˏkɔrəˋleʃən] *n.* 相互關係，關聯

片 a correlation between A and B
A 和 B 之間的關聯

衍 correlate [ˋkɔrəˏlet] *vi.* 關聯 & *vt.* 使有關聯

衍 connection [kəˋnɛkʃən] *n.* 關聯 ②

▸ There is definitely a correlation between happiness and financial success, but not every rich person is happy.

快樂和財務成功**之間**一定**有關聯**，但不是每個有錢人都很快樂。

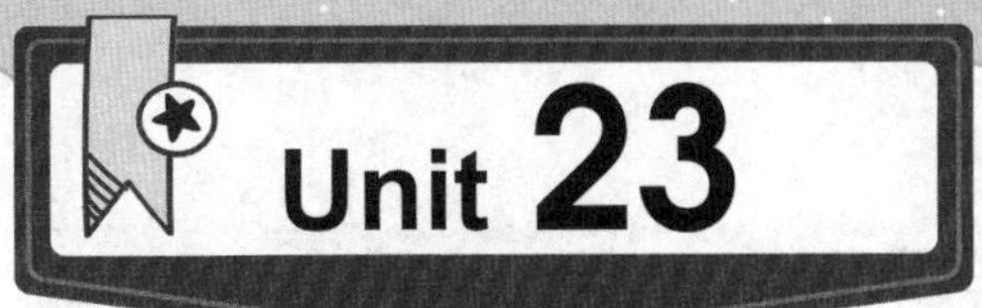

2301-2304

1 **butcher** [ˋbʊtʃɚ] *n.* 屠夫 & *vt.* 屠宰（動物）

▸ My grandfather used to be a butcher who sold meat in the nearby market.
我爺爺曾經是**屠夫**，在附近的市場裡賣肉。

▸ The tribesmen butchered a pig during the ritual.
這些族人在祭典儀式中**屠宰**了一隻豬。

2 **carnival** [ˋkɑrnəvḷ] *n.* 嘉年華，園遊會

似 (1) festival [ˋfɛstəvḷ] *n.* 節，節日 ①
(2) fair [fɛr] *n.* 園遊會 ②

▸ People dressed up in elaborate costumes for the carnival parade.
人們穿著精心設計的服裝參加**嘉年華**遊行。

3 **chef** [ʃɛf] *n.* 廚師

片 a head chef　主廚
似 cook [kʊk] *n.* 做菜的人 ①
延伸 Michelin star　米其林星級（優質餐廳、旅館的評鑑系統）

▸ Rebecca's husband is the head chef in charge of preparing the state banquet.
蕾貝卡的老公就是負責國宴的**主廚**。
*banquet [ˋbæŋkwɪt] *n.* 宴會

cuisine [kwɪˋzin] *n.* 菜餚
片 French / Chinese cuisine　法國菜 / 中華料理

▸ Chinese cuisine is internationally recognized.
中華料理是全世界出名的。

4 **considerate** [kənˋsɪdərət] *a.* 體貼的

片 It's considerate of sb to V　某人做……很體貼
衍 (1) consideration [kən͵sɪdəˋreʃən] *n.* 體貼；考慮 ②
(2) considerable [kənˋsɪdərəbḷ] *a.* 重要的；相當多的 ③
似 (1) thoughtful [ˋθɔtfəl] *a.* 體貼的 ④
(2) understanding [͵ʌndɚˋstændɪŋ] *a.* 體貼的
反 inconsiderate [ɪn͵kənˋsɪdərət] *a.* 不體貼的，缺乏考慮的

▸ It's very considerate of you to lend me a hand in this time of trouble.
你真**體貼**，在這困難的時候對我伸出援手。

2305-2314

5 democrat [ˋdɛmə͵kræt] *n.* (美國) 民主黨員 (首字母大寫)

衍 (1) democratic [͵dɛməˋkrætɪk] *a.* 民主的 ③
(2) democracy [͵dɪˋmɑkrəsɪ] *n.* 民主 ③

▶ Democrats hold very different political views from Republicans.
民主黨員和共和黨員的政治見解很不同。

republican [rɪˋpʌblɪkən] *n.* (美國) 共和黨員 (首字母大寫) & *a.* 共和政體的

衍 republic [rɪˋpʌblɪk] *n.* 共和國，共和政體 ③

▶ As the election drew near, Republicans were worried about the decline in voter support.
選舉將至，選民支持度的下滑讓共和黨員很憂心。

▶ A republican system of government requires upright representatives to maintain the trust of the public.
共和政體制度的政府需要正直的代表來維持公眾的信任。
*upright [ˋʌp͵raɪt] *a.* 正直的

6 descriptive [dɪˋskrɪptɪv] *a.* 描寫的

衍 (1) describe [dɪˋskraɪb] *vt.* 描寫 ②
(2) description [dɪˋskrɪpʃən] *n.* 描寫 ②
be beyond description 非筆墨所能形容

▶ Jack London's novels contain many descriptive passages about life in northern counties.
傑克・倫敦的小說含有許多對於北方幾個郡生活的描寫。
*Jack London 是美國知名作家，生於 1876 年，死於 1916 年。

7 exaggeration [ɪg͵zædʒəˋreʃən] *n.* 誇大

衍 exaggerate [ɪgˋzædʒə͵ret] *vt.* & *vi.* 誇大 ④

▶ It's no exaggeration to say Patrick is a real giant. He is 200 centimeters tall.
說派翠克真的是巨人一點也不誇張。他身高有 200 公分。

8 fad [fæd] *n.* 一時的流行

衍 faddish [ˋfædɪʃ] *a.* 一時流行的
似 craze [krez] *n.* 一時的流行

▶ Some people think Clubhouse is nothing but a fad.
有些人認為 Clubhouse 不過只是一時的流行而已。

9 filter [ˋfɪltɚ] *vt.* 過濾 & *n.* 過濾器

片 a water filter 濾水器
延伸 在許多手機照相功能、IG 限時動態中常看到的『濾鏡』功能，英文正是 filter。

▶ The ozone layer filters harmful UV rays from the sun.
臭氧層過濾掉陽光中有害的紫外線。

▶ Water filters must be replaced regularly.
濾水器要定時更換。

10 gasp [gæsp] *vi.* & *n.* 倒抽一口氣，喘氣

片 (1) gasp for air / breath 大口喘氣
(2) give a gasp of... ……地喘氣

▶ The crowd gasped as the building collapsed before them.
當建築物在他們面前倒下時，群眾倒抽一口氣。

▸ As the lifeguard pulled the drowning man from the ocean, both men were gasping for air.
救生員把溺水的男子從海中拉上岸後，他們倆**大口喘氣**。

▸ The audience gave gasps of astonishment when the magician suddenly appeared on the stage.
當魔術師突然出現在臺上時，觀眾驚訝**地喘息**。

11 glare [glɛr] *vi.* & *n.* 怒視 & *n.* 刺眼強光

片 glare at... 瞪著……

似 stare [stɛr] *vi.* 瞪（與介詞 at 並用）③

▸ Christine could only glare at Timmy as he began teasing her in front of his friends.
當提米在他的朋友面前調侃克莉絲汀時，她只能**怒看著**他。

▸ The teacher's cold glare made Casey realize he had said something very inappropriate.
老師冷冰冰的**瞪視**讓凱西知道他說了非常不恰當的話。

▸ You should wear sunglasses while sailing because the harsh glare of the sun on the water can damage your eyes.
你出海航行時應該要戴上太陽眼鏡，因為水面上刺眼的**陽光**會傷害你的眼睛。

12 warehouse [ˋwɛr͵haus] *n.* 倉庫 & *vt.* 把……放入倉庫

似 depot [ˋdipo / ˋdɛpo] *n.* 倉庫

▸ We need to rent an additional warehouse because we have used up all the storage space in the current one.
我們需要再多租一間**倉庫**，因為目前的儲存空間已經滿了。

▸ The company had to rent storage space to warehouse all of the surplus products.
這間公司得租個儲藏間來**存放**所有剩餘的產品。

13 cognitive [ˋkɑgnətɪv] *a.* 認知的

片 cognitive ability 認知能力

衍 cognition [kɑgˋnɪʃən] *n.* 認知

▸ The disease did not affect the patient's cognitive ability at all; he was still able to think logically.
該疾病一點都沒有影響到這名病人的**認知能力**，他還是能夠有邏輯地思考。

14 collaboration [kə͵læbəˋreʃən] *n.* 合作

片 (1) a collaboration between A and B A 和 B 之間的合作
(2) in collaboration with... 和……合作

▸ The collaborations between John Lennon and Paul McCartney produced some of the best songs in rock and roll history.
約翰．藍儂和保羅．麥卡尼**間的合作**產出了一些搖滾樂史上最棒的歌曲。

2314-2323

衍 (1) collaborate [kə`læbə͵ret] *vi.* 合作
(2) collaborative [kə`læbərətɪv] *a.* 合作的

似 cooperation [ko͵apə`reʃən] *n.* 合作 ④

▶ The company, in collaboration with many experienced software developers, has created several great apps that have become popular.
這間公司和許多有經驗的軟體開發商**合作**，已創造出一些很棒且受歡迎的應用程式。

15 icon [`aɪkɑn] *n.* (電腦) 圖示；偶像；(知名) 代表物

片 a pop icon　流行偶像

衍 iconic [aɪ`kɑnɪk] *a.* 具代表性的；受歡迎的

▶ There are several icons on Kate's computer screen that she has never even bothered to click on.
凱特的電腦螢幕上有一些她從來沒有點進去過的**電腦圖示**。

▶ Lionel Messi is a sporting icon, not only in his home country of Argentina but all around the world.
萊奧．梅西不只在他的祖國阿根廷是體育界的**指標人物**，在全世界也是。

▶ Disney characters such as Mickey and Minnie Mouse are icons that bring joy to kids around the planet.
迪士尼的卡通人物如米奇和米妮老鼠是帶給全球孩童們歡樂的**名角色**。

16 disconnect [͵dɪskə`nɛkt] *vt.* 切斷 (電話、電源)

衍 disconnection [͵dɪskə`nɛkʃən] *n.* 切斷

反 connect [kə`nɛkt] *vt.* 連結 ③

▶ This device automatically disconnects the alarm system once you enter the room.
你一進房間，這個裝置就會自動**切斷**警報系統。

▶ Because I didn't pay my bill, the phone was disconnected.
因我沒有付電話費，所以就被**停話**了。

17 arouse [ə`rauz] *vt.* 激發，引起；喚醒

似 (1) provoke [prə`vok] *vt.* 激起，引起 ⑤
(2) evoke [ɪ`vok] *vt.* 引起 ⑥
(3) wake [wek] *vt.* 喚醒 & *vi.* 醒來 ①
(4) awaken [ə`wekən] *vt.* 喚醒 & *vi.* 醒來 ③

▶ Cindy's bold behavior aroused the interest of the press.
辛蒂大膽的行徑**激起**媒體的興趣。

▶ It was about time to leave, so I aroused my wife from her sleep.
該是動身的時候了，因此我便把我太太從睡夢中**叫醒**。

18 courteous [`kɝtɪəs] *a.* 有禮貌的

似 polite [pə`laɪt] *a.* 有禮貌的 ①

反 discourteous [dɪs`kɝtɪəs] *a.* 失禮的

▶ A courteous and righteous gentleman never does things against his conscience.
有禮的正人君子從不做違背良心的事。
*righteous [`raɪtʃəs] *a.* 正直的

19 risky [`rɪskɪ] *a.* 危險的，有風險的

衍 risk [rɪsk] *n.* 危險，風險 ③

似 (1) dangerous [`dendʒərəs] *a.* 危險的 ①
(2) hazardous [`hæzɚdəs] *a.* 危險的

▸ Investing money can be risky because you can lose money—but you can also make a lot of money.
投資會有風險，因為你可能會賠錢 —— 但也可能大賺一筆。

20 grieve [griv] *vt.* & *vi.* (使) 悲痛

片 grieve over... 為……感到悲傷

衍 grief [grif] *n.* 悲傷，悲痛 ④

▸ Paul grieved his wife's death, yet there was nothing he could do.
= Paul grieved over his wife's death, yet there was nothing he could do.
保羅傷痛妻子的過世，但卻無能為力。

21 terrify [`tɛrə,faɪ] *vt.* (使) 恐懼，(使) 害怕

三 terrify, terrified [`tɛrə,faɪd], terrified

衍 (1) terrified [`tɛrə,faɪd] *a.* 感到害怕的
(2) terrifying [`tɛrə,faɪŋ] *a.* 令人害怕的

似 frighten [`fraɪtn̩] *vt.* 使害怕 ③

▸ The horror movie terrified the children.
這部恐怖電影嚇壞了孩子們。

▸ Tracy's nightmare about a plane crash terrified her to the point that she had to cancel her trip.
崔西做了有關墜機的惡夢，嚇得她必須取消她的旅行。

22 external [ɪk`stɝnl̩] *a.* 外部的 & *n.* 外觀，外形

似 outer [`aʊtɚ] *a.* 外在的；外面的 ③

反 internal [ɪn`tɝnl̩] *a.* 內部的 ②

▸ This ointment is for external use only.
這種軟膏只可外用。
*ointment [`ɔɪntmənt] *n.* 軟膏，藥膏

▸ People should be judged by their character, and not by externals, which are much less important.
應以性格來評斷人，而不是透過較不重要的外表。

23 legacy [`lɛgəsi] *n.* 遺產；歷史遺產

複 legacies [`lɛgəsiz]

片 leave a legacy of... 留下……

衍 (1) inheritance [ɪn`hɛrətəns] *n.* 遺產
(2) heritage [`hɛrətɪdʒ] *n.* 歷史遺產 ⑤

▸ The legacy that Milly was left by her father was enough for her to pay all her debts.
米莉的父親留給她的遺產夠她還清所有債務。

▸ The presidency of Franklin Delano Roosevelt left a legacy of social programs for the American people.
富蘭克林．德拉諾．羅斯福任職總統期間為美國人民留下了社會福利的制度。

2324-2334

24 defendant [dɪˋfɛndənt] *n.* 被告

衍 (1) defend [dɪˋfɛnd] *vt.* 為……辯護 ④
(2) defense [dɪˋfɛns] *n.* 辯護 ④

反 plaintiff [ˋplentɪf] *n.* 原告，起訴人

▸ With a solid alibi on the night of the crime, the defendant was found innocent by the trial jury.
案發當晚，被告有不在場的鐵證，因此被陪審團判定無罪。
*alibi [ˋæləˏbaɪ] *n.* 不在場證明

25 interference [ˏɪntəˋfɪrəns] *n.* 阻礙，干預（不可數）

片 interference in... 干預……

衍 interfere [ˏɪntəˋfɪr] *vi.* 介入，干預 ④

▸ The government's interference in the construction project was criticized by the public.
大眾批評政府介入這項建造計畫。

26 discourse [ˋdɪskors] *n.* 交談，談話；論文，文章

片 a discourse on...
有關……的談話 / 文章

似 (1) conversation [ˏkɑnvəˋseʃən] *n.* 談話 ②
(2) discussion [dɪˋskʌʃən] *n.* 談論 ②
(3) essay [ˋɛse] *n.* 論文 ②

▸ The host and his guests sat in the living room and enjoyed pleasant discourse until late into the evening.
這名主人和他的客人們坐在客廳愉快地交談一直到很晚的時候。

▸ In addition to *Gulliver's Travels*, Jonathan Swift is known for writing many interesting discourses on a variety of subjects.
除了《格列佛遊記》，強納森．史威夫特亦以撰寫許多不同主題、饒富趣味的文章聞名。

27 portfolio [pɔrtˋfolɪˏo] *n.* 公事包；（藝術家的）作品集；投資組合

▸ Janet put her artwork in a portfolio and carried it with her to the job interview.
珍妮特把她的藝術作品放進公事包裡，帶著它去工作面試。

▸ The photographer's portfolio contained photos from all over the world, including the war zones of Iraq and Afghanistan.
這名攝影師的作品集裡含有在世界各地拍攝的照片，包括伊拉克和阿富汗的戰區。

▸ The financial advisor told his client to make sure to include some energy stocks in his portfolio.
該理財顧問告訴他的客戶務必在他的投資組合中包含一些能源股。

28 predator [ˋprɛdətə] *n.* 捕食者，掠食者

衍 predatory [ˋprɛdəˏtɔrɪ] *a.* 捕食的

反 prey [pre] *n.* 獵物 ⑤

▸ With teeth that are razor-sharp, the shark is a dangerous predator of many marine animals.
鯊魚有著尖銳的牙齒，是掠食許多海洋動物的危險生物。
*razor-sharp [ˋrezəˋʃɑrp] *a.* 銳利的

29 provision [prəˋvɪʒən] *n.* 準備；供應；糧食 (恆用複數)

片 make provision for... 為……作準備

似 (1) preparation [ˌprɛpəˋreʃən] *n.* 準備 ③

(2) supply [səˋplaɪ] *n.* 供給；補給品 (恆用複數) ②

▸ Farsighted parents should make provision for their children's education.
有遠見的父母應為子女的教育作準備。

▸ The company manages provisions for accommodations, but transportation is up to the employees.
該公司供應員工住處，但交通就得由員工自行處理。

▸ They had plenty of provisions.
他們有充裕的糧食。

30 recite [rɪˋsaɪt] *vt.* 背誦

衍 recitation [ˌrɛsəˋteʃən] *n.* 背誦
a recitation contest 背誦比賽

▸ "You should all recite this short article," said the teacher.
老師說：『你們大家都要把這篇短文背起來』。

31 escalator [ˋɛskəˌletɚ] *n.* 電扶梯

衍 escalate [ˋɛskəˌlet] *vt.* & *vi.* (使) 逐步上升

▸ The escalator is out of order.
這臺電扶梯壞了。

32 honorable [ˋɑnərəbl̩] *a.* 值得尊敬的；品德高尚的

似 honorary [ˋɑnəˌrɛrɪ] *a.* 名譽的 ⑥
an honorary chairman 名譽主席

▸ John wants to be a singer, but his father doesn't think it's an honorable profession.
約翰想當歌手，可是他爸爸卻認為唱歌不是光榮的職業。

▸ An honorable person would tell the truth and would not shy away from facing it, either.
品德高尚的人會說實話，也不會不敢面對事實。
*shy away from sth （因不喜歡、害怕等）逃避某事

33 reservoir [ˋrɛzɚˌvwɑr] *n.* 蓄水池，水庫

比 dam [dæm] *n.* 水壩 ③
dam 指的是用來攔阻水流的巨大鋼筋水泥設施，而 reservoir 則是水流經攔阻之後所形成的水池。

▸ When the water in the reservoir got too low in 2020, the city began to ration water.
2020 年水庫蓄水量嚴重不足時，全市開始實施配水。
*ration [ˋræʃən] *vt.* 對……實行配給

34 fiscal [ˋfɪskl̩] *a.* 財務的，會計的

似 financial [faɪˋnænʃəl] *a.* 財務的；財政的 ④

▸ The nation's debt was a major fiscal problem that could not be ignored and needed to be paid down.
該國的債務是主要的財務問題，不容忽視且需要償還。

2335-2339

35 judicial [dʒuˋdɪʃəl] *a.* 司法的；法庭 (判定) 的

片 the judicial system 司法系統

▸ Judges and courts are part of the judicial system and must fairly administer justice without political interference.
法官和法庭是**司法系統**的一部分，且一定要不受政治干預公平地執法。

▸ The judicial decision was reported word for word in the leading national newspaper and widely read by the country's citizens.
法院裁定的決議已一字不漏地發布在該國最大宗的報紙上，並已被該國人民廣泛閱讀。

36 liability [ˏlaɪəˋbɪlətɪ] *n.* (法律上的) 責任，義務；債務，負債；麻煩

複 liabilities [ˏlaɪəˋbɪlətiz]
片 have (no) liability for...
對……(沒) 有責任
衍 liable [ˋlaɪəbl̩] *a.* 負有 (法律) 責任的 ⑥
似 (1) responsibility [rɪˏspansəˋbɪlətɪ] *n.* 責任 ③
(2) debt [dɛt] *n.* 債務 ②

▸ The judge ruled the restaurant had no liability for the accident and was not required to pay any money.
法官判定該餐廳**不用為**這起意外**負責**，因此不需要付任何錢。

▸ Because the company's liabilities far exceeded its assets, it was in danger of going bankrupt.
因為這間公司的**負債**遠超過其資產，它面臨破產的危機。

▸ Out of work and 50 years old, Burt knew his age was a liability in finding new employment.
伯特失業且 50 歲了，他知道自己的年紀在找新工作上會是個**麻煩**。

37 premise [ˋprɛmɪs] *n.* 前提，假定；建築物及周圍所屬土地，場所 (恆用複數)

似 (1) assumption [əˋsʌmpʃən] *a.* 假定 ⑤
(2) proposition [ˏprɑpəˋzɪʃən] *n.* 陳述，主張

▸ The premise that disagreeing with the government means one is not patriotic is unfair and unjustified.
一個人不贊同政府就代表他不愛國的**假定**既不公平也不正確。

▸ The business owner was hoping to move his store to new premises that were larger and in a better location.
該業主希望可以把店面搬到較大、地點較好的新**場所**。

hypothesis [haɪˋpɑθəsɪs] *n.* 假設，假說

複 hypotheses [haɪˋpɑθəsiz]
似 theory [ˋθiərɪ] *n.* 學說，理論 ③

▸ The scientist conducted an experiment to test his hypothesis, but the results proved his theory to be incorrect.
這名科學家進行一項實驗來試驗他的**假說**，但結果證實他的理論是錯誤的。

38 siege [sidʒ] *n.* 圍攻

片 be under siege
遭到圍攻；不斷遭受批評

▶ Troy had been under siege for ten years before it was finally taken.
特洛伊城**被圍攻**了 10 年之久才被攻下。

▶ After the tapes were leaked to the press, the corporation was under siege by reporters asking for information.
那些影像外流給媒體後，該公司不斷**遭受**記者**抨擊**要求給予資訊。

39 subsidy [ˋsʌbsədɪ] *n.* 補助金，津貼

複 subsidies [ˋsʌbsədiz]

▶ To encourage people to buy electric vehicles, the government offered subsidies to make them cheaper for people to buy.
為了鼓勵大家買電動車，政府提供**補助**讓人們能以更低的金額購買。

Unit 24

2401-2411

1 hairstyle [ˋhɛrˏstaɪl] *n.* 髮型

似 hairdo [ˋhɛrˏdu] *n.* 髮式，髮型

▸ Changing to a short hairstyle in the summertime is comfortable and easy to manage.
夏天時改留一頭短髮的髮型既舒服又容易整理。

2 hockey [ˋhɑkɪ] *n.* 曲棍球

片 ice hockey 冰上曲棍球

▸ If you want to play ice hockey, the first thing you need to learn is how to ice-skate.
你若想要打冰上曲棍球，就要先學習如何溜冰。

3 howl [haʊl] *vi.* & *n.* (狗、狼等的) 嚎叫

▸ The bear howled in pain after being struck by a bullet from the hunter's gun.
這隻熊被獵人槍枝的子彈擊到後痛苦地哀嚎。

▸ The howl of the wolves can be heard from afar.
這些狼的嚎叫聲從遠處就可以聽得見。
*afar [əˋfɑr] *adv.* 從遠方

4 laser [ˋlezɚ] *n.* 雷射

延伸 laser 是 light amplification by stimulated emission of radiation 的縮寫。

▸ Laser surgery can reduce your need for glasses or contact lenses by reshaping your cornea.
雷射手術能藉由角膜改造來減少你對眼鏡或隱形眼鏡的需求。
*cornea [ˋkɔrnɪə] *n.* 角膜

5 massage [məˋsɑʒ] *vt.* & *n.* 按摩

似 message [ˋmɛsɪdʒ] *n.* 信息 ②

▸ My wife massaged my aching back after a long day at the office.
在辦公室一整天後，我太太按摩我疼痛的背部。

▸ Thanks to your massage, I feel much better. The pain seems to have gone.
由於你幫我按摩，我感覺好多了。疼痛似乎已經消失了。

6 masterpiece [ˋmæstɚˏpis] *n.* 傑作

衍 master [ˋmæstɚ] *n.* 名家，大師 ②
似 masterwork [ˋmæstɚˏwɝk] *n.* 傑作

▸ This masterpiece was written by Charles Dickens, whom I think you've heard of.
這部偉大的作品是由查爾斯．狄更斯所著，我想你聽過他的名字。

7 wreath [riθ] *n.* 花環

▸ The widow laid a wreath on her husband's tomb and said a silent prayer.
那位寡婦在她丈夫的墳墓上放了一個花環，然後默禱一番。

8 torch [tɔrtʃ] *n.* 火把 & *vt.* (蓄意) 縱火

片 (1) the Olympic torch 奧林匹克聖火
(2) carry a torch for sb 單戀某人

▸ The athlete carried the torch into the Olympic Stadium during the Opening Ceremony.
這名運動員在開幕典禮時帶著聖火進奧林匹克體育場。

▸ Andrew has carried a torch for Doreen for many years, but she hasn't seemed to notice.
安德魯單戀朵琳多年，但她似乎還沒注意到。

▸ The burglars took what they wanted and then torched the building.
盜竊者拿走他們要的東西後就放火燒了那棟建築。

9 performer [pɚˋfɔrmɚ] *n.* 表演者

衍 (1) perform [pɚˋfɔrm] *vt.* & *vi.* 表演 ③
(2) performance [pɚˋfɔrməns] *n.* 表演 ③

▸ Not only is the singer a talented musician, but she is also an excellent performer that audiences love.
這名歌手不僅是位才華洋溢的音樂家，也是一位備受觀眾喜愛、超棒的表演者。

10 errand [ˋɛrənd] *n.* 差事，出差

片 (1) run errands 跑腿，出差
= be / go on errands
(2) a fool's errand 徒勞

似 (1) task [tæsk] *n.* 工作，任務 ②
(2) chore [tʃɔr] *n.* 雜務 ⑤

▸ I'm afraid I can't go out with you. I have to run some errands for my boss this afternoon.
很抱歉不能和你出去，我下午必須為我老闆辦一些差事。

▸ Kyle is on an errand buying a newspaper for his dad.
凱爾現在正為他老爸跑腿買份報紙。

▸ Dave was sent on a fool's errand to deliver the message, which could have easily been sent electronically.
戴維被派去做傳達訊息徒勞無益的工作，這可以很容易地透過電子方式傳遞。

11 qualify [ˋkwɑlə,faɪ] *vt.* & *vi.* (使) 有資格

片 qualify as / for...
有……的身分資格 / 有資格……

衍 qualification [,kwɑləfəˋkeʃən] *n.* 資格 ⑥

▸ The exam qualifies students to enter this college.
這個考試讓有資格的學生就讀該所大學。

▸ Philip finally qualified as a lawyer.
菲利普終於拿到律師的資格。

2412-2423

12 operational [ˌapəˋreʃənḷ] *a.* 操作上的

衍 (1) operate [ˋapəˌret] *vt.* 操作 ②
(2) operation [ˌapəˋreʃən] *n.* 操作 ③

▸ Should you have any operational problems, just let me know.
你若有任何操作上的問題，請告訴我就可以了。

13 customs [ˋkʌstəmz] *n.* 海關 (恆用複數)

片 go / get through customs 通關
似 custom [ˋkʌstəm] *n.* 習俗 ②

▸ Believe it or not, it took me almost two hours to get through customs.
信不信由你，我花了將近兩小時才通關。

14 spicy [ˋspaɪsi] *a.* (加了香料) 辛辣的

似 spice [spaɪs] *n.* 香料 ③

▸ Richard is crazy about spicy Indian curry.
理查非常愛吃印度辣咖哩。

15 negotiation [nɪˌgoʃɪˋeʃən] *n.* 協商 (常用複數)

片 be under negotiation 有待商談
衍 negotiate [nɪˋgoʃɪˌet] *vt.* & *vi.* 協商 ④
似 talks [tɔlks] *n.* 商談 (恆用複數) ①

▸ We finally reached an agreement after several rounds of negotiations.
經過了好幾回合的談判後，我們終於達成了協議。

▸ Thomas has decided to accept the job offer, but his salary is still under negotiation.
湯瑪斯決定接受那份工作，但他的薪水還有待協商。

16 incorporate [ɪnˋkɔrpəˌret] *vt.* 使結合，合併

片 be incorporated into... 被結合成……
衍 incorporation [ɪnˌkɔrpəˋreʃən] *n.* 合併
似 combine [kəmˋbaɪn] *vt.* 結合 ②

▸ I was glad that our ideas had been incorporated into the project.
我很高興我們的構想被融入本企畫案中。

17 amend [əˋmɛnd] *vt.* 修訂，修正 (法律、文件等)；改善 (錯誤、糟糕的情況等)

衍 amendment [əˋmɛndmənt] *n.* 修正；改善
似 (1) revise [rɪˋvaɪs] *vt.* 修改，修正 ④
(2) modify [ˋmɑdəˌfaɪ] *vt.* 修改 ⑤
(3) improve [ɪmˋpruv] *vt.* & *vi.* 改善 ②

▸ The public pushed the government to amend the law because it was unfair to some people.
大眾促使政府修訂該法令，因為它對某些人不公。

▸ Paul knew that he needed to amend the situation by clarifying what he meant so people wouldn't be offended.
保羅知道他得澄清自己的意思來改善情況，以讓大家不會感到被冒犯。

18 casino [kə`sino] *n.* 賭場

▸ That club has a secret casino upstairs.
那間俱樂部的樓上有個祕密**賭場**。

19 mortgage [`mɔrgɪdʒ] *n.* & *vt.* 典當，抵押

片 pay off a mortgage 還清抵押貸款
似 loan [lon] *n.* 貸款 ④

▸ It will take me nearly twenty-five years to pay off my mortgage. 我必須花快 25 年的時間才能**還清抵押貸款**。
▸ Johnson has to mortgage his house to pay off his debts. 強森必須**抵押**他的房子以償還債務。

20 cripple [`krɪpḷ] *vt.* 使成跛子 & *n.* 跛子（有輕視意味）

似 disable [dɪs`ebḷ] *vt.* 使傷殘 ⑥

▸ The traffic accident crippled John for life.
這場車禍**使**約翰終身**不良於行**。
▸ It is considered impolite to call someone a cripple.
叫別人**跛子**被認為是無禮的。

21 intensify [ɪn`tɛnsə͵faɪ] *vt.* 增強，強化 & *vi.* 加劇

三 intensify, intensified [ɪn`tɛnsə͵faɪd], intensified
衍 intensification [ɪn͵tɛnsəfə`keʃən] *n.* 強化；加劇

▸ John is a determined person. Any failure will only intensify his desire to try again. 約翰是個很有決心的人。任何的失敗只會**加強**他想要再度嘗試的慾望。
▸ The drought intensified and spread.
這個旱災**加劇**並擴散開來。

22 overtake [͵ovɚ`tek] *vt.*（速度、數量或程度上）超越，趕上；（負面事件）突然來襲、降臨

三 overtake, overtook [͵ovɚ`tʊk ], overtaken [ ͵ovɚ`tekən]

▸ Brittany was able to overtake the other runners in the final seconds of the race.
布萊特妮在比賽的最後幾秒**超越**了其他跑者。
▸ South Korea has overtaken Japan as our main overseas market.
南韓已經**超越**日本成為我們海外的主要市場。
▸ The town was overtaken by grief when several members of the high school football team were killed in a bus crash.
該高中橄欖球隊的幾名成員在公車事故中喪生，整個小鎮都**陷入**了悲痛之中。

23 oversee [͵ovɚ`si] *vt.* 監督，監察

三 oversee, oversaw [͵ovɚ`sɔ ], overseen [ ͵ovɚ`sin]
似 supervise [`supɚ͵vaɪz] *vt.* 監督，管理 ⑤

▸ Gloria was promoted to manager and now oversees a total of 25 employees in the marketing department.
葛洛莉雅被升為經理，現在**管理**行銷部門一共 25 位員工。

2424-2432

24 marine [mə`rin] *a.* 海洋的 & *n.* (美國) 海軍陸戰隊士兵

片 (1) marine life 海洋生物
(2) a marine biologist 海洋生物學家
(3) marine biology 海洋生物學
(4) the United States Marine Corps 美國海軍陸戰隊

▶ You'll be able to see a wide variety of marine life in this aquarium.
在這個水族館你將會看到多樣的**海洋生物**。

▶ When negotiations with the terrorists failed, the marines were ordered to attack the camp.
與恐怖分子的協商破裂後，**海軍陸戰隊士兵**被下令攻擊他們的營地。

25 infect [ɪn`fɛkt] *vt.* 使感染

片 be infected with + 疾病 感染某疾病
衍 infectious [ɪn`fɛkʃəs] *a.* 傳染性的 ⑥
an infectious disease 傳染性疾病

▶ The flu can infect a lot of people.
流感會**傳染給**很多人。

▶ A large number of people around the globe were infected with coronavirus after the outbreak of COVID-19.
新冠肺炎爆發後，全球有許多人都**感染**了冠狀病毒。

26 mortality [mɔr`tælətɪ] *n.* 必死 (性)；死亡率 (皆不可數)

衍 mortal [`mɔrtḷ] *a.* 會死的 & *n.* 凡人 ⑥
反 immortality [ˌɪmɔr`tælətɪ] *n.* 永生，不滅

▶ As people get older, they become more aware of their mortality and make preparations for their eventual death.
人隨著年紀漸長會更加意識到人終將**死亡**，並會為此做好準備。

▶ The mortality from the big earthquake continued to climb as more bodies were recovered from collapsed buildings.
隨著從倒塌的建築物中找到更多屍體，這場大地震的**死亡率**不斷上升。

27 compliance [kəm`plaɪəns] *n.* 服從，遵守

片 (in) compliance with... 遵守……
衍 (1) comply [kəm`plaɪ] *vt.* 順從，遵守 ⑤
(2) compliant [kəm`plaɪənt] *a.* 順從的
似 obedience [ə`bidjəns] *n.* 服從，順從 ④

▶ Compliance with the law is necessary; people who violate the rules will face fines of up to NT$10,000.
守法是必要的，違法的人將被處以至多新臺幣 1 萬的罰款。

▶ The secretary submitted the completed forms to the government in compliance with the guidelines established this year.
祕書**遵循**今年制定的準則遞交了已填好的表格給政府。

28 equity [ˋɛkwətɪ] *n.* 公平，公正 (不可數)；資產淨值；股票

複 equities [ˋɛkwətiz]
似 (1) justice [ˋdʒʌstɪs] *n.* 公平 ②
(2) fairness [ˋfɛrnəs] *n.* 公平，公正
(3) value [ˋvælju] *n.* 價值 ②
(4) share [ʃɛr] *n.* 股票 ①
反 inequity [ɪnˋɛkwətɪ] *n.* 不公平

▸ A society without a good degree of equity is not stable because those who are treated unfairly will resist.
沒有一定**公平**程度的社會是不穩定的，因為受到不平待遇的人會反抗。

▸ With every mortgage payment she makes, Lydia builds up more equity in her apartment by the sea.
莉迪雅每付一筆抵押貸款，她海邊公寓的**資產淨值**就會增加一點。

▸ Charlie prefers equities to bonds because the ones he buys give him voting rights in the companies.
比起債券，查理更喜歡**股票**，因為他購買的股票讓他在這些公司中有投票權。

29 envision [ɪnˋvɪʒən] *vt.* 想像

似 (1) imagine [ɪˋmædʒɪn] *vt.* & *vi.* 想像 ②
(2) envisage [ɪnˋvɪzɪdʒ] *vt.* 想像
(3) visualize [ˋvɪʒuə͵laɪz] *vt.* & *vi.* 想像

▸ Carl could not envision himself living anywhere but in the countryside because it is so peaceful and quiet.
卡爾無法**想像**自己住在除了鄉間以外的任何地方，因為鄉間是如此平和寧靜。

30 ideology [͵aɪdɪˋɑlədʒɪ] *n.* 意識形態；思想體系

複 ideologies [͵aɪdɪˋɑlədʒiz]

▸ The two political parties hold completely different ideologies, with one favoring big business and the other the average worker.
這兩個政黨的**意識形態**大相逕庭，一個贊同大企業，另一個則擁護一般勞工。

31 pedal [ˋpɛdḷ] *n.* 踏板 & *vt.* & *vi.* 騎 (自行車)

片 (1) a gas pedal　油門
(2) pedal a bicycle　騎自行車
= ride a bicycle

▸ The driver pushed down on the gas pedal to make the car go.
駕駛踩**油門**，讓車子前進。

▸ John pedals to and from work every day.
約翰每天**騎自行車**上下班。

32 petition [pəˋtɪʃən] *n.* 請願書；申訴書，訴狀 & *vt.* & *vi.* 請願，申訴

片 (1) sign a petition　簽署請願書
(2) file a petition　遞交訴狀
(3) petition sb to V
向某人請願做……

▸ Judy signed a petition that called for an end to the use of nuclear power in her country.
茱蒂簽署一份**請願書**，呼籲她的國家停止使用核能。

2432-2440

(4) petition for sth　請願某事

似 appeal [ə`pil] *vi.* & *n.* 呼籲，請求 ③

▸ The woman filed a petition with the court, requesting that her former husband be prohibited from contacting or approaching her.
這名女子向法庭遞交訴狀，要求她的前夫不要再聯絡或接近她。

▸ The association petitioned the government to enact stronger gun control laws to help prevent future mass killings.
該協會請求政府制定更嚴格的槍枝管制法來防止未來發生大屠殺。
*enact [ɪn`ækt] *vt.* 制定

▸ The bereaved woman is petitioning for changes to the country's drunk-driving laws.
這名失去親人的女子正在請願希望該國能修改酒駕法令。
*bereaved [bɪ`rivd] *a.* 失去親人的

33 quota [`kwotə] *n.* 限額，定額

片 impose quotas on...
對……實行配額限制

▸ To protect the domestic steel industry, the government imposed a quota on steel imports from other nations.
為了保護國內鋼鐵業，政府對從其他國家進口的鋼鐵實行了配額限制。

▸ The sales manager expected the sales representatives to meet or exceed the high quotas he had set.
業務經理期望業務代表可以達成或超出他所訂定的高額度。

34 reassure [ˌriə`ʃʊr] *vt.* 使放心，使消除疑慮

片 reassure sb (that)...
使某人放心……

衍 reassurance [ˌriə`ʃʊrəns] *n.* 安慰，慰藉

▸ Melvin tried to reassure his daughter the dog wouldn't bite her, but she was still afraid of the animal.
馬文試圖讓女兒放心明白這隻狗不會咬她，但她仍很怕牠。

35 array [ə`re] *n.* 一批，一系列

片 an array of...　一連串 / 一大堆……

▸ I was attracted by a wide array of beautiful flowers in the garden.
花園內一大堆美麗的花朵吸引了我。

36 disrupt [dɪs`rʌpt] *vt.* 中斷，擾亂

衍 disruption [dɪs`rʌpʃən] *n.* 中斷

▸ The angry protestors broke into the office and disrupted the meeting that was going on at the time.
憤怒的抗議者闖入辦公室，並擾亂了當時正在進行中的會議。

37 dreadful [ˋdrɛdfəl] *a.* 可怕的；很爛的

似 terrible [ˋtɛrəbl̩] *a.* 可怕的；很爛的 ①

用法 dreadful 不與 very 並用，若要在其前加上副詞修飾，可使用 absolutely、simply 等。

▸ The dreadful explosion killed all the people on the spot.
這起**可怕的**爆炸事件使所有人當場喪生。

▸ This show is dreadful. Can we change to another channel?
這節目**有夠爛**。我們可否轉臺？

38 indigenous [ɪnˋdɪdʒənəs] *a.* 本地的，土生土長的；當地的

片 be indigenous to + 地方
某地當地所有的

似 (1) local [ˋlokl̩] *a.* 本地的；當地的 ②
(2) native [ˋnetɪv] *a.* 土生土長的 ③
(3) aboriginal [ˌæbəˋrɪdʒənl̩] *a.* 土生土長的 ⑥

▸ The new government has vowed to protect the indigenous culture of the island.
新政府誓言保護該島的**本土**文化。

▸ There are some very interesting animals that are indigenous to Australia and not found in any other country.
澳洲**當地**有一些很有趣的動物，在任何其他國家都找不到。

39 mandate [ˋmænˌdet] *n.* 命令，指令；(選民對所選領導者的) 授權，委任 & *vt.* 命令

片 a mandate to V　授權做……

似 order [ˋɔrdɚ] *n.* & *vt.* 命令 ①

▸ If you ignore or violate an official mandate, you could be charged with a crime and possibly go to jail.
如果你忽視或違反官方**命令**，你有可能會被起訴而被關進監獄。

▸ By winning the election, the new government had been given a mandate to take the country in a new direction.
新政府贏得選舉，被**授權**帶領國家走向新方向。

▸ A certain period of military service for all male citizens of the country has been mandated by law.
法律已**規定**，該國所有男性公民在某期間要服兵役。

40 nonprofit [ˌnɑnˋprɑfɪt] *a.* 非營利的

▸ Carol works for a nonprofit organization that collects donations of money and clothing to help children in Africa.
卡蘿在一間收集捐款和衣物捐贈來幫助非洲孩童的**非營利**組織工作。

41 pickup [ˋpɪk͵ʌp] *n.* 接(人);取(物);增加,提高

片 a pickup in... ……增加 / 上漲

衍 pick up... / pick... up
接(人);取(物)

- Bill picks up his wife from work every day.
  比爾每天都去**接**他老婆下班。
- "When are you going to pick up the photos?" Jim asked.
  吉姆問:『你什麼時候去**取**照片?』

- The taxi driver's last pickup that evening was a woman who wanted to go to the opposite side of town.
  該計程車司機那天晚上最後**接**的人是一名想去城鎮另一邊的女子。
- In December, stores in Western countries always experience a significant pickup in business due to Christmas shopping.
  12 月時由於聖誕採購的緣故,西方國家商店的生意都會大幅**增加**。

42 stance [stæns] *n.* 立場;站姿

似 (1) position [pəˋzɪʃən] *n.* 立場 ②
(2) posture [ˋpastʃɚ] *n.* 姿勢 ⑥

- The manager's stance was that no changes were needed to the product, despite some customer complaints about it.
  儘管有些顧客投訴這項商品,但該經理的**立場**是無須做任何改變。
- After standing in an uncomfortable stance while listening to the speech, George's legs started to feel a bit sore.
  喬治以不舒適的**站姿**站著聽演講後,他的雙腿開始感到有些痠痛。

43 thesis [ˋθisɪs] *n.* 論文;論點

複 theses [ˋθisiz]

似 (1) essay [ˋɛse] *n.* 論文 ②
(2) dissertation [͵dɪsɚˋteʃən]
n. (博士學位或專題) 論文

- Kerry is writing her thesis on effective methods of child discipline to earn her master's degree in psychology.
  凱莉正在撰寫有關管教孩子有效方法的**論文**,以拿到心理學的碩士學位。
- In his essay, Terrance developed his thesis that democracy is fragile and open to corruption from dishonest politicians.
  泰倫斯在論文中提出了**論點**,說明民主很脆弱且容易有腐敗政客的貪腐問題。

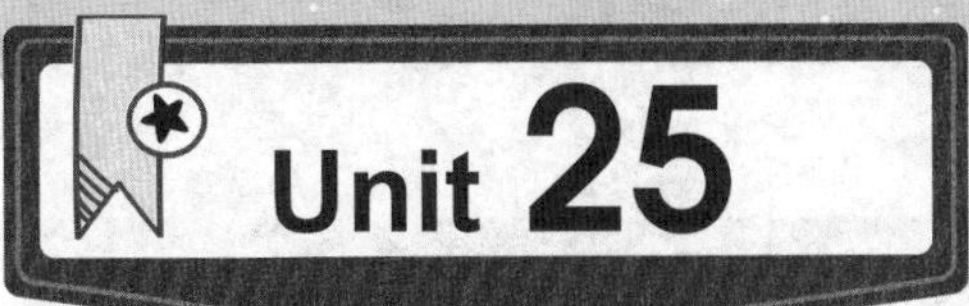

Unit 25

2501-2505

1 passerby [ˌpæsɚˋbaɪ] *n.* 路人

複 passersby [ˌpæsɚzˋbaɪ]
似 pedestrian [pəˋdɛstrɪən] *n.* 行人 ⑤

▸ No passersby paid any attention to the poor beggar.
路人們都沒注意到那個可憐的乞丐。

2 passionate [ˋpæʃənət] *a.* 熱情的，激昂的

片 be passionate about... 熱愛……
衍 passion [ˋpæʃən] *n.* 熱情 ③
have a passion for...
對……很有熱忱

▸ Jenny is passionate about dancing and spends most of her free time practicing.
珍妮很喜歡舞蹈，因此大部分的空閒時間都用來練習跳舞。

compassion [kəmˋpæʃən]
n. 同情（不可數）
片 have / show compassion for...
對……有同情心
似 (1) pity [ˋpɪtɪ] *n.* 同情 ③
(2) sympathy [ˋsɪmpəθɪ] *n.* 同情 ④

▸ You're such a cold fish! You have no compassion for the pain I'm suffering.
你真是冷血動物！你對我經歷的痛苦一點都不感到同情。
*a cold fish 冷血動物

compassionate [kəmˋpæʃənət]
a. 有同情心的
似 sympathetic [ˌsɪmpəˋθɛtɪk]
a. 富有同情心的 ④

▸ The jury's general response to the criminal was compassionate.
陪審團對這名罪犯的普遍反應是富同情心的。

3 pastry [ˋpestrɪ] *n.* 糕點

延伸 (1) pie [paɪ] *n.* 派 ①
(2) tart [tɑrt] *n.* 塔（點心）

▸ This bakery is famous for its large selection of pastries and cakes.
這家麵包店因其糕點及蛋糕種類選擇豐富而聞名。

4 pillar [ˋpɪlɚ] *n.* 柱子

似 column [ˋkɑləm] *n.* 柱子 ③

▸ Beams and pillars are used to support this building.
這棟建築物使用樑柱來支撐。

5 practitioner [prækˋtɪʃənɚ] *n.* 執業醫生 / 律師

片 a medical / legal practitioner
執業醫生 / 律師
衍 practice [ˋpræktɪs] *vt.* 開業從事 ①
practice medicine / law
當執業醫生 / 律師

▸ As a medical practitioner, Nelson has helped countless people regain their health.
= By practicing medicine, Nelson has helped countless people regain their health.
身為一名執業醫生，尼爾森幫助了無數的人重拾健康。

6 prophet [ˋprɑfɪt] *n.* 先知，預言家

衍 prophecy [ˋprɑfəsɪ] *n.* 預言（能力）

▶ A prophet warned us of a catastrophe that would occur by the end of the century.
某位預言家警告在世紀末將有一場大災難發生。
*catastrophe [kəˋtæstrəfɪ] *n.* 災難

7 rack [ræk] *vt.* 使受折磨 & *n.* 架子

片 (1) be racked with / by...
受……折磨 / 所苦
(2) rack one's brain(s) 絞盡腦汁

似 shelf [ʃɛlf] *n.* 架子 ②

延伸 nerve-racking [ˋnɝvˏrækɪŋ] *a.* 使人神經緊張的

▶ Waiting for the exam results to be posted is a nerve-racking experience.
等候考試成績的公布真是一個令人神經緊張的經驗。

▶ The venom from the spider bite racked Patrick's body with pain.
蜘蛛咬傷的毒液讓派翠克的身體受盡疼痛的折磨。
*venom [ˋvɛnəm] *n.* 毒液

▶ I've been racking my brains trying to remember the teacher's name.
我一直絞盡腦汁想要記起這名老師的名字。

▶ You can put your towels and clothes on this rack.
你可以把浴巾和衣物掛在這個架子上。

8 repay [rɪˋpe] *vt.* & *vi.* 償還；報答

三 repay, repaid [rɪˋped], repaid

片 (1) repay sb the money 償還某人錢
(2) repay sb for sth 為某事報答某人

▶ Justin promised to repay me the money I lent him as soon as possible.
賈斯汀答應儘快償還我借他的錢。

▶ I can never repay you for what you have done for me.
你為我做的事我永遠都報答不完。

9 righteous [ˋraɪtʃəs] *a.* 正直的

似 (1) upright [ˋʌpˏraɪt] *a.* 正直的 ⑥
(2) virtuous [ˋvɝtʃuəs] *a.* 品德高尚的

▶ Rev. Robinson was regarded as a righteous man in the neighborhood.
羅賓遜牧師在社區被視為是正直的人。
*Rev. [rɛv] *n.* 牧師（為 reverend [ˋrɛvərənd] 的縮寫，冠於姓氏前，對牧師的尊稱）

10 rod [rɑd] *n.* 棍棒

片 (1) a fishing rod 魚竿
(2) a lightning rod 避雷針

似 stick [stɪk] *n.* 棍子 ②

▶ The prices of fishing rods vary according to the material they are made from.
魚竿的價錢因製造材質的不同而有所差別。

11 sneak [snik] *vi.* 偷偷地走 & *vt.* 偷拿 & *n.* 偷偷摸摸的人

三 sneak, sneaked / snuck [snʌk], sneaked / snuck

片 (1) sneak into... 偷偷溜進……
(2) sneak sth into... 將某物偷偷帶進……

衍 sneaker [ˋsnikɚ] *n.* 運動鞋，球鞋 ⑥
a pair of sneakers 一雙球鞋

▸ Tom sneaked into the classroom in the middle of a lecture without being noticed.
湯姆在課上到一半時偷偷溜進教室沒被發現。

▸ Customers are not allowed to sneak outside food into the movie theater.
電影院不准許顧客把外食偷偷帶進去。

sneaky [ˋsnikɪ] *a.* 鬼鬼祟祟的

似 sly [slaɪ] *a.* 狡猾的 ⑥

▸ The man over there looks sneaky. I wonder what he is up to.
在那裡的男子看起來鬼鬼祟祟的。真不知道他想做什麼。

12 terminal [ˋtɝmənl̩] *n.* 總站；航廈 & *a.* (疾病) 末期的

片 (1) the bus terminal 巴士總站
(2) the air / airport terminal 航廈

衍 (1) terminate [ˋtɝməˏnet] *vt.* & *vi.* 終止
(2) termination [tɝməˋneʃən] *n.* 終止

▸ There's a shuttle service between the airport terminal and the city center.
機場航廈跟市中心之間有接駁車往返的服務。

▸ The family was distraught when they learned Denise's illness was most likely terminal.
該家族得知狄妮絲的病很可能是末期時非常焦慮不安。
*distraught [dɪˋstrɔt] *a.* 極其焦慮不安的

13 toxic [ˋtɑksɪk] *a.* 有毒的

似 poisonous [ˋpɔɪzn̩əs] *a.* 有毒的 ④

▸ Toxic wastes must be disposed of with care.
有毒廢物一定要小心棄置。

14 vacuum [ˋvækjuəm] *vt.* 吸塵 & *n.* 真空

片 (1) a vacuum cleaner 真空吸塵器
(2) a vacuum tube 真空管
(3) in a vacuum 處於真空狀態；與外界隔絕

▸ Barry's mother asked him to vacuum his room before he left for the afternoon.
貝瑞的媽媽請他下午出去前先把自己的房間用吸塵器吸過。

▸ This latest model of vacuum cleaner can move automatically by itself, according to the instructions.
根據使用說明書，這臺最新型的吸塵器可以自動移動。

▸ The learning of social skills does not take place in a vacuum.
社交技能是不能在與外界隔離的環境下習得的。

15 wheelchair [ˋ(h)wilˏtʃɛr] *n.* 輪椅

片 be confined to a wheelchair 坐輪椅

衍 wheel [(h)wil] *n.* 輪子 ②

▸ After the accident, Aaron had to be confined to a wheelchair for the rest of his life.
意外過後，艾倫下半輩子都得坐輪椅了。

2516-2526

16 backyard [ˋbækˌjɑrd] *n.* 後院

▸ Jonas' family hosted a barbecue in their backyard and invited their neighbors for dinner.
喬納斯一家在他們的**後院**辦烤肉派對，並邀請他們的鄰居前來晚餐。

17 chore [tʃɔr] *n.* 雜務

片 (1) do chores　做家務
(2) household chores　家事

▸ Children should be given chores to do in order to teach them responsibility.
家庭雜務應該分配給小孩子，好教會他們責任感。

▸ Mom said that I could go out and play after I did my chores.
媽說我**做完家務**後，就可以到外頭玩了。

18 envious [ˋɛnvɪəs] *a.* 羨慕的

片 be envious of...　羨慕⋯⋯
衍 envy [ˋɛnvɪ] *n.* & *vt.* 羨慕 ③

▸ Everyone is envious of Mary's beauty.
= Mary's beauty is everyone's envy.
= Mary's beauty is the envy of everyone.
= Everyone envies Mary's beauty.
瑪莉的美**羨煞**了每個人。

19 plural [ˋplʊrəl] *a.* 複數的 & *n.* (文法) 複數形

反 singular [ˋsɪŋgjələ] *a.* 單數的 & *n.* (文法) 單數形 ④

▸ *Sheep* is a singular noun, but it can also be used as a plural noun.
sheep 是單數名詞，不過它也可當**複數**名詞使用。

▸ *Wives* is the plural of *wife*.
wives 是 wife 的**複數形**。

20 pirate [ˋpaɪrət] *n.* 海盜 & *vt.* 盜版

衍 pirated [ˋpaɪrətɪd] *a.* 盜版的
a pirated CD / book　盜版 CD / 書

▸ The Vikings were the most famous pirates in medieval Europe.
維京人是中世紀歐洲最著名的**海盜**。
*medieval [ˌmɪdɪˋivəl] *a.* 中世紀的

▸ It's illegal to pirate CDs.
= It's illegal to make pirated CDs.
製作**盜版** CD 是違法的。

21 sophomore [ˋsɑfmɔr] *n.* (大學、高中) 二年級學生

▸ Connie changed her major when she was a sophomore.
康妮**大二**時轉換主修科目。

22 souvenir [ˋsuvə͵nɪr] *n.* 紀念品；紀念物

片 keep sth as a souvenir
保存某物當作紀念品

▸ Mom and Dad brought back several souvenirs from their trip to Spain.
爸媽西班牙之行回來時帶了幾項**紀念品**。

▸ I kept the pen my tour guide gave me as a souvenir.
我**把**導遊送給我的筆**留作紀念**。

23 striking [ˋstraɪkɪŋ] *a.* 明顯的，醒目的

似 (1) noticeable [ˋnotɪsəbḷ] *a.* 顯著的；值得注意的 ⑤
(2) conspicuous [kənˋspɪkjuəs] *a.* 明顯的

▸ There is a striking difference between Liam and Oliver in terms of personality. The former is extroverted, whereas the latter is introverted.
就個性而言，連恩和奧立佛很**明顯**不一樣。前者外向，後者則內向。
*extroverted [ˋɛkstrə͵vɝtɪd] *a.* 外向的
introverted [ˋɪntrə͵vɝtɪd] *a.* 內向的

24 shuttle [ˋʃʌtḷ] *n.* 梭子；往返通勤列車，區間車 & *vt.* 短程運送

片 (1) a space shuttle 太空梭
(2) a shuttle bus 接駁車
(3) a shuttle service 接駁服務

▸ The woman was weaving fabric with a shuttle.
這名女子正在用**梭子**織布。

▸ Is there a shuttle service to and from the airport?
往返機場有**接駁車的服務**嗎？

▸ Our hotel shuttled us to the museum for free.
我們的飯店免費**接送**我們到博物館。

25 output [ˋaut͵put] *n.* 產量；(自電腦、機器) 輸出的東西 & *vt.* (自電腦) 輸出

三 output, output / outputted [ˋaut͵putɪd], output / outputted

似 production [prəˋdʌkʃən] *n.* 生產 ②

反 input [ˋɪn͵put] *n.* 輸入 & *vt.* 把……輸入電腦 ④

▸ The country's agricultural output has doubled in the past year.
該國去年農業**生產**成長了一倍。

▸ Let me tell you what. I run the software, and you check the output.
讓我告訴你怎麼做：我來操作軟體，你來檢查**輸出的資料**。

▸ This special device is used to output information to that machine.
這個特殊的裝置是用來將資料**輸出**到那臺機器。

26 compulsory [kəmˋpʌlsərɪ] *a.* 必須做的，強制性的

似 (1) mandatory [ˋmændə͵torɪ] *a.* 義務的，強制的
(2) obligatory [əˋblɪgə͵torɪ] *a.* 義務的，強制的

▸ In order to graduate, all students must complete the list of compulsory college courses.
為了要畢業，所有學生一定要完成清單上大學的**必修課程**。

2527-2536

反 (1) voluntary [ˋvalən͵tɛrɪ] *a.* 自願的 ④
(2) optional [ˋapʃənḷ] *a.* 可選擇的 ⑤

27 athletics [æθˋlɛtɪks] *n.* 體育運動

衍 (1) athlete [ˋæθlit] *n.* 運動員 ③
(2) athletic [æθˋlɛtɪk] *a.* 運動的，體育的 ④

▸ Brad was never very good at math or science, but he excels in music and athletics.
布萊德從來都不太擅長數學或自然，但他精通音樂和**體育**。

28 shrug [ʃrʌg] *n.* & *vt.* & *vi.* 聳肩

三 shrug, shrugged [ʃrʌgd], shrugged

片 (1) shrug one's shoulders 聳肩
(2) shrug off... 不理會……

▸ In answer to my question, the waitress simply gave me a shrug.
在回答我的問題時，女服務生只是對我**聳了聳肩**。

▸ Don't shrug your shoulders. Give me an answer.
不要只是**聳肩**。給我一個答案。

▸ When Lisa's mother asked why she skipped class, Lisa just shrugged in response.
麗莎的媽媽問她翹課的理由時，麗莎只是**聳了聳肩**回應。

▸ Richard shrugged off allegations that he had cheated the customers.
理查**對於**有關他欺騙顧客的傳言**一笑置之**。
*allegation [͵æləˋgeʃən] *n.* 傳言，斷言

29 inherit [ɪnˋhɛrɪt] *vt.* 繼承；經遺傳而得

片 inherit sth from sb
從某人那裡繼承某物；從某人那裡遺傳到某特徵 / 疾病

衍 inheritance [ɪnˋhɛrətəns] *n.* 繼承

▸ Felicia was surprised to learn that she had inherited a mansion after a distant relative passed away.
費麗莎很驚訝得知她在一位遠親去世後**繼承**了一棟豪宅。

▸ David inherited his big nose and square jaw from his father.
大衛**遺傳**到他爸爸的大鼻子和方下巴。

30 opt [apt] *vi.* 選擇

片 (1) opt for... 選擇……
(2) opt to V 選擇做……
(3) opt in 選擇加入
(4) opt out 選擇不參加

衍 (1) option [ˋapʃən] *n.* 選擇 ④
(2) optional [ˋapʃənḷ] *a.* 可選擇的 ⑤

似 (1) choose [tʃuz] *vt.* & *vi.* 選擇 ①
(2) select [səˋlɛkt] *vt.* & *vi.* 選擇 ②

▸ Despite so many choices on the menu, Tim opted for a simple hamburger and fries.
儘管菜單上有許多品項，提姆**選擇**了一份簡單的漢堡和薯條。

▸ After checking the weather report, Tom and Grace opted to stay home instead of going shopping.
湯姆和葛瑞絲確認天氣預報後，**決定**不要去逛街待在家裡就好。

▸ Donald reluctantly decided to opt in when his friend proposed a mutual investment.
唐納德的朋友提議一項共同投資時，他不情願地**選擇加入**。

▸ We asked our coworkers if they would like to carpool to work, but most people opted out.
我們詢問同事他們是否想要一起共乘車子去上班，但大部分的人都**選擇不要**。
*carpool [ˋkɑr,pul] *vi.* 共乘汽車

31 chapel [ˋtʃæpl̩] *n.* 小禮拜堂

似 a small church 小教堂

▸ Rita had a small but beautiful wedding at the chapel.
瑞塔在一個**小禮拜堂**舉辦了一場小而美的婚禮。

32 infrastructure [ˋɪnfrə,strʌktʃɚ] *n.* 基礎建設

▸ Following years of war, the country's infrastructure was in very poor condition.
經過多年的戰爭，該國的**基礎建設**狀況非常糟糕。

33 entity [ˋɛntətɪ] *n.* 實體

片 a business entity 企業體

▸ The small store separated from its parent company to become an independent business entity.
這間小商店從它的母公司分離出來，變成一個獨立的**企業體**。

34 inning [ˋɪnɪŋ] *n.* (棒球的) 局，回合

▸ Thanks to a string of home runs, the Yankees were able to win the game in the final inning.
由於一連串的全壘打，洋基隊得以在最後一**局**贏得比賽。

35 emission [ɪˋmɪʃən] *n.* (氣體、光線等) 排放 (不可數)；排放物

片 (1) carbon emissions 碳排放
(2) greenhouse gas emissions 溫室氣體排放

▸ The politicians asked people to stop driving their cars in order to limit carbon emissions.
政客們請大眾停止開車以限制**碳排放**。

36 placement [ˋplesmənt] *n.* 放置

衍 place [ples] *n.* 地點 & *vt.* 放置 ①

▸ The family argued for hours over the best placement for the flowers at the wedding ceremony.
這一家人為了婚禮上花朵的最佳**擺放位置**爭執了好幾個小時。

2537-2539

37 theology [θɪˋalədʒɪ] *n.* 神學 (不可數)

衍 theological [ˌθiəˋladʒɪkḷ] *a.* 神學的

▸ After studying Christian theology at university, Marlon eventually decided to become a minister.
馬隆在大學研讀基督**神學**後，最終決定成為一名牧師。

38 supposedly [səˋpozɪdlɪ] *adv.* 大概，可能；據說

衍 (1) suppose [səˋpoz] *vt.* & *vi.* 猜想 ②
(2) supposed [səˋpozd] *a.* 據說的

▸ Trevor heard that a famous Hollywood star had supposedly bought a house in his neighborhood.
崔佛聽聞一名好萊塢明星**據說**在他住的社區買了一棟房子。

39 surveillance [səˋveləns] *n.* 監督，監視

片 (1) a surveillance camera
監視攝影機
(2) keep sb under surveillance
監視某人

似 (1) observation [ˌabzɝˋveʃən]
n. 監視；觀察 ④
(2) supervision [ˌsupɚˋvɪʒən]
n. 監視，監督 ⑤

▸ The army's surveillance of the enemy base suggests there are at least 1,000 soldiers inside.
該軍隊對敵軍基地的**監視**表示裡面至少有 1 千名士兵。

▸ Due to rising crime rates, Mr. Banks purchased several surveillance cameras for his property.
由於犯罪率上升，班克斯先生買了幾臺**監視攝影機**監控自己的房產。

▸ The judge agreed to release the suspect, but police will keep him under surveillance until the trial.
法官同意釋放嫌疑犯，但警方直到審判前會持續**監視**他。

Level 6

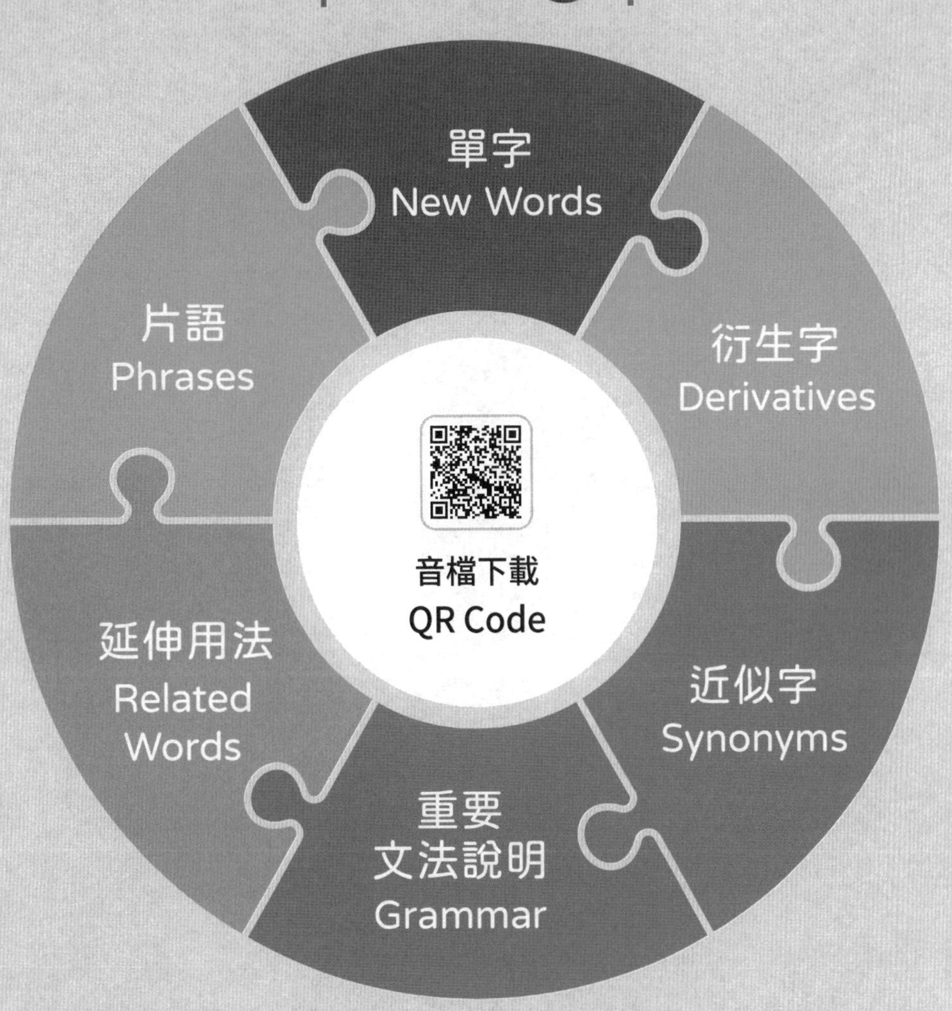
單字
New Words
衍生字
Derivatives
近似字
Synonyms
重要
文法說明
Grammar
延伸用法
Related
Words
片語
Phrases
音檔下載
QR Code

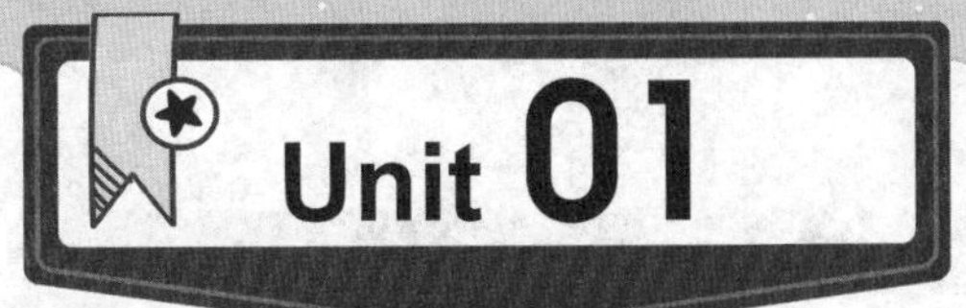

0101-0102

1 administer [əd`mɪnəstɚ ] *vt.* 管理；執行 / 實施（法律等）；給予（藥物、治療等）(= administrate [ əd`mɪnəstret])

片 (1) administer justice / the law 主持正義，執法
(2) administer + 藥物 + to sb 給某人藥物

衍 (1) administrator [əd`mɪnə,stretɚ] *n.* 行政 / 管理人員 ⑤
(2) administrative [əd`mɪnə,stretɪv] *a.* 行政 / 管理的 ⑤

似 manage [`mænɪdʒ] *vt.* 管理 ②

▸ It takes a lot of experience to administer a big company.
= It takes a lot of experience to manage a big company.
管理一間大公司需要很多的經驗。

▸ The duty of a judge is to administer justice.
法官的職責就是**主持正義**。

▸ The doctor administered the vaccine to the villagers.
那位醫師**為**村民**注射**疫苗。
*vaccine [væk`sin] *n.* 疫苗

2 radiate [`redɪ,et ] *vt.* & *vi.* 放射；散發，流露（情感、特質）& [ `redɪət / `redɪ,et] *a.* 輻射狀的

片 A radiates from B 從 B 放射出 A；從 B 散發 / 流露出 A

衍 radiation [,redɪ`eʃən] *n.* 輻射物，放射物；輻射能 ⑤

似 give off... 散發出……

▸ The sun radiates light and heat.
= Light and heat radiate from the sun.
太陽會**散發**光與熱。

▸ One of the car's headlights was broken, so only a single beam of light radiated from the vehicle.
汽車的一個頭燈壞了，所以汽車只**發出**一道光束。

▸ The rock star radiates charm and confidence.
這名搖滾歌手渾身**散發**魅力與自信。

▸ John never fails to look on the bright side of life; optimism positively radiates from him.
約翰都會去看生活中美好的一面。他**很積極樂觀**。

▸ The unusual radiate pattern on the coin meant that it was sought after by many collectors.
這硬幣上獨特的**放射狀**圖案，意味著很多收藏家都很想要。

---

radiant [`redɪənt] *a.* 光芒四射的；容光煥發的 & *n.*（天空中）光點

片 (1) a radiant face 容光煥發的臉龐
(2) be radiant with... 散發出……

▸ Angela announced, with a radiant face, that she was engaged to Brad.
安琪拉**一臉容光煥發**的樣子，宣布她與布萊德訂婚了。

▸ Mary is going to get married next week, and her face is radiant with happiness.
瑪麗下星期要結婚了，她的臉上**洋溢著**喜悅之情。

▸ Our science teacher told us to look toward the radiant, which is where the meteor shower will come from.
我們的科學老師告訴我們要朝**光點**的方向看，因那就是流星雨會來之處。
*a meteor [`mitɪɚ] shower 流星雨

3 originate [əˋrɪdʒə͵net] *vi.* 源自

片 (1) originate in + 時間 / 地方
源自某時 / 某地
(2) originate from sth 源自某物

衍 origin [ˋɔrədʒɪn] *n.* 起源 ②

似 derive [dɪˋraɪv] *vt.* 取得 & *vi.* 源自 ⑤

▸ Automobiles originated in the 19th century.
汽車**源自於** 19 世紀。

▸ My dance teacher told me that the tango originated in both Argentina and Uruguay.
我的舞蹈老師跟我說探戈**起源於**阿根廷與烏拉圭。

▸ Many Christmas traditions are thought to have originated in Germany.
聖誕節的許多傳統被認為是**起源於**德國。

▸ Chinese herbal medicines originate from plants and other natural substances.
中藥**源自**植物以及其他天然物質。
*herbal [ˋɝbl̩ / ˋhɝbl̩] *a.* 草本的
herbal medicine　草藥

4 rash [ræʃ] *n.* 疹子 & *a.* 草率的

片 (1) break out in a rash　開始長疹子
= come out in a rash
(2) a rash decision　草率的決定

似 hasty [ˋhestɪ] *a.* 倉促的，輕率的 ③

▸ I broke out in a rash after eating seafood yesterday.
我昨天吃完海鮮後就**開始長疹子**了。

▸ Think twice, or you're likely to make a rash decision.
你要再三考慮，否則可能會做出**草率的決定**。

5 victor [ˋvɪktɚ] *n.* 勝利者

衍 victory [ˋvɪktərɪ] *n.* 勝利 ②

似 champion [ˋtʃæmpɪən]
n. 冠軍，獲勝的人 ③

▸ Who was the victor in the fencing match?
誰**贏**了這場西洋劍比賽？
*fencing [ˋfɛnsɪŋ] *n.* 劍術

victorious [vɪkˋtɔrɪəs] *a.* 得勝的

似 (1) successful [səkˋsɛsfəl]
a. 成功的 ①
(2) triumphant [traɪˋʌmfənt]
a. 成功的

▸ The victorious team received a hero's welcome in their hometown.
這支**獲勝的**隊伍在他們的家鄉獲得英雄式的歡迎。

6 vocation [voˋkeʃən] *n.* (認為特別適合自己的) 職業；使命

片 have a vocation for...
有……的使命感

似 (1) career [kəˋrɪr] *n.* 職業，生涯
(一生大部分在做的工作) ③

▸ Amy has found her true vocation as a novelist.
艾咪找到真正屬於她的**職業**，就是當個小說家。

▸ Mr. Wilson has a vocation for preaching.
威爾森先生**有**傳道**的使命感**。

(2) occupation [ˌɑkjəˋpeʃən] *n.* 職業（可指短期或長期的工作）(= job) ④
*書面上常用 occupation，而口語上常用 job。
(3) profession [prəˋfɛʃən] *n.*（技術性高的）職業（如醫生、律師）④
(4) vacation [veˋkeʃən] *n.* 假期 ②

---

vocational [voˋkeʃənḷ] *a.* 職業的

片 (1) vocational education / training 在職教育 / 訓練；職業教育 / 訓練
(2) a vocational school 職業學校

▸ Laura is taking vocational training to learn to be a hairdresser.
蘿拉正在接受成為美髮師的**在職訓練**。

▸ George decided to attend the culinary vocational school, rather than the academic school, because he's more interested in cooking.
喬治決定就讀餐飲**職業學校**，而不是著重學術的學校，因為他對烹飪更感興趣。
*culinary [ˋkʌləˌnɛrɪ / ˋkjuləˌnɛrɪ] *a.* 烹飪的

7 abbreviate [əˋbrivɪˌet] *vt.* 縮寫

片 abbreviate A to B 將 A 縮寫為 B
衍 abbreviation [əˌbrivɪˋeʃən] *n.* 縮寫詞，縮略形式
似 shorten [ˋʃɔrtṇ] *vt.* 使變短 ③

▸ You could abbreviate the word "Monday" to "Mon."
你可以把『Monday』這個字**縮寫成**『Mon.』。

8 precede [priˋsid] *vt.* 在……之前

片 A be preceded by B A 之前有 B
衍 preceding [priˋsidɪŋ] *a.* 在前的，前面的
the preceding lesson / chapter 前一課 / 章

▸ Lunch will be preceded by a discussion session.
午餐**之前會有**一場討論會。

---

precedent [ˋprɛsədənt] *n.* 先例，前例

片 set a precedent for... 開……的先例

▸ The bill set a precedent for human rights legislation.
這個法案**開**人權立法**的先例**。

---

unprecedented [ʌnˋprɛsəˌdɛntɪd] *a.* 史無前例的

▸ The mayor was elected for an unprecedented fourth term.
這位市長**史無前例地**於第 4 屆連任選舉中獲勝。

9 blunt [blʌnt] *a.* 鈍的，不利的；直言不諱的 & *vt.* 使變鈍；使（情感）減弱

片 to be blunt　坦白說
= to be frank
= frankly speaking

反 sharp [ʃɑrp] *a.* 鋒利的 ①

▸ My pencil is blunt. Can you help me sharpen it?
我的鉛筆鈍了。你可以幫我把它削尖嗎？

▸ To be blunt, the quality of David's work is terrible.
坦白說，大衛的工作品質真差。

▸ By using it to cut through the rock-hard bread, Cindy blunted her favorite knife.
辛蒂用她最喜歡的刀子來切開如石頭般堅硬的麵包，結果弄鈍了這刀子。

▸ Listening to those boring lectures on medieval history has blunted my enthusiasm for the subject as a whole.
聽那些關於中世紀歷史的無聊講座，降低了我對這整個主題的熱情。

10 abide [əˋbaɪd] *vi.* 遵守

三 abide, abided / abode [əˋbod], abided

片 abide by...　遵守……

衍 law-abiding [ˋlɔə͵baɪdɪŋ] *a.* 守法的

似 abode [əˋbod] *n.* 住所

▸ Welcome to my humble abode!
歡迎光臨寒舍！

▸ Those who do not abide by the captain's orders will be thrown into the sea.
凡不聽從船長號令的人將被丟到海裡。

11 banquet [ˋbæŋkwɪt] *n.* 盛宴（正式場合的大型宴會）& *vi.* 舉辦宴會；參加宴會 & *vt.* 宴請

片 a state banquet　國宴

比 feast [fist] *n.* 盛宴（私人的小型宴會）④
a wedding feast　婚宴

▸ A state banquet will be held this evening in honor of the visiting President of the United States.
今晚將爲來訪的美國總統舉辦國宴。

▸ It is a tradition in our family to banquet on the first Saturday of every month.
我們家的傳統是每月的第一個星期六會舉辦宴會。

▸ Every evening, the fat king and queen would banquet until they could physically eat no more.
每天晚上，胖國王和王后都會參加宴會，直到他們再也吃不下任何東西為止。

▸ The president and first lady will be banqueting their guests in the White House.
總統和第一夫人將在白宮宴請賓客。

12 beep [bip] *n.* 嗶嗶聲 & *vi.* 發出嗶嗶聲

延伸 ding-dong [ˋdɪŋ͵dɔŋ]
n. (鐘或鈴發出的) 叮噹聲

▸ The alarm's beeps almost drove me nuts.
警報器的**嗶嗶聲**快把我給逼瘋了。

▸ Frank shut down his computer because it kept beeping.
法蘭克把電腦關機，因為它不斷**發出嗶嗶聲**。

13 climax [ˋklaɪmæks] *vi.* 達到最高峰 & *n.* 最精彩處，最高潮 (常用單數)

片 (1) climax in / with...
在……時達到最高潮
(2) at the climax of...
在……的最高潮 / 最精彩處
(3) reach a climax
(故事 / 情況等) 達到最高潮

▸ Mr. Wilson's career as a politician climaxed in his being elected president.
魏爾遜先生的政治生涯**在**當選總統**時達到最高峰**。

▸ At the climax of the story, the killer reveals himself.
= As the story reaches its climax, the killer reveals himself.
這故事**到了最高潮**時，凶手暴露其身分。

14 fury [ˋfjʊrɪ] *n.* 震怒

片 to one's fury 令某人憤怒的是
衍 furious [ˋfjʊrɪəs] *a.* 暴怒的 ④
似 (1) anger [ˋæŋgɚ] *n.* 生氣 ②
(2) rage [redʒ] *n.* 憤怒 ④

▸ Much to the manager's fury, our secret was leaked to another company.
令經理相當**震怒**的是，我們的機密被洩漏給了另一家公司。

15 downward [ˋdaʊn͵wɚd] *a.* 往下的

▸ Farmers are worried that the downward trend of vegetable prices will continue for a long time to come.
農民們很擔心菜價**下跌**的趨勢會持續好一陣子。

downward(s) [ˋdaʊn͵wɚd(z)]
adv. 向下地

▸ The road goes downwards before going upwards again.
這條路會先**下坡**，然後又會上坡。

upward [ˋʌpwɚd] *a.* 往上的

▸ The upward movement in vegetable prices was caused mainly by the recent cold fronts.
蔬菜價格**上漲**主要是因為最近冷鋒來襲。
*a cold front 冷鋒

upward(s) [ˋʌpwɚd(z)]
adv. 向上地

▸ With the economy going strong, property prices are moving upwards again.
經濟趨強之後，房地產的價格再度**上漲**。

0115-0123

outward [ˋaʊtwɚd] *a.* 向外的；外表的
反 inward [ˋɪnwɚd] *a.* 向內的

▸ Robert managed to hide his anger and showed no outward sign of it.
羅伯特掩藏了自己的憤怒，沒有表現出任何**外表的**異樣。

outward(s) [ˋaʊtwɚd(z)]
adv. 向外地
反 inwards [ˋɪnwɚd(z)] *adv.* 向內地

▸ Without proper management, it's dangerous for the company to expand outwards at this rapid rate.
沒有適當的管理，這家公司以如此快速的速度**向外**擴張是很危險的一件事。

16 instinctive [ɪnˋstɪŋktɪv] *a.* 本能的，直覺的

衍 instinct [ˋɪnstɪŋkt] *n.* 本能，直覺 ④
似 (1) natural [ˋnætʃərəl] *a.* 自然的 ②
(2) intuitive [ɪnˋt(j)uɪtɪv] *a.* 直覺的

▸ The spinning of webs is instinctive in spiders.
結網是蜘蛛的**本能**。

▸ The girl has an instinctive flair for design.
這個女孩子對設計有**直覺般的**天賦。

17 distress [dɪˋstrɛs] *n.* 痛苦，危難（不可數）& *vt.* 使極痛苦、悲傷

片 (1) be in distress
身處苦難，萬分痛苦
(2) a damsel in distress
處於困境而急需援助的少女
*damsel [ˋdæmzl̩] *n.* 少女
衍 distressed [dɪˋstrɛst] *a.* 憂慮的

▸ I can tell from Gina's face that she is in distress and badly in need of help.
我從吉娜臉上看出她**萬分痛苦**，急需援助。

▸ Elizabeth played the role of a damsel in distress in the film.
依莉莎白在該片中扮演一名**處於困境而急需援助的少女**。

▸ Sean isn't in a good mood because what the teacher said yesterday deeply distressed him.
尚恩心情不好，因為老師昨天說的話讓他**很難過**。

18 fuse [fjuz] *n.* 保險絲；引線，導火線 & *vt.* & *vi.* 融合；(使) 熔合

片 have a short fuse 易怒
似 blend [blɛnd] *vt.* & *vi.* 融合 ④

▸ I have no idea how to fix the fuse, so I'll have to call an electrician.
我不知道怎麼修理**保險絲**，所以我必須要打電話給電工。

▸ Peter lit the fuse on the expensive firework, but sadly, it failed to light up the sky.
彼得點燃了造價昂貴的煙火上的**引線**，但遺憾的是，煙火沒能照亮天空。

▸ Don't say anything stupid during the meeting, or the boss will eat you alive. He has a really short fuse.
開會的時候不要說錯話，不然老闆會痛罵你。他真的**很容易生氣**。

▸ The musician successfully fused together two contradictory styles in her music.
這音樂家成功地在她的音樂裡**融入**兩種相互衝突的風格。

▸ The intense heat inside the machine had caused the two pieces of metal to fuse together.
機器內的高溫使兩塊金屬熔在一起。

19 coastline [ˋkost͵laɪn] *n.* 海岸線

似 shoreline [ˋʃɔr͵laɪn] *n.* 海岸線

▸ We went for a beautiful scenic drive along the coastline.
我們沿著**海岸線**開車，欣賞沿途美麗的景色。
*go for a drive　開車兜風

20 ivy [ˋaɪvɪ] *n.* 常春藤

延伸 the Ivy League [lig]　常春藤盟校（指位於美東地區的八所具頂尖學術傳統的知名學府，包括布朗大學、哥倫比亞大學、康乃爾大學、達特茅斯學院、哈佛大學、賓夕法尼亞大學、普林斯頓大學、耶魯大學。）

▸ Several pots of ivy were hung on the walls to decorate the house.
房子牆上掛滿了一盆盆的**常春藤**作裝飾。

21 dormitory [ˋdɔrmə͵torɪ] *n.* 宿舍 (= dorm [dɔrm])

▸ I stayed in a dormitory and had three roommates when I was in college.
我大學時住在學校**宿舍**，有 3 個室友。

22 itch [ɪtʃ] *n.* 癢；渴望 & *vt.* & *vi.* (使) 發癢

片 (1) have an itch　癢
(2) have an itch for sth
渴望得到某物
= have a strong desire for sth
= have a burning desire for sth
(3) have an itch to + V
渴望做……
= have a strong desire to + V
= have a burning desire to + V

▸ I have an itch on the left side of my back. Can you scratch it for me?
我左背在**癢**。你可以幫我抓一下嗎？

▸ I have an itch for a good vacation.
我**好想**度個愉快的假期。

▸ I have an itch to go to Kenting for a visit.
我**好想**到墾丁去玩一趟。

▸ The fabric of the vest itches me.
這件背心的布料**讓**我很**癢**。

▸ My nose itches, and I can't concentrate.
我的鼻子很**癢**，所以我無法專心。

23 reproduce [͵riprəˋd(j)us] *vi.* & *vt.* 生殖，繁殖 & *vt.* 複製，翻印

片 reproduce oneself　自我繁殖
衍 produce [prəˋd(j)us] *vt.* 生產 ②

▸ Rabbits are known to reproduce at an extraordinary rate.
兔子以**繁殖**迅速著稱。

0123-0130

似 (1) breed [brid] *vi.* 繁殖 & *vt.* 飼養 ④
(2) procreate [ˋprokrɪˏet] *vt.* & *vi.* 繁殖，生育

▶ According to the scientists, the viruses can't reproduce themselves unless there is a host.
根據科學家的說法，除非有宿主，否則病毒無法**自我繁殖**。

▶ Many of the painter's major works were exquisitely reproduced in this reference book.
該畫家的許多重要作品都被精美地**翻印**在這本工具書裡。
*exquisitely [ɪkˋskwɪzɪtlɪ / ɛkˋskwɪzɪtlɪ] *adv.* 精美 / 緻地

reproduction [ˏripreˋdʌkʃən] *n.* 生殖，繁殖；複製品

衍 production [prəˋdʌkʃən] *n.* 生產 ②
似 (1) breeding [ˋbridɪŋ] *n.* 繁殖
(2) replica [ˋrɛplɪkə] *n.* 複製品

▶ The reproduction method of this newly discovered species of beetle is not yet clear to scientists.
科學家仍不清楚該新發現的甲蟲類是以什麼方式**繁殖**的。

▶ The connoisseur told me that the painting I bought wasn't an original work of Picasso but merely a reproduction.
行家告訴我，我買的畫不是畢卡索的真跡，而只是**複製品**而已。
*connoisseur [ˏkɑnəˋsʊr/ ˏkɑnəˋsɝ] *n.* (藝術、美食或音樂等的) 行家

24 headphones [ˋhɛdˏfonz] *n.* (掛在頭上的) 耳機 (恆用複數)

片 a set of headphones 一副耳機
= a headset [ˋhɛdˏsɛt]
似 earphones [ˋɪrˏfonz] *n.* (掛在頭上或塞入耳朵內的) 耳機 (恆用複數) ④

▶ Bob always has his headphones on when listening to music so that he won't disturb others with the high volume.
鮑伯聽音樂時總是帶上**耳機**，這樣他那大聲的音量就不會吵到別人。
*disturb [dɪsˋtɝb] *vt.* 干擾

25 stray [stre] *vi.* 偏離原路，走失；入歧途 & *a.* 走失的；散落的，零星的

片 a stray dog / cat 流浪狗 / 貓

▶ We strayed off the path and got lost in the mountains.
我們**偏離**了小徑，迷失在山中。

▶ Helen's daughter has strayed from the good path she was on; she dropped out of school and started taking drugs.
海倫的女兒**誤入歧途**；她輟學並開始吸毒。

▶ A stray hair at the crime scene led to the arrest of the local politician for murder.
犯罪現場一根**散落的**頭髮導致當地的政治家因謀殺案而被捕。

26 trifle [ˋtraɪfl̩] *n.* 瑣事 (可數) & *vi.* 小看，怠慢

片 trifle with... 怠慢 / 小看……

▶ Such a trifle is not worth discussing during the meeting.
這種**瑣事**不值得在會議中討論。

▶ Rebecca is my only daughter and is very precious to me; she is not someone to be trifled with.
麗蓓嘉是我的獨生女，對我來說非常寶貴；她不該被**怠慢**。

trifling [ˋtraɪflɪŋ] *a.* 不重要的
似 trivial [ˋtrɪvɪəl] *a.* 不重要的 ⑤

▶ The thing that bothers me about our manager is that she often loses her temper over trifling matters.
我受不了我們經理的地方是她常因**瑣**事而發脾氣。
*lose one's temper　某人發脾氣

27 outskirts [ˋaut͵skɝts] *n.* 郊區（恆用複數）

片 on the outskirts of...　在……的郊區
= in the suburbs of...
似 suburb [ˋsʌbɝb] *n.* 郊區 ③

▶ The value of real estate is lower on the outskirts of Taipei than in the central area.
臺北**郊區**的房地產較市中心的便宜。
*real estate [ˋrɪəl ɪs͵tet]　房地產（集合名詞，不可數）

28 ripple [ˋrɪpl̩] *n.* 漣漪 & *vt.* & *vi.*（使）起漣漪

比 wave [wev] *n.* 浪潮 ①

▶ On a boring Sunday afternoon, I skipped stones alone in the park, causing lots of ripples to spread across the pond.
一個無聊的星期天下午，我在公園自個兒玩打水漂，讓池塘起了陣陣**漣漪**。
*skip [skɪp] *vt.* 扔（石塊）打水漂
skip stones　用石頭打水漂

▶ A gentle breeze rippled the water.
微風在水上**吹出了漣漪**。

▶ The water rippled when the wind blew.
風吹時，水面**起了陣陣漣漪**。

29 uprising [ˋʌp͵raɪzɪŋ] *n.* 起義，暴動（= rebellion [rɪˋbɛljən]）

▶ The government tried and failed to stop the uprising by the angry citizens.
政府試圖阻止憤怒的人民**起義**，但沒有成功。

30 operative [ˋɑpərətɪv] *a.* 使用中的；和手術有關的（= operational [͵ɑpəˋreʃənl̩]）

衍 (1) operate [ˋɑpə͵ret]
vi. 運作 & *vt.* 操作 ②
(2) operation [͵ɑpəˋreʃən]
n. 運作；手術 ③
反 inoperative [ɪnˋɑpərətɪv]
a. 不能正常運轉的

▶ The factory employees work in three shifts around the clock, so the machinery is operative 24 hours a day.
工廠員工全天分三班工作，因此機器一天 24 小時都在**運轉**。

▶ The surgeon has developed a new operative technique that will benefit lots of people.
這名外科醫生開發了一種新的**手術**技術，將使許多人受益。

31 shuffle [ˋʃʌfḷ] *vi.* 拖著腳走 & *vi.* & *vt.* (因緊張等而) 坐立不安；洗 (牌)

片 shuffle one's feet
坐立不安，不停地擺動雙腳

▶ Tired from a long day at the office, Ben shuffled along the sidewalk on his way home.
在辦公室待了一天很累，班在回家的路上**拖著步伐**走在人行道上。

▶ Mike shuffled uneasily on the sofa because he was about to have an important job interview.
邁克**不安**地坐在沙發上，因為他即將要參加一個重要的工作面試。

▶ While waiting to see the dentist, Paul shuffled his feet nervously as he sat on the chair.
保羅在等著看牙醫時，在椅子上**坐立不安**。

▶ Tom, it's your turn to be the dealer. Quickly shuffle and give each of us five cards.
湯姆，該你發牌了。快點**洗牌**並給我們每個人五張牌。

▶ Because the young girl's hands were too small to shuffle the cards, she asked her father do it for her.
因為這個小女孩的手太小，不能**洗牌**，她要她的父親幫她洗牌。

32 invariably [ɪnˋvɛrɪəblɪ] *adv.* 總是，不變地

衍 (1) vary [ˋvɛrɪ] *vi.* & *vt.* (使) 不同 ③
(2) various [ˋvɛrɪəs] *a.* 各種各樣的 ③
(3) variable [ˋvɛrɪəbḷ] *a.* 多變的 ⑤
(4) invariable [ɪnˋvɛrɪəbḷ] *a.* 不變的

反 variably [ˋvɛrɪəblɪ] *adv.* 易變地

▶ Roger is much better at tennis than Janice, so he invariably wins whenever they play together.
羅傑網球打得比珍妮絲好得多，所以每當他們一起打網球時，羅傑**總是**贏。

33 imminent [ˋɪmənənt] *a.* (尤指不愉快的事) 即將發生的，逼近的

衍 imminence [ˋɪmənəns] *n.* 迫近

▶ Looking at the dark clouds, Gina could tell that rain was imminent, but she had left her umbrella at home.
看著烏雲，吉娜可以看出**要**下雨了，但她把傘放在家裡了。

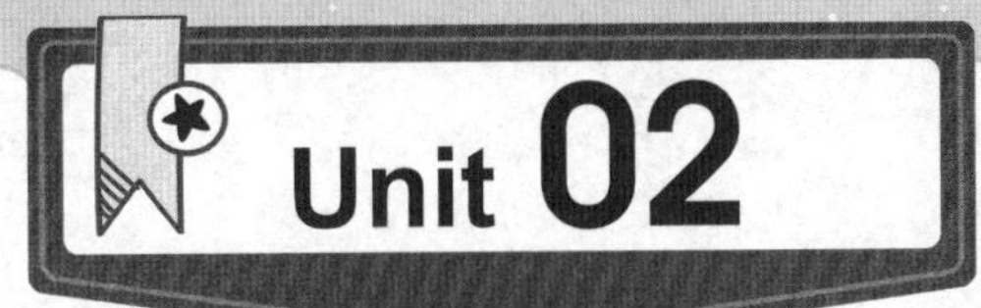

0201-0205

1 honorary [ˋɑnə͵rɛrɪ] *a.* (學位) 名譽上的

片 (1) an honorary degree 名譽學位
(2) an honorary chair 榮譽主席
(3) an honorary doctorate [ˋdɑktərət] 名譽博士學位

衍 (1) honor [ˋɑnɚ] *n.* & *vt.* 榮譽 ③
(2) honorable [ˋɑnərəbḷ] *a.* 值得尊敬的 ⑤

▸ The politician had received an honorary degree from the university.
該政治人物獲得了那間大學所頒的榮譽學位。

2 hunch [hʌntʃ] *n.* 預感，直覺 & *vi.* & *vt.* (使) 背部隆起

片 (1) have a hunch that... 有……的預感
= have a feeling that...
(2) hunch over... 把背隆起緊靠著……

衍 hunchback [ˋhʌntʃ͵bæk] *n.* 駝背；駝背者

▸ I have a hunch that it will rain this afternoon.
我有預感今天下午會下雨。

▸ Linda hunched over her desk as she studied.
琳達念書時把背隆起緊靠著書桌。

3 anticipation [æn͵tɪsəˋpeʃən] *n.* 期待，預期

片 in anticipation of... 期待……
= in expectation of...

衍 anticipate [ænˋtɪsə͵pet] *vt.* 期待，預期 ⑤

▸ Reporters packed the theater in anticipation of the actor's arrival.
記者擠滿了戲院，期待著該演員的到來。

4 mischievous [ˋmɪstʃəvəs] *a.* 惡作劇的，頑皮的

片 a mischievous smile / grin [grɪn] / look 惡作劇的微笑 / 咧嘴笑 / 神色

衍 mischief [ˋmɪstʃɪf] *n.* 惡作劇 ④

似 naughty [ˋnɔtɪ] *a.* 調皮的 ②

▸ The student looked at the teacher with a mischievous smile.
學生對老師露出了惡作劇的微笑。

5 expenditure [ɪkˋspɛndətʃɚ] *n.* (政府或個人的) 開支，開銷 (與介詞 on 並用)

片 a reduction in public / government expenditure 公共 / 政府開支調降

似 (1) expense [ɪkˋspɛns] *n.* 花費，支出 ②
(2) spending [ˋspɛndɪŋ] *n.* (政府、組織等的) 花費，開銷

▸ Make sure our expenditure on research doesn't exceed our budget.
要確定我們的研究開銷不會超過預算。

0206-0213

反 (1) income [ˋɪnˏkʌm] *n.* 收入 ②
(2) revenue [ˋrɛvən(j)u] *n.* 收入，歲入 ⑤

6 simultaneous [ˏsaɪmḷˋtenɪəs / ˏsɪmḷˋtenɪəs] *a.* 同步的

片 simultaneous interpretation
同步口譯

▸ About 1,500 users can have simultaneous access to our system.
本系統可以容納約 1,500 個使用者**同時**上線。

▸ Simultaneous interpretation is incredibly difficult, as you have to translate from one language to another in real time.
同步口譯是非常困難的，因為你必須即時地將一種語言翻譯成另一種語言。

7 eyesight [ˋaɪˏsaɪt] *n.* 視力（不可數）

片 have good / poor eyesight
眼力好 / 不好

延伸 hearing [ˋhɪrɪŋ] *n.* 聽力（不可數）；公聽會（可數）

▸ John has had poor eyesight ever since he was born.
約翰自出生**視力**就很差。

8 outlook [ˋautˏluk] *n.* 展望（與介詞 for 並用，常用單數）

似 prediction [prɪˋdɪkʃən] *n.* 預料 ④

延伸 prospect [ˋprɑspɛkt] *n.* 前景，成功的機會（與介詞 for 或 of 並用，恆用複數）⑤

▸ The outlook for this company is very bright.
該公司的**前景**大好。

9 safeguard [ˋsefˏgɑrd] *vt.* & *vi.* & *n.* 保護，防衛（皆與介詞 against 並用）

片 safeguard (A) against B
保護 (A) 免受 B 所害

▸ The government was praised for working hard and fast to safeguard the country against the virus.
該政府因努力又迅速地**保護**國家**免受**病毒**侵害**而受到讚揚。

▸ Regular exercise can help safeguard against chronic illnesses.
規律運動可幫助**預防**慢性病。
*chronic [ˋkrɑnɪk] *a.* 慢性病的

▸ Senator Presley introduced this bill many years ago as a safeguard against domestic violence.
普利司理議員多年前引進這項法案來**防止**家暴發生。
*domestic [dəˋmɛstɪk] *a.* 家庭的；國內的

10 designate [ˋdɛzɪg,net] *vt.* 指派；把……定名為，標明

片 (1) designate sb to + V
指派某人做……
(2) designate A (as) B　指派 A 當 B；
把 A 定名為 B，標明 A 為 B
(3) a designated hitter
(棒球) 指定代打，指定打擊

衍 designation [,dɛzɪgˋneʃən] *n.* 命名

▶ The official designated his aide to act for him at the conference.
這位官員**指派**助手代理他出席該會議。
*aide [ed] *n.* 助手

▶ Mr. Johnson has been designated (as) chairman of the campaign's fundraising activities.
強森先生已被**指派為**競選募款活動的主席。
*fundraising [ˋfʌnd,rezɪŋ] *n.* 募款

▶ In the UK, several parts of the countryside have been designated (as) Areas of Outstanding Natural Beauty.
在英國，一些鄉村地區被**指定為**「傑出自然風景區」。

11 academy [əˋkædəmɪ] *n.* (專門培養專才的) 學院 (如藝術學院、攝影學院等)

片 (1) a military academy　軍校
(2) the Royal Academy of Music
(英國) 皇家音樂學院

衍 academic [,ækəˋdɛmɪk] *a.* 學術的 ④

延伸 cadet [kəˋdɛt] *n.* 軍校學生

▶ It's my dream to get admitted to West Point Military Academy.
獲得西點**軍校**的入學許可是我的夢想。

12 barbarian [bɑrˋbɛrɪən] *n.* 野蠻人；未開化的人，沒教養的人 & *a.* 野蠻的；未開化的

衍 barbarous [ˋbɑrbərəs] *a.* 野蠻的

似 savage [ˋsævɪdʒ] *n.* 野蠻人 ⑥

反 civilized [ˋsɪvə,laɪzd]
a. 有文化的，開化的

▶ The ancient Greeks and Romans considered the inhabitants of all other nations to be barbarians.
古希臘羅馬人認為所有其他國家的居民都是**野蠻人**。

▶ To our disgust, the barbarian picked his nose at the elegant dinner in that fancy restaurant.
令我們反感的是，這**沒教養的人**在那家高級餐廳裡享用雅緻的晚餐時竟挖鼻孔。

▶ The barbarian invaders burned all the city's buildings to the ground while the citizens were still inside.
野蠻入侵者在該市的市民仍在屋內時，將城內的所有建物都燒毀。

▶ Please don't invite that barbarian guy who doesn't even know which silverware to use at the dinner table!
請不要邀請那**沒教養的**人，他甚至不知道用餐時要用哪種餐具！

13 frantic [ˋfræntɪk] *a.* 發狂似的

似 hysterical [hɪsˋtɛrɪkḷ] *a.* 歇斯底里的

▶ Mary's mother was frantic because her daughter had been missing for several days.
瑪麗失蹤好幾天了，她的母親焦慮地快**抓狂**了。

0214-0224

14 commonplace [ˋkamən,ples] *a.* 普通的

衍 common [ˋkamən]
a. 常見的；普通的 ①

▶ Thanks to the invention of the internet, buying goods online is now commonplace.
由於網路的發明，現在線上購物已經是**很普遍**了。

15 coupon [ˋkupan] *n.* 折價券，優惠券

似 voucher [ˋvautʃɚ] *n.* 兌換券 ⑤

▶ My mother likes to collect coupons from newspapers so she can save money on food.
媽媽喜歡蒐集報紙上的**折價券**，這樣在食物的花費上可以省點錢。

16 garment [ˋgarmənt] *n.* 衣服（可數）

似 clothing [ˋkloðɪŋ]
n. 衣服，服裝（不可數）②

用法
可　說：a garment、two garments (○)
不可說：a clothing、two clothings (×)
可　說：a piece of clothing、two pieces of clothing (○)

▶ This garment must be hand-washed and air-dried.
這件**衣服**一定要手洗並晾乾。

17 interpreter [ɪnˋtɝprɪtɚ] *n.* 口譯人員

似 translator [trænsˋletɚ] *n.* 翻譯人員（尤指筆譯）④

▶ Nicole acted as an interpreter at the international conference.
妮可在這次國際會議中擔任**口譯**。

18 doze [doz] *vi.* 小睡，打瞌睡

片 doze / nod off　小睡，打瞌睡

▶ Grandfather dozed off in the middle of the TV show.
電視節目看到一半爺爺就**打起瞌睡**了。

19 jade [dʒed] *n.* 玉（不可數）

▶ Linda likes wearing earrings made of jade.
琳達喜歡戴**玉**製的耳環。

20 gallop [ˋgæləp] *vi.* & *n.*（馬的）奔馳

片 break into a gallop　突然奔馳起來

▶ The white horse galloped elegantly along the beach.
這匹白馬優雅地**奔馳**過這片沙灘。

▶ The horse broke into a gallop when it heard the gun shot.
馬匹聽到槍聲時，就**開始全力衝刺**。

21 dispose [dɪˋspoz] *vi.* 處置（與介詞 of 並用）

片 dispose of... 處理掉……
= get rid of...

▸ Most countries have difficulties in disposing of nuclear waste.
大部分的國家都面臨**處理**核廢料的困境。

disposable [dɪˋspozəbḷ]
a. 用完即丟棄的

片 (1) a disposable diaper 紙尿布
*diaper [ˋdaɪəpɚ] *n.* 尿布
(2) a disposable chopstick
免洗筷（常用複數）

▸ There has been a lot of debate over the impact of disposable diapers on the environment.
已有很多關於**紙尿布**對環境所造成的影響的爭論。

disposal [dɪˋspozḷ] *n.* 處理，清除

片 at sb's disposal 任由某人支配
似 removal [rɪˋmuvḷ] *n.* 丟棄 ⑤

▸ The disposal of waste is a serious issue to consider when dealing with pollution.
在處理汙染時，廢物**處理**是一項要考慮的重要議題。

▸ It will be a lot more convenient for you to get around the city if you have a car at your disposal.
如果你**隨時**有車可以開的話，在城市裡四處逛逛就會方便得多了。

22 peek [pik] *vi.* 偷窺（與介詞 at 並用）（= peep [pip]）

片 peek at... 偷窺……
延伸 peek-a-boo [ˋpikə͵bu]
n. & *interj.* 躲貓貓（喊著 "peek-a-boo" 並反覆遮臉又露臉的逗小孩遊戲）

▸ The actor peeked at the audience from behind the curtain before the play started.
演員在戲劇開始之前從布幕後面**偷瞄**了觀眾席。

23 comet [ˋkamɪt] *n.* 彗星

片 Halley's Comet 哈雷彗星
延伸 a shooting star
流星（= meteor [ˋmitɪɚ]）

▸ Halley's Comet was named after the astronomer Edmond Halley.
哈雷彗星是以天文學家愛德蒙．哈雷而命名。
*name A after B 以 B 來命名 A
astronomer [əˋstrɑnəmɚ] *n.* 天文學家

24 rivalry [ˋraɪvḷrɪ] *n.* 競爭

衍 rival [ˋraɪvḷ] *n.* 競爭對手 ⑤
似 competition [͵kɑmpəˋtɪʃən]
n. 競爭 ④

▸ There has always been fierce rivalry between the two companies for larger market shares.
這兩家公司之間對於誰能有較大的市場占有率**競爭**總是很激烈。
*fierce [fɪrs] *a.* 激烈的
market share 市場占有率

0225-0233

25 gay [ge] *a.* 快樂的；男同性戀的 & *n.* 男同性戀

似 (1) happy [ˋhæpɪ] *a.* 快樂的 ①
(2) merry [ˋmɛrɪ] *a.* 歡樂的 ③
(3) homosexual [ˏhoməˋsɛkʃuəl] *a.*（尤指男）同性戀的 & *n.*（尤指男）同性戀 ⑥

用法 gay 一字原意為『歡樂的』，但自 1970 年以後由於美國舊金山等地的同志運動蓬勃發展，該字被廣泛用來指稱『男同性戀』。而現今指『歡樂的』則多用 happy 或 merry 替代。

延伸 come out of the closet
出櫃（即公開同性戀身分）

▶ All the guests were happy and gay at the party.
宴會上，所有的來賓都很**盡興**。

▶ That movie star is very popular among gay people.
該電影明星在**同志**群中很受歡迎。

▶ Nowadays, it is considered offensive to say, "He is a gay." It is preferable to say, "He is a gay man."
現今人們認為說『他是個**同性戀**』是冒犯之語，最好說『他是男同志。』

26 duration [djuˋreʃən] *n.* 期間

片 for the duration of + 一段時間
為期……

似 meantime [ˋminˏtaɪm] *n.* 期間 ⑤

▶ The farm was used as a concentration camp for the duration of the war.
戰爭**期間**這座農場被用來當作集中營。
*concentration [ˏkɑnsənˋtreʃən] *n.* 集中

27 surge [sɝdʒ] *vi.* & *n.* 激增，上揚；急衝，湧入

片 (1) a surge in / of...
……激增；……湧入
(2) feel a surge of excitement
突然興奮起來
(3) feel a surge of fury
突然狂怒起來

似 rise [raɪz] *vi.* & *n.* 上升 ①

▶ Adrenalin surges when one feels one's life is in great danger.
當人覺得生命受到很大威脅時，腎上腺素便會**激增**。
*adrenalin [ædˋrɛnḷɪn] *n.* 腎上腺素

▶ Many families are affected by the recent surge in food prices.
最近食物價格**大漲**，許多家庭都受到影響。

▶ When my favorite band appeared on stage, I felt a surge of excitement and couldn't resist screaming!
我最喜歡的樂團出現在舞臺上時，我**感到異常興奮**，忍不住尖叫了起來！

▶ Angelina felt a surge of fury and hung up on Frank.
安潔莉娜**突然一陣怒火上來**，掛了法蘭克電話。

▶ Protesters attempted to surge through the gates but were stopped by the police.
抗議群眾試圖**湧進**大門內，但被警察擋下了。

▶ Now that summer is coming, local folks are expecting a surge of visitors from all over the world.
由於夏日將至，當地人都引頸期待即將由世界各地**湧入**的觀光客。

28 isle [aɪl] *n.* (小) 島 (文學用語或常用於島名)

似 island [ˋaɪlənd] *n.* (大) 島 ①

▸ Few humans have ever set foot on the isle, so it is still very pristine.
幾乎沒什麼人來過這個小島，所以它仍很原始。
*pristine [prɪˋstin / ˋprɪstin] *a.* 原始的

29 intonation [ˌɪntoˋneʃən] *n.* 語調

衍 tone [ton] *n.* 聲調 ②

▸ We usually finish a sentence with a falling intonation.
我們通常會用降低的語調來結束句子。

30 dwarf [dwɔrf] *n.* 侏儒 & *vt.* 使顯得矮小

複 dwarfs / dwarves

▸ *Snow White and the Seven Dwarfs* is a household fairy tale.
《白雪公主與七矮人》是家喻戶曉的童話故事。
*household [ˋhaʊsˌhold] *a.* 家喻戶曉的

▸ At 508 meters, Taipei 101 dwarfs virtually all the other buildings in Taipei.
臺北 101 大樓高達 508 公尺，幾乎使臺北市所有其他的建築相形見絀。

31 gangster [ˋgæŋstɚ] *n.* 幫派分子

延伸 (1) thug [θʌg] *n.* 惡棍，罪犯
(2) hooligan [ˋhulɪgən] *n.* 流氓
(3) hoodlum [ˋhudləm] *n.* 流氓

▸ In the gunfight, two gangsters were killed and three were severely wounded.
槍戰中，有 2 名幫派分子被殺，3 名受到重傷。

32 innumerable [ɪˋn(j)umərəbl̩] *a.* 無數的

衍 (1) number [ˋnʌmbɚ] *n.* 數字 ①
(2) numerous [ˋn(j)umərəs] *a.* 很多的 ④
(3) numeral [ˋn(j)umərəl] *n.* 數字

似 countless [ˋkaʊntləs] *a.* 數不清的

▸ The stars in the galaxy are innumerable.
銀河系中的星星數也數不清。

33 infectious [ɪnˋfɛkʃəs] *a.* 傳染的

衍 (1) infection [ɪnˋfɛkʃən] *n.* 感染 ④
(2) infect [ɪnˋfɛkt] *vt.* 感染 ⑤

似 (1) contagious [kənˋtedʒəs] *a.* 有傳染性的 ⑤
(2) epidemic [ˌɛpəˋdɛmɪk] *a.* 傳染的，肆虐的 ⑤

▸ This disease is dangerous because it is highly infectious.
這種疾病很危險，因為它的傳染力很強。

34 utter [ˋʌtɚ] *a.* 完全的 & *vt.* 說 (= say)

片 (1) not utter a word　不發一語
(2) utter / heave a sigh　歎一口氣
*heave [hiv] *vt.* 發出 (歎息)

似 complete [kəmˋplit] *a.* 完全的 ②

▸ Diana thinks the three-hour board meeting was an utter waste of time.
黛安娜覺得這 3 個小時的董事會會議完全是浪費時間。

▸ The accused sat through the whole court session without uttering a word.
被告在整個開庭過程都不發一語。
*session [ˋsɛʃən] *n.* (法庭) 開庭

utterly [ˋʌtɚlɪ] *adv.* 完全地

似 (1) completely [kəmˋplitlɪ] *adv.* 完全地
(2) entirely [ɪnˋtaɪrlɪ] *adv.* 完全地
(3) totally [ˋtotl̩ɪ] *adv.* 徹底地

▸ The driver's explanation of how the accident happened is utterly unacceptable.
這位駕駛人對意外發生原因的解釋讓人完全無法接受。

35 roam [rom] *vi.* & *vt.* & *n.* 漫步

片 roam about...　漫步於⋯⋯

似 (1) wander [ˋwɑndɚ] *vi.* & *vt.* 閒逛 ③
(2) rove [rov] *vi.* 到處遊走

▸ My father always says that the best way to experience a new city is to simply roam.
我父親總是說，體驗一座新城市最好的方式就是去漫遊。

▸ Every afternoon, the philosopher would roam about the lake, contemplating life.
每天下午，這位哲學家會在湖邊散步，思考人生。
*contemplate [ˋkɑntəm͵plet] *vt.* 思考

▸ Betty and her friends roamed the streets of the new city, wondering where they should go next.
貝蒂和她的朋友在新城市的街道上漫步，在想他們下個地方要去哪裡。

▸ I'm going for a roam around the village before dinner. Would you like to join me?
晚餐前我要在村子裡晃晃。你想一起去嗎？

36 perch [pɝtʃ] *vi.* 棲息 / 停留於 & *n.* 鳥類的棲木

片 perch on / in...
棲息在⋯⋯上面 / 之內

▸ Little birds are perching on the buffalo's back to eat ticks.
小鳥棲息在水牛背上吃蝨子。
*buffalo [ˋbʌfl̩͵o] *n.* 水牛
tick [tɪk] *n.* 小蝨子

▸ Every morning the birds would sit on the perch outside my bedroom window and sing.
每天早上都會有小鳥在我房間窗外的棲木上唱歌。

37 jasmine [ˋdʒæsmən] *n.* 茉莉

延伸 lily [ˋlɪlɪ] *n.* 百合（花）③

▸ Jasmine is my favorite flower.
茉莉是我最喜歡的花。

38 vanity [ˋvænətɪ] *n.* 虛榮

衍 vain [ven] *a.* 虛榮的 ④
in vain 白費功夫
= to no avail
= to no purpose
*avail [əˋvel] *n.* 效用

▸ Out of vanity, Paul drives expensive cars and wears designer clothes.
因為**愛慕虛榮**，保羅開昂貴的名車以及穿名牌服飾。
*designer [dɪˋzaɪnɚ] *n.* 設計師
a designer shirt 名牌襯衫
比較：a brand-name shirt 有牌子的襯衫（未必是名牌）

39 withhold [wɪðˋhold] *vt.* 拒絕給與

三 withhold, withheld [wɪðˋhɛld], withheld

片 withhold sth from sb
拒絕給與某人某物

▸ Because the worker did not fulfill the terms of the contract, the company withheld payment from him.
由於那員工沒有履行契約的條款，公司**扣留**了要給他的款項。

40 strait [stret] *n.* 海峽；（常指因缺錢而有的）困境（此意恆用複數）

片 (1) Taiwan / Formosa Strait
臺灣海峽
(2) be in dire / difficult straits
（錢財方面）很窘迫
*dire [daɪr] *a.* 危急的

▸ The Taiwan Strait lies between Taiwan and Mainland China and is also named Formosa Strait by many Westerners.
臺灣海峽位於臺灣和中國大陸之間，也被許多西方人稱為福爾摩沙海峽。

▸ Not long after losing his job, Hank was in dire straits and didn't know what to do.
漢克丟掉工作不久，就**處境很窘迫**而不知道該怎麼辦才好。

41 lavish [ˋlævɪʃ] *a.* 鋪張奢華的，（花費）揮霍的；（讚美等）慷慨給予的 & *vt.* 慷慨（或過分）地給予

片 lavish sb with sth 給某人很多某物

▸ To celebrate his success, Roger held a lavish party at his home with champagne and expensive food.
為了慶祝他的成功，羅傑在家裡開了一個**鋪張奢華的**派對，喝香檳又吃很昂貴的食物。

▸ The guest speaker was quite embarrassed by the lavish praise that the host gave her as he introduced her to the audience.
當主持人把這位演講嘉賓介紹給觀眾時，這演講嘉賓對主持人的**大肆**讚揚感到相當地尷尬。

▸ Lucy expected her boyfriend to lavish her with gifts and flowers, but he rarely did anything like that.
露西希望她男友**送**她**很多**禮物和鮮花，但他很少這樣做。

0242-0243

42 junction [ˋdʒʌnkʃən] *n.* 交叉路口；匯合處，樞紐站 (= intersection [ˏɪntɚˋsɛkʃən] = crossroads [ˋkrɔsˏrodz] (恆用複數))

▶ When Trevor arrived at the junction, he couldn't remember if he should turn left or right to get to his friend's house.

當崔佛到達交叉路口時，他不記得他該左轉還是右轉才能到他朋友家。

43 incur [ɪnˋkɝ] *vt.* 招致，遭受

三 incur, incurred [ɪnˋkɝd], incurred
(現在分詞為 incurring [ɪnˋkɝɪŋ])

似 occur [əˋkɝ] *vi.* 發生 ②
三態為：occur, occurred [əˋkɝd], occurred

▶ James incurred his boss' anger after being late for work several days in a row.

詹姆士連續幾天都遲到，使老闆很生氣。

*in a row　連續地

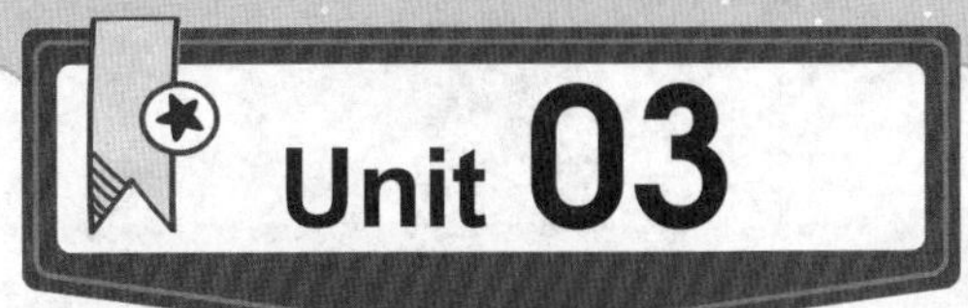

Unit 03

0301-0305

1 equate [ɪ`kwet] *vt.* 使相等（與介詞 with 並用）

片 equate A with B　將 A 與 B 視為相等

衍 (1) equation [ɪ`kweʃən] *n.* 方程式，等式 ⑤
(2) equivalent [ɪ`kwɪvələnt] *a.* 相等的 & *n.* 相等物 ⑤

▶ It's a human tendency to equate wealth and fame with success in life.
將財富、名望和人生的成功劃上等號是人之常情。
*tendency [`tɛndənsɪ] *n.* 傾向

2 attain [ə`ten] *vt.* 達到；獲得

片 attain / achieve one's / a goal　達到目標

▶ Through hard work, Mr. Wilson eventually attained his goal of becoming the greatest writer in his country.
魏爾遜先生經由努力，終於達到目標，成為他國家最偉大的作家。

▶ Frank attained a high score on the English test.
法蘭克這次英文考試拿到了高分。

attainment [ə`tenmənt] *n.* 獲得

▶ The attainment of a doctoral degree is impossible without years of hard work.
沒有多年的努力是無法獲得博士學位的。

3 covet [`kʌvɪt] *vt.* 貪圖

似 crave [krev] *vt.* 渴望獲得

▶ Coveting what other people have will only make your life bitter.
貪圖他人所擁有的東西只會讓你的生活更痛苦。
*bitter [`bɪtɚ] *a.* 痛苦的

4 warfare [`wɔr,fɛr] *n.* 戰爭，交戰狀態（不可數）

片 (1) chemical and biological warfare　生化戰
(2) germ warfare　細菌戰

延伸 (1) truce [trus] *n.* 休戰，停戰
(2) militant [`mɪlətənt] *a.* 好戰的；激進的 & *n.* 好鬥者；激進分子

▶ They're trying to prevent the situation from erupting into open warfare.
他們設法防止這情勢爆發成公開的戰事。

▶ The newly elected president accused the rogue state of engaging in chemical and biological warfare.
新當選的總統指責那流氓國家從事生化戰。

5 precision [prɪ`sɪʒən] *n.* 精確性

片 with precision　精準地
= precisely

衍 (1) precise [prɪ`saɪs] *a.* 精確的 ④
(2) precisely [prɪ`saɪslɪ] *adv.* 精確地

▶ The professor chose his words with precision.
這位教授用字遣詞很精準。

6 thereafter [ðɛr`æftɚ] *adv.* 從那之後

片 shortly thereafter 在那之後很快地

似 afterward(s) [`æftɚwɚd(z)] *adv.* 之後 ③

延伸 hereafter [ˌhɪr`æftɚ] *adv.* 今後，此後

▶ Adam got married at the age of 27 and had his first child shortly thereafter.
亞當 27 歲時結婚，之後很快就有了第一個小孩。

7 amplify [`æmpləˌfaɪ] *vt.* 增強（聲音）；詳述

三 amplify, amplified [`æmpləˌfaɪd], amplified

衍 (1) ample [`æmpl̩] *a.* 大量的，充裕的 ⑤
(2) amplifier [`æmpləˌfaɪr] *n.* 音響擴大器
(3) amplification [ˌæmpləfə`keʃən] *n.* 擴大；詳述

▶ This device is used to amplify the sound.
這個裝置是用來擴大聲音的。

▶ Could you please amplify your point for us?
可以請您為我們詳述您的論點嗎？

8 motto [`mɑto] *n.* 座右銘

似 adage [`ædɪdʒ] *n.* 諺語，格言

▶ My motto is, "Where there is a will, there is a way."
我的座右銘是：『有志者，事竟成。』

9 layout [`leˌaut] *n.*（裝潢）擺設；（刊物）版面編排

延伸 lay out... 規劃 / 設計……

▶ A few more sofas will improve the layout of your living room. 再加上一些沙發的話，你客廳的擺設會更好。

▶ I'm quite satisfied with the new layout for the magazine cover.
新的雜誌封面版面編排讓我很滿意。

10 clearance [`klɪrəns] *n.* 清除；空隙；飛機起飛降落許可；正式許可

片 (1) a clearance sale 清倉大拍賣
(2) clearance for... 飛機起飛降落的許可
(3) security clearance 安全審查許可（證）（即進入某地的權限）

▶ The clearance of illegal structures is a big issue in Taipei.
清除違章建築是臺北的一大問題。

▶ Let's go to your favorite clothing store on the weekend. They're having a clearance sale.
我們週末去你最愛的那家服飾店吧。他們正在清倉大拍賣。

▶ The bridge is so narrow that it doesn't provide enough clearance for trucks to cross over it.
這條橋太窄，行駛卡車時空隙不夠大而無法通過。

▶ The pilot requested clearance for an emergency landing at the airport.
飛行員要求在機場緊急迫降的許可。

▶ Matthew was unable to enter the government building because he did not have security clearance.
馬修無法進入這棟政府大樓，因為他沒有安全審查許可。

11 oblige [əˋblaɪdʒ] *vt.* 迫使；使負義務；施加恩惠

片 (1) oblige sb to + V
迫使某人做 / 使某人有義務做……
(2) oblige sb by + V-ing
幫忙某人做……

衍 (1) obliged [əˋblaɪdʒd] *a.* 感激的
be obliged to sb for sth
因某事而感激某人
= be grateful to sb for sth
= be thankful to sb for sth
▶ I'm much obliged to you for your timely help.
我很感激你即時的幫助。
(2) obligation [ˏabləˋgeʃən]
n. (道德上、法律上的) 義務，責任 ⑤

▶ The sex scandal obliged the mayor of New York City to step down.
這樁性醜聞迫使紐約市長下臺。
*step down （政治人物）下臺

▶ The Constitution obliges all citizens to pay taxes.
憲法使所有公民都有納稅的義務。

▶ Jim obliged his friend by driving him to the airport.
吉米幫忙把他朋友載到機場。

12 inclusive [ɪnˋklusɪv] *a.* 包含的

片 inclusive of... 包含……
= including...
= ... included

衍 (1) include [ɪnˋklud] *vt.* 包括 ②
(2) including [ɪnˋkludɪŋ] *prep.* 包括 ④

延伸 exclusive [ɪkˋsklusɪv] *a.* 不包括的；(新聞) 獨家的；(商品) 專用的 ⑤

▶ Five passengers were injured in the accident, inclusive of a pregnant woman.
= Five passengers were injured in the accident, including a pregnant woman.
= Five passengers were injured in the accident, a pregnant woman included.
5 名乘客在此意外中受傷，包括 1 名孕婦在內。

13 hurdle [ˋhɝdl̩] *n.* (賽馬、賽跑) 欄架；障礙 & *vi.* & *vt.* (跑步過程中) 跨過

片 (1) clear a hurdle
成功跨過一個跳欄
(2) overcome / clear a hurdle
克服障礙
= get over a hurdle
(3) the 100-meter hurdles
100 公尺跨欄賽跑

似 (1) obstacle [ˋabstəkl̩] *n.* 障礙 ④
(2) barrier [ˋbærɪɚ] *n.* 障礙 ④
(3) hindrance [ˋhɪndrəns] *n.* 障礙

▶ Steven cleared all the hurdles easily and came in first.
史蒂芬輕鬆地跨過了所有的跨欄，得到了第 1 名。
*come in first / second 贏得第 1 名 / 第 2 名
=win first / second place

▶ We have to overcome many hurdles in order to be successful.
為了成功，我們必須克服許多障礙。

▶ The famous athlete learned to hurdle by jumping over boxes in her father's warehouse.
這位知名運動員是在父親的倉庫裡跳箱子而學會了跨欄。

▸ On hearing her little brother screaming, Susan hurdled the fence and ran off into the woods in search of him.
蘇珊一聽到她弟弟尖叫，就跳過籬笆跑到樹林裡去找他。

14 preside [prɪˋzaɪd] *vi.* 擔任會議主席，主持

片 preside over a meeting　主持會議
= chair a meeting

▸ The chairman presided over a meeting of the finance committee.
主席主持了財務委員會的一場會議。

15 accustom [əˋkʌstəm] *vt.* 使習慣

片 accustom oneself to...
使某人習慣於……
= adjust oneself to...
= adapt oneself to...

衍 accustomed [əˋkʌstəmd] *a.* 習慣的
get accustomed to + N/V-ing
對……漸漸習慣
= get used to + N/V-ing
▸ It isn't easy for a foreigner to get accustomed to the local lifestyle.
對外來者而言，逐漸習慣本地的生活方式並不容易。

▸ It took Sophie a while to accustom herself to the hustle and bustle of the city life.
蘇菲花了一段時間讓自己習慣城市的喧囂與忙碌。
*hustle and bustle　熙來攘往，忙忙碌碌

16 bass [bæs] *n.* 鱸魚 & [bes] *n.* 男低音歌手；低音；低音提琴 & *a.* 低音的

複 單複數同形

衍 a (double) bass　低音提琴

▸ These rivers provide excellent habitats for bass because their temperatures are moderate and they are highly oxygenated.
這些河流的水溫適中且含氧量又高，提供鱸魚絕佳的棲息環境。
*oxygenate [ˋɑksɪˌdʒənet] *vt.* 加氧於

▸ Ladies and gentlemen, let's welcome the famous Italian bass Jake Brown to our show.
各位先生女士，讓我們歡迎著名的義大利男低音傑克．布朗來到我們的節目。

▸ Henry likes to listen to music with the bass turned up.
亨利聽音響時喜歡把低音開大聲。

▸ Sylvia is nervous because it is the first time she will play the double bass in such a large orchestra.
希薇亞很緊張，因為這是她第一次要在這麼大的管弦樂團中演奏低音提琴。

▸ Many people think that The Who's John Entwistle was the greatest bass guitarist of all time.
很多人認為誰人樂隊的約翰．恩特維斯托是有史以來最偉大的低音吉他手。

17 broil [brɔɪl] *vt.* (直接接觸火焰) 烤〔美〕(= grill [grɪl]〔英〕)

似 roast [rost] *vi.* & *vt.* (用烤箱等) 烤 ③

▸ I'm planning on broiling some chicken and potatoes for dinner tonight.
我計劃要烤雞肉和馬鈴薯當今晚的晚餐。

18 clockwise [ˋklɑk͵waɪz] *a.* 順時針的 & *adv.* 順時針地

▸ Turn the screw in a clockwise direction to fasten the shelf to the wall.
把螺絲按順時針方向轉動，好把架子固定在牆上。

▸ Turn the key clockwise to lock the door.
把鑰匙順時針轉好把門鎖上。

counterclockwise
[͵kaʊntɚˋklɑk͵waɪz] *a.* 逆時針的 & *adv.* 逆時針地〔美〕(= anticlockwise [͵æntɪˋklɑk͵waɪz]〔英〕)

▸ The drunk driver lost control of his steering wheel, and the car rotated in a counterclockwise direction.
這酒醉駕駛人的方向盤失去控制，汽車以逆時針的方向打轉。
*rotate [ˋrotet] *vi.* & *vt.* 旋轉

▸ Press down and then turn the lid counterclockwise to open the bottle.
往下壓並把蓋子逆時針轉就可以打開瓶子。

19 jingle [ˋdʒɪŋg!] *vi.* & *vt.* (使) 發出叮噹聲 & *n.* 叮噹聲；(廣播或電視廣告中容易讓人記得的) 短曲，廣告歌

似 ring [rɪŋ] *vt.* & *vi.* 發出鈴 / 鐘聲 & *n.* 鈴 / 鐘聲 ①

▸ We always know when Tony is near because we can hear the coins jingling in his pocket.
我們總是知道湯尼什麼時候在附近，因為我們能聽到他口袋裡的硬幣叮噹作響。

▸ Susan jingled her car keys to try to get her husband's attention, but he ignored her.
蘇珊把她的車鑰匙弄得叮噹作響，試圖引起她丈夫的注意，但他丈夫卻不理睬她。

▸ The dog ran to greet his master when he heard the jingle of keys outside the door.
那隻狗聽到門外有鑰匙的叮咚聲時就跑去迎接主人。

▸ I can't get the jingle from that soap commercial out of my head! It's so frustrating!
那肥皂廣告的短曲一直在我腦海裡揮之不去！真惱人！

20 geometry [dʒi`ɑmətrɪ] n. 幾何學

似 geomancy [`dʒiəˌmænsɪ] n. 風水
*老外亦常說 feng shui [ˌfʌŋ `ʃweɪ]，即中文『風水』的音譯。

▶ Tina is an outstanding student. She is particularly good at geometry.
蒂娜是個傑出的學生。她的**幾何學**尤其好。

21 peril [`pɛrəl] n. 危險 & vt. 使有危險，危及

片 (1) put sb in peril 使某人陷入危險
= put sb in danger
(2) at one's peril 自己要承擔風險

衍 perilous [`pɛrələs] a. 危險的，冒險的

似 danger [`dendʒɚ] n. 危險 ②

▶ Tom put himself in peril to rescue his dog from the fire.
湯姆**不顧**自己**危險**去火場裡救他的狗。

▶ Paul ignores the doctor's warnings at his peril.
保羅要**承擔**不聽醫師警告的**風險**。

▶ Simon periled his life by climbing the mountain without the appropriate safety gear or sufficient water. 賽門在沒有適當安全裝備和足夠用水的情況下爬山，是**有**生命**危險**的。

22 dwell [dwɛl] vi. 居住

三 dwell, dwelt [dwɛlt] / dwelled, dwelt / dwelled

片 (1) dwell in... 居住於……
= reside in...
(2) dwell on... 老想著……

似 reside [rɪ`zaɪd] vi. 居住 ⑥

▶ The people have dwelt in the desert for thousands of years.
= The people have resided in the desert for thousands of years.
該支民族已**居住在**沙漠中有數千年之久。

▶ Stop dwelling on the past and feeling sorry for yourself! You must move on.
別再**老想著**過去自怨自艾了！你要往前走。

dwelling [`dwɛlɪŋ] n. 住處，住宅

似 (1) house [haʊs] n. 房子 ①
(2) residence [`rɛzədəns] n. 住所 ⑤

▶ Mr. Parker's dwelling was basic and clean.
帕克先生的**住處**簡單又乾淨。

23 robust [ro`bʌst] a. 強健的

似 strong [strɔŋ] a. 強壯的 ①

▶ The once robust young man looks pale and lifeless because of the pressure.
那個以往**健壯的**年輕人因壓力太大，而變得臉色蒼白且毫無生氣。

24 geographical [dʒiə`græfɪkḷ] a. 地理的

衍 geography [dʒi`ɑgrəfɪ] n. 地理學 ③

延伸 (1) geological [dʒɪə`lɑdʒɪkḷ] a. 地質學的
(2) geology [dʒi`ɑlədʒɪ] n. 地質學

▶ Scientists have spent many years researching the cause of geographical changes in this area.
科學家已花費多年研究該區**地理上的**改變。

25 rubbish [ˋrʌbɪʃ] *n.* 垃圾（不可數）〔英〕（= garbage [ˋgɑrbɪdʒ] / trash〔美〕）；無意義的話或想法（= nonsense / garbage〔美〕）

片 talk rubbish　說廢話〔英〕
= talk nonsense / garbage〔美〕

用法 a rubbish (×)
a piece of rubbish (○)　一件垃圾

▸ You ought to put your rubbish in the bin.
你應該把垃圾丟到桶子裡。

▸ Would you just stop talking rubbish?
你能不能別再說廢話了？

26 invaluable [ɪnˋvæljuəbḷ] *a.* 無價的

片 be invaluable to / for...
對……是無價的

衍 valuable [ˋvæljuəbḷ] *a.* 有價值的 ②

反 worthless [ˋwɝθləs] *a.* 沒有價值的

▸ Your internship at this top advertising company will be invaluable to your career.
你在這家頂尖廣告公司的實習經驗，會對你的生涯發展很有幫助。
*internship [ˋɪntɝn,ʃɪp] *n.* 實習

27 compass [ˋkʌmpəs] *n.* 羅盤，指南針

衍 compasses [ˋkʌmpəsɪz]
n. 圓規（恆用複數）
a pair of compasses　一副圓規

▸ The compass is a very important tool for navigation.
羅盤是很重要的導航工具。
*navigation [,nævəˋgeʃən] *n.* 導航

28 surgical [ˋsɝdʒɪkḷ] *a.* 外科的，手術的

片 surgical equipment
外科手術器材（集合名詞，不可數）

▸ Many relief materials were rushed to the refugee camps, including surgical equipment.
許多救濟物資被火速送到難民營，包括外科手術器材在內。
*relief [rɪˋlif] *n.* 救濟品
refugee [,rɛfjuˋdʒi] *n.* 難民

29 eclipse [ɪˋklɪps] *n.*（日或月）蝕

片 (1) a solar / lunar eclipse　日 / 月蝕
(2) a total / partial eclipse
全 / 偏蝕

▸ Millions of people around the globe waited to witness the rare occurrence of the total solar eclipse.
全球數以百萬的人等待觀看罕見的日全蝕。
*occurrence [əˋkɝəns] *n.* 事件，發生的事

30 jolly [ˋdʒɑlɪ] *a.* 快樂的 & *adv.* 很，非常 & *vt.*（說好聽的話）哄（某人）& *n.* 尋歡作樂（可數）

片 jolly... along　鼓勵……

似 cheerful [ˋtʃɪrfəl] *a.* 愉快的 ③

▸ Everyone had a jolly time at the banquet.
每個人在宴會上都很盡興。

▸ I wasn't looking forward to going away for the weekend with my girlfriend's parents, but we actually had a jolly good time.
我不想和我女朋友的父母一起去度週末，但我們真的玩得很開心。

▶ The dog didn't want to go for a walk, so we had to jolly it along a little.
這條狗不想去散步，所以我們不得不**鼓勵**它一下。

▶ Tom says he's going on a business trip, but I think we all know it's just a jolly.
湯姆說他要去出差，但我想我們都知道他是**出去玩**。

---

joyous [ˋdʒɔɪəs] *a.* 快樂的（常用來修飾事物、場合等）

片 a joyous occasion　令人開心的場合

衍 (1) joy [dʒɔɪ] *n.* 高興 ①
(2) joyful [ˋdʒɔɪfəl] *a.* 充滿喜悅的（常用來修飾人或其心情）③

▶ A wedding is a joyous occasion.
婚禮是個**令人開心的**場合。

---

rejoice [rɪˋdʒɔɪs] *vi.* 欣喜

片 rejoice in / at sth　因某事感到開心

▶ If we can learn to rejoice in others' success, our own happiness will increase.
我們若能學習為他人的成功**感到開心**，自己也會更快樂。

31 vapor [ˋvepɚ] *n.* 蒸氣

片 water vapor　水蒸氣

衍 vaporize [ˋvepəˌraɪz] *vi.* & *vt.* (使) 蒸發

▶ The blazing sun vaporized the drops of dew on the grass quickly.
炙熱的太陽很快就**蒸發**掉了青草上的露珠。
*blazing [ˋblezɪŋ] *a.* 炎熱的

▶ The doctor used water vapor to treat my sore throat.
醫生用**水蒸氣**來治療我的喉嚨痛。

32 sneeze [sniz] *vi.* 打噴嚏 & *n.* 噴嚏

片 sth be nothing to sneeze at　某事物是不能被輕忽的（喻認為該事物很重要）〔美〕
= be not to be sneezed at〔英〕

比 hiccup [ˋhɪkəp] *vi.* & *n.* 打嗝

▶ After sneezing several times, I realized I was allergic to my friend's cat.
打了幾次**噴嚏**後，我才發現我對朋友的貓過敏。
*allergic [əˋlɝdʒɪk] *a.* 過敏的
be allergic to...　對……過敏

▶ Coughs and sneezes spread flu viruses.
咳嗽和**噴嚏**會散播流感病毒。

▶ For Jane, a weekly wage of five hundred bucks is nothing to sneeze at.
= For Jane, a weekly wage of five hundred bucks is not to be sneezed at.
對珍而言，每週 500 美金的工資是一筆**不可輕忽的**收入。

33 pastime [ˋpæs,taɪm] *n.* 消遣

似 hobby [ˋhɑbɪ] *n.* 嗜好 ①

延伸 此字是由片語 pass the time (消磨 / 打發時間) 而來的。

▸ We always sing songs to pass the time on weekends.
我們週末總是唱歌來殺時間。

▸ Using social media, such as Facebook and Instagram, seems to have become the most popular pastime these days.
使用如臉書和 Instagram 等社群媒體，似乎已成為近來最普遍的消遣。

34 perish [ˋpɛrɪʃ] *vi.* 慘死，猝死

衍 perishable [ˋpɛrɪʃəbḷ] *a.* 易腐敗的

▸ Fresh milk is perishable and must be refrigerated.
鮮奶很容易腐敗，因此必須冷藏。

似 (1) die [daɪ] *vi.* 死亡 ①
(2) decay [dɪˋke] *vi.* & *vt.* & *n.* 腐爛 ⑤

▸ Hundreds of passengers perished in the plane crash.
有好幾百名乘客在此空難中喪生。

35 affiliate [əˋfɪlɪət] *n.* 附屬機構，分公司，分會 & [əˋfɪlɪet] *vt.* 隸屬於

片 A affiliate oneself with / to B
A 隸屬於 B

▸ The organization is made up of a parent company and two affiliates, all of which make products for automobiles.
該組織由一家母公司和兩家**分公司**組成的，皆是在製造汽車用的產品。

▸ In the press conference, the organization claimed that it doesn't affiliate itself with / to that political party.
在新聞記者會上，該組織聲稱它不**隸屬於**那個政黨。

36 workforce [ˋwɝk,fɔrs] *n.* 勞動力 / 人口 (常用單數)

比 staff [stæf] *n.* 全體員工 (不可數或常用單數) ③

▸ Over the past several decades, more and more women around the world have entered the workforce.
在過去的幾十年裡，世界各地越來越多的婦女進入了**勞動**市場。

37 telecommunications [,tɛləkə,mjunəˋkeʃənz] *n.* 電信 / 訊 (恆用複數，不可數)

衍 (1) communicate [kəˋmjunə,ket] *vi.* & *vt.* 溝通 ③
(2) communication [kə,mjunəˋkeʃən] *n.* 溝通 ④
(3) communications [kə,mjunəˋkeʃənz] *n.* 通訊系統 (恆用複數)

▸ Companies that specialize in traditional telecommunications have suffered due to increased use of internet communication tools such as LINE and Zoom.
由於越來越多人使用如『賴』和 Zoom 等網路通訊工具，專門從事傳統**電信**業務的公司受到了影響。

0338-0340

38 subsidize [ˋsʌbsəˏdaɪz] *vt.* 給予……津 / 補貼

衍 subsidy [ˋsʌbsədɪ] *n.* 補助金 ⑤

▸ Although the government doesn't pay the full cost of daycare, it subsidizes it for parents who qualify.
雖然政府不支付小孩日托的全部費用，但對符合條件的父母仍會給予補助。

39 lethal [ˋliθəl] *a.* 致命的

似 fatal [ˋfetḷ] *a.* 致命的 ④

▸ The drug can be lethal if too much of it is taken, so be careful about how much you use.
這藥如果服用太多可能會致命，所以要小心你的用量。

40 intake [ˋɪnˏtek] *n.* 攝取量；吸氣

片 an intake of breath
吸氣（複數為 intakes of breath）

▸ Herman's doctor told him that he should reduce his intake of alcohol and take better care of his health.
赫曼的醫生告訴他他應少喝酒，並更要好好地照顧自己的健康。

▸ There were several sharp intakes of breath in the crowd when the prime minister announced his resignation.
當總理宣布辭職時，人群中聽見了有些人倒抽一口氣。

0401-0403

1 persistent [pɚˋsɪstənt] *a.* (人) 堅持的，執著的；(不喜歡的事) 持續存在的

片 a persistent rumor / cough / problem　持續不斷的謠言 / 咳嗽 / 問題

衍 (1) persist [pɚˋsɪst] *vi.* 頑強堅持；(不喜歡的事) 持續存在 ⑤
(2) persistently [ˏpɚˋsɪstəntlɪ] *adv.* 頑強堅持地；持續地

▸ How did you manage to get rid of that persistent salesman?
你是怎麼擺脫那**糾纏不休**的推銷員的？

▸ There's been a persistent rumor about the singer's sexual orientation.
關於那位歌手性取向的**謠言持續不斷**。
*orientation [ˏɔrɪɛnˋteʃən] *n.* 方向，傾向

persistence [pɚˋsɪstəns]
n. 堅持；(不喜歡的事) 持續 (皆不可數) (與介詞 in 並用)

片 sb's persistence in + N/V-ing　某人對……的堅持

▸ The manager's persistence in carrying out the project finally paid off.
經理**對於**執行該企畫**的堅持**總算開花結果了。
*pay off　有回報，取得成功

▸ The persistence of the baby girl's high fever made her parents deeply concerned.
小女嬰**持續**發高燒，令她的父母親很擔憂。

2 textile [ˋtɛkstaɪl] *n.* 織物，紡織品 (可數) & *a.* 紡織的

片 a textile industry　紡織業

▸ Our company uses high-quality organic cotton textiles to make the clothes, so you don't need to worry about children being affected by chemicals.
我們公司使用高品質的有機棉**織物**來做衣服，所以您不需擔心孩子會受到化學品的影響。

▸ The country's textile industry is facing many new challenges.
該國的**紡織業**正面臨許多新的挑戰。

3 mimic [ˋmɪmɪk] *vt.* 模仿 & *n.* 善於模仿 (他人或動物) 的人

三 mimic, mimicked [ˋmɪmɪkt], mimicked

似 (1) copy [ˋkɑpɪ] *vt.* 模仿 ①
(2) imitate [ˋɪməˏtet] *vt.* 模仿 ④

▸ We all roared with laughter when Tom mimicked Prof. Usher giving a lecture.
看見湯姆**模仿**厄許教授講課，我們全都大笑了起來。

▸ Laura is an excellent mimic. Everyone thinks it's hilarious when she copies the voices and mannerisms of our teachers.
蘿拉很會**模仿**。每個人都認為她學各個老師的聲音舉止都很好笑。
*hilarious [hɪˋlɛrɪəs] *a.* 引人發笑的
mannerism [ˋmænərɪzm] *n.* (某人特有的說話或動作的) 習性

0404-0411

4 inquire [ɪnˋkwaɪr] *vt.* & *vi.* 詢問

片 (1) inquire about... 詢問有關……
(2) inquire + 疑問詞 (when, what, how, where 等) 引導的名詞子句 詢問……
(3) inquire into... 調查……
= look into...
(4) inquire after sb 問候某人的健康狀況
= inquire after sb's health

衍 (1) inquiry [ˋɪnkwərɪ / ɪnˋkwaɪrɪ] *n.* 詢問 (與介詞 about 並用)；調查 (與介詞 into 並用) ⑤
(2) inquisitive [ɪnˋkwɪzətɪv] *a.* 愛打聽的；好奇心重的

▸ When the man walked past, we took the opportunity to inquire the way to the hotel.
當那個人走過去時，我們趁機詢問了去旅館的路。

▸ I'm calling to inquire about the job openings you advertised in the newspaper.
我打電話來是想詢問貴公司報上徵人的廣告。

▸ I inquired why she didn't tell me the truth in the first place.
我問她為何不一開始就說實話。

▸ The police are inquiring into the financial dealings between the two firms.
警方正調查這兩家公司彼此的財務往來。

▸ Rachel inquired after her grandmother.
= Rachel inquired after her grandmother's health.
瑞秋問候她祖母的健康狀況。

5 nationalism [ˋnæʃənḷɪzəm] *n.* 民族 / 國家主義

衍 (1) national [ˋnæʃənḷ] *a.* 國家的；民族的，民族主義的 ①
(2) nation [ˋneʃən] *n.* 國家；民族 ②
(3) nationality [ˌnæʃəˋnælətɪ] *n.* 國籍；民族 ④

似 patriotism [ˋpetrɪətɪzəm] *n.* 愛國主義

▸ A strong sense of nationalism prevailed in Germany under Hitler's rule.
在希特勒領導之下，民族主義盛行於德國。
*prevail [prɪˋvel] *vi.* 盛行

6 socialism [ˋsoʃəlˌɪzəm] *n.* 社會主義

衍 social [ˋsoʃəl] *a.* 社會的；社交的 ②

延伸 (1) communism [ˋkɑmjʊˌnɪzəm] *n.* 共產主義 (字首可大寫) ⑤
(2) capitalism [ˋkæpətḷˌɪzəm] *n.* 資本主義

▸ Socialism is an economic system that aims for an equal distribution of wealth.
社會主義是謀求財富平均分配的一種經濟制度。

socialist [ˋsoʃəlɪst] *n.* 社會主義者 & *a.* 社會主義的

比 sociologist [ˌsoʃɪˋɑlədʒɪst] *n.* 社會學家 (研究並分析社會群體及其互動等的專家)

▸ My grandfather was a radical socialist throughout his life.
我祖父終其一生都是個激進的社會主義者。
*radical [ˋrædɪkḷ] *a.* 激進的

7 editorial [ˌɛdəˋtɔrɪəl] *n.* 社論 & *a.* 編輯的

衍 (1) edit [ˋɛdɪt] *vt.* 編輯 ③
(2) editor [ˋɛdɪtɚ] *n.* 編輯人員 ③

▸ That newspaper's recent editorials have been centering around environmental issues.
那家報社的**社論**最近都圍繞在環境議題上。

▸ The textbook publisher has an editorial staff of 50.
這家教科書出版社有 50 位**編輯**人員。

8 literal [ˋlɪtərəl] *a.* 字面上的；逐字的，直譯的

片 literal translation　逐字翻譯
= word-for-word translation
= verbatim [vɝˋbetɪm] translation
似 word-for-word [ˌwɝdˌfɚˋwɝd]
a. 逐字的
= verbatim

▸ What is the literal meaning of this word?
這個字**字面上**的意思是什麼？

▸ A literal translation of this poem would ruin its intent.
將這首詩**逐字**翻譯會破壞它的原意。
*intent [ɪnˋtɛnt] *n.* 意圖

literally [ˋlɪtərəlɪ]
adv. 照字面地，直譯地；真正 / 確實地
(= word for word)

▸ Do not translate this article literally.
= Do not translate this article word for word.
別**照字面**翻譯這篇文章。

▸ The auditorium was literally packed with people.
大禮堂**真的**是人滿為患。

9 asthma [ˋæzmə] *n.* 氣喘

衍 asthmatic [æzˋmætɪk] *a.* 氣喘的
an asthmatic patient　氣喘病患

▸ Tom had a severe asthma attack in the middle of the test.
湯姆考試考到一半時突然**氣喘**病發。

10 prestige [prɛsˋtiʒ] *n.* 聲望 (不可數)

片 gain / get prestige　贏得聲望
似 reputation [ˌrɛpjəˋteʃən] *n.* 名聲 ④

▸ Bruce has gained considerable prestige from his job as a lawyer for the top company.
布魯斯擔任這間大公司的律師**贏得**了相當高的**聲望**。

prestigious [prɛsˋtɪdʒəs]
a. 有聲望的

片 a highly prestigious university
一所很有聲望的大學

▸ Allen attended a highly prestigious university.
艾倫在一所很**有聲望的**大學念書。

11 exert [ɪgˋzɝt] *vt.* 施加 (影響、壓力等)；盡力 (用於下列片語中)

片 (1) exert A on B　向 B 施加 A
(2) exert oneself
盡力去做，不遺餘力去做

▸ The manager exerted pressure on the employees to get things done more quickly.
經理向員工**施加**壓力，要他們快點把事情做完。

0411-0418

衍 exertion [ɪgˋzɝʃən]
n. 施加（影響、壓力等）；盡力

似 expert [ˋɛkspɝt] *n.* 專家 ②

▸ You'll have to exert yourself if you want to get good grades.
你如果想得到好成績，就必須**盡力**才行。

12 realization [ˏrɪələˋzeʃən] *n.* 瞭解 (= awareness [əˋwɛrnəs])；實現 (= achievement [əˋtʃivmənt])

片 (1) come to the realization that...
領悟到……
(2) realization of sth
對某事的領悟；實現某事
= realize that...

衍 realize [ˋrɪəˏlaɪz] *vt.* 意識到；實現 ②

▸ Sam came to the realization that his lack of education had been preventing him from getting a good job.
山姆後來**領悟到**，因為教育程度不夠，他一直找不到好工作。

▸ As the criminal sat in the jail cell, the sudden realization of what he had done made him sob loudly.
當這罪犯坐在監獄牢房裡時，他突然**意識到**自己所做的事而大聲啜泣。

▸ The realization of your dreams depends on whether you work hard.
夢想的**實現**取決於你是否努力。

13 fuss [fʌs] *vi.* 大驚小怪 & *n.* 小題大作；抱怨

片 (1) fuss about sth
對某事物大驚小怪
= make a fuss about sth
(2) fuss over...
對……寵愛有加 / 關愛備至
= make a fuss over...

▸ My mother always fusses about trivial problems.
= My mother always makes a fuss about trivial problems.
我媽媽總是**對**枝微末節的問題**大驚小怪**。
*trivial [ˋtrɪvɪəl] *a.* 瑣碎的

▸ The little girl fusses over the dog that she and her parents adopted from the animal shelter.
= The little girl makes a fuss over the dog that she and her parents adopted from the animal shelter.
小女孩**對**她和父母從動物收容所領養出來的狗**寵愛有加**。

▸ There was a fuss among the students when the teacher canceled the field trip.
當老師把遠足取消時，學生都在**抱怨**。

---

fussy [ˋfʌsɪ] *a.* 挑剔的

片 be fussy about...　對……很挑剔
= be picky about...
= be particular about...
= be choosy about...

似 fuzzy [ˋfʌzɪ]
a. (聲音、圖像等) 不清晰的

▸ We all dislike the manager because he is extremely fussy about details.
我們都不喜歡這經理，因為他**對**細節太**挑剔**了。

14 batter [ˋbætɚ] *n.* (棒球) 打擊手 & *vt.* 連續猛打

片 batter sb to death with sth
用某物把某人打死

似 beat [bit] *vi.* & *vt.* 打 ②

▸ John wished he could one day become a batter in Major League Baseball.
約翰希望他有一天能成為美國職棒大聯盟的**打擊手**。
*league [lig] *n.* 聯盟

▸ The news that the mobsters battered a policeman to death with baseball bats shocked the public.
歹徒**用**棒球棒**把**一名警察**毆打致死**的新聞震驚了社會。
*mobster [ˋmɑbstɚ] *n.* 歹徒，黑社會成員

15 brook [brʊk] *n.* 小溪流，小河

似 (1) river [ˋrɪvɚ] *n.* 河 ①
(2) stream [strim] *n.* 小溪 / 河 ②
(3) creek [krik] *n.* 小溪 / 河 ⑤

▸ There used to be fish in the brook, but there's only trash now.
這條**小溪**本來有魚，現在只有垃圾了。

16 kindle [ˋkɪndḷ] *vt.* 點燃；激起 (興趣等)

片 kindle / arouse / spark one's interest 激發 (起) 某人的興趣

▸ At the campground, we kindled a fire and sat in a circle, chatting about nothing in particular.
我們在營區**燃起**了火圍成一圈坐下，漫無邊際地閒聊。

▸ His grandfather's stories of life in the navy kindled John's lifelong interest in sailing.
約翰的爺爺在海軍生活的故事，**激發**了約翰一生對航海的**興趣**。

17 permissible [pɚˋmɪsəbḷ] *a.* 可允許的

衍 (1) permit [pɝˋmɪt] *vt.* 允許 ③
(2) permission [pɝˋmɪʃən] *n.* 允許 ③
without permission 未經許可

似 allowable [əˋlaʊəbḷ] *a.* 可允許的

▸ Hunting wild ducks is not permissible in this protected area.
= Hunting wild ducks is not permitted in this protected area.
在這塊保護區內，獵殺野鴨是不被**允許**的。

18 glacier [ˋgleʃɚ] *n.* 冰河

延伸 iceberg [ˋaɪsˏbɝg] *n.* 冰山 ⑥

▸ The glacier is moving at a rate of 1 meter a year.
該**冰河**以每年 1 公尺的速度移動。
*at a rate of... 以……的速度

19 rugged [ˋrʌgɪd] *a.* 崎嶇不平的；堅固耐用的

衍 rug [rʌg] *n.* 小地毯 ③
似 sturdy [ˋstɝdɪ] *a.* 堅固的 ⑤
反 smooth [smuð] *a.* 平滑的 ②

▸ The eastern part of the island is known for its rugged terrain and rocky coastline.
這座島的東部以其崎嶇不平的地形以及岩岸著名。
*terrain [təˋren] *n.* 地形
coastline [ˋkost,laɪn] *n.* 海岸線

▸ Justin is purchasing a rugged mountain bike to ride on his journey around the island.
賈斯汀準備要買一臺堅固耐用的登山自行車騎去環島旅行。

20 compute [kəmˋpjut] *vt.* 計算

衍 computer [kəmˋpjutɚ] *n.* 電腦 ①
似 (1) count [kaʊnt] *vt.* 計算 ①
(2) calculate [ˋkælkjə,let] *vt.* 計算 ④

▸ Make sure these figures are accurately computed, or we could invite trouble.
這些數據務必要精確計算，否則我們可能會招來麻煩。

computerize [kəmˋpjutə,raɪz] *vt.* 使電腦化

▸ The company is spending thousands of dollars to computerize all of its old files.
該公司正花費數千美元將其所有舊文件進行電腦化處理。

21 knowledgeable [ˋnɑlɪdʒəbl̩] *a.* 博學的

片 be knowledgeable about sth
對某事懂得很多
衍 knowledge [ˋnɑlɪdʒ] *n.* 知識 ①
似 learned [ˋlɝnɪd] *a.* 博學的 ④

▸ James is very knowledgeable about English literature and classical music.
詹姆士對英國文學以及古典音樂很有研究。

22 surname [ˋsɝ,nem] *n.* 姓 (= a family / last name) & *vt.* 給與……姓氏（常用被動）

延伸 a first name 名
= a given name

▸ My English teacher's surname is Wang, and his first name is Shui-Tien.
我的英文老師姓王，名水田。

▸ A thirty-year-old man (who is) surnamed Lai was arrested for drug trafficking early this morning.
今天凌晨一名 30 歲賴姓男子因販毒遭逮捕。

23 electrician [ɪ,lɛkˋtrɪʃən] *n.* 電工

衍 (1) electric [ɪˋlɛktrɪk]
a. 用電力（發動）的 ②
(2) electrical [ɪˋlɛktrɪkl̩]
a. 與電有關的 ②
(3) electricity [ɪ,lɛkˋtrɪsətɪ]
n. 電（能）③

▸ We'll send an electrician to help you with the installation immediately.
我們會立刻派一位電工協助你們安裝。

比 (1) plumber [ˋplʌmɚ] *n.* 水管工 ④
(2) technician [tɛkˋnɪʃən] *n.* (科學或工程學的) 技術人員，技工 ④

24 veto [ˋvito] *vt.* 否決 & *n.* 否決權

片 veto a bill　否決法案

延伸 ballot [ˋbælət] *n.* (無記名) 選票 & *vt.* 進行無記名投票 (或表決) ⑤

▸ The President of the United States may veto a bill that has been passed by both houses of Congress.
美國總統可以否決參眾兩院均已通過的議案。

▸ The power of veto over this bill is held by the President.
這項法案的否決權握在總統手裡。

25 salute [səˋlut] *vt.* & *vi.* (尤指軍中將右手指尖觸碰眉毛末端的) 敬禮，致敬 & *n.* 敬禮

片 (1) give (sb) a salute　向 (某人) 敬禮
(2) a 21-gun salute　21 響禮炮

比 bow [baʊ] *vi.* & *vt.* & *n.* 鞠躬敬禮 ①
bow to sb　向某人鞠躬
take a bow　鞠躬

▸ A line of soldiers stood at attention and saluted the officer as he walked past.
一排士兵立正站好，並在該官員經過時向他敬禮。
*stand at / to attention　立正

▸ The first thing the soldiers learned was that whenever they see an officer, they must salute.
士兵學到的第一件事情是每當看見長官時，就得敬禮。

▸ We gave our commanding officer a final salute on the day he retired.
我們指揮官退休的那一天，我們向他致敬最後一次。

26 lad [læd] *n.* 男孩〔英〕

似 boy [bɔɪ] *n.* 男孩 ①

反 (1) girl [gɝl] *n.* 女孩 ①
(2) lass [læs] *n.* 女孩〔英〕

▸ When Martin was just a lad, his greatest wish was to go to sea.
馬丁還是個小男孩時，他最大的願望就是去當水手。
*go to sea　當水手

27 vigor [ˋvɪgɚ] *n.* 活力 (= vitality [vaɪˋtælətɪ])

片 (1) with vigor　充滿活力地
(2) be full of vigor　充滿活力

▸ After a cup of coffee, Jim began to work with renewed vigor.
喝完一杯咖啡之後，吉姆又恢復活力開始工作。

▸ Grandpa is over eighty but is still healthy and full of vigor.
祖父已年逾 80，但身體仍很硬朗且充滿活力。

0427-0434

vigorous [ˋvɪgərəs] *a.* 健壯的；強有力的；(體育活動) 劇烈的

似 energetic [ˏɛnəˋdʒɛtɪk] *a.* 精力十足的 ③

▶ Kyle is such a vigorous young man: Every year he takes part in at least two marathons.
凱爾是個如此健壯的年輕人：每年他至少參加兩次馬拉松比賽。

▶ Sean's suggestion provoked a vigorous debate among the directors.
尚恩的提議引發董事之間的激辯。
*provoke [prəˋvok] *vt.* 引 / 激起

▶ Melvin has asthma, and that's why he seldom does vigorous exercise.
馬文有氣喘，這就是為什麼他很少做劇烈的運動。

28 suspense [səˋspɛns] *n.* 懸疑，擔心，掛慮

片 (1) keep / leave sb in suspense 吊某人胃口，(故意) 使某人著急 / 焦慮
(2) a suspense story 懸疑故事

似 mystery [ˋmɪstrɪ] *n.* 神祕 ③

▶ There were elements of suspense and mystery in the novel.
這本小說裡有些許懸疑和神祕的情節。

▶ Don't keep me in suspense! Tell me what happened when you asked her to marry you!
不要吊我胃口了！告訴我你向她求婚時發生了什麼事！

▶ Jack is writing a suspense story that he hopes will get published and make him famous.
傑克正在寫一個懸疑故事，他希望這故事能出版，並讓他因此成名。

suspension [səˋspɛnʃən]
n. 中止，暫停；(車輛的) 懸載系統，減震裝置

片 a suspension bridge 吊橋

▶ The government ordered an immediate suspension of all beef imports from that country after the outbreak of the disease.
那個國家爆發疫情之後，政府立刻下令中止從該國進口任何牛肉。

▶ The mechanic knew right away that there was a problem with the car's front suspension.
修車技師馬上就知道是汽車的前懸架有問題。

▶ The Golden Gate Bridge in San Francisco is a famous suspension bridge which attracts a huge number of tourists every year.
舊金山的金門大橋是座著名的吊橋，每年都吸引大量的觀光客來訪。

29 pianist [pɪˋænɪst / ˋpiənɪst] *n.* 鋼琴家

衍 piano [pɪˋæno] *n.* 鋼琴 ①

▶ This film is about a legendary pianist who grew up on the ship.
這部電影是有關一個傳奇性的鋼琴家在船上長大的故事。
*legendary [ˋlɛdʒəndˏɛrɪ] *a.* 傳奇的

violinist [ˌvaɪəˋlɪnɪst]
n. 小提琴家 / 手

衍 violin [ˌvaɪəˋlɪn] *n.* 小提琴 ①

▸ It's my understanding that Joshua Bell is one of the world's greatest violinists.
就我所知，約書亞．貝爾是世上最棒的**小提琴手**之一。

30 reminiscent [ˌrɛməˋnɪsn̩t] *a.* 使人想起的

片 A be reminiscent of B
A 讓人想到 B

▸ The song on the radio was new, but it was reminiscent of an old song that I liked.
收音機放的這首歌是新的，但它**讓**我**想起**了我喜歡的一首老歌。

31 unconditional [ˌʌnkənˋdɪʃənl̩] *a.* 無條件的

衍 condition [kənˋdɪʃən]
n. 條件；狀況 ②

反 conditional [kənˋdɪʃənl̩]
a. 有前提條件的

▸ Our staff's willingness to work overtime isn't unconditional; we give them overtime pay, which is quite high.
我們的員工願意加班並非是**無條件的**；我們給他們相當高的加班費。

32 reliant [rɪˋlaɪənt] *a.* 依賴的

片 A be reliant on B　A 依賴 B

衍 rely [rɪˋlaɪ] *vi.* 依賴 ③
rely on...　依賴……

▸ A human baby, unlike other newborn mammals that can stand up immediately after birth, is totally reliant on his or her parents.
人類的嬰兒並不像其他剛出生的哺乳類動物一樣出生後可以立即站起來，人類的嬰兒是完全要**依賴**父母的。

33 lonesome [ˋlonsəm] *a.* 孤獨的；荒涼的 (= lonely)

衍 lone [lon] *a.* 單獨的 ②

▸ Ever since Rick's girlfriend broke up with him, he has been a very lonesome young man.
自從瑞克的女朋友和他分手後，他就一直是個非常**寂寞**的年輕人。

▸ The regions in northern Canada are extremely remote and the living conditions are harsh; that's why they are quite lonesome places.
加拿大的北部地區非常偏遠，生活條件又惡劣；這就是為什麼那些是相當**荒涼**的地方。

34 trillion [ˋtrɪljən] *n.* 兆 (即「萬億」)

延伸 (1) million [ˋmɪljən] *n.* 百萬 ①
(2) billion [ˋbɪljən] *n.* 十億 ②

▸ The universe is a vast place where distance is measured in light-years and stars are counted in their trillions.
宇宙是一個很大的地方，在那裡距離是以光年來測量的，而恒星是以**兆**來計算的。

35 orthodox [ˋɔrθəˏdɑks] *a.* 正統的，廣為接受的；(人) 傳統的，循規蹈矩的

反 (1) casual [ˋkæʒuəl] *a.* (服裝) 休閒的 ③
(2) informal [ɪnˋfɔrml̩] *a.* 非正式的
(3) unorthodox [ʌnˋɔrθəˏdɑks] *a.* 非正統的

▸ The school uses orthodox teaching methods only, rather than any unusual, alternative, or experimental ways.

這學校只使用**正統的**教學方法，而不是使用任何罕見、另類或實驗性的方法。

▸ My students asked me whether it is true that some orthodox Catholics are not likely to accept new interpretations of the Bible.

我的學生問我，一些**傳統**天主教徒是否不太可能接受對《聖經》的新解釋。

*interpretation [ɪnˏtɝprəˋteʃən] *n.* 解釋

36 intrigue [ˋɪnˏtrig] *n.* 陰謀 & [ˏɪnˋtrig] *vt.* 激起……的好奇心

衍 intriguing [ˋɪnˏtrigɪŋ] *a.* 非常有趣的

▸ The murder mystery novel is full of intrigue and suspense, which makes it appealing to readers.

這部謀殺懸疑小說充滿了**陰謀**和懸疑，這些都很吸引讀者。

▸ The man's story intrigued me, and I couldn't wait for him to tell me more interesting details.

這人的故事**引起了我的好奇心**，我迫不及待要他告訴我更多有趣的細節。

Unit 05

0501-0503

1 qualification [ˌkwɑləfəˋkeʃən] *n.* 資格，條件

衍 qualify [ˋkwɑləfaɪ] *vt.* & *vi.* (使)有資格 ⑤

qualify as + 職位
(通過考試) 取得……的資格

qualify A for B　A 有權利獲得 B

似 quality [ˋkwɑlətɪ] *n.* 品質 & *a.* 優良的 ②

quality control　品質管制，品管

反 disqualification [dɪsˏkwɑləfəˋkeʃən] *n.* 取消資格

▶ Two years of teaching experience is a necessary qualification for this job.
兩年的教學經驗是應徵這工作的必要**條件**。

2 credible [ˋkrɛdəbḷ] *a.* 可信 / 靠的

衍 (1) credit [ˋkrɛdɪt] *n.* 讚揚，認可 & *vt.* 將功勞歸因於…… ③
(2) credibility [ˌkrɛdəˋbɪlətɪ] *n.* 可信度，可靠性 (不可數) ⑤

似 convincing [kənˋvɪnsɪŋ] *a.* 令人信服的

反 incredible [ɪnˋkrɛdəbḷ] *a.* 難以置信的 ④

▶ The British Police don't have credible evidence against the suspect.
英國警方找不到**可靠的**證據去定這名嫌犯的罪。
*suspect [ˋsʌspɛkt] *n.* 嫌犯

3 accordance [əˋkɔrdəns] *n.* 依據 (用於下列片語中)

片 in accordance with...　依據……

衍 accord [əˋkɔrd] *n.* 協定 ⑤

▶ Make sure you use this product in accordance with the instructions.
務必**依照**操作手冊使用此產品。
*instructions [ɪnˋstrʌkʃənz] *n.* 操作手冊，使用說明 (恆用複數)

accordingly [əˋkɔrdɪŋlɪ]
adv. 照著，相應地；因此 (= therefore)

▶ My roommate asked me to turn down the music and I acted accordingly.
我室友要我把音樂關小聲一點，我就**照著**做。

▶ The cost of raw materials rose 10%. Accordingly, we have to increase our price.
= The cost of raw materials rose 10%. Therefore, we have to increase our price.
原物料上漲了百分之 10。**因此**，我們必須調漲價格。

0504-0510

4 ambiguity [ˌæmbɪˋgjuətɪ] *n.* 含糊不清

衍 ambiguous [æmˋbɪgjuəs] *a.* 模稜兩可的 ④

似 vagueness [ˋvegnəs] *n.* 含糊

▸ We need to be careful with our choice of words in our composition to avoid ambiguity.
我們在寫作時必須小心選擇用字，以避免**語意不清**。

5 outing [ˋaʊtɪŋ] *n.* (團體的) 遠足，短途旅行

片 go on an outing to + 地方
去某地遠足

似 (1) excursion [ɪkˋskɝʒən] *n.* 遠足
(2) a field trip （學生）實地考察旅行

▸ Our class went on an outing to the National Palace Museum yesterday.
我們班昨天去國立故宮博物院**遠足**。

6 concession [kənˋsɛʃən] *n.* 讓步

片 make a concession 讓步

衍 concede [kənˋsid] *vt.* 讓步 ⑤

▸ When negotiating, sometimes you need to make some concessions to reach an agreement.
談判時，有時你需要**讓步**才能達成協議。

7 incline [ɪnˋklaɪn] *vi.* & *vt.* (使) 傾向 & [ˋɪnklaɪn] *n.* 斜坡

片 (1) incline to + V / sth
傾向於做⋯⋯ / 贊同某事
(2) incline sb to + V / sth
讓某人傾向於做⋯⋯ / 贊同某事

衍 inclined [ɪnˋklaɪnd] *a.* 傾向於⋯⋯的
be inclined to + V / sth
傾向於做⋯⋯ / 易於做⋯⋯ / 贊同某事
= incline to + V / sth
= be apt to + V
= be prone to + V
= tend to + V

▸ Melvin is inclined to lie, which is why I don't trust him.
梅爾文**老愛**說謊，這也就是我不信任他的原因。

▸ Steve is inclined to optimism. He always thinks the best of people and gives them the benefit of the doubt.
史蒂夫**生性**樂觀。他總是認為人性本善，且也會都把人們往好處想。
*give sb the benefit of the doubt
把某人往好處想

▸ I incline to agree with Michael on this matter, even though we disagree on most things.
儘管我和麥可在大多數事情上的意見都不同，但對於這件事情，我**傾向於**同意邁可的意見。

▸ Samantha inclines to the view that low taxes are the best way to stimulate an economy.
莎曼珊**傾向於**認為低稅收是刺激經濟的最佳途徑。

▸ The "certified organic" label on the product inclined me to believe that it was healthy.
這產品上的『有機認證』標籤使我**易於**相信它是健康的。

▸ The promise of huge profits and an early retirement inclined Paul to a career in banking.
銀行業的巨額利潤和可提前退休的承諾**使**保羅**傾向於**從事該行業。

▸ There is a steep incline toward the end of the walk, so you should be prepared.
散步的盡頭有個陡峭的**斜坡**，所以你應要做好準備。

inclination [ˌɪnkləˋneʃən] *n.* 傾向

片 have an inclination to + V
有做……的傾向
= have a tendency to + V
= tend to + V
= be inclined to + V / sth
= incline to + V / sth

▸ James doesn't seem to have an inclination to devote himself to a long-term relationship.
詹姆士似乎不想將自己投入在一段長期的戀愛關係中。

8 dedication [ˌdɛdəˋkeʃən] *n.* 奉獻（不可數）（與介詞 to 並用）

片 show dedication to...
對……展現出奉獻

衍 dedicate [ˋdɛdəˌket] *vt.* 奉獻 ⑤

似 devotion [dɪˋvoʃən]
n. 奉獻（與介詞 to 並用）⑤

▸ Frank has always shown great dedication to his work and family.
法蘭克總是展現出對工作及家庭極大的奉獻。

9 outright [ˋautˌraɪt] *a.* 完全的；直接的 & [ˌautˋraɪt] *adv.* 完全地；直接地

似 (1) completely [kəmˋplitlɪ]
adv. 完全地
(2) directly [dəˋrɛktlɪ] *adv.* 直接地

▸ No political party is expected to gain the outright majority in this election.
這次選舉中沒有政黨被預期會獲得絕對多數。

▸ Without warning, the soldiers launched an outright attack on their enemy, thus breaking the ceasefire.
士兵們毫無預警地直接攻擊敵人，因此破壞了停火協定。

▸ James and his brother are of the opinion that cigarette smoking should be banned outright.
詹姆士和他的兄弟認為應該徹底禁止吸菸。

▸ If Ben asked me outright, I'd tell him the truth.
要是班直接來問我，我就會告訴他實情。

10 relay [ˋrile] *n.* 接力賽 (= a relay race) & [rɪˋle] / ˋrile] *vt.* 轉達 (= pass on)；轉播

片 relay sth to sb　將某事轉達某人

▸ John is quite nervous because he's running the last leg of the relay race tomorrow.
約翰很緊張，因為他明天要跑接力賽的最後一棒。

▸ I was told the news first and relayed it to my friends by phone.
我首先被告知這個消息，接著就用電話轉告我朋友。

▸ Satellites will be used to relay footage of the celebrity wedding to every corner of the globe.
會用衛星將這名人婚禮的影片片段轉播到全球各個角落。

11 successive [sək`sɛsɪv] *a.* 連續的

似 consecutive [kən`sɛkjətɪv] *a.* 連續的 ⑤

衍 (1) succeed [sək`sid] *vi.* & *vt.* 在……之後；繼承 & *vi.* 成功 ②

succeed sb as + 職位
接替某人的職位

succeed to the throne
繼承王位

(2) successor [sək`sɛsɚ] *n.* 繼承者（與介詞 to 並用）⑤

▸ After it had been weakened by successive storms, the bridge was no longer safe.
這座橋被**連續**幾個暴風雨侵襲削弱後，已經不安全了。

succession [sək`sɛʃən] *n.* 連續；繼承

片 (1) in succession 連續地
= in a row
= successively
(2) a succession of... 一連串的……
(3) in a line of succession 繼承的排序上

▸ The basketball team has won the championship three times in succession.
這支籃球隊已經**連續** 3 次贏得總冠軍。

▸ A succession of financial scandals ruined the official's reputation.
一連串的財金醜聞破壞了該官員的名聲。

▸ Prince George follows his father, Prince William, in the British royal family's line of succession.
在英國王室的**繼承順序上**，喬治王子是排在他的父親威廉王子之後。

12 contestant [kən`tɛstənt] *n.* 參賽者，競爭者

衍 contest [`kantɛst ] *n.* 競爭；競賽 & [ kən`tɛst] *vt.* 爭奪 ④

似 competitor [kəm`pɛtətɚ] *n.* 競爭者 ④

▸ Two contestants dropped out of the race for personal reasons.
兩名**參賽者**因個人因素而退賽了。

13 predicament [prɪ`dɪkəmənt] *n.* 困境

片 in a predicament 處於困境中

▸ Robin and I found ourselves in an awkward predicament when neither of us had enough to pay the bill.
羅賓和我都帶不夠錢付帳時，我們發現我們倆**處在很尷尬的情況之下**。
*awkward [`ɔkwɚd] *a.* 尷尬的；難處理的

14 plight [plaɪt] *n.* 困 / 苦境

似 crisis [`kraɪsɪs] *n.* 危機 ②

▸ The plight of the poor laborers has aroused concern.
貧苦勞工的**困境**已引起了關懷。

15 descent [dɪˋsɛnt] n. 下降；血統

片 (1) descent to / from...
下降至⋯⋯ / 從⋯⋯開始下降
(2) be of + adj. + descent
有⋯⋯的血統

衍 descend [dɪˋsɛnd] vi. & vt. 下降 ⑤

反 ascent [əˋsɛnt] n. 上升

▶ Our flight will begin its descent to the airport in 30 minutes.
我們的班機將於 30 分鐘後開始要**降落**到機場。

▶ The descent from the top of the mountain took the hikers a surprisingly long time.
從山頂上走**下來**所花的時間出乎意料地花了這些健行者很長的時間。

▶ The majority of the students in our class are of Asian descent.
我們班上大部分的學生都是**亞裔**人。

16 beautify [ˋbjutə͵faɪ] vt. 美化

三 beautify, beautified [ˋbjutə͵faɪd], beautified

衍 beauty [ˋbjutɪ] n. 美（不可數）；美女（可數）②

▶ Mom beautified the backyard by planting a lot of flowers.
媽媽種了許多花來**美化**後院。

17 calculator [ˋkælkjəletɚ] n. 計算機

衍 (1) calculate [ˋkælkjə͵let] vt. 計算 ④
(2) calculation [͵kælkjəˋleʃən] n. 計算 ④

▶ In the United States, many students can't do calculations without using a calculator.
在美國，許多學生沒有**計算機**就不會計算。

18 landlady [ˋlænd͵ledɪ] n. 女房東

似 (1) landlord [ˋlænd͵lɔrd] n.（男 / 女）房東 ⑤
(2) a property owner
房（地）產所有人

▶ My landlady comes to collect the rent on the first of every month.
我的**女房東**每個月 1 號都會來收房租。

tenant [ˋtɛnənt] n. 房客 & vt. 以租賃方式居住於 (= inhabit [ɪnˋhæbɪt])

似 lodger [ˋlɑdʒɚ] n. 房客，寄宿者
= roomer
= boarder [ˋbɔrdɚ]

▶ Tenants are not allowed to keep pets inside the apartment.
公寓內禁止**房客**養寵物。

▶ Most of the warehouses in this area are tenanted by an international company that is based in the Netherlands.
這區大部分的倉庫是一家設於荷蘭的國際公司所**租用**的。

19 pickpocket [ˋpɪk͵pɑkɪt] n. 扒手

似 thief [θif] n. 小偷 ②

▶ Watch out for pickpockets while you're traveling.
旅行時小心**扒手**。

0520-0528

20 congressman [ˋkaŋgrəsmən] *n.* (美國) 國會 (男) 議員

似 congresswoman [ˋkaŋgrəs,wumən] *n.* 國會女議員 ⑥

▸ William is stepping down as a congressman after 6 years.
6 年任期後，威廉即將從國會議員職務卸任。

21 scorn [skɔrn] *vt.* & *n.* 不屑

片 with scorn　帶著不屑的態度
衍 scornful [ˋskɔrnfəl] *a.* 輕蔑的
be scornful of...　輕蔑 / 瞧不起……
似 contempt [kəmˋtɛmpt] *n.* 鄙視 ⑤

▸ John was scorned by his friends for speaking ill of them behind their backs.
約翰的同學很不屑他，因為約翰都在背後說他們的壞話。
*speak ill of sb behind sb's back　在背後說某人的壞話

▸ Thinking that the question I asked was very stupid, Leo answered me with scorn.
里歐認為我問的問題很白痴，用很不屑的口氣回答我。

22 swamp [swamp] *vt.* 使忙碌，使應接不暇 & *n.* 沼澤 (地)

片 be swamped with / by sth
忙著做某事
= be occupied with sth
似 bog [bag] *n.* 沼澤 (地)

▸ I'm so swamped with work at the moment that I can't discuss the matter with you.
我此刻工作忙死了，沒空跟你討論這件事。

▸ This tropical swamp is filled with many rare species of plants and animals.
此熱帶沼澤地充滿了各式各樣稀有的動植物物種。

23 glide [glaɪd] *vi.* & *n.* 滑行；(鳥、飛機等) 滑翔

片 glide over...　滑行過……；滑翔飛過……
衍 (1) glider [ˋglaɪdɚ] *n.* 滑翔機
(2) a hang-glider　滑翔翼

▸ The couple glided gracefully over the dance floor and wowed us all with their performance.
這對夫妻優雅地滑過舞池，他們的表演使我們所有的人都讚歎不已。
*wow [waʊ] *vt.* 使驚豔

▸ A huge eagle glided over the area, looking for prey.
一隻大老鷹滑翔飛過這區域尋找獵物。
*prey [pre] *n.* 獵物 (集合名詞，不可數)

▸ The ice skater's smooth glide ended abruptly when another skater crashed into her.
這名溜冰者的平順滑行在另一名溜冰者撞上她後嘎然而止。

▸ Although both of the airplane's engines failed, the pilot quickly took it into a glide and landed it safely.
雖然飛機的兩個引擎都故障了，但那飛行員很快將飛機帶入無動力滑行並安全著陸。

24 gleam [glim] *vi.* & *n.* (某物) 閃爍；(眼神) 閃爍

片 (1) gleam with...
(眼神) 閃爍著 (某情感等)
= glisten with...
(2) a gleam of...
一絲 / 線……，少許……

衍 glisten [ˋglɪsn̩] *vi.* 閃耀 & *n.* 閃光

▸ The mermaid took a rest on a rock near the shore, and her blue hair gleamed in the moonlight.
美人魚在岸邊的一塊岩石上休息，她藍色的頭髮在月光下閃閃發光。

▸ Cathy's eyes gleamed with love whenever she looked at her baby son.
每當凱西看著她的小男嬰時，眼神都**閃爍著**母愛。

▸ A gleam of hope appeared just as Roger was on the verge of giving up.
當羅傑就要放棄時，出現了**一絲**希望。
*verge [vɝdʒ] *n.* 邊緣
be on the verge of... 瀕於……

25 elevate [ˋɛlə͵vet] *vt.* 上升，提升

片 be elevated to... 被晉升爲……

衍 elevator [ˋɛlə͵vetɚ] *n.* 電梯 ③

似 (1) raise [rez] *vt.* 提高 ①
(2) promote [prəˋmot] *vt.* 晉升 ③

▸ To Carter's amazement, he was elevated to manager due to his outstanding performance at work.
令卡特驚訝的是，他因為工作表現很傑出而**被晉升爲**經理。

26 villa [ˋvɪlə] *n.* 別墅

似 chateau [ʃæˋto] *n.* (尤指法國的) 別墅

▸ Whoever owns that villa must be stinking rich.
那棟**別墅**的主人一定超有錢的。
*be stinking rich 非常有錢，滿身都是銅臭味 (為貶義)
(= be extremely rich)

27 latitude [ˋlætə͵t(j)ud] *n.* 緯度

片 at latitude + 數字 + degree(s) south / north 在南 / 北緯……度

▸ The island is located at longitude 121.7 degrees east and latitude 25 degrees north.
這座島位在東經 121.7 度，**北緯** 25 **度**。

longitude [ˋlɑndʒə͵t(j)ud] *n.* 經度

片 at longitude + 數字 + degree(s) east / west 在東 / 西經……度

▸ The small town lies at longitude 13 degrees west.
這座小鎮**位於西經** 13 **度**。

28 pilgrim [ˋpɪlgrɪm] *n.* 朝聖者

▸ Upon arriving in Mecca, the pilgrim performed a series of rituals.
這名**朝聖者**一抵達麥加便進行了一連串的儀式。
*ritual [ˋrɪtʃuəl] *n.* 儀式

0528-0537

pilgrimage [ˋpɪlgrəmɪdʒ] *n.* 朝聖

片 go on a pilgrimage 前往朝聖
= make a pilgrimage

▸ All adult Muslims are required to go on a pilgrimage to Mecca at least once in their lifetime.
所有成年回教徒都被要求一生至少要去麥加**朝聖**一次。

29 unpack [ʌnˋpæk] *vi.* & *vt.* 打開（行李、包裹等）

反 pack [pæk] *vt.* 打包 ①

▸ I have been so busy that I haven't had time to unpack since returning from my trip.
我忙到旅行回來的東西都沒有時間**打開**整理。

▸ When Tim stayed in his rich auntie's house, he didn't bother unpacking his suitcase because her servants had prepared all his clothes and toiletries.
當提姆待在他有錢的阿姨家時，他懶得**打開**手提箱，因為阿姨的僕人已經準備好了他所有的衣服和洗漱用品。
*toiletries [ˋtɔɪlətrɪz] *n.* 洗漱用品（恆用複數）

30 legislator [ˋlɛdʒɪs͵letɚ] *n.* 立法委員

衍 (1) legislation [͵lɛdʒɪsˋleʃən] *n.* 制定法律 ⑤
(2) legislative [ˋlɛdʒɪs͵letɪv] *a.* 立法的 ⑤

似 lawmaker [ˋlɔ͵mekɚ] *n.* 立法者 ⑤

▸ In the US Congress, the legislators are either Senators or Representatives.
美國國會裡，**立法委員**不是參議員就是眾議員。

31 commence [kəˋmɛns] *vt.* & *vi.* 開始

片 (1) commence + N/V-ing 開始……
(2) commence with sth 以某事開始

似 (1) start [stɑrt] *vt.* & *vi.* 開始 ①
(2) begin [bɪˋgɪn] *vt.* & *vi.* 開始 ①

▸ Our company commenced business in January of last year. 我們公司去年元月**開始**營業。

▸ We'll commence renovating the lecture hall in August.
我們會在 8 月時**開始**重新整修演講廳。
*renovate [ˋrɛnə͵vet] *vt.* 整修

▸ The celebration commenced with fireworks and a parade. 慶典以煙火和遊行活動**展開序幕**。

32 hamper [ˋhæmpɚ] *vt.* 妨礙

似 (1) restrict [rɪˋstrɪkt] *vt.* 限制，妨礙 ③
(2) hinder [ˋhɪndɚ] *vt.* 妨礙

▸ The tennis player's sore foot hampered him during the match, and that's why he lost the game.
這網球選手腳痛**妨礙**了他比賽，這就是他輸掉比賽的原因。

33 miscellaneous [͵mɪsəˋlenɪəs] *a.* 各式各樣的

似 (1) various [ˋvɛrɪəs] *a.* 各種各樣的 ③
(2) varied [ˋvɛrɪd] *a.* 各種各樣的
(3) mixed [ˋmɪkst] *a.* 混合的

▸ There were many miscellaneous matters to be discussed in the meeting before the main topic could be covered.
在討論主要議題之前，會議將先討論許多**雜項**。

34 lucrative [ˋlukrətɪv] *a.* 獲利多的

似 (1) profitable [ˋprɑfɪtəbḷ]
a. 有利潤的 ④
(2) rewarding [rɪˋwɔrdɪŋ]
a. 有益的；值得的

▸ In the beginning, Simon's business proved to be lucrative, but recently he hasn't made much money from it.
起初，西蒙的生意證明是**賺錢的**，但最近他並沒有從中賺很多錢。

35 detention [dɪˋtɛnʃən] *n.* (尤指因政治因素而) 拘留；(懲罰不乖學生) 放學後留校

片 be held / kept in detention
被拘留，被關押

▸ When the Russian man returned to his home country, he was held in detention for a long time because he was regarded as a traitor.
當這位俄羅斯男子回到其祖國時，他因為被視為叛徒而**被長期拘留**。

▸ Due to his naughty behavior in class, Rudy was given two detentions by the teacher.
由於魯迪在課堂上很頑皮，所以他被老師罰**留校察看**兩次。

36 align [əˋlaɪn] *vt.* 與……聯合 / 結盟；使成一直線，對準 / 齊

片 align oneself with...
與……聯合 / 結盟

▸ A lot of politicians aligned themselves with this presidential candidate because many members of the American public supported him.
許多政治人物都**支持**這位總統候選人，因為許多美國民眾支持他。

▸ The volunteers carefully aligned the chairs in the hall in preparation for the famous novelist's speech tomorrow.
志工小心翼翼地把大廳裡的椅子**對齊**好，為明天知名小說家的演講做準備。

37 default [dɪˋfɔlt] *n.* & *vi.* 不履行，未支付

片 (1) in default on sth
不履行 / 未支付某事物
(2) by default
自動地 (因可能阻止或改變結果之事未發生)
(3) default on sth
不履行 / 未支付某事物

▸ Due to financial difficulties, Sam was in default on the car loan, and the bank threatened to take the vehicle.
山姆由於經濟困難而**付不出**汽車貸款，銀行便威脅著要拿走這臺車。

▸ According to the rules set out by the organization, John will win this game by default if his opponent doesn't show up in time.
根據該組織所定的規則，如果約翰的對手不及時出現，他將**自動**勝出。

▸ In the contract, certain penalties were specified in case the company defaulted on any of its obligations.
在此合約中規定了某些罰則，以防該公司**不履行**任何義務。

0538-0539

38 advisory [ədˋvaɪzərɪ] *a.* 提供諮詢的 & *n.* (關於天氣、疾病等的) 公告，警告

衍 (1) advice [ədˋvaɪs] *n.* 忠告 ②
(2) advise [ədˋvaɪz] *vi.* & *vt.* 勸告 ③

▸ Because of his experience in the field of medicine, Dr. Peterson was named to a special advisory committee.
由於彼得森博士在醫學領域的經驗，所以他被任命為特別顧問委員會的成員。

▸ The weather forecaster issued a heavy rain advisory, warning people living in mountainous areas to be especially careful.
天氣預報員發布了大雨**特報**，警告住在山區的人要特別小心。

39 definitive [dɪˋfɪnətɪv] *a.* 明確的，不可更改的；(書籍等) 最佳的，最具權威的

衍 definitely [ˋdɛfənətlɪ] *adv.* 肯定，當然

▸ Even though Mark was asked to clarify his response to the question, he refused to give a definitive answer.
儘管馬克被要求清楚闡述他對此問題的答覆，但他拒絕給予**明確的**答案。

▸ *The Works of William Shakespeare* is said to be the definitive collection of the English playwright's writing.
《威廉．莎士比亞的作品》據說是此英國劇作家**最具權威的**作品集。

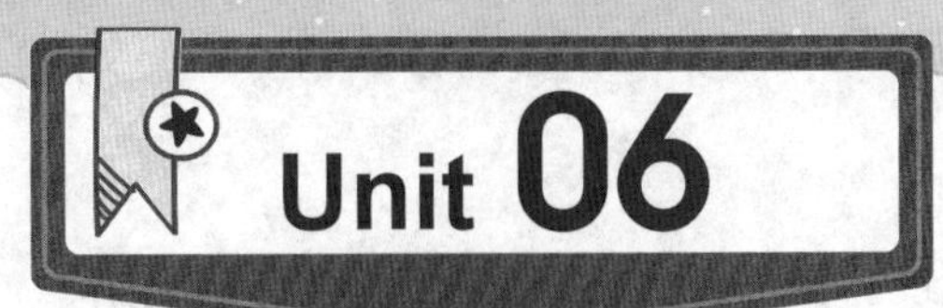

0601-0605

1 imperative [ɪm`pɛrətɪv] *a.* 必須的，緊要的 & *n.* 必要的事，緊急的事

片 (1) It is imperative that...
……是有必要的
(2) It is imperative (for sb) to + V
……是有必要的
(3) a moral imperative
道義上必須要做的事

▸ It is imperative that the movie star's itinerary be kept confidential as he does not want to be spotted by paparazzi.
這名影星的行程**一定要**保密，因為他不希望被狗仔隊看到。
*itinerary [aɪ`tɪnə͵rɛrɪ] *n.* 行程
paparazzi [͵pɑpə`rɑtsɪ / ͵pɑpə`rætsɪ] *n.* 狗仔隊（視作複數）

▸ It is imperative for us to conduct a market survey to understand consumer needs before designing a new product.
在研發新商品之前，我們**一定要**先做市場調查以了解顧客的需求。

▸ According to the prime minister, accommodating the refugees fleeing from that war-torn country is a moral imperative.
該首相認為，收容那些逃離那飽受戰爭蹂躪的國家的難民，**是道義上的責任**。
*accommodate [ə`kɑmə͵det] *vt.* 為……提供住宿

2 hemisphere [`hɛməs͵fɪr] *n.* （地球）半球

片 the northern / southern hemisphere 北 / 南半球
衍 sphere [sfɪr] *n.* 球體；領域 ⑤

▸ Most penguins, such as the emperor penguin, live in the southern hemisphere.
大部分的企鵝，如皇帝企鵝，是住在**南半球**。

3 rampant [`ræmpənt] *a.* （負面的事）蔓延的，猖獗的

似 widespread [͵waɪd`sprɛd] *a.* 普遍的 ⑤

▸ Starvation was rampant in the area after the war.
戰後這個地區人民饑餓現象十分**猖獗**。
*starvation [stɑr`veʃən] *n.* 飢餓

4 symbolize [`sɪmbl̩͵aɪz] *vt.* 象徵，代表

衍 (1) symbolic [͵sɪm`bɑlɪk] *a.* 象徵性的 ⑤
(2) symbol [`sɪmbl̩] *n.* 象徵 ②
似 represent [͵rɛprɪ`zɛnt] *vt.* 代表 ③

▸ In the Bible, lambs symbolize people, and a shepherd symbolizes Jesus.
在《聖經》裡，小羊**代表**人民，牧羊人則**代表**耶穌。
*shepherd [`ʃɛpəd] *n.* 牧羊人

5 refresh [rɪ`frɛʃ] *vt.* 使提振精神 & *vi.* & *vt.* 更新（網頁）

片 refresh oneself (with sth)
（用某事物）使某人提振精神

▸ John refreshed himself with a cup of coffee during the break time.
約翰在休息時間喝了一杯咖啡**提神**。

0605-0611

衍 (1) refreshing [rɪˋfrɛʃɪŋ]
a. 使人提神的
(2) refreshed [rɪˋfrɛʃt]
a. 已恢復精神的

▸ After you access the website, don't forget to refresh to get the latest information about the exam.
你上這網站後，不要忘記要**更新**網頁以獲得有關該考試的最新資訊。

▸ Try to refresh the website every 5 minutes to see if the answers of the exam have been uploaded by the organization.
試著每 5 分鐘**刷新**一次那網站，以看看考試的答案是否已由該組織上傳了。

---

refreshment [rɪˋfrɛʃmənt]
n. 食物飲料；精力恢復（皆不可數）

▸ Josh was finally willing to stop for refreshment after we had been hiking for more than three hours.
我們健步走了 3 個多小時後，喬許終於願意停下來**吃點東西**了。

▸ After working hard for many days, Joe's body ached, and he sought refreshment by visiting a hot spring resort.
喬努力工作很多天後身體很酸痛，便去一個溫泉度假勝地來**恢復精力**。

---

refreshments [rɪˋfrɛʃmənts]
n.（會議或宴會時所供應的）茶點
（恆用複數）

▸ Refreshments will be served at the back of the meeting room during the break.
中場休息期間，會議室後面備有**茶點**供應。

6 inventory [ˋɪnvən͵tɔrɪ] *n.* 存貨清單；存貨；盤點（存貨）

複 inventories [ˋɪnvən͵tɔrɪz]
片 (1) make an inventory of...
將……列成清單
(2) take an inventory 盤點（存貨）

▸ We made an inventory of everything in our warehouse.
我們**將**倉庫裡的所有東西**列了張清單**。

▸ Every month, we take an inventory of our stock in the store.
每月我們都**盤點**店裡的存貨。

7 discharge [dɪsˋtʃɑrdʒ] *vt.* & *n.* 允許離開（軍隊、醫院等）；排放（液體、氣體等）

片 (1) be discharged from the army / a hospital 從軍中退伍 / 出院
(2) discharge A into B
將 A 排放至 B 中
(3) discharge from the army / a hospital 從軍中退伍 / 出院
(4) discharge of sth 排放某物

▸ Tom was discharged from the army due to his mental breakdown.
湯姆因為精神崩潰而**從軍中退伍**。

▸ The factory was fined for discharging industrial waste water directly into the ocean.
這家工廠因為直接**將**工業廢水**排放至**海裡而被罰款。

▸ Mr. Thompson still has to go to see a doctor on a weekly basis after his discharge from the hospital.
湯普遜先生**出院**後，每週仍要去看醫生。

▶ Because of the factory's discharge of foul air, a lot of people have moved out of this area.
由於這工廠**排放**髒空氣，很多人都搬離了此地區。
*foul [faʊl] *a.* 惡臭的

8 remainder [rɪˋmendɚ] *n.* 餘額；剩餘部分

片 the remainder (of sth)
(某物) 剩餘的部分

衍 remain [rɪˋmen] *vi.* 剩餘；保持 ③

▶ The clerk said that I could pay the remainder of the money when I get the cellphone.
店員說，我可以拿到手機後再付**剩下的**款項。

9 vice [vaɪs] *n.* 罪惡；(尤指與色情業相關的) 犯罪活動 & *prefix* 副的

衍 vicious [ˋvɪʃəs] *a.* 殘忍的，惡毒的 ⑤

似 sin [sɪn] *n.* 罪惡，原罪 ③

反 virtue [ˋvɝtʃu] *n.* 美德 ④

▶ The fable told us that greed is a vice and greedy people will eventually be punished.
這則寓言告訴我們，貪婪是種**罪**，貪心的人總有一天會得到懲罰的。

▶ The mayor pledged to fight against vice among teenagers.
市長誓言要掃除青少年間的**犯罪活動**。
*pledge [plɛdʒ] *vt.* 發誓

▶ It is the first time that a female, black vice president has been elected in this country.
這是這國家第一次選出一位黑人女**副**總統。

10 malicious [məˋlɪʃəs] *a.* 惡毒的

反 benign [bɪˋnaɪn] *a.* 和藹的；良性的
a benign tumor　良性腫瘤

▶ Kate spread malicious rumors about her ex-boyfriend because he had been cheating on her.
凱特散布關於前男友的**惡毒**謠言，因為她前男友對她不忠。

11 closure [ˋkloʒɚ] *n.* (工廠、商店等永久) 倒閉；(道路、邊界等短暫) 封閉

片 closure of sth　(短暫) 封閉某物

衍 close [kloz] *n.* 結束 & *vi.* & *vt.* 關閉 ①

▶ There have been two factory closures in the past three weeks due to recession.
因為經濟不景氣，過去 3 個星期已有兩家工廠**倒閉**了。
*recession [rɪˋsɛʃən] *n.* 經濟不景氣

▶ The closure of this canal will hinder trade with nearby nations.
關閉此運河將會阻礙到和附近各國之間的貿易。
*hinder [ˋhɪndɚ] *vt.* 阻礙

disclosure [dɪsˋkloʒɚ] *n.* 揭露 / 公開（不可數）；被揭露 / 公開的事（可數）

片 disclosure of sth　揭露 / 公開某事

衍 disclose [dɪsˋkloz] *vt.* 揭露，公開 ⑤

似 revelation [ˌrɛvḷˋeʃən] *n.* 揭露（不可數）；被揭示的真相（可數）⑥

▸ The disclosure of the senator's scandal has ruined his reputation.
該參議員的醜聞被揭露使他身敗名裂。
*senator [ˋsɛnətɚ] *n.* 參議員
reputation [ˌrɛpjəˋteʃən] *n.* 聲望

▸ The sensational disclosures about the finance minister's extramarital affair have embarrassed his political party, and he has been forced to resign.
財政部長婚外情的聳動消息被披露，其所屬的政黨臉上無光，他因而被迫辭職。
*extramarital [ˌɛkstrəˋmærətḷ] *a.* 婚外的

12 formulate [ˋfɔrmjəˌlet] *vt.* 想出（計畫等）；制定配方

衍 (1) formula [ˋfɔrmjələ] *n.* 配方；公式，方程式；配方奶 ④
(2) formulation [ˌfɔrmjəˋleʃən] *n.* 規畫，制定

▸ The manager formulated a marketing plan for the coming year.
經理想出了明年的行銷計畫。

▸ According to the news report, the scientists formulated various ingredients into an effective allergy medication.
根據這篇新聞報導，科學家將幾種不同的成分混合調配出一種有效治療過敏的藥。
*medication [ˌmɛdəˋkeʃən] *n.* 藥物

13 excerpt [ˋɛksɝpt] *n.* 摘錄（可數）& [ɪkˋsɝpt / ɛkˋsɝpt] *vt.* 摘錄

片 (1) an excerpt from...
從……的摘錄
(2) be excerpted from...
從……摘錄下來

▸ An excerpt from his speech was published in the newspaper.
他演講的一段話被刊登在報紙上。

▸ The following passage is excerpted from Shakespeare's *Tempest*.
以下段落摘錄自莎士比亞的《暴風雨》。

14 adolescence [ædəˋlɛsṇs] *n.* 青春期

片 during / in one's adolescence
當某人青春期的時候

似 puberty [ˋpjubɚtɪ] *n.* 青春期
at puberty　青春期的時候

▸ I left home during my adolescence.
我青少年的時候就離開家自己生活了。

15 beforehand [bɪˋfɔrˌhænd] *adv.* 預先，提前

似 in advance　預先 ①

反 afterward(s) [ˋæftɚwɚd(z)] *adv.* 之後 ③

▸ A hurricane is coming, so I think we'd better reinforce our house a bit beforehand.
颶風就要來了，我認為我們最好事先把房子補強一下。
*reinforce [ˌriɪnˋfɔrs] *vt.* 加強

16 calligraphy [kəˋlɪgrəfɪ] *n.* 書法

片 Chinese calligraphy 中國書法

延伸 handwriting [ˋhænd,raɪtɪŋ]
n. 字跡；書寫 ④

▶ Peter's handwriting is illegible.
彼得的**字跡**潦草到無法辨識。
*illegible [ɪˋlɛdʒəbḷ] *a.* (字跡) 難辨識的
legible [ˋlɛdʒəbḷ] *a.* (字跡) 可辨識的

▶ There's more to Chinese calligraphy than meets the eye. Without years of practice, you can't master this art.
中國書法並非眼見的那麼簡單。沒有多年練習是無法精通這門藝術的。
*There's more to sth than meets the eye.
某事物非外表那麼簡單。

17 endeavor [ɪnˋdɛvɚ] *n.* & *vi.* 努力

片 endeavor to + V 努力去做……
= make an endeavor to + V
= make an attempt to + V
= make an effort to + V

▶ The manager endeavored to get to the bottom of their poor sales performance.
= The manager made an endeavor to get to the bottom of their poor sales performance.
經理**費心**追究業績表現不佳的原因。
*get to the bottom of sth
弄清某事，根究某事 (發生的原因)

18 landslide [ˋlænd,slaɪd] *n.* (指泥土與石頭滑動而造成的) 坍方 (可數)

似 mudslide [ˋmʌd,slaɪd]
n. (指河水挾雜泥土緩緩流動的) 土石流 (可數)

▶ The typhoon caused several landslides in mountain villages.
這次颱風造成山區村落多處**坍方**。

19 gloom [glum] *n.* 陰暗；沮喪 & *vi.* 陰暗；感到沮喪

似 (1) darkness [ˋdɑrknəs] *n.* 黑暗
(2) depression [dɪˋprɛʃən] *n.* 憂鬱 ④
(3) bloom [blum] *n.* 花 & *vi.* 開花 ④

▶ Mrs. Jones looked up at the gathering gloom in the sky, wondering if her husband had brought an umbrella with him.
瓊斯太太抬頭望著天空逐漸聚攏的**陰霾**，想知道先生是否帶了傘。

▶ It's been torturous reading this book as it fills me with nothing but gloom and despair.
這本書讀起來痛苦死了，帶給我的只有**沮喪**跟絕望。

▶ The morning was bright and sunny, but in the afternoon, clouds began to gloom overhead.
早晨陽光明媚，但到了下午，頭頂上的雲開始**陰沉**了下來。

▶ After his team lost the big game, Ricky became depressed and gloomed about the loss for a week.
瑞奇的球隊輸掉了這場大賽後，他整整一週情緒低落、對輸球**感到很沮喪**。

0620-0627

20 pimple [ˋpɪmpḷ] *n.* 面皰，粉刺（可數）

▸ Many teenagers are bothered by pimples on their faces.
許多青少年為臉上的**青春痘**而感到很困擾。

acne [ˋæknɪ] *n.* 粉刺，青春痘（為病症，不可數）

▸ The doctor prescribed some ointment for my acne problem.
醫師開藥膏給我治療**青春痘**。
*ointment [ˋɔɪntmənt] *n.* 藥膏

21 console [kənˋsol] *vt.* 安慰

片 console sb　安慰某人
似 comfort [ˋkʌmfɚt] *vt.* & *n.* 安慰 ③

▸ We tried to console Andy after his house was destroyed in the earthquake.
安迪的房子被地震摧毀後，我們試著要**安慰**他。

consolation [ˌkɑnsəˋleʃən] *n.* 安慰

▸ The only consolation for Tom is that none of his family was hurt in the earthquake.
湯姆唯一的**安慰**就是這次地震他家人全都平安無事。

22 scrape [skrep] *vt.* 刮落，削掉；擦傷 & *n.* 輕微擦傷

片 scrape by　勉強餬口
= make ends meet
似 bruise [bruz] *n.* 瘀傷 & *vi.* & *vt.* 撞傷 ⑤

▸ Could you help me scrape the ice off the windscreen?
你能不能幫我把擋風玻璃上的冰**刮掉**？

▸ I scraped my elbow while playing basketball.
我打籃球的時候**擦傷**了我的手肘。

▸ Matthew earns just enough money to scrape by.
= Matthew earns just enough money to make ends meet.
馬修所得僅能**勉強餬口**。

▸ Brandy got some scrapes when she bumped into the utility pole and fell off her bike.
布蘭迪撞上電線桿後從腳踏車上摔下來，受了點**輕微擦傷**。
*a utility [juˋtɪlətɪ] pole　電線杆

23 lesbian [ˋlɛzbɪən] *n.* 女同性戀 & *a.* 女同性戀的

似 gay [ge] *a.*（尤指男）同性戀的 & *n.*（尤指男）同性戀 ⑥
= homosexual

▸ Maria is 25 years old, works for a major law firm, and identifies as a lesbian.
瑪麗亞今年 25 歲，在一家大的律師事務所工作，並說自己是**女同性戀**。
*identify as...　說自己是（屬於）……

▸ Many governments have approved same-sex marriage for both gay and lesbian couples.
許多政府已同意男同性戀與**女同性戀**情侶的同性婚姻。

24 escort [ɛ`skɔrt ] *vt.* 護送 & [ `ɛskɔrt] *n.* 護送

片 under police escort　在警方護送下
似 accompany [ə`kʌmpənɪ] *vt.* 陪同 ④

▸ The police escorted the president back to his office.
警方**護送**總統回他的辦公室。

▸ After the verdict was announced, the members of the jury left the courthouse under police escort.
判決宣布後，陪審團成員**在警方護送下**離開了法院大樓。
*verdict [`vɝdɪkt] *n.* 判決

25 swarm [swɔrm] *vt.* & *vi.* 擠滿 & *n.* 一群

片 (1) 地方 + be swarming with...
某地擠滿了……
= 地方 + be crowded with...
(2) a swarm of...　一群……

▸ Tourists swarmed the famous attraction and kept taking pictures.
遊客**擠滿**了該知名景點，一直在拍照。

▸ The rock concert was swarming with teenagers.
那場搖滾演唱會**擠滿**了青少年。

▸ A swarm of locusts ate all the crops in the area.
一大群蝗蟲把這地區所有的農作物都吃光了。
*locust [`lokəst] *n.* 蝗蟲

26 villain [`vɪlən] *n.* 惡棍，流氓；(戲劇、小說中) 反派角色

似 (1) hoodlum [`hudləm] *n.* 流氓
(2) hooligan [`hulɪgən] *n.* 流氓

▸ Many people believe that the clothing factories are the real villains and are responsible for the extremely low wages.
很多人認為服飾工廠是真正的**壞蛋**，要對極低的工資負責。

▸ You won't find out who the real villain is until the end of the movie.
你一直到電影結尾才會知道真正的**壞人**是誰。

27 glitter [`glɪtɚ] *vi.* 發光，閃爍；閃現，流露 & *n.* 閃耀

片 (1) sb's eyes glitter with + 情緒
某人的眼睛閃爍著某情緒 / 感
(2) glitter of sth　某物在閃爍
似 (1) sparkle [`sparkḷ] *vi.* & *n.* 閃爍 ⑤
(2) gleam [glim] *vi.* & *n.* 閃爍 ⑥

▸ All that glitters is not gold.
好看的東西未必中用 —— 喻虛有其表。

▸ Irene's eyes glittered with joy when she saw her fiancé walking towards her.
艾琳看見她未婚夫向她走來時，她的眼睛**閃爍著**喜悅。

▸ It'll be hard not to notice Kelly's ring because of the glitter of the big diamond on it.
很難不注意到凱莉的戒指，因為那戒指上的大鑽石**閃閃發光**。

28 sympathize [ˋsɪmpə͵θaɪz] *vi.* 同情

片 sympathize with... 同情……

衍 (1) sympathy [ˋsɪmpəθɪ] *n.* 同情 ④
have sympathy for...
對……感到同情

(2) sympathetic [͵sɪmpəˋθɛtɪk]
a. 富有同情心的 ④
be sympathetic to / toward(s)...
對……感到同情

似 pity [ˋpɪtɪ] *vt.* & *n.* 同情 ③

▸ I can completely sympathize with those who lost their parents in the accident because I myself am an orphan.
我非常同情那些在這起意外中喪失父母的人，因為我自己也是孤兒。
*orphan [ˋɔrfən] *n.* 孤兒

29 enroll [ɪnˋrol] *vi.* & *vt.* 註冊

片 enroll in...
註冊／登記上（學校、課程）

▸ About 100 students enrolled in Professor Johnson's writing course this semester.
這學期約有 100 名學生**報名參加**強森教授的寫作課程。

▸ Since only a limited number of students can take this class, we'd better enroll as soon as possible.
由於能上這門課的學生數量有限，所以我們最好盡快**報名**。

enrollment [ɪnˋrolmənt] *n.* 註冊（不可數）；註冊人數（可數）

▸ Jeremy found the process of enrollment a bit difficult to understand, so he asked his friend to help him.
傑瑞米發現**註冊**過程有點難懂，所以他請朋友幫他忙。

▸ Because the number of babies born each year has been declining, so has enrollment in schools.
因為每年出生的嬰兒數量一直在減少，所以學校的**註冊人數**也在下降。

30 lessen [ˋlɛsn̩] *vt.* & *vi.* 減少

似 (1) decrease [dɪˋkris] *vt.* & *vi.* 減少 ③
(2) reduce [rɪˋd(j)us] *vt.* 減少 ③

▸ A low sodium and low fat diet can lessen the risk of high blood pressure.
低鈉低脂的飲食可以**減少**罹患高血壓的風險。
*sodium [ˋsodɪəm] *n.* 鈉

▸ The deafening noise lessened as the train got farther away.
火車漸漸遠離時，震耳欲聾的噪音就**變小**了。

31 pinch [pɪntʃ] *vt.* 捏 & *n.* 一小撮

片 (1) have to pinch oneself
捏自己一下（以確保不是在做夢）
(2) a pinch of... 一小撮……

▸ When I won the lottery, I had to pinch myself to make sure I wasn't dreaming.
中了樂透時，我**捏了自己一下**確定不是在做夢。

似 squeeze [skwiz] *vt.* & *vi.* & *n.* 捏 ③

▸ Before the soup comes to a boil, add a pinch of salt to it.
在湯還未滾開以前，加一小撮鹽巴進去。
*come to a / the boil 煮沸

32 dictator [ˋdɪk͵tetɚ] *n.* 獨裁者

似 tyrant [ˋtaɪrənt] *n.* 暴君

▸ People nationwide were celebrating the downfall of the dictator.
全國民眾都在慶祝那名**獨裁者**垮臺。
*nationwide [ˋneʃən͵waɪd] *adv.* 在全國 & *a.* 全國的

dictatorship [dɪkˋtetɚ͵ʃɪp]
n. 獨裁統治；獨裁國家

▸ Under the general's dictatorship, people in that country had no rights to speak freely or to vote.
在此將軍的**獨裁統治**下，該國人民沒有言論自由或投票的權利。

▸ People who reside in free countries think it would be horrible to live in a dictatorship such as North Korea.
生活在自由國家的人們認為生活在北韓那樣的**獨裁國家**是很可怕的。

33 iceberg [ˋaɪs͵bɝg] *n.* 冰山（可數）

片 the tip of the iceberg （嚴重問題的）一小部分，冰山一角

衍 ice [aɪs] *n.* 冰 ①

延伸 glacier [ˋgleʃɚ] *n.* 冰河 ⑥

▸ In cold regions, sailors need to be careful not to hit icebergs; if they hit one, it could sink their ships.
在寒帶地區水手需要小心不要撞到冰山；如果撞到冰山，可能會使他們的船沉沒。

▸ John's lie seemed minor, but Flora soon found out it was just the tip of the iceberg regarding his dishonesty.
約翰的謊言似乎微不足道，但芙蘿拉很快發現這只是他謊話連篇的一小部分。

34 moody [ˋmudɪ] *a.* 喜怒無常的，心情不穩的；令人傷感的

衍 mood [mud] *n.* 心情 ②

▸ The boss seemed to be particularly moody that day, getting angry at almost everyone in the office.
那天老闆似乎特別**喜怒無常**，幾乎對辦公室裡的每個人都很生氣。

▸ The director was known for making moody films that explored the dark, depressing side of life.
此導演以製作**感傷的**電影而聞名，這些電影探索了生活中黑暗又壓抑的一面。

35 veil [vel] *n.* 面紗 & *vt.* 掩蓋

似 cover [ˋkʌvɚ] *vt.* 掩蓋 & *n.* 蓋子，掩蓋物 ①

▸ The bridegroom carefully lifted the veil and kissed his bride.
新郎小心翼翼地掀起**面紗**，吻了他的新娘。

▸ The morning fog veiled the mountaintop.
晨霧**掩蓋**住了山頭。

unveil [ʌnˋvel]
vt. 為 (新畫作或雕像等) 揭幕；推出 / 公布 (新產品、計畫等)

▸ Everyone in the room applauded as the artist unveiled his new painting, a scene of a historical battle.
當這位藝術家**為**其新畫作**揭幕**時，房間裡的每個人都鼓掌，此畫呈現的是一場歷史戰役的場景。

▸ Steve Jobs, the former CEO of Apple Inc., often wore a black shirt and blue jeans on stage when he unveiled the newest Apple product.
蘋果公司前執行長史蒂夫．賈伯斯在**推出**最新的蘋果公司產品時，常穿著黑色襯衫和藍色牛仔褲登臺亮相。

36 deduct [dɪˋdʌkt] *vt.* 扣除，減去 (= subtract [sʌbˋtrækt])

片 deduct A from B　從 A 扣除 B

▸ Each month, the company is required by law to deduct a certain amount of income tax from its employees' salaries.
法律規定公司每月**從**員工薪資中**扣除**一定額度的所得稅。

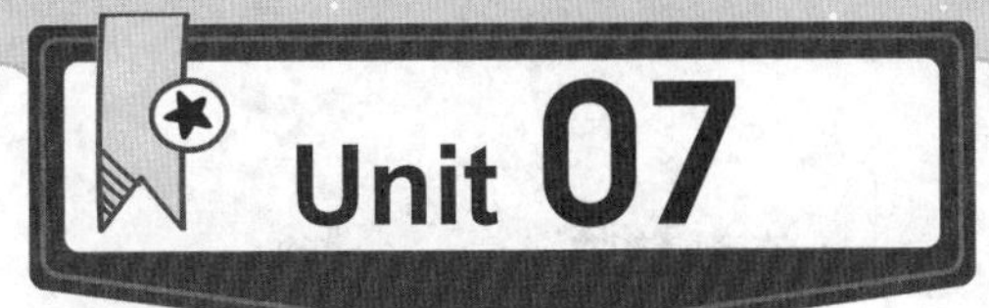

Unit 07

1 resistant [rɪˋzɪstənt] *a.* 抵抗的；對……抵抗力強的

片 be / become resistant to...
抵抗……；對……抵抗力強的

衍 (1) resist [rɪˋzɪst] *vt.* 抵抗，抗拒 ③
(2) disease-resistant [ˌdɪzizrɪˋzɪstənt] *a.* 抗病害的

▸ Botanists have finally succeeded in developing a disease-resistant strain of wheat.
植物學家終於成功培養出能**抗病害的**小麥品種。
*botanist [ˋbɑtənɪst] *n.* 植物學家
strain [stren] *n.* 品種

(3) heat-resistant [ˌhitrɪˋzɪstənt] *a.* 抗熱的

反 irresistible [ˌɪrɪˋzɪstəbl̩] *a.* 無法抗拒的

▸ A lot of conservative people are resistant to radical change and prefer to maintain the status quo.
許多保守派人士**抵拒**激進的改革，寧願維持現狀。
*the status quo [ˌstetəsˋkwo] 現狀

▸ Roaches in our house are becoming resistant to this pesticide.
我們家蟑螂**對**這種殺蟲劑已經漸漸**有抵抗力**了。
*pesticide [ˋpɛstəˌsaɪd] *n.* 殺蟲劑

2 serving [ˋsɝvɪŋ] *n.* (點心、飯菜等的) 一人份 (可數) (= helping)

衍 serve [sɝv] *vt.* 服侍 & *vi.* & *vt.* 供應 (餐飲) ②

▸ There were supposed to be four servings of the vegetable curry, but Rita ate them all by herself.
這道蔬菜咖哩應是 4 **人份**的，但麗塔一個人全吃個精光。

3 liberate [ˋlɪbəˌret] *vt.* 解放，使自由

片 liberate sb from sth
將某人從某事中解放

衍 liberty [ˋlɪbɚtɪ] *n.* 自由 ③

▸ A ten-day trip to Japan temporarily liberated Larry from his daily routine.
10 天的日本之行暫時將賴瑞**從**每天的例行公事裡**解脫**出來。

liberation [ˌlɪbəˋreʃən] *n.* 解放

▸ After the enemy troops retreated and the long siege was over, people took to the streets in celebration of their liberation.
敵軍撤離、包圍結束後，人們走上街頭歡慶**解放**。
*siege [sidʒ] *n.* 包圍，圍攻

4 caffeine [kæˋfin] *n.* 咖啡因

衍 decaffeinated [dɪˋkæfɪˌnetɪd] *a.* 無咖啡因的

▸ An overdose of caffeine could be lethal.
咖啡因過量可能致命。
*lethal [ˋliθəl] *a.* 致命的

0705-0711

5 animate [ˋænəmət] *a.* 活的，有生命的 & [ˋænə͵met] *vt.* 使活動起來

反 inanimate [ɪnˋænəmət]
a. 不會動的，無生命的

衍 animator [ˋænə͵metɚ]
n. 動畫片製作者 / 繪製者

▸ Patty watched the little dark shape on the ground, trying to decide whether it was animate or not.
派蒂看著地上那小小的黑影，試圖確定它是否有生命。

▸ The puppet master animated his puppet with extraordinary skill when minutes ago it was just a lifeless, inanimate object.
人偶師以高超技巧使人偶動了起來，而不過幾分鐘前，它還只是個既無生命又不會動的東西。

animation [͵ænəˋmeʃən]
n. 動畫製作 (技術) (不可數)；動畫 (片) (可數)；活力 (不可數)

片 (1) computer animation
電腦動畫製作技術
(2) a 3-D animation
3D 立體動畫 (片)
(3) with animation　活力十足

▸ This movie is all about computer animation and some eye-catching special effects. There's not much else to be seen.
這部電影全是電腦動畫做的跟一些引人注意的特效。其他就沒啥可看的了。
*eye-catching [ˋaɪ͵kætʃɪŋ] *a.* 引人注目的

▸ Although I love animations, I'm not a big fan of 3-D animations because I always get dizzy when watching them.
儘管我喜歡動畫，但我並不是很喜歡 3D 動畫，因為看 3D 動畫時我總會頭暈。

▸ The author told me with great animation about his plans for the next novel.
該作家活力十足地告訴我他下一部小說的計畫。

6 magnitude [ˋmægnə͵t(j)ud] *n.* 震級；嚴重性

似 seriousness [ˋsɪrɪəsnəs] *n.* 嚴重性

延伸 (1) latitude [ˋlætə͵t(j)ud] *n.* 緯度 ⑥
(2) longitude [ˋlandʒə͵t(j)ud]
n. 經度 ⑥

▸ The earthquake had a magnitude of just 3.2, so fortunately it was not strong enough to cause serious damage.
此地震的震級僅為 3.2，因此幸好這地震的強度不足以造成嚴重的破壞。

▸ We didn't fully understand the magnitude of the problem until it was too late.
我們直到事情已經無法挽回，才徹底了解這問題的嚴重性。

7 diplomacy [dɪˋploməsɪ] *n.* 外交；交際手腕

衍 (1) diplomat [ˋdɪpləmæt]
n. 外交官 ④
(2) diplomatic [͵dɪpləˋmætɪk]
a. 外交的；說話圓滑的 ⑤

▸ If diplomacy failed, we would have no alternative but to resort to military force.
如果外交手段失效，我們就別無選擇，只有走上軍事武力一途。
*alternative [ɔlˋtɝnətɪv] *n.* 可供選擇的東西 / 辦法
have no alternative / choice / option but to + V
除了做……之外別無選擇

▸ To be a leader, the skill of diplomacy is absolutely essential.
要當個領導人，**交際手腕**絕對很重要。

8 insistence [ɪnˋsɪstəns] *n.* 堅持（不可數）

片 (1) at sb's insistence　某人堅持下
(2) insistence on sth　對某事的堅持

衍 insist [ɪnˋsɪst] *vt.* & *vi.* 堅決（與介詞 on 並用）②

▸ At his wife's insistence, Frank started to go to the gym on a regular basis.
在老婆的**堅持之下**，法蘭克開始定時上健身房。

▸ David's insistence on doing everything his way made it impossible to work with him.
大衛**堅持**凡事照他的方法做，讓人覺得沒辦法跟他一起工作。

9 clone [klon] *n.*（以人工繁殖技術）複製的動 / 植物（可數）& *vt.* 人工繁殖技術複製（動 / 植物）

似 replica [ˋrɛplɪkə] *n.* 複製品

▸ Some scientists believe that clones can benefit mankind in many aspects, though there still exist unresolved ethical problems.
有些科學家認為**複製動植物**可以在許多方面造福人類，但目前仍有尚未解決的倫理問題。
*ethical [ˋɛθɪkḷ] *a.* 倫理的

▸ Many people think that cloning animals is an act against nature.
許多人認為**複製**動物是違背自然法則的行為。

10 affectionate [əˋfɛkʃənət] *a.* 充滿深情的（= loving [ˋlʌvɪŋ]）

片 be affectionate toward(s) sb
對某人充滿愛（心）

衍 affection [əˋfɛkʃən] *n.* 鍾愛 ⑤

▸ Frank is very affectionate toward his children. He reads them bedtime stories every night.
法蘭克**對**他的孩子**充滿愛心**。他每天晚上都唸床邊故事給他們聽。
*a bedtime story　床邊故事

11 blaze [blez] *vi.* 熊熊燃燒 & *n.* 大火

似 flame [flem] *n.* 火焰 & *vi.* 燃燒 ③

▸ The house was blazing, but Tony rushed into it to retrieve a portrait of his great grandfather.
房子在**熊熊燃燒**，但湯尼卻衝進去拿他曾祖父的畫像。
*retrieve [rɪˋtriv] *vt.* 取回
portrait [ˋpɔrtret / pɔrtrət] *n.* 畫像，肖像

▸ It took those firefighters about two hours to bring the blaze under control.
這場**大火**花了那些消防員大約 2 小時才控制住。

0712-0720

12 cape [kep] *n.* 斗篷，披風；岬，海角

片 the Cape of Good Hope 好望角

似 cloak [klok] *n.* 斗篷，披風

▸ The magician is wearing a black cape and a top hat.
這名魔術師身穿一件黑斗篷，頭戴一頂大禮帽。

▸ The Cape of Good Hope is near the southern tip of Africa.
好望角位於非洲南端附近。

13 evergreen [ˋɛvɚˏgrin] *n.* 常青 / 綠植物（可數）& *a.*（植物）常青 / 綠的；歷久不衰的

似 (1) permanent [ˋpɝmənənt] *a.* 永久的 ④
(2) lasting [ˋlæstɪŋ] *a.* 永 / 持久的
(3) everlasting [ˏɛvɚˋlæstɪŋ] *a.* 永久的

反 temporary [ˋtɛmpəˏrɛrɪ] *a.* 暫時的 ③

▸ My grandfather told me the tree in his garden was an evergreen.
祖父告訴我他花園裡的那棵樹是一棵常青樹。

▸ Ken's property is huge. There are many large evergreen trees on all sides of it, and they act as a type of fence.
肯的房子很大。四邊都有很多大的常青樹可充當作籬笆。

▸ *Yesterday* by The Beatles is an evergreen song that people enjoy listening to, even though it is decades old.
〈昨日〉是披頭四樂團歷久不衰的歌曲，即使這歌已有幾十年的歷史了，大家仍很喜歡聽。

14 correspondence [ˏkɔrəˋspɑndəns] *n.* 通信（聯繫）；關聯

片 (1) be in correspondence with sb 與某人通信聯繫
(2) a correspondence between A and B A 與 B 有關聯

衍 (1) correspond [ˏkɔrəˋspɑnd] *vi.* 相類似；通信 ④
(2) correspondent [ˏkɔrəˋspɑndənt] *n.*（尤指專門報導某一主題 / 區域新聞的）記者，通訊員 ⑤

▸ My grandfather had been in correspondence with my grandmother for several years when the war broke out.
戰爭爆發時，我祖父母之前就已通信好幾年了。

▸ According to the study, there is a close correspondence between media violence and teenage crime.
根據這項研究，媒體暴力和青少年犯罪之間有著密切的關聯。
*teenage [ˋtinˏedʒ] *a.* 青少年的

15 esteem [ɪˋstim] *n.* & *vt.* 尊敬

片 hold sb in high esteem / regard 很尊敬某人

衍 self-esteem [ˏsɛlfɪˋstim] *n.* 自尊
▸ Getting that job really boosted Michael's self-esteem.
得到那份工作大大提升了麥可的自尊。
*boost [bust] *vt.* 提高

似 respect [rɪˋspɛkt] *n.* & *vt.* 尊敬 ②

▸ Film critics hold the director in high esteem / regard.
影評人都很敬重這位導演。

▸ William Shakespeare's plays and poems are esteemed among literary critics, many of whom believe he was the greatest writer ever.
威廉．莎士比亞的戲劇和詩歌很受到文學評論家的推崇，其中許多文學評論家認為莎士比亞是有史以來最偉大的作家。

16 deafen [ˋdɛfən] *vt.* 使……變聾

衍 (1) deaf [dɛf] *a.* 聾的，失聰的 ②
be deaf to sth　對某事充耳不聞
(2) deafening [ˋdɛfənɪŋ]
a. 震耳欲聾的
a deafening noise
震耳欲聾的噪音

▶ The noise from the nearby construction site almost **deafened** me.
從附近工地傳來的噪音讓我感到震耳欲聾。

17 slump [slʌmp] *vi.* (價格、銷售額等) 暴跌 & *n.* (價格、銷售額等) 暴跌；不景氣

片 (1) a slump in...　……暴跌
(2) be in a slump　不景氣

▶ Sales **slumped** by 40% in the second quarter of the year.
今年第 2 季的業績暴跌了百分之 40。

▶ There's been a **slump** in the demand for new cars due to rising oil prices.
由於油價上漲，市場對新車的需求暴跌。

▶ The tourist industry is in a **slump** because of the global pandemic, which caused most countries to stop international travel.
由於全球爆發流行病，導致大多數國家停止國際間的旅行，因此旅遊業的景氣陷入一片低迷。

18 hoarse [hɔrs] *a.* 沙啞的

片 shout oneself hoarse
某人把嗓子喊啞

似 croaky [ˋkrokɪ] *a.* 低沉而沙啞的

▶ The presidential candidate shouted himself **hoarse**, trying to reassure the voters that the bad days were over.
這名總統候選人一再向選民保證苦日子已經過去了，而把自己的嗓子都喊啞了。

19 spotlight [ˋspɑtˏlaɪt] *n.* 聚光燈 & *vt.* 受到注目，使突出醒目

片 be under / in the spotlight
處於眾人目光的焦點

似 highlight [ˋhaɪˏlaɪt] *vt.* 使醒目，強調 ⑤

▶ The **spotlights** on the stage suddenly went off in the middle of the play.
戲演到一半時，舞臺上的聚光燈突然熄滅了。

▶ I get nervous whenever I am under the **spotlight**.
我每次受到眾人注目都會覺得很緊張。

▶ This incident **spotlighted** the problem of racism.
此事件使種族歧視的問題受到注目。

20 plague [pleg] *vt.* 使難受，受煎熬；(尤指因不停提問而) 糾纏 & *n.* 瘟疫

片 (1) be plagued with / by...
為……所苦，因……而難受

▶ Jerry has been **plagued** with heart problems since he was a child.
傑瑞從小就為心臟方面的問題所苦。

(2) plague sb with sth
用某事物一直糾纏某人

(3) the Plague / plague 鼠疫，黑死病（曾於中古歐洲流行一時，造成重大死傷的傳染病）
= the Black Death
= bubonic plague
*bubonic [bju`banɪk] *a.* 淋巴腺腫的

似 (1) epidemic [ˌɛpəˋdɛmɪk] *n.* (疾病的)流行 ⑤
(2) plaque [plæk] *n.* 匾額

▶ My niece was plaguing me with a lot of questions, but I just wanted to take a rest after work.
我姪女用很多問題一直糾纏著我，但我下班後只想休息一下。

▶ The Plague claimed millions of lives in Europe mainly in the 14th century.
14 世紀時，黑死病在歐洲奪走了數百萬條人命。
*claim a life 奪走一條人命

21 suppress [səˋprɛs] *vt.* 鎮壓；克制（感情或反應）

似 (1) depress [dɪˋprɛs] *vt.* 使沮喪；使蕭條 ⑤
(2) oppress [əˋprɛs] *vt.* 壓迫 ⑥

▶ The army was called in to suppress the prison riots.
軍隊被調來鎮壓監獄暴動。
*riot [ˋraɪət] *n.* 暴動

▶ When Mark told Cindy a funny joke during the serious lecture, she had to suppress a laugh.
馬克在嚴肅的演講期間講了個很好笑的笑話給辛蒂聽，辛蒂得忍住不能笑出聲來。

22 constant [ˋkanstənt] *a.* 持續的；穩定的，持久不變的

衍 constancy [ˋkanstənsɪ] *n.* 恆久不變；忠貞不渝

▶ The constant noise of the machine is driving me crazy.
機器不斷發出的噪音快把我逼瘋了。

▶ According to the weather forecast, the weather will be constant this week.
根據氣象預報，這週的天氣會很穩定。

23 symphony [ˋsɪmfənɪ] *n.* 交響樂；交響樂團（= symphony orchestra [ˋɔrkɪstrə]）

複 symphonies [ˋsɪmfənɪz]

▶ My favorite piece of classical music is Beethoven's Ninth Symphony.
我最喜歡的古典樂是貝多芬的第 9 號交響曲。

24 examinee [ɪgˌzæməˋni] *n.* 應試者，考生

衍 (1) examine [ɪgˋzæmɪn] *vt.* 檢查 ②
(2) examination [ɪgˌzæməˋneʃən] *n.* 檢查；審問；檢驗；考試（= exam）②

▶ The teacher gave the examinees the test booklets.
老師把測驗本發給考生。

examiner [ɪgˋzæmɪnɚ] *n.* (主) 考官

片 a medical examiner 驗屍官

▶ The examiner of my speaking test is a man, and he is quite serious. How about yours?
我的口試官是個男的，他很嚴肅。那你的口試官怎麼樣？

▶ The medical examiner looked for the cause of death of the little boy.
這**驗屍官**查看這小男孩死亡的原因。

25 gorilla [gəˋrɪlə] *n.* 大猩猩

似 guerrilla [gəˋrɪlə] *n.* 游擊隊員

比 (1) chimpanzee [ˌtʃɪmpænˋzi] *n.* 黑猩猩 (比大猩猩小很多) ⑥

(2) orangutan [ɔˋræŋgətæn] *n.* 紅毛猩猩

▶ Thousands of visitors flooded into the zoo, hoping to see the newborn baby gorilla.
數千名群眾湧入動物園，希望可以看到剛出生的**大猩猩寶寶**。
*flood [flʌd] *vi.* & *vt.* 湧進

26 despise [dɪˋspaɪz] *vt.* 鄙視

似 (1) look down on... 鄙視……

(2) despite [dɪˋspaɪt] *prep.* 儘管 ④

反 respect [rɪˋspɛkt] *vt.* 尊敬 ②

▶ Tim despises everyone around him because he has a superiority complex.
提姆因有優越感而**瞧不起**周圍的人。
*superiority [səˌpɪrɪˋɔrətɪ] *n.* 優越
complex [ˋkɑmplɛks] *n.* 情結
a superiority complex 優越感

27 hostel [ˋhɑstl̩] *n.* 便宜的旅社

片 a youth hostel 青年旅社

似 (1) hotel [hoˋtɛl] *n.* 旅館，飯店 ①

(2) inn [ɪn] *n.* 小旅館 ③

(3) motel [moˋtɛl] *n.* 汽車旅館 ③

▶ Most backpackers stay in youth hostels to save money.
為了省錢，大部分的背包客都住**青年旅社**。

28 eternity [ɪˋtɝnətɪ] *n.* 永恆

片 for (all) eternity 永遠
= forever
= for good

▶ I promise I'll love you for all eternity.
我答應我會愛妳直到**永遠**。

29 vine [vaɪn] *n.* 葡萄藤 (= grapevine [ˋgrepˌvaɪn])；藤蔓 (植物)

▶ The vine in our new yard is growing rapidly, and one day soon it will produce fruit.
我們新院子裡的**葡萄藤**長得很快，不久就會結出果實了。

▶ The vines crept over the old mansion, making it all the more creepy at night.
那棟老豪宅因為有**藤蔓**攀爬，讓它在晚上看起來更嚇人。
*mansion [ˋmænʃən] *n.* 豪宅

0729-0738

vineyard [ˋvɪnjəd] *n.* 葡萄園

▸ Andrew owns a vineyard and makes his own wine.
安德魯有座**葡萄園**可以自己釀酒。

30 coral [ˋkɔrəl] *n.* 珊瑚（不可數）& *a.* 橘紅色的，珊瑚色的

片 a coral reef　珊瑚礁

▸ I saw some beautiful coral when I was scuba diving.
我潛水的時候看見了一些美麗的**珊瑚**。

▸ There is a huge coral reef not far from the coast.
距離海岸不遠的地方有一大片**珊瑚礁**。

▸ After the discussion with her roommates, Julia bought two cans of coral paint in order to refurbish the apartment.
茱莉亞在和室友討論後，買了兩罐**橘紅色的**油漆來整修公寓。
⋆refurbish [riˋfɝbɪʃ] *vt.* 翻新 / 整修（建築物或房間）

31 scroll [skrol] *n.* 捲軸 & *vi.* 捲動螢幕 & *vt.* 使滾動或展開

片 (1) a scroll painting　捲軸畫
(2) scroll to...　捲動（螢幕）到⋯⋯

▸ Chinese scroll paintings are one of the most distinct art forms in Chinese culture.
中國的**捲軸畫**是中華文化中最有特色的藝術創作形式之一。
⋆distinct [dɪˋstɪŋkt] *a.* 與眾不同的，別樹一格的

▸ Scroll to the bottom of the page to check the reviews.
滾動到頁面的底部，可以查看評論。

▸ The light breeze scrolled back the layer of sand on the beach table.
微風**捲回**了沙灘桌上的一層沙。

32 lifelong [ˋlaɪf͵lɔŋ] *a.* 終身的

延伸 lifetime [ˋlaɪf͵taɪm] *n.* 終生 ③

▸ Through hard work, the boxer finally achieved his lifelong ambition of becoming the heavyweight champion.
經由努力，這名拳擊手終於達到他成為重量級拳王的**畢生**抱負。
⋆ambition [æmˋbɪʃən] *n.* 抱負，志向

33 syrup [ˋsɪrəp] *n.* 糖漿

片 (1) maple [ˋmepl̩] syrup　楓糖漿
(2) corn syrup　玉米糖漿

▸ My favorite dessert is chocolate ice cream with maple syrup.
我最愛的甜點是巧克力冰淇淋加**楓糖漿**。

34 virgin [ˋvɝdʒɪn] *n.* 處女 / 童男 & *a.* 未開發的

片 (1) a virgin forest　原始森林
(2) extra virgin olive oil
特級初榨橄欖油

▶ Whether Jenny was a virgin or not before she got married is none of your business.
珍妮結婚前是否是個**處女**不關你的事。

▶ These virgin forests are now in danger. We need to do something to prevent them from being exploited.
這些**原始森林**現在正瀕臨危險。我們要做些事情來防止這些森林被開發。

▶ The restaurant is expensive in part because the chef there only uses extra virgin olive oil when he cooks.
這家餐廳很貴，部分是因為那裡的廚師煮菜只使用**特級初榨橄欖油**。

35 plantation [ˏplænˋteʃən] *n.* (熱帶地區種植橡膠、咖啡、甘蔗等) 大農場

衍 plant [plænt] *n.* 植物 ①

▶ All of the banana plantation is in ruins because of the fire last night.
經過了昨晚的火災，整片香蕉**園**滿目瘡痍。
*be in ruins [ˋrʊɪnz]　滿目瘡痍，淪為一片廢墟

36 spokesperson [ˋspoksˏpɝsn̩] *n.* 發言人 (= spokesman [ˋspoksmən] 或 spokeswoman [ˋspoksˏwʊmən])

用法 spokesperson 若依性別來分，男生可用 spokesman，女生則用 spokeswoman。

▶ The government spokesperson refused to comment on the matter.
政府**發言人**拒絕對該事做出評論。

37 defiance [dɪˋfaɪəns] *n.* 違抗

片 in defiance of...　無視……

▶ The general would not allow any defiance of his orders; anyone who refused an order would be punished.
將軍不允許任何**違抗**命令的行為；任何抗命的人都會受到懲罰。

▶ Last night, a large number of people protested outside the city council in defiance of the curfew.
昨晚很多人**無視**宵禁而在市議會外面抗議。
*curfew [ˋkɝf ju] *n.* 宵禁

38 aesthetic [ɛsˋθɛtɪk] *a.* 美 (感) 的，審美的〔英〕(= esthetic [ɛsˋθɛtɪk]〔美〕)

片 aesthetic appeal　美觀

▶ Many critics praised this work of art not only because of its aesthetic appeal but also because of its creativity.
許多評論家讚揚這藝術作品，不僅是因為它外形很**美**，也是因為它很有創意。

0739-0740

39 approximate [ə`prɑksəmət ] *a.* 大概的 & [ ə`prɑksə,met] *vi.* & *vt.* 近似於

片 approximate to... 近似於

▸ Although Kelly didn't know the exact number of people at the event, she gave an approximate figure of 1,500.

雖然凱莉不知道這次活動的確切人數，但她粗估約 1,500 人。

▸ The color of the new paint approximates to the old color of the car, but some of my friends did notice the difference.

新漆的顏色很接近這汽車的舊顏色，但我一些朋友的確有注意到差別。

▸ Try this amazing vegan dish made by Kenny. It really approximates the taste of Thai moon shrimp cake.

嚐嚐肯尼做的這道令人驚豔的素菜。真的很像泰國月亮蝦餅的味道。

40 hierarchy [`haɪə,rɑrkɪ] *n.* 等級制度

複 hierarchies [`haɪə,rɑrkɪz]

▸ A hierarchy is a common system found in many governments and companies around the world.

等級制度是世界各地許多政府和公司常見的制度。

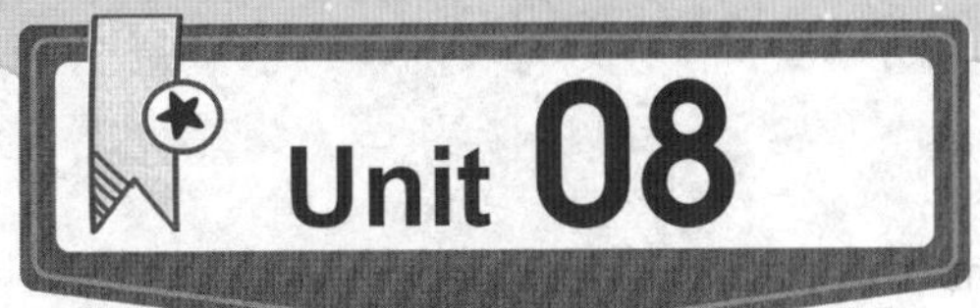

0801-0806

1 reflective [rɪˋflɛktɪv] *a.* 反光的；反映 / 表現……的

片 (1) reflective clothing
有反光材質的衣物
(2) be reflective of...
反映 / 表現出……
= reflect...

衍 (1) reflect [rɪˋflɛkt] *vi.* & *vt.* 反射 & *vt.* 顯示 & *vi.* 沉思 ④
(2) reflection [rɪˋflɛkʃən] *n.* 映照出的影像；反射；沉思 ④

▸ At nights, children should wear reflective clothing to make themselves more visible to automobile drivers.
在深夜，孩童應穿有反光材質的衣物，好讓汽車駕駛人更容易看到自己。

▸ Your taste in music is, to some degree, reflective of your personality.
某種程度來說，你對音樂的品味**反映出**你的個性。

2 vitality [vaɪˋtælətɪ] *n.* 活力，生命力

似 vigor [ˋvɪgɚ] *n.* 活力 ⑥

▸ The process of restructuring the marketing department has injected vitality into the company.
行銷部門改組為該公司注入了一股活力。

3 implicit [ɪmˋplɪsɪt] *a.* 暗指的

似 implied [ɪmˋplaɪd] *a.* 暗示的
反 explicit [ɪkˋsplɪsɪt] *a.* 明確的 ⑤

▸ The politician's remarks contained an implicit criticism of the government.
這名政客的話裡暗藏對政府的批評。

4 lush [lʌʃ] *a.* 鬱鬱蔥蔥的，蒼翠繁茂的，草木茂盛的

似 (1) luxuriant [lʌgˋʒʊrɪənt] *a.* 茂盛的，繁茂的
(2) verdant [ˋvɝdn̩t] *a.* 長滿綠色植物的

▸ We felt so relaxed in the lush mountain range last weekend.
上週末我們在蓊鬱的山林中感到很放鬆。

5 stimulation [ˌstɪmjəˋleʃən] *n.* 激發，刺激

衍 (1) stimulate [ˋstɪmjəˌlet] *vt.* 激勵 & *vi.* & *vt.* 刺激 ⑤
(2) stimulus [ˋstɪmjələs] *n.* 刺激物，促進因素（複數為 stimuli [ˋstɪmjəˌlaɪ]）⑤

▸ The housewife complains of a lack of intellectual stimulation when she is at home looking after her children.
這名家庭主婦抱怨在家顧小孩使她缺乏智力上的激發。

6 skim [skɪm] *vt.* 撇去（液體表面的浮物）& *vi.* & *vt.* 瀏覽（= scan [skæn]）

三 skim, skimmed [skɪmd], skimmed

▸ You'd better skim the fat from the soup before eating it.
你喝湯前最好撇去湯上面的油脂。

0806-0813

片 (1) skim A from / off B
從 B（表面）撇去 A
(2) skim (through / over)...
瀏覽／略讀……

▶ Mandy skims (through) the newspaper every morning while she's having breakfast.
曼蒂每天早上都一邊吃早餐一邊看報紙。

7 bouquet [buˋke / boˋke] *n.* 花束，一束花

片 a bouquet / bunch of flowers
一束花
似 bunch [bʌntʃ] *n.* 一束（花）③

▶ My mom was shocked when my dad, who is usually not romantic, gave her a bouquet of flowers after work today.
我爸這通常並不浪漫的人，今天下班卻給了我媽一束花，她嚇了一跳。

8 affirm [əˋfɝm] *vt.* 證實

片 affirm that... 證實……
衍 affirmation [ˌæfɚˋmeʃən] *n.* 證實
似 confirm [kənˋfɝm] *vt.* 證實 ③

▶ Judy affirmed her intention to apply for the management position.
茱蒂**證實**她將應徵管理階層的職缺。

▶ The spokesman for the government affirmed that a war against terrorism would be necessary.
該政府的發言人**證實**對恐怖主義開戰是必要的。

verify [ˋvɛrəˌfaɪ] *vt.* 證實；確認，核實
三 verify, verified [ˋvɛrəˌfaɪd], verified
片 verify that... 確認……

▶ Unfortunately, there was no witness to verify the suspect's statement.
不幸地，沒有任何證人可以**證明**這名嫌疑犯的說詞。

▶ Please verify that there is sufficient memory available before you download any software.
你下載任何軟體前要**確認**你有足夠的記憶體。

9 teller [ˋtɛlɚ] *n.* 銀行出納員

似 cashier [kæˋʃɪr] *n.*（商店、銀行等的）出納員；收銀員 ⑥

▶ The teller helped clarify the problems I was having with my bank account.
這位**銀行出納員**協助我釐清銀行帳戶的問題。

10 supplement [ˋsʌpləmɛnt] *vt.* 補充 & [ˋsʌpləmənt] *n.* 補充物；（雜誌／報紙的）副刊（皆為可數）

片 (1) supplement A with / by B
用 B 補充 A
(2) a supplement to sth
為某物提供補助，補充某物

▶ Miranda likes to supplement her diet with vitamins.
米蘭達喜歡在飲食裡**補充**維他命。

▶ The money I make from tutoring on weekends is a supplement to my income.
我週末兼家教所賺的錢是**用來貼補**收入所得的。

▶ Interested in buying a new home, Josh looked through the real estate supplement in the newspaper.
喬許對買新房子很感興趣，所以他翻閱了報紙的房地產**副刊**。

11 intervene [ˌɪntɚˋvin] *vi.* 介入，干預

片 intervene in... 干預……
= interfere in...

衍 intervention [ˌɪntɚˋvɛnʃən]
n. 干預 ⑤

▶ The government was urged to intervene in the currency markets in order to stabilize the exchange rate.
政府被要求要**介入干預**貨幣市場以穩定匯率。
*currency [ˋkɝənsɪ] *n.* 貨幣
stabilize [ˋstebḷˌaɪz] *vt.* 使穩定

12 orderly [ˋɔrdɚlɪ] *a.* 整齊的；守秩序的 & *n.* (醫院的) 勤務員 (幫忙移動病患、清潔、抬重物等，工作內容無涉及專業的醫療工作)

複 orderlies [ˋɔrdɚlɪz]

片 in an orderly fashion
以守秩序的方式
= in an orderly way

衍 order [ˋɔrdɚ] *n.* 順序 ①

反 disorderly [dɪsˋɔrdɚlɪ] *a.* 混亂的

▶ The children formed an orderly line before they went into the museum.
這些孩童進入博物館前先排成**整齊的**一排隊伍。

▶ In the event of an emergency, please proceed to the nearest exit in an orderly fashion.
萬一發生緊急事件，請**以有秩序的方式**前往最靠近的出口。
*in the event of... 萬一……
*proceed [prəˋsid] *vi.* (朝某個方向) 前進
proceed to + 地方 向某地前進，到某地

▶ After the pandemic was under control, people were greatly indebted to the doctors, nurses, and orderlies for their help.
在該流行病受到控制後，人們非常感謝醫生、護理師和**醫院勤務員**的幫忙。

---

turmoil [ˋtɝmɔɪl] *n.* 騷動，混亂

片 (1) be in turmoil 陷入 (一片) 混亂
(2) throw... into turmoil
使……陷入混亂

似 chaos [ˋkeɑs] *n.* 混亂 ⑤

▶ Jamie was in turmoil when Gina broke off their engagement.
吉娜解除婚約時，傑米整個人都**亂**了。

▶ Six robberies in one night threw the village into turmoil.
一夜之間有 6 次搶劫**使**該村莊**陷入混亂**。

13 ambush [ˋæmbʊʃ] *n.* 埋伏突襲

片 (1) in an ambush 在埋伏中
(2) lie / wait in ambush
埋伏 (等待攻擊)

▶ Tragically, a group of 20 international aid workers were killed in a terrorist ambush.
不幸的是，一群共 20 名的國際救援人員在恐怖分子的**埋伏突襲中**喪生。

▶ The militia was lying in ambush behind the trees, waiting for the ambassador's car to pass by.
民兵部隊**埋伏**在樹後面，等待大使的車開過去。
*militia [məˋlɪʃə] *n.* 民兵部隊

14 span [spæn] *n.* 一段時間 & *vt.* (時間) 持續，貫穿；包括

目 span, spanned [spænd], spanned
片 a life span　平均壽命
= a life expectancy

▸ Over a span of just one year, the cellphone market has changed dramatically.
光是一年的時間，手機市場就有了大幅改變。

▸ Women tend to have longer life spans than men.
女人一般比男人長壽。

▸ The Great Depression, a time of tremendous difficulty, spanned roughly 10 years.
經濟大蕭條是個非常艱困的時期，大約持續了 10 年。

▸ William Shakespeare's plays span many themes—everything from revenge to love.
威廉．莎士比亞的戲劇涵蓋了許多主題，從復仇到愛情都有。

15 airtight [ˋɛr͵taɪt] *a.* 氣密的；(案件、論點等) 無懈可擊的；(防禦等) 滴水不漏的

片 an airtight case　無懈可擊的案件
似 watertight [ˋwɑtɚ͵taɪt]
a. 無懈可擊的；防水的

▸ Store the cookies in airtight containers and put them in the cupboard, so the cookies won't spoil quickly.
把餅乾放入密閉容器內，再放到櫥櫃裡，這樣它們就不會很快壞掉了。

▸ The lawyer worked hard to develop an airtight case that would prove his client's innocence.
這律師努力構築一個無懈可擊的案件，好證明其委託人無罪。

▸ We have an airtight defense on this military base. With three squads on patrol 24 hours a day, the enemy stands no chance of breaking in by force.
我們基地的防禦滴水不漏。全天候都有 3 個班在巡邏，敵人根本沒機會以武力闖入。
*squad [skwɑd] *n.* (軍隊中的) 班
patrol [pəˋtrol] *n.* 巡邏
on patrol　巡邏

16 bleach [blitʃ] *vt.* 漂白 & *n.* 漂白劑

▸ Laura sometimes bleaches her white clothes to make them look as clean as possible.
蘿拉有時會漂白她的白色衣服，使它們看起來盡可能乾淨。

▸ Besides making clothes whiter, bleach can be used to kill harmful bacteria, too.
除了讓衣服更白之外，漂白水也可用來殺菌。

17 cardboard [ˋkɑrd,bɔrd] *n.* 硬紙板

片 a cardboard box 紙箱

似 cupboard [ˋkʌbɚd] *n.* 碗櫥，櫥櫃 ③

▶ Old newspapers can be recycled and then made into cardboard boxes.
舊報紙可以回收再做成紙箱。
*recycle [riˋsaɪkl̩] *vt.* 回收

carton [ˋkɑrtən] *n.* (裝食物或飲料的) 紙盒，塑膠盒

片 a carton of... 一盒……

▶ Nutritional information must be labeled on milk cartons.
牛奶盒上必須標明營養成分。
*nutritional [n(j)uˋtrɪʃənl̩] *a.* 營養的

▶ Amanda gave her young daughter a carton of juice to drink.
亞曼達給她小女兒一盒果汁喝。

packet [ˋpækɪt] *n.* 小包，小盒裝

片 a packet of... 一小包……

衍 pack [pæk] *n.* 包，盒 & *vt.* 將……打包 ①

▶ Ted tore the sugar packet open and poured it into the coffee.
泰德把糖包撕開，把糖倒進咖啡裡。

▶ Feeling depressed, Ray smoked a packet of cigarettes in just 30 minutes.
雷因為覺得非常沮喪，半個小時內就抽完了一包菸。

18 limp [lɪmp] *vi.* 跛行 & *n.* 跛腳

片 have a limp 跛腳

似 lame [lem] *a.* 跛腳的

▶ The basketball player limped off the court.
那名籃球員一跛一跛地走下球場。

▶ Josh has had a slight limp since the car accident.
賈許自車禍後就略跛。

19 gospel [ˋgɑspl̩] *n.* 福音 (耶穌的啟示和教義)

片 (1) the gospel 福音
(2) preach the gospel 傳福音
(3) gospel music 福音歌曲

▶ Gary is so religious that he preaches the gospel to everyone he meets.
蓋瑞非常虔誠，他向遇到的每個人都傳福音。

▶ These Christians sang gospel music to praise God.
這些基督徒唱福音歌曲讚美主。

20 graze [grez] *vt.* 擦傷 & *vi.* & *vt.* (動物) 吃草 (= graze on the grass)

▶ The little boy tripped over a stone and grazed his knees.
小男孩被石頭絆倒，擦傷了膝蓋。

▶ A herd of cattle were grazing on the grass.
一群牛正在吃著草。

▶ The cattle graze the fields until the frost and snow come.
牛在牧場上**吃草**，直到霜雪降臨。

21 courtyard [ˋkɔrt͵jɑrd] *n.* 庭院，中庭，天井

似 backyard [ˋbæk͵jɑrd] *n.* 後院 ⑤

▶ My grandmother loves to sit on the bench beneath the tree in the courtyard.
我祖母喜歡坐在**中庭**大樹下面的長椅上。

22 playwright [ˋple͵raɪt] *n.* 劇作家

衍 play [ple] *n.* 戲劇，劇本 ①

▶ A: What do you do for a living?
B: I'm a playwright.
A：你靠什麼維生？
B：我是**寫劇本**的。

23 sculptor [ˋskʌlptɚ] *n.* 雕刻家

衍 (1) sculpture [ˋskʌlptʃɚ] *n.* 雕刻（不可數）；雕刻作品（可數）④
(2) sculpt [skʌlpt] *vi.* & *vt.* 雕刻

似 (1) a statue maker 製作雕像的人
(2) carver [ˋkɑrvɚ] *n.* 雕刻師，雕刻愛好者

▶ Michelangelo was an accomplished sculptor from the Renaissance.
米開朗基羅是文藝復興時期一位傑出的**雕刻家**。
*accomplished [əˋkɑmplɪʃt]
a. 傑出的，造詣高的 (= skillful)
the Renaissance [ˋrɛnə͵sɑns] 文藝復興時期

24 grapefruit [ˋgrep͵frut] *n.* 葡萄柚

複 grapefruit / grapefruits
衍 grape [grep] *n.* 葡萄 ②

▶ Would you like some freshly squeezed grapefruit juice?
要不要來點鮮榨**葡萄柚**汁？
*squeeze [skwiz] *vt.* 擠，榨

25 summon [ˋsʌmən] *vt.* 召喚；召集（會議）；鼓起（勇氣）

片 (1) summon sb to + 地方
召喚某人至某地
(2) summon sb to + V
召喚某人做……
(3) summon a meeting / conference 召集會議
(4) summon (up) one's courage
鼓起勇氣
= pluck up one's courage
= work up one's courage

▶ The boss summoned Judy to Seattle for a sudden board meeting.
老闆**召喚**茱蒂到西雅圖參加一個臨時召開的董事會。

▶ The court summoned Justin to give his testimony during the trial next week.
法院**傳喚**賈斯汀在下週的審判中作證。

▶ The minister summoned an emergency meeting to discuss giving aid to the disaster victims.
部長**召集**了一場緊急**會議**討論給災民的援助。

▸ Rex summoned up his courage and asked Catherine out.
= Rex plucked up his courage and asked Catherine out.
= Rex worked up his courage and asked Catherine out.
雷克斯**鼓起勇氣**約凱瑟琳出去約會。

26 linger [ˋlɪŋgɚ] *vi.* 逗留，徘徊；繼續存留

衍 lingering [ˋlɪŋgərɪŋ] *a.* 長時間的
比 (1) roam [rom] *vi.* & *vt.* 漫步 ⑥
(2) stroll [strol] *vt.* 散步 ⑥

▸ After the concert was over, Jessie and her friends lingered outside the theater, hoping to catch sight of the singers.
音樂會結束後，潔西和她朋友在劇院外**徘徊**，希望可以看到這些歌手。
*catch sight of... 看到……

▸ The pleasant childhood memory has lingered in Kelly's mind for a long time.
美好的童年記憶在凱莉的腦海中**留存**了很長一段時間。

27 excel [ɪkˋsɛl] *vi.* 表現優異

三 excel, excelled [ɪkˋsɛld], excelled
片 excel in / at... 在……方面很突出
衍 (1) excellent [ˋɛksələnt] *a.* 出色的 ①
(2) excellence [ˋɛksl̩əns] *n.* 傑出（通常與介詞 in 並用）③

▸ John excels in math.
約翰在數學方面**很拿手**。

▸ David excels at photography, but when it comes to painting, he is all thumbs.
大衛的攝影**很行**，不過說到畫畫時，他就笨手笨腳了。
*be all thumbs 笨手笨腳的

28 selective [səˋlɛktɪv] *a.* 很挑剔，嚴格篩選的

片 be selective about... 對……很挑剔
衍 (1) select [səˋlɛkt] *vt.* 挑選 ②
(2) selection [səˋlɛkʃən] *n.* 選擇 ②
似 choosy [ˋtʃuzɪ] *a.* 挑剔的

▸ Tom was very selective about who he worked with.
湯姆**對**共事的對象都**很挑剔**。

29 superstitious [ˌsupɚˋstɪʃəs] *a.* 迷信的

片 be superstitious about sth 迷信某事
衍 superstition [ˌsupɚˋstɪʃən] *n.* 迷信 ⑤

▸ A large number of Westerners are superstitious about Friday the thirteenth.
很多西方人**很迷信** 13 號星期五這個日子。

30 excess [ɪkˋsɛs / ˋɛkˌsɛs] *n.* 過量 & [ˋɛkˌsɛs] *a.* 過多的

片 (1) an excess of... 過量的……

▸ An excess of vitamins can be harmful to your health.
過量的維他命可能對健康有害。

(2) in excess of... 超過……
(3) V + to excess 過度做……

衍 exceed [ɪkˋsid] *vt.* 超過 ⑤

似 surplus [ˋsɝpləs] *n.* 過量 & *a.* 過量的 ⑤

▸ It is unwise to do a job that is in excess of one's ability.
做自己能力所不及的工作是不智的。

▸ Roger loves drinking beer at his leisure, but he never does it to excess.
羅傑閒暇時喜歡喝啤酒，但他從不過度。

▸ You can donate your excess food to the local food bank to help the homeless.
你可以把多餘的食物捐給當地的食物銀行，來幫助街友。

31 tan [tæn] *vi.* & *vt.* 晒黑，晒成古銅色 & *a.* 古銅色的 (= tanned = suntanned) & *n.* 晒成古銅膚色 (= suntan)

延伸 (1) sunburn [ˋsʌnˏbɝn] *n.* 晒傷
(2) sunburned [ˋsʌnˏbɝnd] *a.* 晒傷的 (= sunburnt [ˋsʌnˏbɝnt])

▸ Some people's skin does not tan easily.
有些人皮膚不容易晒黑。

▸ Many people like to tan their bodies by lying on the beach on a hot day.
很多人喜歡在炎熱的天氣躺在海灘上把身體晒黑。

▸ Vincent's face was tan and radiant after he returned from summer vacation.
放完暑假回來後，文生的臉晒成了古銅色，容光煥發。
* radiant [ˋredɪənt] *a.* 容光煥發的

▸ Mary got a nice tan by spending the summer vacation on the beach.
瑪麗暑假都在沙灘上度過，因而晒了一身漂亮的古銅色。

32 vowel [ˋvaʊəl] *n.* 母音

▸ There are two vowels in the word "hopeful."
『hopeful』這個字有兩個母音。

consonant [ˋkɑnsənənt] *n.* 子音

▸ There are three consonants and two vowels in my name.
我的名字裡有 3 個子音和 2 個母音。

33 livestock [ˋlaɪvˏstɑk] *n.* (統指馴養的牛、羊、馬等) 牲口 (為複數)

延伸 (1) poultry [ˋpoltrɪ] *n.* 家禽；家禽肉 (皆不可數) ⑥
(2) fowl [faʊl] *n.* 家禽 (複數為 fowl / fowls) ⑥

▸ The farmer gave his livestock injections to prevent them from getting infections.
農夫替牲口打針以防感染。
* injection [ɪnˋdʒɛkʃən] *n.* 注射
infection [ɪnˋfɛkʃən] *n.* 傳染

34 tempo [ˋtɛmpo] *n.* 節奏；步調

似 (1) rhythm [ˋrɪðəm] *n.* 節奏 ④
(2) pace [pes] *n.* 步調 ④

▶ When I try to relax, I turn down the lights and listen to music with a slow tempo.
我試著要放鬆時，我會把燈光調暗，然後聽慢**節奏**的音樂。

▶ Howard is still not accustomed to the slow tempo of life in Vancouver.
霍華對於溫哥華緩慢的生活**步調**還是不適應。

35 broth [brɑθ] *n.* (常加入蔬菜或米的) 肉湯，湯

似 soup [sup] *n.* 湯 ①

▶ The chef boiled all the ingredients together to make the beef broth.
廚師將所有的材料放進這鍋牛肉湯裡煮。

▶ Too many cooks spoil the broth.
太多廚師會煮壞了湯。/ 人多手雜。—— 諺語

36 lizard [ˋlɪzɚd] *n.* 蜥蜴

延伸 reptile [ˋrɛptaɪl] *n.* 爬蟲類 ⑥

▶ The scientist discovered a rare species of lizard in the jungle.
這名科學家在叢林裡發現一隻稀有品種的**蜥蜴**。
*species [ˋspiʃiz] *n.* 物種 (單複數同形)

37 lodge [lɑdʒ] *vi.* 寄宿，租住 *vt.* 安置，收容 & *vi.* & *vt.* 卡住 & *n.* 小屋，度假屋

片 (1) be lodged in / at + 地方
被安置在某處
(2) a hunting / ski lodge
狩獵 / 滑雪度假屋

▶ While he studied in England, Raymond lodged in a home near his university.
在英國留學期間，雷蒙**寄宿**在他大學附近的一戶人家家裡。

▶ The little boy was temporarily lodged in the local orphanage.
小男孩**被**暫時**安置在**當地的孤兒院裡。

▶ The fishbone lodged in my throat, and I started to choke.
那根魚刺**卡**在我的喉嚨裡，讓我開始覺得呼吸困難。

▶ There are several lodges by the lake, and you can stay in one of them for a reasonable price.
湖附近有幾間**旅社**價格還挺划算，你可以在那裡過夜。

▶ Rescuers spent the night at the hunting lodge and set off early next morning to continue their search for the missing hiker.
搜救人員在**狩獵度假屋**度過一晚，隔天早上又再度出發尋找失蹤的登山客。

lodging [ˋlɑdʒɪŋ] *n.* 寄宿的地方（不可數）

片 board and lodging　食宿
= room and board
*board [bord] *n.* 伙食；薄木板

▶ The sign near the school reads, "Board and lodging for students: $500 per month."
學校附近有一則廣告說：『學生膳宿：每月 500 美元。』

38 exclusion [ɪkˋskluʒən] *n.* 把……排除在外（不可數）；被排除在外的事物（可數）；不予考慮（不可數）

片 (1) exclusion from...　把……排除在外
(2) exclusion of...　不(予)考慮……，排除……

衍 (1) exclude [ɪkˋsklud] *vt.* 排除 ⑤
(2) exclusive [ɪkˋsklusɪv] *a.* 除外的 ⑤

▶ Jeremy wondered if his exclusion from the dinner invitation list was a sign that Mary didn't like him.
傑瑞米想知道他被排除在晚宴邀請名單之外，是否表示瑪麗不喜歡他。

▶ One of the exclusions in the guarantee was that damage caused by the customer was not covered.
保證書的排除條款之一是用戶所造成的損害並不適用。

▶ Because of the poor economy, the company's exclusion of some workers from the bonus program was understandable.
由於經濟不景氣，公司不考慮給一些員工獎金是可以理解的。

39 archaeology [ˏɑrkɪˋɑlədʒɪ] *n.* 考古學〔英〕(= archeology〔美〕)

衍 (1) archaeologist [ˏɑrkɪˋɑlədʒɪst] *n.* 考古學家
(2) archaeological [ˏɑrkɪəˋlɑdʒɪkḷ] *a.* 考古學的

▶ Linda's interest in history and ancient civilizations led her to choose archaeology as her major.
琳達對歷史和古代文明很有興趣，而促使她選了考古學作為主修。

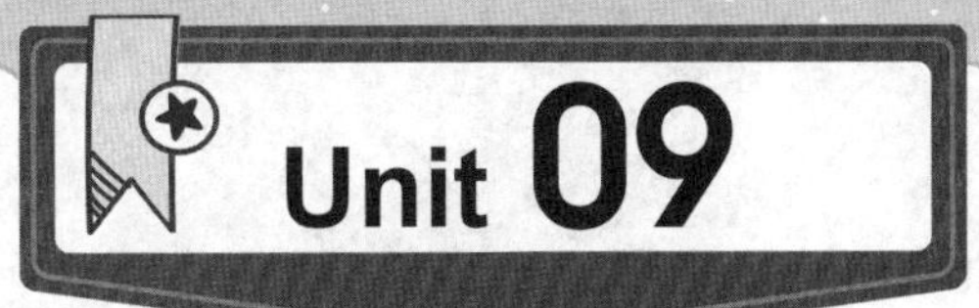

Unit 09

0901-0904

1 glamour [ˋglæmɚ] *n.* 魅力，吸引力〔英〕(= glamor〔美〕)

似 appeal [əˋpil] *n.* 吸引力 ③

▸ A lot of people were attracted by the movie star's glamour.
許多人深受這名影星的**魅力**所吸引。

glamorous [ˋglæmərəs] *a.* 有魅力的

似 (1) gorgeous [ˋgɔrdʒəs] *a.* 性感漂亮的 ⑤
(2) wonderful [ˋwʌndɚfəl] *a.* 很棒的 ①
(3) fabulous [ˋfæbjələs] *a.* 很棒的 ⑤

▸ Scarlett Johansson is a glamorous movie star.
史嘉蕾．喬韓森是位**有魅力的**電影明星。

2 foresee [fɔrˋsi] *vt.* 預見，預測

三 foresee, foresaw [fɔrˋsɔ], foreseen [fɔrˋsin]

片 (1) foresee + 疑問詞 (如：how / what / why... 引導的名詞子句) 預測如何 / 怎麼 / 為何……
(2) foresee that... 預測……

似 (1) predict [prɪˋdɪkt] *vt.* 預測 ④
(2) forecast [ˋfɔr͵kæst] *vt.* 預報 (天氣) ④
三態為：forecast, forecast / forecasted [ˋfɔr͵kæstɪd], forecast / forecasted

▸ None of us foresaw what the boss was going to do with this financial crisis.
我們都無法**預測**老闆將如何處理這次的財務危機。

▸ Few analysts foresaw that natural gas prices would rise steeply.
沒幾個分析師**預測**到天然氣價格會急遽攀升。
*steeply [ˋstiplɪ] *adv.* 急遽地

3 spontaneous [spɑnˋtenɪəs] *a.* 不由自主的，自發的；未事先準備的，即席的

衍 spontaneity [͵spɑntəˋneətɪ / ͵spɑntəˋniətɪ] *n.* 自然發生

似 impulsive [ɪmˋpʌlsɪv] *a.* 衝動的

▸ The crowd broke into spontaneous applause when the speech was over.
演講結束時，群眾**不由自主**發出熱烈掌聲。

▸ I was a bit nervous when they asked me to give a spontaneous speech as tonight's guest of honor.
當他們要我以今晚貴賓的身分發表**即席**演說時，我有一點緊張。

4 casualty [ˋkæʒjuəltɪ] *n.* 傷亡人數 (可數)

複 casualties [ˋkæʒjuəltɪz]

片 (1) cause / suffer heavy casualties 造成 / 受到慘重傷亡

▸ The suicide bombing in a busy shopping street caused heavy casualties.
發生在熱鬧購物街上的自殺炸彈攻擊，造成了重大傷亡。

(2) a road casualty　道路意外傷亡

似 toll [tol] *n.* (傷亡) 總數，損失；過路費 & *vt.* 敲鐘 & *vi.* 鐘聲響起 ⑤

▸ In this country, the number of road casualties increased by 10% last summer.
這國家去年夏天道路意外的傷亡人數增加了 10%。

5 comprehensive [ˌkamprɪˋhɛnsɪv] *a.* 廣泛的，詳盡的，全面的

片 (1) a comprehensive study / guide / survey
全面的研究 / 指南 / 調查

(2) comprehensive insurance
綜合保險〔英〕

似 (1) complete [kəmˋplit] *a.* 徹底的 ②

(2) thorough [ˋθɝo] *a.* 徹底的 ④

▸ Our team is now conducting a comprehensive study on the effects of global warming.
我們小組正在對全球暖化的影響做全面性的研究。

▸ Since Terry had bought comprehensive insurance, he didn't have to pay to get his car fixed after the accident.
由於泰瑞已經買了綜合保險，因此在那事故發生後，他修車不必付錢。

6 disturbance [dɪsˋtɝbəns] *n.* 干擾；(群眾的) 騷動，衝突

片 cause / create a disturbance
妨礙 (公眾) 秩序

衍 disturb [dɪsˋtɝb] *vt.* 打擾 ④

▸ Phone calls in the middle of a movie can be a great disturbance.
電影看到一半電話響起會是一大干擾。

▸ A few football fans were arrested for causing a disturbance during the game.
有幾個橄欖球迷在比賽途中因為妨礙秩序而被逮捕。

▸ There was a disturbance between the protesters and the riot police, but fortunately no one was injured.
抗議者跟鎮暴警察間有衝突，所幸無人受傷。

7 intimacy [ˋɪntəməsɪ] *n.* 親密 (關係) (不可數)

片 intimacy between A and B
A 和 B 之間親密的關係

衍 intimate [ˋɪntəmət] *a.* 親密的 ④

▸ The intimacy between Ben and Holly was obvious whenever they held hands, hugged, or even just looked at each other.
每當班和波莉牽手、擁抱，甚至只是看著彼此時，他們之間的親密關係是很明顯的。

8 drastic [ˋdræstɪk] *a.* 激烈的

片 take drastic action / measures
採取激烈的行動 / 手段

衍 (1) drastically [ˋdræstɪklɪ] *adv.* 激烈地

▸ The number of wild rhinos all over the world has dwindled drastically.
全球野生犀牛的數目已急遽下降。
*rhino [ˋraɪno] *n.* 犀牛
dwindle [ˋdwɪndḷ] *vi.* 減少

▸ The union threatened to take drastic action if its demands were not met.
工會揚言若達不到其訴求的話，便會採取激烈的行動。

似 radical [ˋrædɪkḷ] *a.* 激進的；基本的 & *n.* 激進分子，(漢字的) 部首 ⑤

9 catastrophe [kəˋtæstrəfɪ] *n.* 災難

片 (1) a nuclear / an economic / an environmental catastrophe 核子 / 經濟 / 環境災難

(2) prevent a catastrophe 預防一場災難

衍 catastrophic [ˏkætəˋstrɑfɪk] *a.* 引起重大災難的，災難的

▸ The catastrophic typhoon destroyed the entire village.
引起重大災難的颱風摧毀了整座村莊。

似 disaster [dɪˋzæstɚ] *n.* 災難 ④

▸ The recent cyclone in Bangladesh was a real catastrophe.
最近在孟加拉的那場颶風真是一場大**災難**。

▸ I can't imagine what a catastrophe it will be if we lose Mr. Hank, our most important client.
我無法想像要是我們失去最重要的客戶漢克先生的話，那將會是一場什麼樣的**災難**。

▸ A huge earthquake and tsunami in March 2011 caused a nuclear catastrophe in Fukushima, Japan.
2011 年 3 月在日本福島發生的大地震和海嘯造成了**核子災難**。

▸ The organization of this historic building said that several safety measures were in place to prevent a catastrophe, such as a huge earthquake, from damaging the structure.
這座歷史建築的機構表示已採取多項安全措施，以**防**大地震等**災難**破壞此建築物。

---

tornado [tɔrˋnedo] *n.* 龍捲風

複 tornados / tornadoes

似 twister [ˋtwɪstɚ] *n.* 龍捲風

比 (1) typhoon [taɪˋfun] *n.* 颱風 (發生於西太平洋沿岸的風暴) ②

(2) cyclone [ˋsaɪklon] *n.* 氣旋，旋風 (發生於南太平洋和印度洋沿岸的風暴)

(3) hurricane [ˋhɝˏken] *n.* 颶風 (發生於北大西洋沿岸的風暴) ④

*以上 3 字其實皆指『颱風』，只是在不同的地區有不同的名稱。

▸ The tornado destroyed everything in its path.
這陣**龍捲風**所經之處一切皆被摧毀。

---

tsunami [tsuˋnɑmi] *n.* 海嘯 (可數) (= a tidal wave)

延伸 本字原為日語，英文中的海嘯原是 a tidal wave，現今多用 tsunami。

▸ A tsunami is often caused by an earthquake.
海嘯經常是地震所引起的。

10 denounce [dɪˋnaʊns] *vt.* (公然) 譴責；告發，檢舉

片 (1) denounce A as B　譴責 A 為 B
= A be denounced as B
(2) denounce A to B　向 B 告發 A

衍 denunciation [dɪ͵nʌnsɪˋeʃən]
n. 譴責；告發，檢舉

似 condemn [kənˋdɛm] *vt.* 譴責 ⑤

▸ Senator Louis was denounced as a liar by one of his opponents.
路易斯議員被一位他的反對者斥為騙徒。

▸ A former employee of John's denounced him to the police.
約翰之前的一位職員向警方告發他。

11 apprentice [əˋprɛntɪs] *n.* 學徒

片 (1) be an apprentice to sb
作為某人的學徒
(2) an apprentice chef / electrician / carpenter
助理廚師 / 電工學徒 / 木匠學徒

似 pupil [ˋpjupḷ] *n.* 學徒；小學生 ②

▸ Marvin was one of the apprentices to the famous carpenter.
馬文是這位著名木匠的學徒之一。

▸ After graduating from cooking school, Martin got a job as an apprentice chef at a large international hotel.
馬丁從餐飲學校畢業後，就在一家大型的國際飯店找到了助理廚師的工作。

12 sovereign [ˋsɑvrɪn] *a.* 有最高統治權的；主權獨立的 & *n.* 君主，最高統治者

片 (1) sovereign power　最高統治權
(2) a sovereign country / nation
主權獨立的國家

似 sovereignty [ˋsɑvrəntɪ] *n.* 統治權，主權 (皆不可數) ⑤

▸ In this country, sovereign power lies with the Parliament, which represent the people.
在這個國家，最高統治權落在代表人民的國會手中。

▸ Vietnam used to be a colony, but now it is a sovereign country.
越南過去是個殖民地，但現在是個主權獨立的國家。

▸ Queen Elizabeth II has been the sovereign of the United Kingdom since she was crowned in 1953.
伊麗莎白女王二世自 1953 年加冕以來，就一直是英國的女王。

13 mar [mɑr] *vt.* 損毀

三 mar, marred [mɑrd], marred

似 spoil [spɔɪl] *vt.* 毀損 ③

▸ That baseball player's career was marred by drugs.
該名棒球員的生涯因吸食毒品而蒙上了陰影。

14 outlaw [ˋaʊt͵lɔ] *n.* 逃犯，亡命之徒 & *vt.* 使……不合法，禁止

似 ban [bæn] *vt.* 禁止 ⑤

▸ Police were informed that a group of outlaws were hiding in the forest.
警方被告知有一群逃犯躲在森林裡。

▸ Many states in the US no longer outlaw the use of marijuana for medical purposes.
美國許多州已不再將用作醫療用途的大麻列為非法。

15 superintendent [ˌsupərɪn`tɛndənt] *n.* 主管；(大樓的) 管理員

似 (1) caretaker [`kɛrˌtekə] *n.* 管理員 ⑥
(2) janitor [`dʒænətə] *n.* 管理員 ⑥

▸ The superintendent of our department is young and full of stamina.
我們部門的**主管**年輕又很有毅力。
*stamina [`stæmənə] *n.* 毅力，耐力

▸ Harry was angry because the superintendent still hadn't repaired the sink in his bathroom despite his many requests.
哈利很生氣，因為儘管他請求了很多次，**管理員**仍沒有修理他浴室的水槽。

16 astronaut [`æstrəˌnɔt] *n.* 太空人

▸ Astronauts must complete many years of training before they can actually travel into space.
太空人必須完成多年的訓練，才能進入太空旅行。

astronomy [ə`strɑnəmɪ] *n.* 天文學
比 astrology [ə`strɑlədʒɪ] *n.* 占星學

▸ Martin was deeply interested in astronomy and wanted to be an astronaut one day.
馬丁對**天文學**很感興趣，而且夢想有朝一日能當太空人。

astronomer [ə`strɑnəmə] *n.* 天文學家
比 astrologer [ə`strɑlədʒə] *n.* 占星師

▸ I was too fat to be an astronaut, so I decided to be an astronomer instead.
我太胖了當不了太空人，所以我下決心當個**天文學家**。

17 blond(e) [blɑnd] *a.* 金髮的 & *n.* 金髮女郎

延伸 (1) brunette [bru`nɛt] *n.* 深褐 / 黑色頭髮的白人女性 (= brunet)
(2) redhead [`rɛdˌhɛd] *n.* 紅頭髮的人 (尤指女性)

▸ Heather's long, sleek, blonde hair attracts many men.
海瑟那一頭又長又柔順的**金髮**，吸引很多男人的目光。
*sleek [slik] *a.* 光滑柔順的

▸ The basic plot of the movie is that the hero saves the blonde.
這部電影的劇情基本上就是英雄救**金髮女郎**。

18 carefree [`kɛrˌfrɪ] *a.* 無憂無慮的

似 (1) happy-go-lucky [ˌhæpɪgo`lʌkɪ] *a.* 無憂無慮的，逍遙自在的
(2) lighthearted [ˌlaɪt`hɑrtɪd] *a.* 放鬆的，無憂無慮的

▸ Many people reminisce about their carefree days as students.
許多人會憶起他們學生時代**無憂無慮的**生活。
*reminisce [ˌrɛmə`nɪs] *vi.* 追憶，回想 (與介詞 about 並用)

19 eyelash [`aɪˌlæʃ] *n.* 睫毛 (因人臉上有兩組睫毛故常用複數) (= lash)

延伸 eyebrow [`aɪˌbraʊ] *n.* 眉毛 (因人臉上有兩道眉毛，故常用複數) (= brow) ②

▸ Ella's big eyes and long eyelashes make her look very charming.
艾拉的大眼睛加上長**睫毛**使她看來很有魅力。

eyelid [ˋaɪˏlɪd] *n.* 眼皮，眼瞼
（因人臉上有兩個眼皮，故常用複數）

▸ Cathy was in the habit of closing her eyelids when making important decisions.
凱西做重大決定時習慣闔上眼皮。

20 lofty [ˋlɔftɪ] *a.* 崇高的；高傲的

片 have a lofty air 一副很高傲的樣子
衍 loft [lɔft] *n.* 閣樓
似 (1) noble [ˋnobl̩] *a.* 高尚的 ④
(2) haughty [ˋhɔtɪ] *a.* 高傲的

▸ Many young people have lofty ideals, but they often don't know how to realize them.
許多年輕人有崇高的理想，卻不知道如何將其付諸實現。

▸ The actress always has a lofty air. No wonder she has very few suitors.
這位女星總是一副很高傲的樣子。難怪她乏人追求。

21 polar [ˋpolɚ] *a.* (近) 極地的

片 a polar bear 北極熊
衍 pole [pol] *n.* 極地；杆 ③
the North / South Pole 北 / 南極
延伸 (1) Arctic [ˋɑrktɪk] *a.* 北極的
the Arctic 北極 (地區)
(2) Antarctic [ænˋtɑrktɪk] *a.* 南極的
the Antarctic 南極 (地區)
(3) Antarctica [ænˋtærktɪkə] *n.* 南極洲

▸ Polar bears live in the North Pole, whereas most penguins live in the South Pole.
北極熊棲息於北極，而企鵝則住在南極。
*penguin [ˋpɛngwɪn] *n.* 企鵝

22 cowardly [ˋkaʊɚdlɪ] *a.* 膽小的

似 (1) yellow [ˋjɛlo] *a.* (非正式) 膽小的 ①
(2) chicken [ˋtʃɪkɪn] *a.* (非正式) 膽小的 & *n.* (非正式) 膽小鬼 ①
(3) timid [ˋtɪmɪd] *a.* 膽小的 ④

▸ Peter is cowardly because he tends to panic at the sight of a small bug.
彼得看到小蟲就容易驚慌，因此很膽小。
*panic [ˋpænɪk] *vi.* 驚恐

cowardice [ˋkaʊɚdɪs] *n.* 膽小
片 an act of cowardice 膽小的行為
衍 coward [ˋkaʊɚd] *n.* 膽小鬼 (可數) ④
反 (1) bravery [ˋbrevərɪ] *n.* 勇敢 ③
(2) courage [ˋkɝɪdʒ] *n.* 勇氣 ②

▸ It would be an act of cowardice not to stand up and protect your family in the face of danger.
面對危險時如果不站出來保護家人會被視為是膽小的行為。

23 serial [ˋsɪrɪəl] *a.* 連續的 & *n.* 連續劇

片 (1) a serial number 序號
(2) a serial killer 連續殺人犯
(3) a TV serial 電視連續劇

▸ To fill out the product's warranty form, Robert looked on the back of his computer to find the serial number.
為了填寫產品保證書，羅伯特看了看電腦的背面，找到了序號。

衍 series [ˋsɪrɪz] *n.* (廣播 / 電視的) 系列節目，系列片 ⑤

延伸 episode [ˋɛpə͵sod] *n.* 連續劇中的一集 ⑤

▶ The serial killer will face trial this Thursday for the murder of 8 teenage girls.
這名連續殺人犯這週四將因謀殺 8 名少女而接受法庭審判。
*trial [ˋtraɪəl] *n.* 審判

▶ The TV serial *Charming Betty* last night was incredibly boring.
昨晚播出的電視連續劇《迷人的貝蒂》非常很無聊。

24 tentative [ˋtɛntətɪv] *a.* 暫時性的

似 temporary [ˋtɛmpə͵rɛrɪ] *a.* 暫時性的 ③

▶ This tentative schedule is for reference only. The finalized version will be given to you next week.
這份暫定的行程表只是參考用的。確定的版本會在下星期發給大家。
*version [ˋvɝʒən] *n.* 版本

25 logo [ˋlogo] *n.* 商標

似 trademark [ˋtred͵mɑrk] *n.* 商標 ⑥

▶ The three circles in our company logo symbolize stability, honesty, and unity.
我們公司商標的三個圓代表了穩定、誠信與團結。
*stability [stəˋbɪlətɪ] *n.* 穩定

26 falter [ˋfɔltɚ] *vi.* (說話) 吞吞吐吐，遲疑；動搖，畏縮不前

似 (1) stutter [ˋstʌtɚ] *vi.* 結結巴巴地說，結巴 ⑥
(2) filter [ˋfɪltɚ] *vt.* 過濾 ⑤

▶ Larry's voice faltered when he tried to talk to the beautiful girl.
賴瑞試著跟那美女說話時，聲音就變得吞吞吐吐的。

▶ We shall not falter in the face of adversity.
我們面對逆境也不應動搖。
*adversity [ədˋvɝsətɪ] *n.* 逆境

27 grease [gris] *n.* (機器、食物的) 油 & *vt.* 給……加潤滑油，為……塗 / 抹油

片 elbow grease 費力的工作

衍 greasy [ˋgrisɪ] *a.* 油膩的 ④
a greasy spoon 廉價小吃店

▶ Jamison's hands were covered with grease after he fixed the bike.
傑米森修完腳踏車後雙手沾滿了油。

▶ The kitchen floor was filthy, but with a little elbow grease, I made it shine.
廚房地板原本很髒，但在我稍微費力打掃之後，就閃閃發亮了。
*filthy [ˋfɪlθɪ] *a.* 骯髒的

▶ Sharon greased the pan with butter before placing the cookie dough on it.
雪倫先在烤盤抹上奶油，再把餅乾麵團放在烤盤上。

0928-0936

28 lighten [ˋlaɪtn̩] *vi.* & *vt.* (使) 變亮，(使) 明亮；減輕 (負擔等)；舒緩

片 (1) one's mood lightens
某人心情變得輕鬆
(2) lighten up　放鬆心情

衍 light [laɪt] *vt.* 點亮；使明亮 & *vi.* & *vt.* 點燃 & *n.* 光線；燈光 & *a.* 明亮的；輕鬆愉快的；輕的 ①

似 lightning [ˋlaɪtnɪŋ] *n.* 閃電 ③
a bolt of lightning　一道閃電
*lighten (變亮) 的動名詞是 lightening。

▸ The sky began to lighten after the shower.
陣雨過後，天空開始放晴。

▸ Dad painted the walls white to lighten the room.
老爸把牆壁漆成白色使房間明亮起來。

▸ The load in the truck lightened after the deliveryman sent out almost all of the packages.
送貨員發完幾乎所有的包裹後，卡車的負荷量就減輕了。

▸ My mood lightened when I learned my son had come back safe and sound.
我獲知我兒子安全無恙歸來時，心中大石落了地。

▸ Thank you for giving us a hand. Your help lightened our workload.
謝謝你伸出援手。你的幫忙減輕了我們的工作量。

▸ The conversation became very serious, so to lighten the atmosphere, Jerry decided to tell a short joke.
談話變得很嚴肅，所以傑瑞為了舒緩氣氛，決定講個簡短的笑話。

▸ Lighten up! You're always so serious.
輕鬆一下嘛！你總是那麼嚴肅。

29 lotion [ˋloʃən] *n.* 乳液

片 (1) apply lotion to...
將乳液塗在……
(2) suntan lotion　防曬乳液
*suntan [ˋsʌntæn] *n.* 曬成的古銅色皮膚

▸ Apply some suntan lotion to your skin in case you get sunburned.
皮膚塗點防曬乳液以免被曬傷了。

30 superficial [ˏsupɚˋfɪʃəl] *a.* 表面的；膚淺的

似 shallow [ˋʃælo] *a.* 膚淺的；淺的 ③

▸ The book shows only a superficial understanding of Einstein's theory of relativity.
這本書對於愛因斯坦相對論的了解只是皮毛而已。

▸ Mary is so superficial that she only cares about a person's looks.
瑪麗很膚淺，她只在乎人的外表。

31 tremor [ˋtrɛmɚ] *n.* 輕微地震；顫抖

似 earthquake [ˋɝθˏkwek] *n.* 地震 ②

▸ We felt a tremor while in the office this morning.
我們今早在辦公室有感覺到輕微的地震。

▸ There was a tremor of fear in her voice.
她的聲音因為恐懼而微微顫動。

32 lottery [ˋlɑtərɪ] *n.* 樂透，抽獎

片 (1) win a lottery　中樂透
(2) a lottery ticket　彩券

▸ I will buy my parents a new house if I win the lottery.
如果我中了樂透，就會買棟新房子給我父母。

▸ I've bought lots of lottery tickets, but I've never won any prizes.
我買過很多張彩券，但卻從沒中過獎。

33 sermon [ˋsɝmən] *n.* 布道；冗長訓話 (可數)

片 preach / give / deliver a sermon on sth　就某主題布道

似 (1) lecture [ˋlɛktʃɚ] *n.* 訓話，告誡；(在大學等的) 演說 ④
(2) speech [spitʃ] *n.* 演說 ②

▸ Reverend Lewis preached a sermon on love and compassion.
路易斯牧師就愛與同情心這個主題**布道**。
*Reverend [ˋrɛvərənd] *n.* (牧師 / 主教等) 大人 (置於姓氏前，為對牧師等的尊稱，縮寫為 Rev. / Revd.)
compassion [kəmˋpæʃən] *n.* 同情

▸ After dropping the cup and breaking it, Tiffany had to listen to a sermon from her mother about being careful.
蒂芬妮不小心把杯子打碎，只好聽她母親**說教**，訓她要小心才是。

34 uphold [ʌpˋhold] *vt.* 支持；維持 (原判)

三 uphold, upheld [ʌpˋhɛld], upheld

片 (1) uphold a law / human rights
支持某法律 / 人權
(2) uphold a conviction
維持定 / 判罪

衍 upholder [ʌpˋholdɚ] *n.* 支持者

似 support [səˋpɔrt] *vt.* 支持 ②

▸ My journalist friends fight to uphold the laws concerning the freedom of the press.
我的新聞記者朋友竭力**支持**有關新聞自由的法律。

▸ The Supreme Court ruled that the former governor's conviction of corruption be upheld.
最高法院決議**維持**前任州長的貪汙罪。

35 pony [ˋponɪ] *n.* 小馬

衍 ponytail [ˋponɪˏtel] *n.* 馬尾式髮型

▸ The boy got hurt while riding a pony.
這男孩在騎**小馬**時受傷了。

36 deplete [dɪˋplit] *vt.* (大量) 減少

衍 depletion [dɪˋpliʃən] *n.* 減少

似 (1) reduce [rɪˋd(j)us] *vi.* & *vt.* 減少 ③
(2) decrease [dɪˋkris] *vi.* & *vt.* 減少 ③

▸ Due to the hot weather and lack of rain, the nation's water supply was depleted.
由於天氣炎熱又不下雨，全國的供水量**大大減少**。

37 archive [ˋɑrkaɪv] *n.* 史料，檔案；檔案館 / 室；(電腦) 壓縮檔

▸ The old library had a local archive that was hugely admired by scholars.

這座歷史悠久的圖書館有當地的**史料**，備受學者高度讚賞。

▸ Earlier this morning, George went into the archives to do some research on the town's history.

今天稍早，喬治走進了**檔案館**，對該鎮的歷史做了一些研究。

▸ Frank knew that the file was somewhere in the computer's archive, but he couldn't find it.

法蘭克知道這檔案就在電腦的**壓縮檔**裡，但他卻找不到。

1001-1003

1 customary [ˋkʌstəm,ɛrɪ] *a.* 按慣例的，習俗的；慣常的

片 It is customary (for sb) to + V
(某人) 按慣例 / 習俗要做……

衍 custom [ˋkʌstəm] *n.* 習俗 ②

似 usual [ˋjuʒuəl] *a.* 通 / 慣常的 ②

▸ In America, it is customary to tip the bellboy after he takes your baggage to your room.
在美國，當行李員把行李拿到你房間後，按慣例是要給他小費的。
*bellboy [ˋbɛl,bɔɪ] *n.* 行李員

▸ We sat down at the table and were greeted by the waiter's customary smile.
我們在餐桌前坐下，服務生以他慣有的微笑歡迎我們。

2 decisive [dɪˋsaɪsɪv] *a.* 決定性的；果決的；確定的

片 (1) play a decisive role
扮演決定性的角色
(2) a decisive factor 決定性的因素
(3) a decisive victory
壓倒性 / 確定的勝利

衍 (1) decide [dɪˋsaɪd] *vt.* 決定 ①
(2) decision [dɪˋsɪʒən] *n.* 決定 ②
make a decision 做決定

▸ David's excellent performance during the basketball game played a decisive role in the team's victory.
大衛在籃球賽中出色的表現是球隊勝利的致勝關鍵。

▸ What was the decisive factor that changed the judge's mind?
改變法官想法的決定性因素是什麼？

▸ We all regard our manager as a strong and decisive leader.
我們都認為經理是位堅強又果決的領袖。

▸ The team earned a decisive victory, winning 20 to nothing.
這支隊伍以 20 比 0 的分數取得了壓倒性的勝利。

indecisive [,ɪndɪˋsaɪsɪv]
a. 優柔寡斷的

▸ Andrew is so indecisive. It takes him a long time to make almost any choice.
安德魯很優柔寡斷。他幾乎做任何選擇都要花上很久的時間。

3 aboriginal [,æbəˋrɪdʒənl̩] *n.* 澳洲原住民（字首常大寫）& *a.* 澳洲原住民的（字首常大寫）；原住民的

衍 aborigine [,æbəˋrɪdʒənɪ]
n. 澳洲原住民（字首大寫）；原住民

似 indigenous [ɪnˋdɪdʒənəs]
a. 本土的，土生土長的 ⑤

▸ In the past, the government did not treat the Aboriginals with the fairness that they deserved.
過去，該政府並沒有公平對待澳洲原住民，而公平對待是他們應得的。

▸ When she visited Australia, Katherine enjoyed seeing all the Aboriginal art there and bought some to take home with her.
當凱薩琳去澳洲玩時，她很喜歡看那裡澳洲原住民的藝術品，就買了一些帶回家。

▸ The mayor decided to build a museum to preserve aboriginal culture.
市長決定要蓋一座博物館以保存**原住民**文化。
*preserve [prɪˋzɝv] *vt.* 保存

4 familiarity [fəˏmɪlɪˋærətɪ] *n.* 通曉，熟悉；親近（皆為不可數）

片 one's familiarity with sth
某人通曉某事

衍 (1) familiar [fəˋmɪljɚ] *a.* 熟悉的 ③
be familiar with... 熟悉……
(2) familiarize [fəˋmɪljəˏraɪz]
vt. 使熟悉

▸ Alan's familiarity with Japan made it easy for us to travel from city to city.
艾倫對日本很**熟悉**，因此我們可以很輕鬆地穿梭在各個城市之間。

▸ The familiarity of this restaurant made me feel at home.
這家餐廳很**親切**，讓我有賓至如歸的感覺。

▸ Familiarity breeds contempt.
相處過於親密，就會生侮慢之心。——諺語
*breed [brid] *vt.* 產生

5 adaptation [ˏædæpˋteʃən] *n.* 適應（與介詞 to 並用）；改編（與介詞 of 並用）（= adaption [əˋdæpʃən]）

衍 adapt [əˋdæpt] *vt.* & *vi.* (使) 適應；改編 ④
adapt to sth 適應某事物
adapt A for B 將 A 改編成 B

似 adopt [əˋdɑpt] *vt.* & *vi.* 領養 & *vt.* 採用 ④

▸ John is quite incapable of adaptation to any new environment, in part because his parents spoiled him too much in childhood.
約翰完全不能**適應**任何新環境，部分原因是他父母在他小時候寵壞他了。

▸ The director is working on a film adaptation of this short novel.
導演正在拍攝這部短篇小說**改編**的電影。

6 medieval [ˏmɪdɪˋivḷ] *a.* 中世紀的

片 in medieval times 在中世紀時
= in the Middle Ages

延伸 (1) ancient [ˋenʃənt] *a.* 古代的 ②
(2) modern [ˋmɑdɚn] *a.* 現代的 ①
(3) contemporary [kənˋtɛmpəˏrɛrɪ]
a. 當代的，現代的 ⑤

▸ The concept of personal hygiene nowadays is very different from that in medieval times.
中世紀的個人衛生概念和現在差很多。
*hygiene [ˋhaɪdʒin] *n.* 衛生

7 hacker [ˋhækɚ] *n.* 駭客

衍 hack [hæk] *vt.* & *vi.* 劈，砍；入侵電腦系統

▸ A hacker got into the computer system and stole some important information from the company.
駭客潛入電腦系統偷走了公司的一些重要資料。

8 illuminate [ɪˋlumə͵net] *vt.* 照亮

似 light up... 照亮……

▶ The street lamps illuminated the road as we walked home.
我們走回家時，街燈**照亮**了道路。

illuminating [ɪˋlumə͵netɪŋ]
a. 有啟發性的

衍 illuminated [ɪˋlumə͵netɪd]
a. 被照亮的，發光的

似 inspiring [ɪnˋspaɪrɪŋ] *a.* 鼓舞人心的

▶ The documentary about global warming is very illuminating.
這部有關地球暖化的紀錄片極具**啟發性**。
*documentary [͵dɑkjəˋmɛntərɪ] *n.* 紀錄片

9 extract [ɪkˋstrækt] *vt.* 提煉；摘錄；獲取（情報、錢）& [ˋɛkstrækt] *n.* 萃取物

片 extract A from B
從 B 提煉 A；從 B 摘錄 A

似 excerpt [ɪkˋsɝpt] *vt.* 摘錄 ⑥

▶ Our olive oil is extracted from fine olives and processed in our own factory.
我們的橄欖油是**由**精選的橄欖中所**提煉**出來，然後在我們自己的工廠內加工的。

▶ The following paragraph was extracted from the writer's latest book.
下面這段話**摘錄自**該作者最新的書。

▶ The gangsters may torture Tommy in order to extract information about the whereabouts of his brother, who owed them a fortune.
這些黑幫成員可能會對湯米進行刑求，以**得知**他哥哥的下落，而他哥哥欠了這幫人一大筆錢。
*torture [ˋtɔrtʃɚ] *vt.* 拷問，折磨

▶ This facial cream is made from natural plant extracts and is suitable for sensitive skin.
這面霜是由天然植物**萃取物**做的，適合敏感性肌膚。

10 endurance [ɪnˋd(j)urəns] *n.* 耐力，忍受力

衍 endure [ɪnˋd(j)ʊr] *vt.* 忍受 ④

▶ Jogging can help train one's willpower and endurance.
慢跑可以訓練一個人的毅力和**耐力**。
*willpower [ˋwɪl͵paʊɚ] *n.* 毅力

11 deem [dim] *vt.* 認為

片 (1) deem A (to be) B 認為 A 是 B
= consider A (to be) B
(2) deem that... 認為……

似 consider [kənˋsɪdɚ] *vt.* 認為 ②

▶ I deem it an honor to be chosen to attend the ceremony.
= I consider it an honor to be chosen to attend the ceremony.
我**認為**獲選參加該典禮是一項榮譽。

▸ The inspectors deemed that the playground was not safe for children.
稽查員認為該遊樂場不安全，不適合孩童玩耍。
*inspector [ɪnˋspɛktɚ] *n.* 稽查員

12 defect [ˋdifɛkt] *n.* (生理) 缺陷；瑕疵 & [dɪˋfɛkt] *vi.* 叛逃

片 (1) a genetic defect 基因缺陷
*genetic [dʒəˋnɛtɪk] *a.* 基因上的
(2) defect from A to B
從 A 叛逃到 B 去

衍 defective [dɪˋfɛktɪv] *a.* 有缺點的

似 flaw [flɔ] *n.* 缺陷 ⑥

▸ The child's deformity was caused by a genetic defect.
這孩子的畸形與基因缺陷有關。
*deformity [dɪˋfɔrmətɪ] *n.* (身體的) 畸形

▸ Sarah found a defect in the bag she just bought, so she took it back to the store and asked for a replacement.
莎拉發現她新買的包包有瑕疵，所以拿回店裡去要求換貨。
*replacement [rɪˋplesmənt] *n.* 更換

▸ Many people defected from the Soviet Union to the West in the 1960s.
1960 年代，許多人從蘇聯叛逃到西方國家去。

13 posture [ˋpastʃɚ] *n.* 姿勢；立場，態度 & *vi.* 裝模作樣

片 (1) poor / bad posture 姿勢不良
good posture 姿勢端正
(2) adopt a(n) + adj. + posture toward(s)...
對……採取……的立場 / 態度

似 (1) pose [poz] *n.* (為拍照等擺) 姿勢 & *vi.* (為拍照等) 擺姿勢；裝腔作勢 ②
pose for a picture 擺姿勢拍照
(2) stance [stæns] *n.* 立場，態度 ⑤

▸ Cindy's poor posture led to her recurring back problems.
辛蒂姿勢不良造成她的背部毛病經常發作。
*recurring [rɪˋkɝɪŋ] *a.* 一再復發的

▸ The governor has adopted a neutral posture toward gay marriage.
該州長對同性婚姻採取中立的態度。

▸ Most people thought the politician was not being sincere; they believed he was posturing to get votes.
大多數人認為這政治人物不真誠；他們認為他是為了爭取選票而在裝模作樣。

14 contradict [ˌkantrəˋdɪkt] *vt.* 與……相矛盾 & *vi.* & *vt.* 反駁

片 (1) contradict each other 互相矛盾
(2) contradict oneself
自己反駁自己，自相矛盾

衍 (1) contradiction [kantrəˋdɪkʃən] *n.* 矛盾 ⑤
(2) contradictory [ˌkantrəˋdɪktərɪ] *a.* 矛盾的

▸ Since the two statements contradict each other, one must be a lie.
因為兩項陳述互相矛盾，其中一個必定是謊言。

▸ When the boss says something, you'd better not contradict him, or he'll get very furious.
當老闆說了什麼，你最好不要反駁他，不然他會很生氣。

▸ John contradicted himself many times during our argument.
我們在爭論時，約翰好幾次說話都自相矛盾。

15 narrate [ˋnæret / nəˋret] *vt.* 敘述，描述

衍 (1) narrative [ˋnærətɪv] *a.* 敘事的 ⑤
(2) narration [næˋreʃən / nəˋreʃən] *n.* 敘述

▶ The story was narrated by a Japanese man with a strong accent.
該故事是由一位口音濃重的日本人所**口述**的。
*accent [ˋæksənt] *n.* 口音

▶ Mike is narrating a story based on the four pictures.
邁可正根據這 4 幅圖片**講**故事。

narrator [nəˋretɚ / ˋnæretɚ] *n.* 敘事者，旁白者

▶ The narrator of the novel is a Jewish girl whose parents died in the Holocaust.
這本小說的**敘事者**是一名雙親死於納粹大屠殺的猶太女孩。
*the Holocaust [ˋhɑlə͵kɔst] （二次大戰時納粹對猶太民族的）大屠殺

16 intersection [͵ɪntɚˋsɛkʃən] *n.* 交叉 (點)；十字路口 (可數)

似 crossroads [ˋkrɔs͵rodz] *n.* 十字路口 (單複數同形)
*此字原就有加 “s”。

▶ Nelly drew two lines and then made a small circle at the intersection of the lines.
娜莉畫了兩條線，然後在這些線的**交叉點**畫了個小圓圈。

▶ Many traffic accidents occurred at this busy intersection.
這繁忙的**十字路口**發生過很多交通事故。

17 counterpart [ˋkauntɚ͵pɑrt] *n.* 相對應的人 / 事 / 物

片 one's counterpart 某人對應的人 / 事 / 物

▶ Our general manager will discuss the agreement with his Japanese counterpart tomorrow.
我們總經理明天將與日方的**總經理**談論合約事宜。

18 upright [ˋʌp͵raɪt] *a.* 垂直的，直立的；正直的 & *adv.* 垂直地，直立地 & *n.* 立柱；直立式鋼琴 (= upright piano)

片 sit / stand upright 坐直 / 站直

▶ The plane is landing. Please return your seats to an upright position.
飛機要降落了，請將您的座椅**調正**。

▶ We like Walter because he is upright and dependable.
我們喜歡華特，因為他**正直**又可靠。

▶ Louise sat upright as soon as she heard a scream coming from the kitchen.
一聽到廚房傳來尖叫聲，露易絲就馬上**坐直**了起來。

▶ Judy wanted to buy the nice bed, but she thought the uprights were a bit too large.
茱蒂想買那張好床，但她認為這張床的床**柱**有點太大了。

1018-1029

▸ Because upright pianos take up less space than grand pianos, they are good for homes and schools.
因為**直立式鋼琴**會比平臺鋼琴用到較少的空間，所以適合住家和學校。

19 alligator [ˋæləˏgetɚ] *n.* 短吻鱷

▸ In some places in the United States, such as Florida, people need to be careful of alligators.
在美國一些如佛羅里達州的地方，人們得要小心**短吻鱷**。

crocodile [ˋkrɑkəˏdaɪl] *n.* 長吻鱷

片 shed crocodile tears
貓哭耗子假慈悲

▸ Jason was warned not to swim in the river because crocodiles had been spotted in the area.
傑森被警告不要在河裡游泳，因為這地區有發現過**長吻鱷**。

▸ Sean has lost the tennis game. Don't shed crocodile tears for him. I know you're happy he lost.
尚恩網球比賽輸了。你不用**貓哭耗子假慈悲**了。我知道你很高興他輸了。

20 blot [blɑt] *n.* 汙漬 & *vt.* 吸乾，擦乾

三 blot, blotted [ˋblɑtɪd], blotted

衍 inkblot [ˋɪŋkˏblɑt] *n.* 墨水漬

▸ The pen was a bit leaky and therefore left some messy blots on the piece of paper.
這支筆有點漏水，因此在紙上留下了一些淩亂的**墨跡**。

▸ Gary used some paper towel to blot the surface of the table where he had spilled a bit of water.
蓋瑞用紙巾**擦乾**桌子的表面，他之前在這裡灑出了一些水。

21 caretaker [ˋkɛrˏtekɚ] *n.* (學校、公寓等的) 管理員〔英〕(= janitor [ˋdʒænətɚ]〔美〕)；看護

似 superintendent [ˏsupərɪnˋtɛndənt] *n.* 管理員 ⑥

▸ After coming to London from Southeast Asia, Mr. Li worked as a caretaker for a luxury apartment building.
李先生從東南亞來到倫敦後，就在一間豪華的公寓大樓當**管理員**。

▸ Bill hired a caretaker for his aging mother after she could no longer walk on her own.
老母再也無法靠自己走動時，比爾便為她僱了一名**看護**。

22 poultry [ˋpoltrɪ] *n.* 家禽 (指雞、鴨、鵝等飼養的動物) (不可數)

似 fowl [faʊl] *n.* 家禽 (複數為 fowl / fowls) ⑥

延伸 livestock [ˋlaɪvˏstɑk] *n.* (統稱馴養的牛、羊、馬等) 牲口 (為複數) ⑥

▸ Experts warned that the recent outbreak of bird flu could infect the poultry in this area.
專家警告最近暴發的禽流感將會對此區的**家禽類動物**造成影響。

23 lotus [ˋlotəs] *n.* 蓮花

複 lotuses [ˋlotəsɪz]

▸ Lotuses need to grow in water.
蓮花要在水裡才會生長。

24 shabby [ˋʃæbɪ] *a.* 破爛的

似 derelict [ˋdɛrə͵lɪkt] *a.* 破舊的

▸ The house looks somewhat shabby from the outside, but inside it is quite pleasant.
這房子外觀看來有些**破爛**，但裡頭還挺不錯的。

25 cozy [ˋkozɪ] *a.* 舒適溫暖的〔美〕(= cosy〔英〕)

似 comfortable [ˋkʌmf(ɚ)təbl̩] *a.* 舒適的 ①

▸ The big fireplace and the couch make the living room so cozy in winter.
這個大壁爐和沙發讓客廳在冬天時很**舒適溫暖**。

26 stylish [ˋstaɪlɪʃ] *a.* 格調優雅的

衍 style [staɪl] *n.* 風格 ②

▸ Many celebrities like to dine in this stylish French restaurant.
許多名人喜歡在這間**格調優雅的**法國餐廳用餐。
*dine [daɪn] *vi.* 用餐

27 fascination [͵fæsn̩ˋeʃən] *n.* 迷戀，著迷

片 in fascination 著迷地

衍 fascinate [ˋfæsn̩͵et] *vt.* 使著迷 ⑤

▸ The children watched the magic show in fascination.
孩子們**著迷地**看著這場魔術表演。

28 tilt [tɪlt] *vt.* & *vi.* (使) 傾斜 & *n.* 傾斜

片 tilt toward...
傾向於 (某種意見 / 情況等) ……

▸ The girl tilted the little makeup mirror on the table so she could see herself more clearly.
這女孩**傾斜**桌上小化妝鏡的角度，這樣她就能更清楚地看到自己。

▸ Government spending has tilted toward social welfare.
政府支出已**朝向**以社會福利為主。

▸ The dining table had a slight tilt to it because one leg was shorter than the other three.
餐桌稍微**傾斜**了一點，因為一隻桌腳比另外三隻桌腳短。

29 suitcase [ˋsut͵kes] *n.* (有把手的) 行李箱

似 baggage [ˋbægɪdʒ] *n.* 行李箱〔美〕
(= luggage〔英〕) ③

▸ Can you keep an eye on my suitcase while I go to the bathroom?
我去上個廁所，你可以幫我看行李嗎？

1030-1037

30 loudspeaker [ˋlaʊd͵spikɚ] *n.* 擴音器，喇叭 (= speaker)

▶ Every morning, announcements are made to students over the loudspeaker, but sometimes they are difficult to hear clearly.
每天早上，會有人透過擴音器向學生公告事情，但有時很難聽得清楚。

31 lullaby [ˋlʌlə͵baɪ] *n.* 搖籃曲

複 lullabies [ˋlʌlə͵baɪz]
衍 lull [lʌl] *vt.* 使入睡，使安靜
lull a child / baby to sleep
哄小朋友 / 小寶寶入睡

▶ My grandma usually sang a lullaby before I went to sleep when I was little.
小時候我奶奶在我睡前常會唱搖籃曲。

32 caterpillar [ˋkætɚ͵pɪlɚ] *n.* 毛毛蟲 (蝶或蛾的幼蟲)

延伸 (1) butterfly [ˋbʌtɚ͵flaɪ] *n.* 蝴蝶 ①
(2) pupa [ˋpjupə] *n.* 蛹
(3) cocoon [kəˋkun] *n.* 繭

▶ I wonder what kind of butterfly this caterpillar will become.
我很好奇這隻毛毛蟲會變成什麼樣的蝴蝶。

33 deficient [dɪˋfɪʃənt] *a.* 缺乏的；有缺陷的

片 be deficient in... 在……方面不足
衍 deficiency [dɪˋfɪʃənsɪ]
n. 不足 (與介詞 of 並用)；缺陷 (與介詞 in 並用)
反 sufficient [səˋfɪʃənt] *a.* 足夠的 ③

▶ Wendy's diet is deficient in Vitamin C, so I suggest that she take supplements on a daily basis.
溫蒂的飲食缺少維他命 C，因此我建議她每天攝取補充品。
*supplement [ˋsʌpləmənt] *n.* 補充品

▶ The deficient product inspection process resulted in a high rate of returned products.
產品檢驗過程有缺失，造成高比例的退貨量。

34 preach [pritʃ] *vi.* & *vt.* 傳教，布道 & *vi.* 說教

片 (1) preach the gospel 傳福音
*the gospel [ˋgɑspḷ] 福音
(2) preach about sth 說教某事物
似 lecture [ˋlɛktʃɚ] *vt.* 訓斥 & *vi.* 講課 ④

▶ The minister at the church preaches every Sunday morning for Chinese language speakers and every Sunday afternoon for English language speakers.
教堂的牧師每週日早上為講中文的人布道，而每週日下午為講英文的人布道。

▶ John's father is a pastor who preaches the gospel at a small church.
約翰的父親是在小教堂傳福音的牧師。

▶ Every time he makes a mistake, Jerry has to listen to his father preach about the importance of being careful.
每次傑瑞犯錯時，他都得要聽他父親說教，說小心是很重要的。

preacher [ˋpritʃɚ] *n.* 傳教士，牧師
似 missionary [ˋmɪʃən͵ɛrɪ] *n.* 傳教士 ⑤

▸ I'm always inspired by the religious talks that the preacher gives.
這名**傳教士**的講道總是給我許多啟示。

35 drawback [ˋdrɔ͵bæk] *n.* 缺點

片 a drawback to / of + N/V-ing
……的缺點
似 (1) disadvantage [͵dɪsədˋvæntɪdʒ] *n.* 缺點 ④
(2) shortcoming [ˋʃɔrt͵kʌmɪŋ] *n.* 缺點 ⑥

▸ The main drawback to the project is its high cost.
這計畫的主要**缺點**就是成本太高。

36 audit [ˋɔdɪt] *n.* 查(帳)，審計 & *vt.* 查帳，審計；旁聽

衍 auditor [ˋɔdɪtɚ] *n.* 查帳 / 審計員

▸ The company was informed that the government would be doing an audit on them next week.
該公司被告知政府下週要**查**他們的**帳**。

▸ The head office routinely audited the accounts of all of its branches around the world.
總部定期**稽查**其在世界各地所有分部的**帳目**。

▸ Gina decided to audit the class before officially enrolling in it to see if it suited her.
吉娜決定在正式註冊之前**旁聽**這門課，看看這門課適不適合她。

auditorium [͵ɔdəˋtɔrɪəm] *n.* 禮堂

▸ Our high school auditorium has a seating capacity of 2,000.
我們高中的**禮堂**可容納 2,000 個人。
*capacity [kəˋpæsətɪ] *n.* 容量

37 unify [ˋjunə͵faɪ] *vt.* (使) 統一；(使) 結合

三 unify, unified [ˋjunə͵faɪd], unified
似 (1) unite [juˋnaɪt] *vt.* 使團結 ③
(2) combine [kəmˋbaɪn] *vt.* 使結合 ②
反 divide [dɪˋvaɪd] *vt.* 使對立 & *vi.* & *vt.* (使) 分開 ②

▸ The leader unified the different racial groups and ended the civil war.
這名領導人**統合**了不同的種族團體，結束了內戰。
*civil [ˋsɪvḷ] *a.* 國內的，國民的

▸ The architecture perfectly unifies Western and Eastern styles.
這棟建築完美地**結合**了東西方的風格。

unification [͵junɪfɪˋkeʃən] *n.* 聯合，統一

▸ The unification of the country was difficult due to all the fighting between the different races.
由於不同種族之間彼此鬥爭，全國要**統一**是很困難的。

Notes

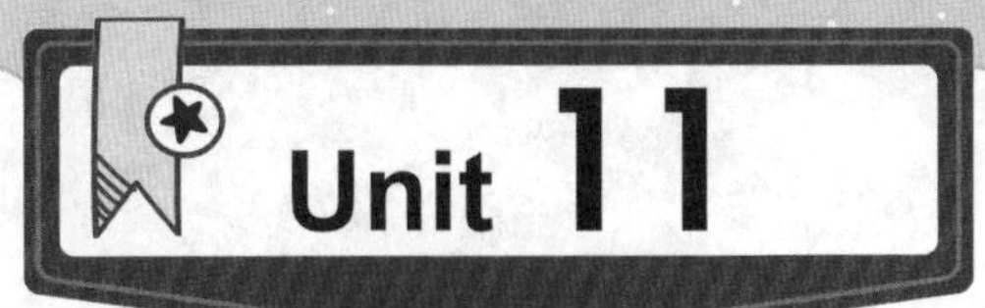

1101-1104

1 liable [ˋlaɪəbḷ] *a.* 有……傾向的，可能……的

片 be liable to + N/V 可能……
= be prone to + N/V

似 prone [pron] *a.* 有……的傾向，易於……；俯臥的 ⑤

▸ These areas near the river are liable to flood.
這條河附近的地區**經常淹水**。

▸ Ralph is liable to fail history if he keeps skipping class.
如果雷夫繼續翹課，他**有可能**歷史科會被當掉。

2 deter [dɪˋtɝ] *vt.* 阻止

三 deter, deterred [dɪˋtɝd], deterred

片 deter sb from + N/V-ing
阻止某人……

衍 deterrence [dɪˋtɝrəns] *n.* 制止

似 hinder [ˋhɪndɚ] *vt.* 阻礙

▸ Several security cameras were installed to deter customers from shoplifting.
幾臺監視器被安裝來**防止**顧客偷竊。
*shoplift [ˋʃɑpˏlɪft] *vi.* & *vt.* 在商店中偷竊

3 prohibition [ˏproəˋbɪʃən / ˏproɪˋbɪʃən] *n.* 禁令（可數）

片 (1) lift a prohibition 解除禁令
(2) a prohibition on / against sth
關於某事物的禁令
= a ban on sth

衍 prohibit [prəˋhɪbɪt] *vt.* 禁止 ⑤

似 forbiddance [fɚˋbɪdṇs] *n.* 禁止

▸ In December 1933, the US government lifted a prohibition on the sale and consumption of alcohol.
1933 年 12 月，美國政府**解除**了禁止銷售和喝酒的**禁令**。

▸ The government announced a prohibition against smoking in public places several years ago.
政府數年前已頒布在公共場所禁止吸菸的**禁令**。

4 outset [ˋaʊtˏsɛt] *n.* 開始

片 from / at the outset 從一開始
= from the beginning

似 (1) beginning [bɪˋgɪnɪŋ] *n.* 開始
(2) onset [ˋɑnˏsɛt] *n.* (不愉快事物的) 開始

延伸 outset 是由片語動詞 set out 衍生而成的名詞。
set out (to + V) 開始（做……）
set out (for + 地方) 啟程（至某地方）

▸ Todd set out to discover a cure for the rare disease.
陶德**開始著手**找尋此罕見疾病的療法。

▸ The machine malfunctioned from the outset.
這臺機器**從一開始**就故障了。
*malfunction [mælˋfʌŋkʃən] *vi.* 故障

▸ I told the salesperson I wasn't interested in his product from the outset.
我告訴這名推銷員我**從一開始**就對他的產品不感興趣。

1105-1109

▸ Milly set out for the station before dawn.
= Milly left / departed for the station before dawn.
蜜莉在天還沒亮的時候便出發前往車站。

5 conspiracy [kən`spɪrəsɪ] *n.* 陰謀

複 conspiracies [kən`spɪrəsɪz]

片 a conspiracy against...
對……圖謀不軌

衍 conspire [kən`spaɪr] *vi.* 密謀

▸ It is said that these soldiers conspired to overthrow the government.
據說這些士兵密謀推翻政府。

▸ There have been rumors of conspiracies against the president since last September.
自去年 9 月以來，就一直有傳言有人要密謀不利於總統。

6 populate [`pɑpjə,let] *vt.* 居住（常用被動語態）

片 a densely / sparsely populated city （居住）人口密度高 / 低的城市

衍 (1) population [,pɑpjə`leʃən] *n.* 人口 ②
(2) populous [`pɑpjələs] *a.* 人口眾多的

似 inhabit [ɪn`hæbɪt] *vt.* 居住於 ⑥

▸ This neighborhood is populated by a lot of celebrities.
這社區住很多名人。

▸ Taipei is one of the most densely populated cities in the world.
臺北是世界人口密度最高的城市之一。（populated 為過去分詞作形容詞用）

---

inhabit [ɪn`hæbɪt] *vt.* 居住於；棲息於

片 inhabit + 地方　居住 / 棲息於某地
= live in / at + 地方
= dwell in / at + 地方
= reside in / at + 地方

▸ That area is inhabited mostly by highly educated people.
那地區居住的大多是高級知識分子。

▸ Many rare animals inhabit that rain forest.
那片雨林棲息了許多稀有的動物。

---

inhabitant [ɪn`hæbɪtənt] *n.* 居民；居住於某地的動物

片 a city of + 數字 + inhabitants
一座有若干人的城市

似 (1) resident [`rɛzədənt] *n.* 居民 ⑤
(2) dweller [`dwɛlɚ] *n.* 居民
(3) habitat [`hæbə,tæt] *n.*（動植物）棲息地 ⑤

▸ Almost one third of the inhabitants of this town are Chinese Americans.
這個小鎮幾乎有 3 分之 1 的居民是華裔美國人。

▸ Vienna, a city of about 2 million inhabitants, is the beautiful capital of Austria.
維也納是個約有 200 萬居民的城市，也是奧地利美麗的首都。

7 applicable [ˋæplɪkəbḷ] *a.* 適用的

片 be applicable to... 適用於……

衍 (1) apply [əˋplaɪ] *vi.* 申請；應用 ②
apply for sth 申請獲得某物
(2) application [ˏæpləˋkeʃən]
n. 申請；應用 ④

▸ This section of the form is only applicable to foreigners residing in Taiwan.
表格的這部分只適用於定居臺灣的外國人。

8 simplicity [sɪmˋplɪsətɪ] *n.* 簡單；簡樸 (皆不可數)

衍 simple [ˋsɪmpḷ] *a.* 簡單的 ①

似 plainness [ˋplennəs] *n.* 簡樸

▸ English grammar is not known for its simplicity; in fact, it can be quite difficult for learners to understand.
英文文法並不簡單；事實上，它對學習者來說可能相當困難。

▸ I want to move to the countryside and lead a life of simplicity.
我想搬到鄉下去過簡樸的生活。

simplify [ˋsɪmpləˏfaɪ]
vt. 簡化，使簡單

三 simplify, simplified [ˋsɪmpləˏfaɪd], simplified

衍 simplification [ˏsɪmpləfəˋkeʃən]
n. 簡單化

▸ The professor tried to simplify the theory for the younger students.
為了這些年紀較小的學生，教授試著將此理論簡化。

9 disgrace [dɪsˋgres] *n.* 恥辱 (不可數)；令人可恥的事 (恆為單數) & *vt.* 使丟臉

片 (1) bring disgrace on sb
使某人蒙羞
(2) in disgrace 不光彩地
(3) be a disgrace to...
對……來說是 (個) 恥辱
(4) disgrace oneself by + V-ing
因做……而使自己蒙羞

似 shame [ʃem] *n.* 羞愧 & *vt.* 使丟臉 ②

▸ The official's involvement in the scandal has brought disgrace on his family.
這位官員涉及醜聞而使家人蒙羞。

▸ I'd rather die than live in disgrace.
我寧死也不願苟活。

▸ Paul is a disgrace to his family: He is a gangster who is in jail for the crimes he committed.
保羅對他家人來說是個恥辱：他是個因犯罪而被關在監獄的幫派分子。

▸ Jim disgraced himself by getting drunk heavily and making a scene at the party.
吉姆在派對上酩酊大醉，當眾大吵大鬧而使自己蒙羞。
*make a scene 當眾大吵大鬧

1109-1117

disgraceful [dɪsˋgresfəl]
a. 丟臉的，可恥的

片 It is disgraceful that...
……真是可恥

似 shameful [ˋʃemfəl] *a.* 丟臉的 ④

▶ Mike's disgraceful behavior embarrassed the entire company.
邁可丟臉的行為使整個公司蒙羞。

▶ It is disgraceful that Larry sold drugs to school kids to make money.
賴瑞為了賺錢而向學童販售毒品，真是令人可恥。

10 friction [ˋfrɪkʃən] *n.* 摩擦（力）；衝突（皆不可數）

片 (1) cause / create friction
造成摩擦 / 衝突
(2) a source of friction between A and B　A 和 B 產生衝突的原因

似 (1) conflict [ˋkɑnflɪkt] *n.* 衝突 ②
(2) clash [klæʃ] *n.* 衝突 ④

▶ When you rub your hands together, the friction produces heat.
摩擦雙手時，摩擦力會生熱。

▶ Religious issues caused constant friction between the two countries.
宗教議題經常造成這兩個國家之間起衝突。

▶ The economic problems were a source of friction between David and his business partners.
經濟問題是大衛和他生意夥伴之間產生摩擦的起因。

11 deprive [dɪˋpraɪv] *vt.* 剝奪

片 deprive sb of sth　剝奪某人的某物

延伸 類似的句構還有：
(1) rob sb of sth　搶奪某人的某物

▶ The gangsters robbed Judy of her money.
那些歹徒搶了茱蒂的錢。

(2) relieve sb of + sb's duties / post　解除某人的職務

▶ The general relieved Captain Smith of his duties.
將軍解除了史密斯上尉的職務。

▶ The court deprived the man of his civil rights.
法庭判處該男子褫奪公權。

12 detergent [dɪˋtɝdʒənt] *n.* 洗潔劑（用來洗衣服或洗碗等）

片 (1) laundry detergent　洗衣精
(2) dish detergent　洗碗精
= dishwashing liquid

延伸 soap [sop] *n.* 肥皂 ②
a bar / cake of soap　一塊肥皂

▶ This laundry detergent can effectively remove stains from clothes.
這種洗衣精可以有效去除衣服上的汙漬。
*stain [sten] *n.* 汙點

▶ Because Mandy put too much dish detergent into the water, there were too many bubbles.
因為曼蒂在水裡放了太多洗碗精，所以有太多泡泡了。

13 detach [dɪˋtætʃ] *vt.* 使分開

片 detach A from B　把 A 從 B 分開

反 attach [əˋtætʃ] *vt.* 附帶；連結 ④

attach A to B　把 A 附加在 B

▶ Please detach the form from the booklet, fill it out, and send it to us.

請將表格從小冊裡**撕下來**，填寫完畢後寄給我們。

detached [dɪˋtætʃt] *a.* 冷漠的，不帶情感的；(房屋) 獨立式的

反 attached [əˋtætʃt] *a.* 附帶的

▶ The attached files are for reference during the meeting.

附件是供開會時參考用的。

▶ I suggest you look at the event from a more detached point of view.

我建議你以更**客觀的**觀點來看這件事。

▶ Housing prices are high in San Francisco, so Jeff can't afford to buy a detached house there.

舊金山的房價很高，所以傑夫在那裡買不起**獨棟的**房子。

14 altitude [ˋæltə,t(j)ud] *n.* (海拔) 高度

片 at an altitude of + 數字

在……的高度

似 attitude [ˋætət(j)ud] *n.* 態度

(與介詞 to / toward(s) 並用) ③

▶ The airplane is now cruising at an altitude of 30,000 feet.

這架飛機正在 3 萬英尺**高空**飛行。

*cruise [kruz] *vi.* 以平穩的速度行駛

15 bodily [ˋbadɪlɪ] *a.* 身體的 & *adv.* 整個身體地

衍 body [ˋbadɪ] *n.* 身體 ①

▶ The police charged the man with inflicting serious bodily harm on the vendor.

警方起訴該男子對這小販造成嚴重的**身體**傷害。

*inflict [ɪnˋflɪkt] *vt.* 使遭受 (損傷等)

inflict sth on sb　使某人遭受某 (負面的) 事物

vendor [ˋvɛndɚ] *n.* 小販

▶ The football player was pushed bodily to the ground by another player who was running quickly.

這名美式橄欖球運動員被另一名跑得很快的球員**整個身體**被推倒在地。

16 celery [ˋsɛlərɪ] *n.* 芹菜 (不可數)

似 salary [ˋsælərɪ] *n.* (按月發放的) 薪水 ③

▶ Celery is high in fiber but low in calories, which makes it a good snack for people on a diet.

芹菜富含纖維、卡路里低，對節食的人來說是很好的點心。

*fiber [ˋfaɪbɚ] *n.* 纖維

calorie [ˋkælərɪ] *n.* 卡路里

17 grumble [ˋgrʌmbḷ] *vi.* & *vt.* & *n.* 抱怨 (常用複數)

片 grumble about sth　抱怨某事

= complain about sth

= whine about sth

▶ That old man grumbles about everything. Just ignore him.

那個老頭什麼都可以**抱怨**。別管他了。

1117-1127

似 (1) complain [kəm`plen] *vt.* & *vi.* 抱怨 ③
(2) whine [(h)waɪn] *vt.* & *vi.* 抱怨，發牢騷 & *n.* 抱怨，牢騷 ⑤

▶ "You never listen to what I say," Maria grumbled.
瑪麗亞抱怨道：『你從不好好聽我說話。』

▶ We'll be in big trouble if the boss hears our grumbles.
要是老闆聽見我們發牢騷，我們麻煩可大了。

18 lunar [`lunɚ] *a.* 月亮的，與月亮有關的

片 a lunar calendar 農 / 陰曆
反 solar [`solɚ] *a.* 太陽的，與太陽有關的 ④

▶ Chinese New Year falls on the first day of the first lunar month.
華人新年是在農曆正月初一。

▶ A solar eclipse is rarer than a lunar eclipse.
日蝕比月蝕更稀奇。
*eclipse [ɪ`klɪps] *n.* (日) 蝕，(月) 蝕

19 feeble [`fibḷ] *a.* 虛弱的

似 (1) weak [wik] *a.* 弱的 ①
(2) frail [frel] *a.* 虛弱的

▶ Bob was too feeble to talk right after the operation.
鮑伯手術完後太過虛弱而無法講話。

20 handicap [`hændɪˏkæp] *vt.* 使有障礙 & *n.* 不利的條件

三 handicap, handicapped [`hændɪˏkæpt], handicapped
似 disadvantage [ˏdɪsəd`væntɪdʒ] *n.* 不利的條件，劣勢 ④

▶ Our project was handicapped by lack of funding.
我們的企畫因缺乏資金而在執行上有困難。

▶ Luke's criminal record will be a handicap when they consider him for the job.
他們在考慮是否給路克這份工作時，他的犯罪紀錄將成為一大不利條件。

21 prehistoric [ˏprihɪs`tɔrɪk] *a.* 史前的

片 in prehistoric times 在史前時代

▶ We can tell by these fossils what human life was like in prehistoric times.
從這些化石我們可看出史前時代人類生活是什麼模樣。

22 crackdown [`krækˏdaun] *n.* 制裁 / 鎮壓 (不法行為等)

片 a crackdown on sth 制裁 / 鎮壓某事物
衍 crack down on... 制裁 / 鎮壓 / 整頓……
似 (1) clampdown [`klæmpˏdaun] *n.* 取締，鎮壓
(2) control [kən`trol] *n.* & *vt.* 控制 ②
(3) restriction [rɪ`strɪkʃən] *n.* 限制，約束 ④

▶ A crackdown on drunk driving was urgently called for after the tragic accident.
這件悲劇意外發生後，政府急需取締酒駕。
*call for... 要求 / 呼籲……

23 sharpen [ˋʃɑrpn̩] *vt.* 削尖；改善

衍 sharp [ʃɑrp] *a.* 尖銳的 ①

似 improve [ɪmˋpruv] *vt.* 增進 ②

▸ The artist sharpened his pencil and then started drawing.
這位藝術家把鉛筆削尖，接著開始畫畫。

▸ I enrolled in the class in the hope that it would sharpen my writing ability.
我報名這堂課為了想要加強我的寫作能力。
*enroll [ɪnˋrol] *vi.* 註冊（與介詞 in 並用）

24 bribe [braɪb] *n.* & *vt.* 賄賂

片 (1) bribe sb to + V　賄賂某人做……
(2) bribe sb with sth
用某物賄賂某人
(3) accept / take a bribe　收受賄賂

衍 bribery [ˋbraɪbərɪ] *n.* 賄賂的行為

似 bride [braɪd] *n.* 新娘 ③

▸ The candidate bribed those people to vote for him.
候選人向那些人賄賂選票。

▸ Greg bribed the prison guard with some money.
葛瑞格用一些錢賄賂了獄警。

▸ The judge will never accept your bribe.
那法官絕不會收受你的賄賂。

25 tiptoe [ˋtɪp͵to] *vi.* 踮起腳尖走 & *n.* 腳尖

片 on tiptoe(s)　踮起腳走

▸ Victoria tiptoed quietly out of the room so as not to wake up her sleeping parents.
維多利亞踮起腳尖走出房間以避免吵醒她沉睡中的父母。

▸ I had to stand on tiptoe to reach the pill bottle on the top shelf.
我得踮起腳尖站著才能伸手拿到架子頂層的藥罐。

26 feminine [ˋfɛmənɪn] *a.* 女性化的 & *n.* (文法) 陰性 (詞)

似 female [ˋfimel] *n.* 女性 & *a.* 女性的 ②

反 masculine [ˋmæskjəlɪn] *a.* 男性的，男子氣概的，陽剛的 & *n.* (文法) 陽性 (詞) ⑤

延伸 gender [ˋdʒɛndɚ] *n.* 性別 ④

▸ That red dress made Daisy look very feminine.
那件紅洋裝讓黛西看起來很有女人味。

▸ Many nouns in French are categorized as feminine, which means they use "la," rather than "le," in front of them.
法文中的許多名詞被歸類為陰性，這意味著在這些名詞前面使用『la』，而不是『le』。

27 token [ˋtokən] *n.* 代幣；(情感的) 表示

片 (1) as a token of sb's appreciation / gratitude　表示某人的感謝
(2) by the same token　同樣地
= likewise [ˋlaɪk͵waɪz] ⑤

▸ Kevin changed his coins into tokens in order to play air hockey.
為了要玩桌上氣墊球遊戲，凱文把他的錢幣換成了代幣。

似 symbol [ˋsɪmbl̩] *n.* 象徵；符號 ②
a symbol of... ……的象徵

▸ Please accept this small gift as a token of my appreciation for your help.
請接受這份小禮以**表示**我很**感激**你的幫忙。

▸ I always respect others' privacy. By the same token, I want no one to invade my own privacy.
我總是很尊重他人隱私，**同樣地**，我不希望有人侵犯我的隱私。
*invade [ɪnˋved] *vt.* 侵犯

28 magnify [ˋmægnə͵faɪ] *vt.* 放大；加強，加劇

三 magnify, magnified [ˋmægnə͵faɪd], magnified

似 exaggerate [ɪgˋzædʒə͵ret] *vt.* & *vi.* 誇大 ④

延伸 a magnifying glass 放大鏡

▸ The professor used a magnifying glass to read the book, which had very small print on its pages.
教授用**放大鏡**看這本書，這本書上的字印得很小。

▸ Mr. Burns told the students that the microscope can magnify an object up to 10 times its original size.
伯恩斯先生告訴學生，顯微鏡可以將物體**放大**至 10 倍。

▸ Without any curtains, furniture, or rugs in the room, the bare walls magnified echoes.
房裡沒有窗簾、傢俱或地毯，光禿禿的牆壁**讓**回音**很大聲**。

29 priceless [ˋpraɪsləs] *a.* 無價的

衍 price [praɪs] *n.* 價錢 ①

似 (1) invaluable [ɪnˋvæljuəbl̩] *a.* 無價的 ⑥
(2) valuable [ˋvæljuəbl̩] *a.* 貴重的 ②

反 valueless [ˋvæljʊləs] *a.* 沒有價值的

▸ The trip may have been expensive, but the opportunity to behold such a spectacular view was priceless.
這趟旅行或許很貴，但能目睹這片美景的機會是**無價的**。
*behold [bɪˋhold] *vt.* 看

30 madam [ˋmædəm] *n.* (對女性的禮貌稱呼) 女士 (= ma'am [mæm])

▸ The clerk said, "What can I do for you, madam?"
店員說：『**女士**，可以幫您什麼忙嗎？』

---

maiden [ˋmedn̩] *n.* 少女 & *a.* (航 / 飛行) 初次的

片 (1) a maiden voyage / flight 首航 / 飛
(2) a maiden name (女子) 婚前姓氏

▸ In the story, the knight woos and wins the heart of a fair maiden.
在這故事中，騎士追求並贏得了一位美麗**少女**的芳心。
*woo [wu] *vt.* 追求

▸ It was surprising that the Titanic sank into the middle of the Atlantic Ocean during her maiden voyage.
鐵達尼號**首航**便沉入了大西洋裡，令人很意外。

mistress [ˋmɪstrəs] *n.* 情婦

似 concubine [ˋkɑŋkjuˏbaɪn] *n.* 情婦，妾

▶ There has been speculation that Susan is the billionaire's mistress.
有人一直在猜測蘇珊可能就是那億萬富翁的**情婦**。
⋆speculation [ˏspɛkjəˋleʃən] *n.* 猜測，推論

31 checkup [ˋtʃɛkʌp] *n.* 健康檢查

片 (1) a (physical) checkup 健康檢查
= a physical
(2) a routine checkup
定期健康檢查

▶ John was suspected of having liver cancer after a physical checkup.
約翰做完**健康檢查**後，被懷疑罹患肝癌。

32 tiresome [ˋtaɪrsəm] *a.* 令人厭倦的

衍 (1) tired [taɪrd] *a.* 感到疲倦的；感到厭煩的 ①
(2) tire [taɪr] *vt.* & *vi.* 使疲累 ②

似 boring [ˋbɔrɪŋ] *a.* 令人厭煩的 ①

▶ The speech was tiresome to everyone.
這場演講使每個人都感到**厭煩**。

weary [ˋwɪrɪ] *a.* 疲勞的

似 tired [taɪrd] *a.* 勞累的 ①

片 be weary of + N/V-ing
對……感到很厭倦
= be tired of + N/V-ing

▶ William is weary of doing the same job day after day, so he is ready to retire.
威廉已**厭倦**了每天一成不變的工作，所以他準備要退休了。

33 preview [ˋpriˏvju] *n.* 試映，預演 / 展 & *vt.* 預先觀看為 (書 / 電影等) 寫報導、預評等

似 review [ˏrɪˋvju] *vt.* 評論 & *vi.* & *vt.* 複習 (功課) & *n.* 評論 ②

▶ The preview of the film has met with great success.
這部電影的**試映**非常成功。

▶ The reporter was given a copy of the book before it went on sale so that she could preview it.
在這本書上市之前，這記者拿到了一本，如此她就能**先看**這本書**好寫報導**。

34 bosom [ˋbʊzəm] *n.* 胸

片 a bosom friend 知心朋友

似 chest [tʃɛst] *n.* 胸 ③

▶ The mother held her baby to her bosom and sang him a lullaby.
母親把她的寶寶抱在**胸**前，對他唱著搖籃曲。

▶ Erica is my bosom friend. We share each other's ups and downs.
艾芮卡是我的**知己**。我們彼此分享生活的起起落落。

🔊 1135-1136

35 dissent [dɪˋsɛnt] *n.* 意見相左 / 分歧 & *vi.* 不同意

反 assent [əˋsɛnt] *n.* & *vi.* 同意

▸ The two political parties are so divided that dissent is common between them; in fact, they almost never agree.

這兩個政黨很不合，以至於常見他們之間意見相左；事實上，這兩個政黨幾乎從來沒有意見相同過。

▸ The council approved the new regulations, with only one member of the city government dissenting.

議會批准了新的條例，只有一名市府成員持異議。

36 avert [əˋvɝt] *vt.* 阻止；轉移（目光等）

片 avert one's eyes / gaze
轉移某人的目光

▸ Fortunately, emergency workers were able to avert disaster by cooling down the nuclear power plant so that it didn't go into meltdown.

幸好緊急救援人員能夠冷卻核電廠避免爐心熔毀，阻止了災難發生。

* meltdown [ˋmɛlt͵daʊn] *n.*（核能電廠）爐心熔毀

▸ The shy boy gazed at the girl from a distance, but he averted his eyes when she looked at him.

那害羞的男孩遠遠地看著那女孩，但當女孩看著他時，他卻把目光轉向一邊。

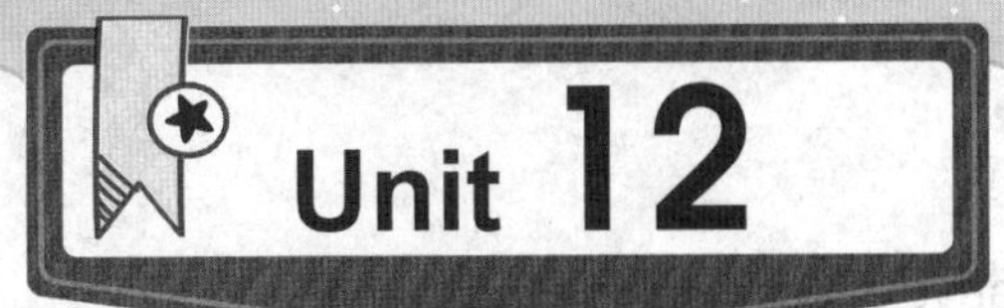

1201-1202

1 breakdown [ˋbrekˏdaʊn] n. (機器) 故障

片 have a nervous breakdown
精神衰弱

延伸 此字源自片語動詞 break down (故障)。

▶ I had to have my car towed after it broke down on the highway.
車子在公路上故障後，我得叫人來把它拖走。

▶ After five breakdowns in two months, Ralph decided he would be better off just buying a new car.
兩個月內發生 5 次**故障**後，雷夫決定買輛新車會比較好。
*be better off + V-ing　做……會比較好

▶ Joe had a nervous breakdown in his late twenties.
喬年近三十時變得**精神衰弱**。

---

breakup [ˋbrekˏʌp] n. 分手，終止

延伸 此字源自片語動詞 break up (終止、分手)。

▶ Nina just broke up with her boyfriend.
妮娜剛和她男朋友分手。

▶ Oliver's midlife crisis led to the breakup of his first marriage.
奧利佛的中年危機導致他第一段婚姻因而**破裂**。

---

outbreak [ˋaʊtˏbrek] n. 爆發

延伸 此字源自片語動詞 break out (疾病、戰爭的爆發)。

▶ Vicky and her family escaped to the United States shortly before war broke out.
維琪和她家人在戰爭爆發前不久逃去了美國。

▶ Doctors and other health experts worked hard to try to limit the spread of the disease outbreak.
醫生和其他衛生專家努力試圖限制該疾病**爆發**蔓延開來。

2 accumulate [əˋkjumjəˏlet] vt. & vi. 累積

片 pile up...　堆積……
= amass...
= build up...

▶ Samuel quickly accumulated a large fortune by investing in the stock market.
薩姆爾藉由投資股票市場而**累積**了一大筆財富。

▶ A thick layer of dust accumulated on my desk because I hadn't cleaned it for a year.
一層厚厚的灰塵**積**在我桌上，因為我已一年沒清理過桌子了。

---

accumulation [əˏkjumjəˋleʃən] n. 累積

▶ There is more to learning than the accumulation of knowledge.
學習並不只是知識的**累積**。

1202-1209

cumulative [ˋkjumjələtɪv]
a. 累積的

片 a cumulative effect of...
……所累積的影響

▸ The cumulative effect of taking too much medicine finally took a heavy toll on Jim's vital organs.
服用過多藥物所累積的影響最終對吉姆的重要器官造成嚴重損害。
*toll [tol] *n.* 損失；死傷
take a heavy toll on... 對……造成嚴重損害

3 injustice [ɪnˋdʒʌstɪs] *n.* 不公平

片 do sb an injustice 待某人不公道，不公地判斷某人

似 unfairness [ʌnˋfɛrnəs] *n.* 不公平

反 justice [ˋdʒʌstɪs] *n.* 公平，正義 ②
do... justice 為……說句公道話
▸ To do Peter justice, we must admit that he meant no harm.
為彼得說句公道話，我們必須承認他本來無意傷害任何人。

▸ Superman, Batman, and most other superheroes are known for fighting against any and every injustice in the world.
超人、蝙蝠俠和大多數其他超級英雄都以對抗世界上任何的不公不義而聞名。

▸ Mary complained that we had done her an injustice by firing her.
瑪麗抱怨說我們把她開除是對她不公。

4 disastrous [dɪˋzæstrəs] *a.* 災難的

衍 disaster [dɪˋzæstɚ] *n.* 災難 ④

似 (1) catastrophic [ˌkætəˋstrɑfɪk]
a. 災難的
(2) devastating [ˋdɛvəsˌtetɪŋ]
a. 毀滅性的

▸ This policy turned out to have a disastrous effect on our economy.
這項政策結果對我們的經濟產生了浩劫性的影響。

devastating [ˋdɛvəsˌtetɪŋ]
a. 毀滅性的

衍 devastate [ˋdɛvəsˌtet] *vt.* 破壞
▸ The war devastated much of the old part of the city.
這場戰爭摧毀了這座城市大部分歷史悠久的地區。

▸ It will deal a devastating blow to the local economy if the factory closes.
這家工廠如果關閉的話，將會重創地方經濟。
*deal a blow to... 對……打擊

5 peninsula [pəˋnɪnsələ] *n.* 半島 (大部分環海但部分連接陸地)

比 island [ˋaɪlənd] *n.* 島嶼 (四面環海) ①

▸ The Italian peninsula, which stretches to the Mediterranean Sea, has the nickname "the boot" because of its distinct shape.
延伸到地中海的義大利半島，因其獨特的形狀而有個『靴子』的綽號。

6 stabilize [ˋstebḷ,aɪz] *vt.* & *vi.* (使) 穩固

衍 (1) stable [ˋstebḷ] *a.* 穩定的 ③
(2) stability [stəˋbɪlətɪ] *n.* 穩定 (性) ⑤

▶ Many people will join a big demonstration this weekend in protest against the government's failure to stabilize housing prices.
本週末將會有許多人參加大規模示威活動，以抗議政府未能**穩定**房價。

▶ John suffered a heart attack three days ago, but his condition has stabilized now.
= John suffered a heart attack three days ago, but he is now in stable condition.
約翰三天前心臟病突發，但現在情況**已穩定**了。

7 forsake [fɚˋsek] *vt.* 遺棄

三 forsake, forsook [fɚˋsuk], forsaken [fɚˋsekən]
似 abandon [əˋbændən] *vt.* 放棄 (= give up) ④

▶ Eric told me he was an orphan and wanted to know why his parents had forsaken him.
艾瑞克告訴我他是個孤兒，他想知道為什麼他父母**拋棄**了他。

8 slum [slʌm] *n.* 貧民區

片 a slum area 貧民區

▶ Tommy was brought up by his mother in the slums of Brooklyn.
湯米是在布魯克林的**貧民窟**由母親一手扶養長大的。

ghetto [ˋgɛto] *n.* (某特定民族) 居住區，貧民區
複 ghettos / ghettoes

▶ Nicholas comes from one of the poorest ghettos in New York.
尼可拉斯來自於紐約其中一個最貧窮的**貧民區**。

9 subscribe [səbˋskraɪb] *vi.* 訂閱

片 subscribe to sth 訂閱某 (刊) 物

▶ You can subscribe to the magazine for as little as $25 a year.
你能以每年 25 美元的低價**訂閱**到這本雜誌。

subscription [səbˋskrɪpʃən] *n.* 訂閱
片 (1) a subscription to sth (刊) 物
(2) take out a subscription to sth 辦理訂閱某 (刊) 物
(3) cancel / renew a subscription 取消 / 更新訂閱

▶ My subscription to *The New York Times* expired last month.
我**訂閱**的《紐約時報》上個月到期。
*expire [ɪkˋspaɪr] *vi.* 期限終止

▶ If you're interested in taking out a subscription to *The Economist*, please fill out this form online.
你若有興趣**辦理訂閱**《經濟學人》雜誌，請上網填寫表格。

10 serene [səˋrin] *a.* 寧靜的

衍 serenity [səˋrɛnətɪ] *n.* 寧靜

似 (1) peaceful [ˋpisfəl] *a.* 寧靜的 ②
(2) tranquil [ˋtræŋkwɪl] *a.* 寧靜的

▸ With the 3D animated screensaver, you'll experience the serene atmosphere of a winter night.
有了這個 3D 的動畫螢幕保護程式，你將體會到冬天夜晚的**寧靜**氣氛。

11 stature [ˋstætʃɚ] *n.* 身高，身材

似 (1) statue [ˋstætʃu] *n.* 雕像 ③
(2) statute [ˋstætʃut] *n.* 法令 ⑥

▸ Most professional basketball players are tall in stature.
大部分的職籃球員**身材**都很高大。

12 parliament [ˋpɑrləmənt] *n.* 議會，國會；(英國) 國會 (字首大寫)

比 congress [ˋkɑŋgrəs]
n. 代表大會；(美國) 國會 (字首大寫) ④

▸ Many countries—such as England, Canada, Australia, and New Zealand—have democratic parliaments.
很多國家 —— 如英國、加拿大、澳洲和紐西蘭等 —— 都有民主**議會**。

▸ The British Parliament consists of the House of Lords and the House of Commons.
英國**國會**由上議院和下議院所組成。

13 allege [əˋlɛdʒ] *vt.* (無證據的) 宣稱

片 (1) allege that... 宣 / 據稱……
(2) It is alleged that... 宣 / 據稱……

衍 (1) alleged [əˋlɛdʒd] *a.* 被指控的，據稱的
(2) allegedly [əˋlɛdʒɪdlɪ] *adv.* 據稱

▸ The money was allegedly stolen by an insider.
這筆錢失竊，**據傳**是內賊所為。

▸ An anonymous caller alleged that a bomb had been planted on the aircraft.
一匿名者打電話，**宣稱**飛機上有炸彈。
*anonymous [əˋnɑnəməs] *a.* 匿名的

▸ It was alleged that prisoners held at Guantanamo Bay were mistreated.
據稱被關在關塔那摩灣的犯人被虐待。
*mistreat [mɪsˋtrit] *vt.* 虐待

allegation [ˏæləˋgeʃən]
n. (無證據的) 指控

似 accusation [ˏækjəˋzeʃən] *n.* 指控 ⑥

▸ The allegations of sexual assault against Mr. Wilson are serious, but they haven't been proven in court yet.
對威爾森先生的性侵**指控**很嚴重，但這些指控尚未在法庭上得到證實。

14 abstraction [æbˋstrækʃən] *n.* 抽象

衍 abstract [ˋæbstrækt] *a.* 抽象的 ④

▸ What you said is an abstraction. I really can't understand that.
你剛剛說的話真**抽象**，我實在聽不懂。

15 surpass [sɚˋpæs] *vt.* 超越

似 outdo [ˌaʊtˋdu] *vt.* 勝過

▶ Jason always tries to outdo everybody else in his class.
傑森總是努力要比班上其他人表現**更**好。

▶ The album's huge success has surpassed everyone's expectations.
這張專輯熱賣的程度**超乎**所有人的預料。

16 unanimous [juˋnænəməs] *a.* 全體一致的

片 be unanimous in + N/V-ing
在……方面全體意見一致

衍 unanimously [juˋnænəməslɪ] *adv.* 全體一致地

▶ James was elected chairman by a unanimous vote.
大家**一致**推選詹姆士為主席。
* be elected (as) chairman / mayor... 被選為主席 / 市長等

▶ The local people were unanimous in their opposition to the construction of a nuclear plant in their area.
當地民眾**一致**反對在他們那區興建核電廠。

17 complement [ˋkampləmənt] *n.* 補足物 & [ˋkampləˌmɛnt] *vt.* 補足

片 A is a complement to B
A 為 B 的補充，A 襯托出 B

衍 complementary [ˌkampləˋmɛntərɪ] *a.* 互補的
a complementary color 互補色

似 compliment [ˋkampləmənt] *n.* & [ˋkampləˌmɛnt] *vt.* 讚美
(發音和 complement 相同) ⑤

▶ The new lamps are ideal complements to the oil painting.
這些新燈完美的**襯托出**這幅油畫。

▶ The delicate sauce and the grilled fish complement each other perfectly.
這個可口的醬料和烤魚**搭配**得好極了。

18 fortify [ˋfɔrtəˌfaɪ] *vt.* 加強

三 fortify, fortified [ˋfɔrtəˌfaɪd], fortified

片 fortify oneself (against A) with B
用 B 加強自己的體力 / 心智 (以抵禦 A)

衍 fort [fɔrt] *n.* 堡壘 ④

似 (1) strengthen [ˋstrɛŋθən] *vt.* 加強 ④
(2) reinforce [ˌriɪnˋfɔrs] *vt.* 加強 ⑤

▶ Knowing that the enemy was approaching, the king ordered the soldiers to fortify the castle against attack.
國王知道敵人正在逼近，就命令士兵**加強**城堡防禦以抵制敵人進攻。

▶ Marcus fortified himself against the cold weather with a glass of whisky.
馬克斯喝了杯威士忌**禦**寒。

19 firecracker [ˋfaɪrˌkrækɚ] *n.* 鞭炮 (可數)

片 set off a firecracker 放鞭炮

似 firework [ˋfaɪrˌwɝk] *n.* 煙火 (常用複數) ③
set off fireworks 放煙火

▶ In Chinese communities throughout the world, people set off firecrackers in celebration of the Lunar New Year.
在世界各地的華人社區，大家都會**放鞭炮**慶祝農曆新年。

20 mourn [mɔrn] *vt.* & *vi.* 哀悼

片 (1) mourn sb's death
哀悼某人的亡故
(2) mourn for sb　為某人哀悼

似 grieve [griv] *vt.* & *vi.* 哀悼 ⑤
grieve over / for sth　哀悼某事

▸ So many years have passed, but Carl still mourns his wife's death.
這麼多年過去了，凱爾仍在**哀悼**妻子**的過世**。

▸ Today, we come here to mourn for our beloved neighbor Mary.
今日，我們前來**悼念**我們親愛的鄰居瑪麗。

mournful [ˋmɔrnfḷ] *a.* 憂傷的

片 a mournful eye　憂傷的眼神

▸ The girl with those mournful eyes somehow looks familiar, giving me a strange sense of déjà vu.
那有著**憂傷眼神**的女孩看來有些眼熟，給我一種似曾相似的奇怪感覺。
*déjà vu [ˏdeʒɑˋvu] *n.* 似曾相識感

21 fertility [fɝˋtɪlətɪ] *n.* 肥沃；生育力

衍 (1) fertile [ˋfɝtḷ] *a.* (土地) 肥沃的；能生育的 ④
(2) fertilize [ˋfɝtḷˏaɪz] *vt.* 施肥

反 infertility [ˏɪnfɝˋtɪlətɪ] *n.* 不孕

▸ The fertility of the land offered the farmer a decent life.
這**肥沃**的土地使這農夫的日子過得不錯。
*decent [ˋdisṇt] *a.* 不錯的，像樣的

▸ Maria took medicine to increase her fertility.
瑪麗亞吃藥以增進**生育能力**。

fertilizer [ˋfɝtḷˏaɪzɚ] *n.* 肥料

▸ Organic fertilizers are much better than chemical fertilizers for the environment.
有機**肥料**要比化學**肥料**對環境更有益。

22 handicraft [ˋhændɪˏkræft] *n.* 手工藝，技藝 (可數) (= craft [kræft])；手工藝品 (常用複數)

延伸 (1) craftsman [ˋkræftsmən] *n.* 工匠
(2) craftswoman [ˋkræftsˏwumən] *n.* 女工匠

▸ Nowadays, few locals are capable of performing this traditional handicraft.
當地人如今幾乎都不會這門**手工藝**了。

▸ Vivian learned how to make several kinds of handicrafts from her grandmother.
薇薇安從她祖母那兒學會了做幾樣**手工藝品**。

23 probe [prob] *n.* & *vi.* 調查

片 (1) a probe into...　對⋯⋯調查
(2) probe into...　調查⋯⋯
= look into...

▸ The media called for a probe into the robbery.
媒體呼籲**對**該搶案展開**調查**。

▸ The FBI has been called in to probe into the case.
聯邦調查局被召來**調查**這樁案子。

24 publicize [ˋpʌbləˏsaɪz] vt. 宣傳，廣告

似 advertise [ˋædvəˏtaɪz] vt. 宣傳，廣告 ③

▸ The company bought ads on Facebook to publicize their grand opening event that would take place in two months.
該公司在臉書上買廣告，以**宣傳**他們兩個月後會舉辦的盛大開幕活動。

25 shaver [ˋʃevɚ] n. 電動刮鬍刀 (= electric shaver = electric razor)

衍 shave [ʃev] vi. & vt. 剃 (毛髮) ④
比 razor [ˋrezɚ] n. (常指非電動的) 剃刀，刮鬍刀 ③

▸ This electric shaver is rechargeable.
這把電動**刮鬍刀**是可充電的。
*rechargeable [riˋtʃɑrdʒəbl̩] a. 可充電的

26 stun [stʌn] vt. 使吃驚 (常用被動語態)

三 stun, stunned [stʌnd], stunned
似 (1) shock [ʃɑk] vt. 使吃驚 ②
(2) astound [əˋstaund] vt. 使震驚 (常用被動語態)

▸ My aunt was stunned by the death of her husband.
姨丈的死訊**使**我阿姨**震驚不已**。

---

stunning [ˋstʌnɪŋ] a. 令人吃驚的
似 astonishing [əˋstɑnɪʃɪŋ] a. 令人吃驚的

▸ I was impressed with the actress' stunning debut performance.
我對這名女演員初次登臺的**精彩**表演印象深刻。
*debut [ˋdebju / deˋbju] n. 初次登臺

27 mainland [ˋmenˏlænd] n. (指與附近島嶼相對的) 大陸，本土

片 (1) mainland Europe 歐洲大陸
(2) mainland China 中國大陸
= the Chinese mainland
比 island [ˋaɪlənd] n. 島嶼 ①

▸ Since British people live on islands not attached to mainland Europe, some of them don't feel strongly connected to the European continent.
因為英國人住在沒和**歐洲大陸**相連的島嶼上，他們其中有些人並不覺得自己與歐洲大陸的關聯很緊密。

▸ Previously, Austin taught English in mainland China; then he moved to South Korea and later Taiwan to teach.
之前奧斯丁在**中國大陸**教英文；然後他搬到了韓國，後來又搬到了臺灣教書。

28 majesty [ˋmædʒəstɪ] n. 雄偉；陛下 (字首大寫)

複 majesties [ˋmædʒəstɪz]
片 Your / His / Her Majesty 國王陛下 / 皇后陛下

▸ Tourists were all impressed by the majesty of this Buddhist temple.
遊客對這座佛教寺廟的**雄偉**印象很深刻。

1228-1232

似 highness [ˋhaɪnəs] *n.* 很高；殿下（對除了國王和皇后以外的王室成員之尊稱，字首大寫）
Your / His / Her Highness　殿下

▸ Your Highness, I'm afraid Her Majesty won't allow you to go into this room.
殿下，恐怕皇后陛下不會允許您進入這個房間。

▸ How do you like your dinner to be served, Your Majesty?
國王陛下，您晚餐想吃什麼呢？

---

majestic [məˋdʒɛstɪk] *a.* 雄偉的
似 (1) grand [grænd] *a.* 雄偉的 ②
(2) spectacular [spɛkˋtækjələ] *a.* 壯觀的 ⑤

▸ We stood in awe before the majestic Westminster Abbey.
我們敬畏地站在**雄偉的**西敏寺前。
*awe [ɔ] *n.* 敬畏
stand in awe　敬畏地站立

---

monarch [ˋmɑnɑrk] *n.* 君主，國王，女王
衍 monarchy [ˋmɑnəkɪ] *n.* 君主政體
似 (1) king [kɪŋ] *n.* 國王 ①
(2) queen [kwin] *n.* 女王 ①
(3) ruler [ˋrulə] *n.* 統治者 ①
(4) emperor [ˋɛmpərə] *n.* 皇帝 ③
(5) sovereign [ˋsɑvrɪn] *n.* 最高統治者，君主 ⑥

▸ The representative of the monarch had a close relationship with the royal family.
該**君主**的代表人與皇室有密切的關係。

29 proverb [ˋprɑvəb] *n.* 諺語

似 (1) saying [ˋseɪŋ] *n.* 諺語，格言
(2) adage [ˋædɪdʒ] *n.* 諺語，格言
(3) maxim [ˋmæksɪm] *n.* 格言

▸ One of Robert's favorite proverbs is "better safe than sorry," which advises people to be careful.
羅伯特最喜歡的**諺語**之一是『有備無患』，此諺語建議人們要謹慎小心。

30 cement [səˋmɛnt] *n.* 水泥 & *vt.* 使強固

似 (1) strengthen [ˋstrɛŋθən] *vt.* 加強，鞏固 ④
(2) fortify [ˋfɔrtə,faɪ] *vt.* 加強 ⑥
延伸 concrete [ˋkɑnkrit] *n.* 混凝土（水泥、沙、水混合而成）④

▸ Cement is a very common material used in the construction of buildings, bridges, and so on.
水泥是一種很常見的材料，會用於建造建築物、橋樑等。

▸ A good friendship is cemented in sincerity and honesty.
真摯和誠實是能**強固**友誼的基石。

31 recreational [ˌrɛkrɪˋeʃənl̩] *a.* 休閒的，娛樂的

衍 recreation [ˌrɛkrɪˋeʃən] *n.* 娛樂 ④

▶ Ken has been so busy lately that he hasn't had any time to enjoy recreational activities such as playing games.
肯最近很忙，忙到沒時間去享受如玩遊戲等**休閒**活動。

32 bilateral [baɪˋlætərəl] *a.* (談判、協定等) 雙邊的

片 a bilateral agreement　雙邊協定

衍 (1) lateral [ˋlætərəl] *a.* 側面的
(2) unilateral [ˌjunɪˋlætərəl] *a.* 單方 / 邊的
(3) multilateral [ˌmʌltɪˋlætərəl] *a.* 多方 (參加) 的

▶ The bilateral trade agreement was between the United Kingdom and the United States; no other country was included in it.
此**雙邊**貿易**協定**是英國和美國雙方簽訂的；不包含其他國家。

Unit 13

1301-1307

1 superiority [səpɪrɪˋarətɪ] *n.* 優勢；優越

片 a sense of superiority　優越感
(= a superiority complex)

衍 superior [səˋpɪrɪɚ] *a.* 優越的；較上等的 ③

反 inferiority [ɪnfɪrɪˋarətɪ] *n.* 劣等；自卑
a sense of inferiority　自卑感
(= an inferiority complex)

▸ South Korea has been quick to establish air and naval superiority.
南韓迅速建立海空**優勢**。
*naval [ˋnevḷ] *a.* 海軍的

▸ Speaking French fluently gave Adam a sense of superiority over most of his classmates.
說得一口流利的法語讓亞當**覺得**自己比大部分的同學來得**優越**。

2 wardrobe [ˋwɔrd,rob] *n.* 衣櫃〔英〕；(某人的) 全部衣物 (皆可數)

片 a summer / winter wardrobe
夏季 / 冬季衣物

似 closet [ˋklazɪt] *n.* 衣櫥〔美〕③

▸ My grandmother kept coats and blankets in a giant oak wardrobe.
奶奶把外套和毯子收在一個很大的橡木**衣櫥**裡。

▸ I feel that my winter wardrobe is somewhat lacking in style.
我覺得我**冬天的衣物**款式不太流行了。

3 transmit [trænsˋmɪt] *vt.* 傳送 (電視、廣播等)；傳播 (疾病或能量)

三 transmit, transmitted [trænsˋmɪtɪd], transmitted

片 (1) transmit sth (from A) to B
將某物 (從 A) 傳送到 B
(2) a sexually transmitted disease
性病

衍 transmission [trænsˋmɪʃən] *n.* 傳送 (電視、廣播等)；傳播 (疾病) ⑤

▸ The show is transmitted live by satellite to over 26 countries across the world.
本節目透過衛星**傳送**，在全世界超過 26 個國家現場播出。
*satellite [ˋsætḷ,aɪt] *n.* 衛星

▸ The flu is transmitted from one person to another through the air.
流行性感冒藉由空氣在人與人**之間相互傳染**。

▸ To make sure he didn't have a sexually transmitted disease, Brandon made an appointment to get tested at a clinic.
布蘭登為了確保他沒有**性病**，就約好要去診所接受檢查。(transmitted 為過去分詞作形容詞用)

4 nurture [ˋnɝtʃɚ] *vt.* & *n.* 養育；培育 (不可數)

似 foster [ˋfɔstɚ] *vt.* 養育；培育 ⑤

▸ Animals nurtured by their own kind are usually healthier than those raised by humans.
通常由同類**撫育**長大的動物，會比被人類豢養的來得健康。

▸ As a teacher, it is Hank's job to nurture the talents of his young students.
身為老師，漢克的工作就是**培養**他年輕學生的才能。

▶ Scientists debate how we are affected by nature and nurture.
科學家們展開辯論，探討天性和後天的**培育**如何影響我們。

5 cultivate [ˋkʌltəˏvet] *vt.* 培養；建立（關係、友誼等）；耕種

片 cultivate a good relationship with... 與……培養良好的關係

衍 cultivated [ˋkʌltəˏvetɪd] *a.* 有教養的；耕種的

似 nourish [ˋnɝɪʃ] *vt.* 培育，滋養 ⑥

▶ Cindy cultivates her knowledge of art by reading magazines.
辛蒂藉由閱讀雜誌**增進**她的藝術知識。

▶ The singer has had difficulty cultivating a good relationship with the press.
這名歌手沒辦法**跟**媒體**打好關係**。
*the press 媒體，新聞界

▶ This farmland is too infertile to cultivate.
這塊農田太貧瘠了，無法**耕種**。
*infertile [ɪnˋfɝtḷ] *a.* 不肥沃的

6 abound [əˋbaund] *vi.* 充滿

片 abound in / with... 充滿 / 富於……

▶ Mr. Jackson's poetry abounds in love for nature.
傑克遜先生的詩**充滿**了對大自然的愛。

▶ The pond abounds with fish and frogs.
池塘裡**有很多**魚和青蛙。

abundance [əˋbʌndəns] *n.* 豐富，充裕

片 (1) an abundance of... 充分的……
(2) in abundance 大量地
= in profusion
= in large quantities

衍 abundant [əˋbʌndənt] *a.* 充裕的 ⑤

似 profusion [prəˋfjuʒən] *n.* 充分，豐富

▶ Lily has an abundance of friends of all ages.
莉莉有**很多**朋友，且各個年齡層都有。

▶ The supermarket at the corner provides its customers with fruits in abundance at low prices.
街角那家超市以低價提供顧客**大量**的水果。

7 feasible [ˋfizəbḷ] *a.* 可行的

片 (1) a feasible suggestion / plan / idea 可行的建議 / 計畫 / 想法
(2) economically / technically feasible 經濟 / 技術上可行的
(3) It is feasible (for sb) to + V （某人）做……是可行的

▶ Raymond thought Vicky had made a feasible suggestion and urged her to discuss it with the boss.
雷蒙認為維琪提出了一個**可行的建議**，就力勸她和老闆討論一下。

▶ It's not economically feasible for this grocery store to be open 24 hours a day.
24 小時營業對這間雜貨店來說不**符經濟效益**。

▸ Stella told Bill it wasn't feasible for him to buy an expensive apartment because his salary was too low.
史黛拉告訴比爾，因他薪水太低，要他買昂貴的公寓是行不通的。

plausible [ˋplɔzəbḷ] *a.* 似乎有理的

片 a plausible explanation / excuse / story　看似合理的解釋／藉口／說法

反 implausible [ɪmˋplɔzəbḷ] *a.* 難以置信的

▸ Diane's story sounded perfectly plausible, so no one suspected she had lied.
黛安的說法聽來毫無破綻，所以沒有人懷疑她在說謊。

8 urgency [ˋɝdʒənsɪ] *n.* 緊急（不可數）

片 a matter of (great) urgency　（十分）緊急的事

衍 (1) urge [ɝdʒ] *vt.* 催促 ④
(2) urgent [ˋɝdʒənt] *a.* 緊急的 ④

▸ Please get Mr. Johnson on the phone right now. It's a matter of great urgency.
麻煩請強生先生聽電話。這是件十萬火急的事。

9 dictate [ˋdɪktet] *vt.* & *vi.* 口述；指定，規定

片 (1) dictate a letter / memo to sb　向某人口述一封信／一則備忘錄
(2) dictate to sb　命令某人

▸ The manager just dictated a letter to his secretary.
經理剛才向祕書口述一封信函。

▸ The committee didn't dictate how the money should be spent.
委員會並未規定這筆錢應該怎麼花。

▸ The government shouldn't be dictated to by the mass media.
政府不該被大眾媒體所操控。

dictation [dɪkˋteʃən] *n.* 口述；指定，命令

片 (1) take dictation　作口述紀錄，記下口述內容
(2) at sb's dictation　在某人的口述之下

▸ Great typing skills are required to take dictation in a courtroom.
在法庭作口述紀錄需要很棒的打字技術。

▸ The secretary typed up the formal letter at her boss' dictation, pausing to ask him a question or two.
祕書在老闆的口述之下把正式信件打成文字，也停下來問他一兩個問題。

▸ It's not in Raphael's nature to accept dictation.
接受命令不是拉斐爾的本性。

10 static [ˋstætɪk] *a.* 停滯不動的；靜電的

片 static electricity 靜電

反 dynamic [daɪˋnæmɪk] *a.* 活躍的；有活力的 ④

▸ Gold prices have remained static for the past few weeks.
過去幾週以來黃金的價格停滯不前。

▸ Rubbing your feet on the floor can cause a build-up of static electricity.
把腳放在地板上摩擦可以造成靜電增加。
*build-up [ˋbɪldˏʌp] *n.* 增大

11 revelation [ˏrɛvəˋleʃən] *n.* 被揭露的內情 / 真相 (可數)；披 / 揭露 (不可數)

片 (1) a revelation about / concerning sth 有關某事的內幕
(2) a revelation that... ……的內幕
(3) revelation of sth 披 / 揭露某事

衍 reveal [rɪˋvil] *vt.* 揭露 ③

似 disclosure [dɪsˋkloʒɚ] *n.* 揭發 ⑥

▸ The mayor resigned soon after revelations about the embezzlement.
市長挪用公款一事被披露後不久就辭職了。
*embezzlement [ɪmˋbɛzḷmənt] *n.* 挪用公款

▸ Everyone on the basketball team was surprised by the revelation that the star player was retiring.
籃球隊的每個人都對這位明星球員要退休的消息感到很驚訝。

▸ The basketball team was waiting for the revelation of their new coach.
這支籃球隊正在等待新教練的人選揭曉。

12 thermometer [θɚˋmɑmətɚ] *n.* 溫度計

似 barometer [bəˋrɑmətɚ] *n.* 氣壓計；顯示 (態度等) 變化的指標

▸ According to the thermometer on the wall, the temperature is now 36 degrees Celsius.
根據牆上的溫度計顯示，目前氣溫為攝氏 36 度。

13 mobilize [ˋmoblˏaɪz] *vt.* 動員

衍 mobilization [ˏmoblәˋzeʃən] *n.* 動員

似 rally [ˋrælɪ] *vt.* 召集 ⑤

▸ The labor union launched a campaign to mobilize support for the strike.
工會發起活動，動員群眾支持這次的罷工。

14 subjective [səbˋdʒɛktɪv] *a.* 主觀的 & *n.* 主格

片 a highly subjective judgment 非常主觀的判斷

衍 subjectivity [ˏsʌbdʒɛkˋtɪvətɪ] *n.* 主觀性

反 objective [əbˋdʒɛktɪv] *a.* 客觀的 ④

▸ In my view, the decision was based on a highly subjective judgment.
在我看來，這決定是出於非常主觀的判斷。

15 cardinal [ˋkɑrdn̩əl] *n.* 樞機 / 紅衣主教（羅馬天主教會位階非常高的神父）& *a.* 重要的；根本的

片 be of cardinal significance / importance 極為重要

▸ The cardinal released a statement on Monday that explained the reason for his stepping down.
那位**樞機主教**在週一發表聲明，解釋他為何辭職下臺。

▸ Washing your hands before eating is a cardinal rule of personal hygiene.
飯前洗手是個人衛生的**基本**準則。
*hygiene [ˋhaɪdʒin] *n.* 衛生

▸ The case was of cardinal significance to the police.
這個案件對警方來說**極為重要**。

16 renaissance [ˋrɛnə͵sɑns] *n.* 復興

片 the Renaissance 文藝復興時期

▸ Following a long period of unpopularity due to the invention of CDs, records have experienced a renaissance recently.
由於 CD 的發明，唱片有很長一段時間都一直不受歡迎，但最近卻死灰**復燃**。

▸ Leonardo da Vinci was a famous painter, sculptor, inventor, and scientist in the Renaissance.
李奧納多．達文西是**文藝復興時期**著名的畫家、雕刻家、發明家兼科學家。

17 corpse [kɔrps] *n.*（尤指人類的）屍體

似 (1) carcass [ˋkɑrkəs] *n.*（尤指動物的）屍體
(2) corps [kɔr] *n.* 軍團，特種部隊
the Marine Corps
美國海軍陸戰隊

▸ General Woodward was promoted to commandant of the Marine Corps.
伍德沃德上將獲晉升為**海軍陸戰隊**司令。
*commandant [ˋkɑmənd͵ænt / ͵kɑmənˋdænt] *n.* 指揮官

▸ According to the latest news, a decayed corpse of a woman was found in the woods.
根據最新消息，在這座森林裡發現了一具腐爛的女**屍**。
*decayed [dɪˋked] *a.* 腐爛的

18 cramp [kræmp] *n.* 抽筋 & *vt.* 束縛

片 (1) get / have a cramp 抽筋
(2) cramp sb's style
限制某人而使某人掃興

▸ The tennis player got a sudden cramp in the middle of the game.
這名網球選手在比賽進行到一半時腳突然**抽筋**。

▸ Patrick didn't want Sandy to go to the party with him because she would cramp his style.
派翠克不希望珊蒂跟他一起去派對，因為她會**處處限制**他而**讓他掃興**。

19 fracture [ˋfræktʃɚ] *n.* 斷裂，骨折 & *vi.* & *vt.* 使斷裂；使分裂

片 (1) fracture one's leg / rib / arm 某人摔斷腿 / 肋骨 / 手臂
(2) fracture A into B 分裂 A 成 B

▸ While taking a shower, Vincent slipped in the bathroom and ended up with a hairline fracture in his arm.
文森在浴室洗澡的時候滑倒，結果手臂的骨頭出現一條很細的**裂痕**。

▸ Be careful. This material is prone to fracture when placed under pressure.
小心。這種材料被壓到時很容易**破裂**。

▸ Susan fractured her right arm and three ribs when she was thrown from her horse.
蘇珊摔下馬時，**摔斷**了右**臂**和 3 根**肋骨**。

▸ If the couple continues ignoring each other's wishes and keeps criticizing each other, their marriage will fracture.
如果這對夫妻繼續無視對方的期望又繼續互相批評，那麼他們的婚姻是會**破裂**的。

▸ The political party was fractured into three smaller groups because of the scandal.
此政黨因為該醜聞而**分裂成** 3 個小團體。

20 rotate [ˋrotet] *vt.* & *vi.* (地球) 自轉；輪職 & *vt.* 輪耕

片 rotate crops 輪耕作物
比 revolve [rɪˋvɑlv] *vi.* & *vt.* (地球) 公轉；(使) 旋轉 ⑥

▸ It takes the Earth 24 hours to rotate once.
地球**自轉**一周需要 24 小時。

▸ The company's employees rotate their working hours twice a month.
這家公司的員工每個月**輪換**兩次工作時間。

▸ Farmers agree that rotating crops each year prevents nutrients in soil from being depleted.
農夫同意每年**輪耕作物**可避免土壤中的養分消耗殆盡。
*deplete [dɪˋplit] *vt.* 消耗

rotation [roˋteʃən] *n.* 旋轉；輪流

片 (1) rotation of the Earth 地球自轉

▸ The scientist spent three years recording day-to-day changes in the rotation of the Earth.
這名科學家花了 3 年記錄**地球自轉**每日的變化。

1320-1327

(2) job rotation （為使員工熟悉不同工作內容而進行的）工作輪調
(3) crop rotation　作物輪耕
(4) in rotation　輪流

似 revolution [ˏrɛvəˋluʃən] *n.* 旋轉；公轉；革命 ④

▸ Frequent job rotation has proven to be beneficial to both the employer and the employees.
經過證明，頻繁的**工作輪調**對僱主與職員都有好處。

▸ With more advanced skills and better crop rotation, the farmers are expecting a good harvest this year.
有了更先進的技術和更有效率地**輪耕作物**後，農夫都希望今年能大豐收。

▸ The teacher asked the students questions in rotation so that all of them had a chance to talk.
老師**輪流**問學生問題，如此他們所有人都有發言的機會。

21 anthem [ˋænθəm] *n.* 聖歌；國歌

片 a national anthem　國歌

▸ When the choir sang an anthem about God's love, Megan felt so calm and peaceful.
當唱詩班唱起一首關於上帝之愛的**聖歌**時，梅根感到非常安寧平靜。
*choir [kwaɪr] *n.* 唱詩班；合唱團

▸ Citizens of a country are expected to stand up whenever their national anthem is played.
一國的公民在奏其**國歌**時都應要起立。

22 boulevard [ˋbuləˏvard] *n.* 大道（字首大寫，用於道路名稱，縮寫為 Blvd.）；林蔭大道

▸ Our office is located on Sunset Boulevard.
我們的辦公室就座落在日落**大道**上。

▸ Phil turned right onto the boulevard and drove along the road towards his grandparents' house.
菲爾右轉到**林蔭大道**上，沿著這條路開往他的祖父母家。

23 ceramic [səˋræmɪk] *n.* 陶瓷作品（常用複數）& *a.* 陶瓷的

▸ There is an exhibition of Japanese ceramics in the museum now.
博物館現正展出日本的**陶瓷作品**。

▸ Sharon prefers ceramic bowls to plastic bowls.
比起塑膠碗，雪倫更喜歡**陶瓷**碗。

24 fiancé / fiancée [ˏfianˋse / fɪˋanse] *n.* 未婚夫 / 未婚妻

延伸 兩字源自法語，發音完全相同（皆有兩種發音），差別在『未婚妻』字尾需多加一個 e，而『未婚夫』則不必。

▸ Alice was brokenhearted when she saw her fiancé kissing another woman.
愛麗斯看見她**未婚夫**親吻別的女人時，心整個碎了。

25 harden [ˋhardn̩] *vt.* & *vi.* (使) 變硬，硬化

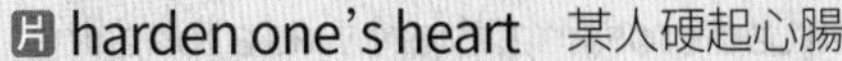

片 harden one's heart　某人硬起心腸

衍 hard [hard] *a.* 硬的 ①

反 soften [ˋsɔfn̩] *vt.* & *vi.* (使) 變柔軟，軟化 ⑤

▸ Jane's husband kept cheating on her, so she finally hardened her heart and left him for good.
珍的老公不斷劈腿，最後她終於**硬起心腸**永遠離他而去。
*cheat on sb　對某人感情不忠
for good　永遠 (= forever)

▸ The power glue will harden in an instant, so make sure you know where on your shoes you want to put it.
三秒膠會在瞬間**變硬**，所以確保你知道要把三秒膠塗在鞋子何處。

harness [ˋharnəs] *n.* 馬具，挽具；登山安全帶 & *vt.* 利用

似 make use of...　利用……
= take advantage of...

▸ The cowboy put the harness on his horse so that it could pull a cart of wood.
這牛仔把**馬具**放在他的馬上面，這樣這匹馬就能拉一車的木頭了。

▸ Make sure your harness is not broken, or you'll fall off the mountain.
要確保你的**登山安全帶**沒有斷掉，不然你會從山上掉下來。

▸ This device can harness the power of the wind to generate electricity for this building.
這個裝置能**利用**風力為這棟建築物提供電力。

26 cram [kræm] *vt.* 硬塞 & *vi.* 填鴨，惡補 & *n.* 死記硬背

三 cram, crammed [kræmd], crammed

片 (1) cram A into B　把 A 硬塞進 B 中
(2) cram for a test / an exam　考試臨時抱佛腳
(3) a cram school　補習班

▸ Sam crammed his school books into a small backpack and went home.
山姆**把**課本都**塞進**一個小背包，然後就回家了。

▸ By cramming for a test, you might get a high score, but it doesn't mean you have learned what you've been taught.
考試臨時抱佛腳也許可讓你得高分，不過這並不表示老師教過的東西你都學會了。

▸ Kelly's parents send her to a cram school so that she can improve her English.
凱莉的父母送她去**補習班**，這樣她的英文就能進步。

27 maple [ˋmepl̩] *n.* 楓樹 (= maple tree)

片 maple syrup　楓糖漿
*syrup [ˋsɪrəp] *n.* 糖漿

▸ Maple syrup is a sweetener made from the sap of maple trees.
楓糖漿是一種由**楓樹**樹汁所製成的甜味劑。
*sweetener [ˋswitn̩ɚ] *n.* 甜味劑，糖精
sap [sæp] *n.* (植物的) 汁

28 crossing [ˋkrɔsɪŋ] *n.* (道路的) 十字路口

片 (1) a railroad / grade crossing
(鐵路) 平交道〔美〕
= a level crossing〔英〕
(2) take a pedestrian crossing
走行人穿越道 (過馬路)〔英〕
*pedestrian [pəˋdɛstrɪən] *n.* 行人

延伸 (1) sidewalk [ˋsaɪdˏwɔk]
n. 人行道〔美〕②
= pavement [ˋpevmənt]〔英〕
(2) a pedestrian / zebra crossing
斑馬線〔英〕
= a crosswalk〔美〕

▶ In front of the railroad crossing, there was a long line of cars waiting for a train to pass by.
在**鐵路平交道**前，有一排長長的車列在等著火車經過。

▶ You should take the pedestrian crossing. It's safer this way.
你應該**走行人穿越道過馬路**。這樣比較安全。

29 shortcoming [ˋʃɔrtˏkʌmɪŋ] *n.* (個性上的) 缺點

似 (1) defect [ˋdifɛkt] *n.* (東西的) 缺點，瑕疵 ⑥
(2) drawback [ˋdrɔˏbæk] *n.* (事情的) 缺點

▶ The drawback to your idea is that it's not practical.
你那想法的**缺點**在於它並不實用。

▶ My girlfriend always makes me aware of my own shortcomings.
我女友總能讓我瞭解到自己的**缺點**。

30 stroll [strol] *vi.* & *n.* 散步

片 take a stroll 散步
= go for a stroll
= take a walk
= go for a walk

▶ Jessica strolled around the old town and came to a church that was over a hundred years old.
潔西卡**散步**到舊城裡，來到一座有百年以上歷史的教堂。

▶ We took a stroll around the picturesque city of Prague and enjoyed its relaxing atmosphere.
我們在風景如畫的布拉格城裡**散步**，享受它悠閒的氣氛。
*picturesque [ˏpɪktʃəˋrɛsk] *a.* 風景如畫的

31 radish [ˋrædɪʃ] *n.* 蘿蔔

複 radishes [ˋrædɪʃɪz]

▶ These radishes and tomatoes are fresh from our garden.
這些**蘿蔔**和番茄都是我們園子裡現採的。

32 marginal [ˋmɑrdʒənl̩] *a.* 些微的，少量的

衍 margin [ˋmɑrdʒən] *n.* 邊緣 ④
似 slight [slaɪt] *a.* 少量的 ④

▶ The manager was worried because there was only a marginal increase in sales last month.
上個月的銷售額只有**些微的**成長，因此經理很擔心。

33 quake [kwek] *vi.* 顫抖；搖晃 & *n.* 地震 (= earthquake)

片 quake with cold / fear / anger
冷得 / 嚇得 / 氣得發抖

似 (1) shake [ʃek] *vi.* 搖晃 ①
(2) tremble [ˋtrɛmbḷ] *vi.* 顫抖 ④

▶ Most retailers would quake at the thought of competing with such a corporate giant.
多數零售商一想到要跟這麼大的企業競爭便**膽顫心驚**。
*corporate [ˋkɔrpərət] *a.* 公司的
a corporate giant　大公司

▶ The homeless people on the streets were quaking with cold.
街上的流浪漢**冷得發抖**。

▶ The powerful earthquake made the building quake, but fortunately it did not fall down.
強烈的地震使這棟建築物**搖晃**，但幸好沒有倒塌下來。

▶ Japan is usually hit with small quakes.
日本常有小**地震**發生。

34 trademark [ˋtred͵mark] *n.* 商標

片 register a trademark　註冊商標

▶ The Coca-Cola company registered its trademark to prevent it from being copied by the competition.
可口可樂公司**註冊**其**商標**以防止同行仿冒。
*the competition　競爭對手

35 martial [ˋmarʃəl] *a.* 戰爭的，打鬥的

片 (1) martial law　戒嚴法 (不可數)
(2) martial art　武術 (常用複數)

▶ After the foreign troops captured the capital, martial law was imposed on the country to prevent rioting.
外國部隊占領該首都後，就對全國強行**戒嚴法**以防止暴亂。
*impose A on B　將 A 強加於 B

▶ Leo is an expert in martial arts and specializes in karate.
李歐是個**武術**專家，專長是空手道。
*karate [kəˋratɪ] *n.* 空手道

36 doom [dum] *n.* 劫數，厄運 & *vt.* 使在劫難逃，註定

片 doom... to failure　使……注定失敗

▶ Sensing that he was about to get fired, Arthur walked into the boss' office with a feeling of doom.
亞瑟感到自己要被解僱了，於是他帶著一種**劫數**難逃的感覺走進了老闆的辦公室。

▶ The general's terrible decision on the battlefield doomed his army to failure.
該將軍在戰場上所做的決定很糟糕，而使其軍隊**注定要打敗仗**。

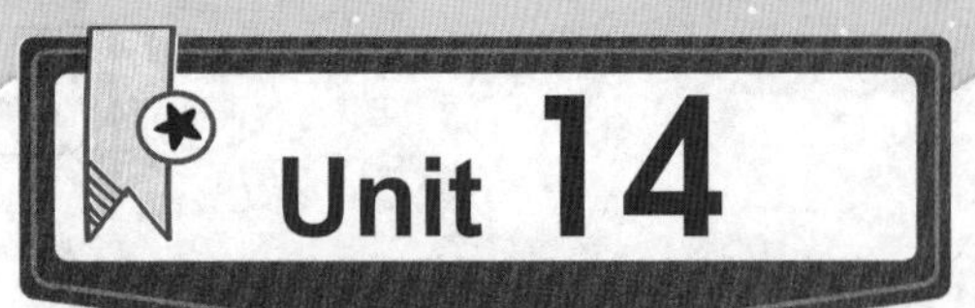

1 warrant [ˋwɔrənt] *n.* 授權令

片 (1) an arrest warrant 逮捕令
(2) a search warrant 搜查令

▶ The judge issued an arrest warrant for the boxer after he failed to show up in court for the murder case.
該拳擊手未出席謀殺案的開庭審理後，法官發布了一張逮捕令。

warranty [ˋwɔrəntɪ] *n.* 保證書

片 be under warranty 在保固期內
= be under guarantee

似 guarantee [ˌgærənˋti] *n.* & *vt.* 保證 ④

▶ You seem to have endless problems with this car. Is it still under warranty?
你這輛車似乎有沒完沒了的問題。它還在保固期內嗎？

2 morale [məˋræl] *n.* 士氣 (不可數)

片 (1) low / high morale 低迷 / 高昂的士氣
(2) raise / boost / improve morale 提升士氣

似 moral [ˋmɔrəl] *a.* 道德的 & *n.* 寓意 ③

▶ The troops were suffering from low morale, which is why they were easily defeated.
部隊士氣低落，這就是為什麼他們這麼容易就被打敗的原因。

▶ The most effective way to boost staff morale is to provide a good working environment.
提振員工士氣最有效的辦法就是提供他們好的工作環境。

3 intrude [ɪnˋtrud] *vi.* 入侵；侵擾

片 (1) intrude into... 入侵 / 闖入……
(2) intrude on / into... 打 / 侵擾……
= encroach [ɪnˋkrotʃ] on...
= infringe [ɪnˋfrɪndʒ] on...

▶ Some strangers intruded into Tom's home while he was out.
湯姆外出時有幾個陌生人闖入他家。

▶ Local newspapers are being urged not to intrude on celebrities' private lives.
地方報紙被強烈要求不要去打擾名人的私生活。

intruder [ɪnˋtrudɚ] *n.* 入侵者

▶ The intruders in my house were arrested soon after the police came.
警方到達後立刻把入侵我家的人逮捕。

4 tropic [ˋtrɑpɪk] *n.* (南、北) 回歸線 & *a.* 熱帶的 (= tropical [ˋtrɑpɪkḷ])

片 (1) the Tropic of Cancer [ˋkænsɚ] 北回歸線
the Tropic of Capricorn [ˋkæprɪkɔrn] 南回歸線

▶ The Tropic of Cancer runs directly through Taiwan, and there is a monument showing its location in Hualien County.
北回歸線直接穿過臺灣，在花蓮縣有座紀念碑標示出其位置。

(2) the tropics 熱帶（地區）（恆用複數）

▸ The scientist has spent a couple of years researching in the tropics.
這位科學家已花了幾年的時間在**熱帶地區**做研究。

▸ During the cold winters in Canada, Martin often thinks about taking a vacation to some beautiful tropic location.
在加拿大寒冷的冬天，馬丁經常在想要去某個美麗的**熱帶**地區度假。

5 oppress [əˋprɛs] *vt.* 壓迫

反 liberate [ˋlɪbə͵ret] *vt.* 解放 ⑥

▸ That regime was accused of brutally oppressing ethnic and religious minorities.
該政權被控殘忍地**壓迫**少數民族及宗教少數派人士。
*regime [rəˋdʒim / reˋdʒim] *n.* 政權
ethnic [ˋɛθnɪk] *a.* 種族的

oppression [əˋprɛʃən] *n.* 壓抑，壓迫（不可數）

▸ The feminist told the poor girl, "Although you are a woman, you are also a human, who has the right to freedom from oppression."
此女權主義者對那可憐的女孩說：『雖然你是一名女子，但你也是個人，而人都有權不受**壓迫**。』

6 analytical [͵ænəˋlɪtɪkḷ] *a.* 分析的

衍 (1) analyze [ˋænə͵laɪz] *vt.* 分析 ④
(2) analysis [əˋnæləsɪs] *n.* 分析
（複數為 analyses [əˋnæləsiz]）④
(3) analyst [ˋænḷɪst] *n.* 分析師 ⑤

▸ We encourage you to develop your analytical skills during the course.
我們鼓勵你們在這堂課裡培養**分析的**能力。

7 restoration [͵rɛstəˋreʃən] *n.* 修復（建築物、畫）；恢復

衍 restore [rɪˋstɔr] *vt.* 恢復 ④
似 renovation [͵rɛnəˋveʃən] *n.* 整修，翻新

▸ The museum is closed temporarily for restoration and is scheduled to reopen to the public on May 1st.
這間博物館暫時關閉進行**維修**，預計5月1日重新對大眾開放。

▸ The first task after the war was the restoration of public order.
戰後的首要工作就是**恢復**公共秩序。

rehabilitate [͵rihəˋbɪlə͵tet] *vt.* 使（病人、罪犯等）重新過上正常生活

▸ The aim of this program is to rehabilitate the prisoners so that they can turn over a new leaf when they are released.
本計畫的目的是要使受刑人**重新學習做人**，以便出獄後能展開新的生活。

rehabilitation [ˌrihəˌbɪlə`teʃən]
n. (病人、罪犯等) 恢復 (正常生活)

片 a drug rehabilitation center
戒毒所

▸ John has been addicted to drugs since college. It would be wise of him to go to a drug rehabilitation center.
約翰自大學時就一直犯毒癮。到**戒毒所**對他來說會是個明智的選擇。

8 inflict [ɪn`flɪkt] *vt.* 施加 (傷害、打擊)

片 inflict A on B 將 (不好的) A 加諸於 B

▸ The typhoon inflicted severe damage on the coastal villages.
颱風**對於**沿海的村莊**造成**極大的損害。

ordeal [ɔr`dil] *n.* 嚴酷考驗，煎熬

片 go through the ordeal of...
經歷……的痛苦經驗

似 torment [`tɔrmənt] *n.* 痛苦 ⑤

▸ After Nancy went through the ordeal of a divorce, she didn't want to fall in love with another man.
南西**經歷**離婚的**煎熬**後，就不想跟其他男人談戀愛了。

9 comparative [kəm`pærətɪv] *a.* 比較的，相對 (而言) 的

衍 (1) comparable [`kɑmpərəbḷ]
a. 可相比的 ⑤
(2) comparatively [kəm`pærətɪvlɪ]
adv. 比較起來說，相對地

似 relative [`rɛlətɪv] *a.* 相對的 ①

▸ The scholar is engaged in a comparative study of the economic systems of India and South Korea.
這位學者正忙於從事一項研究，**比較**印度和南韓兩國的經濟體系。

▸ This company is a comparative newcomer to the home appliances market.
這家公司是家電市場上**比較**新的公司。

10 compile [kəm`paɪl] *vt.* 彙編 (成冊)

片 compile a dictionary / list
彙編字典 / 名單

比 edit [`ɛdɪt] *vt.* 編輯 (文字、版面) ③

▸ Seventeen linguists spent nearly seven years compiling this dictionary.
17 位語言學家花了近 7 年**彙編**這本字典。

11 civilize [`sɪvəˌlaɪz] *vt.* 使文明 / 有教養

衍 civilization [ˌsɪvələ`zeʃən]
n. 文明 (不可數) ④

▸ From my grandmother's point of view, everyone should civilize themselves through the arts.
我奶奶認為每個人都應該用藝術**教化**自己。

civilized [`sɪvəˌlaɪzd] *a.* 文明的；有教養的

反 barbarous [`bɑrbərəs] *a.* 野蠻的，未開化的

▸ One of the main characteristics of a civilized society is that it has laws that are fair for everyone.
文明社會的主要特徵之一是其法律對所有的人都公平。

▶ To my dismay, our manager is rude and doesn't know how to communicate with others in a civilized manner.
令我沮喪的是，我們的經理很粗魯，他不知道如何**有教養**地與人溝通。
*dismay [dɪsˋme] *n.* 沮喪，氣餒

12 enhance [ɪnˋhæns] *vt.* 增強

似 beef up... 加強……

▶ The teacher tried many ways to enhance his students' enthusiasm for studying.
老師嘗試過很多方法試圖**提高**學生學習的熱忱。

enhancement [ɪnˋhænsmənt] *n.* 增強，提升
似 improvement [ɪmˋpruvmənt] *n.* 改善

▶ To survive in business, constant enhancement of your products is a must.
想要在商場生存，就得不斷**強化**自己的產品。

13 applaud [əˋplɔd] *vi.* & *vt.* 鼓掌

片 applaud sb for sth 因某事而為某人鼓掌
衍 applause [əˋplɔz] *n.* 掌聲 ⑤
似 clap [klæp] *vi.* 鼓掌 ②

▶ The audience all stood up and applauded when the show was over.
表演結束時，所有觀眾都起身**鼓掌**。

▶ John's classmates applauded him for his great performance in the speech contest.
約翰在演講比賽中表現優異，**獲得**同學的**掌聲**。

14 boxing [ˋbɑksɪŋ] *n.* 拳擊

片 a boxing ring 拳擊臺
衍 boxer [ˋbɑksɚ] *n.* 拳擊手 ⑤
延伸 wrestling [ˋrɛslɪŋ] *n.* 摔角

▶ Nick took up boxing as a way to increase his self-confidence.
尼克開始打**拳擊**是為了要增加自信心。
*take up + N/V-ing 開始……

▶ As soon as the champion boxer stepped into the boxing ring, members of the audience started to cheer.
那冠軍拳擊手一走進**拳擊臺**，觀眾就開始歡呼了起來。

15 certify [ˋsɝtə͵faɪ] *vt.* 證明

三 certify, certified [ˋsɝtə͵faɪd], certified
片 certify that... 證明……
似 confirm [kənˋfɝm] *vt.* 證實 ③

▶ The psychiatrist certified the patient's sanity.
心理醫生**證明**那位病人心智正常。
*sanity [ˋsænətɪ] *n.* 精神正常

▶ This diploma certifies that you have finished high school.
這份文憑**證明**你已完成高中學業。
*diploma [dɪˋplomə] *n.* 畢業文憑

16 marvel [ˋmɑrvḷ] *vi.* 驚訝 & *n.* 奇蹟

片 marvel at... 對……感到驚奇
= be amazed at...

衍 marvelous [ˋmɑrvələs] *a.* 令人驚嘆的 ③

似 wonder [ˋwʌndɚ] *n.* 奇跡，奇觀 ②

▸ The tourists marveled at the magnificent old buildings in Rome.
觀光客**對**羅馬宏偉又歷史悠久的建築物**大表驚嘆**。

▸ The space shuttle is a marvel of modern technology.
= The space shuttle is a wonder of modern technology.
太空梭是現代科技的一項**奇蹟**。

17 harmonica [hɑrˋmɑnɪkə] *n.* 口琴 (= mouth organ)

片 (1) play the harmonica 吹口琴
(2) glass harmonica 玻璃琴
= armonica [ɑrˋmɑnɪkə]

▸ After my grandfather passed away, I was given his old harmonica.
爺爺過世後，他的舊**口琴**就給了我。

▸ John plays the harmonica very well.
約翰**口琴**吹得很棒。

18 shred [ʃrɛd] *n.* 碎片 & *vt.* 切成碎片 / 細條

三 shred, shredded [ˋʃrɛdɪd], shredded

片 a shred of... 一絲……

衍 shredder [ˋʃrɛdɚ] *n.* 碎紙機

▸ The police could not find a shred of evidence to support Mr. Lee's accusation.
警方找不到**一絲**證據證實李先生的指控。

▸ Mandy shredded some cheese and put it into a bowl; then she added some tomato sauce and an egg.
曼蒂把一些起司**切成細條**放進碗裡；然後加了一些番茄醬和一顆蛋。

19 radius [ˋredɪəs] *n.* 半徑；(半徑) 範圍

複 radii [ˋredɪˏaɪ]

片 within a... radius 在……範圍之內

延伸 diameter [daɪˋæmətɚ] *n.* 直徑 ⑤

▸ The radius of this circle is five centimeters.
這個圓形的**半徑**是 5 公分。

▸ We provide delivery services to people living within a 5-mile radius of our store.
我們提供外送服務給住**在**本店**半徑** 5 英里**範圍內**的民眾。

20 crater [ˋkretɚ] *n.* 火山口 & *vt.* 使成坑

延伸 volcano [vɑlˋkeno] *n.* 火山 ⑤

▸ The scientists are observing the crater for possible volcanic activity.
科學家們在觀察**火山口**有無可能會有火山活動。
*volcanic [vɑlˋkænɪk] *a.* 火山的

▸ A huge rock from space cratered the earth 66 million years ago, and many believe this event killed the dinosaurs.
6,600 萬年前，從太空來的一顆巨大岩石把地球**撞**了個**大凹洞**，很多人認為此一事件使恐龍滅絕。

21 stride [straɪd] *vi.* 跨大步走 & *n.* 步伐

三 stride, strode [strod], stridden [ˋstrɪdn̩]

片 make great / giant strides in... 在……方面有極大的進步

似 (1) step [stɛp] *vi.* 跨步 & *n.* 步伐 ②
(2) march [mɑrtʃ] *vi.* 快步走 ③

▸ The superstar strode across the hallway, got into a limousine, and rode off.
這名巨星大步走過大廳，進了加長型禮車，然後就離開了。
*limousine [ˏlɪməˋzin / ˋlɪməˏzin] *n.* 加長型禮車

▸ Scientists have made great strides in genetic engineering.
科學家在基因工程方面已有極大的進步。
*genetic [dʒəˋnɛtɪk] *a.* 基因上的

22 fin [fɪn] *n.* 魚鰭

片 a shark fin　魚翅，鯊魚鰭

▸ We could see the fins of the sharks sticking out of the water as they swam around the boat.
鯊魚群在船附近游動時，我們可以看到牠們的鰭都露出了水面。
*stick [stɪk] *vi.* 伸出

▸ To protect sharks, we should refuse to eat any shark fins and encourage our friends to do the same.
為了保護鯊魚，我們應要拒吃魚翅，並鼓勵我們的朋友也這樣做。

23 haunt [hɔnt] *vt.* (鬼魂) 常出沒於；不斷困擾

片 (1) 鬼 + haunt + 建物
某建物有鬼魂出沒
= 建物 + be haunted by + 鬼
(2) haunt sb
在某人的腦海中揮之不去

衍 haunted [ˋhɔntɪd] *a.* 鬧鬼的
a haunted house　鬼屋

▸ It's said that two ghosts haunt the house.
= It's said that the house is haunted by two ghosts.
據說這棟房子有兩隻鬼出沒。

▸ The residents are constantly haunted by the fear of an explosion of a nuclear power plant.
這些居民經常提心吊膽，深怕核電廠爆炸。

24 groan [gron] *vi.* 哀嚎 & *vi.* & *vt.* 抱怨 & *n.* 哀嚎聲；抱怨聲

似 moan [mon] *vi.* 哀嚎 *vi.* & *vt.* 抱怨 & *n.* 哀嚎聲；抱怨聲 ⑤

▸ We all groaned when Daddy announced he'd do the cooking for tonight.
當老爸宣布今晚要下廚時，我們都哀嚎起來。

▸ "How long are you going to hog the bathroom?" Nicole groaned.
『你還要霸占廁所多久啊？』妮可抱怨道。

▸ Mark let out a groan when Mom asked him to take care of the piles of dirty dishes.
當媽媽叫馬克負責處理那堆髒碗盤時，馬克發出哀嚎聲。

1424-1434

▸ Zach doesn't like to visit Kathy because he is tired of listening to her groans about her difficult life.
查克不喜歡去看望凱西，因為他厭倦了聽她抱怨她艱困的生活。

25 torrent [ˋtɔrənt] *n.* 洪流

片 fall in torrents 傾流而下
= come down in torrents
衍 torrential [təˋrɛnʃəl] *a.* 急流般的
torrential rain 豪雨

▸ After the thunder, the rain started to fall in torrents.
= After the thunder, the rain started to come down in torrents.
打雷之後，就開始下起了傾盆大雨。

26 mingle [ˋmɪŋgḷ] *vi.* 混合，融入 & *vt.* 混合

片 (1) mingle with... 與……打成一片
(2) mingle A with B
將 A 與 B 混在一起

▸ At the party, Bill walked around and mingled with other guests.
在派對上，比爾四處走動，與其他客人打成一片。

似 mix [mɪks] *vt.* & *vi.* 混合 ②

▸ A businessperson should never mingle business funds with personal funds.
生意人不該把生意上的款項和個人款項混用。

27 whiskey [ˋwɪskɪ] *n.* 威士忌酒 (= whisky〔英〕)

複 whiskeys (= whiskies〔英〕)

▸ Mike pulled a bottle of whiskey off the shelf and poured some into a glass.
邁可把一瓶威士忌酒從架子上拿下來，並且倒了一些在玻璃杯裡。

28 rap [ræp] *n.* 饒舌樂 & *vi.* & *vt.* 敲擊 & *vt.* 批評，責備

三 rap, rapped [ræpt], rapped
片 (1) rap music 饒舌樂
(2) rap on / at... 敲打……
(3) rap sb for sth 為某事批評某人
= criticize sb for sth
衍 rapper [ˋræpɚ] *n.* 饒舌歌手

▸ James is very much into rap music.
詹姆士非常喜歡饒舌樂。

▸ Oliver rapped on Helena's door, but there was no answer because she was not at home.
奧利弗敲打著海倫娜的門，但沒人應門，因海倫娜並不在家。

▸ When Linda got nervous, she would rap the table.
琳達緊張時就會敲桌子。

▸ The critics rapped the writer for his new book.
書評家抨擊那名作家的新書。

29 mermaid [ˋmɝ͵med] *n.* 美人魚

反 merman [ˋmɝ͵mæn] *n.* 雄人魚

▸ Thousands of tourists go to Copenhagen, Denmark to see the statue of *The Little Mermaid*.
數以千計的遊客都到丹麥的哥本哈根欣賞**小美人魚**的雕像。

30 mediate [ˋmidɪ͵et] *vt.* & *vi.* 居中調解

片 mediate (sth) between A and B 替 A 和 B 居中調解 (某事物)

衍 mediator [ˋmidɪ͵etɚ] *n.* 調停者

似 negotiate [nɪˋgoʃɪet] *vt.* & *vi.* 談判 ④

▸ A UN delegation was dispatched to mediate the peace talks between the guerilla leaders and the government officials.
聯合國代表被派往**居中協調**游擊隊領導人**及**政府官員**之間**的和平會議。
*dispatch [dɪˋspætʃ] *vt.* 派遣
guerilla [gəˋrɪlə] *n.* 游擊隊員

31 bombard [bɑmˋbɑrd] *vt.* 砲轟；向……連續提出問題

片 bombard sb with sth 不斷向某人提出 (問題或批評)

衍 (1) bomb [bɑm] *n.* 炸彈 & *vt.* 轟炸 ③
(2) bomber [ˋbɑmɚ] *n.* 投擲炸彈者；轟炸機

▸ The city was heavily bombarded by the enemy for six months in a row.
此城市連續 6 個月遭敵軍嚴重**轟炸**。

▸ The city councilors bombarded the mayor with various questions during the session yesterday.
昨天在會議上，市議員**向**市長**不斷提出**各種問題。
*session [ˋsɛʃən] *n.* (議會等的) 會議

32 treasury [ˋtrɛʒərɪ] *n.* 寶庫

衍 (1) treasure [ˋtrɛʒɚ] *n.* 寶物 & *vt.* 珍惜 ②
(2) treasurer [ˋtrɛʒərɚ] *n.* 出納；會計；財務主管

▸ The king's money was kept in a treasury that had thick doors and strong locks to keep his fortune safe.
國王的錢存放在**寶庫**中，寶庫的門厚實，鎖具又堅固，可確保他的財產很安全。

33 radioactive [͵redɪoˋæktɪv] *a.* 放射性的，有輻射的

▸ One of the main problems with nuclear energy is what should be done with its radioactive waste.
核能的主要問題之一是應要如何處理其**放射性**廢料。

34 equalize [ˋikwəl͵aɪz] *vt.* 使平等

衍 equal [ˋikwəl] *vt.* 相等 & *a.* 相等的 ②

▸ The new rules passed by the government were meant to equalize the employment situation in the country, making conditions fairer.
政府通過的新規定旨在**使**該國的就業狀況**均等**，並使情況更加公平。

1435-1436

35 draught [dræft] *n.* (通風) 氣流〔英〕(= draft〔美〕)；一大口〔英〕(= draft〔美〕)；西洋跳棋 (恆用複數)〔英〕(= checkers〔美〕)

片 a draught of... 一大口……

似 drought [draʊt] *n.* 乾旱 ⑤

▸ Feeling an uncomfortable, cold draught from the open window, Sam got up to close it.

山姆感到有股不舒服的冷風從敞開著的窗戶吹進來，所以他站起來把窗戶關上。

▸ Bill was already drunk, but he still took another draught of beer and sang loudly.

比爾已經喝醉了，但他還是又喝了一大口啤酒，還大聲唱歌。

▸ The game of checkers is known by another name in the United Kingdom; there, it is called draughts.

西洋跳棋遊戲在英國也有另一個名稱；在那裡西洋跳棋叫做draughts。

36 bureaucrat [ˋbjurə͵kræt] *n.* 官員 / 僚 (貶義)

衍 bureaucracy [bjuˋrɑkrəsɪ] *n.* 官僚主義 / 體制 ⑤

▸ Nancy handed the documents to the government bureaucrat for certification, but he said more information was required.

南希將文件交給了政府官員以進行認證，但他卻說還需要更多的資料。

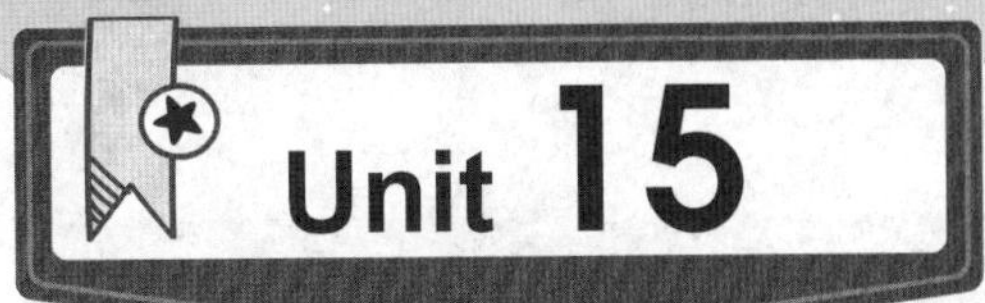

1501-1505

1 lengthy [ˋlɛŋθɪ] *a.* 冗長的

衍 (1) length [lɛŋθ] *n.* 長度 ②
(2) lengthen [ˋlɛŋθən] *vt.* & *vi.* 加長 ④

反 brief [brif] *a.* 簡短的 ②

▸ The board of directors finally reached a consensus on the issue after a lengthy discussion.
董事會在**冗長的**討論後，終於針對該議題達成了共識。
*consensus [kənˋsɛnsəs] *n.* 共識

2 conserve [kənˋsɝv] *vt.* 節約（能源）；保護（環境）& [ˋkɑnsɝv] *n.* 果醬（= jam）

片 conserve electricity / water / energy 節約用電 / 用水 / 能源

衍 conservation [ˏkɑnsɚˋveʃən] *n.* 保護；節約（不可數）⑤

似 (1) converse [kənˋvɝs] *vi.*（和……）交談 ④
(2) reserve [rɪˋzɝv] *vt.* 預訂（房間、位子等）③
(3) preserve [prɪˋzɝv] *vt.* 保存（食物）④

▸ To conserve electricity, make sure you turn off the lights before you leave the office.
為了要**省電**，離開辦公室前一定要把燈都關掉。

▸ New laws have been enacted to conserve wildlife in that mountain area.
政府已制定新法規以**保護**該山區的野生動植物。

▸ I have fond memories of my grandmother making strawberry conserve in her kitchen when I was young.
我有關於我奶奶的美好回憶，我小時候她會在廚房做草莓**果醬**。

3 setback [ˋsɛtˏbæk] *n.* 挫折（可數）

衍 frustration [frʌsˋtreʃən] *n.* 挫折 ④

▸ Although Tim has suffered several setbacks in business, he's always managed to bounce back.
雖然提姆在事業上屢遭**挫折**，但他總能成功重新出發。
*bounce [baʊns] *vi.* 彈跳

4 manuscript [ˋmænjəˏskrɪpt] *n.* 手稿

衍 script [skrɪpt] *n.*（戲劇、廣播）底稿 ⑤

▸ Norman sent his manuscript to several publishers, but there has been no response from any of them so far.
諾曼把他的**手稿**寄給了幾家出版社，但到目前為止，沒有任何一家有回應。

5 transcript [ˋtrænˏskrɪpt] *n.*（根據錄音、影片、演講等而整理的）逐字稿，文字本（= transcription）；成績單〔美〕

衍 transcribe [trænˋskraɪb] *vt.* 抄寫；謄寫
▸ The recordings of the interview were transcribed by the secretary.
這段訪問的錄音由祕書將其**抄寫**下來。

▸ Mr. Hill had his secretary send him the video transcript.
希爾先生要他的秘書寄影片的**逐字稿**給他。

▸ You can download our official transcript request form on the website.
你可以從網站下載正式的**成績單**申請表格。

6 soothe [suð] *vt.* 安慰，使鎮定；減輕 (疼痛)

衍 soothing [ˋsuðɪŋ] *a.* 撫慰的

似 (1) calm [kɑm] *vt.* 使鎮定 ②
(2) relieve [rɪˋliv] *vt.* 減輕 (疼痛) ④

▸ A security guard in the shopping mall came to soothe a little girl who had got lost and was crying loudly for her mom.
購物中心的保全前來**安慰**一個小女孩，她迷路了，還大聲哭著要媽媽。

▸ Lucy applied some ointment on my bruised knee to soothe the pain.
露西在我瘀青的膝蓋上塗了些藥膏以**減輕**疼痛。
*ointment [ˋɔɪntmənt] *n.* 軟膏，藥膏

7 attendant [əˋtɛndənt] *n.* 服務生

片 a flight attendant 空服員

衍 attend [əˋtɛnd] *vt.* 照顧 & *vi.* & *vt.* 出席 ②

▸ I had never thought that my dream of becoming a flight attendant would one day come true.
我從沒想過我成為**空服員**的夢想，有一天竟能成真。

8 preventive [prɪˋvɛntɪv] *a.* 預防的 & *n.* 可預防的藥 / 措施等

片 take preventive measures to + V
採取預防措施以……
= take precautions to + V

衍 prevent [prɪˋvɛnt] *vt.* 預防 ③

▸ We should take preventive measures to stop a pandemic from breaking out.
我們應當採取**預防措施以**防止流行病爆發。
*pandemic [pænˋdɛmɪk] *n.* 大流行病

▸ To avoid a big disaster, there were several preventives in place at the nuclear power plant.
為了避免一場大災難，此核電廠已採取了幾項**預防措施**。
*in place （政策等）正在運作，就位

9 purity [ˋpjʊrətɪ] *n.* 純淨

衍 pure [pjʊr] *a.* 純潔的 ③

似 clarity [ˋklærətɪ] *n.* 清澈度 ⑤

反 impurity [ɪmˋpjʊrətɪ] *n.* 不純淨
▸ There were complaints about the impurity of the milk from the farm.
有人抱怨那座農場出產的牛奶**不純**。

▸ A white rose is a symbol of purity, whereas a red rose symbolizes passion.
白玫瑰是**純潔**的象徵，而紅玫瑰則象徵熱情。

---

purify [ˋpjʊrə͵faɪ] *vt.* 淨化

三 purify, purified [ˋpjʊrə͵faɪd], purified

衍 purification [͵pjʊrəfəˋkeʃən] *n.* 淨化

似 cleanse [klɛnz] *vt.* 使清潔

▸ The kidneys are the organs that purify the blood and are responsible for producing urine.
腎臟是**淨化**血液的器官，另外也負責製造尿液。
*urine [ˋjʊrɪn] *n.* 尿液

▸ John is in charge of water purification for the city.
約翰負責該市的水質**淨化**工作。

10 synthetic [sɪnˋθɛtɪk] *a.* 合成的 & *n.* 合成物 / 纖維（常用複數）

片 synthetic / artificial fiber 合成纖維

衍 synthesize [ˋsɪnθə͵saɪz] *vt.* 綜合

似 artificial [͵ɑrtəˋfɪʃəl] *a.* 人造的 ④

▸ Many people prefer wearing natural material to synthetic material.
許多人喜歡穿天然布料，而較不喜歡穿**合成的**布料。

▸ Although the shirt looked nice, Teddy didn't buy it because it was made of synthetic fiber, rather than cotton.
雖然這件襯衫看起來不錯，但泰迪沒有買，因為這襯衫是用**合成纖維**做的，而不是棉製的。

▸ The shoes look fantastic; no one would ever guess that they are made of synthetics, rather than real leather.
這鞋看起來棒極了；沒人會猜到這鞋是用**合成材料**做的，而不是用真皮做的。

synthesis [ˋsɪnθəsɪs] *n.* 綜合

複 syntheses [ˋsɪnθəsiz]

▸ The Japanese American author describes his childhood as a synthesis of Western and Eastern values.
這名日裔美籍作家描述其童年是**綜合**了東西方的價值觀。

11 diversify [daɪˋvɝsə͵faɪ / dɪˋvɝsə͵faɪ] *vt.* & *vi.* 使多樣化

衍 (1) diverse [daɪˋvɝs / dɪˋvɝs]
a. 多樣的 ④
(2) diversity [daɪˋvɝsətɪ / dɪˋvɝsətɪ]
n. 多樣性（不可數）④

▸ To reduce the risk of losing money, you should diversify your investments.
為了減低金錢損失的風險，你應將投資**多樣化**。

12 elite [ɪˋlit] *n.* （一群）菁英分子（可數）& *a.* 菁英的

片 the social elite 社會菁英分子

用法 此字可用單數或複數動詞，而用複數動詞較常見。

▸ The social elite are willing to join us in raising funds for orphans.
社會菁英分子願意加入我們為孤兒籌募基金的行列。

▸ A small elite group of people can travel by private jet whenever they please.
少數**菁英**族群可隨時搭乘私人噴射機旅行。

13 prosecute [ˋprɑsə͵kjut] *vt.* 起訴

片 prosecute sb for + N/V-ing
因……起訴某人

衍 (1) prosecution [͵prɑsəˋkjuʃən]
n. 起訴 ⑤
(2) prosecutor [ˋprɑsə͵kjutɚ]
n. 檢察官

▸ The multinational chain store was prosecuted for exploiting its workers by forcing them to work overtime.
這家跨國連鎖商店因強迫員工超時工作，而被**以**剝削勞工罪名**起訴**。
*exploit [ɪkˋsplɔɪt] *vt.* 剝削

1514-1519

似 charge sb with sth　指控某人某罪行

▸ To our shock, our neighbor Steve was charged with murder.
令我們震驚的是我們的鄰居史帝夫竟被控謀殺罪。

14 formidable [ˋfɔrmɪdəbḷ] *a.* 可怕的，難對付的

片 a formidable task / opponent
艱困的任務 / 難對付的對手

似 (1) difficult [ˋdɪfə͵kəlt] *a.* 艱困的 ①
(2) redoubtable [rɪˋdautəbḷ] *a.* 令人敬畏的

▸ The linguists are undertaking the formidable task of compiling a comprehensive English dictionary.
這些語言學家正著手進行一個艱困的任務，他們要彙編一本內容詳盡的英文字典。
*linguist [ˋlɪŋgwɪst] *n.* 語言學家

15 colloquial [kəˋlokwɪəl] *a.* 口語的，會話的

片 a colloquial expression　口語用字

似 (1) spoken [ˋspokən] *a.* 口語的
(2) oral [ˋɔrəl] *a.* 口頭的，口述的 ③

▸ It would not be appropriate to use colloquial words and phrases in a formal business letter.
正式的商業書信不宜使用口語的字眼和片語。

▸ Many colloquial expressions are fine to be used in everyday conversation, but not in formal writing.
許多口語用字可以在日常對話中使用，但不能用於正式寫作中。

slang [slæŋ] *n.* 俚語（集合名詞，不可數）& *vt.* 用粗話罵，謾罵〔英〕

片 a slang expression / word / term
俚語字眼

用法 slang 為不可數，故：
▸ He knows many slangs. (×)
▸ He knows a lot of slang. (○)
= He knows many slang expressions.

▸ "Pot" and "dope" are slang for marijuana.
= "Pot" and "dope" are slang expressions for marijuana.
『pot』和『dope』這兩個字都是『大麻』的俚語。
*marijuana [͵mærəˋ(h)wɑnə] *n.* 大麻

▸ After hearing that her best friend Elaine had an affair with her husband, Ivy slanged Elaine in front of others during the dinner party.
艾薇在聽說她最好的朋友伊蓮和丈夫有染之後，就在晚宴上謾罵伊蓮。

16 alienate [ˋelɪən͵et] *vt.* 使疏離

片 alienate A from B　使 A 和 B 疏離

衍 (1) alien [ˋelɪən] *n.* 外國人；外星人 ⑤
(2) alienation [͵elɪənˋeʃən] *n.* 疏離（感）

▸ Jack's promotion to the post of vice president alienated him from his former colleagues.
傑克高升為副總裁的職位後，使他和原來的同事疏離了。

17 wrestle [ˋrɛsl̩] *vi.* & *vt.* (與……) 摔角 & *vi.* 努力解決 & *n.* 搏鬥

片 wrestle with...
與……摔角；努力解決……

衍 (1) wrestler [ˋrɛslɚ] *n.* 摔角手
(2) wrestling [ˋrɛslɪŋ] *n.* 摔角 (運動)

▶ The two boys wrestled with each other.
這兩個男孩**扭打**在一起。

▶ The police officer tackled the robber and wrestled him to the ground.
警官抓住搶匪，並把他**摔**到地上。
*tackle [ˋtækl̩] *vt.* 抓住

▶ Kenny spent the whole weekend wrestling with the problem.
肯尼花了整個週末的時間**全力應付**這個問題。

▶ For kids who have difficulty learning things quickly, attending school can be a real wrestle.
對於那些難以快速學習的孩子來說，去上學真是個**煎熬**。

18 slash [slæʃ] *vt.* 削減 & *n.* 斜線 (表有其他選擇)；(長又深的) 砍痕

似 reduce [rɪˋd(j)us] *vt.* 減少 ③

▶ Although prices had already been slashed significantly for the sale, many prospective buyers still thought the items were too expensive.
雖然這次拍賣的價格已大幅**調降**，但很多潛在買家仍覺得這些東西太貴了。

▶ Rick has several part-time jobs, but mostly he is an editor-slash-teacher at a couple of companies.
瑞克有幾個兼職工作，但通常他是幾家公司的編輯**兼**老師。

▶ During the fight with the robber, Greg suffered a long, painful slash on one of his arms.
葛瑞格在與強匪搏鬥的時候，他一隻手臂遭劃傷，**傷口**很長又很痛。

pierce [pɪrs] *vt.* 刺穿

似 piece [pis] *n.* 片，塊 ①

▶ Vicky had her ears pierced so that she could wear beautiful earrings.
薇琪**穿**了耳洞，好配戴漂亮的耳環。

19 brace [bres] *vt.* 使防備 & *n.* 牙套 (恆用複數)

片 brace oneself for sth
使自己準備好接受 (不好的事)

延伸 bucktooth [ˋbʌkˌtuθ] *n.* 暴牙

▶ The passengers were told to brace themselves for a crash landing.
乘客被告知要**準備**緊急迫降。

▶ My younger sister has to wear braces on her teeth.
我妹妹得戴**牙套**。

1520-1526

20 chairperson [ˋtʃɛr,pɝsn̩] *n.* 主席 (= chair = chairman [ˋtʃɛrmən] 或 chairwoman [ˋtʃɛr,wumən])

衍 chair [tʃɛr] *vt.* 主持 (會議等) & *n.* 主席；椅子 ①

▸ Peter was unanimously elected as chairperson of the committee.
彼得獲得全體一致投票通過，獲選為委員會主席。
*unanimously [juˋnænəməslɪ] *adv.* 全體一致地

21 monstrous [ˋmɑnstrəs] *a.* 可怕的

衍 monster [ˋmɑnstɚ] *n.* 怪物 ③

▸ The monstrous fire burned the whole building to the ground.
可怕的大火焚毀了整棟大樓。

22 reap [rip] *vt.* 收割；獲得 (好處、利益)

似 harvest [ˋhɑrvɪst] *vt.* & *vi.* & *n.* 收成 ③

▸ It's usually autumn when farmers begin to reap their harvest.
通常秋天是農夫開始收成的季節。

▸ It was Luke again who reaped all the profits while we did all the hard work.
又是路克獲得好處，而我們卻得做所有困難的活。

▸ They that sow in tears shall reap in joy.
辛勤工作方能歡樂收成。/ 先苦後甘。—— 諺語

23 finite [ˋfaɪnaɪt] *a.* 有限的

似 limited [ˋlɪmɪtɪd] *a.* 有限的
反 infinite [ˋɪnfənɪt] *a.* 無限的 ⑤

▸ It's worrying that the earth's finite resources are being exploited at an alarming rate.
地球上有限的資源正以驚人的速度被開發利用，這點令人很擔憂。
*alarming [əˋlɑrmɪŋ] *a.* 驚人的，令人擔憂的
at an alarming rate　以驚人的速度

24 puff [pʌf] *vi.* 喘氣 & *vt.* & *vi.* 抽 (菸) & *n.* 抽菸；一陣 (風或煙)；泡芙

片 (1) puff (on) a cigarette　抽菸
= smoke a cigarette
(2) take a puff　吸口菸
(3) in a puff of smoke　一陣煙之中

似 (1) gasp [gæsp] *vi.* 喘氣 ⑤
(2) smoke [smok] *vt.* & *vi.* & *n.* 抽菸 ①

▸ Jimmy didn't even puff after the intense game.
在那場激烈的比賽過後，吉米甚至氣都沒有喘一下。

▸ Randy sat in the living room, puffing a cigarette until his wife told him to stop smoking.
蘭迪坐在客廳抽菸，直到妻子告訴他不要抽菸了。

▸ If you want to puff on your cigarette, you need to go outside.
如果你想抽菸，就必須去外面。

▸ The old man slowly took a puff and then began to tell us his story.
那老人慢慢地吸了一口菸，然後開始告訴我們他的故事。

▸ The magician disappeared in a puff of smoke.
那魔術師消失在一陣煙之中。

▸ One of Steve's favorite snacks is cream puffs.
史提夫最喜歡吃的點心之一就是奶油泡芙。

25 shriek [ʃrik] *vi.* & *n.* 尖叫

片 let out a shriek
尖叫了一聲，發出一聲尖叫聲

似 scream [skrim] *vi.* & *n.* 尖叫 ③

▸ Betty shrieked when she saw a shadow move behind her bedroom door.
貝蒂看到一個影子從她臥房門後移動時，嚇得尖叫出聲。

▸ Wendy let out a shriek when her little brother tapped her on the back.
溫蒂的弟弟從背後拍她時，她嚇得尖叫了一聲。
*tap [tæp] *vt.* 輕拍

26 overdo [ˌovɚˋdu] *vt.* 超過

三 overdo, overdid [ˌovɚˋdɪd], overdone [ˌovɚˋdʌn]

片 overdo it 做某事做得太過分

▸ Adding imaginative illustrations will help liven this book up, but don't overdo it.
在這本書裡加入富想像力的插畫可以讓書看起來更有趣，但可不要加過頭。
*illustration [ˌɪləsˋtreʃən] *n.* 插圖
liven [ˋlaɪvən] *vt.* 使活潑
liven sth up 使某物看起來更有趣，使某物活潑起來

overflow [ˌovɚˋflo] *vi.* & *vt.* 溢出 & *vi.* 充滿，洋溢 & [ˋovɚˌflo] *n.* 容納不下的東西 / 人

片 overflow with... 滿溢著……
= brim with...
= be filled with...
= be full of...

▸ The river overflowed because of the heavy rainfall all week.
因為整星期下大雨，所以這條河的水就溢出來了。

▸ Not paying attention, Yolanda poured so much orange juice into the cup that it overflowed the edge.
尤蘭達並沒注意到，結果她往杯裡倒了太多的柳橙汁溢了出來了。

▸ When Amy heard of the death of her father, her eyes overflowed with tears.
當艾美得知父親過世時，她的眼中充滿了淚水。

▸ I put a bucket underneath the water tank to catch the overflow.
我在水槽底下擺了一個水桶來裝溢出來的水。

overwork [ˏovɚˋwɝk]
n. & *vi.* 工作過度

似 overtime [ˋovɚˏtaɪm] *n.* 加班；加班時數 & *adv.* 加班
work overtime　加班工作

▸ Overwork will decrease work efficiency.
工作過度會降低工作效率。

▸ Jimmy has been overworking for a while since one of his colleagues left.
因為一名同事離職的關係，吉米已經**加班**好一陣子了。

overhear [ˏovɚˋhɪr] *vt.* 無意中聽到

三 overhear, overheard [ˏovɚˋhɝd], overheard

比 eavesdrop [ˋivzˏdrɑp] *vi.* 竊聽（與介詞 on 並用）

▸ I overheard a couple next to me saying that they didn't like the meal.
我**無意間聽到**坐我隔壁的那對情侶說他們不喜歡這裡的食物。

27 wholesale [ˋholˏsel] *n.* 批發（價）& *a.* 批發的 & *adv.* 批發地 & *vt.* 批發（貨物）

片 at wholesale　以批發價

衍 wholesaler [ˋholˏselɚ] *n.* 批發商

反 retail [ˋritel] *n.* & *vt.* & *vi.* 零售 & *a.* 零售的 ⑤
retailer [ˋritelɚ] *n.* 零售商

▸ We buy plain T-shirts at wholesale, add some decorations to them, and then sell at retail prices.
我們**以批發價**買進素色 T 恤，加上一些裝飾後再以零售價賣出。

▸ Wholesale prices of roses increased by 20 percent before Valentine's Day.
情人節之前，玫瑰花的**批發價格**上漲了 20%。

▸ The farmer sells his produce wholesale to supermarkets, but he also runs a stall of his own.
這農民把他的農產品**批發**給超市，但他也有經營自己的攤位。
*produce [ˋprɑd(j)us] *n.* 農產品

▸ The supplier only wholesales computers and other related items to other companies; he doesn't sell directly to the public at all.
此供應商只向其他公司**批發**電腦及其他相關產品；他並不直接向大眾銷售產品。

28 mortal [ˋmɔrtḷ] *a.* 凡人的；嚴重的，致命的 & *n.* 凡人

片 (1) a mortal man　凡人
(2) a mortal blow / wound to...　對……是致命的一擊
(3) a mortal enemy　不共戴天的仇敵，死敵

衍 (1) mortality [mɔrˋtælətɪ] *n.* 必死 ⑤
mortality rate　死亡率
(2) immortality [ˏɪmɔrˋtælətɪ] *n.* 不朽

▸ Greek mythology is about the gods living on Mt. Olympus and their interactions with mortal men.
希臘神話是關於居住在奧林帕司山上的神祇與**凡人**之間的來往互動。
*mythology [mɪˋθɑlədʒɪ] *n.* 神話（集合名詞，不可數）

▸ Losing the contract was a mortal blow to our company.
失去該合約**對**我們公司**是一大打擊**。

▸ The scientist had a sudden heart attack just when he was one step away from figuring out the secret of immortality.
該科學家在即將解開**長生不老**祕密的前一刻，突然心臟病發。

似 lethal [ˋliθḷ] *a.* 致命的 ⑥

反 immortal [ɪˋmɔrtḷ] *a.* 不死的；不朽的

▸ I didn't mean to step on Joe's foot, but he stared at me as if I were his mortal enemy.
我並非故意踩到喬的腳，但他瞪我的樣子就好像我是他**不共戴天的仇人**。

▸ Superman is a well-known comic book character that is much more powerful than any mortal.
超人是個很有名的漫畫人物，他比任何一個**凡人**都要強大得多。

29 mound [maʊnd] *n.* (大) 堆 & *vt.* 堆起

片 a mound / heap / pile of sth
一 (大) 堆某物

似 (1) heap [hip] *n.* 一堆 ③
(2) pile [paɪl] *n.* 一堆 ③

▸ I've got mounds of paperwork to do before leaving for lunch.
= I've got piles of paperwork to do before leaving for lunch.
我去吃中餐之前有**很多**文書工作要做。

▸ As the workers dug the deep hole, they mounded the dirt all around the circle of the opening.
當工人挖那個深洞時，他們把泥土**堆**滿在洞口的周圍。

30 resolute [ˋrɛzə͵lut] *a.* 堅決的

片 be resolute in... 堅決……

衍 (1) resolve [rɪˋzɑlv] *vt.* 決心 ④
(2) resolution [͵rɛzəˋluʃən] *n.* 決心 ④
make a resolution to + V
決心要做……

似 determined [dɪˋtɝmɪnd] *a.* 堅決的

▸ Max is resolute in his attempt to break the record for the 100-meter dash.
麥克斯**堅決**想要打破百米短跑的紀錄。
*dash [dæʃ] *n.* 短跑

31 well-being [͵wɛlˋbiɪŋ] *n.* 幸福 (不可數)

片 a sense of well-being 幸福感

似 welfare [ˋwɛl͵fɛr] *n.* 幸福 ④

▸ Walking with his sweetheart in the sunshine gave Tom a sense of well-being.
湯姆和愛人在陽光下漫步，這讓他心中興起一陣**幸福感**。

32 reckless [ˋrɛkləs] *a.* 魯莽的，不負責任的

片 reckless driving 危險駕駛

衍 recklessly [ˋrɛkləslɪ] *adv.* 魯莽地

似 (1) careless [ˋkɛrləs] *a.* 粗心的
(2) irresponsible [͵ɪrɪˋspɑnsəbḷ] *a.* 不負責任的

▸ The reckless driver was pulled out of the car and arrested.
那**魯莽的**駕駛從車裡被拉出來並且被逮捕。

1533-1536

33 ascend [əˋsɛnd] *vi.* & *vt.* 上升 & *vt.* 登上(王位)

片 (1) ascend to... 上升至……
(2) ascend the throne [θron] 登上王位

似 (1) lift [lɪft] *vt.* 向上移動 ②
(2) climb [klaɪm] *vi.* & *vt.* 爬升 ①

反 descend [dɪˋsɛnd] *vi.* 下降 & *vt.* 走下 ⑤

▸ There is a long flight of stairs ascending to the main gate of the cathedral.
有條很長的階梯**向上通往**大教堂的正門。

▸ The air became thinner as we ascended the mountain.
我們**爬上**山時，空氣變得稀薄了起來。

▸ The prince ascended the throne after the death of his father.
王子在父親過世後就**登上了王位**。

34 breadth [brɛdθ] *n.* 寬度；廣泛(性)

片 breadth of... ……很廣，……的廣泛

似 (1) width [wɪdθ] *n.* 寬度 ②
(2) breath [brɛθ] *n.* 呼吸 ③
take a deep breath 深呼吸
catch one's breath 喘口氣，休息一下
can hardly catch one's breath 連喘口氣的時間都沒有，非常忙碌
hold one's breath 閉氣

▸ What is the breadth of this table?
這張桌子**寬**多少？

▸ I was surprised at my grandfather's extraordinary breadth of knowledge.
我對祖父知識的**淵博**感到很驚訝。

35 bypass [ˋbaɪ͵pæs] *n.* (繞過城鎮中心的) 外環路 & *vt.* (道路) 繞過；(為更快實現某事而) 越過，避開

衍 (1) pass [pæs] *vi.* & *vt.* 經過 ①
(2) underpass [ˋʌndɚ͵pæs] *n.* 地下道 ⑥
(3) overpass [ˋovɚ͵pæs] *n.* 天橋

▸ To help improve the traffic situation in the city, the government decided to build a bypass.
政府為了幫助改善此城市的交通狀況，決定修建一條**外環路**。

▸ The new highway will bypass the town entirely, which has some merchants worried they might lose business.
新的公路會完全**繞過**這小鎮，這讓一些商人擔心他們可能會沒有生意。

▸ If you try to bypass your supervisor by talking directly to his superior, it will likely cause problems at work.
如果你試圖**越過**你的上司而直接和他的上司談，這可能會在工作上造成問題。

36 ratify [ˋrætə͵faɪ] *vt.* 正式簽署 / 批准

三 ratify, ratified [ˋrætə͵faɪd], ratified

片 ratify a treaty / agreement 正式簽署條約 / 協定，批准條約 / 協定

▸ It is said that this powerful country is going to ratify a trade agreement with several small countries in the Pacific Ocean.
據說此強國將和太平洋上的幾個小國**正式簽訂**貿易**協定**。

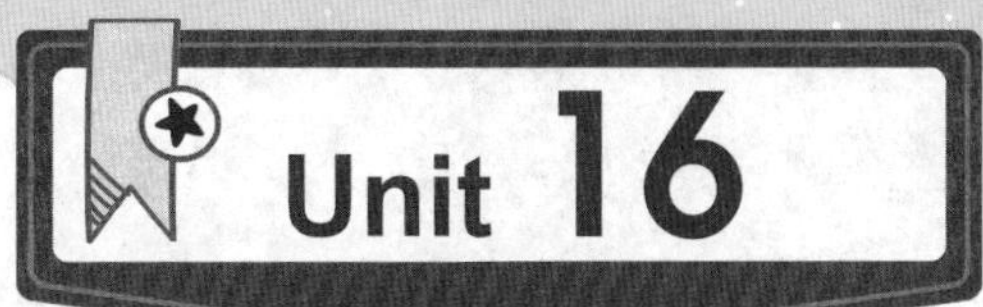

1601-1603

1 brink [brɪŋk] *n.* 邊緣

片 on the brink of... 在……的邊緣
似 edge [ɛdʒ] *n.* 邊緣 ②

▸ Rising antagonism between different ethnic groups in that country has put it on the brink of a civil war.
日益上升的族群對立使該國**處於**內戰爆發**邊緣**。
*antagonism [ænˋtægə,nɪzəm] *n.* 對立

verge [vɝdʒ] *n.* 邊緣
片 be on the verge of... 在……的邊緣
= be on the brink / edge of...

▸ The heavy workload made Tim feel like he was on the verge of a nervous breakdown.
龐大的工作量讓提姆覺得他**在**精神崩潰**邊緣**。

2 divert [daɪˋvɝt / dɪˋvɝt] *vt.* 轉移；轉移注意力

片 (1) divert A into B 將 A 轉移至 B
(2) divert (one's) attention from... 將（某人）注意力由……移轉開來
似 distract [dɪˋstrækt] *vt.* 使分心 ⑤

▸ The top management decided to divert more money into new product development.
管理高層決定**將**更多的錢**轉用在**新產品研發上。

▸ The psychiatrist asked me to divert my attention from work for the moment, saying that it would be good for my health.
精神科醫師要我現階段先**將**注意力**從**工作上**轉移開來**，說這樣對我的健康比較好。

diversion [daɪˋvɝʒən / dɪˋvɝʒən]
n. 分散注意力的事物；消遣，娛樂
衍 (1) diverse [daɪˋvɝs / dɪˋvɝs] *a.* 多元的 ④
(2) diversity [daɪˋvɝsətɪ / dɪˋvɝsətɪ] *n.* 多元性 ④
(3) diversify [daɪˋvɝsə,faɪ / dɪˋvɝsə,faɪ] *vt.* 多元化 ⑥
似 (1) distraction [dɪˋstrækʃən] *n.* 分散注意力的事物；消遣，娛樂 ⑥
(2) pastime [ˋpæs,taɪm] *n.* 消遣 ⑥

▸ The dog Tom brought in created a diversion for everyone in the office.
湯姆帶來的狗讓辦公室裡的每個人都**分**了**心**。

▸ Playing golf is one of my favorite diversions.
高爾夫球是我最喜愛的**消遣**之一。

3 overlap [,ovɚˋlæp] *vi.* & *vt.* 重疊；部分相同 & [ˋovɚ,læp] *n.* 重疊部分

三 overlap, overlapped [,ovɚˋlæpt], overlapped
片 overlap with... 與……部分相同
衍 overlapping [,ovɚˋlæpɪŋ] *a.* 重疊的

▸ Because Toby's two front teeth overlapped a little bit, he wanted to go to see an orthodontist to straighten them.
因為托比的兩顆門牙有點**重疊**到，所以他想去看牙齒矯正醫生來把這兩顆門牙弄直。
*orthodontist [,ɔrθəˋdɑntɪst] *n.* 牙齒科矯正醫生

▸ The tree has grown so much that some of its branches now overlap the neighbor's backyard.
這棵樹長得很茂盛，茂盛到它的一些樹枝現在已經**覆蓋**到鄰居的後院了。

▸ Terry's views on this book overlapped with mine.
泰瑞對這本書的意見**部分跟**我**相同**。

▸ That professor's research fields overlap Professor Johnson's.
那教授研究的領域與詹森教授研究的領域有**部分相同**。

▸ The boss was concerned that there was some overlap in the duties of a few of the employees.
老闆擔心一些員工的職責有**重疊**。

4 yearn [jɝn] *vi.* 渴望；懷念

片 (1) yearn to + V　渴望做……
= long to + V
= desire to + V
= crave to + V
(2) yearn for sth　渴望得到某物
= long for sth
= crave (for) sth

▸ When Sam was 18, he yearned to leave home and live by himself.
山姆 18 歲的時候便**渴望**離開家，自己一個人生活。

▸ William yearns for the peace and quietness that a rural life can offer.
威廉**渴望**鄉村生活能帶來的安寧和平靜。

yearning [ˋjɝnɪŋ] *n.* 渴望，嚮往

片 have a yearning for + N / to + V
對……熱切渴望
= have a desire for + N / to + V
= have a craving for + N / to + V
= have a longing for + N / to + V

▸ Rita has a yearning for a career in show business.
瑞塔**渴望**能從事演藝事業。

▸ Maggie has a strong yearning to become a fashion model.
瑪姬極**渴望**能當時裝模特兒。

5 modernize [ˋmadɚn͵aɪz] *vt.* & *vi.* 使現代化

衍 modern [ˋmadɚn] *a.* 現代的 ①
似 (1) upgrade [ʌpˋgred] *vt.* 升級 ⑤
(2) renovate [ˋrɛnə͵vet] *vt.* 翻新

▸ The school administration has decided to modernize all the student dormitories this summer.
學校管理部門決定這個夏天將所有學生宿舍**現代化**。

▸ The government saw the need to modernize after a series of economic breakdowns.
在一連串的經濟挫敗之後，政府體認到**現代化**的必要性。
*breakdown [ˋbrek͵daʊn] *n.* 失敗

modernization [͵madɚnəˋzeʃən] *n.* 現代化

▸ The modernization of the railway system took the country almost ten years.
該國花了大約十年的時間進行鐵路系統**現代化**。

6 predecessor [ˋprɛdə͵sɛsɚ] *n.* 前輩

反 successor [səkˋsɛsɚ] *n.* 繼任者 ⑤

▸ Rose learned a lot of useful things from her predecessor.
蘿絲從她**前輩**身上學到了很多有用的東西。

7 offspring [ˋɔf͵sprɪŋ] *n.* 後代，子孫

複 單複數同形

似 descendant [dɪˋsɛndənt] *n.* 後代，後裔（可數）

▸ The old couple didn't have any offspring.
這對老夫婦沒有任何**子孫**。

▸ For the well-being of our offspring, we must do the best we can to protect our environment.
為了**子孫**的福祉，我們應盡全力保護我們的環境。
*well-being [͵wɛlˋbiɪŋ] *n.* 幸福

8 indignant [ɪnˋdɪgnənt] *a.* 憤慨的

片 be indignant about / at...
對……感到憤怒
= be angry about / at...

衍 indignation [͵ɪndɪgˋneʃən] *n.* 憤怒

似 (1) angry [ˋæŋgrɪ] *a.* 生氣的 ①
(2) furious [ˋfjʊrɪəs] *a.* 怒不可抑的 ④

▸ Mary was indignant about the discrimination she suffered in the office and decided to make a complaint to her boss.
瑪麗**對**於在辦公室所受的歧視**大感憤慨**，決定向老闆投訴。
*discrimination [dɪ͵skrɪməˋneʃən] *n.* 歧視
make a complaint to sb　向某人投訴

9 harass [həˋræs] *vt.* 騷擾

片 sexually harass sb　對某人性騷擾

▸ Nora angrily told the boss that she was sexually harassed by her supervisor Frank yesterday.
諾拉憤怒地告訴老闆，昨天她的上司法蘭克**性騷擾**她。

harassment [həˋræsmənt] *n.* 騷擾（不可數）

片 sexual harassment　性騷擾

▸ In the workplace, women are much more prone to sexual harassment than men.
在職場上，女性比男性更容易被**性騷擾**。
*be prone to sth　易於遭受某事物之害

10 scenic [ˋsinɪk] *a.* 風景優美的

衍 (1) scene [sin] *n.* 場面；景象 ②
(2) scenery [ˋsinərɪ] *n.* 風景（集合名詞，不可數）④

▸ Doug's home was in a scenic location near a lake, with a great view of the beautiful mountains.
道格的家在湖邊**風景秀麗的**地方，可欣賞美麗的山景。

11 disable [dɪsˋebḷ] *vt.* 使喪失能力，使殘廢；使 (機器) 無法使用

衍 able [ˋebḷ] *a.* 能 ①
be able to + V　能夠做……

反 enable [ɪnˋebḷ] *vt.* 使能夠 ③
enable sb to + V　使某人能夠做……

▸ Although the accident left Cindy disabled and confined to a wheelchair for the rest of her life, she is still very optimistic about the future.
雖然那起意外讓辛蒂身體不良於行且後半生都得在輪椅上度過，但她對未來仍非常樂觀。
*be confined to...　被限制在……

▸ The thief got caught when he was trying to disable the car alarm.
那小偷試圖解除汽車警報器時被逮個正著。

disabled [dɪsˋebḷd] *a.* 殘障的

片 the disabled　行動不便人士

似 handicapped [ˋhændɪ,kæpt] *a.* 殘障的
*現今多以 people with disabilities 代替 physically challenged、the handicapped 或 the disabled。

▸ Many public facilities here don't have proper access for the disabled.
這邊很多公共設施都沒有適合行動不便的人所使用的通道。

disability [,dɪsəˋbɪlətɪ] *n.* 障礙

反 ability [əˋbɪlətɪ] *n.* 能力 ①

▸ I was surprised to know that the accomplished scholar suffered from severe learning disability as a child.
得知那位傑出的學者小時候曾有嚴重的學習障礙時，我很驚訝。
*accomplished [əˋkɑmplɪʃt] *a.* 很有成就的

12 propel [prəˋpɛl] *vt.* 推動，推進

三 propel, propelled [prəˋpɛld], propelled

衍 propeller [prəˋpɛlɚ] *n.* 螺旋槳

似 push [pʊʃ] *vt.* 推 ①

▸ This state-of-the-art sports car is propelled purely by solar energy.
這輛最先進的跑車完全由太陽能所驅動。
*state-of-the-art [,stetəvðiˋɑrt] *a.* 十分先進的

13 ironic [aɪˋrɑnɪk] *a.* 諷刺的

衍 (1) irony [ˋaɪrənɪ] *n.* 諷刺 (不可數) ⑤
(2) ironically [aɪˋrɑnɪklɪ] *adv.* 諷刺地，說來可笑的是

▸ Ironically, that lifeguard cannot swim.
可笑的是，那名救生員不會游泳。

似 sarcastic [sɑrˋkæstɪk] *a.* 諷刺的

▸ I found it rather ironic when the author of the best-selling guidebook to Japan admitted that he had never set foot in that country.
那位暢銷日本旅遊書的作者竟承認他從沒去過日本，我覺得這可真諷刺。

14 hail [hel] *vt.* 讚揚；招呼，呼叫 & *n.* 冰雹

片 (1) hail A as B　將 A 譽為 B
(2) hail a cab / taxi　叫計程車

似 hell [hɛl] *a.* 地獄（字首也可大寫）③

▶ Albert Einstein was hailed as one of the most distinguished scientists in the twentieth century.
阿爾伯特．愛因斯坦被譽為是 20 世紀最傑出的科學家之一。

▶ I hailed Susan from across the street, but apparently she didn't notice me.
我從對街向蘇珊打了聲招呼，但是她似乎沒注意到我。

▶ I think it's going to take ages for the bus to come. Let's hail a cab, shall we?
我想巴士還要等很久才會來。我們叫計程車如何？

▶ Because of the hail, I have three dents on the roof of my car.
由於下冰雹，我的車頂上有三個凹痕。
*dent [dɛnt] *n.* 凹痕 / 陷

15 aspire [ə'spaɪr] *vi.* 渴望，嚮往

片 (1) aspire to + V　渴望做……
(2) aspire to sth　渴望獲得某物
(3) aspire after sth　追求某物

衍 aspiration [ˌæspə'reʃən] *n.* 抱負，志向

似 yearn [jɝn] *vi.* 渴望 ⑥

▶ Mike has aspired to be a scientist since he was a child.
麥可小時候就立志當個科學家。

▶ Lucy used to aspire to a career in the entertainment business, but she ended up becoming a scholar.
露西曾經渴望在娛樂圈發展，但她後來卻變成了一名學者。

▶ All his life, Mr. Wilson aspired after fame and wealth.
威爾遜先生窮其一生都在追求名利。

16 chant [tʃænt] *vi.* & *vt.* 反覆呼喊；吟誦，念（經）& *n.* 不斷重覆的話；（反覆吟誦的）禱文

片 chant a sutra　唸經，誦經
*sutra ['sutrə] *n.* 佛經

▶ As they marched towards the government offices to show their anger at recent decisions, the protesters began to chant loudly.
抗議人士遊行到政府辦公室以示對最近的決定感到憤怒時，他們開始大聲反覆呼喊。

▶ As the president went into the building, his loyal followers chanted, "We support you!"
當總統走進大樓時，他的忠實追隨者一再高呼：『我們支持你！』

▶ During the service in the church, which lasted two hours, people prayed and chanted.
在為期兩小時的教堂儀式上，人們祈禱並吟誦。

▶ The monks chant sutras every morning.
這些和尚每天早上都會唸經。

▸ To show they opposed the Vietnam War, some Americans repeated the chant, "We won't go!" meaning they wouldn't fight.
一些美國人為了表明他們反對越戰，他們**反覆不停地喊**：『我們不會去！』這意味著他們不會去打仗。

▸ The Muslim chants could be heard over speakers in the Middle Eastern town every day at certain times.
在中東小鎮上，每天特定的時間都會在擴音器上聽到穆斯林的**禱文**。

17 reckon [ˋrɛkən] *vt.* & *vi.* 認為，覺得 & *vt.* 計算

片 (1) reckon (that)... 認為 / 覺得……
(2) be reckoned to be...
被認為是……
= be considered / thought to be...
(3) What do you reckon?
你覺得 / 認為呢？(即問對方是否同意)
(4) reckon sth up 算出某物的總數

似 (1) think [θɪŋk] *vt.* & *vi.* 認為 ①
(2) consider [kənˋsɪdɚ] *vt.* & *vi.* 認為 ②

▸ Paul reckoned that he had been fooled and ripped off by the salesperson.
保羅**覺得**他被那推銷員愚弄而且狠敲了一筆。

▸ Mike is reckoned to be the best carpenter in town.
= Mike is considered / thought to be the best carpenter in town.
麥可**被認為是**鎮上最棒的木匠。

▸ I think Amanda wasn't telling the truth. What do you reckon?
我認為亞曼達沒有說實話。**你覺得呢**？

▸ The total amount of money you owe, including interest, is reckoned to be 15 grand.
你欠我的錢加上利息，經過**計算**是 15,000 美元。

▸ Susan reckoned the bill up and noticed that the cashier had given her the wrong change.
蘇珊**把**帳單**金額加起來**後發現收銀員找錯錢了。

18 anchor [ˋæŋkɚ] *n.* 錨；(電視或廣播新聞節目的) 主播；支柱，靠山 & *vi.* & *vt.* 下錨停船

片 drop anchor 下錨

衍 anchorage [ˋæŋkərɪdʒ] *n.* (船隻) 停泊處

似 anchorperson [ˋæŋkɚ͵pɝsn̩] *n.* 主播
= anchorman [ˋæŋkɚ͵mæn]
或 anchorwoman [ˋæŋkɚ͵wʊmən]

▸ The captain ordered us to drop anchor and prepare to land.
船長命令我們**下錨**準備登陸。

▸ Ron and Vicky are the anchors of a nightly news program.
朗恩和薇琪是晚間新聞的**主播**。

▸ Mary's son has been her anchor since her husband died.
瑪麗自從老公過世後，她兒子就成了她的**精神支柱**。

▸ The captain of the fishing boat anchored off the coast of Greece, telling his staff to take a rest.
這漁船的船長在希臘海岸附近**下錨停船**，告訴他的船員去休息一下。

▸ The ship will have to be anchored here due to the coming storm.
因為有暴風雨要來，船得要在此**停泊**。

wharf [(h)wɔrf] *n.* 碼頭

▸ Fisherman's Wharf is one of the most famous tourist attractions in San Francisco.
漁人**碼頭**是舊金山最著名的景點之一。

19 twinkle [ˋtwɪŋkḷ] *vi.* & *n.* 閃爍，發光

片 (1) twinkle with joy / delight
(眼睛) 散發出喜悅的光芒
(2) a twinkle in one's eye
某人眼中流露出的喜悅光芒

似 (1) glitter [ˋglɪtɚ] *vi.* & *n.* 閃耀 ⑥
(2) gleam [glim] *vi.* & *n.* 閃爍 ⑥
(3) glisten [ˋglɪsṇ] *vi.* 閃耀

▸ My girlfriend's eyes twinkle like the stars in the sky.
我女友的眼睛像天上的星星**閃爍發光**。

▸ Judy's eyes twinkled with joy when she saw her boyfriend.
茱蒂看到男友時兩眼**流露出喜悅的光芒**。

▸ I like Kate because she is smiling and there is always a twinkle in her eye.
我喜歡凱特，因為她總是笑臉迎人，**眼神總是流露出開心的光芒**。

20 cracker [ˋkrækɚ] *n.* (鹹) 餅乾

似 cookie [ˋkʊkɪ] *n.* (甜) 餅乾〔美〕①
= biscuit [ˋbɪskɪt]〔英〕②

▸ Danny likes to eat crackers with cheese.
丹尼喜歡吃**鹹餅乾**配起司。

21 crutch [krʌtʃ] *n.* 拐杖

片 be on crutches　拄著柺杖

似 crunch [krʌntʃ] *vi.* 嘎吱地咬 / 走過 & *n.* (食物或東西碎裂) 嘎吱聲

▸ Billy broke his leg in a motorbike accident and has been on crutches for the past few months.
比利在一場機車車禍中摔斷了腿，因此他過去幾個月都得**拄著柺杖**。

22 shrub [ʃrʌb] *n.* 灌木，矮樹

似 bush [bʊʃ] *n.* 灌木 ③

▸ We planted some roses and some shrubs in our backyard.
我們在後院種了一些玫瑰花和**小樹叢**。

23 healthful [ˋhɛlθfəl] *a.* 有益健康的

衍 (1) health [hɛlθ] *n.* 健康 ①
be in good / poor health
身體很好 / 差
(2) healthy [ˋhɛlθɪ] *a.* 健康的；有益健康的 ①
healthy food　健康食品

▸ Regular exercise is healthful to your body.
規律的運動**有益身體健康**。

wholesome [ˋholsəm] *a.* 健康的，有益健康的

▸ A good vacation every now and then is important to a wholesome life.
偶爾好好度個假對**健康的**生活很重要。

24 mow [mo] *vt.* 割（草）

片 mow a lawn　剪草坪
⋆lawn [lɔn] *n.* 草坪 / 地

▸ My brother is responsible for mowing the lawn.
我哥哥負責**剪草坪**。

25 cub [kʌb] *n.*（熊、獅、虎等的）幼獸

▸ It is common for bears to have two cubs.
熊通常會生兩隻**幼熊**。

26 stepchild [ˋstɛpˏtʃaɪld] *n.* 繼子 / 女

複 stepchildren [ˋstɛpˏtʃɪldrən]
比 an adopted child　養子 / 女
⋆adopted [əˋdɑptɪd] *a.* 被領養的

▸ Although Jason is her stepchild, Lydia loves him very much and takes good care of him.
雖然傑森是莉迪亞的**繼子**，但莉迪亞非常愛他，而且很照顧他。

stepfather [ˋstɛpˏfɑðɚ] *n.* 繼父

比 an adoptive father　養父
⋆adoptive [əˋdɑptɪv] *a.* 領養（人）的

▸ I still call my stepfather by his name.
我還是以我**繼父**的名字來稱呼他。

stepmother [ˋstɛpˏmʌðɚ] *n.* 繼母

比 an adoptive mother　養母

▸ Cinderella has a mean stepmother and two stepsisters, all of whom are jealous of her.
灰姑娘有一個心腸險惡的**繼母**和兩個同父異母的姐姐，她們都很忌妒她。

27 reef [rif] *n.* 礁

片 (1) a coral reef　珊瑚礁
(2) Great Barrier Reef　大堡礁（位於澳洲）

▸ There is a huge coral reef not far from the coast.
距離海岸不遠處有一大片**珊瑚礁**。

28 muse [mjuz] *vi.* 沉思 & *n.* 靈感（來源）

片 muse about / on sth　沉思某事
似 ponder [ˋpɑndɚ] *vi.* 仔細考慮 ⑥

▸ I sat alone on the sofa, musing about the possibility of starting my own business.
我獨自坐在沙發上，**沉思**著自行創業的可能性。

▸ The poet told the reporter that his muse was his girlfriend, who inspired him to write great works.
這詩人告訴記者，他的**靈感來源**是他的女友，他女友激發他寫出了很棒的作品。

29 tuck [tʌk] *vt.* 把……塞入

片 tuck A into B　把 A 塞入／進 B 中

似 truck [trʌk] *n.* 卡車，貨車 & *vt.* 用卡／貨車裝運 ①

▸ The material was delivered hundreds of miles by train before being trucked to customers in various parts of the state.

此材料用火車運送了數百英里之後，再**用卡車運送**到該州各地的客戶手中。

▸ Ashley asked her son to tuck his shirt into his pants before he left for school.

艾希莉要她兒子去學校前**把**襯衫**塞進**褲子裡。

30 endowment [ɪnˋdaumənt] *n.* 捐款，資助；天賦（皆可數）

衍 endow [ɪnˋdau] *vt.* 捐款，資助

▸ The rich man left a large endowment worth millions of dollars to the university in his will.

這位有錢人在遺囑中留下了價值數百萬美元的鉅額**捐款**給那所大學。

*in one's will　在某人的遺囑中

▸ Among Britney's many artistic endowments were singing, acting, dancing, and painting

在布蘭妮的眾多藝術**天賦**中，就包括唱歌、表演、舞蹈和繪畫。

31 cellular [ˋsɛljələ˞] *a.* 細胞的

片 cellular phone　手機〔美〕

= cellphone〔美〕①

= mobile [ˋmobil / ˋmobaɪl] phone〔英〕

衍 cell [sɛl] *n.* 細胞 ②

▸ The doctor was worried that the disease had already done much cellular damage to the patient.

醫生擔心這種疾病已經對病患造成了很多**細胞**損傷。

▸ Modern cellular phones are called smartphones because they have computing power that allows them to perform many functions.

現代**手機**被稱為智慧型手機，因為它們具有計算機處理能力，可以執行很多功能。

32 dividend [ˋdɪvə͵dɛnd] *n.* 紅利，股利（可數）

衍 divide [dɪˋvaɪd] *vi.* & *vt.* (使) 分開 & *n.* 分歧 ②

▸ Because the company had a poor year, it was not able to give dividends to investors.

該公司由於今年業績不佳，無法給投資者**分紅**。

Unit 17

1701-1709

1 hygiene [ˋhaɪdʒin] *n.* 衛生(不可數)

片 (1) personal hygiene　個人衛生
(2) a hygiene standard　衛生標準

衍 hygienic [haɪˋdʒɛnɪk / haɪˋdʒinɪk] *a.* 衛生的

▸ Tim's personal hygiene is terrible. He seldom brushes his teeth and never likes to take a shower.
提姆的**個人衛生**很糟糕。他很少刷牙，也不喜歡洗澡。

▸ Weak food hygiene standards were the main reasons for the restaurant's closure.
食物**衛生標準**很差是這家餐廳關門大吉的主因。

sanitation [ˌsænəˋteʃən] *n.* 公共衛生系統(不可數)

衍 sanitary [ˋsænətɛrɪ] *a.* 衛生的

▸ Poor sanitation is a widespread problem in this country.
公衛系統很差在此國是個普遍存在的問題。

2 trek [trɛk] *n.* & *vi.* 長途跋涉

三 trek [trɛk], trekked [trɛkt], trekked

似 hike [haɪk] *n.* & *vi.* 遠足，健行 ②

▸ It's a bit of a trek from here to the train station.
從這兒**走**到火車站有一小段**路**。

▸ It took the hiking team 9 hours to trek across the forest.
這支健行隊花了 9 小時才**走**出這座森林。

3 solidarity [sɑləˋdærətɪ] *n.* 團結

片 show / express one's solidarity with sb　展現與某人團結一致的心意

▸ The politician joined the strike to show his solidarity with the protesters.
該政治人物加入罷工，以**展現與**抗議者**團結一致的心意**。

4 momentum [moˋmɛntəm] *n.* 動力，衝勁；(物理學) 動能(皆不可數)

片 gain / gather momentum
取得氣勢；獲得動能

▸ The petition against the housing development at the historical site has gained momentum, as several famous stars have strongly supported the petition in public.
反對在此歷史遺跡上蓋住宅區的請願**勢頭強勁**，因為有幾位知名的明星大力公開支持此請願。

▸ The car gained momentum as it went downhill.
車往下坡開時**獲得動能**。

5 refine [rɪˋfaɪn] *vt.* 提煉；改良

片 refine oil / sugar　提煉石油 / 糖

衍 (1) refined [rɪˋfaɪnd] *a.* 精煉 / 製的
(2) refinery [rɪˋfaɪnərɪ] *n.* 提煉廠

▸ The country refined 3 million barrels of crude oil every year to make plastic bags.
該國每年**提煉** 3 百萬桶原油來製造塑膠袋。

▸ We refined our working process for better efficiency.
為了更有效率，我們**改善**了工作的步驟。

refinement [rɪˋfaɪnmənt] *n.* 改良；改良品

片 a refinement of sth　某物的改良品

▸ It seems that our plan still needs some refinements, since the boss' brow kept wrinkling when he was reading our plan.
看來我們的計畫還需要一些**改進**，因為老闆在讀我們的計畫時眉頭一直皺著。

▸ This version of the plan is a refinement of the one that Joey brought in to the meeting last week.
這個版本的計畫是依喬伊上週在會議提出的計畫**所改良而成的**。

6 reliance [rɪˋlaɪəns] *n.* 依賴 (與介詞 on 並用)

片 place too much reliance on sth
過分信賴某物

衍 (1) rely [rɪˋlaɪ] *vi.* 依賴 ③
rely on...　依靠……
= depend on...
= count on...
(2) reliant [rɪˋlaɪənt] *a.* 信賴的；依賴的 ⑥
be reliant on...　依賴……

▸ Economists predict that over the next five years, this country will increase its reliance on renewable energy to 33%.
經濟學家預測，未來 5 年此國家**對**可再生能源**的仰賴**程度將增加到 33%。

▸ The reporter knew he shouldn't place too much reliance on his memory and that he should always check the facts.
這記者知道他不應該**太相信**自己的記憶，也知道他應要一直查核事實。

7 coalition [ˏkoəˋlɪʃən] *n.* 聯合

片 in coalition with sb　與某人聯合

似 ally [ˋælaɪ] *n.* 同盟國 ⑤

▸ The political party has been trying to work in coalition with other parties.
此政黨一直以來都試著要**聯合**其他政黨。

8 layman [ˋlemən] *n.* 門外漢 (= layperson [ˋleˏpɝsn̩])

複 laymen [ˋlemən]

片 in layman's terms　用簡單淺顯的語言表達

反 expert [ˋɛkspɝt] *n.* 專家 ②

▸ Lucy asked the doctor to explain her condition in layman's terms.
露西請醫生**用淺白的話**來解釋她的病情。

9 sociology [ˏsoʃɪˋɑlədʒɪ] *n.* 社會學

衍 sociological [ˏsoʃɪəˋlɑdʒɪkl̩]
a. 社會學的

▸ Miss Wang is a professor of sociology and criminology at Stanford University.
王小姐是史丹佛大學的**社會學**及犯罪學教授。
*criminology [ˏkrɪməˋnɑlədʒɪ] *n.* 犯罪學

socialize [ˋsoʃəˏlaɪz] *vi.* 與人交際

片 socialize with sb　與某人交際

▸ Duke wasn't interested in socializing with other classmates.
杜克對要**和**其他同學**交朋友**並不感興趣。

sociable [ˋsoʃəbl̩] *a.* 擅交際的

反 unsociable [ʌnˋsoʃəbl̩] *a.* 不擅交際的

▸ Bonnie and Tom are the most sociable couple I know.
邦妮和湯姆是我認識的人之中，最擅長交際的一對情侶。

10 potent [ˋpotn̩t] *a.* (藥物) 強效的

片 a potent drug　強效藥品

衍 potency [ˋpotn̩sɪ] *n.* 影響力；藥效

▸ For years, Luke has been taking a potent drug that makes his heart beat regularly.
好幾年來路克一直在服用強效藥品，以讓心臟正常跳動。

11 subordinate [səˋbɔrdn̩ət] *n.* 部屬 & *a.* 次要的 & [səˋbɔrdn̩et] *vt.* 使居次要地位

片 (1) be subordinate to sb/sth
次要於某人 / 某物
(2) subordinate A to B
將 B 的優先次序置於 A 之上

▸ Tanya has a good relationship with her subordinates.
譚雅和她的部屬關係良好。

▸ In the past, women were usually subordinate to men in the workplace.
過去女性在職場上的位階通常低於男性。

▸ Tiffany has subordinated her dream to her family's expectations.
蒂芬妮把家人對她的期待擺在第一位，自己的夢想則為次要。

12 mastery [ˋmæstərɪ] *n.* 熟練 (不可數)

片 one's mastery of sth　某人熟練某事

衍 master [ˋmæstɚ] *vt.* 精通 ②

▸ Todd's mastery of Spanish enabled him to get this good job.
由於陶德精通西班牙文，所以得到了這份好工作。

13 accessory [ækˋsɛsərɪ] *n.* 附加物件；衣物配件 (皆常用複數) & *a.* 附加的，附屬的

片 fashion accessories　流行 (時尚) 配件

▸ Gina's accessories matched her purple silk gown perfectly.
吉娜的配件和她的紫色絲質禮服極為相襯。

▸ The boutique around the corner sells jewelry and other fashion accessories.
街角那家精品店販售珠寶和其他的流行時尚配件。

▸ Liver, a kind of accessory organ, helps the digestive system work properly, but doesn't get access to food.
肝臟是一種輔助器官，它可以幫助消化系統正常運作，但並沒有接觸到食物。

14 acclaim [əˋklem] *vt.* & *n.* 稱讚 (不可數)

片 (1) be acclaimed for sth
因某事受到讚賞
= be praised for sth

▸ Dr. Smith was widely acclaimed for having published a brilliant academic paper.
史密斯博士因發表了一份優秀的學術報告而廣受讚揚。

(2) receive acclaim 受到讚揚

▸ Though in his late 40s, Alex still receives great acclaim as one of the most dominant pitchers ever.

即使快 50 歲了，艾力克斯依舊廣受讚揚為有史以來最重要的投手之一。

15 accountable [əˋkauntəbl̩] *a.* (對人 / 事) 應負責的

片 (1) be held accountable for sth 應對某事負責

= be held responsible for sth

(2) be accountable to sb 應對某人負責

▸ This student should be held accountable for his role in spreading the fake news.

= This student should be held responsible for his role in spreading the fake news.

這學生應要為自己散播假新聞一事負責。

▸ A school should be accountable to the students who pay tuition to attend it.

學校應對有交學費念書的學生負責。

16 accusation [ˏækjəˋzeʃən] *n.* 控告

片 (1) make an accusation 提出控告

(2) an accusation against sb 控告某人

衍 accuse [əˋkjuz] *vt.* 指控 ④

be accused of sth 因某事遭到指控

▸ Patricia made an accusation against her coworker Simon, saying that he hit her. However, this hasn't been proven yet.

派翠莎控告她同事賽門打了她。但這還沒得到證實。

▸ Mr. Blake's accusation against Mr. Collins was proved false.

布雷克先生對柯林斯先生的控訴被證明是不實的。

17 astray [əˋstre] *adv.* & *a.* 偏離正途地

片 (1) go astray 誤入歧途

(2) lead sb astray 使某人誤入歧途

▸ Tom's younger brother went astray and became a gangster.

湯姆的弟弟誤入歧途而變成了幫派分子。

▸ Adolescents are easily led astray by bad companions.

青少年很容易被壞朋友帶壞。

*adolescent [ædl̩ˋɛsn̩t] *n.* 青少年

18 growl [graul] *vi.* (動物生氣時的) 低吼 & *vi.* & *vt.* (人) 咆哮 & *n.* (動物生氣時的) 低吼；(人) 咆哮

片 growl at... 對著……低吼；對……咆哮

似 snarl [snɑrl] *vi.* & *n.* (動物呲牙裂嘴地發出) 低吼；(人) 咆哮

▸ The dog growled at the mailman and then snapped at his ankle.

這隻狗對郵差發出低吼，接著便朝他腳踝咬了下去。

*snap [snæp] *vi.* 咬 (人)

- My boss growled at me for being late.
  我遲到了，所以老闆**怒罵**我。
- "Don't touch me. Leave me alone," the sad girl growled.
  那悲傷的女孩**咆哮**著：『別碰我。別煩我。』
- Animals such as dogs, tigers, lions, and bears use a growl to express their anger and to threaten.
  狗、老虎、獅子和熊等動物用**咆哮**來表達憤怒和表示威脅。
- The general gave his orders with a growl, staring at his soldiers, all of whom were fearful of him.
  將軍**咆哮**著發號施令，並盯著他的士兵，這些士兵都很怕他。

19 stutter [ˋstʌtɚ] *vi.* & *n.* 結巴

似 stammer [ˋstæmɚ] *vi.* & *n.* 結巴，口吃

- Nelson was often teased at school because he stuttered.
  尼爾森因為講話會**結巴**，在學校常常被取笑。
- The shy young man talked with a slight stutter because of his nervousness.
  這害羞的年輕人因為緊張而講話有一點**結巴**。

20 mustache [ˋmʌstæʃ] *n.* 八字鬍，小鬍子〔美〕(= moustache〔英〕)

片 wear a beard / mustache / goatee 留鬍鬚 / 八字鬍 / 山羊鬍

似 (1) beard [bɪrd] *n.* 下巴及兩耳下方的鬍鬚 ②
(2) goatee [goˋti] *n.* 山羊鬍

- After wearing a mustache for ten years, Dan finally decided to shave it off.
  蓄鬍 10 年後，阿丹終於決定把它剃掉。

21 referee [ˌrɛfəˋri] *n.* (足球、籃球、拳擊等) 裁判 (在比賽中來回走動)

比 umpire [ˋʌmpaɪr] *n.* (棒球等) 裁判 (在比賽中常靜止不動)

- Both teams were happy with the referee's decision.
  兩支隊伍對**裁判**的決定都很滿意。

22 hearty [ˋhɑrtɪ] *a.* 熱情的，興高采烈的；(食物) 豐盛的

片 (1) give sb a hearty welcome 衷心歡迎某人
(2) a hearty breakfast 豐盛的早餐

似 sincere [sɪnˋsɪr] *a.* 誠心的 ③

- The host gave us a hearty welcome when we arrived.
  我們抵達時，主人**衷心歡迎**我們。
- After a hearty breakfast, Brad and his friends set out to climb the mountain.
  吃了**豐盛的早餐**之後，布萊德和他朋友就出發去登山了。

23 shutter [ˋʃʌtɚ] *n.* 百葉門窗（恆用複數）；相機的快門

片 open / close a shutter
打開 / 關上百葉窗

▸ Open the shutters, please. It's so dark in here.
麻煩你把**百葉窗打開**。這裡面很暗。

▸ This camera is completely automatic, which means there is no way to adjust the speed of the shutter by yourself.
這相機是完全自動的，這意味著我們沒辦法自己調整**快門**的速度。

24 cucumber [ˋkjukəmbɚ] *n.* 黃瓜

片 (1) be / remain as cool as a cucumber 十分冷靜
(2) a sea cucumber 海參

▸ I made a salad with smoked chicken and cucumber.
我做了一個燻雞肉加**黃瓜**的沙拉。

▸ The suspect remained as cool as a cucumber during the lie detector test.
在接受測謊時，嫌犯**仍然十分冷靜**。
*detector [dɪˋtɛktɚ] *n.* 偵測器
a lie detector 測謊機

▸ Ricky's friends encouraged him to eat the sea cucumber. However, because he hated seafood, he wouldn't even try it.
瑞奇的朋友鼓勵他吃**海參**。但因為他討厭海鮮，他甚至都不想嚐。

25 hedge [hɛdʒ] *n.* 樹籬笆；屏障，防範措施 & *vt.* 用樹籬笆圍住 & *vi.* 防範 / 備

片 (1) be a hedge against...
是對抗……的屏障 / 防備手段
(2) hedge against... 防範 / 備……

比 fence [fɛns] *n.* (鐵製或木頭製的) 籬笆 ③

▸ Miranda's investments in overseas funds were a hedge against inflation.
米蘭達投資海外基金**是**用來**防範**通貨膨脹的。

▸ The back yard is hedged by evergreen bushes, which don't offer much privacy but look nice.
後院以常綠灌木**圍住**，雖然這些常綠灌木未能提供太多隱私，但卻看起來很漂亮。

▸ As a way of hedging against losses in his investments, Paul buys a variety of stocks, rather than just a single stock.
保羅購買了各種股票，而不是只買單一股票，來作為一種**防範**虧損的方法。

26 statesman [ˋstetsmən] *n.* (尤指受人尊敬的) 政治家

複 statesmen [ˋstetsmən]

似 politician [ˌpɑləˋtɪʃən] *n.* 政客，政治人物 ③

▸ Abraham Lincoln was a great statesman.
亞伯拉罕．林肯是一位偉大的**政治家**。

27 fishery [ˋfɪʃərɪ] *n.* 漁場；漁業

複 fisheries [ˋfɪʃərɪz]

衍 (1) fish [fɪʃ] *n.* 魚 ①

(2) fisherman [ˋfɪʃɚˌmən] *n.* 漁夫 ②

▸ The fishery has been polluted so seriously that many fish species are endangered.

該漁場受到嚴重汙染而使很多魚類瀕臨絕種。

▸ Due to restrictions placed on catching fish, many people involved in the fishery have struggled to make a living.

由於對捕魚所設的限制，許多從事漁業相關的人都很難謀生。

28 underneath [ˌʌndɚˋniθ] *prep.* & *adv.* 在……之下 & *n.* 底部，下面 & *a.* 下面的

似 (1) below [bəˋlo] *prep.* 在……之下 ①

(2) beneath [bɪˋniθ]

prep. 在……之下 ③

▸ Police sent a bomb squad to defuse the bomb underneath the ambassador's car.

警方派遣了一支防爆小組去拆除大使座車底下的一枚炸彈。

*a bomb squad [ˋbɑm ˌskwɑd] 防爆小組

defuse [dɪˋfjuz] *vt.* 拆除（炸彈等）的引信

ambassador [æmˋbæsədɚ] *n.* 大使

▸ Kelly was disgusted when she lifted the log in the garden and saw many worms and cockroaches underneath.

當凱莉抬起花園裡的木頭看到下面有許多蟲和蟑螂時，她覺得很噁心。

▸ In the movie, the gangster had taped a gun to the underneath of the table so he could use it any time.

在這部電影裡，那黑幫成員把槍用膠帶貼在桌子下面，這樣他就可以隨時使用了。

▸ On the underneath part of the ring that Julia's husband bought for her are the words, "To my loving wife."

在茱莉亞的丈夫買給她的戒指下面寫著：『給我親愛的妻子。』

29 nag [næg] *vt.* & *vi.* 嘮叨，不斷抱怨 & *n.* 好嘮叨的人

三 nag, nagged [nægd], nagged

片 (1) nag sb to + V

嘮叨地要某人做……

(2) nag sb about sth 某人嘮叨某事

(3) nag at sb 對某人喋喋不休

衍 nagging [ˋnægɪŋ] *a.* 喋喋不休的，抱怨的 & *n.* 嘮叨；抱怨

▸ The children have been nagging their parents to take them to Disneyland.

小孩們一直喋喋不休地吵著要爸媽帶他們去迪士尼樂園玩。

▸ My girlfriend kept nagging me about my weight, so I decided to go to the gym and work out a bit.

我女友一直批評我的體重，所以我決定去健身房運動一下。

▸ Will you stop nagging at me? I'd really appreciate it if you left me in peace for a moment.

你可以別再對我嘮叨了嗎？如果你能讓我清靜一下，我會真的很感激。

▸ Henry felt reluctant to go home and face his nagging wife.
亨利很不想回家面對他**嘮叨的**太太。

▸ David dumped Alice because he was fed up with her nagging.
大衛甩了愛麗絲，因為他真是受夠她的**嘮叨**了。

▸ Carl considers his mother a big nag, but he loves her despite the fact she often bothers him.
卡爾認為他母親是個**很愛嘮叨的人**，但他很愛他母親，儘管他母親經常來煩他。

30 widow [ˋwɪdo] *n.* 寡婦

▸ The poor widow had to raise 3 children all by herself after her husband died of lung cancer.
丈夫肺癌過世後，那可憐的**寡婦**必須獨自撫養 3 個孩子。

widower [ˋwɪdoɚ] *n.* 鰥夫

▸ After his wife died, the widower moved into the mountains and led a secluded life there.
妻子過世後，那**鰥夫**搬到山中，在那兒過著與世隔絕的生活。
*secluded [səˋkludɪd] *a.* 隔絕的，退隱的

31 terrace [ˋtɛrəs] *n.* 陽臺；梯田 & *vt.* 使……成梯田

似 balcony [ˋbælkənɪ] *n.* 陽臺 ②

延伸 terrace 與 balcony 皆可指『陽臺』，但前者指較寬敞平坦的『露天大陽臺』，後者則為附著在二樓以上公寓外圍的『窄小陽臺』。

▸ After dinner, David and I stood silently on the terrace, watching the starry sky.
晚飯後，大衛和我不發一語站在**陽臺**上，仰望星空。

▸ The black tea is grown on terraces on the side of the mountain, and the leaves are picked regularly.
紅茶生長在這山坡的**梯田**上，都會定期採摘其葉子。

▸ The act of terracing land is an effective way of conserving water for crops.
讓土地**變成梯田**是為作物節約用水的有效方法。

32 bulky [ˋbʌlkɪ] *a.* 笨重的；體型龐大的

似 (1) large [lɑrdʒ] *a.* 大的 ①
(2) huge [hjudʒ] *a.* 龐大的 ②
(3) immense [ɪˋmɛns] *a.* 巨大的 ⑤

▸ I prefer a laptop because a desktop is bulky and difficult to move.
我比較喜歡筆電，因為桌上型電腦既**笨重**又難以搬動。
*laptop [ˋlæp,tɑp] *n.* 筆電，筆記型電腦

▸ My brother is very bulky, while I'm as thin as a stick.
我哥哥**體型龐大**，但我瘦得跟竹竿似的。

33 pending [ˋpɛndɪŋ] *a.* 待決定的 / 處理的；即將發生的

▸ With his court date pending, Trevor was not allowed by law to leave the country for any reason.
由於崔佛的開庭日期**還不確定**，依法他不許以任何理由出國。

▶ In the TV show, the three political commentators were talking about their country's pending election.
在這電視節目中，三位政治評論員正在談論他們國家**即將到來的**選舉。

34 goodwill [gʊdˋwɪl] *n.* 友善

▶ Since Gordon has done many favors for his friends, he has established a lot of goodwill with them.
由於戈登幫了朋友很多忙，所以他們都對他很**友善**。

35 Celsius [ˋsɛlsɪəs] *n.* 攝氏溫度（縮寫為 C）

▶ In summer, the temperature can get as high as nearly 40 degrees Celsius in this area, but in winter it's much colder.
夏天時，這地區的氣溫可能高達**攝氏**近 40 度，但冬天時這裡天氣變得更冷。

Fahrenheit [ˋfærən,haɪt] *n.* 華氏溫度（縮寫為 F）

▶ The temperature this afternoon will rise to about ninety degrees Fahrenheit.
今天下午的溫度會上升到大約**華氏** 90 度。

36 psychiatry [saɪˋkaɪətrɪ] *n.* 精神病學

衍 psychiatrist [saɪˋkaɪətrɪst] *n.* 精神科醫生

▶ Norman studied psychiatry in university and became a famous psychiatrist around the world after he got his PhD.
諾曼在大學是學**精神病學**，並在拿到博士學位後成了一名世界知名的精神科醫生。

psychic [ˋsaɪkɪk] *a.* 精神的；通靈的
(= psychical [ˋsaɪkɪkḷ])

衍 psycho [ˋsaɪko] *n.* 精神失常的人

▶ The doctor told Mrs. Brown that she should deal with her psychic problems, rather than physical ones.
醫生告訴布朗太太，她應該處理她**精神方面**的問題，而不是身體上的問題。

▶ Some people thought the fortune teller had amazing psychic powers, but others thought he was just very good at guessing.
有些人認為這算命先生有驚人的**通靈**能力，但另一些人則認為他只是很會猜而已。

psychotherapy [saɪkoˋθɛrəpɪ] *n.* 心理 / 精神治療

▶ Psychotherapy techniques attempt to help people to deal with their problems and to try to overcome them.
心理治療技術試圖幫助人們處理他們的問題，並試圖克服這些問題。

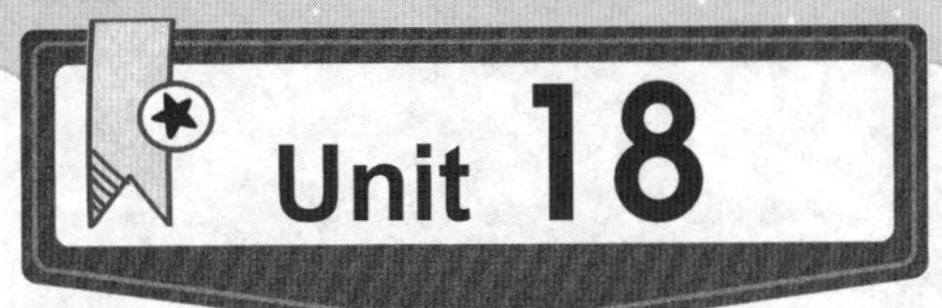

Unit 18

1801-1802

1 brochure [broˋʃur] *n.* 小冊子

片 a travel brochure　旅遊小冊子

似 booklet [ˋbuklət] *n.* 小冊子 ⑥

▸ The beautiful pictures of the Italian countryside in the travel brochure tempted us to go on vacation there.
旅行手冊上義大利鄉下的美麗照片讓我們很想去那裡度假。

pamphlet [ˋpæmflət] *n.* 小冊子

比 leaflet [ˋliflət] *n.* (單頁) 傳單

▸ This is a free pamphlet promoting the importance of conserving energy and resources.
這是一本倡導節約能源與資源重要性的免費手冊。
*conserve [kənˋsɝv] *vt.* 節約使用

2 addiction [əˋdɪkʃən] *n.* 上癮 (與介詞 to 並用)

片 addiction to alcohol　對酒 (精) 上癮

衍 (1) addict [əˋdɪkt] *vt.* 使上癮 (與介詞 to 並用) & [ˋædɪkt] *n.* 上癮的人 ④
(2) addictive [əˋdɪktɪv] *a.* 上癮的

▸ Mark's addiction to alcohol has ruined his career.
馬克的酒癮毀了他的職涯。

eccentric [ɪkˋsɛntrɪk] *a.* 古怪的 & *n.* 古怪的人

似 (1) strange [strendʒ] *a.* 奇怪的 ①
(2) odd [ɑd] *a.* 奇怪的 ③
(3) bizarre [bɪˋzɑr] *a.* 奇異的 ⑤

▸ Nelson's eccentric behavior makes him unpopular with his classmates.
尼爾森怪異的行徑讓他並不受同學歡迎。

▸ Mr. Danforth is an eccentric who rarely talks to anyone and likes to collect the labels from packages.
丹福斯先生是個古怪的人，他很少和任何人交談，而他還喜歡收集包裹上的標籤。

freak [frik] *n.* 怪胎；(對某事物的) 狂熱愛好者 & *vi.* & *vt.* (使) 吃驚 / 不安 / 惱怒

似 (1) enthusiast [ɪnˋθ(j)uzɪ͵æst] *n.* 熱衷者
(2) fanatic [fəˋnætɪk] *n.* 狂熱者

▸ Women that wore pants when going outside used to be regarded as freaks.
以前出門穿褲子的女人被認為是怪胎。

▸ Tim is a comic book freak. He often dresses himself up like the characters from the comic books.
提姆是個漫畫狂。他經常把自己打扮成漫畫人物的樣子。

▸ Sally freaked on the street when she suddenly saw the man who had yelled at her and threatened to hit her.
莎莉突然在街上看到那個對她大叫又威脅要打她的人的時，她嚇壞了。

▸ The sight of a flying cockroach in the living room caught Jerome by surprise and totally freaked him.
傑羅姆一看到客廳裡有一隻會飛的蟑螂，大吃一驚嚇壞了。

1803-1810

3 aviation [ˌevɪˋeʃən] *n.* 航空業

衍 avian [ˋevɪən] *a.* 鳥類的
avian flu　禽流感
= bird flu

似 aerospace [ˋeroˌspes] *n.* 航太(業)(研究火箭、太空船等的行業) & *a.* 航太工業的

▸ My friend has a career in aviation as a pilot for China Airlines.
我朋友任職航空業，擔任華航的飛行員。

4 capsule [ˋkæpsḷ] *n.* 膠囊；太空艙，座艙

片 (1) a time capsule　時光膠囊(將某時代的一些代表性物品封存起來，讓後世能藉由這些物品認識此時代)
(2) a space capsule　太空艙

比 (1) pill [pɪl] *n.* 藥丸；避孕藥 ③
(2) tablet [ˋtæblət] *n.* 藥片 ③

▸ This bottle of vitamin C supplements contains 200 capsules.
這瓶維他命 C 補充劑含有 200 粒膠囊。

▸ Are you interested in burying a time capsule so future generations can know what our time was like?
你有興趣埋一個時光膠囊，這樣後代子孫可以知道我們的時代是什麼樣子嗎？

▸ The astronauts spend many hours in machines that simulate space capsules before their actual mission into space.
太空人在實際出任務之前，會先在一個模擬太空艙環境的機器裡待好幾個小時。
*astronaut [ˋæstrəˌnɔt] *n.* 太空人
simulate [ˋsɪmjəˌlet] *vt.* 模擬

5 annoyance [əˋnɔɪəns] *n.* 惱怒(不可數)；煩人的人或物(可數)

片 to one's annoyance
令某人惱怒的是

衍 (1) annoy [əˋnɔɪ] *vt.* 使生氣 ④
(2) annoying [əˋnɔɪɪŋ] *a.* 令人討厭的

似 nuisance [ˋn(j)usəns]
n. 討厭的人或物(可數名詞)

▸ Much to my annoyance, Melinda canceled our dinner date without letting me know in advance.
令我非常生氣的是，梅琳達事先沒有告訴我就取消了我們的晚餐約會。

▸ It is such an annoyance when someone's cellphone rings in the middle of a movie.
電影演到一半有人的手機卻響了，這真是件令人討厭的事。

6 antibiotic [ˌæntɪbaɪˋɑtɪk] *n.* 抗生素 & *a.* 抗生素的

延伸 (1) antibody [ˋæntɪˌbɑdɪ] *n.* 抗體
(2) antidote [ˋæntɪˌdot] *n.* 解毒藥(與介詞 to 並用)；克服的方法

▸ The doctor prescribed some antibiotics for my ear infection.
醫師開了些抗生素給我治療耳朵發炎。
*infection [ɪnˋfɛkʃən] *n.* 感染

▸ The doctor gave Sandra some antibiotic pills and told her to take them three times a day.
醫生給了珊卓一些抗生素的藥，並告訴她每天服用三次。

7 assassinate [ə`sæsən,et] *vt.* 暗殺（常用被動語態）

似 murder [`mɝdɚ] *vt.* 謀殺 ③

▸ Security tightened amid rumors that the president would be assassinated.
總統會遭暗殺的謠言紛傳，而使維安措施更加嚴密。

assassination [ə,sæsə`neʃən] *n.* 暗殺

▸ The assassination of the president led to a bloody power struggle in that country.
該國總統被暗殺，引起了國內一場血腥的權力鬥爭。

assassin [ə`sæsɪn] *n.* 刺客，暗殺者

▸ According to the news report, that man is a professional assassin for a radical political group.
根據新聞報導，那名男子是激進政治團體僱用的職業殺手。
*radical [`rædɪkḷ] *a.* 激進的

8 boycott [`bɔɪ,kɑt] *vt.* & *n.* 聯合抵制

片 call for a boycott against...
呼籲抵制……

▸ People are boycotting this store because of its unreasonable selling prices.
大家在聯合抵制這家商店，因其售價很不合理。

▸ Animal rights activists call for a boycott against all products that are tested on animals.
動物保育人士呼籲抵制任何使用動物做測試的產品。

9 caption [`kæpʃən] *n.* （圖片下的）文字說明 & *vt.* 加（圖片的）說明於

比 title [`taɪtḷ] *n.* 新聞標題 ②

▸ I just came up with a funny caption for this picture of us at the beach.
我剛想到為我們這張在海邊拍的照片加個有趣的說明。

▸ All the pictures are captioned and dated so that they can be sorted later.
所有的圖片都加了說明和日期，方便日後整理。

10 captive [`kæptɪv] *a.* 被俘虜的；被關在籠內的 & *n.* 俘虜

片 (1) be taken captive　被俘虜
(2) a captive animal
關在籠子裡養的動物

衍 capture [`kæptʃɚ] *vt.* & *n.* 俘獲 ③
capture a thief　抓賊
the capture of a thief　抓賊

▸ Fifteen British sailors were taken captive by Iranian naval officers last week.
上星期有 15 名英國水手被伊朗海軍官員俘虜。

▸ Beth cannot bear to see captive animals, so she never visits the zoo.
看到動物被關在籠子裡貝絲會受不了，因此她從未去過動物園。

▸ The pirates took many captives and sold them as slaves.
海盜們抓了許多俘虜拿去當奴隸賣。

captivity [kæpˋtɪvətɪ] *n.* 監禁

片 be held in captivity 被監禁

似 captivate [ˋkæptə͵vet] *vt.* 使著迷

▸ I was totally captivated by Mary's beauty the first time I met her.
我第一次見到瑪麗就被她的美完全給迷住了。

▸ Shortly after the civil war broke out, more than three thousand people were held in captivity by the rebel troops.
內戰爆發不久，便有 3 千多人遭到叛軍軍隊監禁。

11 algebra [ˋældʒəbrə] *n.* 代數

延伸 mathematics [͵mæθəˋmætɪks] *n.* 數學 ①

▸ Algebra is a closed book to me.
我對代數一竅不通。
*be a closed book to sb 某人對……一竅不通

12 wag [wæg] *vi.* & *vt.* & *n.* 搖動

三 wag, wagged [wægd], wagged

片 (1) wag a tail 搖尾巴
(2) the tail wagging the dog
本末倒置

▸ When a dog's tail wags, the animal is happy, but when a cat's tail wags, it is annoyed.
當狗的尾巴搖動時，牠心情是很快樂的，但當貓的尾巴搖動時，牠可就生氣了。

▸ Mr. Cobain's dog sat up and wagged its tail cheerfully when it saw him coming.
柯本先生的狗一看見他過來就坐了起來，還興高采烈地搖起尾巴來。

▸ Stacy thinks she should buy a new gown to match her new necklace, but I think it's a case of the tail wagging the dog.
史黛西認為她應該要買件新禮服來搭配她的新項鍊，但我覺得那根本就是本末倒置。

▸ With a wag of his finger, the king dismissed the servants.
國王搖了一下手指，叫僕人退下去。
*dismiss [dɪsˋmɪs] *vt.* 讓……離去，解散

13 porter [ˋpɔrtɚ] *n.* 搬運工，挑夫

衍 port [pɔrt] *n.* 港 ②
a port city 港都

▸ A porter's job is to help carry people's boxes or suitcases.
搬運工的工作就是幫大家搬箱子或行李。

14 chemist [ˋkɛmɪst] *n.* 化學家

衍 chemistry [ˋkɛmɪstrɪ] *n.* 化學 ④

▸ That chemist is working on a new experiment.
那位化學家正在進行一項新實驗。

15 navigate [ˋnævə͵get] *vt.* & *vi.* 導航（船、飛機、車等），確定（船、飛機、車等的）路線

衍 navigator [ˋnævə͵getɚ]
n. 領／導航員

▸ The captain navigated his ship through the rough waters during the storm.
船長引領船隻駛過暴風雨中驚濤駭浪的海域。
*waters [ˋwɑtɚz] *n.* 水域，海域（恆用複數）

▸ The equipment is used to help sailors navigate, especially during foggy conditions when it is difficult to see.
這設備是用來協助船員**確定航行方向**的，特別是在有霧的時候，此時視線並不佳。

navigation [͵nævəˋgeʃən] *n.* 導航

▸ Mechanics discovered that there were some problems with the plane's navigation system.
技工發現這架飛機的導航系統發生了一些問題。

16 flake [flek] *vi.* （油漆）成片剝落 & *n.* 小薄片

片 (1) flake (off)　剝落
(2) a flake of...　一小片……

衍 (1) cornflakes [ˋkɔrnfleks]
n. 玉米片（恆用複數）
(2) snowflake [ˋsno͵flek] *n.* 雪花（可數）

▸ The snowflakes disappeared right after they fell onto the ground.
雪花一落到地上就消失了。

▸ You need to apply more paint to the wall; otherwise it will flake off pretty soon.
你必須在牆上多塗點油漆，要不然油漆很快就會剝落。

▸ It is a truly amazing fact of nature that no two flakes of snow are exactly the same.
沒有兩片雪花是完全一模一樣的，這真是自然界令人驚奇的事情。

17 refute [rɪˋf jut] *vt.* 反駁，駁斥

似 deny [dɪˋnaɪ] *vt.* & *vi.* 否認 ②

▸ The idea that human beings evolved from monkeys has not been refuted.
人類是從猴子進化而來的理論從未遭到反駁。
*evolve [ɪˋvɑlv] *vt.* 進化

18 heighten [ˋhaɪtn̩] *vt.* 提高

衍 (1) high [haɪ] *a.* 高的 ①
(2) height [haɪt] *n.* 高度 ①

▸ A symphony orchestra is always used to heighten the dramatic effect of the opera.
歌劇一直用交響樂團來增加其戲劇效果。

▸ The result of the election heightened the tension between the two ethnic groups.
選舉的結果造成這兩個不同族群間的關係更加緊張。

19 stagger [ˋstægɚ] *vi.* & *n.* 蹣跚而行，搖晃

似 stumble [ˋstʌmbḷ] *vi.* 蹣跚而行；跌倒 ⑤

▶ The drunken man staggered out of the bar and hailed a taxi to take him home.
這名醉漢**蹣跚地走**出酒吧，然後叫了輛計程車回家。
*hail a taxi / cab　叫計程車

▶ After being stabbed in the back, the ninja was in pain and walked with a stagger.
那忍者背後被刺後，痛苦不堪，走路都走**不穩**。
*ninja [ˋnɪndʒə] *n.* 忍者

20 curb [kɝb] *vt.* 抑制 & *n.* 人行道路邊

似 restrain [rɪˋstren] *vt.* 抑制 ⑥

▶ The government should introduce some new policies to curb inflation.
政府應該實施一些新政策來**抑制**通貨膨脹。

▶ The car skidded into the curb, nearly hitting a pedestrian.
這輛車打滑開上**人行道路邊**，差點撞上一名行人。
*skid [skɪd] *vi.* 打滑
pedestrian [pəˋdɛstrɪən] *n.* 行人

21 notable [ˋnotəbḷ] *a.* 值得注意的 & *n.* 名人，顯要人物

衍 (1) note [not] *vt.* 注意 ①
(2) noticeable [ˋnotɪsəbḷ] *a.* 值得注意的；顯要的 ⑤

▶ The *Mona Lisa* is one of the notable paintings on display at the Louvre museum.
《蒙娜麗莎》是羅浮宮展出的**著名**畫作之一。

▶ Among the notables at the event were several Hollywood actors, some popular singers, and a few politicians.
此活動中的**名人**包括幾位好萊塢演員、一些流行歌手和幾位政治人物。

notably [ˋnotəblɪ] *adv.* 特別地；明顯地

似 especially [əˋspɛʃəlɪ] *adv.* 特別是 ②

▶ Lisa is good at several outdoor activities, most notably scuba diving.
麗莎擅長一些戶外活動，**特別是**潛水。

▶ The media's stance is notably biased against women.
媒體的立場**很明顯地**對婦女有偏見。
*stance [stæns] *n.* 立場，態度

22 flaw [flɔ] *n.* 缺陷，缺點 (可數) & *vt.* 使有缺陷

衍 flawed [flɔd] *a.* 有缺點的

似 defect [ˋdifɛkt] *n.* 缺陷，缺點 ⑥

▶ Mark's design is rejected because there is a flaw.
= Mark's design is rejected because it is flawed.
馬克的設計作品因為**有缺陷**而被否決了。

23 heroic [hɪˋroɪk] *a.* 英雄的，英勇的 & *n.* 英勇果斷的行為；逞英雄的行為（皆恆用複數）

片 a heroic figure 英雄人物

衍 (1) hero [ˋhɪro] *n.* 英雄 ②
(2) heroine [ˋhɛro͵ɪn] *n.*（女）英雄 ②

似 heroin [ˋhɛro͵ɪn] *n.* 海洛因（不可數）⑥

▶ Because of his heroic deeds, Jerry was awarded a medal.
因為傑瑞很**英勇的**行為，所以他得到了一枚獎章。

▶ Victor was given a medal for his heroics in saving a young boy from a house fire last month.
維克多上個月把一名小男孩從失火的房子中救出來，他因其**英勇的行為**而獲得了勳章。

▶ Police warn that if people witness a robbery, they should not engage in heroics such as tackling the robber.
員警警告，如果大家看到搶劫，不要做像對付搶劫犯這樣**逞英雄的行為**。
*tackle [ˋtækḷ] *vt.* 對付，處理

24 underpass [ˋʌndɚ͵pæs] *n.* 地下道

片 take an underpass / overpass
走地下道 / 天橋，過地下道 / 天橋

衍 overpass [ˋovɚ͵pæs] *n.* 天橋

▶ My family and I hid in the underpass during the tornado.
龍捲風來襲時我和家人躲在**地下道**裡。

▶ For safety's sake, you'd better take the underpass instead of walking across the street.
為了安全起見，你最好**走地下道**。而不要步行過街。

25 curry [ˋkʌrɪ] *n.* 咖哩 & *vt.* 巴結（用於下列片語中）

片 (1) chicken / beef curry
咖哩雞肉 / 牛肉
(2) curry favor with sb 巴結某人

▶ Curry dishes are a staple of Indian cuisine.
咖哩料理是印度菜的主食。
*staple [ˋstepḷ] *n.* 主食

▶ Melissa made some chicken curry for her husband, but he didn't think it was spicy enough.
梅麗莎為她老公做了一些**咖哩雞肉**，但她老公認為不夠辣。

▶ Gary made attempts to curry favor with the manager, hoping he would get promoted.
蓋瑞試著**巴結**經理，希望可以讓他升官。

26 nearsighted [͵nɪrˋsaɪtɪd] *a.* 近視的〔美〕

似 myopia [maɪˋopɪə] *n.* 近視（醫）

反 farsighted [͵fɑrˋsaɪtɪd] *a.* 遠視的；眼光遠的

▶ Do not read in dim light, or you're likely to become nearsighted.
別在暗淡的光線下看書，否則你可能會得**近視**。
*dim [dɪm] *a.* 暗淡的

1826-1834

shortsighted [ʃɔrt`saɪtɪd]
a. 近視的〔英〕；目光短淺的

▸ Because he is quite shortsighted, Brian can hardly see anything clearly without his glasses and must wear them regularly.
因為布萊恩近視，所以他沒戴眼鏡幾乎看不清楚任何東西，因此他得常戴眼鏡。

▸ Monica is short-sighted, and she never plans ahead.
莫妮卡短視近利，她從不先做計劃。

27 slaughter [`slɔtɚ] *vt.* & *n.* 屠宰（動物）；屠殺（人類）

似 (1) butcher [`bʊtʃɚ] *vt.* 屠宰（動物）& *n.* 屠夫 ⑤
(2) massacre [`mæsəkɚ] *vt.* & *n.* 屠殺（人類）

▸ The villagers slaughtered a pig in preparation for the summer festival.
村民宰殺一頭豬以籌備夏日節慶。

▸ It is said that a large number of people in that city were slaughtered by rebel soldiers.
據說在那城市有很多人被叛兵屠殺。
*rebel [`rɛbl̩] *a.* 反叛的 & *n.* 反叛者

▸ Zoe has been a vegetarian for a long time because she is opposed to the slaughter of animals.
柔伊長期以來一直是素食主義者，因為她反對宰殺動物。

▸ On the site where numerous innocent civilians were killed, there is a monument to remember the terrible slaughter.
在這曾經有許多無辜平民被殺的地方，有一座紀念碑在此要人們牢記那次可怕的屠殺。

slay [sle] *vt.* 殺害
三 slay, slew [slu], slain [slen]
似 kill [kɪl] *vt.* 殺害

▸ According to the latest news, two passengers were slain by the hijacker because they tried to stop him.
根據最新的新聞，有兩名乘客因試圖阻止劫機犯而被殺了。

28 nostril [`nɑstrəl] *n.* 鼻孔

▸ When a horse is startled, it will have upright ears and flared nostrils.
當馬受到驚嚇時，牠的耳朵會豎起，鼻孔會放大。
*flare [flɛr] *vi.* & *vt.* (使) 撐開（鼻孔等）

29 woe [wo] *n.* 悲痛

衍 woeful [`wofəl] *a.* 悲傷的

▸ The story Ken told me about his childhood was a real tale of woe.
= The story Ken told me about his childhood was really woeful.
肯告訴我關於他童年的事，那真是個充滿悲痛的故事。

30 broaden [ˋbrɔdən] *vt.* 拓寬；擴大(眼界)

片 broaden one's horizons
開拓某人的眼界
*horizon [həˋraɪzn̩] *n.* 範圍，眼界，見識(常用複數)；地平線(恆用單數)

衍 broad [brɔd] *a.* 寬的 ②

似 widen [ˋwaɪdn̩] *vt.* & *vi.* 變寬 ③

▸ To bring more visitors in, the city government decided to broaden the road that led to the seaside resort.
為了吸引更多觀光客前來，市府決定**拓寬**通往該海濱度假勝地的道路。
*seaside [ˋsiˌsaɪd] *n.* 海濱 / 邊
resort [rɪˋzɔrt] *n.* 度假勝地

▸ The scholar's informative speech really broadened my horizons.
這位學者資訊豐富的演說真令我**開了眼界**。

31 reign [ren] *vi.* & *n.* 統治

片 reign over... 統治……

似 rule [rul] *vt.* & *vi.* & *n.* 統治 ①

▸ We feel nostalgic about the days when our last emperor reigned.
我們都很懷念上一位國王**統治**的日子。
*nostalgic [nɑsˋtældʒɪk] *a.* 使人懷念過去的
be nostalgic about... 對……很懷念

▸ Many important reforms were carried out during the reign of the last emperor.
許多重要的改革都是上一位國王**在位**時所實施的。

32 evoke [ɪˋvok] *vt.* 喚起，引起

▸ The smell of cigarette smoke evoked a memory in Ralph of his father, who was a heavy smoker.
香菸的味道**喚起**了雷夫對他父親的回憶，因他父親是個老菸槍。

33 champagne [ʃæmˋpen] *n.* 香檳

▸ Many people like to celebrate special events, like New Year's Eve, by opening a bottle of champagne.
很多人喜歡開**香檳**來慶祝如除夕夜等特別的活動。

34 provisional [prəˋvɪʒənl̩] *a.* 暫定的

衍 provision [prəˋvɪʒən] *n.* 提供；準備；條款；糧食，物資(此意恆用複數) ⑤
the provision of... 提供……
make provision for...
對……預先作準備 / 安排

▸ The manager stressed that the date for the meeting was only provisional; it might be changed in the future.
經理強調會議的日期只是**暫定**；日後可能會變。

35 prototype [ˋprotə͵taɪp] *n.* 雛型，樣本；典型

片 the prototype of a(n)...
……的典 / 模範

▸ The engineers developed a prototype first before working on a finished version of the new product.
工程師先開發一個雛型，然後再研究新產品的最終版本。

▸ Dan Jacobson is the prototype of a salesperson: he is very outgoing, talkative, and extremely persuasive.
丹・雅各布松是典型的銷售人員：他非常外向、健談又極具說服力。

*outgoing [ˋaʊt͵goɪŋ] *a.* 外向的，開朗的

Unit 19

1901-1905

1 encyclopedia [ɪnˏsaɪklə`pidɪə] *n.* 百科全書

片 a walking encyclopedia
百科通（比喻某人某方面知識非常豐富）
a walking dictionary
活字典，單字懂得很多的人

衍 encyclopedic [ɪnˏsaɪklə`pidɪk] *a.* 知識廣博的
▸ Lena has an encyclopedic knowledge of reptiles.
莉娜擁有極為豐富的爬蟲類相關知識。

▸ You can refer to the encyclopedia for more information.
你可以參考**百科全書**以得到更多資訊。

▸ Ask Tim if you have any questions about vegetables. He's a walking encyclopedia.
如果你有任何跟蔬菜相關的問題，問提姆就對了。他是個百科通。

2 enrich [ɪn`rɪtʃ] *vt.* 使富庶，使豐富

衍 rich [rɪtʃ] *n.* 富有的 ①

▸ Reading can greatly enrich your life.
閱讀可以大大豐富你的生命。

enrichment [ɪn`rɪtʃmənt] *n.* 富足

▸ Many people thought that the politician was mainly interested in his own enrichment, not in helping the public.
很多人認為這位政治人物主要是對自己發財有興趣，而不是對幫助大眾有興趣。

3 heroin [`hɛroˏɪn] *n.* 海洛英

似 heroine [`hɛroˏɪn] *n.* 女英雄 ②
延伸 cocaine [ko`ken] *n.* 古柯鹼 ⑤

▸ Schoolchildren are warned to stay away from heroin.
學童被告誡要遠離海洛英。

4 edible [`ɛdəbḷ] *a.* 可食用的

似 eatable [`itəbḷ] *a.* 可食用的
延伸 (1) drinkable [`drɪŋkəbḷ] *a.* 可飲用的
(2) potable [`potəbḷ] *a.* 可飲用的

▸ Some mushrooms are edible, while some are highly poisonous.
有些蘑菇是可食用的，然而有些深具毒性。

5 cholesterol [kə`lɛstəˏrol] *n.* 膽固醇

比 steroid [`stɛrɔɪd] *n.* 類固醇
▸ The boxer received a 10-match suspension for taking steroids.
該拳擊手因服用類固醇遭禁賽 10 回。
*suspension [sə`spɛnʃən] *n.* 中止，停賽

▸ Too much cholesterol in your body will increase the risk of heart disease.
體內有太多膽固醇會增加心臟方面疾病的風險。

obesity [o`bisətɪ] *n.* 肥胖症

衍 obese [o`bis] *a.* 肥胖的

▶ Obese people run a higher risk of cardiovascular disease.
肥胖的人得到心血管疾病的風險較高。
*cardiovascular [,kɑrdɪo`væskjulɚ] *a.* 心血管的

▶ Obesity is a problem affecting 2/3 of the US population.
肥胖問題影響著 3 分之 2 的美國人口。

---

diabetes [,daɪə`bitiz] *n.* 糖尿病（不可數）

衍 diabetic [,daɪə`bɛtɪk] *a.* 糖尿病的 & *n.* 糖尿病患者

▶ Susan has had to take regular insulin injections since she was diagnosed with diabetes three months ago.
自從 3 個月前被診斷出糖尿病之後，蘇珊必須定期注射胰島素。
*insulin [`ɪnsəlɪn] *n.* 胰島素

6 cashier [kæ`ʃɪr] *n.*（商店）收銀員

衍 cash [kæʃ] *n.* 現金 ②

似 teller [`tɛlɚ] *n.*（銀行）出納員 ⑥
an automated teller machine
自動提款機（縮寫為 ATM）

延伸 a cash register　收銀機

▶ The cashier told the police that she did not see the suspect's face, but she could recognize his voice.
收銀員告訴警方她沒看到嫌疑犯的臉，但她能認出他的聲音。

7 conscientious [,kɑnʃɪ`ɛnʃəs] *a.* 克盡職責的

衍 conscience [`kɑnʃəns] *n.* 良心；善惡觀念 ④

似 dutiful [`d(j)utɪfəl] *a.* 盡忠職守的

▶ Hillary's supervisor considered her to be a conscientious worker because she always finished her work on time.
希拉蕊的主管認為她是個盡忠職守的員工，因她總能準時完成工作。

8 census [`sɛnsəs] *n.* 人口普查；（官方的）統計調查

似 censor [`sɛnsɚ] *n.*（對出版物或電視電影的）審查員 & *vt.* 審查

▶ There is a national census in that country every ten years.
那國家每 10 年就作一次全國人口普查。

▶ Some staffers from City Hall are taking a traffic census to find out how many cars use this road per day.
有些市政府的員工正在做交通流量統計調查，以了解每天有多少車輛使用這道路。

9 dental [ˋdɛntḷ] *a.* 牙齒的

片 (1) a dental clinic　牙科診所
(2) dental / tooth decay
蛀牙的現象

衍 dentist [ˋdɛntɪst] *n.* 牙醫 ②

▸ If you have dental problems, you should go to see a dentist.
如果你有牙齒方面的問題，應該去看牙醫。

▸ The experienced dentist works at a dental clinic and also sometimes lectures at a national university.
此經驗豐富的牙醫在某間牙科診所工作，有時也會到在國立大學講課。

▸ Since Kent didn't look after his teeth properly when he was younger, he suffered a lot of dental decay.
由於肯特在他年輕時就沒有好好地顧好自己的牙齒，所以他有很多蛀牙。

cavity [ˋkævətɪ] *n.* (牙齒的) 蛀洞

複 cavities [ˋkævətɪz]

片 get / have a (tooth) cavity filled
把蛀洞補起來，補蛀牙

似 a decayed tooth　蛀牙

▸ You should get that cavity filled as soon as possible.
你應該快去把那顆蛀牙補起來。

10 discomfort [dɪsˋkʌmfɚt] *n.* 不舒適，不適 & *vt.* 使不舒服

反 comfort [ˋkʌmfɚt] *n.* 舒適 & *vt.* 安慰 ③

▸ I apologize if what I said caused you any discomfort.
如果我說的話傷了你，那真的很抱歉。

▸ Ruby was slightly discomforted by her friend Emma's indifferent attitude toward the whole matter.
露比見她朋友艾瑪對這整件事一副事不關己的模樣，心裡有點不太舒服。
*indifferent [ɪnˋdɪfərənt] *a.* 漠不關心的

11 pebble [ˋpɛbḷ] *n.* 鵝卵石

似 paddle [ˋpædḷ] *n.* (船) 槳 ⑥

▸ The west coast has many pebble beaches.
西海岸有很多滿是鵝卵石的海濱。

12 oasis [oˋesɪs] *n.* 綠洲；樂土

複 oases [oˋesiz]

▸ The city of Las Vegas was built upon an oasis.
拉斯維加斯市是蓋在綠洲之上。

▸ The park is an oasis of peace amid the hustle and bustle of the big city.
該座公園是這喧囂城市的一塊寧靜樂土。
*hustle and bustle　喧鬧

13 dismay [dɪsˋme] *vt.* 使憂慮，氣餒 & *n.* 驚慌，沮喪，氣餒

片 to sb's dismay 令某人失望的是

▶ Judy was dismayed when her best friend Helen told her she couldn't make it to her wedding.
茱蒂覺得很沮喪，因為她最好的朋友海倫跟她說沒辦法參加她的婚禮。

▶ To Jerry's great dismay, his parents won't be able to attend his graduation ceremony.
傑瑞的父母沒辦法出席他的畢業典禮，讓他非常失望。

14 emigrate [ˋɛmə͵gret] *vi.* 移居國外

片 emigrate from A to B 從 A 移居到 B

衍 (1) immigrate [ˋɪmə͵gret]
vi. 由外移民國內 ④
(2) immigrant [ˋɪmə͵grənt]
n. (外來) 移民，僑民 ④
(3) immigration [͵ɪməˋgreʃən]
n. 由外移民國內 ④
(4) migrate [ˋmaɪgret]
vi. (人為找工作等暫時) 移居；(動物隨季節變化) 遷徙
(5) migration [maɪˋgreʃən]
n. 遷移，(動物) 遷徙 ⑤
(6) migrant [ˋmaɪgrənt]
n. (為找工作而遷徙的) 移居者；遷徙的動物 ⑥

比 emigrate、immigrate、migrate 三者均表『移居』，emigrate 指從本國移出，而 immigrate 則指從他國移入，另外 migrate 多指候鳥的遷移或人因工作目的而進行的移居。

▶ Many people are emigrating from Taiwan to countries like Canada, the US, and Australia.
有很多人從臺灣移民到加拿大、美國、澳洲等國家。

emigration [͵ɛməˋgreʃən]
n. 移居國外

▶ Massive levels of emigration could cause serious worker shortages in our country.
大量的人移民到國外會使本國的勞工嚴重短缺。

▶ At the height of emigration, many people in this country moved to Canada.
移民高峰期，此國家很多人搬到了加拿大。

emigrant [ˋɛməgrənt] *n.* 移民 (由內移出者)

▶ It is often difficult for emigrants to find good employment in the countries they move to.
外來移民往往很難在他們移居的國家找到很好的就業機會。

15 dual [`djuəl] *a.* 雙重的

延伸 dual citizenship 雙重國籍

▶ The fact that some government officials hold dual citizenship has attracted a lot of criticism.
某些政府官員持有**雙重國籍**而引來了一片撻伐。

16 enlighten [ɪn`laɪtn̩] *vt.* 啟發，教導；說明

片 enlighten sb on sth 啟發某人某事；為某人說明某事

衍 (1) enlightening [ɪn`laɪtn̩ɪŋ] *a.* 有啟發性的

▸ That was a really enlightening speech.
那場演講真是**啟發人心**。

(2) enlightened [ɪn`laɪtn̩d] *a.* 開明的

▸ Gordon's parents hold enlightened views on education.
戈登的父母對教育的看法很**開明**。

似 (1) instruct [ɪn`strʌkt] *vt.* 教導 ④
(2) explain [ɪk`splen] *vt.* 解釋 ①

▶ Mr. Brown's lecture enlightened us on the importance of environmental protection.
布朗先生的演講**啟發**了我們認知環保的重要性。

▶ I don't understand your plan. Can you enlighten me on it further?
我不懂你的計畫。你可以就該計畫進一步**為我說明**嗎？

enlightenment [ɪn`laɪtn̩mənt] *n.* 清楚知曉，開通

似 explanation [ˌɛksplə`neʃən] *n.* 解釋 ④

▶ The news anchor provided little enlightenment about the background to this situation.
這新聞主播對這情形的背景資料說得不是很**清楚**。
*anchor [`æŋkɚ] *n.* (新聞節目等) 主播 (= anchorman / anchorwoman)

17 expire [ɪk`spaɪr] *vi.* 期滿，過期

似 come to an end 結束

▶ My passport is going to expire in another two weeks.
我的護照再兩個禮拜就**過期**了。

expiration [ˌɛkspə`reʃən] *n.* 期滿

片 an expiration date 保存期限

▶ To be on the safe side, always check the expiration date on the food package before you buy it.
為了保險起見，買東西前都要先查看一下食物包裝上的**保存期限**。

18 screwdriver [`skruˌdraɪvɚ] *n.* 螺絲起子

衍 screw [skru] *n.* 螺絲 & *vt.* 用螺絲旋緊 ③

▶ Do you have a screwdriver? I want to tighten the screws of the shelf I put up yesterday.
你有**螺絲起子**嗎？我想把我昨天架好的架子上的螺絲拴緊。

1919-1927

19 plow [plaʊ] *n.* 犁 & *vt.* 犁 / 耕（田）（= plough〔英〕）

似 cultivate [ˋkʌltə͵vet] *vt.* 耕種 ⑥

▸ The ox pulled the plow to turn the soil over and thus made it easier for the crops to grow.
那頭牛拖著犁翻土，好讓穀物更容易生長。

▸ If you want to be a farmer, you have to know how to plow.
你想當農夫的話就得知道怎麼犁田。

20 chestnut [ˋtʃɛs͵nʌt] *n.* 栗子

延伸 (1) peanut [ˋpi͵nʌt] *n.* 花生 ③
(2) cashew [ˋkæʃu] *n.* 腰果（= cashew nut）
(3) pine nut [ˋpaɪ͵nʌt] *n.* 松子

▸ Mother made my favorite chestnut cake for my birthday.
媽媽為了我的生日做了我最愛吃的栗子蛋糕。

walnut [ˋwɔlnət] *n.* 胡桃

▸ I love chocolates with walnuts inside.
我喜歡巧克力裡面有胡桃。

21 heterosexual [͵hɛtəroˋsɛkʃʊəl] *a.* 異性戀的 & *n.* 異性戀者

似 straight [stret] *a.* 異性戀的 & *n.* 異性戀者（皆口語）①

▸ According to a study, only some of the younger generation see themselves as exclusively heterosexual.
根據一項調查，年輕世代中只有某些人認為他們是百分之百的異性戀。

▸ Ben lived as a heterosexual for many years before coming out in his 50s.
班以異性戀的身份生活了很多年，直到 50 多歲才出櫃。

homosexual [͵homəˋsɛkʃʊəl]
a.（尤指男）同性戀的 & *n.*（尤指男）同性戀

似 (1) gay [ge] *a.* 同性戀的 ⑥
*本字常做形容詞用，多說 “He is gay.” 而不說 “He is a gay.”。
(2) homo [ˋhomo] *n.* 男同性戀者（貶義，應避免使用）
(3) lesbian [ˋlɛzbɪən] *n.* 女同性戀 & *a.* 女同性戀的 ⑥

反 bisexual [baɪˋsɛkʃʊəl] *n.* 雙性戀 & *a.* 雙性戀的

延伸 come out (of the closet)　出櫃（第一次向外界表示自己為同性戀者）

▸ This famous actor acknowledged his homosexual orientation to the public.
這位知名演員向大家承認自己有同性戀傾向。

▸ Bruce's mother has accepted that her son is a homosexual, but his father still struggles with that fact.
布魯斯的母親已接受她兒子是個同性戀了，但布魯斯的父親對這一事實仍在掙扎中。

22 dazzle [ˋdæzl̩] *vt.* 使目眩 & *n.* (光的) 炫目，耀眼

▸ The neon signs along the shopping street dazzled me.
這條購物街上的霓虹燈廣告牌讓我眼花撩亂。
*a neon sign [ˋniˏɑn ˏsaɪn] 霓虹燈廣告牌

▸ The boys enjoyed swimming in the lake and seeing the dazzle of the sun on the surface of the water.
這些男孩喜歡在那湖裡游泳，也喜歡看水面上耀眼的陽光。

dazzling [ˋdæzlɪŋ] *a.* 令人目眩的

▸ The sun was so dazzling that I had to wear sunglasses while walking on the street.
陽光太強了，我上街得戴太陽眼鏡才行。

23 novice [ˋnɑvɪs] *n.* 新手 (與介詞 at 並用)

似 beginner [bɪˋgɪnɚ] *n.* 初學者 ②
反 expert [ˋɛkspɝt] *n.* 專家 ②

▸ I've never surfed before. I'm a complete novice at surfing.
我之前從未衝過浪。我在衝浪上完全是個新手。

24 sloppy [ˋslɑpɪ] *a.* 草率的

似 slipshod [ˋslipˏʃɑd] *a.* (尤指工作) 馬虎的

▸ I can't put up with Mike's sloppy work anymore. I'll have to let him go.
我再也受不了邁可馬虎的工作表現了。我得炒他魷魚。

25 relic [ˋrɛlɪk] *n.* 古物

▸ The archaeologists dug out a relic from the Greek ruin.
考古學家在一處希臘廢墟裡挖到了一個古物。
*archaeologist [ˏɑrkɪˋɑlədʒɪst] *n.* 考古學家
dig [dɪg] *vt.* 挖掘
三態為：dig, dug [dʌg], dug

26 spur [spɝ] *n.* 馬刺 & *vt.* 鼓勵

三 spur, spurred [spɝd], spurred
片 (1) on the spur of the moment 心血來潮
(2) spur sb (on) to + V 鼓勵某人做⋯⋯
似 encourage [ɪnˋkɝɪdʒ] *vt.* 鼓勵 ②

▸ After the cocktail party, my friends and I took a walk to the beach on the spur of the moment.
雞尾酒會後，我和朋友一時興起散步到海灘。

▸ What Kevin had said spurred Rick to ask the beautiful girl out.
凱文說的話激勵了瑞克去約那漂亮的女孩出來。

27 nucleus [ˋn(j)uklɪəs] *n.* (原子) 核；核心

複 nuclei [ˋn(j)uklɪˏaɪ] / nucleuses
片 the nucleus of sth ⋯⋯的核心
似 core [kɔr] *n.* 核心 ⑤

▸ An atomic nucleus is made up of protons and neutrons.
原子核是由質子和中子所組成的。
*proton [ˋprotɑn] *n.* 質子
neutron [ˋn(j)utrɑn] *n.* 中子

延伸 (1) nuclear [ˋn(j)uklɪr] *a.* 核能的 ④
a nuclear war 核子戰爭
a nuclear bomb 核子彈
(2) nuke [njuk] *n.* 核武（口語）

▸ Susan and Richard will form the nucleus of the sales team for this project.
蘇珊和瑞奇將是這項計畫銷售組的核心人物。

28 flourish [ˋflɝɪʃ] *vi.* 茂盛；興旺 & *n.* (為引人注意的) 誇張動作

片 with a flourish 動作誇張地
似 (1) prosper [ˋprɑspɚ] *vi.* 繁榮 ④
(2) boom [bum] *vi.* 繁榮 ⑤
(3) thrive [θraɪv] *vi.* 興旺 ⑤

▸ The company began to flourish after the new manager took charge.
新的經理接管後，公司的業務蒸蒸日上。
*take charge (of...) 負責／管理……

▸ Calvin entered the room with a flourish, wearing very colorful clothes and waving to everyone in sight.
卡文動作誇張地走進房間，穿著五顏六色的衣服，向他看到的人都揮手致意。

29 underway [ˌʌndɚˋwe] *adv.* & *a.* 在進行中（不用於修飾名詞）

似 (1) in progress 正在進行中的
(2) in business 在經營中
(3) in operation 正在運作
(4) underwear [ˋʌndɚˌwɛr] *n.* 內衣（不可數）③
(5) underweight [ˌʌndɚˋwet] *a.* 體重不足的

▸ By the time Jenny and Frank arrived at the stadium, the baseball game was already underway.
當珍妮和法蘭克到體育場時，棒球比賽已經開始了。

30 directive [dəˋrɛktɪv] *n.* 指示，命令

衍 direct [dəˋrɛkt] *a.* 直達的 ②
似 (1) order [ˋɔrdɚ] *n.* 命令 ①
(2) command [kəˋmænd] *n.* 命令 ②
(3) regulation [ˌrɛgjəˋleʃən] *n.* 規則 ④

▸ According to the government directive, everyone who takes public transportation is required to wear a mask.
根據政府指令，每個搭公共交通工具的人都必須戴口罩。

31 collision [kəˋlɪʒən] *n.* 相撞；(不同文化等的) 碰撞，衝突

衍 collide [kəˋlaɪd] *vi.* 相撞

▸ Due to the poor weather, there were some major collisions on the nation's highways that resulted in serious injuries.
由於天候惡劣，國道發生了一些嚴重的撞車事故，造成很多人受傷。

▸ Every time Debbie and her French boyfriend have a discussion, a collision of cultures occurs, which usually results in an argument.
每次黛比和她法國男友討論事情時，都會有文化衝突，而通常這都會讓他們吵架。

32 privatize [ˋpraɪvətaɪz] *vt.* 使私有化

衍 (1) private [ˋpraɪvət] *a.* 私人的 ②
(2) privacy [ˋpraɪvəsɪ] *n.* 隱私權 ④

似 denationalize [diˋnæʃənḷ͵aɪz] *vt.* 使私有化

反 nationalize [ˋnæʃənḷ͵aɪz] *vt.* 使國有化

▶ Up until two years ago, it was a fully government-owned corporation, but it has since been privatized.
在兩年前，這是一家完全是國營的公司，但後來這家公司已私有化了。

Unit 20

2001-2006

1 infer [ɪnˋfɝ] *vt.* 推論

三 infer, inferred [ɪnˋfɝd], inferred

片 (1) infer A from B　從 B 推論出 A
(2) infer that...　推論出……

似 (1) refer [rɪˋfɝ] *vi.* 提及；參考（與介詞 to 並用）④
refer to...　提及……；參考……
(2) transfer [trænsˋfɝ] *vt.* & *vi.* 調動 & *n.* [ˋtrænfɝ] *n.* 調動 ④
(3) confer [kənˋfɝ] *vi.* 協調 & *vt.* 授與（學位、文憑）
confer with sb　與某人協商
confer a degree / diploma on sb　授與某人學位 / 文憑

▸ The president often confers with his advisers on important issues.
總統常與他的顧問們商議重大議題。

▸ The president of Yale University conferred an honorary doctorate on Rita last Friday.
上星期五耶魯大學校長頒授麗塔榮譽博士學位。

▸ You may infer one's family background from the way he or she eats at a dining table.
您可以從一個人在餐桌上吃飯的方式來推斷其家庭背景。

▸ From the evidence we've found, we can infer that the victim has a close relationship with the killer.
從我們找到的這些證據可推論，受害者與凶手之間的關係很親密。

inference [ˋɪnfərəns] *n.* 推論

片 make / draw an inference　做出結論

似 conclusion [kənˋkluʒən] *n.* 結論 ③

▸ According to the data, we are able to make the inference that global warming is endangering the habitat of polar bears.
根據這些資料，我們可以推論全球暖化正威脅到北極熊的棲息地。

2 starvation [starˋveʃən] *n.* 飢餓

衍 (1) starve [starv] *vi.* 挨餓 & *vt.* 使飢餓 ③
(2) starving [ˋstarvɪŋ] *a.* 飢餓的
be starving to death　快餓死了

▸ Thousands of children in Africa are dying from starvation each day.
每天非洲有上千名孩童餓死。

famine [ˋfæmɪn] *n.* 飢荒

似 feminine [ˋfɛmənɪn] *a.* 女性的 ⑥

▸ The long drought in that country has caused widespread famine.
該國長期乾旱造成飢荒遍野。
*drought [draut] *n.* 乾旱

3 hospitable [haˋspɪtəbḷ] *a.* 好客的；(氣候、環境等) 適宜的

似 generous [ˋdʒɛnərəs] *a.* 慷慨的 ②
反 inhospitable [ɪnhaˋspɪtəbḷ]
a. 不好客的

▸ When I first arrived in America, my aunt was very hospitable and made me feel at home.
我第一次到美國時，我阿姨很好客，讓我覺得賓至如歸。

▸ The weather in this region is very hospitable.
這地區的天氣非常宜人。

hospitality [ˌhaspɪˋtælətɪ] *n.* 好客

▸ This is just a small present to thank you for your hospitality.
這只是一份小禮物，感謝你們的殷勤招待。

4 hospitalize [ˋhaspɪtḷˌaɪz] *vt.* 使住院治療 (通常用被動語態)

衍 hospital [ˋhaspɪtḷ] *n.* 醫院 ①

▸ The wounded soldier was hospitalized for several weeks.
那受傷的士兵被送到醫院去治療了好幾個星期。

5 irritate [ˋɪrəˌtet] *vt.* 使憤怒；使過敏

似 provoke [prəˋvok] *vt.* 激怒 ⑤

▸ The noise Norman made when he was eating irritated me.
諾曼吃飯的聲音讓我很討厭。

▸ This brand of cream irritates my skin.
這牌子的乳液讓我的皮膚過敏。

irritable [ˋɪrəˌtəbḷ] *a.* 易怒的
似 short-tempered [ˌʃɔrtˋtɛmpɚd]
a. 脾氣壞的，很快就動怒的

▸ Gary didn't get much sleep last night so he was rather irritable today.
蓋瑞昨晚沒睡什麼覺，因此他今天很容易動怒。

irritation [ˌɪrəˋteʃən] *n.* 生氣；發炎
片 irritation at + N/V-ing 對……生氣
似 allergy [ˋælɚdʒɪ] *n.* 過敏 ⑤

▸ We could feel Father's irritation at being stuck in the traffic jam.
被困在車陣中時，我們都可以感覺到爸爸的怒氣。

▸ This ointment may cause irritation to sensitive skin.
這藥膏可能造成敏感性肌膚發炎。

6 fireproof [ˋfaɪrˌpruf] *a.* 防火的

似 bulletproof [ˋbulɪtˌpruf] *a.* 防彈的
a bulletproof vest 防彈背心

▸ Most of the buildings constructed these days are made with fireproof materials.
現今建造的房子大多使用防火材質。

waterproof [ˋwɔtɚˌpruf]
a. 防水的 & *vt.* 對……進行防水處理

▸ I can swim with my watch on because it is waterproof.
我可以戴手錶游泳，因為那是防水的。

似 water-resistant [ˋwɔtə·rɪˏzɪstənt]
a. 防 / 抗水的

▸ To protect the wooden furniture from the rain, George waterproofed it with an expensive paint he ordered online.
喬治為了保護木製家具免受雨淋，他用他在網上訂購的昂貴油漆對木製家具做了防水處理。

7 splendor [ˋsplɛndɚ] *n.* 壯麗，光彩

衍 splendid [ˋsplɛndɪd] *a.* 壯麗的；極好的 ④

▸ The tourists marveled at the splendor of the palace.
觀光客對此皇宮的輝煌讚嘆不已。

8 humiliate [hjuˋmɪlɪˏet] *vt.* 使丟臉，使羞辱

似 embarrass [ɪmˋbærəs] *vt.* 使尷尬 ④

▸ Getting involved in the scandal humiliated the politician and his family.
這名政客因涉及醜聞而使自己與家人蒙羞。

humiliating [hjuˋmɪlɪˏetɪŋ]
a. 丟臉的，羞辱的

衍 embarrassing [ɪmˋbærəsɪŋ]
a. 令人尷尬的

▸ It was humiliating to be reprimanded by the principal in front of the whole school.
當著全校的面被校長罵是非常丟臉的事。
*reprimand [ˏrɛprəˋmænd] *vt.* 責罵

humiliation [hjuˏmɪlɪˋeʃən] *n.* 羞辱

似 embarrassment [ɪmˋbærəsmənt]
n. 尷尬 ④

▸ The mayor could not bear the pressure from the press and resigned in humiliation.
該市長無法承受媒體的壓力，因而羞愧辭職。

9 imprison [ɪmˋprɪzn̩] *vt.* 監禁

衍 (1) prison [ˋprɪzn̩] *n.* 監牢 ②
(2) prisoner [ˋprɪzn̩ɚ] *n.* 犯人 ②

似 (1) jail [dʒel] *vt.* 監禁 & *n.* 監牢 ③
(2) put sb in prison
把某人關進監牢裡

▸ The man will be imprisoned for at least 10 years for theft.
這名男子因偷竊罪至少得坐牢 10 年。
*theft [θɛft] *n.* 偷竊罪

imprisonment [ɪmˋprɪzn̩mənt]
n. 監禁

片 life imprisonment 終身監禁

▸ Matt was sentenced to life imprisonment for committing a series of murders.
麥特因犯下好幾起謀殺案而被判終身監禁。

10 intimidate [ɪnˋtɪməˏdet] *vt.* 威嚇，脅迫

片 intimidate sb into + N/V-ing
脅迫某人……

似 threaten [ˋθrɛtn̩] *vt.* 威脅 ③

▸ The thug intimidated me into giving him all my money.
那個惡棍脅迫我把所有的錢給他。
*thug [θʌg] *n.* 惡棍，罪犯

11 extinguisher [ɪkˋstɪŋgwɪʃɚ] *n.* 滅火器

片 a fire extinguisher　滅火器

衍 extinguish [ɪkˋstɪŋgwɪʃ] *vt.* 撲滅（火）

▸ Everyone should have a fire extinguisher at home as a safety precaution.
為了安全起見，每個人家裡都應要有**滅火器**。
*precaution [prɪˋkɔʃən] *n.* 預防措施

12 spiral [ˋspaɪrļ] *n.* 螺旋 & *a.* 螺旋的 & *vi.* 盤旋著生長 / 移動

片 in a downward / upward spiral
不斷減少 / 增加

似 spire [spaɪr] *n.*（教堂上方）錐形尖塔

▸ Since John retired, his health has been in a downward spiral.
自從約翰退休後，他的健康情況就**持續惡化**。

▸ In art class, Heather learned how to make complicated spiral shapes and created such a beautiful painting.
在美術課上，希瑟學會了如何畫複雜的**螺旋**形狀，並創作出了這樣一幅美麗的畫。

▸ The large staircase spiraled to the top floor, with so many steps that people became tired and dizzy.
大樓梯**盤旋**到樓頂，而臺階太多了，多到令人頭昏眼花。
*staircase [ˋstɛrˏkes] *n.* 樓梯

13 nude [n(j)ud] *a.* 裸體的 & *n.* 裸體藝術作品；裸體（用於下列片語中）

片 (1) a nude beach　裸體海灘
(2) in the nude　裸體地

似 naked [ˋnekɪd] *a.* 裸體的 ③

▸ The movie starts with a nude scene where the leading actor is taking a shower.
這部電影開始時是男主角正在淋浴的**裸體**場景。

▸ Edward was too embarrassed to remove his swimsuit, despite the fact that he was sitting on a nude beach.
儘管愛德華坐在**裸體沙灘**上，但他還是尷尬到無法脫下泳衣。

▸ Research shows that men are twice as likely as women to sleep in the nude.
調查指出男性**裸**睡的比例是女性的兩倍。

14 hijack [ˋhaɪˏdʒæk] *vt.* & *n.* 劫持（飛機）

衍 hijacker [ˋhaɪˏdʒækɚ] *n.* 劫機犯

似 carjack [ˋkɑrˏdʒæk] *vt.* & *n.* 劫持車輛
carjacker [ˋkɑrˏdʒækɚ] *n.* 劫車者

▸ Passengers screamed in terror when the terrorists took out their guns in an attempt to hijack the plane.
當恐怖分子掏出槍來企圖**劫機**時，機上乘客全都尖叫嚇壞了。

▸ The security was tightened because of the recent hijack.
因為最近的**劫機**事件，所以安全措施加強了。

15 reptile [ˋrɛptaɪl] *n.* 爬蟲類

延伸 (1) mammal [ˋmæml̩] *n.* 哺乳類 ⑤
(2) amphibian [æmˋfɪbɪən] *n.* 兩棲類

▸ Reptiles are the oldest creatures living on earth.
爬蟲類是地球上最早的生物。

16 lieutenant [luˋtɛnənt] *n.* 中尉（縮寫為 Lt.）

▸ Lt. Smith is our platoon leader.
史密斯中尉是我們的排長。
*platoon [pləˋtun] *n.* （常由中尉指揮的）排

sergeant [ˋsɑrdʒənt] *n.* 中士（縮寫為 Sgt.）

▸ The sergeant is very strict with us, but in general he is a good man.
那中士對我們很嚴厲，但基本上他人還不賴。

admiral [ˋædmərəl] *n.* 海軍將軍／上將

似 general [ˋdʒɛnərəl] *n.* 將軍 ②

▸ The admiral gave us a pep talk this morning to boost our morale.
將軍在今晨給我們精神訓話以激勵我們的士氣。
*a pep [pɛp] talk 鼓舞士氣的話
boost [bust] *vt.* 推動
morale [məˋræl] *n.* 士氣

colonel [ˋkɝnl̩] *n.* （陸／空）上校（縮寫為 Col.）

似 captain [ˋkæptɪn] *n.* 海軍上校（縮寫為 cpt.）③

▸ We all respect Col. Sanders very much because of his great leadership.
山德斯上校領導有方，因此我們都很尊敬他。

17 continuity [ˌkɑntəˋn(j)uətɪ] *n.* 連貫性（不可數）

衍 (1) continue [kənˋtɪnju] *vt.* & *vi.* 繼續 ②
(2) continuous [kənˋtɪnjuəs] *a.* （不間斷）持續的 ④
(3) continual [kənˋtɪnjuəl] *a.* （偶有間歇）持續的 ④

▸ There is no continuity between the start of this story and the end of it.
這則故事的開頭和結尾沒什麼連貫性。

18 goalkeeper [ˋgolˌkipɚ] *n.* 守門員

▸ A goalkeeper's job is to try to stop the ball from going into the goal.
守門員的工作就是要設法阻止球進入球門之內。

19 ward [wɔrd] *vt.* 避開 & *n.* 病房

片 (1) ward off... 避開……
= get rid of...

▸ I need to drink some wine to ward off the cold.
我得喝點酒來驅寒一下。

(2) a maternity ward 產科病房
*maternity [məˋtɝnətɪ] *a.* 產婦的

▸ Hannah is a nurse working in the maternity ward.
漢娜是在**產科病房**工作的護士。

20 flunk [flʌŋk] *vt.* & *vi.* (某科) 考不及格 & *vt.* 使 (某人) 不及格

片 flunk out of school (被) 退學
= withdraw from school

▸ Not well prepared, Ray flunked the history test yesterday.
雷因為沒有好好準備，所以昨天歷史**沒有考及格**。

▸ I did poorly on my English test, so I was flunked by my teacher.
我英文考試考得很差，所以老師就把我**當掉**了。

▸ Because of his poor academic performance, Todd flunked out of college a year before he was supposed to graduate.
陶德因為學業表現極差，他在原定畢業的前一年**被退學**了。

21 resent [rɪˋzɛnt] *vt.* 怨恨

片 resent + N/V-ing 怨恨……
衍 resentful [rɪˋzɛntfəl] *a.* 令人怨恨的
似 hate [het] *vt.* 憎恨 ①

▸ Mary bitterly resented her father for walking away from their family when she was very young.
瑪麗**憎恨**她父親，因為他在她小時候就拋棄了家庭。
*bitterly [ˋbɪtəlɪ] *adv.* 激烈地

▸ Dennis resents getting up early.
= Dennis hates getting up early.
= Dennis hates to get up early.
丹尼斯**討厭**早起。

resentment [rɪˋzɛntmənt]
n. 怨恨，不滿

片 have resentment toward(s)...
對……有怨恨 / 不滿

▸ Many people have resentment toward the new policy.
許多人**對**新政策**感到不滿**。

22 awesome [ˋɔsəm] *a.* 令人敬畏的；很棒的

比 awful [ˋɔfəl] *a.* 可怕的 ③

▸ Looking down from the cliff to the wild sea below, Clark was treated to an awesome view of nature.
克拉克從懸崖往下看，看到下面波濤洶湧的海洋，他覺得大自然賞賜了給他這**絕妙的**景色。
*A be treated to B 以 B (樂事等) 賞賜給 A

▸ The girl in a mini-skirt has an awesome figure.
那位穿著迷你裙的女生身材**很棒**。

23 brotherhood [ˋbrʌðɚ,hʊd] *n.* 手足之情

▸ The staff in this department has a strong sense of brotherhood and excels at working as a team to overcome obstacles.

該部門的員工有著強烈如同手足般的情誼，擅長以團隊合作來克服障礙。

⋆excel [ɪkˋsɛl] *vi.* 擅長（與介詞 at 並用）

motherhood [ˋmʌðɚ,hʊd]
n. 母親的身分

反 fatherhood [ˋfɑðɚ,hʊd]
n. 父親的身分

▸ Cindy had a hard time combining motherhood and her career as an accountant.

辛蒂很難兼顧母親的身分和會計師的職業。

⋆combine [kəmˋbaɪn] *vt.* 使結合

24 chili [ˋtʃɪlɪ] *n.* 辣椒〔美〕(= chilli〔英〕)

複 chilies（= chillies〔英〕）

似 pepper [ˋpɛpɚ] *n.* 胡椒；甜椒 ③
black pepper 黑胡椒
a red pepper 紅椒
a green pepper 青椒

似 (1) chilly [ˋtʃɪlɪ] *a.* 冷颼颼的 ③
(2) Chile [ˋtʃɪlɪ] *n.* 智利（一南美洲國家）

▸ Add some chili to the beef stew to give it a spicy flavor.

在這鍋燉牛肉裡再加些辣椒讓它有辣味。

⋆stew [stju] *n.* 燉菜

25 oath [oθ] *n.* 誓言

片 take an oath 發誓句句屬實

▸ The witness was asked to take the oath before giving evidence.

此證人在作證前被要求發誓。

⋆give evidence （就某案件）提供證詞

26 nickel [ˋnɪkḷ] *n.* 鎳；（美國和加拿大的）5 分鎳幣

延伸 (1) quarter [ˋkwɔrtɚ] *n.*（美國和加拿大的）25 分硬幣；4 分之 1 ①
(2) dime [daɪm] *n.*（美國和加拿大的）10 分硬幣 ③

▸ The company owns a nickel mine, which supplies raw material for its production of stainless steel.

此公司擁有一個鎳礦坑，可為生產不鏽鋼提供原料。

⋆stainless [ˋstenləs] *a.* 不生鏽的，沒有汙點的
stainless steel 不鏽鋼

▸ It is interesting that American and Canadian nickels, which look similar to each other, also resemble a $5 Taiwanese coin.

有趣的是，看起來都很像的美國和加拿大 5 分鎳幣，也和臺灣的 5 元硬幣長得很像。

nickel-and-dime [ˌnɪklənˋdaɪm] *vt.* (因金錢上的逐步索取而) 一點一滴地耗損

▸ With all of the extra fees charged, some customers feel the company is nickeling-and-diming them.
因為這家公司收取了所有額外的費用，一些客戶覺到這公司在一點一滴地榨窮他們。

27 contention [kənˋtɛnʃən] *n.* 看法，觀點；爭吵

片 (1) sb's contention that...
某人的看法 / 觀點是……
(2) be in / out of contention for sth
(在體育運動中) 有 / 沒有機會贏得某事物

▸ The judge disagreed with the lawyer's contention that the man must be guilty because of the evidence presented.
法官不同意律師的看法，即因為所提出的證據，就認定該男子有罪。

▸ Due to their different lifestyles, attitudes, and expectations, there is a lot of contention between Julie and Robert.
由於茱莉和羅伯特的生活方式、態度和期望有所不同，所以他們常爭吵。

▸ The team lost an important game, which meant that they were out of contention for the trophy.
這球隊輸掉了一場重要比賽，這意味著他們沒有機會贏得獎盃。

28 gauge [gedʒ] *vt.* (用某儀器) 測量；判斷，判定 & *n.* 測量儀器

似 (1) measure [ˋmɛʒɚ] *vt.* 測量 ②
(2) judge [dʒʌdʒ] *vi.* & *vt.* 判斷 ②
(3) evaluate [ɪˋvæljuˌet] *vt.* 評估 ④

▸ It is common for police officers to gauge the speed of motor vehicles through the use of radar.
警察常用雷達來測量出汽車的速度。

▸ The interviewer asked Morris a difficult question and then observed him to gauge his reaction.
面試官問莫里斯一個難題，然後觀察他，以衡量他的反應。

▸ Rufus usually keeps a tire gauge in his car to measure the air pressure in his tires.
魯弗斯通常在車上放一個胎壓計，以測量輪胎的氣壓。

29 commonwealth [ˋkɑmənˌwɛlθ] *n.* 英聯邦；聯邦 (用於正式名稱中)

片 the Commonwealth of Nations
大英國協
= the (British) Commonwealth

▸ As members of the Commonwealth of Nations, many Canadians feel a special connection to the United Kingdom.
加拿大身為大英國協的成員，很多加拿大人覺得與英國有特殊的聯繫。

▸ The official name of the country is the Commonwealth of Australia, but most people simply refer to it as Australia.
此國的官方名稱是澳洲聯邦，但大多數人就只稱其為澳洲。

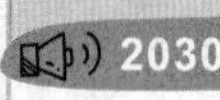
2030

30 premiere [prɪˋmɪr] *n.* 首映 / 演 & *vi.* & *vt.* (使) 首映 / 演

似 premier [prɪˋmɪr] *a.* 最重要的 & *n.* 總理，首相 ⑤

▸ Nancy invited her boyfriend to the premiere of the play she was in, but he had to work that night.
南希邀請她男友去參加她所演出的戲劇首演，但那一晚她男友得上班。

▸ When the film premiered, the audience was completely surprised when the hero died at the end of the movie.
當這部電影首映時，觀眾很詫異電影最後男主角竟然死掉了。

▸ Only a few theaters premiered the movie because it was not expected to be a big hit.
只有幾家影院首映了這部電影，因為預計這電影並不會大受歡迎。

2101-2104

1 migrant [ˋmaɪgrənt] *n.* (為找工作等而遷徙的) 移居者，隨季節遷移的動物 & *a.* 遷移的

片 a migrant worker 移工

衍 migration [maɪˋgreʃən] *n.* 遷移 / 徙 ⑤

▶ It can be difficult for governments to keep track of the movement of migrants, especially during national holidays.

政府可能會很難追蹤移工的動向，特別是在國定假日期間。

*keep track of... 追蹤……的動向，掌握……的最新消息

▶ Hawaii used to have a large number of migrant workers, who worked on pineapple and coffee plantations during harvest time.

夏威夷曾有許多移工，他們在鳳梨和咖啡園收成時前來工作。

*plantation [plænˋteʃən] *n.* 農園

migrate [ˋmaɪgret] *vi.* (動物隨季節或人因找工作等而) 遷徙

▶ In September, these birds migrate 5,000 miles south to a warmer climate to spend the winter.

9 月時，這些鳥往南遷移 5,000 英里到氣候較暖和的地方過冬。

2 punctual [ˋpʌŋktʃuəl] *a.* 準時的

衍 punctuality [ˌpʌŋktʃuˋælətɪ] *n.* 準時

似 be punctual 準 / 守時
= be on time

▶ Jeremy prides himself on always being punctual.

傑若米對於他總是準時而感到自豪。

*pride oneself on + N/V-ing 某人對於……感到自豪

3 melancholy [ˋmɛlənˌkalɪ] *n.* 憂鬱 & *a.* 憂鬱的

似 (1) gloomy [ˋglumɪ] *a.* 憂鬱的 ⑤
(2) downhearted [ˌdaunˋhartɪd] *a.* 沮喪的

▶ Recalling all the problems he had faced recently, Paul felt melancholy so deep and strong.

回想起所有他最近遇到的問題，保羅感到的憂傷既深刻又強烈。

▶ After feeling melancholy all day, Ted decided to take himself out to a movie and a nice dinner.

泰德一整天都感到很憂鬱後，他決定讓自己出去看場電影、吃頓很棒的晚餐。

4 pharmacy [ˋfarməsɪ] *n.* 藥局 (可數)

似 drugstore [ˋdrʌgˌstor] *n.* 藥妝店 ③

▶ I have a prescription from my family doctor. Can I have it filled at your pharmacy?

我有一份家庭醫師開的處方箋。我可以在你們藥局領藥嗎？

*prescription [prɪˋskrɪpʃən] *n.* 處方

pharmacist [ˋfɑrməsɪst] *n.* 藥劑師

延伸 fill a prescription
(藥劑師) 給處方的藥

▸ The pharmacist refused to fill the woman's prescription because it had expired.
藥劑師拒絕依照該處方箋為這女子配藥，因為那處方箋已經過期了。

5 mentality [mɛnˋtælətɪ] *n.* 心態

衍 mental [ˋmɛntḷ] *a.* 心理的；精神的 ③
似 mindset [ˋmaɪndˏsɛt] *n.* 心態

▸ I just cannot understand the mentality of people who abuse animals.
我就是無法了解那些虐待動物的人的心態。
*abuse [əˋbjuz] *vt.* 虐待

6 proficiency [prəˋfɪʃənsɪ] *n.* 精通 (不可數)

片 proficiency in... 精通……
衍 proficient [prəˋfɪʃənt] *a.* 精通的
be proficient in / at + N/V-ing
精通……
= be adept in / at + N/V-ing
= be skilled in / at + N/V-ing
= be good at + N/V-ing

▸ Tiffany's proficiency in five different foreign languages qualified her for the job.
蒂芬妮精通 5 種不同外語的能力，這使她有資格能夠勝任這份工作。

7 literate [ˋlɪtərət] *a.* 識字的 & *n.* 識字者

片 a computer literate 懂電腦的人
反 illiterate [ɪˋlɪtərət] *a.* 不識字的 & *n.* 不識字的人
computer-illiterate
[kəmˏpjutəɪˋlɪtərət] *a.* 不會用電腦的
technologically illiterate
不會使用科技產品的

▸ Increasing the number of literate youngsters is a top priority for that country.
增加識字青年的數量是此國家首要的工作。

▸ The old man said, "Young people these days are computer literates; I always ask my granddaughter questions when I have difficulty using a laptop."
老人說：『現在的年輕人很懂電腦。我用筆電有困難時，都會問我孫女問題。』

literacy [ˋlɪtərəsɪ] *n.* 識字

片 a literacy / illiteracy rate
識字率 / 文盲比率
反 illiteracy [ɪˋlɪtərəsɪ] *n.* 不識字

▸ India's literacy rate has shown steady increase over the past few years thanks to a national literacy campaign.
印度由於推行全國識字運動，因而在過去幾年間識字率有穩定的提升。

8 liter [ˋlitɚ] *n.* 公升〔美〕(= litre〔英〕)

似 litter [ˋlɪtɚ] *n.* 一窩 (小豬、小狗等) & *vt.* & *vi.* 亂扔 (垃圾) ③
a litter of puppies 一窩小狗

▸ Doris won the contest by drinking a 2-liter bottle of Coke faster than any other competitor.
桃樂斯比其他參賽者還快喝完一瓶兩公升的可樂而贏得了比賽。

9 vaccine [væk`sin] *n.* 疫苗

衍 (1) vaccinate [`væksə,net] *vt.* 接種（疫苗）

▸ Many schoolchildren have been vaccinated against hepatitis.
許多學童已**注射**過肝炎**疫苗**。
*hepatitis [,hɛpə`taɪtəs] *n.* 肝炎

(2) vaccination [,væksə`neʃən] *n.* 疫苗接種

▸ Most schools require students to receive certain vaccinations before they're allowed to attend.
大部分學校會要求學生入學前先接受特定的**疫苗接種**。

▸ No effective vaccine has yet been developed for HIV.
目前尚未培育出對抗愛滋病病毒的**疫苗**。
*HIV 愛滋病病毒
（為 human immunodeficiency [ɪmjənodɪ`fɪʃənsɪ] virus 的縮寫）

10 lease [lis] *n.* 租約 & *vt.* 租借

片 lease sth to sb 將某物租借給某人

似 rent [rɛnt] *vt.* 出租 & *n.* 租金 ②

▸ Under the terms of the lease, we are not allowed to have pets in this apartment.
租約的條約中有規定，我們不得在公寓內養寵物。

▸ The business center contains thirty-five rooms, about two-thirds of which are leased to the city government.
這棟商業中心有 35 房，其中大約 3 分之 2 已**租借給**市政府。

11 merchandise [`mɝtʃən,daɪs / `mɝtʃən,daɪz] *n.* 商品（集合名詞，不可數）& [`mɝtʃən,daɪz] *vt.* 推銷

用法 此字為集合名詞，故不可說：
a merchandise (×)
two merchandises (×)
而應說：
a piece of merchandise (○)
two pieces of merchandise (○)
a lot of merchandise (○)

▸ This chain store has a wide selection of merchandise on sale to celebrate its 5th anniversary.
這家連鎖商店為了慶祝其 5 週年慶，有很多**商品**在特價。

▸ Companies need to merchandise their products; otherwise, customers won't know these items are even available for sale.
公司都需要**推銷**其商品；不然顧客甚至不知道這些商品已有銷售。

12 pneumonia [n(j)u`monjə] *n.* 肺炎（不可數）

延伸 (1) malaria [mə`lɛrɪə] *n.* 瘧疾（不可數）
(2) smallpox [`smɔl,pɑks] *n.* 天花
(3) tuberculosis [t(j)u,bɝkjə`losɪs] *n.* 肺結核（不可數，常縮寫為 TB）
(4) panacea [,pænə`sɪə] *n.* 萬靈藥

▸ Pneumonia is the leading cause of death among children under 5 years of age in that country.
在該國，**肺炎**是 5 歲以下孩童死亡的主因。

13 paralyze [ˋpærə͵laɪz] *vt.* 使癱瘓（常用於被動語態）

衍 paralysis [pəˋræləsɪs] *n.* 癱瘓（不可數）

▸ The serious car accident left Tommy paralyzed from the neck down.
這場嚴重的車禍使湯米從脖子以下癱瘓了。

▸ Because of the blackout, all public facilities were paralyzed.
因為停電，所有的公共設施都癱瘓了。
*blackout [ˋblæk͵aʊt] *n.* 停電

14 persevere [͵pɝsəˋvɪr] *vi.* 堅持不懈

片 persevere in + N/V-ing　堅持……
衍 perseverant [͵pɝsəˋvɪərənt] *a.* 堅忍的
似 persist [pɚˋsɪst] *vi.* 堅持 ⑤

▸ Despite a number of setbacks, the two travelers persevered in their attempts to bike all the way from Spain to the southern end of Africa.
儘管有一些挫折，這兩名旅行者仍堅持要從西班牙一路騎腳踏車到非洲南端。
*setback [ˋsɛt͵bæk] *n.* 挫折

perseverance [͵pɝsəˋvɪrəns] *n.* 毅力

▸ Ned always shows great perseverance in the face of difficulty.
奈德面對困難時總是展現出堅強的毅力。
*in the face of...　面對……

15 prose [proz] *n.* 散文（集合名詞，不可數）

▸ Vincent wrote several books of prose before retiring to the Italian countryside.
文森退隱到義大利的鄉下之前，寫了幾本散文書。

16 perplex [pɚˋplɛks] *vt.* 使困惑（= confuse）

片 be perplexed about...
對……感到很困惑
衍 (1) perplexed [pɚˋplɛkst]
a. 感到困惑的
（= confused = puzzled）
(2) perplexing [pɚˋplɛksɪŋ]
a. 令人困惑的
（= confusing = puzzling）
▸ I found your explanation extremely perplexing.
我覺得你的解釋很令人困惑。
似 puzzle [ˋpʌzḷ] *vt.* 使困惑 ②

▸ The students were perplexed about the grammar rule, so the teacher explained it once again.
學生對於那文法規則感到很困惑，所以老師又解釋了一遍。

17 panorama [ˌpænəˋræmə] *n.* 全景

片 a panorama of... ……的全景

衍 panoramic [ˌpænəˋræmɪk] *a.* 全景的

a panoramic view of sth

某物的全景

▶ The luxury hotel located on the mountaintop offers a breathtaking panorama of the city.

坐落於山頂的那家豪華飯店提供令人讚嘆的城市全景。

*breathtaking [ˋbrɛθˏtekɪŋ] *a.* 驚人的，令人震懾的

18 pesticide [ˋpɛstəˏsaɪd] *n.* 殺蟲劑

衍 pest [pɛst] *n.* 害蟲 ④

似 insecticide [ɪnˋsɛktəˏsaɪd] *n.* 殺蟲劑

▶ There are many natural alternatives you can use instead of pesticides to keep your vegetable plants healthy.

除了殺蟲劑之外，你還有很多天然的替代方案來維持蔬菜的健康。

19 pious [ˋpaɪəs] *a.* 虔誠

似 (1) religious [rɪˋlɪdʒəs] *a.* 虔誠的 ③

(2) devout [dɪˋvaʊt] *a.* 虔誠的

▶ Jack is a pious follower of Christianity. He dedicates all his spare time to reading the Bible and praying.

傑克是基督教的虔誠信徒。他把所有空閒時間拿來唸《聖經》和禱告。

20 Xerox [ˋzɪrɑks] *vt.* (以靜電複印機) 複印 (字首可小寫) & *n.* 全錄牌影印機 (商標名)

片 a Xerox machine 複印機

= a photocopier [ˋfotəˏkɑpɪɚ]

似 (1) copy [ˋkɑpɪ] *vt.* 影印 ①

(2) photocopy [ˋfotəˏkɑpɪ] *vt.* 影印

▶ I'm going to xerox a few copies of this brochure for this afternoon's meeting.

我要去影印幾份小冊子以便下午的會議上使用。

*brochure [broˋʃʊr] *n.* 小冊子

▶ A thief broke into the office last night but only stole one Xerox machine.

昨夜小偷有闖進辦公室，但卻只偷走了一臺影印機。

21 obstinate [ˋɑbstənət] *a.* 頑固的

似 stubborn [ˋstʌbɚn] *a.* 頑固的 ③

▶ Stop being so obstinate and self-righteous! There's some truth in what Mary said.

別再這麼頑固跟自以為是了！瑪麗說的話的確有幾分道理。

*self-righteous [ˏsɛlfˋraɪtʃəs] *a.* 自以為是的

22 sly [slaɪ] *a.* 奸詐的

似 (1) cunning [ˋkʌnɪŋ] *a.* 奸詐的 ④

(2) foxy [ˋfɑksɪ] *a.* 狡猾的

反 (1) direct [dəˋrɛkt] *a.* 坦率的 ②

(2) frank [fræŋk] *a.* 坦率的 ③

▶ Beware of that man. He can be very sly!

小心那男人。他可能很狡詐！

23 reside [rɪˋzaɪd] *vi.* 居住

片 reside in... 住在……

似 (1) dwell [dwɛl] *vi.* 居住
(與介詞 in 並用) ⑥
三態為：dwell, dwelt [dwɛlt], dwelt
(2) inhabit [ɪnˋhæbɪt] *vt.* 居住於；
(動物) 棲息於 (之後直接接受詞) ⑥

▶ Though he has become a famous artist, Eddie still resides in the poor community where he was brought up.
艾迪雖然已成了知名的藝術家，但他卻仍住在他從小長大的貧窮社區裡。

24 foe [fo] *n.* 敵人

似 enemy [ˋɛnəmɪ] *n.* 敵人 ②

反 friend [frɛnd] *n.* 朋友 ①

▶ The leader urged everyone to unite against their common foe.
領導人力勸大家團結起來對抗他們共同的敵人。

25 hover [ˋhʌvɚ] *vi.* (鳥、直升機) 盤旋

片 hover over... 在……上空盤旋

▶ When I arrived at school this morning, I noticed a police helicopter hovering overhead.
我今早到學校時，看到有架警用直升機在我頭上空盤旋。
*overhead [ˋovɚ͵hɛd] *adv.* 在頭頂上的，在上面的

▶ A hawk hovered over the prairie, searching for prey.
一隻鷹在大草原上盤旋，尋找獵物。
*prairie [ˋprɛrɪ] *n.* 大草原
prey [pre] *n.* 獵物 (集合名詞，不可數)

26 destined [ˋdɛstɪnd] *a.* 注定的

片 (1) be destined to + V 注定要做……
= be bound to + V
(2) be destined for + 地方
預定前往某地
= be bound for + 地方

▶ The author is young but has published over 10 books. He seems destined to become a great writer.
該作者年紀輕輕，但已出版超過 10 本書了。看來他注定會成為一位偉大的作家。

▶ All flights destined for Sydney today are canceled because of the storm.
因為暴風雨的關係，今天預定前往雪梨的所有班機全被取消了。

27 spectacle [ˋspɛktəkl̩] *n.* 奇觀

片 make a spectacle of oneself
出洋相

衍 spectacular [spɛkˋtækjəlɚ]
a. 壯觀的 ⑤

▶ Niagara Falls is a real spectacle.
尼加拉瀑布真是個奇景。

▶ Wayne made a spectacle of himself after he got drunk at a dinner party.
韋恩在晚宴上喝醉，出了洋相。

28 chimpanzee [ˌtʃɪmpænˋzi] *n.* 黑猩猩（比大猩猩小很多）（= chimp [tʃɪmp]）

比 (1) gorilla [gəˋrɪlə] *n.* 大猩猩 ⑥
(2) orangutan [oˋræŋgəˌtæn] *n.* 紅毛猩猩

▸ Genetically, chimpanzees are very similar to human beings.
就基因上來說，黑猩猩跟人類非常相似。
*genetically [dʒəˋnɛtɪklɪ] *adv.* 從基因 / 遺傳學而言

29 restrain [rɪˋstren] *vt.* 抑止

片 restrain... from + V-ing 制止……做……
= stop... from + V-ing

▸ The authorities are doing their best to restrain the spread of the disease.
有關當局正傾全力抑制疾病蔓延。

▸ The shrink advised Eliot to restrain himself from overworking.
精神科醫生建議艾略特應避免工作過度。
*shrink [ʃrɪŋk] *n.* 精神科醫生（口語）
= psychiatrist [saɪˋkaɪətrɪst]（正式）

restraint [rɪˋstrent] *n.* 自制（力）

似 self-control [ˌsɛlfkənˋtrol] *n.* 自制力

▸ Betty showed great restraint by not responding to George's insulting remarks about her looks.
喬治侮辱貝蒂的長相，而貝蒂並未做回應，展現了極佳的自制力。

30 sportsman [ˋspɔrtsmən] *n.*（男）運動員 / 家

複 sportsmen [ˋspɔrtsmən]
似 (1) athlete [ˋæθlit] *n.* 運動員 ③
(2) sportswoman [ˋspɔrtsˌwʊmən] *n.*（女）運動員 / 家（複數為 sportswomen [ˋspɔrtsˌwɪmɪn]）⑥

▸ The equipment will help disabled sportsmen or sportswomen build physical strength.
這項器材可以幫助有身心障礙的男女運動員增強體力。

sportsmanship [ˋspɔrtsmənˌʃɪp] *n.* 運動家精神

似 honesty [ˋɑnəstɪ] *n.* 誠實 ③

▸ The player was taken out of the game because of poor sportsmanship.
這運動員因為沒有運動家精神而被踢出了比賽。

31 awhile [əˋ(h)waɪl] *adv.* 片刻

片 stay awhile 暫留 / 稍停片刻
似 for a while 一會兒
= for a short time

▸ Stay awhile if you can. I have something important to tell you.
可以的話，請暫留片刻。我有重要的事要跟你說。

▸ I will wait here awhile.
= I will wait here for a while.
我會在這裡稍等片刻。

32 oatmeal [ˋot͵mil] *n.* 燕麥粉；燕麥粥

似 porridge [ˋpɔrɪdʒ] *n.* 麥片粥〔英〕

▸ Have you tried these oatmeal cookies? They're very yummy. Most importantly, they're gluten-free.
你嚐過這些燕麥餅乾嗎？它們很好吃。最重要的是，它們不含麩質。
*gluten [ˋglutən] *n.* 麩質

▸ Studies show that oatmeal can lower blood cholesterol, thus reducing the risk of heart disease.
研究指出，燕麥粥可以降低血中的膽固醇，因此可降低罹患心臟病的風險。
*cholesterol [kəˋlɛstə͵rol] *n.* 膽固醇

33 analogy [əˋnælədʒɪ] *n.* 相似，類似

片 draw / make an analogy between A and B　把 A 比作 B

▸ To help the audience understand him better, Phillip drew an analogy between a child's mind and a sponge.
菲利普為了幫助聽眾更好地理解他，他把孩童的心智比作像一塊海綿。

34 monetary [ˋmʌnə͵tɛrɪ] *a.* 貨幣的，金融的

▸ Some countries have strict monetary policies in place to protect the value of their currencies.
一些國家設有嚴格的貨幣政策來保護其貨幣的價值。
*in place　就位，正在運作

35 comrade [ˋkɑmræd] *n.* (常指共患難的) 朋友

▸ Oliver was looking forward to meeting his old college comrades over the weekend for dinner and drinks.
奧利弗期待週末與他的大學老友見面，一起吃晚餐和喝酒。

36 petroleum [pəˋtrolɪəm] *n.* 石油 (可提煉汽油、柴油或煤油)

▸ Many common substances, like gasoline and kerosene, are made from petroleum.
很多像是汽油和煤油等常見的東西，都是由石油提煉而成的。
*kerosene [ˋkɛrə͵sin] *n.* 煤油

petrol [ˋpɛtrəl] *n.* 汽油〔英〕
(= gasoline [ˋgæsə͵lin]〔美〕= gas〔美〕)

▸ Since Jerry's car was running low on petrol, he needed to find a petrol station soon.
由於傑瑞車子快沒油了，他得盡快找到加油站才行。
*run low on...　……快沒了

diesel [ˋdizḷ] *n.* 柴油

▸ Some cars don't use gasoline; rather, they run on diesel, which costs motorists less to purchase in Taiwan.

有些車子不使用汽油，而是使用柴油為動力，而在臺灣柴油的價錢較低。

*run on... 以……為動力

motorist [ˋmotərɪst] *n.* 開汽車的人

37 fable [ˋfebḷ] *n.* 寓言故事

片 Aesop's Fables 伊索寓言

似 parable [ˋpærəbḷ] *n.* (宗教類的) 寓言故事

延伸 (1) folklore [ˋfok,lɔr] *n.* 民間傳說 (集合名詞，不可數) ⑥

(2) a fairy tale 童話故事

▸ Children can learn a lot from reading fables.

孩子可從閱讀寓言故事中學到很多東西。

▸ When I was a child, my mom used to read one of Aesop's Fables to me before I went to sleep.

我小時候，我媽會在我睡覺前讀一篇伊索寓言給我聽。

38 locker [ˋlakɚ] *n.* 置物櫃

片 a locker room (健身房內有置物櫃的) 更衣間

衍 lock [lak] *n.* 鎖 ③

▸ Please put your belongings in the lockers by the entrance.

請把東西放在入口處旁的置物櫃裡。

*belongings [bɪˋlɔŋɪŋz] *n.* 所有物，(隨身)財物 (恆用複數)

▸ I may have left my keys in the locker room in the gym. I'd better call the gym.

我可能把鑰匙留在健身房的更衣室裡了。我最好打電話給健身房一下。

Unit 22

2201-2207

1 reconcile [ˋrɛkən͵saɪl] *vt.* 調停；使和解

片 (1) reconcile A with B　使 A 與 B 調解
(2) be reconciled (with sb)
與（某人）和解

衍 reconciliation [rɛkən͵sɪlɪˋeʃən]
n. 和解

▸ David found it difficult to reconcile his love for writing with the need to support his family.
大衛感到很難**調和**他對寫作的喜好**和**養家的義務。

▸ Bob and Andy were finally reconciled with each other after Bob offered his apology.
在鮑伯提出道歉後，他和安迪兩個終於**和解**了。

2 renowned [rɪˋnaund] *a.* 有名的

片 (1) be renowned for...
因……而出名
= be famous for...
= be famed for...
= be noted for...
(2) be renowned as...
以……的身分而聞名
= be famous as...
= be known as...

▸ This diplomat is renowned for his negotiation skills.
這名外交官**以**談判技巧**而聞名**。

▸ George is renowned as a top pastry chef.
喬治是個**著名的**頂級糕餅師傅。
*pastry [ˋpestrɪ] *n.* 油酥糕點

notorious [noˋtorɪəs]
a. 惡名昭彰的

片 (1) be notorious for...
因……而臭名遠揚
(2) be notorious as...
以……的身分而臭名遠揚

似 infamous [ˋɪnfəməs] *a.* 聲名狼藉的

▸ Jim is notorious for his bad breath.
吉姆的口臭**臭名遠揚**。

▸ John is notorious as a womanizer.
約翰花花公子的**臭名遠揚**。
*womanizer [ˋwumən͵aɪzɚ] *n.* 玩弄女性的人

3 shoplift [ˋʃɑp͵lɪft] *vi.* & *vt.* (在商家) 順手牽羊

衍 shoplifter [ˋʃɑp͵lɪftɚ] *n.* 偷走店家貨物的扒手

似 steal [stil] *vi.* & *vt.* 偷 ③
三態為：steal, stole [stol], stolen [ˋstolən]

延伸 pickpocket [ˋpɪk͵pɑkɪt] *n.* 扒手 ⑥

▸ The Hollywood film star was caught on the spot while shoplifting.
這好萊塢影星在店內**順手牽羊**被逮個正著。
*on the spot　當場，立即

▸ Brandon knew he was in big trouble when he was caught shoplifting some comic books from a store.
當布蘭登被抓到從店裡**偷**了一些漫畫時，他知道他麻煩可大了。

4 seduce [sə`d(j)us] *vt.* (性的) 勾引，挑逗；引誘

片 seduce sb into + V-ing
引誘某人做……
= lure sb into + V-ing

衍 (1) seduction [sə`dʌkʃən] *n.* 引誘；吸引
(2) seductive [sə`dʌktɪv] *a.* 誘惑的，有魅力的

似 tempt [tɛmpt] *vt.* 引誘 ⑤

▸ The manager got fired for attempting to seduce his female subordinates.
經理由於試圖**勾引**他的女部屬而遭解僱。
*subordinate [sə`bɔrdn̩ət] *n.* 部屬

▸ With provocative commercials, the company seduced its consumers into buying its weight-loss pills.
這間公司以煽動性的廣告**引誘**消費者購買其減肥藥。
*provocative [prə`vɑkətɪv] *a.* 煽動性的

lure [lʊr] *vt.* 引誘 & *n.* 誘惑

片 lure sb into + N/V-ing
引誘某人……

▸ Advertisements lure consumers into buying things they don't necessarily need.
廣告會**引誘**消費者購買他們不見得需要的東西。

▸ Although Ada was on a diet, the lure of the chocolate cake was too strong, and she ate it quickly.
儘管艾達在節食，但巧克力蛋糕的**誘惑**太大了，然後艾達很快就把它吃掉了。

5 versatile [`vɝsətl̩] *a.* 多才多藝的

衍 versatility [ˌvɝsə`tɪlətɪ] *n.* 多才多藝

▸ John is very versatile; he is a painter, a musician, an engineer, and a scientist.
約翰非常**多才多藝**，他是個畫家、音樂家、工程師兼科學家。

6 usher [`ʌʃɚ] *n.* 帶路的人，引座員 & *vt.* 帶路

片 (1) usher sb in / into / to...
帶領某人至……
(2) usher in...
帶來了 (革命、新時代等)

▸ The usher helped me find my seat.
引座員幫我找到了座位。

▸ The servant ushered me into the guest room.
那佣人為我**引路至**客房。

▸ The invention of the copy machine ushered in a revolution in the printing industry.
影印機的發明**帶來了**印刷業的革新。

7 vibrate [`vaɪbret] *vt.* 使震動 & *vi.* 震動

似 vibrant [`vaɪbrənt] *a.* 充滿活力的；(顏色) 明亮的

▸ John has a vibrant personality.
約翰是個很有活力的人。

▸ The explosion two miles away vibrated the windows of my house.
兩英里外的爆炸**震動**了我家的窗戶。

▸ A guitar string vibrates when it is plucked.
吉他的弦一撥就會**震動**。
*pluck [plʌk] *vt.* & *vi.* 撥 (弦)

vibration [vaɪˋbreʃən] *n.* 震動

▸ Vibrations could still be felt 20 minutes after the earthquake took place.
地震過後 20 分鐘仍可感覺到**震動**。

8 referendum [ˌrɛfəˋrɛndəm] *n.* 公投

片 hold a referendum on...
舉辦……的公投

▸ The government agreed to hold a referendum on the issue soon.
政府同意於近期內為該議題**舉辦公投**。

9 rehearse [rɪˋhɝs] *vt.* & *vi.* 排演

衍 rehearsal [rɪˋhɝsl̩] *n.* 排演 ⑤
似 practice [ˋpræktɪs] *vt.* & *vi.* 練習 ①

▸ We've rehearsed this scene many times.
這一幕我們已經**排演**很多次了。

▸ With a hectic schedule like this, there's not much time left for us to rehearse for the upcoming tour.
行程這麼緊湊，我們已沒什麼時間**彩排**即將來臨的巡演了。
*hectic [ˋhɛktɪk] *a.* 忙碌的
upcoming [ˋʌpkʌmɪŋ] *a.* 即將來臨的

10 rigorous [ˋrɪgərəs] *a.* 嚴格的

似 difficult [ˋdɪfəˌkəlt] *a.* 困難的 ①

▸ Before you are qualified as a lifeguard, you will be given a rigorous training course.
在成為合格的救生員之前，你將接受非常**嚴格的**訓練。

▸ This truck didn't pass the rigorous vehicle emissions test.
這部卡車沒通過**嚴格的**車輛廢氣排放檢測。

11 strangle [ˋstræŋgl̩] *vt.* 勒死

▸ The forensic examination showed that the man had been poisoned before he was strangled to death.
法醫檢驗結果發現該名男子在被**勒死**之前曾遭下毒。
*forensic [fəˋrɛnsɪk / fəˋrɛnzɪk] *a.* 法醫的

suffocate [ˋsʌfəˌket] *vt.* 使窒息 & *vi.* 窒息

▸ The unpleasant cigarette smoke almost suffocated me.
這令人討厭的菸味讓我快要**沒辦法呼吸**。

▸ Infants risk suffocating while sleeping on adult mattresses.
嬰兒若睡在成人的床墊上會有**窒息**的危險。
*risk + V-ing　可能會有……的風險
mattress [ˋmætrəs] *n.* 床墊

smother [ˋsmʌðɚ] *vt.* 悶死；(把火) 悶熄

▸ According to the newspaper, the murderer smothered the man and then dumped the body into the river.
根據報紙所述，凶手**悶死**那名男子後再將屍體丟入河中。

▸ Daniel tried to smother the fire with a blanket.
丹尼爾試著以毯子將火**悶熄**。

12 synonym [ˋsɪnə͵nɪm] *n.* 同義字 / 詞

片 a synonym for / of... ……的同義字
衍 synonymous [sɪˋnɑnəməs] *a.* 同義的

▸ "Uprising" is a synonym for "revolution."
『暴動』是『革命』的**同義字**。

antonym [ˋæntə͵nɪm] *n.* 反義字 / 詞
衍 antonymous [ænˋtɑnəməs] *a.* 反義的

▸ "Strong" and "weak" are antonyms.
『強壯』和『虛弱』是**反義字**。

13 stationery [ˋsteʃən͵ɛrɪ] *n.* 文具 (集合名詞，不可數)

似 stationary [ˋsteʃən͵ɛrɪ] *a.* 固定式的 (與 stationery 發音完全相同) ⑥
a stationary bike
(在健身房等內的) 固定式腳踏車

▸ The shop sells a lot of books, magazines, and imported stationery.
這家店賣很多書、雜誌以及進口**文具**。

14 liner [ˋlaɪnɚ] *n.* (大型) 郵輪

似 (1) cruiser [ˋkruzɚ] *n.* 郵輪
延伸 (1) warship [ˋwɔr͵ʃɪp] *n.* 軍艦
(2) raft [ræft] *n.* 竹筏；橡皮艇

▸ We went to the harbor to see the gigantic ocean liners arriving and departing.
我們到海港去看大型**郵輪**進出港口。

15 retort [rɪˋtɔrt] *vt.* & *n.* 回嘴，反駁

似 (1) answer [ˋænsɚ] *vt.* & *vi.* & *n.* 回答 ①
(2) reply [rɪˋplaɪ] *vt.* & *vi.* & *n.* 回答 ②

▸ "Where I want to go is none of your business!" Jim retorted angrily.
吉姆生氣地**回嘴**：『我想去哪裡你管不著！』
*be none of sb's business 和某人無關

▸ Everyone was surprised at Henry's sudden, sharp retort.
大家對亨利突如其來的尖銳**反駁**感到很驚訝。

16 acre [ˋekɚ] *n.* 英畝 (約 4,047 平方公尺)

▸ Mr. Brown just bought 200 acres of land in Southern India.
伯朗先生剛在印度南部買了 200 **英畝**的地。

17 chirp [tʃɝp] *vi.* (鳥) 發出啾啾叫聲

似 (1) twitter [ˋtwɪtɚ] *vi.* (鳥) 發出啾啾叫聲
(2) tweet [twit] *vi.* (鳥) 發出啾啾叫聲

▸ Every morning I wake up to the sound of birds chirping in the trees.
每天早晨我醒來時都會聽到鳥兒在樹上鳴叫的聲音。

18 sneaker [ˋsnikɚ] *n.* (一隻) 運動鞋

片 a pair of sneakers　一雙運動鞋

▸ Wearing a nice pair of sneakers will help you perform well in the race.
穿上一雙好的運動鞋會讓你在比賽時有好表現。

19 imposing [ɪmˋpozɪŋ] *a.* 壯觀的；印象深刻的

似 impressive [ɪmˋprɛsɪv] *a.* 印象深刻的 ②

衍 impose [ɪmˋpoz] *vt.* 強加於 ④

▸ I was held in awe by the imposing view of the Grand Canyon.
我被大峽谷壯觀的景色給震懾住了。
*awe [ɔ] *n.* 敬畏
hold sb in awe　使某人敬畏 / 震懾

20 spacecraft [ˋspes,kræft] *n.* 太空船 (= spaceship [ˋspes,ʃɪp])

複 單複數同形

用法 『太空船』有兩種說法 (spacecraft 及 spaceship)，若為 spacecraft 則單複數同形，即 a spacecraft、two spacecraft；但 spaceship 複數要加 s，即 a spaceship、two spaceships。而飛機也有兩種說法 (aircraft 及 airplane)，若為 aircraft 則單複數同形，如：an aircraft、two aircraft，分別等於 an airplane、two airplanes。

▸ The launching of the spacecraft was postponed due to an approaching storm.
太空船的發射因有暴風雨即將到來而被延期。

21 folklore [ˋfok,lɔr] *n.* 民間傳說 (不可數)

似 legend [ˋlɛdʒənd] *n.* 傳說 ④

▸ In folklore, foxes often represent cunning and evil.
民間傳說裡，狐狸通常象徵狡猾與邪惡。

22 devour [dɪˋvaur] *vt.* 吞食

片 devour sth　狼吞虎嚥地吃
= gulp sth down
= wolf sth down

▸ The hungry boy devoured the hamburger in no time.
那個飢腸轆轆的男孩一下子就把漢堡吃掉了。

▸ In a short time, the wooden building was devoured by the flames.
沒多久這座木造建築就被大火吞噬了。

23 imperial [ɪm`pɪrɪəl] *a.* 帝國的

衍 (1) empire [`ɛmpaɪr] *n.* 帝國 ④
(2) emperor [`ɛmpərɚ] *n.* 皇帝 ③
(3) empress [`ɛmprɪs] *n.* 女皇

▸ The Forbidden City is a reminder of China's imperial past.
紫禁城會讓人們想起中國的帝制時期。
*reminder [rɪ`maɪndɚ] *n.* 提醒物
a reminder of... 使人想起……

24 occurrence [ə`kɝəns] *n.* 發生（不可數）；發生的事件（可數）

片 an unexpected / a frequent / a rare / a common occurrence
意外 / 經常 / 罕見 / 普通的事情
衍 occur [ə`kɝ] *vi.* 發生 ②
似 incident [`ɪnsədənt] *n.* 事件 ④

▸ The occurrence of stomachaches is often linked with pressure.
胃痛發作往往與壓力有關。
▸ An unexpected occurrence threw John into despair.
一件意外事件使約翰陷入絕望之中。
*despair [dɪ`spɛr] *n.* 絕望

25 drizzle [`drɪzl̩] *n.* 毛毛雨 & *vi.* 下毛毛雨

反 (1) pour [pɔr] *vi.* 下大雨 ③
(2) downpour [`daʊnˏpɔr] *n.* 傾盆大雨

▸ You'd better carry an umbrella with you in case the drizzle turns into a pouring rain.
你最好隨身帶把傘，以免這毛毛雨變成傾盆大雨。
▸ It was drizzling when we walked to school.
= It was raining lightly when we walked to school.
我們走去上學時，天空正飄著細雨。

26 disbelief [ˏdɪsbə`lif] *n.* 不相信

片 in disbelief 不可置信地
反 belief [bə`lif] *n.* 相信 ②

▸ The audience stared at the magician in disbelief.
觀眾不可置信地盯著魔術師看。

disbelieve [ˏdɪsbə`lɪv] *vt.* 不信，懷疑
反 believe [bə`liv] *vt.* 相信 ①

▸ Willy has always been an honest man. Why should I disbelieve his words?
威利一直是個很誠實的人。為什麼我不該相信他說的話呢？

27 octopus [`ɑktəpəs] *n.* 章魚

複 octopi [`ɑktəpaɪ ] / octopuses [ `ɑktəpəˏsɪz]
延伸 squid [skwɪd] *n.* 烏賊

▸ An octopus uses its tentacles to grab its prey.
章魚會用牠的觸角捕捉獵物。
*tentacle [`tɛntəkl̩] *n.* 觸角

oyster [`ɔɪstɚ] *n.* 牡蠣，蠔
片 the world is sb's oyster
世界是屬於某人的，某人可隨心所欲地做想做之事

▸ My stomach began to feel funny after I gulped down some oysters.
我大口吞下幾枚生蠔之後胃開始覺得怪怪的。
*gulp [gʌlp] *vt.* 大口吞嚥（與 down 並用）

似 shellfish [ˋʃɛl,fɪʃ] *n.* 甲殼類海生動物（如螃蟹，龍蝦，蛤蠣等）

▸ Mary is young, beautiful, and talented. The world is her oyster.
瑪麗年輕貌美又有才華。**世界是**她的**舞臺，任由**她翱翔。

clam [klæm] *n.* 蛤蠣
片 be as happy as a clam 樂翻天

▸ I was as happy as a clam when the team that I supported won the baseball game.
當我所支持的球隊贏了棒球比賽時，我**樂翻天**了。

trout [traʊt] *n.* 鱒魚
複 trout / trouts

▸ The fishermen are excited about the approaching trout season.
漁夫們對於即將來臨的**鱒魚**季感到很興奮。

28 taboo [tæˋbu / təˋbu] *n.* 禁忌 & *a.* 禁忌的

複 taboos [təˋbuz]

▸ Premarital sex is considered a taboo by some people.
有人認為婚前性行為是個**禁忌**。
*premarital [priˋmærətḷ] *a.* 婚前的

▸ Homosexuality is still viewed as a taboo subject in some countries.
在一些國家同性戀仍是個**禁忌**話題。

tattoo [tæˋtu] *vt.* & *n.* 刺青
複 tattoos [tæˋtuz]
片 (1) a tattoo parlor 刺青店
*parlor [ˋpɑrlɚ] *n.* 店鋪
(2) a tattoo artist 刺青藝術家

▸ The gangster has a dragon tattooed on his back.
這流氓在背上**刺**了一條龍。

▸ It will be very expensive and time-consuming to remove all of these tattoos.
要把這些**刺青**移除會花很多錢且也很耗時。

▸ Niki told her mother she was going to the library, but in fact she had an appointment at a tattoo parlor.
妮基告訴她母親說她要去圖書館，但實際上她是跟**刺青店**有了約。

▸ Amanda asked the tattoo artist to draw a flower on her left arm and a snake on her right.
亞曼達要求**刺青藝術家**在她左臂上畫一朵花，然後在右臂上畫一條蛇。

29 confederation [kən,fɛdəˋreʃən] *n.* 聯盟，同盟 (= alliance [əˋlaɪəns])

似 federation [,fɛdəˋreʃən] *n.* 聯盟，同盟

▸ The confederation of states that fought against the US government during the American Civil War was known as "the Confederacy."
在美國內戰期間，一些州組成**聯盟**，一起對抗美國政府，此**聯盟**被稱為『美利堅邦聯』。
*the Confederacy [kənˋfɛdərəsɪ] 美利堅邦聯

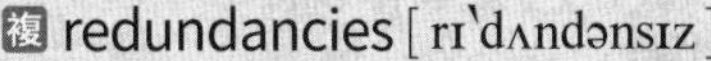

30 redundancy [rɪˋdʌndənsɪ] *n.* (尤指詞等) 多餘，累贅 (不可數)；失業，被解僱 (常用複數)〔英〕

複 redundancies [rɪˋdʌndənsɪz]

片 make redundancies　裁員〔英〕

▸ Ms. Pritchard informed her students that redundancy is something they should avoid in both their writing and speaking.

普里查德老師告訴她學生，在寫作和口語上都應要避免累贅的詞彙。

▸ The poor economy forced the company to consider making redundancies, though the general manager hoped to avoid that.

經濟不景氣迫使此公司考慮裁員，雖然總經理希望能避免這種情況。

redundant [rɪˋdʌndənt] *a.* 多餘的

似 (1) surplus [ˋsɝpləs] *a.* 多餘的 ⑤
(2) superfluous [suˋpɝfluəs] *a.* 多餘的

反 (1) necessary [ˋnɛsə͵sɛrɪ] *a.* 必需的 ②
(2) essential [ɪˋsɛnʃəl] *a.* 必要的 ④

▸ These three sentences are redundant. Your composition would be better without them.

這 3 個句子是多餘的。沒了這些句子你的文章會更好。

31 relentless [rɪˋlɛntləs] *a.* 不間斷的 (= endless)；不屈不撓的

衍 relent [rɪˋlɛnt] *vi.* 變溫和

▸ Conrad's severe headache was relentless—it never went away and seemed to get worse by the hour.

康拉德的頭一直很痛 —— 這頭痛從未消失過，而且似乎一直越來越痛。

*go away　消失
by the hour　一直，持續地

▸ Despite the heavy rain and cold, Roger was relentless, climbing higher and higher up the steep mountain.

儘管下大雨且又很冷，羅傑還是不屈不撓，不斷攀爬著這座陡峭的山。

32 procession [prəˋsɛʃən] *n.* 行列，隊伍

片 (1) march in procession　成排行進
(2) a procession of...　一長串的⋯⋯

衍 proceed [prəˋsid] *vi.* 繼續進行 ④

▸ Thousands of people marched in procession toward the square.

數千名群眾成排朝廣場行進。

▸ A procession of black limousines drove through the city in a farewell to the superstar.

一行黑色禮車開經本市，向這位巨星告別。

*limousine [lɪməˋzin] *n.* 加長型禮車 (= limo [ˋlɪmo])

33 prospective [prə`spɛktɪv] *a.* 可能成為的

片 a prospective buyer / client
可能的買家 / 客戶，未來的買家 / 客戶

衍 prospect [`prɑspɛkt] *n.* 可能性 ⑤

似 potential [pə`tɛnʃəl] *a.* 可能的 ④

▶ The real estate agent showed three prospective buyers around the house.

這房屋仲介帶了 3 位可能的買家來參觀這棟房子。

*estate [ɪ`stet] *n.* 地產
real estate 房地產
a real estate agent （房地產）仲介
show sb around 帶領某人參觀

Unit 23

2301-2306

1 complexion [kəmˋplɛkʃən] *n.* 膚色

片 a dark / fair complexion
深 / 淺色膚色

▶ Sophie has a darker complexion than her twin sister.
蘇菲的膚色較她的雙胞胎姐姐深。

2 distraction [dɪˋstrækʃən] *n.* 分散注意力的事物

衍 distract [dɪˋstrækt] *vt.* 使分心 ⑤

▶ Any distraction you encounter while driving might result in serious accidents.
開車時一分心就可能引起嚴重事故。
*encounter [ɪnˋkaʊntɚ] *vt.* 遇到

3 condense [kənˋdɛns] *vt.* 縮減 & *vi.* (使) 凝結

片 (1) condense A into B　把 A 縮減為 B
(2) condense into...　凝結成……

▶ The student condensed a great deal of material into a 10-page report.
那學生把大量的資料縮減成一篇 10 頁的報告。

▶ Steam condenses into water when it cools.
蒸氣冷卻時凝結為水。

4 dissident [ˋdɪsədənt] *n.* 異議分子

衍 dissent [dɪˋsɛnt] *vi.* & *n.* 不同意 ⑥

▶ In a dictatorial regime, dissidents are not accepted and are often exiled.
在獨裁政權下，異議分子是不被接納的，很多也因此遭流放。
*dictatorial [ˏdɪktəˋtɔrɪəl] *a.* 獨裁的
exile [ˋɛksaɪl / ˋɛgzsaɪl] *vt.* 流放

5 differentiate [ˏdɪfəˋrɛnʃɪˏet] *vt.* & *vi.* 區別

片 differentiate A from B
區別 A 和 B 的不同
= differentiate between A and B
= tell A from B
= tell between A and B

似 distinguish [dɪˋstɪŋgwɪʃ] *vt.* 區分 ④
distinguish A from B
分辨 A 與 B 的不同
= distinguish between A and B

▶ I can't differentiate the genuine bag from the fake one because they look so much alike.
我分不清真的名牌包跟仿冒品，因為它們看起來太像了。
*genuine [ˋdʒɛnjʊɪn] *a.* 真的，真貨的

▶ A good journalist can differentiate between facts and opinions.
好的記者要能分辨事實與意見的不同。

6 beverage [ˋbɛvərɪdʒ] *n.* 飲料

似 drink [drɪŋk] *n.* 飲料 ①

▶ You have to be at least 20 years old to buy alcoholic beverages in this country.
在這國家你要滿 20 歲才可以買酒精類飲料。

2307-2315

7 cater [ˋketɚ] *vi.* & *vt.* 承辦宴席 & *vi.* 迎合

片 (1) cater for...
承辦……的宴席，為……提供飲食
(2) cater to...
滿足 / 提供……的需求……〔美〕

衍 caterer [ˋketərɚ] *n.* 承辦宴席的人

▸ Mary runs a small business that caters for private parties and some small public events.
瑪麗經營一家小公司，是為私人派對和一些小型的公開活動來承辦宴席的公司。

▸ Sky Restaurant catered the meal. The food they prepared is quite delicious, isn't it?
天空餐廳提供這次的餐點。他們準備的食物很好吃，對吧？

▸ This brand of clothing caters to athletes, especially runners and cyclists.
此服裝品牌滿足了運動員的需求，尤其是跑者和騎腳踏車的人。

8 charitable [ˋtʃærətəbḷ] *a.* 慈善的

衍 charity [ˋtʃærətɪ] *n.* 博愛；施捨（不可數）；慈善機構（可數）；慈善事業（不可數）④

似 (1) generous [ˋdʒɛnərəs] *a.* 慷慨的 ②
(2) benevolent [bəˋnɛvələnt] *a.* 仁慈的

反 uncharitable [ʌnˋtʃærətəbḷ] *a.* 不寬厚的

▸ The charitable foundation is raising money for victims of the earthquake.
該慈善基金會目前正為地震受災戶募捐。

9 communicative [kəˋmjunə,ketɪv] *a.* 善溝通的；對話的

衍 (1) communicate [kəˋmjunəket] *vt.* 傳達 & *vi.* 溝通 ③
(2) communication [kə,mjunəˋkeʃən] *n.* 聯絡；通訊 ④

▸ A good leader is not only communicative but also willing to listen.
好的領導人不只要善於溝通也要願意傾聽。

▸ I took some conversation classes to increase my communicative abilities in English.
我上了一些會話課來提升我英文對話的能力。

10 concise [kənˋsaɪs] *a.* 簡明的，精簡的

似 brief [brif] *a.* 簡要的 ②

▸ A summary should be as clear and concise as possible.
一篇綱要要盡量簡要清楚。

11 conquest [ˋkaŋkwɛst] *n.* 征服

衍 (1) conquer [ˋkaŋkɚ] *vt.* 征服 ④
(2) conqueror [ˋkaŋkərɚ] *n.* 征服者

▸ The Spanish conquest of the Inca Empire took about forty years to complete.
西班牙人花了約 40 年的時間才征服印加帝國。

12 cosmetic [kɑzˋmɛtɪk] *a.* 化妝的

▸ Cosmetic products are supposed to make their users more beautiful and attractive.
化妝類產品應是讓其使用者變得更漂亮、更迷人。

cosmetics [kɑzˋmɛtɪks] *n.* 化妝品（恆用複數）

似 makeup [ˋmek͵ʌp] *n.* 化妝品（不可數）④

▸ Mary didn't wear any makeup today.
瑪麗今天沒有上妝。
不可說：
Mary didn't wear any cosmetics today. (×)

▸ The doctor suggested I use oil-free cosmetics because I have acne problems.
因為我有青春痘的問題，所以醫師建議我使用不含油的**化妝品**。
*acne [ˋæknɪ] *n.* 青春痘（醫學名稱）

13 dismantle [dɪsˋmæntl̩] *vt.* 拆卸；解散

片 dismantle sth 拆卸某物
= take sth apart
= disassemble sth

似 crumble [ˋkrʌmbl̩] *vi.* 碎裂

▸ Eric dismantled his bike but could not put it back together again.
艾瑞克把腳踏車**拆**了，但卻不會組裝回去。

▸ The new minister dismantled the old health care system soon after he was sworn in.
新任部長就職不久後馬上就**廢除**了舊有的健保制度。
*swear sb in 帶領某人宣誓就職
be sworn in 宣誓就職

14 curfew [ˋkɝf ju] *n.* 宵禁

片 impose (a) curfew 實施宵禁

▸ The government will impose a curfew across the country.
政府將在全國**實施宵禁**。

15 skeptical [ˋskɛptɪkl̩] *a.* 懷疑的（= sceptical [ˋskɛptɪkl̩]〔英〕）

片 be skeptical about...
對……表示質疑

衍 (1) skeptic [ˋskɛptɪk] *n.* 懷疑者
(2) skepticism [ˋskɛptə͵sɪzm̩]
n. 懷疑論；懷疑的態度

▸ Economists are highly skeptical about the government's economic reforms.
經濟學家對於政府的經濟改革大**表質疑**。

cynical [ˋsɪnɪkl̩] *a.* 懷疑（人的真善）的；挖苦的，憤世嫉俗的

▸ The union members were cynical about the management's promises.
工會成員對資方的承諾**心存懷疑**。

Level 6 Unit 23

片 be cynical about... 不相信……

衍 cynicism [ˋsɪnə,sɪzm̩] *n.* 譏諷作風；犬儒主義

▸ Harry's cynical tone was pretty offensive.
哈利嘲諷的口吻相當得罪人。
*offensive [əˋfɛnsɪv] *a.* 冒犯的，得罪人的

dubious [ˋd(j)ubɪəs] *a.* 猶豫不決的；可疑的

片 be dubious about + N/V-ing 猶豫是否該……

衍 doubtful [ˋdaʊtfəl] *a.* 起疑的 ③

▸ Mary is dubious about accepting the job offer.
瑪麗猶豫是否該接受這份工作。

▸ That man who sneaked into the backdoor of the building looked dubious.
那個潛入大樓後門的男子看起來很可疑。

16 dusk [dʌsk] *n.* 傍晚

片 from dawn to dusk 從早到晚

反 (1) dawn [dɔn] *n.* 黎明；開端 & *vi.* 開始明白 ③
(2) daybreak [ˋde,brek] *n.* 黎明

▸ The peasants worked from dawn to dusk, striving to earn a living.
這些農夫們從早工作到晚，努力維持溫飽。
*peasant [ˋpɛzn̩t] *n.* 農夫

twilight [ˋtwaɪ,laɪt] *n.* 黃昏；幕光

片 at twilight 黃昏的時候

▸ We were enchanted by the city at twilight as we walked.
我們散步時，這城市黃昏時分的景象把我們給迷住了。

▸ Randy enjoys watching twilight fall over the sleepy town each evening from his porch.
蘭迪喜歡每天傍晚從走廊上看著暮光降臨到這寂靜的小鎮上。

17 detain [dɪˋten] *vt.* 拘留；使耽擱

似 (1) maintain [menˋten] *vt.* 維持 ②
(2) contain [kənˋten] *vt.* 包含，容納 ②
(3) sustain [səˋsten] *vt.* 維持（生命）⑤

▸ Six robbery suspects were detained by the police.
六名涉及搶案的嫌犯遭到警方拘留。

▸ We were detained at the airport due to possible thundershowers.
由於可能會有大雷雨，所以我們暫時被困在機場。

18 disciplinary [ˋdɪsəplɪn,ɛrɪ] *a.* 懲戒的

片 (1) a disciplinary committee 懲戒委員會
(2) disciplinary action 懲戒處分 / 行動

衍 discipline [ˋdɪsəplɪn] *n.* 紀律 & *vt.* 懲戒 ④

▸ The students that were caught fighting at school were referred to the disciplinary committee for punishment.
那些學生在學校被抓到在打架，他們已被轉到懲戒委員會去做處分了。

▸ Paul may face disciplinary action because he was found with drugs at school.
保羅在學校裡被發現攜帶毒品，因此可能將接受懲戒處分。

19 discreet [dɪ`skrit] *a.* 謹慎的

衍 discretion [dɪ`skrɛʃən] *n.* 謹慎，考慮周到

似 (1) careful [`kɛrfəl] *a.* 小心的 ①
(2) cautious [`kɔʃəs] *a.* 謹慎的 ⑤
(3) prudent [`prudn̩t] *a.* 謹慎的

反 indiscreet [ˌɪndɪ`skrit] *a.* 不謹慎的

▸ Darren is too discreet a person to tell you about his problems.
戴倫是個過於謹慎的人，所以他不會告訴你有關他的問題。

20 bachelor [`bætʃələ] *n.* 單身漢；(大學) 學士

片 a bachelor's degree　學士學位

反 spinster [`spɪnstə] *n.* 老處女，未婚中 / 老年女子 (此字極為不雅，應少用)

▸ Kevin remained a bachelor until he was in his 40s.
凱文直到四十幾歲才結束單身。

▸ Where did you get your bachelor's degree?
你是在那兒拿到學士學位的？

21 aluminum [ə`lumɪnəm] *n.* 鋁

▸ All aluminum cans should be recycled.
所有的鋁罐都應回收。

22 cigar [sɪ`gɑr] *n.* 雪茄

似 cigarette [`sɪgərɛt] *n.* 香菸 ③

▸ Steve is puffing away on his cigar, thinking about what to write next for his novel.
史提夫抽著雪茄，想著小說接下來該寫什麼。

23 odor [`odə] *n.* (不好的) 氣味

片 body odor　體味

衍 (1) odorous [`odərəs] *a.* 難聞的
(2) deodorant [di`odərənt] *n.* 除臭劑

似 smell [smɛl] *n.* 氣味 ①

反 fragrance [`fregrəns] *n.* 芬芳 ⑥

▸ The pile of garbage in front of the traditional market emitted a pungent odor.
傳統市場前面那堆垃圾發出了刺鼻的臭味。
*pungent [`pʌndʒənt] *a.* 刺鼻的，氣味重的

ozone [`ozon] *n.* 臭氧

片 the ozone layer　臭氧層

▸ The ozone layer blocks out most of the sun's harmful ultraviolet rays.
臭氧層隔絕大部分太陽有害的紫外線。
*ultraviolet [ˌʌltrə`vaɪələt] *a.* 紫外線的

24 fowl [faul] *n.* 家禽 (指雞、鴨、鵝等動物)

複 fowls / fowl

▸ Unfortunately, the outbreak of bird flu led to the killing of thousands of fowls in this nation.
不幸的是，禽流感的爆發導致此國上千隻家禽類動物被屠殺。

25 indifference [ɪnˋdɪfərəns] *n.* 漠不關心，冷漠

片 indifference to sth
對某事物漠不關心

反 concern [kənˋsɝn] *n.* 關心，擔心 ②

▸ The boy's indifference to his schoolwork worried his parents.
這男孩對學業漠不關心，這點令他父母很擔憂。

26 discard [dɪsˋkɑrd] *vt.* 丟棄 & *n.* 不要的東西（可數）

似 throw away... 丟棄……
= get rid of...

▸ Please discard your trash in the provided trash cans before you leave the campsite.
離開營地之前，請把垃圾丟到我們所提供的垃圾桶內。

▸ The woodworker's shop was littered with discards from his most recent creation.
這木工的店裡散落著他最近創作作品的廢棄物。

27 paradox [ˋpærədɑks] *n.* 自相矛盾

衍 paradoxical [ˌpærəˋdɑksɪkḷ]
a. 矛盾的

似 inconsistency [ˌɪnkənˋsɪstənsɪ]
n. 矛盾

▸ It's a paradox that professional comedians often have unhappy personal lives.
職業喜劇演員私下的生活通常都不快樂，這可很矛盾。

28 sneaky [ˋsnikɪ] *a.* 鬼鬼祟祟的

衍 sneak [snik] *vi.* & *vt.* 偷偷地走；
偷拿 ⑤

似 sly [slaɪ] *a.* 狡猾的 ⑥

▸ He looks sneaky. I wonder what he is up to.
他看起來鬼鬼祟祟的。我想知道他在做什麼。
*be up to sth （尤指偷偷地）正在做（不法之事）

29 paddle [ˋpædḷ] *n.* 槳 & *vt.* & *vi.* 用槳划

似 peddle [ˋpɛdḷ] *vt.* 到處叫賣，兜售

▸ Paddles are used to control the movement and direction of a canoe.
槳是用來控制獨木舟划行與行進方向的。

▸ Tom and Jerry paddled their canoe as hard as they could in order not to fall over the waterfall.
湯姆與傑瑞盡全力划船，以免掉下瀑布。

▸ Because the fishing boat's engine ran out of gas, the boat had to be paddled back to shore.
因為這艘漁船的引擎汽油已耗盡，因此得將船划回岸邊。

30 revive [rɪˋvaɪv] *vi.* & *vt.*（使）復甦，（使）有精神

似 restore [rɪˋstɔr] *vt.* 使恢復

▸ You look dead tired. A hot bath might help you revive a bit.
妳看起來累極了。洗個熱水澡可能有助妳提振一下精神。

▸ The government should spare no effort to revive our economy.
政府應不遺餘力振興我們的經濟。

revival [rɪˋvaɪvl̩] *n.* 復甦
似 renaissance [ˋrɛnə͵sɑns] *n.* 復興

▸ There has been a revival of interest in impressionist paintings in recent years.
近幾年大家對印象派畫作又重新燃起興趣。
*impressionist [ɪmˋprɛʃənɪst] *n.* 印象派的

31 orient [ˋorɪənt] *vt.* 使適應 & *n.* 東方 (國家) (字首大寫)

片 (1) orient A to B　使 A 適應 B
= accustom A to B
(2) the Orient　東方 (國家)
衍 oriented [ˋorɪəntɪd] *a.*
以……為方向的，重視……的
a money-oriented society
以金錢為導向的社會，一個只顧賺錢的社會
an exam-oriented educational system　以升學為導向的教育制度
反 the Occident [ˋɑksədənt]　西方

▸ The school handbook will help you orient yourself to university life.
這本學校手冊能助你適應大學生活。

▸ Marco Polo first set off to explore the Orient in the 13th century.
13 世紀，馬可波羅第一次前往東方探索。

oriental [͵orɪˋɛntl̩] *a.* 東方的，亞洲的 (字首可大寫) & *n.* 東方 / 亞洲人 (貶義，字首大寫)
反 occidental [͵ɑksəˋdɛntl̩] *a.* 西方的，西洋的 (字首可大寫) & *n.* 西方人 (字首大寫)

▸ Vicky loves Japanese culture, and that's why her house is decorated in an oriental style.
維琪很喜歡日本文化，那就是為什麼她家的裝潢帶有東方色彩的風格。

▸ According to the author, the Europeans at that time regarded Orientals as barbarous.
根據此作者的說法，當時的歐洲人認為東方人是很野蠻的。
*barbarous [ˋbɑrbərəs] *a.* 野蠻的

32 sorrowful [ˋsɔrəfəl] *a.* 悲傷的

似 sad [sæd] *a.* 悲傷的，難過的 ①

▸ The sorrowful old man missed his wife, who recently passed away.
那位悲傷的老先生很思念他最近過世的老伴。

33 zoom [zum] *vi.* (鏡頭) 拉近 / 遠 & *n.* 可變焦距鏡頭，變焦鏡頭 (= zoom lens)

片 (1) zoom in on...
對……做鏡頭特寫，把……的畫面縮小

▸ The camera zoomed in on the mayor's face during the speech.
市長演講的時候，攝影機拉近，對他的臉部做了特寫。

2333-2339

(2) zoom out
將鏡頭拉遠，把畫面放大

▸ After getting off of the bus at the wrong stop, Lindsey zoomed out on the Google Maps app to check her location.
琳姿公車下錯站後，她就**放大**了在谷歌地圖應用程式上的地圖，以查看她現在在哪裡。

▸ This camera has an incredible zoom feature that can take clear photos from over 50 meters away.
這款相機有非常棒的**變焦鏡頭**，可以從 50 多公尺外拍攝到清晰的照片。

34 airway [ˋɛrˏwe] *n.* 呼吸道；航線；航空（公司）（常用於公司名，常用複數）

衍 air [ɛr] *n.* 空氣 ①
似 airline [ˋɛrˏlaɪn] *n.* 航空公司 ③

▸ After catching the dangerous disease, Richard had trouble breathing because his airways were partly blocked.
感染了這種危險的疾病後，理查因**呼吸道**部分阻塞而變得呼吸有困難。

▸ The airway from London to New York equals a total distance of more than 5,550 kilometers.
從倫敦到紐約的**航線**總距離超過 5,550 公里。

▸ One of the airlines that travels the route from Vancouver to Taipei is called EVA Airways Corporation.
從溫哥華到臺北的航空公司中有一家叫做『長榮**航空**』。

35 trustee [trʌˋsti] *n.* （財產）受託人，託管人

衍 trust [trʌst] *vi.* & *vt.* 信任 ②

▸ In her father's will, Melanie was left $1 million, which would be controlled by a trustee until she turned 18.
在父親的遺囑中，他留了 100 萬美元給梅蘭妮，而這筆錢將由**受託人**管理，直到梅蘭妮 18 歲為止。

36 paperback [ˋpepɚˏbæk] *n.* 平裝本

反 hardcover [ˋhardˏkʌvɚ] *n.* 精裝（硬皮）書

▸ While Gabby saw several expensive hardcover copies of the novel, she was unable to locate any of the paperbacks.
加比雖然有看到幾本這小說昂貴的精裝本，但她卻找不到任何的**平裝本**。

37 lining [ˋlaɪnɪŋ] *n.* （衣服等的）襯裡，襯料

片 every cloud has a silver lining
黑暗中總有一線光明

▸ Cynthia likes her new jacket because it has a fur lining that can keep her very warm in winter.
辛西亞很喜歡她的新外套，因為這外套毛皮**襯裡**可讓她在冬天時很暖和。

▶ Jasmine's mother used to cheer her up by telling her that every cloud has a silver lining.
潔絲敏的母親過去常告訴她，**黑暗中總有一線光明**，好讓潔絲敏振作起來。
*cheer (sb) up　使（某人）振作起來 / 打起精神來

38 provincial [prəˋvɪnʃəl] *a.* 省的 & *n.* 鄉下 / 外地人，首都以外的人（貶義）

片 a provincial government　省政府
衍 province [ˋprɑvɪns] *n.* 省 ⑤

▶ The provincial government is providing help to address the problem of the gap between the rich and the poor.
省政府正提供協助以解決貧富差距的問題。

▶ Ken is just a provincial; never mind what he said. He doesn't know how to appreciate your abstract painting.
肯只是個**鄉下人**，別管他說了什麼。他不知道如何欣賞你的抽象畫。

39 respective [rɪˋspɛktɪv] *a.* 各自的

衍 (1) respect [rɪˋspɛkt] *vt.* & *n.* 尊重 ②
(2) respectful [rɪˋspɛktfəl]
a. 滿懷敬意的 ④
(3) respectable [rɪˋspɛktəbl̩]
a. 值得尊敬的 ④

▶ We attended the keynote speech first, and then we went to our respective workshops.
我們先參加了主題演講，接著前往**各自的**專題研討會。
*a keynote speech　主題演講

Unit 24

2401-2409

1 intellect [ˋɪntḷ͵ɛkt] *n.* 智力

衍 (1) intelligence [ɪnˋtɛlədʒəns] *n.* 聰明才智；情報 ④
(2) intellectual [͵ɪntḷˋɛktʃuəl] *a.* 智力的 & *n.* 知識分子 ④

▸ I enjoy Amanda's company because she is a woman of considerable intellect and great personal charm.
我喜歡和雅曼達在一起，因為她是個很有智慧又很有個人魅力的女性。
*company [ˋkʌmpənɪ] *n.* 陪伴

2 miraculous [məˋrækjələs] *a.* 奇蹟的，不可思議的

衍 (1) miracle [ˋmɪrəkḷ] *n.* 奇蹟 ③
work / perform miracles 有奇效
(2) miraculously [məˋrækjələslɪ] *adv.* 奇蹟地

▸ Jeremy made a miraculous recovery from a nearly fatal heart attack.
那心臟病幾乎致傑瑞米於死地，但他卻奇蹟般地復原了。

3 forthcoming [͵fɔrθˋkʌmɪŋ] *a.* 即將到來的

似 (1) imminent [ˋɪmənənt] *a.* 即將到來的 ⑥
(2) approaching [əˋprotʃɪŋ] *a.* 即將到來的

▸ The forthcoming presidential election in Ukraine has stirred great interest around the world.
烏克蘭即將來臨的總統選舉引起全世界強烈的關注。
*stir [stɝ] *vt.* 引起

4 extracurricular [͵ɛkstrəkəˋrɪkjələ˞] *a.* 課外的

片 an extracurricular activity 課外活動

▸ Johnson took part in many extracurricular activities while in college.
強森念大學時參加了很多課外活動。

5 ponder [ˋpandə˞] *vi.* & *vt.* 仔細考慮，沉思

似 (1) consider [kənˋsɪdə˞] *vt.* 仔細考慮 ②
(2) contemplate [ˋkantəm͵plet] *vt.* 仔細考慮 ⑤

▸ Having earned his master's degree from New York University, Charles is now pondering what his next move should be.
查爾斯在紐約大學取得碩士學位後，他現在正仔細考慮下一步該怎麼走。

▸ The mysteries of the universe have been pondered for centuries by human beings.
好幾世紀以來，人類一直在思考宇宙的奧秘。

meditate [ˋmɛdə͵tet] *vi.* 深思熟慮；冥想，打坐

片 meditate on / upon sth 深思某事

▸ Donald meditated on which college to apply to on his teacher's advice.
唐納德按照老師的建議仔細考慮要申請哪些大學。

▸ The monk meditates under that tree every morning.
每天早上這和尚都會在那棵樹下打坐。

meditation [ˌmɛdəˋteʃən] *n.* 沉思；冥想，打坐

片 in meditation 在沉思

▶ Rita saw her grandmother looking out of the window, deep in meditation.
麗塔看到她奶奶看著窗外，陷入了沉思。

▶ Karen found inner peace by practicing yoga and meditation.
凱倫藉由練習瑜珈和打坐得到了內心的平靜。

6 evacuate [ɪˋvækjʊˌet] *vi.* & *vt.* 撤離

片 (1) evacuate sb from + 地方
將某人從某地方撤離
(2) evacuate sb to + 地方
將某人撤離至某地方

衍 evacuation [ɪˌvækjʊˋeʃən]
n. 撤離，避難

▶ The government ordered five buildings to be evacuated after the gas leak was discovered.
在發現瓦斯漏氣後，政府下令居民從這五棟建築物撤離。

▶ A large number of people were evacuated from the village following the outbreak of the disease.
這疾病爆發後，很多人從那村莊被撤離。

▶ The residents were evacuated to safe areas before the volcano erupted.
火山爆發前，居民已經被撤離到安全地區。

7 exempt [ɪgˋzɛmpt] *a.* 被豁免的 & *vt.* 使豁免

片 (1) be exempt from... 豁免於……
(2) exempt A from B 使 A 豁免於 B

▶ Franklin is exempt from military service because he has dual citizenship.
法蘭克林不用服兵役，因為他有雙重國籍。

▶ Frank's bad eyesight exempted him from military service.
法蘭克視力不佳使他不用服兵役。

8 faction [ˋfækʃən] *n.* (大團體中的) 派系

▶ Rumor has it that a powerful faction of the military intends to overthrow the king.
有傳言軍方一個強大的派系打算推翻國王。

9 hypocrite [ˋhɪpəkrɪt] *n.* 偽君子

似 double-dealer [ˌdʌblˋdilɚ]
n. 口是心非的人，偽君子〔英〕

▶ It's a torment to have to associate with a hypocrite, who says one thing but does another.
必須結交那種言行不一的偽君子真是一種折磨。
*torment [ˋtɔrmɛnt] *n.* 折磨

hypocritical [ˌhɪpəˋkrɪtɪkl]
a. 虛偽的，言行不一的

似 insincere [ˌɪnsɪnˋsɪr] *a.* 沒誠意的

▶ It would be hypocritical of you to have a church wedding if you don't believe in God.
如果你不信神卻在教會結婚，這麼做是很虛偽的。

2409-2417

hypocrisy [hɪˋpɑkrəsɪ] *n.* 虛偽

反 sincerity [sɪnˋsɛrətɪ] *n.* 誠懇 ④

▸ Many people felt the congressman's attendance at the fundraiser was an act of hypocrisy.

許多人認為那國會議員出席這場資金籌募活動根本就是一種虛偽的行為。

*attendance [əˋtɛndəns] *n.* 出席
fundraiser [ˋfʌndˌrezɚ] *n.* 募款活動

10 tedious [ˋtidɪəs] *a.* 沉悶的

似 (1) boring [ˋbɔrɪŋ] *a.* 無聊的 ①
(2) dull [dʌl] *a.* 無聊的 ②
(3) monotonous [məˋnɑtənəs] *a.* 單調的，沉悶的

▸ Brandon's job is so tedious that he often falls asleep in the middle of working.

布蘭登的工作很無聊，因此他常工作到一半時就睡著了。

11 monotony [məˋnɑtənɪ] *n.* 單調

似 boredom [ˋbɔrdəm] *n.* 無聊 ⑤

▸ Taking half a day off work occasionally is a nice way to break the monotony of everyday life.

偶而請假半天不上班是個讓每天生活不再單調的好方法。

12 longevity [lɑnˋdʒɛvətɪ] *n.* 長壽（不可數）

似 permanence [ˋpɝmənəns] *n.* 永久，持久

▸ Ned attributes his longevity to regular exercise, a balanced diet, and a carefree lifestyle.

奈德認為他會長壽是因為他有定期運動、有均衡的飲食以及無憂無慮的生活方式。

13 mute [mjut] *a.* 無聲的；啞巴的 & *vt.* 降低（音量）& *n.* 靜音裝置 / 按鈕（= mute button）

似 silent [ˋsaɪlənt] *a.* 沉默的 ②

▸ The governor has remained mute about his stance with regard to the new laws for migrant workers.

這位州長對於自己對移工新法條的立場仍保持沉默。

*stance [stæns] *n.* 立場
with regard to... 關於……

▸ Contrary to popular belief, not all deaf people are mute.

與大多數人所想的不一樣，其實並非所有耳聾的人都是啞巴。

▸ Noise from outside was muted after we installed the soundproof windows at the office.

我們在辦公室裝了隔音窗後，外面的噪音就減弱了。

▸ In order not to disturb his roommates, Chris turned on the subtitles and watched the film on mute.

克理斯為了不打擾他室友，就把字幕打開，以靜音模式看這部電影。

14 backbone [ˋbæk͵bon] *n.* 脊椎骨 (= spine)；支柱；勇氣，決心

片 (1) be the backbone of sth
為某物的支柱 / 棟樑
(2) have no backbone to + V
沒有勇氣 / 膽量做……

▸ My backbone hurts from long hours of sitting. I need to stretch my legs.
我坐太久，**脊椎**好痛。我得活動活動筋骨。

▸ The state-of-the-art computer industry is the backbone of this country's economy.
先進的電腦產業是該國的經濟**支柱**。
*state-of-the-art [͵stetəvðɪˋart] *a.* 先進的

▸ Andrew has no backbone to tell his parents what he really wants to be in the future.
安德魯**沒有勇氣**告訴父母他未來真正想當什麼。

15 amid [əˋmɪd] *prep.* 在其中 (= amidst [əˋmɪdst])

似 (1) among [əˋmʌŋ]
prep. 在……之中 ②
(2) in the middle of... 在……之中
= in the midst [mɪdst] of...

▸ The singer stood singing amid a crowd of his fans.
= The singer stood singing among a crowd of his fans.
這位歌手站在一群歌迷**中間**唱歌。

▸ The politician fled the country amid rumors that he was involved in a bribery scandal.
這政客涉及了一項行賄醜聞的謠言**正在傳開之時**，他就逃出國了。
*bribery [ˋbraɪbərɪ] *n.* 賄賂

16 kin [kɪn] *n.* 親戚 & *a.* 相似的，相關的

片 (1) next of kin
最親的家 / 親屬，直系血親 (單複數同形)
(2) be kin to... 和……有相似 / 關

▸ I wrote my sister's name and number down when the hospital asked for next of kin.
當院方問到**最親的家屬**時，我寫下了我妹妹的名字和電話號碼。

▸ Lance learned from his grandfather that he is distant kin to the Swedish royal family.
蘭斯從他爺爺那裡得知，他是瑞典王室的**遠親**。

17 fragrant [ˋfregrənt] *a.* 芬芳的

似 (1) perfumed [pɚˋfjumd] *a.* 芳香的
(2) scented [ˋsɛntɪd] *a.* 芳香的
(3) aromatic [͵ærəˋmætɪk] *a.* 芬芳的

▸ These fragrant flowers bloom all year round.
這些**芬芳的**花朵一年到頭都會綻放。

fragrance [ˋfregrəns] *n.* 香味

似 (1) perfume [pɚˋfjum] *n.* 香味；香水 ④
(2) scent [sɛnt] *n.* 香味 ⑤
(3) aroma [əˋromə] *n.* 香味，芬芳

▸ I like the fragrance of jasmine.
我喜歡茉莉的**香味**。
*jasmine [ˋdʒæzmən] *n.* 茉莉

18 ornament [ˋɔrnəmənt] *n.* 裝飾品 & *vt.* 裝飾

片 be ornamented with sth
用某物做 / 來裝飾
= be decorated with sth

似 (1) decorate [ˋdɛkə͵ret] *vt.* 裝飾 ③
(2) decoration [͵dɛkəˋreʃən] *n.* 裝飾 ④

▸ The department stores are decorated with Christmas ornaments during the holiday season.
聖誕假期期間，百貨公司裝飾著聖誕飾品。
*the holiday season　從感恩節一直到新曆新年這段假期

▸ This seaside café is painted blue and ornamented with shells.
這間海邊的咖啡館被漆成藍色，用了很多貝殼做裝飾。

19 revolt [rɪˋvolt] *vi.* 造反 & *vt.* 反感，厭惡 & *n.* 叛變

片 (1) revolt against sb　對某人造反
(2) be in revolt against sth
起而反抗某事物

衍 revolution [͵rɛvəˋluʃən] *n.* 革命 ④

似 rebel [rɪˋbɛl] *vi.* 造反 ④
三態為：rebel, rebelled [rɪˋbɛld], rebelled

▸ The people revolted against the dictator and established their own government.
人民起義反抗這獨裁者，並建立了自己的政府。
*dictator [ˋdɪk͵tetɚ] *n.* 獨裁者

▸ The dirt and mess in Hank's house revolted me.
漢克房子裡的灰塵和髒亂讓我很反感。

▸ The town's people are in revolt against the raising of taxes.
鎮民起而反抗增稅一事。

20 disciple [dɪˋsaɪpl̩] *n.* 門徒，跟隨者

似 (1) follower [ˋfɑloɚ] *n.* 信徒；跟隨者 ③
(2) believer [bɪˋlivɚ] *n.* 信徒

▸ It is said that Confucius—a Chinese philosopher and teacher—had 3,000 disciples.
據說身兼中國哲學家及教師的孔子有 3,000 名弟子。

21 solitary [ˋsɑlə͵tɛrɪ] *a.* 單獨的

似 lonely [ˋlonlɪ] *a.* 寂寞的 ①
反 sociable [ˋsoʃəbl̩] *a.* 合群的 ⑥

▸ Herman has been living a solitary life in the mountains since his wife passed away.
赫曼自從老婆去世後，就一直獨自一人在山裡生活。

solitude [ˋsɑlə͵t(j)ud] *n.* 獨處

片 in solitude　獨處地

▸ The old man is looking for a place where he can live in solitude.
這老人正在尋找一個可以讓他獨居的地方。

22 induce [ɪnˋd(j)us] *vt.* 誘使，勸說

片 induce sb to + V
誘使 / 勸說某人做……

似 (1) persuade [pɚˋswed] *vt.* 說服 ③
(2) tempt [tɛmpt] *vt.* 引誘 ⑤

▸ The salesperson induced me to buy this second-hand car, which he claimed to be in perfect condition.
該業務員誘使我買下這輛二手車，宣稱該車的車況極佳。
*claim sth to + V　宣稱某事物……

23 velvet [ˋvɛlvɪt] *n.* 絲絨

▸ You should dry-clean this evening gown because it's made of velvet.
你應把這件晚禮服拿去乾洗，因為它是絲絨製的。

24 industrialize [ɪnˋdʌstrɪəl͵aɪz] *vt.* & *vi.* (使) 工業化

衍 (1) industry [ˋɪndʌstrɪ] *n.* 工業 ②
(2) industrial [ɪnˋdʌstrɪəl]
a. 工業的 ③
(3) industrialist [ɪnˋdʌstrɪəlɪst]
n. 企業家，實業家

▸ The government is trying hard to make this region industrialized.
政府正努力要讓此地區工業化。

▸ After the discovery of oil and natural gas deposits, the small nation industrialized very quickly.
在發現了石油和天然氣礦藏之後，這小國很快就工業化了。

25 dispense [dɪˋspɛns] *vt.* 分配；配藥

片 (1) dispense A to B　將 A 分給 B
(2) dispense medicine　配藥

衍 (1) dispenser [dɪˋspɛnsɚ] *n.* 投幣機
(2) dispensary [dɪˋspɛnsərɪ]
n. (附屬於醫院的) 藥局，配藥處

▸ The hospitable villagers dispensed hot tea to thirsty mountain climbers.
好客的村民提供熱茶給口渴的登山客。

▸ Pharmacists can't be too careful when dispensing medicines.
藥劑師配藥時再小心也不為過。
*pharmacist [ˋfɑrməsɪst] *n.* 藥劑師
can't be too careful when...
當……時再小心也不為過，當……時越小心越好

---

dispensable [dɪˋspɛnsəbl̩]
a. 用不到的，不必要的

似 unnecessary [ʌnˋnɛsə͵sɛrɪ]
a. 不必要的

反 indispensable [͵ɪndɪˋspɛnsəbl̩]
a. 不可或缺的 ⑤

▸ Harold was worried about his position in the company when he found that his job was dispensable.
哈洛德發現他的工作並非不可或缺時，他開始擔心他在公司裡的職位。

26 yogurt [ˋjogɚt] *n.* 優格 (= yoghurt)

似 yoga [ˋjogə] *n.* 瑜珈 ⑥

▸ Maggie usually eats fruit and yogurt for breakfast.
瑪琪早餐通常吃水果和優格。

27 patriot [ˋpetrɪət] *n.* 愛國者

衍 patriotism [ˋpetrɪətɪzm̩] *n.* 愛國心；愛國主義

▸ The patriots formed a militia to drive away the invading army.
這群愛國的人組成民兵擊退入侵的軍隊。
*militia [məˋlɪʃə] *n.* 民兵

patriotic [ˌpetrɪˋɑtɪk] *a.* 愛國的

▸ Singing the national anthem proudly is a great way to be patriotic.
驕傲地唱著國歌是表現愛國的好方式。

28 outgoing [ˋaʊtˌgoɪŋ] *a.* 外向的

似 extrovert [ˋɛkstrəˌvɝt] *a.* 外向的 (= extroverted)

反 (1) shy [ʃaɪ] *a.* 害羞的 ②
(2) introvert [ˋɪntrəˌvɝt] *a.* 內向的 (= introverted)

▸ Jason's good interpersonal skills and outgoing personality qualify him as a great sales rep.
傑森良好的人際關係技巧以及外向的個性，讓他有資格當個優秀的推銷員。
*rep [rɛp] *n.* 推銷員，業務員 (= sales rep / representative)

29 orphanage [ˋɔrfənɪdʒ] *n.* 孤兒院

衍 orphan [ˋɔrfən] *n.* 孤兒 ④

▸ Robin's parents died in an accident, so he was raised in an orphanage.
羅賓的父母親死於一場意外，因此他是在孤兒院長大的。

30 hybrid [ˋhaɪbrɪd] *n.* (動 / 植) 混種；混合物；油電混合動力車 & *a.* (動 / 植) 混種的；混合的；油電混合動力車的

似 (1) cross [krɔs] *n.* 混合物；混血兒 ①
(2) mixture [ˋmɪkstʃɚ] *n.* 混合物 ②
(3) compound [ˋkɑmpaʊnd] *n.* 混合物；化合物 & *a.* 混合的 & [kəmˋpaʊnd] *vt.* 使混合 ⑤

▸ Would you like to try this delicious fruit? It's a hybrid of a tangerine and an orange.
你想嚐嚐這美味的水果嗎？它是橘子和柳丁的混種。

▸ Gordon uses a management style that is a hybrid of two famous theories, and it is quite effective.
戈登使用的管理風格是結合了兩種知名的理論，而這混合過的理論非常有效。

▸ Today, some cars are completely electric, but hybrids that use both gas and electricity are still more common.
現在有些汽車完全是電動的，但同時使用汽油和電力的油電混合動力車仍更常見。

▸ Mason's dog is a hybrid breed—it is a cross between a poodle and a cocker spaniel.
梅森的狗是混種，是貴賓犬和可卡長毛獵犬的混種狗。
*poodle [ˋpudḷ] *n.* 貴賓狗
cocker spaniel [ˌkɑkɚ ˋspænjəl] *n.* 可卡長毛獵犬

▸ In order to come up with a hybrid solution that would satisfy everyone, Henry considered suggestions from various managers.
亨利為了提出一個每個人都滿意的混合解決方案，他認真考慮了不同經理們的建議。

▸ One of the most popular hybrid vehicles is the Prius, which has been manufactured by Toyota since 1997.
普銳斯是最受歡迎的**油電混合動力**車之一，豐田從 1997 年開始生產此車款。

31 convene [kən`vin] *vi.* & *vt.* 召開（會議等）

似 (1) gather [`gæðɚ] *vi.* 聚集 ②
(2) assemble [ə`sɛmbḷ] *vi.* & *vt.* 聚集 ④
(3) summon [`sʌmən] *vt.* 召集 ⑥

▸ An urgent board meeting of the company convened soon after several of its top managers were involved in a bribery case.
此公司的幾位高級管理人員捲入賄賂案後不久，該公司馬上**召開**了緊急董事會會議。

▸ To deal with the urgent problem, Mr. Foster convened an emergency meeting on Saturday morning in the boardroom.
為了解決此一緊迫問題，福斯特先生於週六上午在紐約董事會會議室**召開**了一次緊急會議。

32 scrutiny [`skrutənɪ] *n.* 詳細的檢 / 審查

片 under scrutiny
受到密切關注，接受審查

▸ Roland found himself under scrutiny by the police after he visited a friend who died mysteriously the next day.
羅蘭曾探訪了一位朋友，這位朋友第二天卻離奇死亡，之後羅蘭發現他**遭到**了警方**密切關注**。

33 salvage [`sælvɪdʒ] *vt.* 搶救（財物等）；挽救（= save）& *n.*（對財物等的）搶救；搶救出的物品（皆不可數）

片 a salvage operation 搶救行動

▸ Many of Ben's possessions were destroyed in the fire, but he was able to salvage some things.
班的很多財產在大火中被摧毀，但他還有**搶救**一些東西回來。

▸ Despite losing so much money, Lanny managed to salvage his business by getting a loan from the bank.
儘管蘭尼損失了這麼多錢，但他還是設法向銀行貸到了錢來**挽救**自己的生意。

▸ A salvage operation was launched after a cargo train was derailed last night.
昨晚一列貨運列車出軌後，**搶救行動**就開始了。

▸ Unfortunately for Norman, the salvage from the building that was flooded was much less than he had expected.
不幸的是，對於諾曼來說，從那棟被洪水淹沒的建築物中所**搶救出來的東西**，比他預期的要少得多。

Level 6 Unit 24

2433-2435

savage [ˋsævɪdʒ] *n.* 野蠻人 & *a.* 野蠻的，粗俗的 & *vt.* (動物) 兇猛地攻擊；猛烈抨擊

似 (1) uncivilized [ʌnˋsɪvḷ͵aɪzd] *a.* 野蠻的，未開化的
(2) violent [ˋvaɪələnt] *a.* 暴力的 ③

▸ Tom is rude and mean. He is not unlike a savage.
湯姆人很粗魯，心腸又壞。他跟野蠻人沒什麼兩樣。

▸ Cannibalism is considered savage behavior.
吃人肉被視為是野蠻的行為。
*cannibalism [ˋkænəbḷ͵ɪzəm] *n.* 吃人（肉）

▸ After learning that Sam was going to hike in some remote mountains, his mother got worried because she was afraid he would be savaged by a bear.
山姆的母親在得知山姆要去一些偏遠的山林裡去徒步旅行後，她很擔心，因為她怕他會被熊攻擊。

▸ Even though the comedian's remarks were made in jest, he was savaged by the national press.
雖然這喜劇演員的言論是開玩笑的，但他卻受到了全國新聞界的抨擊。
*in jest 開玩笑地

34 ruthless [ˋruθləs] *a.* 無情的

似 (1) cruel [ˋkruəl] *a.* 殘忍的 ③
(2) merciless [ˋmɝsɪləs] *a.* 無情的

▸ The lawyer told the jury they shouldn't be fooled by the criminal's smile—he was actually a ruthless killer.
律師告訴陪審團，他們不應該被那罪犯的微笑給矇騙了——他實際上是個很無情的殺手。
*jury [ˋdʒʊrɪ] *n.* 陪審團

35 organizer [ˋɔrgə͵naɪzɚ] *n.* 籌辦人

似 organize [ˋɔrgə͵naɪz] *vt.* 組織 ③

▸ The journalist had an interview with the organizer of the trade show and wrote an article in the newspaper to promote the events.
這記者採訪了此貿易展的籌辦人，並在報紙上寫了篇文章來宣傳此展覽的活動。

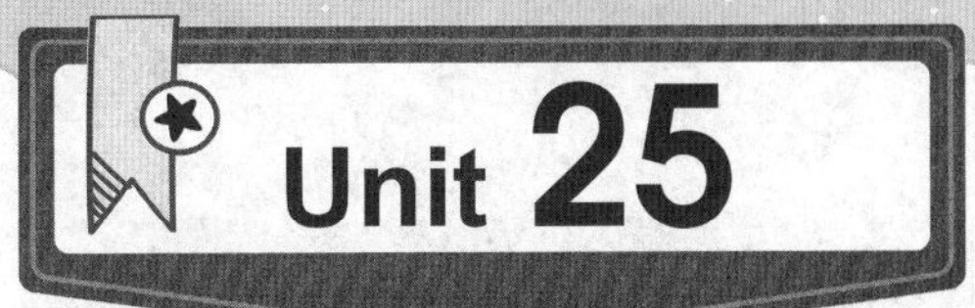

2501-2503

1 transplant [træns`plænt ] *vt.* 移植 & [ `træns,plænt] *n.* 移植

片 (1) transplant A to B　把 A 移至 B
(2) a liver / heart transplant
肝 / 心臟移植

衍 transplantation [,trænsplæn`teʃən] *n.* 移植

▸ That tree is tall enough to be transplanted to the garden.
那棵樹已經長得夠高，能夠**移植**到花園裡去了。

▸ The patient requires a liver transplant immediately.
這病人需要馬上接受**肝臟移植**。

2 nourish [`nɝɪʃ] *vt.* 餵養，給……提供營養

衍 nourishing [`nɝɪʃɪŋ] *a.* 有營養的

似 (1) feed [fid] *vt.* 餵養 ①
(2) sustain [səs`ten] *vt.* 供養 ⑤

▸ Lisa is thin and small because she was not properly nourished as a child.
莉莎會這麼瘦小是因為她小時候沒有得到適當的營養。

nourishment [`nɝɪʃmənt]
n. 營養 (不可數)

似 (1) nutrition [n(j)u`trɪʃən] *n.* 營養 (不可數) ⑤
(2) nutrient [`n(j)utrɪənt] *n.* 養分 (可數) ⑤

▸ Breast milk can provide all the basic nourishment a baby needs.
母乳可提供嬰兒所需的基本營養。

3 outnumber [aut`nʌmbɚ] *vt.* (數量上) 勝過

衍 number [`nʌmbɚ] *n.* 數字 & *vt.* 給……編號 ①

延伸 某些字可與 out 結合形成及物動詞，表『在某方面勝過……』，如：
(1) outwit [aut`wɪt] *vt.* 以機智勝過，智勝
(2) outsmart [aut`smɑrt] *vt.* 以機智勝過，智勝
(3) outdistance [aut`dɪstəns] *vt.* 超越，拉開距離
(4) outlive [aut`lɪv] *vt.* 活得比……久

▸ Women usually outlive their husbands.
女人通常比她們的老公長壽。

(5) outshine [aut`ʃaɪn] *vt.* 光芒強過，聲勢勝過

▸ New Zealand is a country where the sheep population outnumbers the human population.
紐西蘭是一個羊群數目多於人的國家。

4 underestimate [ˌʌndɚˋɛstəˌmet] *vt.* 低估 & [ˌʌndɚˋɛstəmət] *n.* 低估

衍 estimate [ˋɛstəmet] *vt.* 估計 ④

反 overestimate [ˌovɚˋɛstəˌmet] *vt.* 高估 & [ˌovɚˋɛstəˌmət] *n.* 高估

▸ The influence of gossip on decision-making should not be underestimated.
流言對決策的影響不應被低估。

▸ The jeweler said the ring was worth about US$500, but Bill insists that is an underestimate.
這珠寶商說這枚戒指價值約 500 美元，但比爾堅持說這價值被低估了。

5 vanilla [vəˋnɪlə] *n.* 香草

片 vanilla ice cream　香草冰淇淋

▸ Vanilla extract is often used for flavor in baking.
香草精常用於烘培時提味用。
*extract [ˋɛkstrækt] *n.* 萃取物，精華

▸ Everyone else in my family prefers chocolate treats, but my favorite will always be vanilla ice cream.
我家其它人都喜歡巧克力點心，但我最喜歡的永遠是香草冰淇淋。

6 utensil [juˋtɛnsḷ] *n.* 器具；用具

片 a kitchen utensil　廚房用具

▸ A whisk is a kitchen utensil for beating eggs and cream.
攪拌器是一種用來打蛋和奶油的廚房用具。
*whisk [(h)wɪsk] *n.* 攪拌器

7 outrage [ˋaʊtˌredʒ] *vt.* 使憤慨 & *n.* 令人憤慨的事

似 (1) anger [ˋæŋgɚ] *vt.* 使發怒 ②
(2) infuriate [ɪnˋfjʊrɪˌet] *vt.* 使大怒

▸ People were outraged by the increasing food prices.
民眾對於物價上漲感到憤怒。

▸ The scandal caused public outrage.
該醜聞令大眾憤慨。

outrageous [aʊtˋredʒəs]
a. 令人無法接受的，駭人的

似 shocking [ˋʃɑkɪŋ] *a.* 令人震驚的

▸ It's outrageous that such a cold-blooded murderer should be released on parole after only 10 months in prison.
這冷血殺人犯竟然坐牢 10 個月就獲假釋，這真是令人無法接受。
*parole [pəˋrol] *n.* 假釋
be on parole　在假釋中

8 retrieve [rɪˋtriv] *vt.* 重新找回

衍 retriever [rɪˋtrivɚ] *n.* 獵犬
(能尋回獵獲物的一種獵狗)
a golden retriever　黃金獵犬

▸ Many people wonder if the police chief will retrieve the billionaire's money that was stolen.
許多人懷疑這警察局局長是否能找回那億萬富翁失竊的錢。

9 royalty [ˋrɔɪəltɪ] *n.* 皇室（集合名詞，不可數）；版稅（常用複數）

複 royalties [ˋrɔɪəltɪz]

片 (1) a member of the royalty
一名皇室成員

(2) receive royalties on sth
獲得某物的版稅

衍 royal [ˋrɔɪəl] *a.* 皇家的，皇室的 ②

▶ Annie discovered that her grandmother was a member of the royalty.
安妮發現她外婆是**皇室成員**。

▶ The author received 5% royalties on each copy sold.
這名作家每賣出一本書，就可抽 5% 的**版稅**。

10 smuggle [ˋsmʌgl̩] *vt.* 走私

片 (1) smuggle sth into + 地方
把某物走私到某地方

(2) smuggle sth out of + 地方
把某物從某地方走私出去

衍 smuggler [ˋsmʌglɚ] *n.* 走私者

▶ The man was arrested for smuggling drugs into Malaysia.
這名男子因**走私**毒品到馬來西亞而遭逮捕。

▶ Tim was caught at customs trying to smuggle 30 kilos of heroin out of the country.
提姆在海關被抓到要**走私** 30 公斤的海洛英**出**國。

11 escalate [ˋɛskə͵let] *vt.* & *vi.* (使) 逐步上升，(使) 惡化

衍 escalator [ˋɛskə͵letɚ] *n.* 手扶梯 ⑤

似 (1) soar [sɔr] *vi.* 急升，飛漲；翱翔 ⑤
(2) elevate [ˋɛlə͵vet] *vt.* 使上升 ⑥

▶ The general escalated the war by sending in more troops.
將軍派出更多軍隊而**讓**戰事**升高**。

▶ The situation was only escalated by Joe's refusal to apologize to Brad.
情況因為喬拒絕向布萊德道歉而**變得更糟糕**。

12 stationary [ˋsteʃən͵ɛrɪ] *a.* 固定的

似 stationery [ˋsteʃən͵ɛrɪ] *n.* 文具（集合名詞，不可數）(與 stationary 發音完全相同) ⑥

▶ Those stationary bikes are the latest equipment in the gym.
那些**固定**腳踏車是健身房裡最新的設備。

13 staple [ˋstepl̩] *n.* 釘書針；主食 & *vt.* 用釘書機釘

衍 stapler [ˋsteplɚ] *n.* 釘書機

▶ Remember to remove the staples from the papers before you photocopy them.
在影印文件前，記得要把**釘書針**拿起來。

▶ Pasta is the staple of Italian cooking.
義大利麵食是義大利菜的**主食**。
*pasta [ˋpɑstə] *n.* 義大利麵食

▶ When you turn in your application pack, please do not staple the pages together.
當你繳交你的申請文件包時，請不要將頁面裝**釘**在一起。

14 symmetry [ˋsɪmətrɪ] *n.* 對稱

衍 symmetrical [sɪˋmɛtrɪkḷ] *adj.* 對稱的
反 asymmetry [eˋsɪmətrɪ] *n.* 不對稱

▶ In esthetics, symmetry is one of the most basic rules.
就美學而言，對稱是最基本的原則之一。
*esthetics [ɛsˋθɛtɪks] *n.* 美學〔美〕(= aesthetics〔英〕)

15 veterinarian [ˌvɛt(ə)rəˋnɛrɪən] *n.* 獸醫(常簡寫為 vet [vɛt])

似 veteran [ˋvɛtərən] *n.* 退役軍人，老兵 ⑤

▶ The veterinarian checked the cat's ears carefully.
獸醫細心地檢查貓咪的耳朵。

16 ounce [auns] *n.* 盎司(約等於 28 公克，縮寫為 oz)

比 pound [paund] *n.* 磅(等於 454 公克，縮寫為 lb) ②

▶ Most people drink around 40 ounces of water per day, but experts recommend more than twice that amount.
大多數人每天喝大約 40 盎司的水，但專家建議要喝這水量的兩倍以上。

▶ An ounce of prevention is worth a pound of cure.
一盎司的預防等於一磅的治療。/ 預防勝於治療。── 諺語

17 snore [snɔr] *n.* 打呼聲(可數) & *vi.* 打呼

延伸 yawn [jɔn] *n.* 哈欠 & *vi.* 打哈欠 ④

▶ I tossed and turned last night because of my friend's loud snores.
我昨晚翻來覆去睡不著，因為我朋友的打呼聲很大。

▶ I don't usually snore except after an exhausting day.
除非一整天下來很累，否則我通常不會打呼。

18 badge [bædʒ] *n.* 徽章

片 a badge of honor 榮譽勳章

▶ Captain Walter was awarded a badge of honor for his courageous actions in the war.
華特上尉因為戰爭時的英勇行為獲頒榮譽勳章。

19 arithmetic [əˋrɪθmətɪk] *n.* 算術；計算

片 do arithmetic 算算數

▶ We learn arithmetic right after we enter kindergarten.
我們進幼稚園後就開始學算術了。

▶ When it comes to doing arithmetic, Mark is a genius.
說到算算數，馬克是天才。

20 clasp [klæsp] *vt.* & *n.* 緊握

似 (1) hold [hold] *vt.* 抓住 ①
(2) grasp [græsp] *vt.* 抓緊 ③
(3) grip [grɪp] *vi.* & *vt.* 緊握 ⑤

▶ Throughout the long journey, the mother clasped her baby tightly to her chest.
在漫長的旅途中，那位母親緊緊把她的嬰兒抱在胸前。

▶ Ashley held her grandfather's hand in a firm clasp, hoping that he would recover soon.
艾希莉緊**握住**她爺爺的手，希望他能很快好起來。

21 bra [brɑ] *n.* 內衣，胸罩 (= brassiere [brəˋzɪr])

比 underwear [ˋʌndɚ͵wɛr] *n.* 內衣（集合名詞，不可數）③

▶ My younger sister felt quite embarrassed when she went bra shopping with my mother for the first time.
我妹妹第一次和我媽去買**內衣**時，她覺得很尷尬。

22 solemn [ˋsɑləm] *a.* 嚴肅的，莊嚴的

衍 (1) solemnity [səˋlɛmnətɪ] *n.* 嚴肅
(2) solemnly [ˋsɑləmlɪ] *adv.* 莊嚴地

▶ You're not supposed to laugh out loud on such a solemn occasion. If you laugh one more time, I'll have to show you the door.
這種**嚴肅**的場合你不應當笑出聲來。如果你再笑一次的話，我就得讓你離開。

23 janitor [ˋdʒænətɚ] *n.* (學校、大棟建築物等的) 工友，管理員

似 (1) caretaker [ˋkɛr͵tekɚ] *n.* (大樓的) 管理員 ⑥
(2) superintendent [͵supərɪnˋtɛndənt] *n.* (大樓) 管理員 ⑥

▶ The school janitor cleaned and waxed the basketball court before the tournament.
學校**工友**在錦標賽之前把籃球場清理乾淨還打了蠟。
*tournament [ˋtɝnəmənt / ˋturnəmənt] *n.* 錦標賽，比賽

24 wrinkle [ˋrɪŋkḷ] *n.* 皺紋 & *vi.* & *vt.* 使起皺紋

片 wrinkle (up) one's nose 皺鼻子 (表不喜歡)

衍 wrinkled [ˋrɪŋkḷd] *a.* 有皺紋的
a wrinkled face 滿是皺紋的臉

▶ No one can live to old age without getting wrinkles.
任何人老了都會有**皺紋**。

▶ Since his son often tells tall tales, Chuck's forehead wrinkled in suspicion as the boy began his latest story.
由於查克的兒子經常講荒誕不經的故事，所以當這男孩開始說他最近的事時，查克因懷疑而**眉頭深鎖**。
*a tall tale 荒誕不經的故事

▶ My sister wrinkled her nose when she smelled something bad.
我妹妹聞到有臭味的東西就會**皺鼻子**。

25 dresser [ˋdrɛsɚ] *n.* 矮衣櫃

似 (1) closet [ˋklɑzɪt] *n.* 衣櫥 ③
(2) wardrobe [ˋwɔrd͵rob] *n.* 衣櫥〔英〕⑥

▶ This dresser has many drawers in which I store clothes and accessories.
這**矮衣櫃**有很多抽屜讓我放衣服和配件。

dressing [ˋdrɛsɪŋ] *n.* 沙拉醬

延伸 (1) sauce [sɔs] *n.* 醬（拌食物用的）③
(2) seasoning [ˋsizṇɪŋ] *n.* 調味料，佐料（鹽、胡椒粉、香料等）
(3) condiment [ˋkɑndəmənt] *n.* 調味品（鹽、胡椒、芥末等）

▸ I always get Thousand Island dressing when I order salads.
我點沙拉時總是會用千島醬。

26 freeway [ˋfrɪˏwe] *n.* 高速公路

似 expressway [ɪkˋsprɛsˏwe] *n.* 高速公路

▸ While traveling on the freeway, you must obey the speed limit.
在高速公路上行駛，你得要遵守速限規定。

27 inland [ˋɪnlænd] *a.* 內陸的，內地的 & *adv.* 內陸地 & *n.* 內陸

片 an inland city 內陸都市

▸ Judy has lived in an inland city all her life; she has never seen the ocean.
茱蒂一直都是住在內陸城市；她從未見過海洋。

▸ The troops began to march inland after they had taken several important military posts along the coast.
部隊在占領了幾個沿海重要軍事據點後，開始向內陸挺進。

▸ After the goods are unloaded at the harbor, they'll be delivered to the country's inland.
貨物在港口卸貨後，會被送到此國的內陸地區。

28 yoga [ˋjogə] *n.* 瑜珈

片 do yoga 做瑜珈
似 yogurt [ˋjogɚt] *n.* 優格，酸奶

▸ Doing yoga regularly can help improve your health.
定期做瑜珈有益改善健康。

29 fume [fjum] *n.* 煙（常用複數）& *vi.* & *vt.* 發怒

片 (1) car exhaust fumes 汽車排放的廢氣
(2) fume about / over... 對……發怒
似 (1) smoke [smok] *n.* 煙 ①
(2) gas [gæs] *n.* 氣體 ③

▸ Car exhaust fumes have become one of the major sources of pollution in the city.
汽車排放的廢氣在該城市已成為汙染的主要來源之一。

▸ Judy was still fuming about my being late even after I apologized to her and promised that I'd never do it again.
我為我遲到了向茱蒂道歉，還保證絕不再犯，但她還是很氣我遲到。

▸ "How dare she stand me up again!" my roommate fumed.
我的室友發怒道：『她怎麼敢放我鴿子！』。
*stand sb up 放某人鴿子

30 pact [pækt] *n.* 條約，協定

似 (1) agreement [əˋgrimənt] *n.* 協定，協議 ①
(2) treaty [ˋtritɪ] *n.* 條約，協議 ⑤
(3) contract [ˋkɑntrækt] *n.* 合約 ②

▸ The two countries signed a free-trade pact.
這兩個國家簽訂了自由貿易**協定**。

31 pollutant [pəˋlutənt] *n.* 汙染物（可數）

衍 (1) pollute [pəˋlut] *v.* 汙染；弄髒 ③
(2) pollution [pəˋluʃən] *n.* 汙染（不可數）③
reduce pollution 減少汙染

▸ Air and water pollutants may cause some cancers.
空氣和水**汙染物**可能導致某些癌症。

32 revolve [rɪˋvɑlv] *vi.* 旋轉；公轉

片 revolve around... 繞著……轉；以……為中心

衍 revolution [ˌrɛvəˋluʃən] *n.* 旋轉；（天體的）公轉；革命 ④

比 rotate [ˋrotet] *vi.* & *vt.*（使）旋轉；地球自轉；輪流做 ⑥
rotation [roˋteʃən] *n.* 旋轉；地球自轉；輪作 ⑥

▸ It takes the Earth about 365 days to revolve around the sun.
地球繞太陽**公轉**一次大約要花 365 天。

▸ Brian's whole life revolves around his family.
布萊恩一生都以家人為**中心**。

33 woodpecker [ˋwudˌpɛkɚ] *n.* 啄木鳥

衍 peck [pɛk] *vi.* & *vt.* 啄
peck at... 啄……

▸ Because woodpeckers peck at tree trunks to find food, such as insects that do damage to trees, these birds are nicknamed tree doctors.
因為**啄木鳥**會啄食樹幹尋找食物 —— 例如像是對樹木造成傷害的昆蟲，所以這些鳥被暱稱為樹醫生。

peacock [ˋpiˌkɑk] *n.* 公孔雀

反 peahen [ˋpiˌhɛn] *n.* 母孔雀

▸ The peacock has beautiful feathers on its back.
公孔雀背上有美麗的羽毛。

seagull [ˋsigʌl] *n.* 海鷗
（= gull [gʌl]）

▸ David spied a few seagulls in the backyard of his house.
大衛在他家後院發現了幾隻**海鷗**。
*spy [spaɪ] *vt.* 注意 / 察覺到（= notice）

sparrow [ˋspæro] *n.* 麻雀

▸ A few sparrows were standing on the lamppost.
有幾隻**麻雀**站在街燈柱上。
*lamppost [ˋlæmpˌpost] *n.* 街燈柱

2534-2538

34 statute [ˋstætʃut] *n.* 成文法，法令

似 (1) statue [ˋstætʃu] *n.* 雕像 ③
(2) stature [ˋstætʃɚ] *n.* 身高 ⑥

▶ The new statute will severely punish those who drive under the influence.
新法規將嚴懲那些酒駕的人。
*drive under the influence 酒駕

35 jockey [ˋdʒɑkɪ] *n.* 賽馬騎師 & *vi.* 激烈競爭

似 (1) rider [ˋraɪdɚ] *n.* 騎馬者；騎車者
(2) compete [kəmˋpit] *vi.* 競爭 ③

▶ Stanley used to be teased for his short stature, but he went on to find success as a jockey.
史丹利以前因身材矮小而被取笑，但他後來成功地成為了一名賽馬騎師。

▶ Upon hearing that the CEO planned to retire, several people began jockeying to take the position.
當聽說執行長計劃要退休時，幾個人開始激烈競爭這個職位。

36 offshore [ˌɔfˋʃɔr] *a.* 離岸的，海上的；(投資 / 公司等) 設在海外的

比 inshore [ˋɪnˌʃɔr] *a.* 近岸的
反 onshore [ˋɑnˌʃɔr] *a.* 陸上的

▶ Have you been to any of Taiwan's offshore islands, such as Green Island or Orchid Island?
你去過臺灣任何如綠島或蘭嶼等離島嗎？
*orchid [ˋɔrkɪd] *n.* 蘭花

▶ Albert was caught stealing money from the company and depositing it in an offshore bank account.
亞伯特被抓到偷了公司的錢，還把錢存入了海外銀行的帳戶。

37 obsess [əbˋsɛs] *vt.* (使) 著迷；(使) 心神不寧 & *vi.* 過分在意

片 (1) be obsessed with...
著迷於……；因……而心神不寧
(2) obsess about...
糾結於……，過分在意……

▶ My younger sister is completely obsessed with K-pop. She could sing along to the songs all day long.
我妹妹完全沉迷於韓國流行音樂。她可以整天一直跟著那些歌一起唱。

▶ A lot of young girls today are obsessed with the idea of losing weight.
現今許多女孩子滿腦子想的都是減肥。

▶ Emma, please stop obsessing about your weight. You're the most beautiful girl I've ever seen.
艾瑪，別再糾結於你的體重了。妳是我見過最漂亮的女孩。

obsession [əbˋsɛʃən] *n.* 執著，著迷 (與 with 並用)

▶ John's obsession with gambling finally cost him his life savings.
約翰沉迷於賭博，最後失去了他所有的存款。
*cost sb sth 使某人失去某物

38 booklet [ˋbʊklət] *n.* 小冊子

似 (1) brochure [broˋʃʊr] *n.* 小冊子 ⑥
(2) pamphlet [ˋpæmflət] *n.* 小冊子

延伸 (1) guide [gaɪd] *n.* 指南，手冊；旅遊指南 ②
(2) manual [ˋmænjuəl] *n.* 使用手冊，說明書 ④
(3) handbook [ˋhændˏbʊk] *n.* 手冊，說明書

▸ When he started university, Paul was given a booklet containing rules and other useful information about the school.

保羅大學剛入學時，他拿到了一本小冊子，裡面寫著有關這所學校的規定及其他有用的資訊。

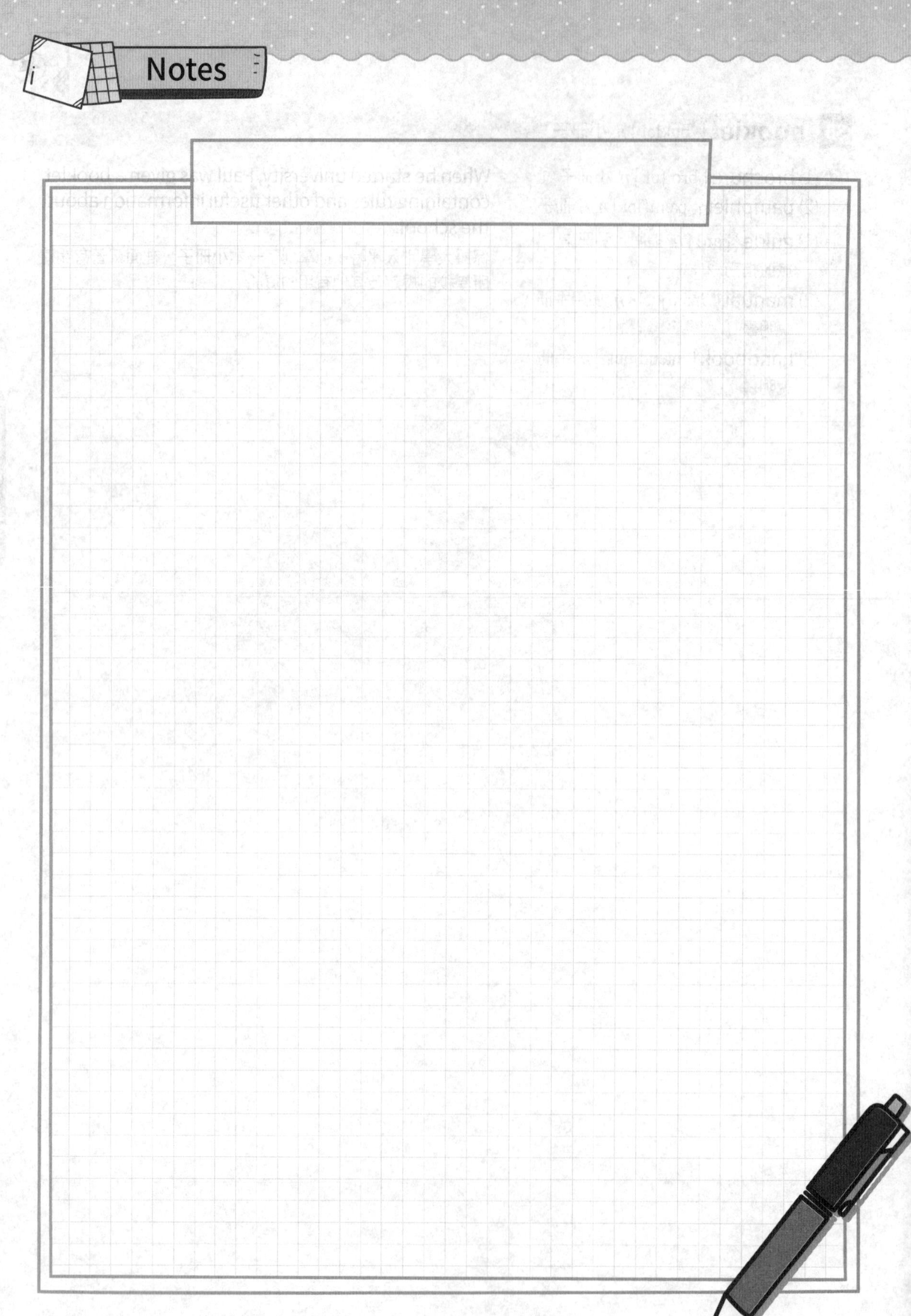
Notes

索引

A

abbreviate 237
abide 238
abnormal 8
abolish 8
aboriginal 325
abortion 7
abound 355
abrupt 67
abstraction 348
absurd 104
abundance 355
abundant 157
abuse 109
academy 247
accelerate 34
accessible 175
accessory 394
acclaim 394
accommodate 27
accommodation 27
accord 77
accordance 275
accordingly 275
accountable 395
accounting 176
accumulate 345
accumulation 345
accusation 395
accustom 258
acknowledge 40
acknowledgement 41
acne 290
acquaint 202
acquisition 146
acre 441
activist 193
acute 146
adaptation 326
addiction 401
administer 235
administration 35
administrative 35
administrator 36
admiral 424
adolescence 288
adolescent 152
adorable 7
adore 6
adverse 177
advisory 284
advocate 157
aesthetic 303
affection 59
affectionate 297
affiliate 263
affirm 306
agenda 155
aggression 160
agony 115
agricultural 50
airtight 308
airway 454
aisle 156
alcoholic 177
algebra 404
alien 136
alienate 376
align 283
allegation 348
allege 348
allergic 156
allergy 156
alliance 59
alligator 330
allocate 174
ally 58
alongside 177
alter 12
alteration 12
alternate 56
altitude 339
aluminum 451
ambiguity 276
ambush 307
amend 218
amid 459
ample 82
amplify 256
analogy 436
analyst 160
analytical 365
anchor 388
animate 296
animation 296
annoyance 402
anonymous 141
anthem 360
antibiotic 402
anticipate 54
anticipation 245
antique 161
antonym 441
applaud 367
applause 116

appliance 202
applicable 337
apprentice 318
approximate 304
apt 108
archaeology 314
architect 30
architecture 30
archive 324
arena 135
arithmetic 468
arouse 210
array 222
arrogant 177
articulate 178
artifact 109
ascend 382
aspire 387
ass 161
assassin 403
assassinate 403
assassination 403
assault 117
assert 55
assess 111
assessment 111
asset 133
assumption 37
asthma 267
astonish 161
astonishment 161
astray 395
astronaut 319
astronomer 319
astronomy 319
athletics 230
attain 255
attainment 255
attendance 155
attendant 374
attic 112
attorney 28
attribute 18
auction 176
audit 333
auditorium 333
authorize 73
autonomy 160
avert 344
aviation 402
awe 17
awesome 425
awhile 435

B

bachelor 451
backbone 459
backyard 228
badge 468
ballot 162
ban 162
banner 53
banquet 238
barbarian 247
barefoot 7
barren 17
bass 258
batch 82
batter 269
beautify 279
beep 239
beforehand 288
behalf 95
belongings 162
beloved 104
beneficial 162
betray 127
beverage 447
beware 163
bias 202
bid 125
bilateral 353
biological 159
bizarre 27
blast 108
blaze 297
bleach 308
blond(e) 319
blot 330
blueprint 163
blunt 238
blur 39
blush 27
bodily 339
bodyguard 200
bolt 163
bombard 371
bonus 163
booklet 473
boom 164
boost 27
booth 153
boredom 53
bosom 343
boulevard 360
bound 49

boundary	50
boundless	50
bouquet	306
boxer	164
boxing	367
boycott	403
bra	469
brace	377
braid	137
breadth	382
breakdown	345
breakthrough	148
breakup	345
bribe	341
briefcase	114
brink	383
broaden	409
brochure	401
broil	259
bronze	135
brook	269
broth	313
brotherhood	426
browse	200
bruise	107
bulk	106
bulky	399
bully	164
bureau	20
bureaucracy	20
bureaucrat	372
burial	159
butcher	207
bypass	382
C	
caffeine	295
calcium	178
calculator	279
calligraphy	289
canal	164
canvas	75
capability	102
cape	298
capsule	402
caption	403
captive	403
captivity	404
carbon	116
cardboard	309
cardinal	358
carefree	319
caretaker	330
carnival	207
carton	309
cashier	412
casino	219
casualty	315
catastrophe	317
categorize	20
cater	448
caterpillar	332
cathedral	137
caution	97
cautious	97
cavity	413
celebrity	165
celery	339
cellular	391
Celsius	400
cement	352
cemetery	158
census	412
ceramic	360
ceremony	44
certainty	112
certificate	165
certify	367
chairperson	378
champagne	409
chant	387
chaos	121
chapel	231
characterize	83
charitable	448
check-in	165
checkout	165
checkup	343
chef	207
chemist	404
chestnut	416
chili	426
chimpanzee	435
chirp	442
choir	155
cholesterol	411
chord	155
chore	228
chronic	147
chubby	53
chunk	194
cigar	451
circuit	43
cite	15
citizenship	81
civic	81

索　引

civilize 366
civilized 366
clam 444
clarity 89
clasp 468
clause 170
clearance 256
climax 239
cling 40
clinical 126
clockwise 259
clone 297
closure 287
cluster 133
coalition 393
coastline 241
cocaine 179
coffin 158
cognitive 209
coherent 145
coincidence 111
collaboration 209
collective 83
collector 83
collision 418
colloquial 376
colonel 424
colonial 68
columnist 184
combat 77
comedian 170
comet 249
commence 282
commentary 8
commentator 8
commission 2
commitment 74
commodity 96
commonplace 248
commonwealth 427
communicative 448
communism 4
communist 4
commute 113
commuter 113
compact 152
comparable 166
comparative 366
compass 261
compassion 225
compassionate 225
compatible 157
compel 58
compensate 28
compensation 28
competence 93
competent 93
compile 366
complement 349
complexion 447
complexity 127
compliance 220
complication 127
compliment 170
comply 113
component 36
compound 88
comprehend 171
comprehension 171
comprehensive 316
comprise 84
compromise 107
compulsory 229
compute 270
computerize 270
comrade 436
conceal 98
concede 90
conceive 46
conception 46
concession 276
concise 448
condemn 44
condense 447
conduct 2
confederation 444
confession 89
confidential 158
confine 205
conform 113
confront 5
confrontation 5
congressman 280
conquest 448
conscientious 412
consecutive 185
consensus 185
consent 114
conservation 166
conserve 373
considerate 207
consolation 290
console 290
consonant 312
conspiracy 336

constant	300	corridor	33	cucumber	397
constitutional	60	corrupt	117	cuisine	207
constraint	206	corruption	117	cultivate	355
consultation	149	cosmetic	449	cumulative	346
consumption	131	cosmetics	449	curb	406
contagious	143	counsel	123	curfew	449
contaminate	171	counselor	123	currency	122
contemplate	86	counterclockwise	259	curriculum	87
contemporary	11	counterpart	329	curry	407
contempt	98	coupon	248	custody	171
contend	62	courteous	210	customary	325
contention	427	courtyard	310	customs	218
contestant	278	coverage	129	cynical	449
continental	104	covet	255	**D**	
continuity	424	cowardice	320	dazzle	417
contractor	194	cowardly	320	dazzling	417
contradict	328	cozy	331	deadly	28
contradiction	139	crackdown	340	deafen	299
controversial	63	cracker	389	debris	185
controversy	63	cram	361	debut	185
convene	463	cramp	358	decay	143
conversion	39	crater	368	deceive	171
convert	39	credibility	84	decent	130
convict	48	credible	275	deception	172
conviction	48	creek	124	deceptive	172
coordinate	90	cripple	219	decisive	325
copyright	52	criterion	101	declaration	59
coral	302	crocodile	330	decline	46
core	57	crossing	362	dedicate	91
corporate	2	crucial	166	dedication	277
corporation	2	crude	137	deduct	294
corpse	358	cruise	178	deem	327
correlation	206	crutch	389	default	283
correspondence	298	crystal	67	defect	328
correspondent	49	cub	390	defendant	212

索　引

defiance	303	detergent	338	disclose	99
deficient	332	devastating	346	disclosure	288
deficit	90	devotion	68	discomfort	413
definitive	284	devour	442	disconnect	210
defy	206	diabetes	412	discourse	212
delegate	124	diagnose	156	discreet	451
delegation	125	diagnosis	157	discriminate	94
deliberate	74	dialect	124	discrimination	94
democrat	208	diameter	50	disgrace	337
denial	58	diaper	9	disgraceful	338
denounce	318	dictate	356	dismantle	449
density	102	dictation	356	dismay	414
dental	413	dictator	293	dispensable	461
depict	139	dictatorship	293	dispense	461
deplete	323	diesel	437	disposable	249
deploy	172	differentiate	447	disposal	249
depress	202	digestion	35	dispose	249
deprive	338	dilemma	92	disrupt	222
deputy	112	dimension	56	dissent	344
derive	36	diminish	102	dissident	447
descend	92	diplomacy	296	dissolve	111
descent	279	diplomatic	8	distinction	5
descriptive	208	directive	418	distinctive	5
designate	247	directory	179	distract	193
despair	70	disability	386	distraction	447
despise	301	disable	386	distress	240
destination	72	disabled	386	disturbance	316
destined	434	disapprove	147	diversify	375
destiny	72	disastrous	346	diversion	383
destructive	78	disbelief	443	divert	383
detach	339	disbelieve	443	dividend	391
detached	339	discard	452	doctrine	65
detain	450	discharge	286	document	41
detention	283	disciple	460	documentary	41
deter	335	disciplinary	450	domain	168

dome	118	ego	116	episode	118
donate	149	elaborate	51	equalize	371
donation	150	electrician	270	equate	255
donor	150	elevate	281	equation	64
doom	363	eligible	194	equity	221
doorway	108	elite	375	equivalent	64
dormitory	241	eloquent	178	erect	62
dough	152	embrace	70	erection	62
downward	239	emigrant	414	errand	217
downward(s)	239	emigrate	414	erupt	103
doze	248	emigration	414	escalate	467
drastic	316	emission	231	escalator	213
draught	372	enchant	172	escort	291
drawback	333	encyclopedia	411	essence	29
dreadful	223	endeavor	289	estate	13
dresser	469	endorse	176	esteem	298
dressing	470	endorsement	176	eternal	49
driveway	108	endowment	391	eternity	301
drizzle	443	endurance	327	ethic	59
drought	186	enhance	367	ethical	59
dual	415	enhancement	367	ethics	59
dubious	450	enlighten	415	evacuate	457
duration	250	enlightenment	415	evergreen	298
dusk	450	enrich	411	evoke	409
dwarf	251	enrichment	411	evolution	141
dwell	260	enroll	292	evolve	140
dwelling	260	enrollment	292	exaggeration	208
E		enterprise	23	examinee	300
eccentric	401	enthusiastic	43	examiner	301
eclipse	261	entitle	6	exceed	33
ecological	178	entity	231	excel	311
ecology	178	entrepreneur	24	exceptional	87
ecosystem	179	envious	228	excerpt	288
edible	411	envision	221	excess	311
editorial	267	epidemic	28	excessive	33

索引

exclaim	86
exclude	79
excluding	79
exclusion	314
exclusive	80
execute	12
execution	13
executive	12
exempt	457
exert	267
exile	180
exotic	35
expedition	140
expenditure	245
expertise	185
expiration	415
expire	415
explicit	119
exploit	128
exploration	93
extension	21
extensive	21
exterior	14
external	211
extinct	180
extinction	180
extinguisher	423
extract	327
extracurricular	456
extraordinary	32
eyelash	319
eyelid	320
eyesight	246
F	
fable	437
fabric	26
fabulous	126
facilitate	186
faction	457
faculty	37
fad	208
Fahrenheit	400
falter	321
familiarity	326
famine	420
fascinate	85
fascinating	85
fascination	331
fatigue	98
feasible	355
federal	1
feeble	340
feminine	341
fertility	350
fertilizer	350
fiancé / fiancée	360
fiber	49
filter	208
fin	369
finite	378
firecracker	349
fireproof	421
fiscal	213
fishery	398
flake	405
flaw	406
flawless	33
fleet	145
flexibility	203
flip	72
flourish	418
fluency	7
fluid	110
flunk	425
foe	434
folklore	442
foresee	315
forge	204
format	180
formidable	376
formulate	288
forsake	347
forthcoming	456
fortify	349
forum	186
foster	147
foul	7
fowl	451
fraction	51
fracture	359
fragment	145
fragrance	459
fragrant	459
framework	142
franchise	204
frantic	247
fraud	195
freak	401
freeway	470
freight	58
friction	338
frontier	42
fume	470
fury	239
fuse	240

fuss 268
fussy 268

G

galaxy 29
gallop 248
gangster 251
garment 248
gasp 208
gathering 49
gauge 427
gay 250
generate 34
generator 34
genetic 186
genetics 186
genre 202
geographical 260
geometry 260
ghetto 347
glacier 269
glamorous 315
glamour 315
glare 209
gleam 281
glee 117
glide 280
glitter 291
gloom 289
gloomy 181
goalkeeper 424
goodwill 400
gorgeous 181
gorilla 301
gospel 309
grant 3
grapefruit 310
graphic 174
gravity 181
graze 309
grease 321
greed 181
grieve 211
grill 187
grim 126
grip 40
groan 369
gross 50
growl 395
grumble 339
guideline 182
gut 164

H

habitat 145
hacker 326
hail 387
hairstyle 216
hamper 282
handicap 340
handicapped 182
handicraft 350
harass 385
harassment 385
harden 361
harmonica 368
harness 361
haul 106
haunt 369
hazard 110
headphones 242
healthful 389
hearty 396
hedge 397
heighten 405
heir 183
hemisphere 285
hence 16
herb 183
heritage 103
heroic 407
heroin 411
heterosexual 416
hierarchy 304
highlight 65
hijack 423
hoarse 299
hockey 216
homosexual 416
honorable 213
honorary 245
horizontal 123
hormone 194
hospitable 421
hospitality 421
hospitalize 421
hostage 183
hostel 301
hostile 114
hostility 115
housing 77
hover 434
howl 216
humiliate 422
humiliating 422
humiliation 422
hunch 245

hurdle 257
hybrid 462
hygiene 392
hypocrisy 458
hypocrite 457
hypocritical 457
hypothesis 214

I

iceberg 293
icon 210
ideology 221
idiot 183
illuminate 327
illuminating 327
illusion 64
immense 116
imminent 244
immune 186
imperative 285
imperial 443
implement 187
implication 65
implicit 305
imposing 442
imprison 422
imprisonment 422
impulse 32
incentive 157
inclination 277
incline 276
inclusive 257
incorporate 218
incur 254
indecisive 325
index 24
indifference 452
indifferent 97
indigenous 223
indignant 385
indispensable 85
induce 460
indulge 114
industrialize 461
inevitable 47
infect 220
infectious 251
infer 420
inference 420
infinite 99
inflict 366
infrastructure 231
inhabit 336
inhabitant 336
inherent 109
inherit 230
initiate 76
initiative 76
inject 175
injection 176
injustice 346
inland 470
inning 231
innovation 9
innovative 9
innumerable 251
inquire 266
inquiry 82
insane 187
insecure 25
insight 65
insistence 297
installation 129
instinctive 240
institute 35
institution 35
intact 145
intake 264
integrate 55
integration 55
integrity 57
intellect 456
intensify 219
intent 134
interference 212
interior 14
interpretation 4
interpreter 248
intersection 329
interval 55
intervene 307
intervention 120
intimacy 316
intimidate 422
intonation 251
intrigue 274
intrude 364
intruder 364
invaluable 261
invariably 244
inventory 286
investigator 149
ironic 386
irony 168
irritable 421
irritate 421

irritation 421
isle 251
itch 241
ivy 241

J

jade 248
janitor 469
jasmine 253
jingle 259
jockey 472
jolly 261
journalism 133
journalist 133
joyous 262
judicial 214
jug 108
junction 254
jury 48
justification 11
justify 10
juvenile 152

K

kidnap 186
kin 459
kindle 269
knowledgeable 270

L

lad 271
lame 183
landlady 279
landlord 189
landslide 289
laser 216
latitude 281
lavish 253
lawmaker 22
lawsuit 130
layer 69
layman 393
layout 256
league 11
lease 431
legacy 211
legendary 119
legislation 22
legislative 22
legislator 282
legitimate 128
lengthy 373
lesbian 290
lessen 292
lest 72
lethal 264
liability 214
liable 335
liberate 295
liberation 295
lieutenant 424
lifelong 302
lighten 322
likelihood 122
likewise 130
limp 309
liner 441
linger 311
lining 454
liter 430
literacy 430
literal 267
literally 267
literate 430
livestock 312
lizard 313
locker 437
lodge 313
lodging 314
lofty 320
logo 321
lonesome 273
longevity 458
longitude 281
loop 87
lotion 322
lottery 323
lotus 331
loudspeaker 332
lounge 194
lucrative 283
lullaby 332
lumber 79
lump 34
lunar 340
lure 439
lush 305

M

madam 342
magnify 342
magnitude 296
maiden 342
mainland 351
mainstream 97
maintenance 10
majestic 352
majesty 351
malicious 287

索引

索引

mammal	172
mandate	223
manifest	113
manipulate	195
mansion	189
manuscript	373
maple	361
mar	318
marginal	362
marine	220
martial	363
marvel	368
masculine	189
massage	216
massive	21
masterpiece	216
mastery	394
mattress	82
meantime	6
mechanism	75
meddle	45
mediate	371
medication	188
medieval	326
meditate	456
meditation	457
melancholy	429
memo	45
mentality	430
mentor	189
merchandise	431
merge	101
mermaid	371
metaphor	146
metropolitan	76
midst	68
migrant	429
migrate	429
migration	188
milestone	199
mimic	265
mingle	370
miniature	84
minimal	118
minimize	118
mint	184
miraculous	456
miscellaneous	282
mischievous	245
missionary	129
mistress	343
moan	181
mobilize	357
mock	134
mode	79
modernization	384
modernize	384
modification	69
modify	69
molecule	26
momentum	392
monarch	352
monetary	436
monopoly	128
monotony	458
monstrous	378
moody	293
morale	364
morality	82
mortal	380
mortality	220
mortgage	219
motherhood	426
motive	31
motto	256
mound	381
mount	4
mourn	350
mournful	350
mow	390
mumble	78
municipal	84
muscular	115
muse	390
mustache	396
mustard	170
mute	458
myth	43
N	
nag	398
naïve	18
narrate	329
narrative	139
narrator	329
nasty	189
nationalism	266
navigate	405
navigation	405
nearsighted	407
negotiation	218
neutral	64
nickel	426
nickel-and-dime	427
nobility	154
nominate	136

nomination	136
nominee	136
nonetheless	30
nonprofit	223
norm	101
nostril	408
notable	406
notably	406
noticeable	133
notify	142
notion	11
notorious	438
nourish	465
nourishment	465
novelty	143
novice	417
nowhere	30
nucleus	417
nude	423
nurture	354
nutrient	188
nutrition	187
O	
oasis	413
oath	426
oatmeal	436
obesity	412
obligation	73
oblige	257
obscure	138
observer	24
obsess	472
obsession	472
obstinate	433
occurrence	443
octopus	443
odds	107
odor	451
offering	121
offshore	472
offspring	385
olive	63
operational	218
operative	243
opponent	56
opposition	56
oppress	365
oppression	365
opt	230
optimism	96
optional	188
orchard	106
ordeal	366
orderly	307
organism	119
organizer	464
orient	453
oriental	453
originality	36
originate	236
ornament	460
orphanage	462
orthodox	274
ounce	468
outbreak	345
outfit	168
outgoing	462
outing	276
outlaw	318
outlet	158
outlook	246
outnumber	465
output	229
outrage	466
outrageous	466
outright	277
outset	335
outsider	143
outskirts	243
outward	240
outward(s)	240
overall	17
overdo	379
overflow	379
overhead	89
overhear	380
overlap	383
oversee	219
overtake	219
overturn	195
overwhelm	70
overwhelming	70
overwork	380
oyster	443
ozone	451
P	
packet	309
pact	471
paddle	452
pamphlet	401
panorama	433
paperback	454
paradox	452
parallel	132
paralyze	432

索引

parliament	348	persevere	432	plea	61
participant	190	persist	75	plead	61
particle	26	persistence	265	pledge	99
partly	14	persistent	265	plight	278
passerby	225	personnel	5	plow	416
passionate	225	perspective	53	plunge	80
pastime	263	pessimism	96	plural	228
pastry	225	pesticide	433	pneumonia	431
patch	67	petition	221	poetic	52
patent	52	petrol	436	poke	85
pathetic	196	petroleum	436	polar	320
patriot	461	petty	167	pollutant	471
patriotic	462	pharmacist	430	ponder	456
patrol	71	pharmacy	429	pony	323
patron	106	phase	38	populate	336
peacock	471	photographic	174	porch	33
peasant	98	pianist	272	porter	404
pebble	413	pickpocket	279	portfolio	212
pedal	221	pickup	224	posture	328
pedestrian	196	pier	99	potent	394
peek	249	pierce	377	poultry	330
pending	399	pilgrim	281	practitioner	225
penetrate	88	pilgrimage	282	preach	332
penetration	88	pillar	225	preacher	333
peninsula	346	pimple	290	precaution	97
pension	147	pinch	292	precede	237
perceive	9	pious	433	precedent	237
perception	9	pipeline	196	precision	255
perch	252	pirate	228	predator	212
performer	217	pitcher	139	predecessor	385
peril	260	placement	231	predicament	278
perish	263	plague	299	preference	105
permissible	269	plantation	303	prehistoric	340
perplex	432	plausible	356	prejudice	148
perseverance	432	playwright	310	preliminary	93

premature	195
premier	191
premiere	428
premise	214
premium	175
prescribe	119
prescription	119
preside	258
presidency	73
presidential	73
prestige	267
prestigious	267
presumably	37
presume	37
prevail	16
prevailing	16
preventive	374
preview	343
prey	72
priceless	342
prior	25
privatize	419
probe	350
procession	445
proclaim	9
prodigy	201
productivity	131
proficiency	430
profile	125
profound	74
progressive	138
prohibit	144
prohibition	335
projection	167
prolong	81
prone	140
propaganda	102
propel	386
prophet	226
proportion	15
prose	432
prosecute	375
prosecution	167
prospect	10
prospective	446
prototype	410
proverb	352
province	60
provincial	455
provision	213
provisional	409
provoke	149
prune	135
psychiatry	400
psychic	400
psychotherapy	400
publicize	351
puff	378
pulse	190
punctual	429
purchase	15
purify	374
purity	374
pyramid	34
Q	
quake	363
qualification	275
qualify	217
quest	115
questionnaire	138
quiver	122
quota	222
R	
racism	94
rack	226
radiant	235
radiate	235
radiation	38
radical	127
radioactive	371
radish	362
radius	368
ragged	44
raid	159
rail	44
rally	49
rampant	285
ranch	71
random	100
rap	370
rash	236
ratify	382
ratio	15
rational	130
rattle	201
realism	118
realization	268
realm	79
reap	378
rear	61
reassure	222
rebellion	148
recession	187
recipient	195
recite	213

索 引

reckless 381
reckon 388
recommend 3
recommendation 3
reconcile 438
recreational 353
recruit 103
redundancy 445
redundant 445
reef 390
referee 396
referendum 440
refine 392
refinement 393
reflective 305
refresh 285
refreshment 286
refreshments 286
refuge 191
refute 405
regardless 55
regime 112
rehabilitate 365
rehabilitation 366
rehearsal 192
rehearse 440
reign 409
reinforce 110
rejoice 262
relay 277
relentless 445
reliance 393
reliant 273
relic 417
remainder 287
reminder 190
reminiscent 273
removal 66
renaissance 358
render 57
renowned 438
rental 192
repay 226
reproduce 241
reproduction 242
reptile 424
republican 208
resemblance 150
resent 425
resentment 425
reservoir 213
reside 434
residence 24
resident 24
residential 25
resistant 295
resolute 381
resort 116
respective 455
respondent 151
restoration 365
restrain 435
restraint 435
resumé 23
resume 23
retail 196
retort 441
retrieve 466
revelation 357
revenue 57
reverse 41
revival 453
revive 452
revolt 460
revolve 471
rhetoric 193
rib 154
ridge 71
ridiculous 104
rifle 6
righteous 226
rigid 60
rigorous 440
rim 156
riot 160
rip 144
ripple 243
risky 211
ritual 120
rival 198
rivalry 249
roam 252
robust 260
rod 226
rotate 359
rotation 359
royalty 467
rubbish 261
rugged 270
ruthless 464

S

sacred 32
saddle 4
safeguard 246
saint 2

salmon	142	sentiment	33	shuttle	229
salon	204	sentimental	33	sibling	120
salute	271	sequence	66	siege	215
salvage	463	serene	348	simplicity	337
sandal	198	sergeant	424	simplify	337
sanitation	392	serial	320	simultaneous	246
savage	464	series	1	skeleton	153
scan	96	sermon	323	skeptical	449
scandal	198	server	45	skim	305
scar	80	serving	295	skull	153
scenario	17	session	37	slam	122
scenic	385	setback	373	slang	376
scent	191	setting	25	slap	87
scheme	14	shabby	331	slash	377
scope	92	shareholder	1	slaughter	408
scorn	280	sharpen	341	slavery	109
scramble	44	shatter	82	slay	408
scrap	123	shaver	351	sloppy	417
scrape	290	shed	159	slot	150
screwdriver	415	sheer	145	slum	347
script	166	sheriff	77	slump	299
scroll	302	shield	161	sly	433
scrutiny	463	shiver	122	smash	86
sculptor	310	shoplift	438	smog	204
seagull	471	shortage	71	smother	441
sector	202	shortcoming	362	smuggle	467
seduce	439	shortsighted	408	snatch	40
segment	79	shove	100	sneak	227
selective	311	shred	368	sneaker	442
seminar	193	shrewd	156	sneaky	227, 452
senator	47	shriek	379	sneeze	262
sensation	53	shrub	389	sniff	173
sensational	53	shrug	230	snore	468
sensitivity	52	shuffle	244	soak	134
sensor	203	shutter	397	soar	197

索 引

sob	205	spectator	81	static	357
sober	104	spectrum	120	stationary	467
sociable	394	speculate	165	stationery	441
socialism	266	sphere	100	statistical	59
socialist	266	spicy	218	stature	348
socialize	393	spine	154	statute	472
sociology	393	spiral	423	steer	88
soften	205	splendor	422	stepchild	390
sole	95	spokesperson	303	stepfather	390
solely	95	sponge	191	stepmother	390
solemn	469	sponsor	48	stereotype	136
solidarity	392	sponsorship	48	stew	46
solitary	460	spontaneous	315	stimulate	119
solitude	460	sportsman	435	stimulation	305
solo	95	sportsmanship	435	stimulus	120
soothe	374	spotlight	299	stink	201
sophisticated	18	spouse	192	stinky	201
sophomore	228	sprint	86	stock	1
sorrowful	453	spur	417	storage	41
souvenir	229	squad	167	stout	105
sovereign	318	squash	168	straighten	51
sovereignty	130	squat	124	straightforward	100
sow	107	stability	149	strain	22
spacecraft	442	stabilize	347	strait	253
spacious	103	stack	132	strand	173
span	308	stagger	406	strangle	440
sparkle	203	stain	42	strap	173
sparrow	471	stake	61	strategic	92
specialist	23	stalk	117	stray	242
specialize	23	stall	153	stride	369
specialty	23	stance	224	striking	229
specify	64	staple	467	stroll	362
specimen	43	startle	68	structural	105
spectacle	434	starvation	420	stumble	60
spectacular	126	statesman	397	stun	351

stunning	351
sturdy	105
stutter	396
stylish	331
subjective	357
submission	13
submissive	13
submit	13
subordinate	394
subscribe	347
subscription	347
subsequent	83
subsidize	264
subsidy	215
substantial	10
substitute	52
subtle	111
suburban	91
succession	278
successive	278
successor	92
suffocate	440
suitcase	331
suite	112
summon	310
superb	192
superficial	322
superintendent	319
superiority	354
superstition	198
superstitious	311
supervise	78
supervision	78
supervisor	78
supplement	306
supposedly	232
suppress	300
supreme	12
surge	250
surgical	261
surname	270
surpass	349
surplus	90
surveillance	232
suspend	32
suspense	272
suspension	272
sustain	31
sustainable	31
swamp	280
swap	93
swarm	291
symbolic	101
symbolize	285
symmetry	468
sympathize	292
symphony	300
symptom	137
syndrome	138
synonym	441
synthesis	375
synthetic	375
syrup	302
T	
taboo	444
tackle	198
tactic	92
tan	312
tangle	184
tattoo	444
tedious	458
telecommunications	263
teller	306
tempo	313
tempt	99
temptation	99
tenant	279
tentative	321
terminal	227
terrace	399
terrify	211
testify	203
textile	265
texture	75
theft	192
theology	232
theoretical	139
therapist	167
therapy	167
thereafter	256
thereby	65
thermometer	357
thesis	224
thigh	135
thorn	137
threshold	148
thrill	199
thriller	199
thrive	164
throne	172
thrust	69
tick	144
tile	80
tilt	331
tin	134

tiptoe 341
tiresome 343
token 341
toll 126
torch 217
torment 155
tornado 317
torrent 370
tournament 133
toxic 227
trademark 363
trait 89
traitor 127
transaction 57
transcript 373
transformation 158
transit 18
transition 18
transmission 150
transmit 354
transparent 143
transplant 465
trauma 197
treasury 371
treaty 77
trek 392
tremor 322
tribute 62
trifle 242
trifling 243
trigger 197
trillion 273
trim 135
triple 63
trivial 166
trophy 203
tropic 364
trout 444
trustee 454
tsunami 317
tuck 391
tuition 199
tumor 129
tuna 142
turmoil 307
twilight 450
twinkle 389

U

ultimate 36
unanimous 349
unconditional 273
uncover 91
underestimate 466
undergo 47
undergraduate 142
underline 199
undermine 166
underneath 398
underpass 407
understandable 124
undertake 54
underway 418
undo 192
undoubtedly 42
unemployment 167
unfold 84
unforgettable 199
unification 333
unify 333
unlock 146
unpack 282
unprecedented 18, 237
unveil 294
update 63
upgrade 169
uphold 323
upright 329
uprising 243
upward 239
upward(s) 239
urgency 356
usher 439
utensil 466
utility 73
utilize 74
utter 252
utterly 252

V

vaccine 431
vacuum 227
vague 39
valid 110
vanilla 466
vanity 253
vapor 262
variable 47
variation 47
vegetation 191
veil 294
vein 31
velvet 461
vendor 17
venture 88
venue 205
verbal 98

verdict	197
verge	383
verify	306
versatile	439
version	54
versus	21
vertical	123
veteran	65
veterinarian	468
veto	271
via	106
viable	112
vibrate	439
vibration	440
vice	287
vicious	103
victor	236
victorious	236
viewer	81
viewpoint	81
vigor	271
vigorous	272
villa	281
villain	291
vine	301
vinegar	188
vineyard	302
violinist	273
virgin	303
virtual	64
visa	200
vitality	305
vocal	174
vocation	236
vocational	237
volcano	160
vomit	193
voucher	138
vow	190
vowel	312
vulnerable	140
W	
wag	404
walnut	416
ward	424
wardrobe	354
warehouse	209
warfare	255
warrant	364
warranty	364
warrior	78
wary	163
waterproof	421
weary	343
weird	27
well-being	381
wharf	389
whatsoever	19
wheelchair	227
whereabouts	200
whereas	30
whine	182
whisk	58
whiskey	370
wholesale	380
wholesome	390
widespread	42
widow	399
widower	399
wig	200
wilderness	154
wildlife	154
windshield	131
wither	113
withhold	253
witty	184
woe	408
woodpecker	471
workforce	263
workshop	95
worship	26
worthwhile	68
worthy	67
wreath	217
wrestle	377
wrinkle	469
wrongdoing	143
X	
Xerox	433
Y	
yacht	200
yearn	384
yearning	384
yield	16
yoga	470
yogurt	461
Z	
zoom	453

附　錄

Cardinal Numbers 基數

1. **one** [wʌn] 一
2. **two** [tu] 二
3. **three** [θri] 三
4. **four** [fɔr] 四
5. **five** [faɪv] 五
6. **six** [sɪks] 六
7. **seven** [ˋsɛvən] 七
8. **eight** [et] 八
9. **nine** [naɪn] 九
10. **ten** [tɛn] 十
11. **eleven** [ɪˋlɛvən] 十一
12. **twelve** [twɛlv] 十二
13. **thirteen** [θɝˋtin] 十三
14. **fourteen** [fɔrˋtin] 十四
15. **fifteen** [fɪfˋtin] 十五
16. **sixteen** [sɪksˋtin] 十六
17. **seventeen** [ˏsɛvənˋtin] 十七
18. **eighteen** [eˋtin] 十八
19. **nineteen** [naɪnˋtin] 十九
20. **twenty** [ˋtwɛntɪ] 二十
21. **twenty-one** [ˋtwɛntɪˏwʌn] 二十一
22. **twenty-two** [ˋtwɛntɪˏtu] 二十二
23. **twenty-three** [ˋtwɛntɪˏθri] 二十三
24. **twenty-four** [ˋtwɛntɪˏfɔr] 二十四
25. **twenty-five** [ˋtwɛntɪˏfaɪv] 二十五
26. **thirty** [ˋθɝtɪ] 三十
27. **thirty-one** [ˋθɝtɪˏwʌn] 三十一
28. **thirty-two** [ˋθɝtɪˏtu] 三十二
29. **thirty-three** [ˋθɝtɪˏθri] 三十三
30. **thirty-four** [ˋθɝtɪˏfɔr] 三十四
31. **forty** [ˋfɔrtɪ] 四十
32. **fifty** [ˋfɪftɪ] 五十
33. **sixty** [ˋsɪkstɪ] 六十
34. **seventy** [ˋsɛvəntɪ] 七十
35. **eighty** [ˋetɪ] 八十
36. **ninety** [ˋnaɪntɪ] 九十
37. **one hundred** [wʌn ˋhʌndrəd] 一百
38. **one thousand** [wʌn ˋθaʊzṇd] 一千
39. **one million** [wʌn ˋmɪljən] 一百萬
40. **one billion** [wʌn ˋbɪljən] 十億

Ordinal Numbers 序數

1. **first** [fɝst] 第一
2. **second** [ˋsɛkənd] 第二
3. **third** [θɝd] 第三
4. **fourth** [fɔrθ] 第四
5. **fifth** [fɪfθ] 第五
6. **sixth** [sɪksθ] 第六
7. **seventh** [ˋsɛvənθ] 第七
8. **eighth** [eθ] 第八
9. **ninth** [naɪnθ] 第九
10. **tenth** [tɛnθ] 第十
11. **eleventh** [ɪˋlɛvənθ] 第十一
12. **twelfth** [twɛlfθ] 第十二
13. **thirteenth** [θɝˋtinθ] 第十三
14. **fourteenth** [fɔrˋtinθ] 第十四
15. **fifteenth** [fɪfˋtinθ] 第十五
16. **sixteenth** [sɪksˋtinθ] 第十六

⑰ **seventeenth** [ˌsɛvən`tinθ] 第十七
⑱ **eighteenth** [e`tinθ] 第十八
⑲ **nineteenth** [naɪn`tinθ] 第十九
⑳ **twentieth** [`twɛntɪɪθ] 第二十
㉑ **twenty-first** [`twɛntɪˏfɝst] 第二十一
㉒ **twenty-second** [`twɛntɪˏsɛkənd] 第二十二
㉓ **twenty-third** [`twɛntɪˏθɝd] 第二十三
㉔ **twenty-fourth** [`twɛntɪˏfɔrθ] 第二十四
㉕ **twenty-fifth** [`twɛntɪˏfɪfθ] 第二十五
㉖ **thirtieth** [`θɝtɪɪθ] 第三十
㉗ **fortieth** [`fɔrtɪɪθ] 第四十
㉘ **fiftieth** [`fɪftɪɪθ] 第五十
㉙ **sixtieth** [`sɪkstɪɪθ] 第六十
㉚ **seventieth** [`sɛvəntɪɪθ] 第七十
㉛ **eightieth** [`etɪɪθ] 第八十
㉜ **ninetieth** [`naɪntɪɪθ] 第九十
㉝ **hundredth** [`hʌndrədθ] 第一百
㉞ **thousandth** [`θauzṇdθ] 第一千
㉟ **millionth** [`mɪljənθ] 第一百萬
㊱ **billionth** [`bɪljənθ] 第十億

Days of the Week 一星期

❶ **Monday** [`mʌnde] / **Mon.** 星期一
❷ **Tuesday** [`tjuzde] / **Tue.** 星期二
❸ **Wednesday** [`wɛnzde] / **Wed.** 星期三
❹ **Thursday** [`θɝzde] / **Thu.** 星期四
❺ **Friday** [`fraɪde] / **Fri.** 星期五
❻ **Saturday** [`sætɚde] / **Sat.** 星期六
❼ **Sunday** [`sʌnde] / **Sun.** 星期日

Months 月份

❶ **January** [`dʒænjuˏɛrɪ] / **Jan.** 一月
❷ **February** [`fɛbruˏɛrɪ] / **Feb.** 二月
❸ **March** [martʃ] / **Mar.** 三月
❹ **April** [`eprəl] / **Apr.** 四月
❺ **May** [me] 五月
❻ **June** [dʒun] / **Jun.** 六月
❼ **July** [dʒu`laɪ] / **Jul.** 七月
❽ **August** [`ɔgəst] / **Aug.** 八月
❾ **September** [sɛp`tɛmbɚ] / **Sep.** 九月
❿ **October** [ɑk`tobɚ] / **Oct.** 十月
⓫ **November** [no`vɛmbɚ] / **Nov.** 十一月
⓬ **December** [dɪ`sɛmbɚ] / **Dec.** 十二月

附錄

附 錄

Seasons 季節

❶ **spring** [sprɪŋ] 春天
❷ **summer** [ˋsʌmɚ] 夏天
❸ **autumn** [ˋɔtəm] / **fall** [fɔl] 秋天
❹ **winter** [ˋwɪntɚ] 冬天

Countries and Areas 國家與地區

❶ **Argentina** [ˏɑrdʒənˋtinə] 阿根廷
❷ **Australia** [ɔˋstreljə] 澳洲
❸ **Brazil** [brəˋzɪl] 巴西
❹ **Canada** [ˋkænədə] 加拿大
❺ **China** [ˋtʃaɪnə] 中國
❻ **France** [fræns] 法國
❼ **Germany** [ˋdʒɝmənɪ] 德國
❽ **India** [ˋɪndɪə] 印度
❾ **Indonesia** [ˏɪndoˋniʒə] 印尼
❿ **Italy** [ˋɪtəli] 義大利
⓫ **Japan** [dʒəˋpæn] 日本
⓬ **Malaysia** [məˋleʒə] 馬來西亞
⓭ **Mexico** [ˋmɛksɪˏko] 墨西哥
⓮ **(the) Philippines** [(ðə) ˋfɪləˏpinz] 菲律賓
⓯ **Republic of China** [rɪˋpʌblɪk əv ˋtʃaɪnə] 中華民國
⓰ **Russia** [ˋrʌʃə] 俄羅斯
⓱ **Saudi Arabia** [ˏsaudɪ əˋrebɪə] 沙烏地阿拉伯
⓲ **Singapore** [ˋsɪŋgəˏpor] 新加坡
⓳ **South Africa** [ˏsauθ ˋæfrɪkə] 南非
⓴ **South Korea** [ˏsauθ koˋrɪə] 南韓
㉑ **Spain** [spen] 西班牙
㉒ **Taiwan** [ˏtaɪˋwɑn] 臺灣
㉓ **Thailand** [ˋtaɪlənd] 泰國
㉔ **Turkey** [ˋtɝkɪ] 土耳其
㉕ **(the) United Kingdom** [(ðə) juˏnaɪtɪd ˋkɪŋdəm] 英國
㉖ **(the) United States** [(ðə) juˏnaɪtɪd ˋstets] 美國
㉗ **Vietnam** [ˏvjɛtˋnæm] 越南

Continents 大陸；洲

❶ **Africa** [ˋæfrɪkə] 非洲
❷ **Antarctica** [ænˋtɑrktɪkə] 南極洲
❸ **Asia** [ˋeʒə] 亞洲
❹ **Australia** [ɔˋstreljə] 澳洲
❺ **Europe** [ˋjurəp] 歐洲
❻ **North America** [ˏnɔrθ əˋmɛrɪkə] 北美洲
❼ **South America** [ˏsauθ əˋmɛrɪkə] 南美洲

The Principal Oceans of the World 世界主要海洋

❶ **(the) Arctic Ocean**
[(ði) ˋɑrktɪk ˋoʃən] 北極海

❷ **(the) Atlantic Ocean**
[(ði) ətˋlæntɪk ˋoʃən] 大西洋

❸ **(the) Indian Ocean**
[(ði) ˋɪndɪən ˋoʃən] 印度洋

❹ **(the) Pacific Ocean**
[(ðə) pəˋsɪfɪk ˋoʃən] 太平洋

Religions 宗教

❶ **Buddhism** [ˋbʊdɪzəm] / **Buddhist** [ˋbʊdɪst] 佛教 / 佛教的；佛教徒

❷ **Catholicism** [kəˋθɑlə͵sɪzəm] / **Catholic** [ˋkæθəlɪk] 天主教 / 天主教的；天主教徒

❸ **Christianity** [͵krɪstʃɪˋænətɪ] / **Christian** [ˋkrɪstʃən] 基督教 / 基督教的；基督徒

❹ **Eastern Orthodoxy** [ˋistɚn ˋɔrθə͵dɑksɪ] / **Eastern Orthodox** [ˋistɚn ˋɔrθə͵dɑks] 東正教 / 東正教的

❺ **Hinduism** [ˋhɪndu͵ɪzəm] / **Hindu** [ˋhɪndu] 印度教 / 印度教的；印度教徒

❻ **Islam** [ˋɪsləm] / **Muslim** [ˋmʌz͵lɪm / ˋmʊz͵lɪm] 伊斯蘭教，回教 / 回教的；回教徒

❼ **Judaism** [ˋdʒudɪ͵ɪzəm] / **Jewish** [ˋdʒuɪʃ] 猶太教 / 猶太教的；猶太人

❽ **Taoism** [ˋtaʊ͵ɪzəm] / **Taoist** [ˋtaʊɪst] 道教 / 道教的；道教徒

Parts of Speech 詞性

❶ **adjective** [ˋædʒɪktɪv] / *adj.* 形容詞

❷ **adverb** [ˋædvɝb] / *adv.* 副詞

❸ **article** [ˋɑrtɪkḷ] / *art.* 冠詞

❹ **auxiliary** [ɔgˋzɪljərɪ] / *aux.* 助動詞

❺ **conjunction** [kənˋdʒʌŋkʃən] / *conj.* 連接詞

❻ **noun** [naʊn] / *n.* 名詞

❼ **preposition** [͵prɛpəˋzɪʃən] / *prep.* 介詞

❽ **pronoun** [ˋpronaʊn] / *pron.* 代名詞

❾ **verb** [vɝb] / *v.* 動詞

附錄

Notes

國家圖書館出版品預行編目（CIP）資料

英文字彙王：進階單字 4001-6000 Levels 5 & 6
／賴世雄作. -- 初版. -- 臺北市：
常春藤有聲出版股份有限公司, 2022.01
面； 公分.--（英文字彙王系列；E64）
ISBN 978-626-95430-4-5（平裝）
1. 英語 2. 詞彙
805.12 110020680

英文字彙王系列【E64】

英文字彙王：進階單字 4001-6000 Levels 5 & 6

總 編 審 賴世雄
終　　審 李　端
執行編輯 許嘉華
編輯小組 常春藤中外編輯群
設計組長 王玥琦
封面設計 胡毓芸
排版設計 王穎婕．林桂旭
錄　　音 李鳳君．劉書吟
播音老師 Leah Zimmermann．Tom Brink．Jacob Roth
Stephanie Buckley．Brian Foden．Leila Pereira
法律顧問 北辰著作權事務所蕭雄淋律師
出 版 者 常春藤有聲出版股份有限公司
地　　址 臺北市忠孝西路一段 33 號 5 樓
電　　話 (02) 2331-7600
傳　　真 (02) 2381-0918
網　　址 www.ivy.com.tw
電子信箱 service@ivy.com.tw
郵政劃撥 19714777
戶　　名 常春藤有聲出版股份有限公司
定　　價 480 元